HE WAS THE
– MAN IN AM

'I want to finish this railroad, Charles, because I can't go back. But if there were any way in which I could trade this railroad, and all its locomotives, and all its ties and its spikes and its rails – if there was any way in which I could trade this railroad for one day with Hannah, one more day with Hannah, then I would do it gladly.'

He lifted his head, and when he did so, Charles was shocked to see that he was crying.

'I was prepared to see people die for the sake of this railroad. I was prepared to ruin people's reputations, their happiness, their whole lives. That was the price of progress, I thought.'

Also by Graham Masterton in Sphere Books:

RICH
THE SWEETMAN CURVE
REVENGE OF THE MANITOU
THE WELLS OF HELL
THE DEVILS OF D DAY
CHARNEL HOUSE
FAMINE

Railroad

GRAHAM MASTERTON

SPHERE BOOKS LIMITED
30-32 Gray's Inn Road, London WC1X 8JL

First published in Great Britain by Hamish Hamilton Ltd
Copyright © 1981 by Graham Masterton
Published by Sphere Books Ltd 1981
Reprinted 1982 (twice)

Set in Lasercomp Times

Printed and bound in Great Britain by
©ollins, Glasgow

Dla mej najserdeczniejszej przyjaciólki . . .
mej najbardziej milowanej ukochanej . . .
tej, z którą zawsze będę lącnzie żywić
me nadzieje, me szczęscie, me marzenia,
i której zawsze będę oddany cialem i duszą . . .

Prologue

Collis Edmonds had appeared only twice on the observation platform of his private car between Ogden, Utah, where he had joined the train, and Winnemucca, Nevada; and then only to smoke the last quarter of a burned-down cigar and toss it on to the tracks. Emily had been intrigued, and had asked the black conductor who he was. He looked so lonely, standing by the wrought-iron rail – a tall, thin-faced man with a slight stoop and eyes that seemed to be permanently fixed on some point in the middle distance. He was dressed in black, although on the second occasion that Emily had seen him, he had worn a red fez with a tassel, too – the kind that gentlemen used for smoking and writing.

'That,' the conductor had told her emphatically, 'is The Boss.'

Emily went back to her Pullman sleeping car and sat down on the green plush seat, taking out her notepad and her pencil. Outside the window, through the tapestry curtains, the scrubby sagebrush plain moved past at the astonishing speed of twenty miles per hour.

She wrote, 'I have seen the man the conductors call "The Boss". He travels in his own Pullman car, although for one so wealthy, travelling in only one private car must be "roughing it", as they say out here in the West.'

She paused, biting the end of her pencil. Then she added, 'I believe I can understand how a man who has created this extraordinary railroad – a man who has dramatically changed the fate of the whole nation – can wish to remain a recluse. What he must feel within him for having spanned a continent! What thoughts he must have! He is a handsome yet tormented person, and even though I have glimpsed him but twice, I feel a warmth and compassion for his historic predicament, and his loneliness. I wish very much that I might meet him one day, and impart my feelings (discreetly, of course!).'

She put away her pad. She knew that she ought to write more – about the hazy purple mountain range that sheltered Salt Lake City, about the alkali plains over which they were passing now, with the smoke from the locomotive's stack rolling southward on the wild like tumbleweed. She ought to write about the comforts of the palace car in which she was travelling, the walnut and primavera panels, the plush sofas, and the gorgeous amaranth mouldings. She was, after all, here to represent her journal, *Ladies' Home Notes*, and her New York lady readers would be fascinated to know how food was prepared at twenty miles per hour, and what it was like to eat antelope steak while flying on rails across the very plains on which the animals had been reared.

But the appearance of The Boss had somehow made all these chatty details seem irrelevant. She thought she had seen in his profile something of the terrifying scale of what had been achieved in building the Sierra Pacific Railroad, and something of the depth and darkness of the imagination which had conceived it. She sat for a long time watching the sun set, her eyes turned by its falling light into transparent amber, her curly hair turned into fraying fire, and her thoughts had been miles and years and hundreds of lifetimes away when the grey-uniformed conductor at last touched her arm and told her that dinner was being served.

The next morning, Emily stood on the platform, feeling the warmth of the summer wind and smelling the sagebrush. She tried to glimpse what was going on behind the heavy drawn drapes of The Boss's private car, but all she could see was part of a silver inkstand and the edge of a newspaper. After the train left Reno, however, and began to climb through the foothills of the Sierra Nevada, The Boss appeared outside of his Pullman car more frequently. Emily made a few brief notes about the winding railroad track and the perseverance of the Chinese labourers who had built it, and about how high above sea level they were; but her attention was fixed on the last car of the train, and on the way its single occupant came out for an hour at a time to smoke and drink and stare at the uneven white line in the blue summer sky that marked the snowy peaks of the Sierras.

It was almost noon by the time the train had climbed at last through the stifling darkness of countless snowsheds and had emerged among the blue-green pines that surrounded Donner Lake, close to the very summit of the mountain pass that would take the train into California. Emily wrapped her beaver coat around her and stood in the open, separated from The Boss's private car by nothing more than a few feet of chilly mountain air and a greasy coupling.

The Boss stayed inside, his curtains drawn, right up until the moment when the labouring locomotive hauled the twelve-car train to the summit. Then, quite abruptly, his door opened, and he emerged, wearing a fawn coat with a dark fur collar, his face paler than usual, his eyes tired. He acknowledged Emily with a look that could have been anything from a wince to an unrealised smile, and then he went immediately to the rail, to look out over the Sierras.

At Colfax, after a long and winding descent through the mountains, the train stopped to take on water. It was warmer here, although the air was still quite crisp. Many of the passengers stepped down from the train to stretch their legs, but Emily stayed in the parlour car, writing up some of her notes. She had almost finished, and was blotting the last page, when the parlour door opened and The Boss walked in.

Emily sat up straight and tugged at her bottle-green travelling jacket. 'Good afternoon,' she said, in a high, curious voice. She hadn't really meant to sound so inquisitive, but The Boss didn't appear to notice, or mind. He looked around the car as if he were searching for somebody else, somebody whose face and whose memory somehow eluded him.

'I'm Collis Edmonds,' he said slowly.

'Yes,' she replied.

'And you . . .?' he asked her.

'Miss Emily Van ᴅrugh, from New York.'

Collis Edmonds nodded. His eyes still searched around the parlour.

'Are you enjoying your trip, Miss Van Brugh?'

'Yes, sir. This railroad is more of a marvel than I could have imagined.'

Collis Edmonds nodded again. 'Yes,' he said, as if he were irked by compliments about his achievements. 'A great marvel. A great . . . feat of human . . . what's-its-name . . . endeavour.'

There was an odd, tight silence. Collis Edmonds didn't seem to have anything to say, yet he didn't make any move to leave. At last Emily said cautiously, 'Do you think, Mr Edmonds, I might ask you a few questions?'

'Questions? Of course you may. What do you want to know?'

'I want to know why you built the railroad.'

He turned towards her and focused his eyes on her sharply. 'You want to know *why*?'

'Yes.'

'My dear young lady . . . why on earth do you think?'

'I'm not sure. Having seen you, and now having met you, I'm not at all certain.'

3

He raised his hands. 'Well, for goodness sake, I built it to make money. I built it because it was needed. I built it because – well, I built it because I did, that's all.'

Emily said nothing, but sat framed by the California sunshine that shone through the parlour car's dusty window, her pencil neatly raised in her hand, her notepad unmarked.

'Aren't you going to write that down?' asked Collis Edmonds, after a long pause. 'No? Then what else would you like? Some facts? Some figures? We built thirty-seven miles of snowsheds through these mountains between '68 and '69, using up sixty-five million board feet of timber. There are fifteen tunnels taking the Sierra Pacific through the rock; and on occasions the granite was so hard that we could progress only eight inches in twenty-four hours. Is that the kind of thing? The summit is seven thousand, one hundred and fifty-six feet above mean sea level, and in winter the snow can be anything up to forty feet deep.'

He stopped. Then he said, much more quietly, 'You're not making any notes at all.'

Emily lowered her eyes. Collis Edmonds watched her for a moment, and then came across to her table, drew out a chair, and sat down. He continued to watch her with an expression that was half amused, half intrigued, his chin resting on his fist.

'You really want to know why, don't you?' he asked her.

Emily glanced up. 'You must think I'm being very ill-mannered,' she said. 'But I do believe you had a special purpose. The way you stand on the platform of your car . . . the way you look out at the mountains.'

'You have a very romantic turn of mind,' said Collis Edmonds. 'Why should you suppose that *my* mind works in the same way? I'm a railroad builder. Who could be more pragmatic?'

'Well . . . perhaps I'm mistaken,' Emily replied. 'In which case you must accept my apologies.'

Collis Edmonds sat back and took out an engraved gold pocket watch. He stared at it for a while, then said, 'We have several hours left before we arrive in Sacramento. Would you think it impertinent of me to ask you to come to my parlour, and take a light supper?'

'I'd be honoured,' said Emily.

'Good,' Collis Edmonds told her. 'I believe my cook is preparing a salmon soufflé, and I have some fine champagne. And while we eat, and while we drink, I shall do my best to answer your question

4

for you, honestly, and at length. You want to know why I built the Sierra Pacific Railroad? I shall tell you. But I must warn you ahead of time that some of what occurred may shock you, and some of it may scandalise you, and some of it may make you wonder how low a human being can sink in the pursuit of glory.'

Emily blushed, but only a little. 'I think I can bear tó be shocked, Mr Edmonds, and to be scandalised. I am, after all, a reporter.'

Collis Edmonds grinned and stood up. 'Join me just before the train leaves,' he said. 'I look forward to entertaining you.'

For the next three hours, as the train gradually descended the foothills of the Sierra Nevada, with the sky darkening behind it and the sun sinking ahead of it, Collis Edmonds talked to Emily Van Brugh. The champagne sparkled in lead-crystal glasses; the cutlery that shuddered on the table was solid silver. There was fresh salmon, and asparagus, and peaches, and delicious sharp cheese.

After those hours, Emily returned to her own parlour and packed her clothes in preparation for leaving the train at Sacramento. She never saw Collis Edmonds again, although after the train had reached the terminus, and she was waiting to be taken by carriage to her hotel, she saw his special Pullman car detached from the rest of the train and shunted slowly off into the darkness, its curtains drawn tight.

The story she wrote appeared in *Ladies' Home Notes* on 13 October 1870. It was entitled 'A Modern Ladies' Companion to Railroad Travel Across the Continent, & How the Unaccompanied Lady Is to Manage in California'. It told of the marvels of the Sierra Pacific Railroad; of the deserts and mountains and towering cliffs; of what to eat, and what to eschew; of what clothes to take, and where to stay. It even mentioned the fact that there were thirty-seven miles of snowsheds through the mountains.

It told scarcely anything at all of what Collis Edmonds had said to her during that three-hour supper, because that was one of those stories whose pain and tenderness and fierceness would only have offended Emily's readers – a story that she could only retell in the silence and the quietness of her own memory, and her own heart.

5

Chapter 1

He awoke just after ten o'clock in the morning in a front second-floor room at the Monument Hotel. His head was pounding, and his mouth tasted, in the nauseatingly memorable words of his grandfather, as if he'd been sucking toads all night. He lay there for almost five minutes, blinking up at the decorative plaster moulding on the ceiling, trying to decide what day it was, and what hour it could be, and why the Lord was punishing him this time.

It was plainly a wet day. He could hear the scattering of rain on the windowpanes, and only a dim submarine light strained through the red-and-cream-striped drapes. It was also plainly quite late, because he could hear the wheels of growlers and carriages outside in the square, and a horse with a distinctive cough. Under the shelter of the hotel's portico a newsboy yelped in a voice like a Jew's harp, *'Tribune! Tribune!'*

Something else rapidly became plain, too; and plain in the plainest way. There was a grunt and a sigh beside him, and the grubby green comforter was thrown back by a white freckled arm, revealing on the pillow beside him a tangle of gingery curls. After a further struggle, a girl's pallid face rose into view, with reddened eyes and smudged rouge, and an expression that reminded him of a stranded codfish he had once had to kill with a brick.

'Mother in heaven,' she said, in a strong Irish brogue. 'Is it morning already?'

He didn't answer, but pressed the back of his hand to his thumping forehead. There was no question about it. The Lord was punishing him, yet again, for drinking too many stone fences, smoking too many Virginia cheroots, gambling away too much money, and above all for finishing up his evening's amusement, as he almost always did, with a girl of irredeemably homely looks. He couldn't think why he did it. No matter how pretty and enchanting they appeared by gaslight, when he was dizzy with bourbon and sweet cider and exhilarated by the loss of scores of dollars of his father's money, these girls always emerged from the sheets the following morning tousled and plump, with faces as uncompromising as German mineworkers. The Lord was right, right, right, and

7

he was wrong, wrong, wrong. He only wished the Lord wouldn't keep rubbing it in.

The girl stared at him for a long time. She must have been eighteen or nineteen, and her body was still clothed in that white subcutaneous fat that a man's fingernails could dig into in moments of sexual duress. *Duress* was the only word he could think of. *Ecstasy* seemed out of the question. But she was amiable. She bent forward and kissed his dark tousled hair, and smiled at him with a little twist of her mouth that was almost fetching.

He sat up in bed, accompanied by a chorus of complaining springs, and looked around him. The hotel room was high-ceilinged, and furnished with cheapness and severity. Apart from their large institutional iron bed, the kind of bed to which lunatics were manacled, there was a sawed-oak armchair, a marble-topped washstand, and a grim varnished bureau with an oval mirror on top of it. He let his head drop to his chest and let out a long sigh of resignation.

'You don't have to look so miserable,' the girl said. 'It's only Tuesday.'

He turned his eyes towards her balefully. 'Why shouldn't I be? I feel it.'

He pushed back the comforter and climbed unsteadily out of bed. The threadbare carpet seemed to tilt and yaw like the deck of a small ship. He groped across to the washstand, and held on to it for a while before he poured a basinful of cold water out of the lily-patterned jug.

The girl lay back on the pillow and watched him splash himself. In the milky light, his body was naked and angular, and a little underweight, so that his ribs showed. He had a long face, with dark curly sidewhiskers, and a sharp straight nose, and rather worried-looking eyes. Even when he was winning at cards, with a whole handful of queens and jacks, you would have thought by his eyes that he was right on the verge of throwing in the sponge, or even of slitting his throat.

'You don't *have* to feel miserable,' the girl said. 'You could jump back into bed and feel anything you like.'

He turned and peered at her with one eye closed against the water. He couldn't find a towel, so he pulled the drapes towards him and dried himself on those. She looked back at him with that little twisted smile, admiring his melancholy leanness.

He said in a thick voice, 'The only feeling I want right now, apart

8

from my misery, with which I'm quite content, is the feeling of Bromo Vichy salts down the back of my throat.'

She kept on smiling. 'Misery and Bromo Vichy aren't the two best feelings you could have.'

'I know,' he told her. He went to the oval mirror on top of the bureau and inspected his swollen eyes. 'But they'll do.'

She twisted her frayed red curls around her finger. She didn't say anything for a while, but pouted in what she obviously considered was a sulky and flirtatious manner. 'Last night, you didn't seem satisfied with anything,' she said. 'I would have called you a tiger.'

'What a pair,' he replied absently, as he searched for his cotton combinations. 'The tiger and the hippopotamus.'

'The what?'

He was on his hands and knees, looking under the bed. He raised his head and said: 'The hippopotamus. It's a large beast from Africa, that likes to wallow.'

She stared at him as he abandoned the search for his underwear and went instead to the armchair, where his black evening coat was hanging, and took out a leather case of cheroots. He drew one out, bit off the end, and then sat naked on the end of the bed, his right ankle crossed over his left knee, and lit up. He puffed smoke, spat a shred of tobacco from the tip of his tongue, coughed, and then turned back to the girl.

'You're cruel,' she said. 'That's a cruel thing to say.'

'Is it?'

'You should know that it is. We can't help the way we're made. Didn't your parents ever teach you that?'

'All my parents ever taught me was that the value of the dollar exceeds the value of any and all human principles, and that women who don't wear bonnets are anybody's for the asking.'

The girl sat up in bed revealing breasts that were small and white and chubby. 'You told me last night you loved me.'

He raised an eyebrow.

'You said you loved me, and that you'd marry me as soon as you were able.'

He sucked at his cheroot and grinned. 'Under the influence of fifteen stone fences, a man would say anything. Mind you, I've drunk more. But then, on the other hand, I've said worse things.'

He stood up and put his hands on his hips. 'What I really want to know about last night is where I flung down my long johns.'

She was silent for a moment. Outside, the summer rain lashed

9

against the window and gurgled along the gutters of the parapet. 'What's your name?' she asked him, as he bent over to explore under the bureau.

'Collis,' he told her. 'What's yours?'

'Kathleen Mary.'

'I might have guessed.' Collis reappeared, red-faced but triumphantly holding up his combinations. 'There,' he said. 'The finest suit of French Bon-Bon underwear that ever strode the streets. Guaranteed, in times of emergency or pressing lust, to open in a flash.'

Kathleen Mary dropped her eyes. Even in her profession she considered it indelicate to spend too much time admiring a gentleman's undergarments. She kept her eyes lowered while Collis, his cheroot clenched between his teeth, climbed into the Bon-Bon outfit and buttoned himself up. When he was finished, he looked as if he were about to enter a velocipede race, or swim the Hudson blindfolded. He sat down on the bed again and looked into Kathleen's eyes with that dark, worried expression that may have been worry but was more likely to be pained impatience.

'My dear,' he said, laying a hairy, long-fingered hand over her pale plump hand. 'I am only twenty-five, am more than moderately wealthy, and have most of my life ahead of me. There are wagers to be wagered, drinks to be drunk, ladies to be courted, dances to be danced. There are scores of saloons in New York in which I have yet to fall over. There are dozens of whorehouses whose ill repute I have yet to put to the test. There are oysters to be tasted, champagne to be poured, races to be run. When all these things are done, I shall probably think about taking a wife, but not before, and certainly not you.'

Kathleen Mary reached out and stroked his forehead, pushing the dark curls away from his eyes. She said, in her sorrowful Irish lilt, 'You never meant a word then. What you said about loving me, and wanting to take me away from the streets, you never meant a word of it.'

'It was meant at the time,' Collis put in. 'But you know what it's like when you're . . . happy.'

She shook her head. 'I don't. Happy's just a word as far as I'm concerned. Happy is what other people feel.'

He turned away, discomfited. 'I'm sure nobody's life is that bad. You must have some happy times.'

'In two rooms, in a building on Delancey Street they should have

burned down years ago, with a father who drinks anything from
whisky to lavender water, and a brother of thirty who can't even tie
his own shoelaces?'

'I'm sorry.'

Kathleen Mary knelt up in bed, a pale fat Aphrodite rising from
a seagreen comforter. '*You're* sorry,' she wailed, her breath all
herrings and brandy. 'Well, think how sorry *I* feel.'

Collis grimaced. He tried to get up from the bed, but Kathleen
Mary forced him to sit down again, and he was uncomfortably
aware that she was as strong as she was large, and determined, too.
He was already beginning to have visions of climbing out of the
hotel window in his Bon-Bons, his arm raised against the whipping
rain, in a futile attempt to escape from her clutches.

'You lay in my arms last night, and those were your very words.
"I love you," you said. "I want you to be my bride," you said. And
now it's morning, you're treating me cruel and offhand as can be.'

'I'm sorry,' said Collis, in a tight, strained voice. 'But I really
don't think it's any use your going on about it.'

Kathleen Mary was visibly saddened, and hurt, and she turned
away when she saw how much he really disliked her, and stood by
the half-open drapes, staring out at the dribbling raindrops that
clung to the window.

'I've no right to press you,' she said. 'It isn't your fault, what I
have to suffer.'

He sat up again, rubbing his arms. He had lost his cheroot among
the bedclothes, and he spent a minute or two trying to find it. When
he looked up again, he was surprised to see that Kathleen Mary was
weeping.

He got up from the bed, went to the window, and put his arm
around her. She sniffed, and attempted to smile bravely through her
tears. For a moment or two, they stood without speaking, while she
continued to sniff and he looked at her with those concerned eyes of
his, and outside the clouds must have begun to clear, because the
window was suddenly suffused with bright mother-of-pearl light,
and the raindrops shivered and sparkled on the glass.

'I didn't intend to hurt your feelings,' he said huskily. 'I've gotten
too hard-shelled of late, I guess, what with my family nagging so
much. Why don't you get yourself dressed, and I'll buy you some
breakfast. We can have chicken capitolade down at Sweeney's.'

She wiped her nose with the back of her wrist. 'You don't have to
feel obliged.'

11

Collis shrugged, and took down his pants from where they had been hanging like a Christmas stocking from the end of the bed. As he pulled them on, he said, 'I *do* feel obliged, as a matter of fact. I think you're most likely right, and it's time that I started paying more attention to the feelings of my fellow men and women. Apart from that, it's such damned hard work being as much of a sour-faced bastard as my father, and as much of a tyrant as my mother, and as much of an unctuous hypocrite as my sister Maude, all rolled up into one. I think it's probably easier, and less of a strain on the liver, to be pleasant.'

He reached into his pocket and took out a handful of silver dollars.

Kathleen Mary coloured and looked back at him with uncertainty. 'That's all right,' she said quietly. 'It's two dollars the night, all night, and I don't ask for any more.'

Collis picked out three dollars and handed them to her. 'There's an extra dollar by way of recompense for rudeness.'

She dropped the money into her cheap black leather reticule. Then she took her corsets from the arm of the chair, wrapped them around herself, and proceeded to lace them up, inch by inch, with increasing tightness, until her small-breasted chest was puffed out like a pigeon's, and her hips and thighs swelled out below.

'That's the worst of it over,' she said breathlessly.

Collis pulled his shirt over his head and tucked its voluminous tails into his pants. Then he went to the mirror again to tie up his floppy black necktie. His chin was unshaven and prickly, but shaving would have to wait until he got home. He raked his fingers through his hair and decided he didn't look any worse than most. Kathleen Mary meanwhile was buttoning up her corset cover and struggling into her full-skirted bottle-green dress with the small lace collar.

'Can you wait while I braid my hair?' she asked. 'I won't take more than a few minutes.'

Collis was lacing up his square-toed shoes. 'Take as long as you must. I'm in no hurry.'

Kathleen Mary took out her comb and started to twist her greasy red hair into ringlets. 'You must lose a terrible deal of money,' she said. 'That was a couple of hundred or so I saw you lose last night.'

'I didn't lose it. I spent it. I gambled it.'

'But when you wagered how many bald men would walk through

12

the door in the next ten minutes, for fifty dollars, that was hardly gambling at all. That was just throwing your money away.'

'I don't see that it matters to you,' said Collis. 'And if you really want to know, it doesn't matter to me. It's not my money. It's the price my dear father pays me to stay out of his business and out of his life. I can't throw it away fast enough.'

'But to bet on how many bald men might walk through a door, when there are families who could pay off all of their debts, and buy food like they've never eaten before, and find happiness at last, for the same amount of money, well, don't you think that's wicked?'

Collis laughed. 'You – a whore – you're talking to me of wickedness?'

Kathleen Mary stopped braiding her hair and stood straight. He could see her square, mannish face in the dim oval frame of the mirror on top of the bureau, as if a photographic portrait had come to life and was staring at him accusingly.

'Is whoring a sin when there's no other choice?' she demanded. 'How else can I feed my father? How else can I pay for the doctors my brother needs? Sin is only sin when a person has a chance to live better.'

'Is that the rationale of the streets?' asked Collis, raising a sarcastic eyebrow.

'Let me tell you something,' she said. 'When I was ten years old, I was washing carboys for the Brooklyn Chemical Company. My eyes stung and my hands burned and I earned myself just enough to bring home bread and beer every day to my father and brother, and maybe some cabbage and ribs at the end of the week. Then, when I was twelve, my father took me into his bed one morning, not because he lusted after me, but because he knew what I was going to have to do, and wanted the first time to be gentle. I walked the streets from that day forward, just as I did last night, and just as I will tomorrow.'

Collis said, 'When I promised to marry you –'

'Oh, don't worry.' She smiled. 'It happens all the time. Drunken cabbies, drunken policemen, drunken gentlemen. Perhaps I just took a shine to you, and thought that it might be true.'

He looked at the tip of his cheroot. 'I'm afraid that it can't be. I'm sorry. I must seem like a real bastard.'

'You're not really,' she told him, with that twisted little smile. 'But I still believe you're wasting yourself. You're rich, and your

13

brains are good, and yet here you are with nothing to do but drink and gamble. Don't you know how my father sits by the grate and frets for work? He's a labourer, and he longs to be out in the West, building railroads, which is his own particular calling. He longs to swing a pick, and lay down ties and rails, and yet there's no work to be had. You, though, with all of your money and all of your style, you could go out West and make yourself a fortune.'

Collis affected an expression that was even more worried than usual. 'Out West? Do you know what's *out* there?'

'It always sounds romantic to me,' she said wistfully.

'Romantic? Do you know what Daniel Webster called it?'

'Daniel Webster? He was almost a traitor, wasn't he?'

'He was the greatest doughface who ever lived, but he wasn't stupid. He said the West was nothing but savages and wild beasts, cactus and prairie dogs. You couldn't even find yourself a fresh Maine lobster out in the West, and a life without fresh Maine lobsters doesn't bear thinking about!'

He set his foot on the bed and polished the toe of his shoe with the sheet. 'No thank you,' he said. 'Your father may feel the calling to live in log cabins and eat buffalo meat and work the whole day through till the sweat pops off his brow, but that's not for me. Maybe I lost fifty dollars last night betting on how many bald men would walk into the room, but last week I won seventy dollars betting on how many ladies at dinner would eat their asparagus with their fingers, and how many would not, for fear of lewdness. So it all evens itself out.'

'I'm sorry for you,' she said, quietly.

He finished his shoes and stood tall, tugging his vest straight. But then he saw that the look in her eyes was really sorrow after all, and he felt strangely unsettled.

'You don't have to feel sorry for me,' he said uncomfortably. 'I've got everything I could possibly want.'

'That's exactly the trouble.' She smiled. 'When you've got everything, you've got everything to lose.'

'May God preserve us from tub-thumping tarts,' he said, trying to sound flippant. 'I paid the extra dollar out of courtesy, not to hear an evangelical address.'

She sighed, shrugged, and picked up her reticule. 'Perhaps you're right,' she told him. 'And anyway, it's time for breakfast.'

Collis felt oddly disturbed, as if Kathleen Mary had intruded on the privacy of his life, as if she had walked into the closed house of his head, into the fug of cigar smoke and perfume and midnight gambling clubs, and opened up a dim high skylight.

He sucked hard at his cheroot. 'I could give up gambling tomorrow,' he said. 'Give up drinking, give up going with whores. But where would that lead me? What would I do? I have a good education, I'll grant you. But success depends on ambition, and opportunity. A few people are lucky enough to have both. But I don't think I have either. I would rather pass my days amusing myself, and keeping out of mischief's way, than by trying to tempt disaster by striking out into business. I'm not cut out for it. I'm a man who wagers on bald heads and asparagus, and cats and horses and ladies' underwear besides, and nothing will change me.'

Kathleen Mary listened to these words and then gave Collis a faint smile. 'That's why I'm sorry for you, do you see?'

At that moment, there was the clatter of footsteps along the bareboard corridor outside, and someone hammered heavily on their door. 'Who is it?' cried Collis, without taking his cheroot out of his mouth or his hands out of his pockets.

'You should know who it is!' exclaimed a high, annoyed voice. 'I should think you should damn well know!'

Kathleen Mary glanced at Collis worriedly, but he simply called back, 'I haven't the faintest notion! Is it Arnold Douglas? Is it General Tom Thumb?'

'Open up this door and you'll soon see!' shouted the voice.

'I can't!' responded Collis.

'The devil you can't!' the voice called back.

'My hands are in my pockets,' said Collis, 'and they will only come out to pay my debts or shake hands with my friends. Opening hotel doors for bears with sore heads is not one of their duties.'

'Will you open this door or shall I tear it down?' demanded the voice.

Collis took his cheroot out of his mouth. 'If your stature is as short as your temper, you should be able to walk under it,' he said.

The doorhandle was rattled furiously for a while, and then they heard more footsteps outside, and muffled conversation. It sounded as if the hotel manager had been called, because after a while they heard the jangling of keys.

'Can't a fellow get some sleep?' called Collis. 'This must be the noisiest hotel in New York! Why don't you drive a coach and horses down the corridor, and have done with it?'

There was a gentler rapping, and then Collis heard the manager.

15

'Mr Edmonds, sir, I'm sorry to disturb you.'

'I should think so. Is this a hotel or a circus?'

There was an uncomfortable pause. Collis could imagine the manager, who was a small, punctilious, sensitive man, with highly polished shoes and a shock of brown brilliantined hair, grimacing with displeasure, as if he had just swallowed the slippery black neck of a steamed clam. But then the manager rapped again and said, 'There's a gentleman here who insists on seeing you, Mr Edmonds. He says he will continue to create a disturbance until you do.'

'Then let him. I haven't any wish to see anyone at this moment, particularly a hooligan who bangs on my door and shouts.'

'Mr Edmonds, it might be easier if you were to open the door for just a moment.'

'It might be easier if you all went off and left me alone.'

There was a further pause. Collis and Kathleen Mary could hear a hurried, intense, whispered conversation. Then the manager came back to the door.

'This gentleman says he is the proprietor of the Madison Saloon, sir. He says that last night, while you were visiting his establishment, you managed to break a considerable amount of glassware and bottles, sir. He says, sir, that you were dancing on his tables.'

Collis winked at Kathleen Mary. 'He says that, does he? Well, let him say what dance I was doing.'

More muffled conversation. Then: 'The polka, sir.'

'The polka? What does he think I am, a damned foreign revolutionary? He is lying in his teeth, if he has any. He is simply trying to make me pay for his own clumsiness. It was not a polka at all. It was a waltz, and a waltz never hurt anybody.'

While he was saying this, Collis was signalling to Kathleen Mary that she should open the sashed window. She didn't understand his frantic mime at first, but when he hissed at her, '*The window!*' she nodded, and went across to unfasten it. A fine drizzle was still falling, and the parapet outside was glossy and wet.

'Can't you just pay for the damage?' Kathleen Mary whispered. 'It can't be very much.'

'Of course I can,' Collis retorted. 'But it's much more entertaining to slip out from under their noses, and leave them unpaid.'

The doorhandle was rattled again, and this time it was the proprietor of the Madison who spoke. 'I'm not alone out here!' he

16

called, in his contralto voice. 'I've brought two bruisers to make sure I'm paid!'

'I'm afraid that's true, Mr Edmonds,' added the hotel manager. 'There are two gentlemen of no mean size out here.'

'What's size, compared to genius?' called out Collis, and quietly ushered Kathleen Mary to the open window. 'Climb out on to the parapet,' he told her softly, 'and keep close to the wall. You can walk along to the costume makers next door. They're bound to have their windows open – it's a hot-house in there.'

'How do you know?' Kathleen Mary asked him anxiously.

'I've done this before, my dear, more times than you can count. Now, get going, before the manager unlocks the door. It's quite safe.'

'I'm not at all sure,' said Kathleen Mary. 'It looks an awful long way down to the ground.'

'Just go, will you?' urged Collis. Behind him he could hear the manager's keys in the door.

He bent down and laced his fingers together so that Kathleen Mary could use his hands as a step. Shakily, with her green dress held up, she clambered through the open window and crouched on the parapet on her hands and knees.

'Go on!' said Collis.

'I can't,' she told him in a squeaky voice. 'I'm frightened.'

The bedroom door burst open, and there was the manager in his tailcoat, and the proprietor of the Madison Saloon, a stocky, bluff fellow with wide whiskers and extravagant eyebrows, and behind them both, looming very large, the wide shoulders and the stony, stitched-up face of a Chatham Square bruiser.

'Too late!' Collis grinned and swung out on to the parapet. 'The phantom table waltzer escapes again!'

They rushed across the room towards him, but he slammed down the sash window from the outside and pulled a grotesque, triumphant face. He turned to Kathleen Mary. 'Come on, girl,' he ordered. 'Get yourself moving.'

But Kathleen Mary was unable to move. Her fear of the height had overwhelmed her, and she was still kneeling in an inch of rainwater, her face buried in her hands, her green dress sodden and her lace bonnet already awry. Collis put out a hand and held her shoulder, firm and fat beneath the cotton dress, and he could feel her shivering uncontrollably, the shiver of total hysteria. Already behind him the window was being jerked up again, and he knew that unless Kathleen Mary could be prodded into action, he was probably in for a beating, not to mention the humiliation of having to cough up money for the Madison's broken glassware.

'Up, girl, for the love of God!' he shouted. 'They're right on our tails!'

'I can't, sir!' she panted. 'I simply can't!'

Collis glanced towards the street. It was certainly too far to try jumping, a good thirty feet down to the muddy sidewalk. He could see a cab waiting in the drizzle, the cabbie hunched and caped in canvas, and his mud-streaked horse in a similarly melancholy pose. He could see the newsboy sheltering on the corner, his newsbill flapping wetly around his waist. A policeman was sheltering, too, across the street, and passing the time of day with a portly storekeeper. All around were red-brick hotels and houses, streaked with rain and glistening in the watery daylight.

The sashed window rattled up. 'Right, sir!' said the proprietor of the Madison Saloon. 'Now we have you!'

'*Move!*' bellowed Collis to Kathleen Mary.

She reared up, the poor heavy girl, but as she did so, the window immediately ahead of her banged open, and the second bruiser popped out his head, all shaven scalp and bottle scars. She fell back in surprise and lost her footing. Collis tried to seize her, but all he caught was her dress, which tore with a loud rip. She swayed, stumbled again, reached for the low stone parapet to save herself from toppling, but her hand slipped on the wet green moss which covered it.

Collis scrabbled to reach her again, but to his horror she went over the parapet and the next thing he heard was a tremendous crack as she hit the flagged sidewalk below.

'The woman's fallen!' shouted the bruiser with the shaved head.

Collis leaned over the edge of the parapet and looked wildly down to the street. The policeman was already halfway across the muddy roadway, and people seemed to be running from all directions, their feet splashing in the puddles. He could see Kathleen Mary's white legs, and her boots, but that was all, because four or five people were already bending over her. He balanced back along the parapet and climbed back in through the open window.

The manager was waiting for him, impatient and bulging-eyed. His brilliantined hair was sticking up like a chicken's comb. All through the hotel there was the reverberation of running feet.

18

'Now you've done it, by God,' quivered the manager. 'All your damned fooling about. Now you've done it.'

Collis seized the man's necktie and pushed him back against the doorframe. He stared furiously and intently into the manager's face as if he were ready to hit him, but then he let him go without a word and walked off quickly along the landing and down the stairs. He was too shocked to think of hitting anybody. He could still see Kathleen Mary tumbling over the parapet, and still hear the resounding crack of her impact on the sidewalk.

Collis crossed the hotel lobby, with its worn patterned carpets, its sombre mahogany desk, and its smell of leaking gas. He pushed open the engraved-glass doors and stepped out into the crowd which was gathering around Kathleen Mary. The drizzle had died away altogether now, and the day was uncomfortably bright and warm.

He pushed two or three protesting bystanders out of the way, and there she was, spreadeagled on the flags, her head supported by a tapestry cushion which the hotel doorman had brought out from the lobby. A doctor was already kneeling beside her, a fat bespectacled man in a fawn vest who smelled of whisky, his brown leather bag incontinently opened to reveal an unsanitary collection of linen bandages, tongue depressors, cough candies, and red rubber tubing. He was lifting up her eyelids with his thumb, baring her white naked eyes, and trying to feel for her pulse.

'Is she dead?' asked Collis.

The doctor looked up at him with piggy eyes. 'Is she a friend of yours?' he asked sharply.

'I was there when she fell.'

'Well, she isn't dead,' said the doctor.

Collis closed his eyes for a moment. 'Thank God,' he said quietly.

'Hmph,' said the doctor. 'Considering her calling, she might have been better off dead. She struck her pelvis on the edge of the curbstone, you see, and there's no doubt that it's crushed. She won't go a-whoring again.'

'You knew her?' asked Collis.

The doctor nodded. 'She came to me regular, for babies, and for diseases. I know them all around here. Her name's Kathleen Mary Murphy. Her father's a drunken bum, and her brother's a cretin. The Lord only knows what's going to happen to them.'

Collis looked down at Kathleen Mary's abraded face. Her eyes were closed now, although she was still breathing ir rough, irregular gasps. She could have drowned, or suffocated, she looked so blue. He couldn't believe that only a few minutes before he had been joking and arguing with her, and that last night she had actually lain in his arms.

The policeman elbowed his way through the crowd and tugged at Collis's coatsleeve. His peaked cap was studded with raindrops, and the shoulders of his tightly belted uniform jacket were dark with damp. He wore muttonchop whiskers, fluffed into curls, so that his intent little eyes stared at Collis like a bird from a hedge. He said, 'I want to ask you a question or two, sir, if you'll step out of the crowd.'

Collis shook his head. 'There's nothing to say. She missed her footing and fell.'

'All the same, sir.'

Collis turned back to Kathleen Mary. For a moment he thought he saw her eyelids flutter, and he touched her forehead with his fingertips. But the doctor said, 'She's out cold. Concussed, most like. She won't wake up for a while, and that's if she wakes up at all.'

'All right,' said Collis. He stood up, watched by the jostling crowd around him. 'Do you have a card, so that I could keep in touch with you, to see how she is?'

The doctor didn't look up. 'You'd be better off forgetting about her, if you want my opinion. I mean that. Those that show an interest are admitting a liability, and the last thing a young man like you wants is a family like the Murphys around his neck for the rest of his life. Forget her. It was just one of those accidents, that's all.'

Collis hesitated for a moment, but then the policeman said, 'When you're ready, sir,' and Collis turned away from Kathleen Mary and pushed his way to the edge of the throng. The proprietor of the Madison Saloon was there, one hand rammed deep in his vest pocket, the other twiddling his moustache, and Collis couldn't remember having seen so wheat-coloured and objectionable a man in years. Behind him stood the two thugs, the broad-shouldered bruiser in a tight grey tailcoat, and his shaven-headed friend in a blue sailor's pullover. One of them was whistling between broken teeth.

'These gentlemen say they saw everything,' the policeman said to Collis. 'They saw the woman fall.'

The proprietor of the Madison gave a slanted smile. 'We'll even give evidence in court that it was all an accident, if we're so required. That's if Mr Edmonds plays fair with us.'

20

Collis looked from the saloon proprietor to the policeman, and then at the two bruisers. At the door to the Monument Hotel, the hotel manager stood watching, and he wasn't to be trusted any more than they were. So it was either a question of agreeing to pay for the Madison's breakages, and probably a little bit more besides, or of going to jail under suspicion of having pushed Kathleen Mary off the ledge, for whatever motive these scoundrels could concoct.

'Well,' said Collis, taking out his leather wallet. 'How much fair play do you think you need?'

The policeman said blandly, 'Ten dollars each will suffice for the evidence, sir, plus twenty-three dollars and eight cents for this gentleman's glassware and bottles.'

Collis, without a word, counted out seventy-five dollars in bills and handed them over. 'You can keep the change,' he said dryly.

The policeman openly shared out the money and tucked his own ten-dollar bill into the pocket of his coat. Then, tipping his cap to the proprietor of the Madison, he went across to help clear the crowds away from the black-varnished van which had just arrived to take Kathleen Mary to the hospital. Collis watched, with a feeling of emptiness and exhaustion, as she was lifted from the sidewalk, her legs swinging like an unstrung marionette's, and laid on a narrow bed inside the van's cream-painted interior.

Before they closed the van doors, the doctor waddled across to Collis, snapping shut his leather bag in a shower of tongue depressors, and held his arm. 'I want to tell you that it's no use feeling guilty,' he said. 'It's no use blaming yourself.'

Collis lowered his eyes. 'I still feel responsible,' he said hoarsely.

The doctor shrugged. 'I'm not saying you're *not* responsible. I'm just telling you that if Kathleen Mary hadn't fallen off that parapet today, she would have been knifed in the back, or worse, tomorrow. Whatever happened, this hasn't changed her fate. It's only brought it nearer.'

The doctor gave his arm a brief squeeze, and then went back to the van and climbed aboard. The door was closed, the horses geed up, and the van rumbled and splashed off across the rutted street. Gradually the crowd around the hotel began to disperse. Only Collis remained on the sidewalk, watching the van disappear around the corner; and long after it was gone, he stayed where he was, his face thoughtful and pale.

Collis lit a cheroot, smoked it for a while, then tossed it fizzing

21

into a puddle and hailed a hack. 'Seventy-two East Twenty-first Street,' he wearily instructed.

When he came down from his rooms after two hours' sleep and a shave, his father was just returning home. They met in the dark cavernous hallway, and both of them paused, Collis at the foot of the wide marble staircase and his father by the gilt umbrella stand, suspicious actors from different plays. Their butler, Angus, discreetly took off his father's light-grey spring coat, and then retired on creaking shoes.

'Good afternoon, sir,' said Collis.

His father said nothing, but took a few paces forward on the shiny stone floor and then adopted one of his favourite poses, his legs apart, his hands tucked behind his back under the tails of his coat, his head cocked in unconscious imitation of the President, James Buchanan. He was a stout, white-haired man, with a florid face and heavy white moustache. He had one eye that never quite looked straight, and which had unnerved Collis ever since he was a small boy. He wore a black tailcoat, and a black vest, across which was suspended the longest gold watch chain that Collis had ever seen, and he wore upright collars that were starched as stiff as cuttlefish shells. He walked, his father, as if he were chest-deep in water, and as if it were only his round belly that kept him buoyant. His friends on Wall Street called him the Black Ship, after the Navy's steam-propelled men-of-war; his enemies called him Porky Boy.

'How's the market?' asked Collis guardedly.

'Tolerable, tolerable,' answered his father. He kept his one good eye fixed on Collis, while the other seemed to wander around of its own accord, as if half of his mind wasn't paying attention. 'Cereals are holding their price, though silver's shaky.'

'Well, I'm glad to hear it,' said Collis.

His father remained where he was, immovable. 'I don't have to be pacified, you know,' he said, in a testy tone. 'I don't have to be *humoured.*'

Collis said nothing, but raised his eyebrows slightly, as if to suggest, 'Well, Father, that's what *you* say.'

'I sometimes wonder if you think of me as an ogre,' said his father. 'I'm not, you know. I like my fun as well as the next man.'

Collis shrugged. 'I believe you. If you think that playing

22

backgammon with all your old banker friends is fun, and if you think that entertaining rabid Southern Democrats for dinner is fun, then, sure, I believe you have fun.'

His father's eyes protruded a little, and his chins settled back into his collars like thick pink junket poured from a jug. It was a sure sign that he was displeased, and impatient, and on the very edge of being annoyed. 'You're a damn whippersnapper Yankee, that's your trouble,' he said. 'It's damn whippersnappers like you who will break up the Union. And then don't come around with your hand open, asking for your allowance, because there won't be a crust to be had.'

Collis smiled. 'I suppose you're right, sir. You usually are.'

His father tugged out a large white handkerchief and dabbed at his mouth. Then, tucking it back into his sleeve, he told Collis, 'What you need to learn, young man, is that there is no dishonour in compromise. Compromise is the watchword of an ordered life.'

'Yes, sir,' said Collis. 'Now, I do believe that Mother's waiting for you in the drawing-room.'

'Don't rush me, Collis,' retorted his father irritably. 'It's about time that you and I had a good long talk about your future, and all this political stuff and nonsense you've been flirting with.'

'Father, this is hardly the time or the place. Mother's waiting, and there are hot spiced buns with your afternoon tea. Apart from that, I'm really not in a political frame of mind at the moment. Look – if it makes you feel any better, I'll spend the rest of the day talking like a doughface.'

'I'll be damned if you'll mention that word in this house again!' shouted his father.

Collis turned away with exaggerated weariness and raised his eyes to the huge crystal chandelier which hung over the hallway, as if he were praying that it might drop suddenly on their heads and at least break the monotony of their daily arguments.

'You understand nothing,' said his father, in a tight, blustering voice. 'You don't understand where your money comes from, or what a man has to do for his country in order to earn it. You don't understand about freedom, or democracy, or the guarantees of the Constitution. You don't understand slavery, nor the God-given right of the landowner. You're a wastrel, and a parasite, and if you weren't my natural-born son, and if I didn't believe that one day you'll collect your scattered senses, I'd pay you one penny here and now and kick you out into the street.'

23

Collis tugged down his immaculate grey vest of watered silk and looked at his father with an indulgent smile.

'Yes, Father,' he said. 'I understand.'

His father stared at him for a moment with his one good eye, and Collis knew from experience how much he was boiling up inside, like a steam locomotive with its safety valve closed down. They always had this effect on each other, though, no matter how cordially their conversations began. They were both too stubborn, both too certain that they were absolutely right, not only politically and morally, but on every subject under the sun, from geography to piano-playing.

Collis's father twisted at his thick white moustache and then said, with extreme self-control, 'I see you're in no mood for rational conversation. Let's go in to tea, shall we?'

Collis nodded. 'If you don't mind eating your hot spiced buns with a Black Republican.'

'If I believed that you really were, Collis, I'd wring your neck.'

Collis, with great formality, took his father's elbow. They walked side by side along the gloomy hallway, their shoes clicking on the floors of polished brown marble, until they reached the white-painted double doors that led to the drawing-room. Through amber-tinted windows and elaborately tasselled lace drapes, the warm light of Tuesday evening sifted across the hall, and before they opened the doors, father and son looked at each other, and each was a dim portrait, like a sepia daguerreotype, a portrait grown faded with age and familiarity and vexatious argument.

'There's one thing, sir,' said Collis, his hand hesitating on the doorhandle.

His father looked away. 'I suppose you want money.'

'A hundred would do.'

'A hundred? I gave you seventy-five on Saturday.'

'Well, that's right, sir. But all this Dred Scott business is unsettling the dollar, isn't it, and it hardly buys a decent meal these days.'

Collis's father stared at his son apoplectically. He spoke in a whispering hiss, so that his mother wouldn't hear. 'You dare to ask me for more money because the Supreme Court has done what it should have done years ago, and said that a slave's a slave, and always will be? You dare to invoke the name of that darky Dred Scott to panhandle me for more allowance? You're more than flesh and blood can possibly stand!'

From within the drawing-room came a high, imperious voice. 'Is that you, Makepeace? Why are you muttering so? Come in, for pity's sake.'

Collis's father jerked up his head as if somebody had tugged his shirt-tail. 'Yes, my dear, I'm coming!' he called, reaching into his coat and handing Collis eighty-five dollars in paper and silver. 'Dred Scott,' he said under his breath, as he opened the doors and went in for his tea. Collis counted the money, then pushed it into the slant-cut pocket of his grey coat.

His mother was waiting. She did not like to wait. She was sitting upright in her accustomed chair, a stiff Louis XIV piece of exquisite fluted lines but uncompromising rigidity, her jewelled and liver-spotted hands clasped in her lap, her long neck elevated like that of an inquiring egret, her hooped skirt of coffee-coloured silks spread around her as if it were a voluminous nest on which she was hatching eggs. It was late in the year for her to have remained in the city; usually she was out in the country by now, at their farm upstate. But there had been two late parties which she had wanted to attend, and a long-running scandal which she could hardly bear to leave until fall.

'You must not mutter outside the door, Makepeace,' she said, pulling the crimson cord for the servants. 'It irritates.'

Makepeace flapped up his tails and sat down opposite her, in a rococo chair with a padded tapestry seat. 'No more irritating for you, my dear, than it was for me. Collis insisted on having a political argument in the hallway which I did not wish to bring past the door.'

Ida Edmonds peered severely at her only son, who was still standing, one hand resting on the crochet cover of the grand piano. He bowed a fraction, smiled, and said: 'Mother.' Then he went across to the gilded mirror on the opposite wall and adjusted his flamboyant grey silk necktie. She followed him with her eyes as if he had brought in something offensive on his shoe.

There was an awkward silence, but then Ida was at home with awkward silences. She thrived on the discomfiture of others, and to that end she sang in church in a high, relentless screech; gave dinner parties of crushing formality, at which the faces of the guests were usually as doleful as those of the trout; decorated the family home as if it were the Palace of Versailles, with ormolu clocks and bulging commodes and tapestry-draped tester beds and things that tinkled and chimed and whirred; and most of all held domineering court in her drawing-room, either to her fluttering lady friends in New York society, or to bored politicians, or to the occasional waxen-faced young men who came to court Maude, her daughter, and who had to sit drinking tepid tea and listening to a numbing litany of Maude's mother's virtues. 'Gaze upon the mother today,' she used to say, arching her neck, 'and you will see how the girl may flower.'

Makepeace had met Ida in Boston, at one of the Shottons' parties at Louisburg Square, in 1827, in the days when he was trying to make his fortune as a wholesaler of lobster, and as a financier of fishing fleets. She was the eighth (though not the last) daughter of a Nantucket shipping family, haughty Episcopalians, and she stood an inch taller than Makepeace and had the imperious Roman-nosed face of a daughter of the Revolution. She had demanded that he waltz with her all evening, and by the spring of 1828, to his genuine surprise, they were married.

On the invitation of a friend of Ida's father's, Makepeace liquidated his fishing interests in Boston and joined a merchant bank on Wall Street, I. P. Wolmer's. The Edmondses then bought a massive granite-faced townhouse and while Makepeace settled down to make money, Ida settled down to socialising and child-bearing. In 1832, during a hot August of cholera and dust and garbage in the streets, Collis was born, and while he lay red-faced and wrapped in baby blue in his crib, coal fires were kept constantly alight in his room to cleanse it of possible disease.

Makepeace's bank survived the Panic of 1837 with scarcely a tremble, and prospered. The Edmondses became friends with Philip Hone, the mayor; with Albert Gallatin, the Secretary of the Treasury; and with William Douglass and his daughters; and although they were never socially celestial, they were, at the very least, doughty and indispensable. It would have been unthinkable to hold a *déjeuner à la fourchette* without asking Ida.

Meanwhile little Collis was hardly an asset to the Edmondses' social aspirations. He was a tyrannical baby, crying for hours for no obvious reason, and a worse toddler. They hired a private tutor and a governess, but his pranks wore both of these worthy people down, and they resigned. They sent him to Colonel Wagstaff's Military Academy on St John's Park until he was ten years old, but he never buttoned up his tunic properly and never kept his boots clean, and on the academy's Fourth of July parade (twenty little toy soldiers strutting around the gardens with wooden rifles for the delight of their overindulgent parents) Collis wore a face of thunder and marched resolutely out of step. At the Lincoln Academy, in his adolescent years, he did no better, and played truant three or four times each month. By the time he was seventeen, his parents had despaired of him. Ida declared that he was 'God's most obstreperous creature', and Makepeace, to keep him occupied, took him into the bank.

With his own salary, and a substantial allowance to supplement it, Collis began to explore all the temptations that New York could offer him. He went to concert saloons along Broadway and drank beer and whisky until he was sick. With a crowd of young dogs from similarly wealthy families, he visited brothels on Greene Street and Mercer Street, losing his virginity the day before his eighteenth birthday to one of the 'noctivagous strumpetocracy', a hazel-eyed, well-endowed Czech girl with an extraordinary accent. He became a Broadway dandy himself, gambling on the slightest whim, smoking long cheroots, drinking at the Gem Saloon on Broadway and Worth Street, and having himself regularly shaved and barbered at Phalon's hair-cutting establishment. On the weekends, he cantered his dappled pony. Dollar, up the soft earth verges of Third Avenue, sometimes as far uptown as Fifty-seventh Street, where he would sit for a while and talk to his friends and look out over the shantytowns and rocky hills of northern Manhattan, and then he would race back downtown, sometimes tickling the horses of the street railroads with his crop for the fun of frightening the passengers. Later, he would change and take lunch at the Union Club, the only premises on which Makepeace had ever known him to behave.

'You must not persist in contradicting your father, Collis,' Ida said, stretching her neck. 'You know nothing of politics, and still less about finance. It is your own fault. You have thrown everything that I gave you to the wild winds, without a hint of gratitude.'

'Yes, Mother,' said Collis, turning around and tugging his cuffs straight. He smiled at her benignly, mainly because he knew that she couldn't abide being smiled at when she was in one of her matriarchal moods, but also because he found it hard to take her seriously.

Ida pulled a sour face, and a kind of shiver ran down her neck, but she said nothing. Instead, she pulled the cord for the servants, and within a moment or two, Lettice and Margaret appeared with silver birdcage trays set with silver teapots and Minton cups, and plates of hot raisin buns covered with fresh linen napkins. Lettice, a

27

stout girl with red cheeks and a rolling gait like a cowboy, poured out tea and handed around the cups.

'I wanted you here, Collis, for a special reason,' said Ida at length, setting down her tea.

'Oh?' Collis glanced up at his father and saw at once that his father knew what was coming. Whatever his mother wanted to say, they must have discussed it last night, before retiring to their separate bedrooms. His father coughed and almost choked on a raisin.

'I believe it is high time that you sought a bride,' Ida announced. 'Your father and I have talked the matter over at some length, and we are both of the opinion that a good woman may do something to curb your behaviour and rehabilitate you into a useful and respectable member of the polite society.'

'A *bride?*' asked Collis, incredulously.

'There would be incentives,' put in his father.

'Such as?'

'The incentive of the constant love of a well-brought-up young lady, for one,' answered Ida, in acid tones. 'The incentive of being socially acceptable, for another.'

'I'm perfectly acceptable,' declared Collis. 'In fact, I'm so acceptable that I'm almost growing impatient with myself. Even A. T. Stewart can't get into the Union Club, for all his wonderful department store, and now they want to make me a member of the Yacht Club, too.'

Ida touched her brow with her fingertips as if much more of this conversation would give her a headache. Then she said quietly, 'Whether you want to take this seriously or not, the fact remains that one day, and the sooner the better, you must learn to cope for yourself. New York has enough idlers, enough half-pay officers, enough rich bachelors, and enough waiters on Providence. It is no longer fashionable to behave like a mad dog, Collis, if it ever was. And your first step must be to marry.'

'Is it impossible to be a respectable bachelor?' asked Collis.

There was a silence. The afternoon sunshine suddenly faded from the red-and-blue curlicued carpet, from the gilded occasional tables with their marble tops and their lion's-claw feet, from the tapestry tuffets and sideboards, and from the tall mournful mirrors with their gas brackets and reflected vases of dried flowers. Although it was summer, Ida did not believe in letting the common air of the street into her home, and the room was stagnant and still.

'It appears to be impossible for *you*,' Ida said, at length. 'Although you make no mention of it, I have understood for some years that you nave been a frequenter of certain types of house off Broadway, and even of casual women who walk the streets. I must confess it makes me ill even to speak of it.'

Makepeace leaned forward in his chair. 'Collis,' he said, softly but earnestly, 'we are making a considerable effort on your behalf. I will go so far as to say that if you marry by the spring, I will buy you a house as a wedding gift. There are lots for sale on Park Avenue, at Thirty-sixth Street, and if you say the word I shall bid for one.'

Collis made a steeple of his fingers. 'That's your incentive, is it?'

'That, and I shall consider taking you back into the bank.'

'So what's the catch? Surely marriage alone won't be enough to satisfy you. I might marry one of the casual women of the streets, and then where would we be?'

Ida made a faint sound like a church hassock being knelt upon by someone stout.

'There's no catch at all,' said Collis's father, keeping his voice and his temper under reasonable control. There were bun crumbs in his whiskers. 'All I would say is that we have already made some preliminary inquiries of the young lady in question.'

Collis stared at him, then at his mother.

'You've already selected my bride?'

Makepeace flushed slightly.

'You've already gone out, like two drovers, and roped me in a cow?'

'She is not a cow!' Ida said breathlessly. 'She does not resemble a cow in the slightest!'

'We considered it best,' Makepeace added. 'Since your behaviour didn't appear to be conducive to choosing a respectable young lady by yourself, we took the liberty of doing it for you. And, I must say, she is quite charming.'

Collis buried his face in his hands for a few moments, then let out a loud smothered laugh, sitting up straight in his chair.

'What wonderful parents!' he told them, looking from Ida to Makepeace and back again. 'All my life you have begrudged me affection and understanding, and now, without warning, you are conscientiously taking it upon yourselves to direct the future course of my personal happiness.'

Ida, with hooded eyes, glared back at her son in displeasure. 'You will not lower yourself by employing such cheap sarcasm,' she said. 'It offends.'

'Haven't you considered that your interference into my personal affairs also offends? Haven't you considered that I might care to choose a bride of my own? A girl I love, and actually know?'

'Collis!' bellowed his father. 'This is quite enough!'

He realised how loudly he'd shouted, and was flustered for a second, knowing that the servants would be listening raptly at the doors; but then he raised his whiskery face and glared at Collis with his one controllable eye.

'The girl I wish you to marry is Delphine Spooner.'

'Delphine Spooner? Four feet eleven, with arms like salamis?'

'Don't be so damned impertinent! I wish you to marry her!' snapped Makepeace. 'I wish it!'

Collis stared at his father, and then his mother, and stood up. 'Sir,' he said to his father, 'I find you transparent. I know what Delphine Spooner is, and that is the daughter of George Spooner, of the Ohio Life and Mutual Trust Company. I also happen to know that you have been trying for nearly six months to ally your own interests with those of Ohio Life.'

Makepeace's moustaches twitched. 'What of it?' he demanded.

'What of it?' said Collis. 'I'll tell you what of it! I refuse to be married off to an ugly dumpling for the convenience of your business and for the preservation of Mother's social sensitivities! Not for a hundred partnerships in your seedy bank, and not for all the vacant lots of any avenue you care to mention! As for you, Mother! "The constant love of a well-brought-up young lady, indeed!" All you ever think about, my dear, is your constant love of yourself!'

Makepeace jumped to his feet, all five feet four of him. 'Apologise!' he roared. 'Apologise, or so help me I'll pay you one penny and kick you out in the street!'

Collis stood there rigidly, his jaw clenched tight and his fingers digging into the palms of his hands. His mother was white, white as her Brussels lace cap or the globes of the gaslights. His father's furious panting was the only sound in the room, apart from the chatty ticking of a gilded clock.

'I'm sorry,' Collis said eventually. 'I lost my temper. That was unforgivable. Please accept my apologies.'

Ida patted at her eyes with her handkerchief, as if she had been mortally grieved.

'I suggest you withdraw to your rooms, Collis, and think about what we've discussed,' Makepeace said. 'I also suggest that you consider your future carefully, because if you fail to marry, I shall have to withdraw your allowances. I am not prepared to keep you for very much longer, especially in the style in which you care to live.'

Collis looked at him. 'I see,' he replied gently.

'I trust you do. Now, I think it best if you leave your mother and myself alone.'

Collis gave his mother a small bow and nodded to his father. Then he quickly crossed the room, opening the double doors so smartly that he surprised Lettice and Margaret in the middle of their eavesdropping. Both girls stared at him as he passed by and strode along the hallway to the stairs. His face was engraved with anger.

It was later that evening, not long before he went out, that his father came to his rooms and they talked, fatefully, of lobsters.

Collis had three rooms on the second floor of the house, facing south. One was a bedroom, with a carved light-oak bed, and pale-blue wallpaper. The second was a private bathroom, with a white enamelled tub in a walnut surround, a marble washbasin, and a tubular shower, one of three recently installed and connected to the Croton Reservoir, despite Ida's initial fears that the water was teeming with tadpoles and that after she had bathed in it bullfrogs would grow in her womb. The third room was a study of sorts, with a leather settee, and a leather armchair, and a writing desk, and it was here that Collis was sitting, in his black vest and shirtsleeves, idly smoking and reading a copy of the *Evening Post*, when his father knocked and diffidently stepped in through the door.

'Collis,' he said in his hoarse voice.

Collis turned the page of his newspaper. The smoke from his cheroot rose lazily up to the gas-light, and then swirled around in the heat from the incandescent mantles.

'I'm sorry, sir. I'm just going out for the evening. Urgent appointments.'

Makepeace came across the room and stood over his son, his hands on his hips. He was wearing a blue silk smoking robe, tied around his portly waist, and a matching blue silk hat, like a fez, with a black tassel dangling from it. It was going to be an evening at home, playing checkers with Maude, and listening to Ida's ceaseless tides of self-exaltation.

31

'Collis, in spite of our disagreements, I want you to know that I still regard you fondly.'

Collis looked up. His father smelled slightly of brandy, and he suspected that the old man must have had a quiet nip before coming upstairs. 'Did Mother send you?' he asked.

A muscle tightened in his father's whiskery cheek. Then Makepeace shook his head and said indistinctly, 'No.'

'Why don't you sit down?' asked Collis. 'It's your house, after all. I'm just the temporary lodger.'

'You mustn't take it to heart, Collis.'

'Why not? It appears that my tenancy lasts only as long as my willingness to marry a short fat girl, and what else does that make me, if not a lodger?'

Makepeace sat heavily down in the leather armchair and regarded his son with what Collis could see was a considerable measure of sadness. It was nine o'clock now, and it was growing dusky outside, and Makepeace was tired after his day on Wall Street, and less inclined to bluster. He took off his blue fez. The gaslight gleamed on his bald patch, and shadows masked his eyes.

'I suppose you think I'm an unscrupulous old man,' he said.

Collis shrugged. 'I don't know what to think.'

'Well,' said his father, rubbing his eyes, 'I suppose it's true that if you married Delphine, it would suit my business purposes well. It would certainly suit your mother. But whatever you believe, those weren't our first considerations when we thought of her.'

Collis went to the window and stood with his back to his father, looking out over the twilit width of East Twenty-first Street, and across towards Gramercy Park, where the gaslights twinkled behind the breeze-blown trees. It was a warm, sultry evening, with a feeling of more summer rain, and he was looking forward to a cold beer at the Gem, and then dinner at Delmonico's with his friend Henry Browne. After that – who knew where lust and inebriation would take him? He had tried to suppress the memory of last night, and this morning, and Kathleen Mary's fall from the parapet. The doctor had advised him not to mourn her, not to get involved, and to the best of his ability, he hadn't. But he had decided that he would visit a regular whorehouse tonight. Iris's or Madame Morris's, on Greene Street, and that he would leave the ladies of the streets alone. Particularly the Irish ones, or the ones who called, "Come home with me, sir," with too much anxiety in their eyes. He knew that Kathleen Mary had stirred his conscience, and altered his feelings about himself, although he wasn't sure exactly how.

His father said, 'Your mother and I may not express our feelings exactly right at times, but we both feel concern for your future. We shall be dead some day, you know, and what will you do, then?'

'I expect I shall survive. I shall have to.'

'The wretches of Gotham Court *survive*, Collis. The drunks and the sluts of the Five Points *survive*. But we wish you more than survival. We wish you to build upon the prosperity that I have created throughout my years of work, to work hard yourself, and to become wealthier still.'

'Nobody makes his fortune through hard work these days,' Collis answered. 'Not the way that you did with your fishing fleets. A fellow has to gamble on the stock market these days, or on railroad bonds, or faro. It's all risk, and has nothing to do with effort.'

Makepeace shook his head. 'You're misguided, do you know that? You don't understand how much wealth this nation still possesses, untapped and unexploited. I myself went for one particular resource – lobsters – and I made my first hundred thousand from lobsters. But there is still gold, and silver, and land itself, and all the plants that can be grown on the land and all the animals that can be fed off those plants. There's money out there, Collis – it's just waiting to be fished out of the sea, or dug up from the soil.'

'Very philosophical,' said Collis.

'It's not philosophy, it's *fact*, and the only reason you're sitting on your backside bemoaning your lot is that you've never had the gumption to go see for yourself. I'm a doughface, am I? Well, maybe I damn well am. Maybe I was fishing up thirty-pound lobsters off Maine before you were born, or even thought of, and maybe I'd like to see the Union stay together so that my Southern bills are paid and my Southern investments are safe. What I have, I worked for by my own sweat, and I'll remind you that every morsel of food you eat in this house, and every stick of furniture you sit upon, was paid for by Southern money, and by my own efforts.'

Collis set his cheroot on the edge of a silver ashtray and blew out a last funnel of blue smoke.

'Father,' he said, 'your rhetoric is as overblown as your facts. The day I see a thirty-pound lobster, I shall drop to my knees and beg your forgiveness for doubting you, but until then, I think I shall feel entitled to reserve my judgement. Thirty pounds! A lobster like that could break your leg with one claw!'

Makepeace pulled at his whiskers. 'There are thirty-pound lobsters off Maine, and bigger. I've seen beasts with such claws as would each feed a family of five, and still leave meat enough for patties the following day!'

'Thirty pounds? You're not joking?'

'As big as this,' said Makepeace, stretching his arms out. 'So big they had to be held down by two men, and boiled to death in my partner's wash-house boiler, along with the shirt fronts!'

Collis couldn't resist laughing. 'I wish I'd been there,' he said. 'The sight of you struggling with a thirty-pound lobster would have made my whole life worthwhile.'

'Don't be so damned impertinent,' said his father, but almost benignly. 'Those were hard days, and hard times, and there were none of the conveniences you expect today, like gaslight, and lead plumbing. You should be grateful, you young beggar, because if it weren't for those lobsters, and if it weren't for my training in them, you'd be the poorest soul in New York, and you wouldn't have a pair of shoes to take you up Third Avenue, let alone a horse.'

Collis sat down and looked across at his father seriously, his hands clasped on his lap and his legs crossed. The trouble was, he knew that his father was often right, and that it was time for him to learn how to support himself. These days, in spite of the speculative boom in gold and railroads and real estate, the price of keeping a good house was increasing almost monthly, and the time was going to come when he was going to have to support himself, his wife if he took one, and children if he had any, as well as servants, and horses, and carriages, at a respectable address.

'Father, let me ask you a question.'

'About lobsters?'

'About Delphine.'

'Well, of course. She's a fine girl, you know. A girl of excellent education. And she has a sense of humour, too, which is rare enough in women.'

'You can spare me the eulogies,' Collis said. 'What I want to know is, has she been told that I fancy her?'

'Of course not. I have *some* sense of propriety.'

'In that case, would it interfere too gravely with your carefully prepared schemes if I were to meet her, and have the opportunity of

34

making her acquaintance more thoroughly? All I happen to know about her at the moment is that she is decidedly ample, though short, and that her family paid fifteen hundred dollars for a pew at Grace Church, which strikes me as needless extravagance.'

His father sniffed and looked across. 'You can see her, of course. But you don't have to make it sound as if you're doing us a favour,' he said.

'Why not?' asked Collis. 'I *am*. I would far rather not meet her at all. But I am trying to be sensible, by your lights at least, and to be accommodating. One eye on the future, don't you know? So why don't you talk to your friend George Spooner and ask if Delphine and I might accidentally on purpose encounter each other at a dance, or a lunch, or something of the sort.'

'You mean it?' asked Makepeace. 'You're at least prepared to try?'

Collis shrugged. 'Why not? I have nothing to lose, even if I don't have very much to gain.'

'You have your mother's approbation to gain.'

'That's exactly what I mean.'

Before Makepeace had the chance to make a retort, there was another rap at the door, and Maude appeared, Collis's sister. She was a tall girl for the times, at least five feet five, with a round pudgy face and unnaturally high colouring in her cheeks. This evening she wore a plain gown of unpleasant buff, with a citrine brooch and sleeves that were too tight for her, and an expression to match.

'Father and I were discussing lobsters,' said Collis, leaning back on the settee to look up at her. 'He says that off Maine there are monsters of thirty pounds or more, and we were trying to decide whether one of them could take your head off with one pinch.'

'Don't be repulsive,' said Maude. 'Father, the checker board is ready, and Mother has asked Angus to pour you a glass of sherry wine.'

'Thank you, Maude,' answered Makepeace, a little heavily.

Collis got to his feet. 'Well,' he said, 'since you two have decided on an evening of debauchery, with checkers and the demon drink, I suppose I'd better get me gone to my chapel meeting, so that I can pray for your souls.'

He took a cab downtown, sitting back on the leather-upholstered seat as it rolled noisily over the ruts of Broadway. The cabby was of the fat, greasy-vested, uncommunicative sort. and sat with his shoulders hunched, twitching his whip at his horse's ears as if it irritated him somehow to see a horse with ears, but as if he couldn't stir himself to do very much about it. These days, many of the cabbies were Armenian or Irish, and didn't know the streets of New York any better than the day they had first stepped off the boat, let alone enough English to be able to understand where one wanted to go. But the jam of traffic jostling its way downtown carried the hansom along with it, whether the cabby wanted to go in that direction or not, and that suited Collis, as far as it went.

It was a warm, overcast night, and the rain had held off, so Broadway was thicketed with cabs and stagecoaches and carriages, and the sidewalks were teeming with people. Outside the marble portico of the St Nicholas Hotel, along the gas-lit frontage, from a confusion of coaches with silk-hatted coachmen and well-brushed horses, the fashionable and the well-to-do were alighting for a charity dinner, and then parading two by two into the glittering marble hallway, between settees of tiger and leopard and zebra skins, as if they were the most graceful of creatures admitted to the most elegant of arks.

The night smelled of perfume and gas; of brick dust and horse manure and decaying garbage; a sweetish, sourish, distinctive odour which was at its strongest at this time of year, when food rotted quickly and the sewers were full. Collis barely noticed it, but he did take out his handkerchief to cover his nose and mouth as the cab was halted by a jam of coaches on the corner of Walker Street, where Broadway was obstructed by uprooted flagstones and builder's rubble, because two dead dogs lay in the gutter, awaiting collection by the dead-animal man, and the warmth of the evening made them stunningly high.

They arrived at last outside the Broadway Theatre, and Collis climbed down from the hansom and paid the driver thirty cents. Then, tugging his grey silk vest straight and setting his black silk top hat slightly back on his head, which these days was considered the rakish way of wearing it, he walked through brass-and-mahogany doors to the Gem Saloon. It wasn't crowded yet, as it would become later in the evening, but already one or two of his cronies were there, leaning up against the far end of the bar, next to the elaborately decorated and curtained dining booths. The smoke was thick and the conversation was loud and cheerful.

The Gem Saloon was high-ceilinged, with a polished floor of

checkered marble, and a fine long bar, carved with satyrs and cupids in bas-relief. Behind the white-jacketed backs of the barkeepers, reflecting the gas standards and the jugs and the bottles, and the clientele themselves, was the largest mirror in the whole of New York City, framed in convoluted gilt and crested by a mean-looking eagle. The Gem was still one of the most fashionable bars for young gentlemen and for aspiring New York politicians, although the Tammany hierarchy didn't frequent it as often as they once used to, now that prohibition was becoming an increasingly sensitive issue.

Henry Browne was drinking old-fashioneds and telling a long story about a talking dog. 'Collis!' he called. 'Come and join us! What a fortuitous arrival!'

Jack De Veeart of the coffee-importing De Veearts was there, a ruddy young man whose neckties looked as if they were going to strangle him; and Lewis Dunlop, who had big ears and was often dull-witted, but who was rich, through the grace of his commodity-dealing father, beyond almost all comparison. Henry Browne was older than all of them, twenty-six, and far more self-assured. He had joined the army as a lieutenant, but there had been a marginally scandalous affair involving a colonel and his wife, and he had discreetly left the service, with official approval, after only three years. Subsequently, he had studied for two years, at New York University, though quite what he had studied he claimed he could never recall. He was tall and broad-shouldered, with a head of curly light-brown hair, and Collis always felt about him that he would be a good friend to have around in a fight.

Jimmy the barkeeper asked, 'Mr Edmonds? What will you take, sir?'

'A draught beer, please, and the sooner the better,' said Collis. 'It's as warm as a street sweeper's armpit out there.'

Jimmy took a porter glass out of its bed of ice and poured Collis a beer. Collis drank it gratefully, wiped his mouth, and then set the glass on the bar. Jack De Veeart inquired, 'Better? Back in the land of the living and breathing?'

Collis nodded. 'Good,' said Jack. 'Now Henry can carry on with his story.'

'Ah,' said Henry. 'That was what was so fortuitous about Collis's arrival. I've forgotten the end of the story. I know it was something to do with the dog saying, "You'd walk like this too, if you had four legs," but that's all I can remember.'

'The man's incorrigible,' complained Lewis Dunlop. 'He can never, ever, recall how his stories wind up. It's too damned frustrating for words.'

'Well, it's interesting that you should mention frustrating,' said Henry, 'because an acquaintance of mine mentioned today that a new whorehouse has opened its doors on Leonard Street, and apparently it puts on a very piquant exhibition. I thought after Delmonico's we might wander that way, and see what we can see.'

'That sounds fair,' agreed Lewis. 'By the way, Collis, how did you get on with your latest Gorgon last night? There was a red-headed horror, and no mistake!'

Jack laughed. 'He's quite right, Coll. You do have the most appalling taste in ladies, when you're tiddly. Was she good, being so ugly, or were you too drunk to mind?'

'She was good-natured, in her way,' Collis told them, with unexpected seriousness. 'I don't suppose she ever had the chance in her life to do anything grand, or even anything worthwhile. But she was a thoughtful girl, and I believe that if anyone said that of me, I wouldn't half object.'

Henry lifted one of his shaggy light-brown eyebrows. 'That sounds like an epitaph, my dear boy. You really shouldn't be so sad about a lady of the streets, particularly a lady of the streets who could have gone twenty rounds with the best middleweight in the nation, and won.'

Lewis and Jack laughed, and Jack slapped Collis on the back. Collis sipped a little more beer and tried to look amused.

Henry noticed his expression. 'There's definitely something wrong,' he said. 'You're not yourself.'

'He's all right,' said Lewis. 'If this whorehouse show is anything you say it is, and if Delmonico's is putting on its peppered steak, then we'll soon have him back to normal.'

'No, no,' remarked Henry. 'It's more than that. I detect a thoughtfulness, a silent introspection. What's amiss, Collis? I know it's something.'

Collis shrugged. 'There was an accident this morning. I took the girl to the Monument, you see, because it was nearest, and because they know me there; but in the morning, when I woke up, there were two pugilists at the door, as well as the manager from the Madison Saloon.'

'Oh my God,' said Jack. 'I suppose he wanted paying for the glasses we broke.'

Collis nodded. 'I tried to do my usual, and duck out of the window, but this silly girl didn't manage it, and slipped. She fell three floors.'

'Was she killed?' asked Lewis, with a frown.

'I don't think so. They brought a doctor, and he said her hips were crushed. He told me to forget about it. He said it wasn't my fault, and even if it was, I shouldn't admit any guilt. He said that girls like that are bound to die anyway before their time, and that the worst I'd done was hasten her finish.'

'A sensible man,' commented Jack. 'Most people would have screwed you for ten dollars to keep quiet about it.'

'Most of them did. The manager of the Madison, and the manager of the Monument, and the local officer.'

'So it cost you a pretty penny, last night, as well as your good humour?' asked Henry.

Collis finished his beer and asked Jimmy for a stone fence. 'It's made me think about myself, if that's what you mean, and what I am, and where my money comes from.'

'Money comes from parents,' said Jack. 'It's a known biological fact.'

Collis watched absent-mindedly as Jimmy poured two ounces of bourbon into a tall, frosted glass, clattered in a spoonful of ice cubes, and then topped it up with cider. He said, without looking up at his friends, 'This was almost the first time I've ever thought of a whore as a real person, I guess. When she was lying on the sidewalk, all broken and bruised like that, she wasn't trying to do anything but survive, as all people must.'

'I hope you're not going to be morbid all evening,' said Lewis. 'If you are, then I suggest we cancel the restaurant, and forget about Leonard Street, and go to the cemetery and read the inscriptions on the gravestones until we all feel better.'

'No, I don't think I'm morbid,' Collis told him with a faint smile. 'I just think I'm taking stock of myself. I suppose my father prompted me, too, when we talked this afternoon.'

'Does your father know about the girl?' asked Henry.

'No. You're the first people I've mentioned it to.'

'Then I should make sure it stays that way. To frequent the brothels is one thing, but to let it be *known* that you do is quite another. I quite expect that one half of the Union Club has the clap and that the other half is doing its best to contract it, but in the best society these things are always better left unsaid. And as for letting 'whores fall out of hotel windows . . . well, that does smack of uncaring libertinism, don't you think?'

'Henry,' said Collis, raising his glass, 'I drink to your sense of social delicacy. But there is one thing more.'

'You let another whore fall out of another window?' inquired Jack.

'It's bad enough dodging the slates and the bricks from the demolition work,' put in Lewis.

'No, no,' Collis told them. 'It's what my father broached with me this afternoon. He said he had found me a young lady. Arranged a betrothal, as it were. He is desperately keen to see me married and respectable – or, at the very least, married and apparently respectable.'

Collis blew smoke. 'This is what they call a marriage of convenience, although it seems to be for everyone's convenience except my own. The girl he wants me to marry is Delphine Spooner, who is the daughter of George Spooner, of Ohio Life and Mutual. And guess which Wall Street finance company is interested in joint speculative investments with Ohio Life and Mutual? No prizes for the right solution.'

'Delphine Spooner,' said Jack thoughtfully. 'I met her once at a birthday party, out at Astoria, Long Island. Quite pretty, if I remember, but very, er, *petite*.'

'I've only seen her a couple of times,' said Collis, 'but I remember her arms were unbecoming. Plump, if you know what I mean.'

'Well, that settles it,' said Jack. 'You can't marry a girl with plump arms.'

'Quite right,' said Henry. 'And supposing you don't even like the young lady when you meet her? What then? I really think you're going to have to make a stand here, young Collis. Is a man's destiny his own, or not? You hold our collective fate in your hands.'

'I've already agreed to meet her,' said Collis. 'I'm not entirely sure why, although I guess it has a lot to do with money. I know my father would cut down my allowance if I annoyed him. He might even cut it off altogether. But that isn't the whole reason. Maybe that business with Kathleen Mary this morning made me think twice. Maybe it's time I *was* respectable.'

'Hallelujah,' said Jack. 'The scales have fallen from his eyes. He has been converted to the one true faith, which is to honour thy father and thy mother, marry a virgin, and if at all possible, live no further north than Fourteenth Street.'

'I really don't know what's the matter with you, Collis,' said Lewis. 'I always thought you were a man of the world. A dashing figure. And here you are, considering wedlock with a very drab young lady. It's inadmissible!'

Henry raised a hand to Jimmy, to indicate that they were all ready for another round of drinks. It was growing noisy and bright and hot in the saloon now, as pre-theatre crowds pressed in for a quick beer or whisky before the shows started. Just as Jimmy slid over fresh glasses for them, a tall, sallow young man in a showy silk vest and hyacinthine whiskers came pushing his way through the throng of black top hats and starched white shirt fronts and shook them all by the hand as if he hadn't seen them for seven years.

'I'm so pleased I bumped into you,' he said, blinking his brown, bulging eyes. 'I was thinking of a couple of hours' faro this evening, if you were in the mood.'

'Have a drink, Nathan,' said Henry. 'At the moment we're deciding whether we're in the mood for a wedding or a funeral, or maybe both.'

Nathan Hackett looked from Henry to Collis, and then to Jack and Lewis, and his smile slowly faded. He was the son of Colonel Walter Hackett, who was president of innumerable banks and funds and trusts, but was probably better known for his love of polo and cards and women. Colonel Hackett's only legitimate offspring, Nathan had inherited all of his madcap enjoyment of wagering and gambling; and although Collis considered himself a sharp faro player and a risky kind of a betting man, he knew that Nathan unquestionably had the edge on him. It was Nathan who the previous night had bet on the matter of the bald heads.

'You're welcome to join us,' said Collis. 'I'm afraid I was just starting the evening with some reflective thoughts, and I've made us all miserable. I've had one of those days when you don't know whether to do away with yourself by drowning, which might take the press out of your clothes, or by taking poison, which might disagree with your luncheon.'

'We're going to Delmonico's,' put in Henry. 'And then we're off to Leonard Street to enjoy a slightly exotic entertainment.'

Nathan took his pocket watch out of his vest and peered at it. 'I have to meet the Rodgerses at White's Restaurant,' he said. 'But once that chore's over, I'll come down to Delmonico's and join you.

You know the way the Rodgerses eat. Like lions at the zoo. It should all be devoured in a half-hour.'

'I bet you five dollars they'll take longer,' Collis said.

Nathan grasped his hand. 'Done! Now, I must be off. I'm late already.'

'No force-feeding, mind,' said Jack. 'We don't want you to win this wager by propping open poor old Dorothy Rodgers's mouth with a salt cellar and pouring the soup straight down her gullet.'

Nathan raised his hands as if to protest his innocent intentions and then pushed his way back through the crowd. Henry turned to Collis and remarked, 'Well, that seems to have cheered you up. There's nothing like a wager, I always say. It's almost as exhilarating as getting drunk. How about another stone fence before we go to the restaurant?'

They gathered in the colonnaded porch of the grey Federal house on Leonard Street, under a twinkling red lamp. Nathan Hackett had joined them in time for the coffee and brandy at Delmonico's, and had silently tucked a five-dollar bill into Collis's pocket. Apparently, Mr Rodgers had been to his dentist on Bond Street that morning and his usual gobbling had been slowed to a painful, measured mastication of every bite.

Red lights shone on almost every other house on Leonard Street, and the sidewalks were busy with opera-hatted, bewhiskered gentlemen, many of whom, like Collis and his friends, had walked over from Broadway to complete their evening's entertainment at 'ladies' boardinghouses'. There were shouts and guffaws and drunken laughter, and down at the Broadway end of the street, a street musician was playing the banjo while a scraggly monkey hopped and danced on the end of a chain at his feet.

Henry Browne knocked at the 'boardinghouse' door, and after a while it was opened. The five friends trooped quietly inside, into a red-draped hallway decorated with plush wallpapers and furnished with rococo hallstands in a style that Collis called 'early gin palace'. The door was closed and secured behind them, and their doorman, a tall Negro in a powdered wig and the uniform of an eighteenth-century flunky, offered to take their hats and their canes. From a doorway at the far end of the hall, also draped with tasselled curtains, they could hear flute and cello music, and a sudden spattering of applause.

42

'I'm told this show is splendid,' said Henry, taking out a pair of small spectacles from a blue velvet case and propping them on the bridge of his nose. 'Just the thing after rosemaryed mutton and raspberry ices. Just the thing to put you in the mood.'

'Who's paying?' asked Lewis.

'My treat,' said Collis. 'For the performance, at least. Your lady is your own choice, and for her you can stump up for yourself.'

'That's only because you invariably choose the cheapest,' Jack ribbed him.

Collis pulled a face. 'I pay in other ways, I assure you. I had one devil of a hangover this morning, apart from all the other tribulations.'

Nathan said, 'I bet you my five dollars back that I can pick an uglier girl than you.'

'Done,' said Collis, 'although I'm damned if I know why.'

At that moment, the drapes over the far door parted and a young girl emerged, very pretty and delicate, with dark ringlets and made-up eyes, and wearing nothing more than a pale-blue Empire-style dress of sheerest lawn, through which it was possible to see a host of alluring curves and shadows. 'My name is Gemima,' she said, beckoning. 'Would you come this way, gentlemen, and be seated?'

Henry winked. 'What did I tell you? It looks all very toothsome indeed.'

Collis gave him a wry grin.

Gemima led them through the drapes and then along a shadowy passage to an oak door. The music was louder now, and they could hear the gruff voices of men calling out ribald encouragement. Gemima opened the door and ushered them into a small partitioned-off room, like a private box at the theatre. It was furnished with club armchairs upholstered in purple velvet, and there was a small marble-topped table on which a magnum of French champagne was chilling in an ice bucket.

The front of the box was hung with heavy, dark drapes, so that the occupants were shadowed from the view of other boxes. There must have been five or six boxes altogether around the main room, and each gave its guests an unobstructed view of a scarlet-covered daybed, brightly illuminated by a gas bracket, and of three young lady musicians, all scantily dressed in Grecian-style tunics, who sat on upright chairs beside the daybed with a cello and a flute and a violin.

43

An exhibition nas just finished,' said Gemima in a soft whisper. 'Please sit down, and another will start directly.'

Collis sat at the front, by the polished mahogany rail, and Nathan Hackett sat beside him. While the others drew up their chairs, Gemima poured the champagne for them in tall cold glasses, and they toasted her, with quiet appreciation, before she bowed and left them, closing the door. The girl musicians started to scrape out an uneven version of 'Nymphs and Shepherds, Come Away', but the audience, who were already turning the air grey with cigar smoke, were not overly critical, particularly of the young black-haired cellist, who had to sit with her legs wide apart.

'I must say I like that violinist,' said Collis. 'Now, she's quite fair.'

Nathan touched his knee. 'Just remember our wager. The uglier you pick 'em tonight, the more likely you are to win. So you can forget the fair ones.'

Collis sipped his champagne and sighed. 'I suppose you're right. If I don't marry Delphine, and Father cuts off my money, I'm going to need every dollar I can win.'

'You could always work,' Henry pointed out. 'There are some professions that a young fellow like you could go into without disgrace. I hear that being a speculator in railroad bonds is an amusing way to pass the time.'

'Father believes I should exploit the resources of the earth and the ocean. He made his first hundred thousand from lobsters, and I suppose he believes that what was good enough for him is easily good enough for me.'

'How the devil do you make a hundred thousand from lobsters?' asked Jack. 'Do you send them begging letters, or what?'

Collis coughed. 'You have to bring them up from the bed of the sea, and boil them. That's all. But it all sounds like too much hard work to me. Father said they often caught thirty-pounders, which took two men to hold down, and five hours to boil.'

Henry raised an eyebrow. 'The nearest I've ever seen to a thirty-pound lobster is Isaac Singer, that sewing-machine fellow.'

Nathan Hackett frowned. 'And I've never seen a thirty-pound lobster at all. My dear fellow, a thirty-pound lobster would be the size of a small boy. If you ask me, your dear father's been pulling your leg.'

'He said it was true,' retorted Collis. 'And if he said it was true then it was.'

'Well,' said Nathan, leaning back in his armchair, 'I hate to dispute his word. But if you can find me a thirty-pound lobster, and set it on a plate in front of me, then I will pay you a hundred dollars.'

'Two hundred,' said Collis intently.

Nathan glanced at Henry. 'Young Collis is getting riled up, don't you think, Henry? I didn't think he was on speaking terms with his dear father, let alone ready to fight on his behalf.'

He turned to Collis, smiled, and said, 'Three hundred.'

Collis put out his hand, and they settled the wager with a firm shake.

'I'll have one of those monsters snapping its claws at you within the next six weeks,' he promised. 'Then you can eat your words, and your wager besides.'

Nathan smiled and shrugged. 'I'll believe it when I see it. That's all I can say.'

'Quiet, you two,' said Henry. 'I believe the exhibition's starting.'

'About time too,' grumbled Lewis. 'A fellow can grow weary of "Nymphs and Shepherds", even when it's played in the altogether.'

The three girl musicians faltered into silence, and then an imposing-looking woman, fiftyish and grey-haired, in a sparkling turban and a peacock-blue gown, came out from behind the drapes and stood by the daybed, smiling and nodding in the gaslight.

'Gentlemen, we're so pleased that you're here tonight. I am Mrs Netta de La Paige, and these talented young ladies are my orchestra, the Nightingales. In a moment, I wish to present to you one of the most artistic and instructive of exhibitions, which will feature my Nubian artiste Cornelia and my Aryan artiste Henrietta, together with one of the most magnificent of male physical specimens, the Mighty Marmaduke.'

The Nightingales raised their instruments and began assiduously to scrape and tootle at 'In a Monastery Garden', which caused Jack to guffaw loudly. Then the drapes parted again and out into the circle of light danced a statuesque blonde girl, wound with flowing translucent scarves. By her height and the breadth of her shoulders, Collis guessed she was probably Swedish or Finnish. Her hair was cropped into close curls, and she had the kind of clear-eyed, straight-nosed face that he remembered from illustrations to stories of the Norse gods.

She danced and twirled around the room, pirouetting from box to box, and curtsying coquettishly in front of each. Collis raised his hands and applauded her as she came past his box, and she lowered her shiny green-painted eyelids and ran the tip of her tongue across her bared teeth.

'She likes you, damn it!' Nathan Hackett laughed. 'I swear to God she likes you!'

The blonde girl, having completed her provocative tour of the boxes, arranged herself on the red daybed. Now the three-piece orchestra clumsily changed its tune, this time to some pastiche of an oriental melody, complete with tinkling finger cymbals from the flautist. Out of the drapes, to rough shouts of pleasure and amazement, emerged a Negro girl, as tall as the blonde, wearing nothing but a triangular loincloth of gold coins linked together. Her skin was densely black, as blue-black as writing ink, and her hair had been wound into curling snakes and wrapped with gold leaf. She was slant-eyed and big-lipped and mesmerisingly sensual, and Collis found it was impossible to take his eyes away from her. She swayed past them, snarling at them with her wide white teeth and leaving behind her a musky, arousing perfume.

'Now for the Mighty Marmaduke,' said Nathan. 'I bet you he can't manage both ladies in the next fifteen minutes.'

'Five dollars?' asked Collis.

They shook hands.

The cellist drew her bow across her instrument in a deafening discord. Then the curtains were thrown aside and out stalked a muscular, curly-headed man, six feet two at least, in a leopard-skin costume and black leather knee boots. His face was rugged as a cliff, with a huge shaggy moustache, but it was the prominent bulge in his costume that drew most attention. He could have been an out-of-work actor, or an Irish road-digger, or anything at all, but he walked around the room with an air of arrogance and brutish superiority, because he knew that not one of the gentlemen who were watching him had anything to match, no matter how wealthy they were.

Collis couldn't take his eyes away from the bright-lit circle in the centre of the room as the two girls slunk from the daybed and curled themselves around the shins of the Mighty Marmaduke. Then the blonde girl shed her scarves, one by one.

At that moment, the room was quite hushed, and even the lady instrumentalists put down flute and cello and violin. The Mighty Marmaduke disdainfully released the cords which stayed his costume, and it peeled downward from his broad, coarse-haired chest, until the black girl seized it and tugged it right to his knees. There was another cello chord, and the Mighty Marmaduke stood magnificently revealed.

Henry and Nathan clapped loudly, and Henry even whistled between his teeth, but Collis found himself strangely disinclined to applaud. He was stimulated by what was happening before him, he admitted that much. But somehow the stimulation seemed unconvincing, as if he was becoming awkwardly aware that everything he was seeing, and therefore everything he was feeling, was an erotic charade.

Collis sat for a moment staring at the sexual tableau in front of him, biting his thumbnail. Then, almost as if he had been urgently paged, he drained his champagne glass and stood up.

'Gentlemen,' he said, 'it's been a remarkable evening, in more ways than one, but now I must leave you.'

Henry caught at his sleeve. 'You can't *go*, my dear boy. You haven't seen the best part yet! Look – look at what they're doing now!'

Collis wouldn't look, and shook his head. 'I've had enough, Henry. Perhaps just for this evening, maybe for good. It's beginning to strike me, all this pornographic gimcrackery, as pretty stale stuff.'

'Oh, come on, now,' said Jack. 'Just because you're jealous of the Mighty Marmaduke, there's no need to rush out in a huff.'

Collis turned to him. 'I don't think I need to be jealous. I expect he's jealous of me, being able to leave whenever I like. Don't you think he gets bored, doing that?'

'What a let-down!' said Lewis. 'Where's the Collis we know and admire?'

'He's still here,' said Collis quietly. 'Now, don't let me spoil the exhibition for you. I'll see you tomorrow, maybe, if anybody fancies a drink and some dinner.'

Henry paused, nodded, and then let go of Collis's sleeve. He was beginning to understand what was disturbing his friend. It wasn't so much his father, and his self-centred mother, nor even the plunge that Kathleen Mary had taken off the parapet. Henry knew that Collis had been made to think about himself and his future by what had happened in the past twelve hours; and that, having thought, he was slowly lifting his head from the nightly slough of drinking and gambling and whoring, and scenting the clear, cold wind of something else.

It was something that stimulated more than erotic circus shows, and something that intoxicated quicker than drink. It was ambition.

'Take care, Collis. Let's talk tomorrow,' was all Henry said, but that was all that was needed.

Chapter 2

The 'chance' meeting with Delphine Spooner was carefully orchestrated, the following Thursday lunchtime, at Taylor's. Ida had visited Mrs Spooner at her substantial brownstone house on Second Avenue, and over boudoir biscuits and Lapsangsouchong, the two of them had arranged that Delphine and her mother should go shopping and promenading on Broadway, and should arrive on the corner of Franklin Street, where Taylor's Restaurant stood, at the stroke of midday, and that Mrs Spooner should suggest they go inside for an ice. Coincidentally, of course, Collis would already be there with Ida, and over their light lunchtime refreshment, the two could be introduced.

Collis detested the idea. He would much rather have simply left his card at the Spooners' house and then paid Delphine a visit. But Ida adored intrigue, particularly an intrigue which made everybody uncomfortable except herself, and she insisted on 'a fateful encounter of two like hearts'.

'I don't know why the devil I'm doing this,' Collis told his mother, as they waited in the drawing-room for Steadman to bring around their carriage. 'I feel as if I were ten years old.'

'You're doing it to please *me*,' said Ida. She was dressed in a coffee-coloured gown with a lace-trimmed bodice, and she held her off-white shawl around herself as tightly as if she were sitting in a draught. Her bonnet was overloaded with ribbons and ostrich plumes, and her face was powdered quite white. 'You do very little to please me, as much as I deserve it, but now you can exert yourself, if only slightly, to see that I am happy.'

'Mother,' said Collis, 'I'm not sure that happiness becomes you.'

Ida clucked, and stretched her neck disdainfully. If Collis was going to be impertinent and unappreciative, then she would rather not listen. She had to admit, though, that she was moderately pleased by his agreement to meet Delphine, and she had tried to see him in a less critical light over the past few days. He was a very fine-looking boy, after all; and in his cream-coloured suit with maroon braiding around the edges, and his cream-coloured silk hat, he was a handsome prize for any girl.

She was only sorry that this was the last week that she and the

Spooners were to remain in New York, before retreating for the rest of the summer. It would mean that, once introduced, Collis and Delphine would have to postpone the continuation of their planned romance until the fall. Still, that would give them time to moon and mope over each other, and in Ida's view the best romances were full of a good deal of mooning and moping.

She didn't even consider for a moment, now that Collis had agreed to look Delphine over, that the 'young lovers' might despise each other on sight.

At last the carriage arrived at the front door, and Collis escorted his mother out on to Twenty-first Street. It was a bright, hazy day, with a faint wind blowing from the north-west, which did something to relieve the ripe smell of garbage and horse manure in the streets. The Edmondses had a newish dark-green brougham, and their coachman, Steadman, was holding the door open for them, with his usual inane smile fixed on his face, as if he were about to burst out laughing. They climbed aboard and settled themselves down while Steadman hauled himself up on to the box and snapped his whip at their two well-polished chestnuts, Scylla and Charybdis. They rolled eastward across town, Ida shaded by her fringed parasol and Collis sitting back on his seat with his white gloves on his knee and his worried eyes looking out at the crowded sidewalks as if he were a French nobleman being taken to the Bastille in a tumbril.

'I always think I look more elegant in light brown,' remarked Ida. 'I was wearing light brown when I first met your father.'

'She'd better not be too stout,' said Collis. 'If she's too stout, I'm leaving at once.'

Ida turned to him, offended that he hadn't commented on her elegance in light brown. 'Of course she's not stout,' she said coldly. 'You don't think I would marry you off to anyone stout?'

'I do, as a matter of fact,' said Collis gloomily. 'I think you'd marry me off to anyone, particularly if she looked less elegant in light brown than you do.'

Ida gave a tight, disapproving sniff. 'You're absolutely insufferable, do you know that? I thought you'd changed your ways when you agreed to come today, but now I'm not so certain.'

'I came today because I wanted to,' Collis told her.

She shook her parasol to shoo off the flies. 'I was afraid of that,' she said. 'It was too much to expect that you might have come for my sake.'

Collis sighed. 'Mother, I am only going along with this

50

preposterous arrangement because I agree it's time I started to think about my future, and I have to start somewhere. If I like Delphine, and Delphine likes me, there may be a possibility of our coming to some sort of arrangement; but if we dislike each other, then there really isn't any point in continuing. You may look a picture in light brown and ostrich plumes, but Cupid's wings and little golden bows and arrows really don't suit you at all.'

'Oh, if your father were here,' said Ida.

'If my father were here, there would be very much less room in this carriage than there is now, and that's all. Now do try to calm down, Mother. We're supposed to be on a casual shopping expedition, remember? We don't want to spoil the illusion.'

Ida's neck tensed for a moment, rigid with strings and tendons. Then she turned away with an aggrieved toss of her ostrich plumes and refused to speak another word to Collis until they reached Broadway at Franklin.

Steadman, with one of his old smiles, assisted them to alight outside Taylor's. Collis told him to wait around the corner, and then he and his mother went in through the glass doors to the grand saloon of Broadway's most gilded and decorative restaurant. As usual at this time of day, the pillared saloon was humming and twittering with the conversation of ladies who had withdrawn from the midday heat and the dust and crush of shopping to take ices, omelettes, sandwiches, or coffee. They sat clustered, these ladies, in their fashionable dresses of canary yellow and emerald green and sapphire blue, around an archipelago of more than a hundred black walnut tables, their gloved hands fluttering, their feathered bonnets bobbing, and their laughter chirruping above the background bustle like flocks of birds on park railings.

The maître d', in magnificent muttonchops and a swallow-tailed coat, bowed as Ida stalked in, followed at a diffident distance by Collis. He guided them, in a whole cloud of 'good mornings', and 'pleasant days', and stale perspiration odours, to a table by the mirrored wall on the right-hand side of the restaurant. There he left them in the hands of a rather surly young uniformed waiter, who took their order for coffee and pâté sandwiches in a slow, sloping hand, as if he didn't care if he was going to be able to read it back or not. Taylor's interior decor was celestial, but its service was generally regarded as abysmal.

'Well, Mother?' asked Collis. But Ida shushed him. She had wanted to sit by the mirrors because it was cooler there, away from

51

the windows; and because, more important, she could admire herself in the glass from time to time without seeming vainer than she actually was; and because, even *more* important, she could see Winifred Spooner and Delphine the moment they walked in.

'I hope you're not going to say anything embarrassing, Mother, when you introduce us,' said Collis. He was feeling unaccountably nervous, although he couldn't think why. He had flirted with enough women, both high life and low life, not to be alarmed by a girl like Delphine Spooner. Perhaps it was the fact that he was considering marriage, and settling down, that was giving him such palpitations.

'What do you mean by "embarrassing"?' asked his mother haughtily. 'Do you mean that I should refrain from telling Delphine the truth about you, that you are an insolent scoundrel, and a gambler, and a frequenter of whorehouses?'

A thin elderly woman in black, eating cinnamon cakes at the next table, turned and stared at Ida in alarm, but Ida cut her down with a glare that could have boiled ice.

'I simply mean that I don't want you telling her that I'm soft about her, or anything of that kind. "This is my son – he's been admiring you from afar for years." That kind of thing.'

'A mother has to try her best to save her son from complete dissipation,' retorted Ida.

The waiter brought their coffee, setting the pot down on the walnut table with an insolent clatter. Collis sipped at his cup dejectedly and decided he had never felt so much like a beer in his whole life.

It wasn't long, though, before Ida suddenly seized his arm and almost made him spill the whole cupful on his cream-coloured pants. He looked up, and there, through the glass doors, appeared a plump middle-aged woman in a grey dress and shawl, and just behind her, a short young girl whose face was hidden by the brim of her yellow bonnet. Collis felt a surge of panic. He just knew this was going to be a disaster. If Ida hadn't been clasping his arm so firmly, he would have excused himself from the table and rushed out. He suddenly felt suffocated by all the women around him, asphyxiated by their perfume and choked by their feathers, and tied and trammelled by their fussy female schemes.

'Winifred! My dear!' Ida called. 'What a surprise!'

Winifred Spooner came through the tables with a beatific beam on her face, like a mother superior on a holy errand. Delphine followed obediently behind. Collis rose to take the ladies' hands, and found that he was towering over both mother and daughter, although he was only just six feet in height himself. Embarrassed, he clasped Mrs Spooner's grey-gloved fingers and said, 'It's an enormous pleasure, ma'am,' but then immediately regretted having said 'enormous'.

Winifred Spooner, with an obvious smirk that Collis was quite sure could be plainly interpreted by everybody in the saloon, Delphine included, brought her daughter forward and announced, 'This is Mr Collis Edmonds, my pet. I expect you've heard of him.'

Delphine kept her head lowered, so that all Collis could see of her was the semicircular rim of her lemon-yellow bonnet, and the yellow satin daisies that decorated it. She wore a dress of the same colour, with a silk facing on her bodice, and white lace trim around her skirts. She was very small, there was no question about that, but Collis noted with some relief that her arms, which may have been plump with puppy fat when he first saw her, were now quite slender, and her wrists were attractively childlike.

Collis held out his hand. For a moment, Delphine remained where she was, her head down, and then she reached her own hand out, in its small lemon-coloured glove, and placed it in his. She looked up and whispered, 'I'm very pleased to make your acquaintance, sir.'

She could have said anything. She could have said, 'You have a smut on the tip of your nose.' Collis could do nothing but look at her, and realise, with an extraordinary tight feeling in his upper chest, like a diver rising from the deep, that two years can change a seventeen-year-old girl into a nineteen-year-old woman, and a very remarkable young woman at that.

Delphine Spooner was hypnotisingly pretty. What Collis could see of her dark hair was arranged in little curls, and beneath the curls her forehead was high and pale. Her eyes were quite huge, and they had a dreamy, myopic look about them which he found irresistible. Her nose was short and slightly upturned, and her lips were pink and sulky. She was petite, yes; but her figure was practically perfect: small, high, rounded breasts; an upright back; and a way of standing that made him think, immodestly, of firm thighs and trim little ankles.

He kept hold of her hand, although his grasp was very gentle, and would not release it. He let his usual worried look melt away

53

into a warm expression of interest and intrigue, just as he always did when he flirted with a pretty woman. Then, in his huskiest voice, he said, 'I'm quite devastated to meet you. I think you've just made this the most beautiful and the most surprising day of my life.'

Delphine's cheeks coloured, and she tried to take her hand away, but Collis lifted her fingers to his lips and brushed her glove with a kiss. Then, still holding her tight, he raised his eyes and gazed at her for a full ten seconds in the darkest, most smouldering way he could manage. Delphine returned his gaze for a moment, but then she dropped her eyes and looked away, although Collis could tell by the way she allowed him to keep her hand captive that she didn't disapprove. It was all part of the game of courtship and pretended modesty, and he was pleased and excited that she knew how to play it.

Ida coughed, and Collis suddenly realised that almost everybody at the surrounding tables was staring at them. He released Delphine and busily went around the table to pull out a chair for Mrs Spooner, who thanked him in her lisping, flustered voice as if he had done something quite wonderful for her. Then he pulled out Delphine's chair, and she sat down with a quiet 'Thank you, Mr Edmonds' that left him breathless. He knew this was all quite ridiculous, being made to feel so stimulated by a demure little financier's daughter from Second Avenue, particularly when his mother, of all people, had arranged for them to meet. But when he saw the dark curls which lay on the nape of Delphine's neck, and the curve of her ears with their pearl pendant earrings, he decided, a little wryly perhaps, but without any hesitation, that none of those objections was enough to dampen his interest in her.

'What a *chance*, meeting you here,' said Winifred, as Collis resumed his chair. 'We were shopping for birthday presents for the twins. So *tiresome* of them to be born in the summer, when shopping's so hot and exhausting.'

Ida said, 'That was scarcely their fault, Winifred. Makepeace was born on the Fourth of July, and I gather he was quite advanced in years before he discovered the fireworks and the celebrations weren't all for him. But you know what egotists men are.'

All the time she was speaking, Ida was keeping her eyes fixed on Collis and Delphine. Delphine had her eyes lowered still, but Collis, with his elbow on the table and his chin resting on his upturned hand, was staring at her, completely spellbound.

'You must try the black-currant ice,' Collis said. 'It's very good. They make it with black-currant leaves. It has a very musky flavour.'

'Yes,' said Delphine, 'I do believe I've already tasted it.'

The waiter came to take their order, and huffed and puffed, as if he were mortally offended that they should invite two more people to sit at their table without begging his permission. Winifred asked for tea, and Delphine for a lemon sherbet. Collis kept his gaze on Delphine, and still she sat, straight and self-assured, with her eyes modestly averted.

'It's very surprising to me that we haven't been introduced before,' said Collis. 'I believe that I saw you once at a party on East Seventeenth Street, but that was quite some time ago.'

Delphine looked up. 'There really hasn't been any reason for us to be introduced,' she said. 'We move, as I understand it, in quite different circles.'

Collis was slightly taken aback. What, exactly, did she mean by 'quite different circles'? He hoped she wasn't trying to suggest that he patronised whorehouses and gambling dens, because if she knew about that side of his social life, then he couldn't see that there was very much hope for any kind of love affair between them. Nice young ladies like Delphine didn't keep company with rakes.

'Well,' said Collis cautiously, 'more's the pity.'

'Thank you,' replied Delphine.

There was a minute's silence between them. Ida and Winifred, although they were making sure that they kept half an ear on everything that was going on, were now engaged in running down Esmé Blunt, the wife of the art dealer, for her dreadful taste in dinner guests, and that withering cascade of criticism would occupy them for the next twenty minutes at least.

'Do you ride?' Collis asked Delphine.

She shook her head. 'Not much in the city. But when we go to Larchmont, I like to. I'm looking forward to getting out of New York this year, aren't you?'

'I was until now,' said Collis.

Delphine smiled a little. Her lips were very full and sensual, in spite of her cool manners, and Collis couldn't help imagining what it would be like to press a kiss on them, and then to part them with the tip of his tongue. She was so damned pretty, and now, in the heat of the restaurant, he could smell the fragrance she wore, an

55

essence of jonquils. A flowery, tiny, yellowy fragrance, like Delphine herself.

'You don't have to flatter me for the sake of it,' she said. 'I'm not a child.'

Collis laughed. She had caught him off balance at first, but now he was beginning to understand her. She didn't know much about him, but she could see what kind of a man he was, with his fashionably casual clothes and his suave manner, and she was teasing him. That made him adore her even more. If there was one thing on this earth that aroused him, it was a woman who teased.

'I can see for myself that you're not a child,' he told her. 'You're the most charming young woman I've seen in this city all year, and that's why I'm flattering you.'

'Does this kind of talk work well for you, usually?' she asked.

'Usually?'

'I mean, with other ladies. Are they impressed, or do they simply smile and twirl their parasols and give you coquettish little smiles?'

'The way you are now?'

Delphine smiled. 'Yes, if you like.'

'So you're not impressed?'

'Am I supposed to be?'

Collis grinned. 'Of course you are. You're supposed to swoon at my feet. You're supposed to go home this evening and think about nothing else but me, and how I'm going to call for you on Saturday afternoon and take you riding.'

'I believe my horse is lame. He caught his foot in a railroad line on Hudson Street.'

'I can lend you a mare. I have a beautiful mare called Hopeful.'

'Hopeful?' She smiled. 'That's a perfect name.'

The waiter brought Delphine's ice, and she began to eat it with her long-handled spoon. Collis watched her, and the more he watched her, the more he desired her. He hadn't fallen so immediately and passionately for anyone since he was fifteen years old, when he had sat for hours on the back stairs, hoping to catch a glimpse of their kitchen maid, who was a green-eyed, big-breasted Italian girl, and whose very apron, rustling up the stairs, had made him squeeze his eyes tight shut with frustrated lust. There was more to Delphine than feelings of lust, however. There was a sharp, piquant personality that he knew he was going to have to trounce. She was demure, but she was self-willed and she needed bridling.

'I believe you're suspicious of me,' said Collis.

Delphine licked ice from the bottom of her spoon. 'Suspicious? Why should I be?'

'I don't know. Perhaps you've heard stories about me that made you leery.'

She looked down at her dish. 'You *are* a flatterer, aren't you? First you flatter me, and now you're flattering yourself. Where on earth would I have heard stories about you?'

'I'm not exactly unknown in New York,' replied Collis. 'And you know how stories get about.'

'What sort of stories?'

He shrugged. He definitely felt that he was on the defensive end of this conversation, no matter how much he tried to push her.

'Well . . . stories,' he said. 'Stories of, well, escapades.'

'You have *escapades*?' she asked him. 'Is that what you do during the day, instead of working? You have *escapades*?'

Collis felt slightly hot. 'Yes,' he said, 'sometimes.'

'And people tell stories of your escapades?'

'In a manner of speaking, yes.'

Delphine laid down her spoon and looked at him boldly. 'You're almost a legendary figure then, in your own time?'

He said, tightly: 'You're teasing me.'

'Yes.'

'Why do you want to do that?'

'Because I want to get to know you better,' she said, 'and because there is no quicker way of doing it than to tease. When you tease, people spring to the defence of everything they love dearest, and so you can discover what they love dearest in just a few minutes.'

'Have you found out what I love dearest?'

'Oh, yes,' she said. 'I mean, I guessed it when I first saw you, but now you've told me for yourself.'

Collis leaned forward. 'What is it,' he asked her, 'that I hold so dear?'

Delphine turned towards her mother and Ida, who had paused to listen for a moment. When they saw that she was looking, they immediately plunged back into their conversation like two diners gobbling the same bowl of spaghetti. Delphine looked back at Collis with her amused, entrancing smile. 'They seemed to be pleased that we've got together,' she said. 'Do I sense a plot?'

'Probably,' said Collis. 'But who cares, if the plot has such happy results?'

'I don't know whether it has,' Delphine replied.

57

'You grieve me,' said Collis, trying hard to look grieved.

'No, I don't,' said Delphine. 'I don't think you're capable of being grieved, not for anyone else's sake, anyway. That's because the thing you hold dearest, as I was telling you, is your scandalous reputation. You care for your public notoriety more than anything else, and you would defend it to the death.'

'Then you *have* heard about me,' said Collis. That was bad news. If she accepted his advances at all, he would have a long, uphill struggle trying to convince her that he was reformed, and that he would never gamble or drink or touch the ladies of the night again. A pretty creature like Delphine Spooner certainly wouldn't have to put up with an erratic, erotic, boastful rake. She could pick any one of dozens of respectable young bankers instead, and live happily and substantially ever after.

'Yes, I admit I've heard about you,' Delphine told him. She took another spoonful of ice. 'In fact, your escapades are quite well known.'

'They're very much exaggerated,' said Collis.

'Oh?' she said.

'Oh, yes, indeed. Well, you know how people like to talk, and how a story gets embroidered in the telling. Most of the stories that people tell about me are quite inaccurate. Some of them are downright lies. That was why I suspected you might be suspicious. Anybody would be suspicious if they heard stories like that. But they're not true, I assure you.'

Delphine inclined her head to one side. 'That's a pity,' she said.

Collis stared at her. 'I beg your pardon?'

She turned her eyes towards him. 'I said, "That's a pity."'

'I'm sorry,' he said awkwardly. 'I don't understand what you mean.'

Delphine bent her bonnet confidingly towards him. 'It's a pity,' she said softly, so that Ida and Winifred were unable to hear, no matter how far they inclined themselves in her direction, 'because I have wanted for a very long time to meet you.'

'You have? I'm afraid I still don't understand.'

'You're being very obtuse.'

'My dear young lady, I'm not being obtuse at all. It's you. You're talking in complete riddles.'

She smiled mischievously. 'All riddles have solutions, my dear sir. The solution to my riddle is that I am quite tired of being

58

introduced to worthy young gentlemen with no reputation. I am bored of bankers, and I am fed up with financiers, and if I have to spend the evening being nice to another high-risk insurance broker, I think I shall scream. I want to meet someone dashing, someone perverse, someone with style. I want to meet men like you. Only when I do, what happens? You tell me that all the stories about you are fabricated, and that you're probably just as tedious and worthy as all the rest of them.'

Collis had at first been puzzled, then scandalised, then, gradually, intrigued. Delphine Spooner was a great deal more fascinating than he had first supposed, as well as being prettier. There was something about the way she spoke, about the way she held her head, that made her looks even more compelling. He reached out and laid his hand over hers, oblivious of his mother's sideways glance, and said: 'They're not all lies, you know. Some of them have what you might call a grain of truth.'

Delphine's cheeks coloured again, but she kept her composure. 'You may think me very forward, and I must assure you that I do not normally ask questions of this nature, but have you ever been with strumpets?'

Collis didn't know what to answer at first. Here was a girl who could be devious enough to be tricking him into an admission of immorality, so that she could decide if he was worthy of her or not. But here was a girl, too, who could be spirited and unusual enough to feel the need for a man of experience, a man well acquainted with loose women.

'Is that what the stories say of me?' he said cautiously.

She nodded, almost eagerly. 'Melissa Dunlop, Lewis Dunlop's sister, said that on one occasion you had bedded two ladies at once.'

Ida, leaning across the table with dangling earrings and rustling coffee-coloured silk, said, 'Have you two young people found something in common, Collis?'

Collis said, 'I think so, Mother,' but kept his eyes on Delphine. All around them, Taylor's burbled with conversation, and waiters hurried through the subdued light with trays of coffee and plates of oysters, but he believed, in the few minutes they had been together, that Delphine and he had grown a strange and private understanding. 'Yes,' he said to Delphine, pronouncing the words most carefully, 'that's true.'

Delphine closed her eyes. Her hand stirred under his.

'I don't know whether you've been trying to establish if I'm a

R.—C

59

worthy sort of a man, the sort of man who drinks only one schooner of sherry in three months, and shakes hands with women instead of kissing them; or if you've been trying to find out if I'm a scoundrel, who never wakes up without a hangover, and never in his own bed. But whatever you want me to be, I'll be, because you're very pretty, Miss Spooner, and because I am absolutely enchanted by you.'

She opened her eyes again, and stared at him with those huge hazel eyes, eyes he could have lost himself in. He didn't know for a moment whether she was going to lean forward and kiss him, or whether she was going to slap his face. She did neither. She simply turned to Winifred, her mother, and said clearly, 'Mr Edmonds has kindly invited me to ride with him on Saturday afternoon, Mother. He has a mare that I may borrow, named Hopeful. Do you think I could go?'

Ida looked at Winifred, and Winifred looked back at Ida. Then Winifred said, 'Of course, my pet. I hope you thanked Mr Edmonds for his generosity.'

Delphine turned back to Collis and gave him a smile that made the back of his neck prickle with alarm and desire. 'I shall, Mother. I shall.'

On the way home in the carriage, Collis unexpectedly took his mother's hand, and he said, 'Mother, I've accused you of many misdeeds in the past. We've argued, you and I, over everything and anything. But the evidence of today has absolutely convinced me that, whatever I do, I must never again criticise your taste.'

Ida, shaded under her parasol, said loftily, 'You liked Delphine, then? In spite of the fact that I had to drag you along to meet her like a six-year-old boy?'

Collis couldn't help smiling. 'She is easily the prettiest girl I have seen in two years.'

'Not the prettiest ever?'

'Well, there was Edna Rice Perry.'

Ida shivered and retrieved her hand from her son's grasp. 'I don't know how you can compare Delphine Spooner and that Perry trollop.'

But then she turned to Collis with a softer expression and said, 'Still, if you like Delphine even half as much as you liked Edna, your father and I shall be well satisfied.'

Collis looked back at his mother for a while, saying nothing, but then he settled back on the cushions of his seat, humming quietly to himself, and wishing it were Saturday.

Later that night, Collis knocked at the door of his father's library. He was all dressed up to go to dinner at the Jacobses', on Union Square, but he couldn't resist telling Makepeace what he thought of Delphine Spooner. It was such an unusual feeling for him, to be pleased with his parents, that he was quite revelling in it – although he knew perfectly well that as soon as the novelty of meeting Delphine had worn off a little, they would be back to their old scraps about politics and gambling and good manners.

Collis opened the double oak doors of the gloomy, tobacco-smelling room, to find his father sitting at his desk in the dim, unsteady light of a single oil lamp, a litter of bonds and deeds and stock certificates all around him, his reading spectacles perched on his forehead.

'Sir,' said Collis.

There was a pause while Makepeace ran his pencil down a column of figures. Then he lifted his head and said, 'Ah.'

'If you're busy, sir . . .' said Collis.

His father shook his head. 'Not too busy, my boy. I shall have to spend all night at this in any case. Are you going out this evening?'

'Yes, sir. Eli Jacobs is holding a dinner for some foreign composer.' Collis pulled over a small, heavy chair and sat down. 'But I really wanted to tell you about Delphine Spooner.'

'Delphine? Oh, yes. Your mother said that you seemed to have taken a shine to her. I'm pleased.'

There was a difficult silence. It occurred to Collis that his father didn't look particularly well. His eyes were reddened in the lamplight, and beneath his whiskers his complexion was noticeably pasty. Collis looked around at all the papers strewn on the desk and on the floor, and then he took out a cheroot and carefully bit off the end.

'Is something wrong, Father?'

Makepeace gave a quick, humourless smirk. 'Wrong? What makes you think that?'

'All these papers,' said Collis, striking a match. 'You're generally so tidy.'

'I was . . . looking for something. An old insurance certificate.'

'You don't usually keep insurance certificates in with stocks and bonds, do you?'

61

Makepeace reached across his desk and began to rustle and ruffle through some of the papers. 'You shouldn't concern yourself,' he said. 'You just go off and have dinner with Eli Jacobs, and leave me to do what I can do best.'

'I was going to tell you about Delphine.'

His father looked across at him, his odd eye gazing fixedly at the unlit gas bracket on the wall behind Collis's shoulder. Then, as if he couldn't help himself from speaking the truth, he said, 'I believe Delphine's turned out very pretty. It's a pity that it's probably too late to do us any good.'

'Sir?'

Makepeace shook his head. 'Don't worry about it. Just do whatever you can.'

'Father,' said Collis, dismissing a twisted cloud of cheroot smoke with a wave of his hand, 'I don't know what you're talking about. *What's* too late to do us any good?'

Makepeace was burrowing through a sheaf of legal documents tied up with pink ribbons. 'I suppose it serves me right for being a doughface. It's all just useless speculation. The market's nothing but unsecured credit, puffery, and wind.'

'Sir – will you please talk sense?'

'Sense?' said Makepeace. 'What have *you* ever known about sense? If you'd been the kind of son that a man could rely on, if you'd come into the bank and learned a civilised profession, then we might have avoided this altogether. I was overworked, overstrained. What do you think I do all day, to keep you in liquor and whores? Now the whole damned thing is falling to pieces. It's like a damned hot-air balloon, with a leak.'

'Father,' said Collis, 'will you please tell me what on earth is happening?'

Makepeace took a deep breath, and then got up from his chair. He walked across to the plain marble fireplace, empty and swept now that it was summer, and stood with his back to Collis, his shoulders hunched, and his arms wrapped around his chest. From the dark-panelled library wall, a few feet to his left, a shadowy oil painting of his grandfather, portly and petulant, looked down at him with disapproval.

At last, Makepeace turned his head, so that Collis could see his white whiskers and his blunt nose in profile. 'You've never cared before, Collis,' he said hoarsely, 'and I'm sure that you don't seriously care now. In any event, whatever I told you would be quite beyond your understanding.'

'You're not giving me the opportunity to *try* to understand, are you, sir?'

'Collis – you can spend money like a prodigal, but you don't have the faintest notion how to manage it. The management of money is fraught with risks of cataclysmic proportions. The most cataclysmic thing that ever happened to you was a dose of gonorrhea.'

'Father, I *am* your son.'

'That's what I'm complaining about! Any other son would have given me respect and support, any other son would have taken some of the burden off my shoulders! But not you. You were quite content to thumb your nose at me with one hand and rifle my pockets with the other!'

Collis stood up and crossed the rug to where his father was standing. He could see that a greasy film of perspiration was shining on his father's forehead, and that the old man seemed to be panting, the way he did when he tried to climb more than one flight of stairs at once.

'Father,' Collis said gently.

Makepeace raised his one good eye.

'Well, my boy,' he grumbled after a moment. 'You always said that I was too self-confident, didn't you? You always said that the world couldn't last as it was.'

'What's happened, Father?' asked Collis.

'It's the bank,' said Makepeace. 'We've overstretched ourselves.'

'Seriously?'

Makepeace nodded. 'To the tune of two million dollars.'

'Irrecoverable?'

'Completely. All gone on worthless speculations and frauds. It was only discovered this morning, when Greenbaum heard from his agents in California, and it was a good thing he did, or we would have been taken for another million.'

'What are you going to do?' asked Collis.

Makepeace gestured at all the papers and bonds strewn over his desk. 'That's what I've been trying to work out. With any luck, I may be able to borrow two million for a limited while, and keep things going so that they look normal. But if there's any fluctuation in the market, I could be very heavily pressed. The bank is right on the brink, Collis. Right on the brink.'

63

'You mean you could go bankrupt?'

'It's a possibility. If I were a betting man, like you, I'd say the odds were five to four against us. It depends mostly on finding a two-million-dollar loan.'

'Is that what you meant when you said my meeting with Delphine was too late to do any good?'

Makepeace nodded. He was plainly embarrassed. 'If we could have leaned on Ohio Life and Mutual for a few months, without too many tricky questions being asked, well . . . I wouldn't have liked doing it, but it would have been better than nothing.'

'Have you spoken to George Spooner?'

'Oh, yes. Very guardedly, of course. I didn't tell him anything was wrong. But, even so, I didn't get very far. He really wants to wait until we can present him with a full investment programme later in the year.'

Collis went over to his father's desk and looked down at the pages of figures and frantic notes, all written in that distinctive forward-sloping hand, in black marking ink.

'What happens if you can't find the money?' he asked. 'Is that the end of I. P. Woolmer's Bank?'

'I'm afraid it's more than that.'

'I don't understand. It's not *your* money, is it? It won't do your reputation any good, but you won't be broke.'

Makepeace gave a quick shake of his head. 'You're wrong, Collis. I shall be very broke. I sank a great deal of my own money into these speculations, and worse still, I borrowed from the bank.'

Collis stared at him. 'You borrowed from the bank?'

His father looked away. 'I know it's out of character. It's something I've never done before. But I believed I was right, what with the market so bullish this year. I believed I could make a quick, adventurous profit before the bottom started to fall out. It *must* fall out, of course, and it will. Too many of these speculative investments are built on nothing but clouds and moonshine. But I believed, with all my years of experience, that I could do it.'

'I don't understand why you even wanted to.'

Makepeace returned to his desk and sat himself down. He rubbed his eyes and sighed. 'I'm not a young man, Collis. My liver is weak, and I can't continue to work for very many more years. I wanted to make a few hundred thousand to safeguard my retirement, that was all, and ensure that your mother could live in the kind of luxury to which she is accustomed.'

64

He paused for a moment, tugging at his moustache, and then he said, 'This country is in for some bad times ahead. Maybe sooner, maybe later, I don't know. But if the North continues to bait and persecute the South, the South is going to strike back, and that's going to mean lean times for us all. I just wanted to make some financial hay while the sun was still shining, to store some feed up for the future.'

Collis sat down again too, and watched his father with increasing sadness.

'I guess, to be truthful, I was seeking some selfish excitement out of the speculation, too,' said Makepeace. 'All my life I've been known as a safe, middle-of-the-highway banker. I've been careful, and scrupulously honest, and circumspect. Mr Six Per Cent! But anyone who's spent most of his working life in Wall Street knows what it is to take a financial risk, and win. To pull off the clever coup, that nobody else was on to, or to hold the far-sighted investment that suddenly pays off one thousand times over. Well, I suppose I wanted to do something like that just once before I thought of retiring, so that the Curb would have something to remember me by.'

'You and I, we're more alike than we even know,' said Collis, so softly that he wasn't even sure that his father had heard him.

Makepeace lifted a piece of paper and then let it fall back to his desk again. 'As it turned out, I invested in a bubble,' he said. 'A damned worthless scheme for building a railroad out of Sacramento, the Sacramento Valley Railroad, coupled with a so-called gold mine that turned out to be the richest vein of iron pyrites in the whole state. Fool's gold, appropriately named. There were other speculations as well, on land and commodities, and I salvaged a few thousand dollars out of a sugar deal, but on the whole the bank and I were thoroughly scalped.'

'Does Mother know?' asked Collis.

Makepeace shook his head. There were tears in his eyes, and he brushed them away with the cuff of his smoking jacket.

Collis leaned back in his chair. 'I don't know what to say. I don't even know what I could possibly do to help.'

'Nothing at all,' said Makepeace. 'I'm going to try to work out a scheme for saving the bank, and I'll probably present it to my board tomorrow. They may force me to quit, or they may give me a chance to undo the damage I've done. It's all up to me. As far as you're concerned – well, I've told you what's happened, and you've got a pretty fair idea of what *could* happen, and you'll just have to be more careful with your spending money.'

Collis stayed where he was for a few minutes, while his father went back to his hurried, scratchy writing. He closed his eyes, and he could hear *skritch-skritch-skritch* and then a rattling sound as his father dipped into the silver inkpot. He didn't know whether he felt furious or sorrowful. He could understand what his father meant about the exhilaration of coups on the stock market, because he was a habitual gambler himself. But there was a difference between gambling away your allowance and gambling away your entire family fortune, particularly when that family fortune was keeping Collis in clothes, faro stakes, stone fences, and women. He couldn't imagine what Ida was going to say when she found out.

Collis opened his eyes and watched his father for a while. 'Well, I suppose I'd better be going,' he said. 'I mustn't be late for my dinner party, after all. And I'm sure you've got enough work to keep you busy.'

Makepeace looked up. 'You won't tell your mother? Not until I know what's going to happen, one way or another.'

'No.'

'Thank you,' said his father. 'I have somebody looking for your lobster, you know. An old friend of mine from Belfast, Maine. He promised to send it down on ice as soon as he could.'

Collis took a last look around the paper-strewn library, the wreckage of his father's career, before he went out without another word and closed the doors behind him.

He arrived outside the Spooners' house on Second Avenue the following afternoon, just as the bells of St Mark's Church were beginning to ring a peal. He rode his own dappled pony, Dollar, and led behind him his sleekly groomed chestnut, Hopeful. He was dressed in a dark-green cutaway coat and tight buff riding pants, with gloriously polished brown boots and a dark-green curly-brimmed hat. He still had a pounding headache from Eli Jacobs's dinner party, and his lean face was markedly paler than usual.

Outside the Spooners' fashionable brownstone on the corner of Twelfth Street, under a plane tree, a black stablehand in a white shirt and knee breeches was already holding an elderly-looking grey, which Collis presumed would be ridden by Delphine's chaperone. He closed his eyes for a moment and prayed that she wouldn't be too ugly. He wasn't sure that his aching eyeballs could take it.

Collis dismounted and handed the reins of his horses to the boy. Then he mounted the steps to the black-painted front door and knocked. While he waited, he looked along the length of the avenue, up towards Stuyvesant Square, watching the carriages and the hacks rattling between the tree-lined sidewalks. It was a warm, close afternoon, and the air was filled with dust, and with sparkling chaff from dried horse manure.

At length the front door was opened by a lugubrious footman with shiny bear's-greased hair, who showed Collis into the empty, echoing hallway and then into a small anteroom which smelled of stale pot-pourri. He was requested to wait, and he sat tapping his riding crop against his glossy boot, looking around at glass domes of dried flowers and stuffed birds.

The afternoon sunlight filtered through layers of lace curtains, and he yawned in the cloyingly sweet air. Eli's party had turned into the usual drunken debacle, with Eli walking along the table-top imitating a pelican, and the foreign composer who was his guest falling asleep behind the settee. Collis was beginning to wish he had suggested to Delphine some gentler way of spending the afternoon, like playing checkers.

It wasn't long before he heard the rustling of skirts, and the diminutive Winifred Spooner appeared, all purple satin and fuss, followed by Delphine and a quite pleasant-looking brunette girl dressed in grey.

Collis rose and took Mrs Spooner's hand. But it was Delphine whom he was watching as he kissed Winifred's rings. She looked prettier than she had on Thursday, if that was possible; far prettier in the flesh than in his memory. She wore a plumed black hat and a riding coat of black linen, fastened with grey frogging. Her full black riding skirt was decorated with black silk fringes. The severity of her clothes only served to emphasise her beauty, however, and with her soft, radiant skin and her compelling eyes, she looked to Collis like the perfect female creature about whom every man dreamed.

'You have met Delphine, of course,' said Winifred. Collis bowed and kissed Delphine's black-gloved hand.

'This,' said Winifred, 'is Delphine's cousin from Baltimore, Miss Alice Stride.'

Alice Stride nodded. Her nose was rather too large for her face, but her eyes had that expression of human sympathy and intelligence that Collis looked for in friends. She would plainly make some man an astonishing wife one day, and meanwhile, with luck, she would probably make a discreet and obliging chaperone.

'I'm honoured to make your acquaintance, Miss Stride,' said Collis. 'Are you related, by chance, to any of those Strides who have done so well in Congress?'

'My father is Senator William Stride, sir,' replied Alice boldly.

Collis stared back at her, amused. 'Then we shall have plenty to argue about.'

Delphine asked, 'Have you brought Hopeful, Mr Edmonds? The mare you promised to lend me?'

'She's right outside,' said Collis. 'In her own way, she's looking as groomed and as sweet-tempered as you are.'

He turned to Winifred and added, 'Mostly, when I meet a pretty and charming girl, I find it difficult to discern from her parents how she acquired her looks and her manner. But I only have to look at you, Mrs Spooner, to see where Delphine's inheritance came from.'

Winifred went slightly pink, gave a silly little girlish laugh, and then said, 'Will you take sherry before you ride?'

'No, *no*,' said Delphine. 'Let's be off at once!'

'Mr Edmonds?' asked Winifred.

Collis shook his head politely. Even that small shake was enough to revive his dull headache. 'I am not a great drinker of wine, Mrs Spooner,' he told her.

Winifred fussed them all to the door, where the black stableboy brought up their horses and a set of wooden steps for the ladies to mount. Collis held Hopeful's bridle and stroked her nose while Delphine arranged herself on the mare's saddle, her legs elegantly crossed under her black-fringed skirts, her narrow ankles temptingly sheathed in polished black-leather riding boots.

'Miss Spooner, you look a picture,' said Collis. 'I hope I can remember for ever how you look at this moment.'

Delphine gave him a fey, pretty smile. 'There will be many other times to remember, I trust.'

'Now then, Delphine,' said Alice, mounting her grey, 'I'm supposed to be your chaperone. And that means no forwardness of any kind.'

'Is it forward to wish happy times on yourself?' asked Delphine.

'The way you do it it is,' retorted Alice.

Collis climbed on to Dollar, and with a wave to Winifred Spooner, the three of them trotted close together uptown, through Stuyvesant Square, where the trees shimmered in the sunlight, and three men in shabby evening coats and string-tied pants played German festival tunes on trumpets and fiddles. The brassy off-key music echoed and faded as they turned west on Seventeenth Street and then turned uptown again on Third Avenue.

'I have been thinking of you, Collis,' said Delphine, as they rode side by side.

'And I have been thinking of you,' he replied. He looked across at her and was captivated by the way she sat so upright in the saddle, her black plumes bobbing in the summer breeze.

She turned to him. 'Pleasant thoughts, I hope?'

'Delightful. And yours?'

'Becoming, in the extreme.'

'I'm beginning to feel left out of this already,' Alice said, with a wry smile.

Collis raised his hat to her. 'The fate of all chaperones, I regret But do tell me how your father is keeping.'

'As intent on preserving slavery as ever, if that's what you mean, said Alice.

'And you agree with him?'

Alice made a *moue*. 'It's not as simple as it seems. The whole of Southern life would change so much if the slaves were to be freed. Everything for which the Southerners have given their lives would be lost. My father, for one. How could he run his cotton plantations without slaves?'

'Your father may have given a great deal,' Collis pointed out. 'But he has also received a great deal in return. He is a very rich man these days, by all accounts.'

'Rich, but *very* agreeable,' said Delphine. 'In fact, Alice's father is almost my favourite uncle.'

'Is he in New York now?' asked Collis.

Alice nodded. 'He goes back to Washington next Wednesday. Why, did you wish to meet him?'

'I would be honoured. Could you arrange it?'

They rode northward, past country houses and derelict Dutch farms, as far as Fifty-ninth Street, where they turned westward again towards Central Park. Along the south side of Central Park, with their stove chimneys smoking in the faint wind that blew from the Hudson, stood untidy rows of ramshackle shanties, where dirty

69

children played, and where hard-eyed men and women stood at their doors or paused in their scratchy gardens to watch the wealthy ride by. Collis rode protectively close to Delphine and Alice as they descended the rocky slope to the lake and passed along the muddy bridle paths between the bushes.

When they reached the shoreline, they dismounted, the two young ladies slipping down from their saddles with exquisite aplomb, and they walked along the water's edge and talked.

Discreetly, Alice fell a little behind, so that Delphine and Collis could talk alone. The three of them, and their horses, were reflected in the lake as they walked, and the day passed, hot and clear, over their heads. From the far side of the lake, their voices sounded muted and languorous, mingling with the hum of insects and the chip-chipping of thrushes.

Collis said, 'Are you forward by nature, or is it a game you like to play?'

Delphine smiled. 'I'm not really forward. I'm just inquisitive. There seems to be so much that young ladies are not allowed to know.'

'Such as?'

'Well, anatomy, and things of that kind.'

'Anatomy can be quite tedious.'

Delphine gave him another of her dreamy, short-sighted looks. 'It depends on whose, I suppose?'

Collis coughed. He had never been spoken to like this by any young lady before in his life, whores excepted, and he found it both unsettling and arousing. If she persisted in discussing 'anatomy, and things of that kind', he wasn't sure that he was going to be able to keep his composure, particularly since his riding breeches were so tight. He brought Dollar to a halt and reached out for Delphine's hand. She paused, and then gave it to him.

'You look distressed,' she said. 'What have I done to distress you?'

'Absolutely nothing. But I'm disturbed by your conversation. Wouldn't it be better if we talked about something else, like art, or women's rights, or how they're going to improve this dreadful park?'

'Instead of anatomy, you mean?'

'Yes.'

'But, Collis,' she said coquettishly, 'I know all about art, and I know as much as I want to know about the Amazons, and I was

70

reading only yesterday what the city plans to do with the park. I want to talk about love, and the emotions of love.'

'Delphine,' Collis told her, 'I think you're the most appealing young lady I've met in my whole life. But we must consider the proprieties.'

'Why?'

'*Why?* Well, because we must! We hardly know each other. We've talked for a half-hour over a plate of lemon ice, and that's all. People don't discuss topics of anatomy until they're married, and not often then.'

'You surprise me,' she said, continuing along the path and leading Hopeful after her.

'*I* surprise *you*?' he said, following her.

'I thought you were a man of the world. A sophisticate. I thought I might learn something from you.'

'*I* surprise *you*? Miss Spooner, *you* surprise *me*! I have never discussed such things with a lady before, ever. When I'm with ladies, I talk about riding, and how beautiful it is in South Carolina at this time of year, and sewing. I don't come out as bold as brass and talk about anatomy.'

Delphine stopped again and turned to face him. He looked down at her, and whatever he felt about her frisky and wayward spirit, he knew that he could never resist her prettiness. A little way behind them, Alice stopped as well and studiously looked out towards the lake.

Delphine held out her hand and said, 'You may kiss me.'

Collis swallowed. He glanced all around him, but there was nobody in sight, and it was quite plain that Alice wasn't going to turn around for ten dollars.

Delphine said, 'Come along. You may kiss me.'

He found himself breathing harder than he wanted to. He stood close to her, and she was so tiny that her plumed hat reached only up to his chest. Holding the reins of his pony in one hand, he gently lifted her chin with the other, feeling how soft her skin was, and he gazed down into those wide hazel eyes in pleased bewilderment. Delphine's lips were moist, and slightly parted, and he could see the white tips of her teeth.

'I don't understand you at all,' he said hoarsely.

She smiled. 'You don't have to understand me. Just kiss me.'

Hesitantly, he bent his head and touched his lips to hers.

71

'That's not a kiss,' she whispered. 'Kiss me the way you kiss your strumpets.'

He froze. A fleeting, upsetting thought passed through his mind, the half-seen vision of something difficult and extraordinary. It had some connection with Kathleen Mary falling off the parapet, some link with what he had thought when he had seen her lying on the sidewalk, broken and hurt. Whores were not only whores, but people. Real women, with real lives. Was it possible, then, that they were sisters under the skin with ladies? Could ladies be whorish, too?

'I can't wait here all afternoon, sir,' Delphine said playfully.

Collis kissed her, not as deeply as he would have kissed a whore, always provided her teeth were sound, but with considerable tenderness and affection. Then he stood straight and looked at her for a long time without saying a word.

'You're very handsome,' she said. 'I believe I could grow to love you.'

'You don't even know me.'

'I know. But I don't believe I have to.'

They carried on walking. Alice, behind them, was trilling a song about a lover and his lass. Delphine glanced back and gave Alice a wave.

'Do I frighten you?' Delphine asked Collis.

He shook his head.

'Do I alarm you?'

He shrugged. 'A little.'

'I suppose I get my personality from my grandmother. She was one of the great lady pioneers, you know. In 1796, she was the first lady to ride in John Fitch's steamboat, on the Collect Pond. They say she was a terror, and that she used to scare her suitors so much that two of them emigrated back to England for fear of her.'

'You're a terror yourself. But a beautiful terror.'

'Thank you,' she said. 'I don't really mean to be. It's just that I find gentlemen so interesting, provided they're not stuffy, and I've always wanted to know what it is that makes them so. Is it their freedom to drink what they like, and ride where they will? Or is it their freedom to lie with whores? Is it something that I could share?'

Collis led his pony up to a scrubby tree and tied it up. He took Hopeful, too, and tied her up.

'I don't think that kind of experience makes a man wiser, or more interesting,' he said, taking a cheroot. 'I don't think it makes ladies

72

any more charming, either. All the harlots and the women drinkers that I've come across are as noodle-headed as anyone you could wish to meet. I'm beginning to think that I've been as noodle-headed as the rest of them, because I never got anything out of gambling and whoring and drinking but empty pockets and a sore head.'

'Nothing at all?'

Alice brought her grey over, and Collis tethered it for her. Delphine told her, with a frown, 'Collis says he didn't get anything out of his experiences with strumpets at all but a sore head.'

Alice raised an eyebrow. 'Delphine is fascinated by iniquity at the moment. She's just dying to do something wicked.'

'It's not that at all,' protested Delphine. 'I simply want to find out what being iniquitous is *like* – whether it broadens one's outlook on life.'

Collis struck a light and sucked at his cheroot. For some reason he thought of his father, weary and defeated by ill luck. He said quietly, 'I believe that it's probably all a matter of purpose. I wouldn't have said that a week ago, but my mind has been changed since then. To drink and gamble and whore because you have no other way of filling the hours of your day – well, that's not broadening at all. You live your life in a kind of repetitive dream, and before you know where you are, you're older than you ever imagined you could be, with nothing more to show for all those hours of carousing but a bad liver and a social disease.'

He paused awhile, then added, 'It seems to me that I've lived my life without much purpose, and that it's high time I had one.'

Alice looked at him pointedly. 'Does that mean you're looking for love?'

Delphine's face was worried for a moment, but then she smiled and clapped her hands. 'Do say yes! Do say that you're looking for love!'

'This is all getting too serious,' said Collis tenderly. 'It truly is. Let's ride down to the De Vere Restaurant and take some tea.'

'Shame,' protested Delphine. 'You haven't answered our question.'

'But I shall.' Collis grinned. 'All in good time.'

'I don't know why you're beating around the bush so much,' Alice said airily. 'I do believe that you're both quite taken with each other.'

Collis looked at her, surprised. But she simply shrugged and said,

73

'I'm sorry to be so blunt, sir, but it's plain to see from a mile and a half away.'

Delphine lowered her eyelashes for a moment, but then she looked up at Collis and gave a small, suppressed giggle. 'You've embarrassed him now, Alice,' she said. 'He's been embarrassed enough for one day, with all my forward conversation.'

Collis, quite tickled, blew out a stream of smoke. 'I'm not embarrassed. I'm *intrigued*, I'll admit. I've heard of the bold new etiquette, but I've never yet come across it in a lady. I've heard of women's rights, as well, but I've never yet met a lady who has decided to confer them on herself, regardless of what her friends and her family may think. I've even heard of love at first sight. But I've never yet been introduced to anyone who has carried me away so completely with her grace, and her spirit, and her fascinating manner, all in the space of a single hour.'

Delphine was blushing now, and Alice, pleased, was holding her hand.

Alice reached into her sleeve for a small lace handkerchief and dabbed at her eyes. 'It's so wonderful,' she said. 'I've always been a believer in kindred spirits. I'm sure you two can make each other very happy.'

Collis stepped forward and took Delphine in his arms. Her eyelashes were glistening, and her lips were trembling just a little. 'You and your forward talk,' he said. 'You and your *anatomy*!'

She couldn't help smiling. 'I was so afraid that you were going to feel offended if I talked that way. But I had to know if you were a real man or not. I couldn't have put up with another of Mama's mummified bankers. You've been so understanding, Collis. You're the first man who has ever spoken to me as a woman, as well as a lady.'

Without prompting this time, Collis kissed her. Her lips were soft and moist, and the feel of them stirred him as no other woman's lips ever had. It was a long time, whole seconds, before he opened his eyes, and saw Delphine's hazel eyes so close that he could scarcely focus, and the tears that ran freely down her cheeks. She held him tight for a while, weeping with the delight of knowing him and kissing him; and then she was able to regain herself and stand straight, and borrow Alice's handkerchief.

'I think this is a very special day,' said Alice.

'I think we ought to go take tea,' said Collis.

He untethered the horses and helped Delphine and Alice mount

74

up. They rode back around the edge of the lake and up the sloping path that took them out of the park by the square white-painted houses at the top of Sixth and Seventh Avenues. It was almost three o'clock now, and a veil of high clouds had passed over the sun, so that the air was closer and dustier. They trotted at a fast pace westward to the low farm building at the junction of Broadway and Eighth Avenue, and then they turned downtown and galloped for a while along the hard-baked mud surface of Broadway, overtaking farm carts and stagecoaches.

At last, by Thirty-fourth Street, they slowed down and rode quietly together as if they had been friends all their lives, with no need of conversation. Delphine turned to Collis from time to time and smiled at him, and Alice smiled benignly at them both.

'I've always preferred playing Cupid to playing chaperone,' she said as they arrived at De Vere's and a boy came out to take their horses.

Collis took Alice's hand and gave it a squeeze. He only wished that he could feel as certain about his future with Delphine as she did. Maybe her father could help. But, on the other hand, maybe he couldn't; and maybe all of this day, with its flirtation and its kisses and its misty sunshine, would be the most sadly wasted day he had ever spent.

Senator William Stride was standing by the window of the smoking-room of the Astor Place Hotel, his deeply carved features illuminated only by the red light of the setting sun, reflected from the windows of the buildings across the street. He was a tall, stooping man, with a nose like an eagle's beak, and sidewhiskers of tight silver curls. His collars were always higher and stiffer than anyone else's, and his tailcoats were always darker and more severe. In the Senate he was nicknamed Lucifer, although it wasn't always said unkindly. He might have been a slave-owner, but he was cultured and humane, and his spontaneous contributions to worthy causes were famous. It was considered unwise to cross him, that was all, because when he was crossed he would make life hell.

Collis walked across the smoking-room, between the shiny leather chairs, and held out his hand.

'Senator? I'm Collis Edmonds. I'm pleased to meet you.'

The Senator turned, his hands still clasped behind his back, and lifted a curly grey eyebrow. 'Mr Edmonds? Ah, yes. Alice told me you might be coming.'

He reached out a large, dry hand, as wide as a hoe, and shook hands. 'Won't you sit down? This isn't really my notion of a private meeting place, but I'm afraid I've been very pushed for time. I had a meeting this afternoon with the board of the Erie Railroad, and it went on two hours and ten minutes longer than I had hoped.'

Collis sat in one of the club armchairs, and Senator Stride sat opposite him, his long legs stretched out across the Persian rug and his ankles crossed. His arms seemed to be longer still, and it appeared to Collis that a great deal of complicated folding and bending was required before they were neatly arranged across the Senator's chest.

It was so dark in the smoking-room now, despite the beads of light from the gas-jets, that Senator Stride's face was deep in shadow, and all Collis could see was the tip of his beak and his side-whiskers. Out of this shadow spoke a voice that was deep and educated and unmistakably Southern, a drawl that was almost sinister in the way it coaxed five vowels out of words that had only two, and lingered on every consonant until it had been thoroughly tongued.

'I understand from Alice that you've been paying court to Delphine Spooner,' said Senator Stride. He pronounced 'court' as 'cow-ought'.

'That's true, sir. In a modest way. We've known each other only a very little time.'

'Alice says you're both as keen as chili peppers.'

'Alice is exaggerating a little, sir. But she's not too far wrong. I am very fond of Delphine, and I do believe that my feelings are returned.'

The shadowy head nodded. 'I've known the Spooners for a great number of years, and they're fine people. I was best man at their wedding, did you know that? And I'm Delphine's godfather, too.'

'Yes. Alice told me. They're a very pleasant family.'

A waiter came in with a tray, his white shirt front oddly luminous in the gloom of the smoking-room.

'Would you care for a drink?' asked the Senator.

'A whisky, with a splash of water.'

'And bring me a glass of fresh lime juice,' said Senator Stride. 'Just a small one.' Then he turned back to Collis and added, 'I'm a temperance man, myself. I don't much hold with liquor. But don't let that put you off yours.'

'No, sir,' said Collis uneasily, changing his position in his

76

slippery leather chair. He suddenly began to feel that he might have made a mistake in coming to Senator Stride, and apart from that, his collar seemed distinctly too tight, and his shoes pinched. It was the fashion this year for young men to wear shoes made of what *Life Illustrated* called 'astoundingly *little* sections of patent leather', and in front of the gaunt, plain Senator, with his shoes as big as coal-boxes, Collis felt decidedly foppish.

'Your father's Makepeace Edmonds, isn't he, from I. P. Woolmer's Bank?' asked Senator Stride.

'Er – yes, sir.'

'A man who understands the South and her problems, if I remember.'

'Yes, sir.'

'A view that Alice tells me you don't personally share.'

Collis took a deep breath. 'No, sir. Not entirely.'

'Are you a Black Republican, Mr Edmonds? A free-soil man?'

Collis sat up straighter. 'Sir, I didn't really come to meet you to discuss my politics. What I feel about the South and slavery are not really relevant. I'm still young, anyway, and I expect I'll change my mind when I'm as old and wise as you.'

'Young? At twenty-five? I was in Congress when I was your age, and I haven't changed my mind one whit since. Not about anything.'

Collis tried to smile, and was surprised by how difficult it was. 'I'm sure you haven't, sir. But then you're a professional politician, and I'm nothing more than one of four million voters. We look to you to remain constant, while you look to us to change our minds.'

Senator Stride sat in silence for a while, digesting with disinterest, if not actual displeasure, what Collis had said.

'Well,' he announced, after a few moments, 'I guess you have a way with words, if nothing else.'

'I came to ask you a financial favour, as a matter of fact.'

'You want to borrow *money*?' inquired the Senator, with a dry, incredulous sniff. 'With a bank president for a father?'

'I don't want it for myself, sir.'

'Then what? Are you canvassing on behalf of one of these dim-witted gold speculations? I can assure you, Mr Edmonds, that my money is never thrown away on frivolities.'

'I wouldn't call this a frivolity, sir I. P. Woolmer's Bank is in deep trouble, and they need someone to bail them out.'

There was another pause, while the Senator took stock of what

77

he had just heard. He unfolded one arm and let it hang down beside his chair, his veiny hand swinging just an inch from the carpeted floor. Collis kept his eyes on the Senator's shadowed face.

'They're a sound bank,' said the Senator. 'Real sound. Why should they be in trouble?'

'There's been some speculation.'

'I see. And what do they need?'

'They don't need cash. They just need underwriting for two million dollars until they get themselves back on their keel again.'

'Two million dollars?'

Collis nodded.

Senator Stride twiddled with his whiskers.

'Why did they send you?' asked the Senator, after yet another lengthy pause. 'Why didn't your father approach me himself, or Harry Benedict?'

'They didn't send me.'

'Ah-hah. Then it all becomes clearer. It was your father who decided to speculate. Your father who's gotten his fingers burned. He's told you, but he hasn't told anyone else. He wants two million dollars to shore up the bank while he puts his silly mistakes right.'

Collis bit at his thumbnail. 'If you want to put it that way.'

'It's not how I care to *put* it that's important, Mr Edmonds. It's the way that it *is*.'

'Well, all right. That's the way it is.'

The waiter came in with their drinks. He set the Senator's lime juice on a dark polished mahogany side table, and then asked Collis if he would mind propping his whisky glass on the arm of his chair. Before he left, he went across to the gas brackets and turned up the gas, so that for the first time Collis could see the Senator's deep-set, glittering eyes. The sight of them didn't make him feel any more comfortable.

'What nature of speculations did your father invest in?' asked Senator Stride.

Collis sipped his whisky. 'Railroads, gold. A few commodities.'

'How do I know, if I agreed to underwrite him, that I wouldn't be throwing good money after bad?'

'Because of his reputation, sir. This is the first time he's ever attempted risky speculations. It'll be the last time, too. He did it for personal reasons, because of personal pressures, but he understands now that the only criteria in banking must be security and steady growth. He's made a mistake, admittedly. But he's one of the finest bankers in Wall Street, and your money's as safe in his hands as it is in the deepest vault in the whole country.'

Senator Stride took a drink of his lime juice and pursed his lips against its sourness. 'That's a very fine recommendation, Mr Edmonds. Regrettably, it comes from a source that I have to describe as inordinately biased.'

'It's true, all the same. You know that it is.'

'All right, supposing it *is* true. If I were to risk two million dollars of my own money by underwriting your father's debts at the bank, what would be in it for me?'

'A percentage.'

'Of course, a percentage. But how much percentage? And what guarantee would I have that it would ever be paid?'

'Six per cent per annum. And my word on it.'

'Are you an officer of the bank? An accredited representative?'

'No. But I will give you a written indemnity, once you agree to secure the deficit.'

Senator Stride watched Collis for a while, his wide hands steepled in front of his mouth, blowing thoughtfully between his fingers.

'Your father's on the edge of bankruptcy, is he not?'

'Not personally. Of course not.'

'Then why are you so worried? If it was only a bank deficit, and not a personal deficit, you wouldn't even care. Did your father invest his own money in these worthless speculations?'

'A little.'

'Only a little? You're making a very impassioned plea for only a little.'

'I want to help my father, that's all.'

'What a solicitous son you are. But what are the board members of I. P. Woolmer's going to think when *they* find out? They're bound to, you know.'

Collis nodded. 'Father was going to talk to them on Friday, but he decided to postpone it for a week. He guessed he'd stand more chance of weathering it out if he'd already arranged for the losses to be covered.'

'What happens if he fails?'

'Then they'll probably request his resignation.'

'That won't be much of a hardship. He's due for retirement soon.'

Collis sighed. 'Very well. He's lost a great deal of his own money, too. If he can't sort this out by the board meeting on Thursday, he'll be almost destitute.'

Senator Stride nodded. 'I thought as much. The family rallies around only when their own comfort is threatened.'

'You don't have to be unpleasant about it.'

'Why not? Poverty is a very unpleasant fact of life. I hope you're well prepared for it.'

Collis dropped his gaze. He was beginning to understand why they called Senator Stride after the devil. He had a way of prodding and prodding at you until you fell over the precipice of your own sins and omissions. Nevertheless, he persisted.

'Will you consider helping? Even if you didn't underwrite the whole amount yourself, I'm sure I could find others to join you. The most important thing is discretion. If the word gets out that I. P. Woolmer's has lost two million dollars of investors' money on a cheapjack railroad speculation – well, you can imagine what would follow.'

'I most assuredly can imagine, Mr Edmonds. I saw the Bank of Charleston go down like a brick in '37, taking a reasonable amount of my money along with it. I wouldn't let that occur a second time.'

'Well, then?'

Senator Stride finished his lime juice. When he had done so, he stood up and walked back across to the window. He stared at his own saturnine reflection for a long time before he answered.

'I'm going to have to consider this most carefully, Mr Edmonds. I'm going to have to think over the good points of it and the bad points of it.'

Collis stood up too. 'How long will it take you to make up your mind?' he asked, trying not to sound bitter.

'A day or two. I'd like to speak to some of my brokers first, and George Spooner.'

'Do you have to do that? If the Spooner family think that I'm going to go broke – '

Senator Stride gave Collis a plain home-baked look that meant, 'You've come to me with your cap in your hand, son. Don't start laying down conditions.'

He said quietly, 'George Spooner has to know. If I. P. Woolmer's goes down, then Ohio Life is going to be threatened, too. Ohio Life does a whole lot of its banking through Woolmer's.'

'I've asked you this favour in confidence, Senator Stride. I don't want Mr Spooner to know. Not until it's all settled.'

'Mr Edmonds,' warned the Senator, 'you'd better understand that when you're down in the ditch, anyone can call you Shorty. I won't even think about underwriting your father's mistakes unless I've discussed it with George Spooner first, and if I *don't* underwrite them because you don't want George Spooner to know, then you're stuck anyway.'

'Then I think I'd better go someplace else.'

'I'll still tell George what's happened, whether you go someplace else or not. He's an old, old friend of mine, Mr Edmonds, and your father's horsing around with railroad stocks has put his business at risk.'

'Is that how much I can trust a Southern Democrat?'

'It's how much George Spooner can trust a Southern Democrat. If I was your friend, wouldn't you expect me to do the same?'

Collis sat on the arm of one of the smoking-room chairs and rubbed his eyes. The idea of asking Senator Stride to underwrite I. P. Woolmer's had seemed so simple when he had thought about it over the weekend. But now, nightmarishly, it looked as if the price of saving his father was going to be losing Delphine. He couldn't imagine that the Spooners would allow her to marry a young man whose family had been within a cat's whisker of ignominious bankruptcy. He finished his whisky, and then felt it rise again in the back of his throat. It was Monday evening, and out on the street below he could hear a vendor call out: 'Pineapples, fresh pineapples! Come and buy your lovely pineapples!'

'All right,' said Collis. 'If you have to speak to Mr Spooner, you have to. But please let me know as soon as you can.'

'Oh, I shall assuredly do that,' replied Senator Stride. And, for the first time that evening, he smiled.

Just before eleven o'clock the following morning, Angus the butler came up to Collis's rooms and announced that there was a man to see him in the front room. He had been writing a letter to an old schoolmate of his who had gone to St Louis and made a modest fortune in lumber. He had put down his pen and was rereading what he had written while Angus hovered at the door. Then he crumpled up the sheet of writing paper, and tossed it over his shoulder.

Angus, grey-haired, like a jowly old dog in wire-rimmed spectacles, creaked ahead of him down the stairs and along the corridor and opened the front-room doors for him. From the sound of it, he wore absolutely ferocious stays.

Collis paused in the hallway and lit up a small corona before he entered. He decided he was probably smoking too much; but then, the way things were, he needed some way of settling his nerves. The front room was small and gloomy and decorated in reds and golds, and in a chair by the window he could see the wavy hair of a man who was sitting with his back to Collis, trying to read a copy of the *Herald* by the opal-coloured light that was sieved through the curtains. Collis stood by the door, puffing at his cigar to get it going, and trying to think who on earth this was.

After a few moments, the man turned around; he came across the room with his hand out and a satisfied smile on his face. He was, to Collis's complete disgust, none other than the wheat-complexioned manager of the Madison Saloon, in a loud check suit and tan gloves, and reeking of lavender water.

Collis declined to shake hands. 'Who let you in here?' he said.

'Your butler, sir.' The man grinned. 'He used to work in premises of mine, a good while back.'

'Angus? I was under the impression he'd been in service all his life.'

'No, sir. In his youth he was one of the best dealers in town. He went by the name of Shaker in those days.'

'Well, you surprise me,' said Collis. 'You also annoy me. I thought I'd already paid you off, both for your damned glassware and your silence. And you might as well know that I don't intend to patronise your swinepit of a saloon ever again.'

'There are still enough swine left to give me a reasonable living,' said the manager, still grinning, and showing teeth the colour of old varnished pine.

'Then what do you want?' demanded Collis.

'A glass of Madeira wine wouldn't go down too badly,' the manager suggested.

'Are you serious?'

'Of course, Mr Edmonds. I'm more than serious. I'm distraught. In fact, I was so upset when I heard what had happened that I came around here straight away by cab to offer you my commiserations.'

'Commiserations? What for?'

The manager raised one of his wheaty eyebrows. 'I thought you might have heard.'

'Heard what? If you don't stop playing games with me, I'll kick you out of the house.'

'It's the young lady, sir,' said the manager. 'The young lady who fell from the parapet. She's passed on.'

Collis stared at the man through the smoke of his cigar. He felt giddy, as if he had been spinning around and around, and had suddenly stood still. He went to the carved and polished sideboard and picked up a small silver handbell, which he rang, his eyes still on the wheat-coloured manager, his cigar still smouldering between his teeth.

'I see,' said Collis. 'I suppose you'd better sit down.'

'I'm all right standing, thank you.' The manager smiled.

At that moment, Angus creaked in. He glanced at the manager and tried hard not to look as if he knew him; then he came over to Collis and said, 'Yes, sir?'

'We'd like a Madeira wine, please, *Shaker*,' Collis said, 'and a glass of dry sherry.'

'Shaker, sir?'

'It's all right. Our friend from the Madison here told me something about your past. It's no disgrace. In fact, if you're that good, you might come up to my rooms one night and we'll play a couple of hands.'

Angus coughed. 'Thank you, sir. A Madeira wine and a fino.'

When he was gone, Collis turned back to the manager. 'Suppose you tell me just what it is you're looking for,' he said. 'I'm not the kind of man who likes to thrash around the bushes.'

'Well,' said the manager, feigning embarrassment, 'what I really wanted was some species of agreement. You know the sort of thing I mean. You do me a favour, as it were, and I'll do you a favour in return.'

Collis smoked, and nodded. 'I know the sort of thing you mean. It's usually called blackmail.'

'Oh, no,' said the manager. 'It's nothing like that. Blackmail is when somebody's guilty, and someone else agrees to keep the secret quiet for a price. But I know that you're innocent. All I'm doing is asking for a donation in order to keep my memory in good working order. If you like, I'm looking for a contribution to mental science.'

'How much?' asked Collis bluntly.

The manager shrugged. 'How much is it worth to you to stay out of the courts? You see, now that she's dead, the police are going to have to do something about it, even if it's only to file a report that

83

she died by happenstance. It would be most unfortunate if they decided you pushed her off that parapet on purpose.'

Collis thrust his hands in his pockets. 'Now why should I have wanted to do something like that? There's no motive, you see. That's where your story falls down.'

The wheat-coloured manager beamed. 'It depends if I can remember you shouting at her before she fell, or not.'

'*Shouting* at her?'

'That's right. It could be that I heard you calling her a slut, and a she-devil, and generally expressing your annoyance because she was teasing you for certain disabilities.'

'Are you crazy? I ought to punch you in the nose.'

'You don't have to do that. It would be much better, all around, if you didn't. We don't want the police to think you're a naturally violent man, do we? Not a man who's easily aroused to punching people, or pushing them off parapets.'

Angus appeared at the door with the drinks on a small tray. The two men remained silent while he handed the manager his Madeira and then shuffled across to Collis with his sherry. He sniffed once and left, leaving the door slightly ajar. Collis called, 'Door, Shaker!' and after a slight pause it was closed, with a click.

'I drink to your health,' said the manager, raising his glass.

Collis ignored him. 'Just tell me how much you want,' he said. 'I'm not in the mood for social pleasantries.'

'Well,' said the manager, with the air of a man trying to decide the price of a reasonable horse, 'I'd say that five hundred dollars should settle it.'

'Five hundred dollars? Are you out of your mind?'

'Not that I know of. You have to look at the price objectively, if you see what I mean. At the moment, you're free, and you're walking around at your liberty, and so five hundred dollars seems like a lot. But imagine if you were locked up in a police cell. Imagine being incarcerated with a rabble of felons and drunkards. Five hundred dollars would seem a very small price to pay for your freedom then.'

'It's too much. I didn't kill the girl, and that's all there is to it. I'm not paying five hundred dollars to a scalawag like you to protect myself from the consequences of a crime I didn't commit.'

'You have forty-eight hours to think about it.' The manager smiled.

'Don't you give me deadlines,' warned Collis. 'I'm not paying your damned blackmail now, nor in forty-eight hours, nor ever.'

The manager sipped his Madeira. 'I'm sorry to hear you say that,' he said. 'It could have been a most amicable arrangement for both of us. Most amicable.'

Collis took a quick, angry breath. 'The most amicable thing you can do right now is leave,' he told the manager.

There was a pause. The manager finished his Madeira and laid the glass neatly on the sideboard. He thought for a moment and then looked up at Collis with a cajoling, almost friendly expression.

'You're sure I can't persuade you to change your mind?'

'Out,' Collis said.

'Very well.' The manager nodded. 'I'm sorry to hear you talk that way, but if you feel you can't accommodate me, what more can I do? I'll be around in forty-eight hours in any event, to see if you've decided to pay. I'll bring my two friends from Chatham Square, too, if you'd care to meet them again.'

Collis seized the manager by the sleeve and pulled him roughly towards the door while the manager cried, 'Here! Here! Steady, Mr Edmonds!' But Collis was too furious to stop. He wrenched open the door and shoved the manager out into the hallway. Then he stalked out after him and pushed him again, so that the man fell against the hall-stand and was showered in derbies and silk hats.

'Out!' shouted Collis. 'Out!'

He opened the heavy front door and manhandled the manager on to the front step. Angus, aroused by the noise and the commotion, hurried along the hallway as fast as his corsetry would permit, but he was too late to prevent Collis from kicking the manager right in the seat of his pants, so that the man howled in pain and staggered down the five marble steps to the street clutching his backside.

'Don't come back!' yelled Collis. 'Not you, nor your boxers, nor anybody to do with you!'

'I warn you!' shouted the manager. He was crimson in the face now, and just as angry as Collis.

'Warn all you damn well want!' Collis told him. 'Just make sure you don't try to set foot in this house again!'

Angus, his eyeglasses perched precariously on the end of his nose, stood beside Collis and watched the manager limp to the corner of Gramercy Park and wave for a cab. Outside, it was a warm, dusty day, and a girl in a carriage gave Collis a saucy glance from under her parasol as she and her unimpressible-looking mother rolled by. Collis didn't, and couldn't, take any notice. As he turned away from the open door and walked back across the hallway, he began to understand how much his life had changed in just a few days. A couple of weeks ago, he would have called at once for his horse and contrived to gallop around the block so that he could raise his hat to a girl as pretty as that, and beg her mother for an introduction.

He drew hard at his cigar to rekindle it. Behind him, Angus closed the front door and came shuffling back, shaking his head.

'You look distinctly unhappy,' said Collis.

Angus nodded. 'Every right to be, sir. Not for my own sake, mind you. But I've known that fellow for more than twenty years. I worked in one of his gaming rooms from '32 to '39, and I can tell you straight out that he's one of the hardest nuts in the business. Not a man to cross, sir. Not if you fancy a nose to breathe through.'

'What's his name?'

'Carpenter, sir. Herbert Carpenter. Not a man to cross, by any means.'

'I see,' said Collis, with a sigh of fatigue.

Makepeace came home from Wall Street at seven o'clock, when the sun was beginning to sink into the grainy skies over New Jersey. Collis had heard his carriage draw up outside, and he stood by an upstairs window looking down on his father's rounded shoulders and the top of his black silk hat as the old man was helped down to the sidewalk. He could see by his father's defeated demeanour that no miracles had happened during the day to rescue him from his creditors. He let the diamond-patterned lace curtain fall back into place, and the street outside was veiled in white.

He stood at the head of the stairs as Makepeace came in through the front door, handed his hat and his cane to Angus, and then took out his big white handkerchief and wiped his perspiring forehead. It was still warm and dusty out on the streets.

'Father,' said Collis quietly.

Makepeace looked up. 'Oh, you're there.'

'Yes. Is there any news?'

Makepeace shrugged. 'It depends what kind of news you mean. There's plenty of bad news. Plenty of that. But not much good news at all.'

Collis descended the stairs and came across the hallway. When he saw his father close to, he suddenly appreciated how much this financial disaster had taken out of him. He looked bloated with illness instead of puffed up with pride, and somehow his formal business clothes seemed ill-fitting and incongruous. He smelled of brandy, and Collis guessed that he must have stopped off at the club on the way home to fortify himself after the day's despair.

'Is there no hope at all?' asked Collis.

Makepeace shook his head. 'It's almost impossible. The problem is, I have to keep it quiet. I can't tell anybody what I need the money for. And even the wildest speculator won't underwrite me for two million dollars without having some kind of inkling what he's supposed to guarantee, and why.'

Collis looked at his father sadly for a moment. 'Don't you have any old friends you can turn to? Somebody who owes you a favour? Not after all these years on Wall Street?'

Makepeace raised his head and smiled. 'You'd be surprised how many so-called friendships are dependent on one's solvency. When you're a beggar, my boy, they don't want to know you any more. I talked to three friends of mine at three separate trusts, and none of them would entertain the smallest loan, not even twenty dollars, without papers and guarantees and full details of what I was going to use it for. On Wall Street, your friendships are only as wide as your wallet.'

Collis wondered whether it was time to tell his father about Senator Stride, but he decided against it. If the Senator came up with the guarantee, then everything would be fine and dandy in any case. But if he didn't, and particularly if he told George Spooner all about Makepeace's fruitless speculations, then Makepeace was going to be something less than grateful. Collis considered it was probably wiser to leave the outcome as a surprise, whether it was pleasant, or unpleasant, or downright catastrophic.

'I'm tired now,' said Makepeace. 'I'm going to take a shower bath. Am I going to see you later, or will you be out?'

'I was thinking of meeting some friends for dinner.'

'Well, then, I probably won't.'

Collis laid his arm around his father's shoulders. He said gently, 'I want you to know that I *do* support you. I know we have arguments, and fights; and I know we don't see eye to eye on politics. But if there's anything I can do to help you, well, you only have to let me know.'

His father nodded. 'Thank you,' he said gruffly, as if he was unsure whether to believe Collis or not, but prepared to accept his sympathy for the time being. Then he added, 'By the way, I heard from my friend in Maine today. The fellow who was looking for a thirty-pound lobster for you.'

'Oh, yes?' asked Collis. 'Did he find one?'

Makepeace started to sort through his pockets. 'He didn't exactly find one . . . wait a minute, I have his letter here someplace. He didn't exactly find one . . . but he good as did.'

'What do you mean, he *good* as did? Either you can find a thirty-pound lobster or you can't.'

Makepeace at last found the letter. He unfolded it carefully, peered at it, and then handed it to Collis. 'You can see for yourself,' he said.

Collis held the letter up to the light that came through the crescent-shaped window above the front door. The writing was sloped, even, very old-style New England, like the original penmanship on the Declaration of Independence.

It said:

Belfast, Maine

My dear Makepeace,

Further to y'r inquiry for a 30-pound lobster, I have required my people to ask high and low of lobstermen and to haunt the fishmarkets for you. Regrettably, I have to inform you that the intensity of lobster catching these days is such that beasts of 20 pounds or more are not to be had. Even 12 pounds is considered a very substantial weight. Perhaps I can assist, however, by enclosing the following five affidavits, all legitimately signed by Maine lobstermen, each deposing that they have seen and handled in their time lobsters of 30 pounds in weight.

Cordially,
Jack Foreman

Collis slowly folded the letter up again. This was the damned limit. He had promised Nathan Hackett that he would set a thirty-pound lobster on a plate in front of him. If he couldn't, he was going to be down by $300, and $300 on top of the $500 that Herbert Carpenter of the Madison Saloon was demanding was $800. Where the hell, with his father in perilous debt, was he going to find $800?

He said hoarsely, 'Do you have the depositions?'

Makepeace searched in his pockets again and eventually handed over five soiled and scrappy pieces of paper, smelling of fish. Collis

88

looked quickly through them; some were signed with crosses, others with crude, jagged signatures. Collis examined them all, then sighed.

'It seems that times have changed since I was in the fish business,' said Makepeace with an uneasy smile. 'Lobsters don't get the time to grow that large.'

Collis turned away. 'So much for the lobsters you had to boil in your wash-house. Nothing but windbaggery. *Now* what the hell am I going to do?'

'You can show those depositions.'

'Father, depositions are not lobsters. Depositions can't be cracked and eaten. Depositions can't be set on a plate with pepper sauce, and served up for dinner. I promised lobster, not depositions, and now I'm sunk for three hundred dollars.'

Makepeace coughed and took out his handkerchief. 'I can't let you have three hundred. Not that much. Not just now.'

'So what do you suggest I do? Welch on a bet?'

'You shouldn't have made the bet in the first place. It was ridiculous.'

Collis didn't feel like arguing about it any more. His father was beaten, defeated, and struggling to keep his pride while his whole world collapsed around him, and Collis didn't want to add to the landslide.

Nodding to himself, Makepeace went off down the hallway, to say good evening to Ida, and Collis watched him go with a feeling of desolation and unfamiliar regret. He looked so old and humbled that it was difficult for Collis to stay angry. He just hoped that Nathan Hackett would be equally understanding.

Maude came bustling downstairs, in a nasty medicine-pink dress.

'There's a smell of fish around here,' she said, wrinkling her nose.

Collis smiled. 'It takes a haddock to recognise one,' he told her, and then dodged past her ferociously swung purse to run upstairs and get himself dressed.

Later that evening, he met Henry Browne in the bar of the St Nicholas Hotel. The bar was crowded with gentlemen in white ties and evening dress, like a noisy gathering of black-backed gulls, and the burble of conversation under the gilded ceiling and the glittering gas-light was of horses and money and prize boxing. Henry Browne was sitting at a table in the corner drinking whisky and draught beer, and he seemed distinctly depressed.

A waiter with a curly moustache came over to take Collis's order, and then Collis sat back and took stock of his friend with a sympathetic smile.

'What's your problem?' he asked him. 'You look as though you bought at fifty and sold at five.'

'Well, it's something like that,' said Henry. 'I just heard that a railroad company in which I was foolish enough to invest five thousand dollars has gone very much to the wall. They didn't even get as far as knocking in one single spike.'

'I think everybody's had the same trouble,' said Collis cautiously. 'My father lost a bit of money on a railroad in California. Well, more than a bit. Quite a few thousand, from what he tells me.'

'If you ask me,' said Henry, swallowing a mouthful of whisky with a sharp grimace, 'if you ask me, these railroad fellows are better at milking money out of overenthusiastic speculators than they are at building railroads. My crowd got one hundred and twenty-five thousand dollars out of the government for no more effort than closing their eyes and drawing a supposed railroad line across an inaccurate map. It was conveniently swallowed up when they went bankrupt, of course.'

'I suppose you're rather strapped, then.'

'I will be for a while. Why?'

Collis shrugged. 'Nothing special. I could have done with a loan of a thousand or so, that's all.'

'A thousand? What about your father?'

'I think he's a little – well, *unnerved* at the moment. He hasn't been very free with his spare change.'

'I could lend you a couple of hundred, if that's any use.'

'I'm going to need more than that just to pay off Nathan.'

'You mean you can't find a thirty-pounder?'

Collis nodded.

'Oh,' said Henry. 'That's embarrassing.'

'Yes. And that isn't all.'

'Do you want to tell me?' asked Henry. He took out a long Russian cigarette from a monogrammed silver case and lit it. The air was clouded with the sweet, musky aroma of Turkish and Balkan tobaccos.

Collis was almost tempted to explain all about I. P. Woolmer's

Bank, and his father's disastrous speculations, but he decided against it. His father had trusted him to hold his tongue, and that was the least he could do for the silly old duffer. 'It's too early yet. Perhaps I'll be able to tell you when I hear from my friends in high places.'

'I didn't know you had friends in high places. Apart from tha⁺ dark-haired lady on the top floor of that house in Mercer Street.'

'No, no. This is a Senator.'

Henry ran his hand through his fair brown hair and shook his head. 'Don't talk to me about Senators. Senators are the serpents of the earth. This railroad of mine was headed up by a Senator, and if you ask me he was the trickiest fellow in the whole sorry operation.'

'Have I heard of him?' said Collis.

'I shouldn't think so. A Southern gentleman. Do you want another drink?'

'A Southern gentleman? Not William Stride?'

Henry's expression tightened. 'Yes, that's right. How did you know?'

Collis suddenly felt flushed. The bar around him was bright, but unfocused, a fuzzy vision of talking and laughing faces and sparkling lights. 'What was the name of his railroad company?'

'You look extremely pink, Collis,' Henry said. 'Are you all right?'

'Henry – what was the name of his company?'

'The Sacramento Valley Railroad. But why?'

Collis covered his eyes with his hand. 'My God,' he said. 'He must have thought I was a raving lunatic.'

'Who?'

'It doesn't matter,' Collis told him. 'Well, rather, it does.'

'Collis, I don't know what the blue blazes you're talking about.'

'It's Stride. It's all absolutely ridiculous. If you can imagine the worst possible thing that could happen, it's happened.'

Henry crossed his legs and stared at Collis with an urbanely creased forehead. 'My dear Collis, the worst possible thing that could happen would be to die of heart failure just *before* eating one of Delmonico's stuffed woodcock. Or maybe to fall and fracture one's leg while following Kitty Brough upstairs.'

'Henry,' said Collis, 'what I have to tell you is highly confidential. But I really feel I must confide in someone. The whole damned situation is driving me mad.'

'You know me,' said Henry. 'I'm the essence of secrecy itself.'

'Well, sometimes you are,' Collis replied. 'But this time, I must insist. It's too important to get out. It could ruin hundreds of people, yourself included.'

'In that case,' said Henry, lifting his beer glass, 'I give you my word as a disgraced officer and a disgraceful gentleman.'

Collis leaned forward, so close that Henry recoiled a little, as if he were afraid that Collis might kiss him. But Collis pulled him back again and whispered in his hairy ear: 'My father's bank may be going bust. To the tune of two million dollars.'

'God Almighty,' said Henry.

'God Almighty hasn't helped very much so far. The trouble is, Father hasn't only lost his investors' money, he's lost a whole lot of his own, some of which he borrowed from the bank.'

'That was cavalier of him,' remarked Henry.

'Don't ask me what it was. A brainstorm or something. He's never done anything like it in his life, not until now.'

Henry nodded. 'I know. Your father has an enduring reputation as one of the stodgiest bankers who ever breathed. Lewis swears that he's fashioned out of solid sourdough.'

'Never mind that,' said Collis. 'What I've done has made the whole situation a hundred thousand times worse. When I went out with Delphine, our chaperone was Alice Stride, and it occurred to me that if she introduced me to her father, the well-known and wealthy Senator Stride, I might persuade him to underwrite I. P. Woolmer's for the lost two million. Or some of it, at least.'

He paused, and then he said frustratedly, 'What never entered my damned stupid mind was that Senator Stride could have been party to the very damned speculation by which my father was busted. I should have known he was tied up in some railroad deal or another. Almost every damned politician is these days, from Jeff Davis downward.'

'Awkward,' commented Henry.

'Awkward? I don't know how Senator Stride managed to listen to me cajoling him for money and still keep a straight face. As if he was going to underwrite my father for two million dollars that he'd already gone to considerable pains to gyp out of him.'

Henry stared at Collis from only two or three inches away. They blinked at each other for a while. Then Henry said, 'In my opinion, humble as it may be, you've landed yourself in the creek.'

Collis sat back. 'It's even worse than that. God, this place is hot – why don't they put in some fans? The Senator's going to tell

Delphine's father that my family is flat broke, without any chance of getting ourselves out of it, and that's going to put a stop to my courting Delphine. And God knows what's going to happen when he starts spreading the word around Wall Street that Woolmer's is on the verge of bankruptcy, which he surely will. Father will kill me with his bare hands. That's if Mother doesn't kill us both first.'

Henry slowly and thoughtfully stroked his cheek.

'Do you *like* this Delphine?' he asked Collis.

Collis didn't answer, but swigged back his drink and set the empty glass firmly back on the table.

'I know. Why don't we have another?' said Henry, with the brightness of a man who has suddenly and intuitively solved a complicated problem.

Collis shook his head. 'That won't help. It's the end of the world.'

'I know it won't help.' Henry smiled. 'But I always think life looks so much more manageable when one is lying helplessly on one's back, don't you? At least, that's what the colonel's wife told me.'

The waiter came up and stood beside them, twiddling his moustache. Collis raised his eyes to him wearily and then at last said, 'Oh, very well. We'll have the same again.'

The two bruisers must have been following Collis all evening. As Henry and he left the brightly lit frontage of the St Nicholas and crossed Broadway to the north side of Spring Street, they emerged from a darkened store doorway and crossed the street only a few feet behind.

Collis and Henry were both in better humour. Collis was laughing almost uncontrollably at a long story Henry was relating to him about the time he had been obliged to hide in a brother officer's wardrobe (having already availed himself of the brother officer's bed and the brother officer's wife), and how the brother officer had pulled open the wardrobe door, said, 'Oh, excuse me,' and promptly closed it again. Henry, after seven whiskeys and as many beers, had decided that $5000 probably wasn't too much to pay for a salutary experience; and Collis, after six stone fences, had almost forgotten about his problems with Senator Stride and Delphine Spooner.

They turned into Spring Street, still laughing, but as soon as they were out of the gaslights of Broadway and into the shadows, the two men behind them quickened their footsteps and practically ran to catch up with them.

Collis turned. Henry turned, too. Only a few feet away, as bulky and implacable as two small buildings, were Herbert Carpenter's two Chatham Square toughs, their fists raised and their faces set in those rigid, frowning expressions that men of low intelligence consider obligatory for any tasks of violence.

'What do you want?' said Collis, with as much clarity and resolve as he could muster.

The tough with the shaven scalp and the bottle scars answered. 'Compliments of Mr Carpenter, this is. On account of you kicking him downstairs.'

Henry looked at Collis blurrily. 'Do you *know* these men?'

'Yes,' nodded Collis. 'I think they've come to beat me up.'

Henry tried to stand very straight. In a slurry voice, he announced, 'I think you'd better know that I was boxing champion at West Point, 1849. My left hook broke an instructor's jaw, and my right hook was so deadly that they considered bedding me down in the armoury, along with the Springfield rifles.'

'Well,' answered the tough with the shaven head, 'I don't mind about that. It's *him* we're after, not you.'

'You'll have to fight me first,' said Henry gallantly.

'I don't mind about that,' the tough told him.

Without warning, the other bruiser, with spiky hair and a tight-fitting tailcoat, stepped forward and punched Henry very hard in the face. Collis, in a split second, saw Henry rolling across the street in a flurry of evening dress and horse manure, and then something as fast and heavy as a cantering pony collided with his shoulder and sent him hurtling against the iron railings. He bounced off, as if he were made of India rubber, but his back was bruised and he hit his ear on the sidewalk. He tried to get up, but a huge boot kicked him in the hip, and he felt as if the night was bursting in every direction.

He heard Henry yelling a hoarse drunken yell, and he lifted his head. The tough in the tailcoat had Henry's neck in an armlock and was screwing his knuckles into the side of his temples. Collis tried to pull himself to his feet, and had almost succeeded when a fist as hard as a doorknob punched him in the ear and he pitched over again.

From somewhere, Henry's voice shouted, 'Collis! On your feet! Run!' and somehow he managed to grasp the railings and pull himself upright again, with bright pinpoints of light sparkling in front of his eyes.

The shaven-headed tough called, 'More? You want more?' and charged at him again, his fists revolving like a funfair ride. But then Collis, his left shoe uncomfortably squashed down at the back, his pants torn at the seams, his silk hat crushed over one eye, was up and running. Henry was already halfway down Spring Street, his legs pumping up and down as if he were dancing a very fast polka.

The bruisers came hard behind them, silent and dogged. Collis only once glanced over his shoulder, as they ran across Lafayette Street, dodging between the carriages, and the two toughs were almost close enough to sink their broken teeth into his ear.

'Collis! Follow me!' Henry shouted, and unexpectedly turned down a narrow, pitch-black alley between two dilapidated red-brick houses. Collis ran after him blindly, holding his hands out in front of him in case he struck a wall or a fence in the dark. The alley reeked of damp and sewage, and echoed with the *splank-splank-splank* of running feet.

They turned right, tripping over someone who was lying drunk and asleep on a heap of rubbish. A coarse voice yelled: 'Wake a man up in his bed, would you? Wake a man up in his bed?' but they were running towards the lights of the Bowery now, and all of a sudden they were out of the alley and pushing their way through the crowds that swarmed along the warm sidewalks outside the theatres and the bars and the novelty saloons.

'We can slow down now,' panted Henry. 'They won't attack us here. Not with the Bowery b'hoys around.'

They slowed to a walk, bruised and filthy and still gasping for breath. Behind them, the two pugs emerged from the alley and followed them for a short way, but then, thwarted, they turned off at Stanton Street and were lost in the darkness. Collis and Henry kept walking uptown, making their way as inconspicuously as they could through the parading crowds of hard young men in red shirts and elaborate cravats, with flouncy young bonneted women on their arms. Collis looked firmly ahead of him, avoiding the hostile and curious stares that followed them along the sidewalk, for these were the Bowery b'hoys and girls, and they were just as inclined to and capable of pasting intruders like Collis and Henry as the two Chatham Square bruisers.

At last they found a cab, with the driver asleep on the box. Henry shook the man awake, and he agreed to take them up to the Union

Club. They both felt like a stiff drink and a brush-up before they retired for the night.

Inside the cab, lighting a cigarette, Henry said hoarsely, 'That was no fun. What *have* you been up to, to make a couple of thugs like that so furious?'

Collis was still shaking. He looked across at Henry, whose face was hidden in curling smoke and the shadows of the carriage, and shook his head.

'I don't know. It seems to me that heaven has decided to single me out for some singularly unpleasant punishment. Like Job.'

'How odd,' said Henry. 'Let's just hope you don't get boils on your bottom.'

Chapter 3

His father's fury, the following morning at breakfast, was worse
than boils. The coffee grew cold in the silver urn, the scrambled eggs
went stiff and dark yellow, and the toast curled up in despair. Ida, at
one end of the table, sat mute with shock, her face white and stiff as
a meringue. Maude, sitting opposite Collis, pulled such a variety of
disgusted and disapproving faces that in happier circumstances he
would have had to laugh.

But the circumstances were catastrophic. A torn-open letter lay
on his father's uneaten eggs. His father, dressed for the office in grey
vest and tailcoat, was pacing the rug, popping with anger, while the
ormolu clock on the sideboard chimed the hour at which he should
already have been sitting at his desk.

Collis at least had the diplomacy to keep his head lowered. His
father came around to his side of the table from time to time, and
bent over him, and raged in his ear, and in the face of that kind of
treatment there was very little else he could do.

'I asked you, on your honour, to keep this unfortunate affair to
yourself!' shouted Makepeace. 'I asked for your word! So what did
you promptly do? You went, without consulting me, to one of the
lowest financial rats in the whole of America. You went to the very
man whose bubble had burst and left me destitute! You revealed my
identity to him, and he went straight away to trumpet my disaster
around the breadths of Wall Street! My God, Collis, I thought you
were a fool, but I didn't realise you were an idiot!'

Makepeace wiped his mouth with his napkin. The pause gave
Collis the opportunity to say quietly, 'It was you who lost the
money in the first place, Father. And there was no guarantee that
you could have found anyone to underwrite you. In fact, there was
hardly any chance at all.'

'Don't be so damned impertinent!' shouted Makepeace. 'Until
you stuck your oar in, it was nothing more than a temporary set-
back, a few days' financial difficulty! But now, I'm finished! I'm
going to have to sell the house, and the farm, and the carriages, and
every damned painting and ornament we possess!'

Maude, at that point, burst into tears, her face folding up like a
bright-red umbrella. 'It's so unfair,' wept Maude.

'What's unfair about it?' asked Collis. 'We're all in the same boat.'

'That's what I mean,' Maude sobbed. 'Just because *you've* been thoughtless, I don't see why *I* should have to suffer. I don't know anything about money at all. I simply want to live my life in dignity and grace. Now, I shan't even be able to do that. I'm so ashamed!'

'Oh, well,' said Collis, 'perhaps if you ask the Lord, He will provide for you.'

'Don't blaspheme,' put in Ida. 'You've surpassed yourself this time, you cruel and inconsiderate boy. And I'm not particularly pleased with *you*, Makepeace, for putting our happiness and security at risk.'

'If it hadn't have been for Collis, everything would have worked out perfectly well!' snapped Makepeace. 'Now, it's ruination. I haven't the least idea what we're going to do, but this letter from the bank makes it absolutely clear what I *can't* do. I can't touch any of my invested money, I can't seek loans, I can't authorise any underwriting of debts. I'm finished, and all because of a son I thought I could trust!'

Collis stood up. He was the only one who had eaten, and he patted his lips with his napkin. 'Father,' he said calmly, 'if I am to be blamed for this entire disaster, I think it would probably be better for all of you if I packed my bag and left home for a while.'

The breakfast room was silent. Collis cocked his head to one side, like his father, and gave a faint, regretful smile. Maude sobbed into her wet, screwed-up handkerchief. Makepeace, his face pale and solemn, stood in the far corner of the room, by the heavy net curtains, as motionless as a man carved from ebony and ivory. Ida, in a sudden flurry of skirts and perfume, withdrew from the breakfast table, left the room, and closed the door behind her. They heard a muted mewl, like a cat, as she fled down the hall.

'I think you'd better do as you've suggested, and pack your bag,' fumed Makepeace. 'I'm not sure how much longer I can tolerate your presence around this house.'

Collis finished his coffee. 'Father,' he said, 'I was just thinking the very same thing.'

It was his original intention to stay for a week or two with Henry Browne, until the scandal had blown over; but when he took a cab to Henry's over on Washington Place, he saw to his dismay that

Nathan Hackett was standing on the doorstep, in a smart cream summer coat, and so he reached up and tapped the cabbie on the back with his cane and directed him to carry straight on by. It wasn't that he was ashamed to face Nathan, eventually. It was simply that he would rather postpone their next meeting until he had enough cash in hand to pay off his debt for that accursed lobster. He could never have dreamed of embarrassing Nathan by offering an IOU – not when Nathan and half of New York already knew that Makepeace Edmonds was flat broke and on suspension from I. P. Woolmer's Bank. All in all, the recognised etiquette during times of financial stress was to keep one's head well down and avoid putting one's friends into uncomfortable corners.

It was a close, humid day, and even in his light-grey travelling suit he was feeling sweaty and hot. He tugged his tall grey hat over his face as the cab rattled past the elegant black-painted railings of Henry Browne's house so that Nathan wouldn't recognise him, and he didn't sit up straight again until they had passed the trees and classic Greek Revival houses of Washington Square. He looked back through the small oval window in the back of the cab's hood and saw Nathan stepping inside Henry Browne's front door. For the first time in his life, he felt excluded, a social outcast. He remembered Senator Stride saying, 'Poverty is an unpleasant fact of life. I hope you're well prepared for it.'

His next call was to Second Avenue. He asked the cab to wait on the corner of Twelfth Street, and he left his leather-and-canvas valise on the seat. Then he stepped up to the door of the Spooners' brownstone and rapped the polished brass knocker. He felt ridiculously nervous, and he kept tugging and fiddling with his grey gloves. While he waited, the three-piece raggedy band that he had seen on Saturday, the day when he had gone out riding with Delphine and Alice, came slowly shuffling past, playing a sad oom-pah-pah tune, their frayed pants white with dust.

The mournful footman with the shiny hair answered the door. Collis handed him his card. 'I've come to call on Miss Delphine.'

The footman took the card, sniffed, and said, 'Wait, please, sir.' He closed the door, and Collis heard him calling someone within the house. The band went oom-pah-pah, oom-pah-pah. The cabbie climbed down from his box and fastened a nosebag to his horse. Before he climbed back up again, he gave Collis a long, inexplicable look; the look that plain working people give to the extraordinary and peculiar rich.

If only he knew that I am poorer than he, thought Collis.

It was an interminable three minutes before the footman re-opened the door, just enough to hand back Collis's card, and say, 'I regret Miss Delphine is indisposed. Good morning.'

He was about to close the door for good, but Collis thrust his malacca cane into the opening and jammed it.

'Sir, please!' insisted the footman.

Collis pushed the door wider. 'I don't care whether she's indisposed or not,' he hissed. 'I have to see her. Now, will you go tell her I'm here?'

'My instructions, sir, are simply to –'

'I'm not interested in your instructions. Just go tell her.'

The footman sighed. 'Very well, sir. Please wait a little longer.'

He went back into the house, leaving Collis alone at the door once more. The cab driver, watching him philosophically, lit up a clay pipe and contentedly puffed away at it. If a gentleman was damn fool enough to pay him for sitting here feeding his horse and smoking a fill of tobacco, that was quite all right by him.

It was Winifred Spooner who came to the door next. She was flustered, and dressed in bright emerald green. Collis bowed, and took her hand to kiss it, which flustered her even more.

'Mr Edmonds. How nice to see you. I'm really afraid that Delphine – '

Collis squeezed her hand gently. 'You don't have to make social excuses, Mrs Spooner. I know quite well what's happened. But I do ask that you let me speak to Delphine, if only for just a few moments.'

'I regret that my husband – '

'Please, Mrs Spooner. No one need know.'

Winifred rubbed her hands anxiously and bit at her lips. 'Well, if you promise to be very brief. No more than a few minutes. My husband was quite adamant that you weren't to be let into the house, you see. On no account, he said.'

Collis followed her into the small anteroom where he had waited before. It was very close and warm in there, and he took out his handkerchief to dab the perspiration from his forehead. He supposed there was something to be said for being poor; he wouldn't have to wear a high collar and a vest any more, and spend all his time in suffocating drawing-rooms.

Winifred invited him to sit down, but he was too nervous to do so for long. After she had left to fetch Delphine, he circled the room, measuring the rug as he went, stopping every now and then to pick up an ornament or a book, and put it down again. For a while, he examined himself in the gilded mirror over the fireplace, and he thought how expressionless he looked, compared with how torn and damaged he felt. His white wing collar was immaculate, his grey silk cravat perfect. Perhaps the very perfection of his image was what was wrong. When you were wealthy, when you were confident, you didn't need to look as if you'd stepped from a fashion plate in a quarterly magazine.

He was still staring at himself when a soft voice said, 'Collis,' and he turned around to see Delphine standing at the door. Her dark curls were hanging loose around her shoulders, and she was dressed in a plain day gown of pale-blue silk, decorated only with embroidered flowers around the bodice. The gown was cut quite low, so that the swell of her rounded breasts was showing; and between them, in her cleavage, was resting a small cross of pearls and amethysts.

Collis didn't move. He didn't know whether to embrace her or not. Maybe she felt the same way her father did, that he was a pauper now, and not suitable for a girl like her. After all, he had no way of knowing what Senator Stride had actually told George Spooner, or what unpleasant embellishments he might have added to the tale.

'Thank you for coming down,' said Collis quietly. 'I was afraid for a moment that you wouldn't want to see me.'

She came across the room and stood close to him. Her eyes were as wide and as entrancing as the day he had first met her in Taylor's, and the gown, charged with its own static electricity, clung to the curves of her figure. She reached out her hand and held the grey sleeve of his coat, as if he were a possession that she didn't want to relinquish. 'I heard what happened,' she said, almost inaudibly. 'I'm so sorry. I don't know what else I can say.'

'It wasn't your fault,' said Collis. 'It wasn't even Alice's fault. In any case, everyone seems so determined to blame me that it doesn't matter whose fault it was.'

'What are you going to do?'

'I don't know. I was going to stay with a friend of mine, but I n. not sure about it now. When you're flat busted broke, you suddenly realise that you're an imposition on your old friends.'

'Isn't that what friends are for?' she asked him.

He took her hand between his, pressing it gently. 'There are

101

some good things in life which I would rather not put to the test.'

'Sit down for a moment,' she said. 'Just here, on the chaise longue. Don't worry about Mother. We're having the Cheesmans for dinner tonight, and she's flapping about in the dining-room.'

Collis, awkwardly, sat; and Delphine sat beside him, her knee pressed against his. She took his hand again, and stroked each finger as she spoke, her own little fingers caressing the knuckles, the joints, and the dark hairs that grew around his rings. She kept her eyes lowered as she spoke to him, so quietly that he had to lean forward, until his cheek was almost touching her curly hair, so that he could hear. On the wall behind her, a very pompous-looking portrait of her father in a blue military-style coat looked down at her with unceasing disapproval.

'Are you going to leave New York?' Delphine asked him.

'I'm not sure. I suppose I'll have to.'

'I'm going to miss you, you know. I've been dreaming about you every night.'

He touched her hand.

She gave a small, wistful smile. 'I suppose it's a punishment for both of us. Most of these terrible things are. I've been too forward and you've been too reckless, and the Lord has seen fit to separate us. But I want you to know that I'll wait for you, Collis. However long it takes you to get over this scandal, I'll wait.'

He didn't say anything for a long, breathless minute. Then he told her, 'You mustn't. You hardly know me. And I could be away for years.'

She raised her head. Her eyes were misted with tears. 'If years is what it takes, then years it is.'

'But you hardly know me. And I hardly know you.'

Delphine shook her head. 'Don't deceive yourself, Collis. You knew me well the first time you met me. Just as I knew you. We're two people of the same kind. We're the sort of lovers who can't help but fall in love, because it was ordained by fate, and by whatever it is that makes people what they are. We come alive when we're together, like flour and sugar when you mix them with water. It's yeast, bubbling, living yeast.'

'Delphine . . .'

She raised the tips of her fingers to his lips. 'I know what you're going to say, but don't say it. Don't protest. I love you, Collis, I love you very dearly, and no argument will ever make me change my mind. I'm going to wait for you as long as I can, and even if you say

102

you don't love me, I won't mind, because I know that you're only trying to be kind, and spare me my sadness. I love you, and you love me, and nothing on earth, not money nor politics nor years of separation, will ever alter that.'

Collis felt a crushing misery that almost made it impossible for him to breathe. He leaned forward and kissed Delphine on the forehead, then on her lips, and the tears slid from her eyes and mingled with their kiss. She stroked his cheek, so gently and lovingly, and when he sat back and looked at her, he couldn't speak for the lump in his throat.

'You don't have to say anything,' she whispered. 'I know how you feel.'

'Do you?' he asked her. 'Do you know what it's like to have to leave you? It's the most terrible agony I've ever had to face.'

'You'll come back.'

He took out his handkerchief and wiped his eyes. 'Yes, I suppose I will. Though God knows how I'm ever going to raise enough money to get myself together again. I've been so used to collecting my allowance, and spending it, and going back for more when I've run out.'

'Your father made himself a fortune,' said Delphine. 'So can you.'

'For you, I'll knock down mountains,' said Collis.

The clock chimed, and Delphine said, 'I have to get back to help Mother. I promised I would only stay for two or three minutes. Oh, Collis. Oh, my darling.'

She took his face between her hands and lavished him with kisses. He felt as if he couldn't stand this parting moment any longer, as if the sad ecstasy of it was too much, and yet he couldn't bring himself to push her away from him. He closed his eyes and kissed her, and prayed that this one second would go on for ever, and that he would never have to open his eyes and realise that the time had actually come to say goodbye.

'Oh, Collis,' she panted. 'Oh, Collis, oh my God, I can't bear to see you go. Oh, Collis, my love.'

'Delphine,' he murmured. 'My beautiful Delphine.'

She kissed him more fiercely now, until he could taste blood in his mouth along with the tears and the tantalising perfume she wore. She pressed closer, and her hand worked its way under his vest, so that she could caress him through his thin silk shirt and his cotton underwear.

'Delphine,' he said, trying to push her away. 'Delphine, you mustn't.'

'Mustn't what, my darling? Mustn't what?'

'Your mother – she's bound to come see what you're doing – '

'Nonsense. She's too busy with that stupid cook of ours. Oh, Collis, you're delicious. You taste like nothing I ever tasted before.'

'For God's sake, Delphine, this is more than I can bear.'

Her eyes closed, she took his hand in hers and raised her gown at the side, right above the top of her blue-gartered stockings, until Collis could see the pale skin of her bare thigh. She pressed his hand against it, so that he could feel the soft warmth of her flesh, and she wouldn't let him go. Her neck was arched back now, and she was breathing in soft gasps through her pink, parted lips.

Collis was beyond caring whether Winifred was going to return from the kitchen or not. His blood felt as if it were roaring through his veins, around and around, in a vivifying rush, until his cheeks burned. All he was aware of was Delphine, soft and alive, kissing him as no lady nor whore had ever kissed him before. All he was aware of was her slippery, electrified gown, the warmth of her body, and her perfumed hair. Her pearl and amethyst cross blurred brightly in front of his eyes, as if he were dreaming, and waking, and then dreaming again.

Panting softly, she pulled his captive hand still further, into the warmth between her thighs. He couldn't resist now. He was caught, hypnotised by her rhythmic breathing. The sensation was overwhelming. He couldn't have released himself even if he'd wanted to.

'Collis, my lover,' she said, and her voice shook.

From the doorway, if anyone had seen them, it would have appeared as if they were sitting quietly together, waiting for Winifred to return from the kitchen. But a particularly observant spectator would have seen Delphine close her eyes now and again for no apparent reason, and Collis occasionally reaching out with his right hand as if he were about to take something invisible from out of the air. The morning sunlight faded and then brightened again, casting patterns across the floor and misty aureoles around the lovers' faces. Delphine's eyes looked bright, but blind, as if she was concentrating every ounce of attention on the suppressed explosion that was growing in her mind.

It could have lasted no time at all, or for ever. But then Delphine gripped his thigh so hard that it hurt and she gasped: 'My God. My

104

God, Collis, my God, and her face was flushed and congested. He caressed her even deeper until she made a sound like a sniff, and then sat with her eyes screwed up tight and quaked and quaked.

There were footsteps in the hallway. Collis quickly withdrew his hand and moved himself back on the chaise longue, trying to appear formal and calm and composed all at once, in spite of the emotions that were heaving up inside him. Delphine mouthed a silent word at him, he wasn't even sure what it was, but it looked like a plea for something, for understanding or for love, or for the day and the week and maybe even the world to stop right then and there, so that the sensuality of the past few minutes could stay with her always.

The footsteps passed. It was the footman, answering the door to a caller. Delphine took Collis's hand, the hand that had taken her, and squeezed it tight.

'I'm sorry, Collis,' she whispered. 'It was all my fault. Please don't think badly of me. Please.'

'How could I think badly of you?' he asked her. 'You're like an angel. You're the most beautiful girl I've ever met. You disturb me as nobody else.'

'I didn't mean to do that,' she said. Her wide eyes glistened with tears. 'I didn't mean to behave like a strumpet. But there isn't any more time, is there? No more time for proper courting. And I couldn't let you go without finding out at least what – '

She lowered her head. He could hardly stand to look at the soft curve of her neck, knowing that he was going to lose her. He bit his lip and blinked with sadness.

'At least what kind of a lover you are,' she added huskily. 'At least what kind of a man.'

There was a tremulous pause, and then she began openly to weep, looking at Collis with such regret and desolation that he had to turn away, in case he started to cry too, just as freely.

'I think I'd better leave,' he said.

Delphine held him tight for a moment, as close as she possibly could. 'Go now,' she begged. 'Please, before I ask you to stay longer. I can't bear goodbyes. Just promise me that whatever happens, when you come back to New York, you'll come to find me. I'll be waiting for you, Collis, even if I've married another man, even if I've borne his children. I'll always be waiting for you, right up until the end.'

'I'll come for you,' he promised, kissing her forehead, and

touching her hair for the last time. He tried to smile. 'Even if I have to build my own railroad to get here.'

They kissed once more, and then he took his malacca cane and his hat, and the lugubrious footman showed him to the door. He turned, on the front step, and Delphine was standing in the shadows of the hallway, watching him leave without tears now, but with an expression of tenderness and love that would stay with him, in his mind, for years and years to come. In her pale-blue silk dress, with her hair in soft brown curls, and her eyelashes still wet from crying. He saw Winifred bustling down the passage in the background and he saw Delphine turn towards her, and that was all he saw before the footman closed the door behind him, and he was shut out from the life that, only a few days before, had been naturally and rightly his. By the curb, the cab driver was snoozing on top of his seat, his curly-brimmed hat pulled down over his eyes. Collis tapped his foot with his cane and said, 'Are you ready? We're off.'

The cab driver pushed back his hat and stared at Collis as if he was still dreaming.

He paid one last call, to the public cemetery. Under a sky whisked with cirrus clouds, on a shadowless pathway, he stood in front of the wooden cross which marked the grave of Kathleen Mary Murphy, his hat in his hand, and said a prayer. Her death had boiled up his life like a potful of mulligatawny soup, but he felt she deserved some respect, if only a few words of encouragement to enjoy herself wherever she was now, and to rest in peace. In the distance, by the railings, the cab driver waited for Collis with deadened patience, too overwhelmed with boredom even to smoke his pipe. Collis knelt beside the soft earth of the grave mound and pushed a silver dollar into it.

'You deserve more, Kathleen Mary,' he said, under his breath. 'But I regret that I don't have it to spare. Some other time, perhaps.'

The rough grass and the wild flowers of the cemetery were rippled by a warm summer wind, and the trees bowed, and made a seething sound. Collis raised his head, and knew that the wind was coming from the West.

By six o'clock, the sky was a misty, luminous lilac, and the wind had dropped. Even on the deck of the Atlantic mail steamer *Virginia*, moving slowly out of New York harbour with rhythmically beating paddles, there was only a soft, reluctant breeze, and the flag at the stern hung limp. Collis stood by the rail and watched the trees of the Battery slide past. Beyond, under a haze of humidity, were the clustered rooftops of the city, the spire of Trinity Church, the rows of red-brick and brownstone houses and the higgledy-piggledy slums and tenements and warehouses. The steamer gave a mournful honk as it passed Governors Island, and he turned away from the stern and walked slowly forward on the port promenade deck, excusing himself as he pushed past the passengers who huddled against the rails, balancing himself against the uneven sway of the waves beneath his feet. He didn't want to watch New York disappearing into the evening mist. He would rather sit up front, and smoke a cigar, and look towards the sea.

He was still disturbed and aroused by what had happened with Delphine. For any young lady of breeding to admit to erotic appetites was unheard of, at least in mixed company, and the way she had so urgently demanded his touch was tumultuously unsettling. Her desires had not demeaned her, although he wondered how much more there was to her personality than her sexual precocity. She had said she loved him, and that she would wait for him forever if necessary. But did she really have any idea of what love was? She was only nineteen, and completely inexperienced with men.

The *Virginia* passed a white-painted Cunard paddle steamer, the *Persia*, coming in from England. Its passengers lined the decks and waved, but Collis was not in the mood for waving at anyone. The *Persia* blew her whistle, and the sepia smoke from her tall funnel drifted towards the distant woods of Brooklyn, and Collis wished that he were on her, and about to land in New York. But, like any gambler, he knew when he had overstayed his welcome. It was time to open a fresh game.

As they paddled out to the threshold of the grey-green Atlantic, there was a smell of brine and woodsmoke in the air. Not far away, by the rail, a girl in a white dress was holding her bonnet, her face lit by an angle of late sunlight, her petticoats ruffled by the wind. Suddenly she turned around and caught Collis's eye. She was blonde, with china-blue eyes, and a square, Swedish-looking face. Collis stood up and raised his hat to her, but she turned away without a flicker of acknowledgement and walked off coolly down the deck, until she disappeared from view around behind the lifeboats.

It was two hours before dinner was served, and then the fifty passengers were called into the long lamplit dining-saloon and seated at two narrow varnished maple tables, each passenger in front of a cheap white plate on which a hard roll tumbled from side to side with the pitching and wallowing of the ship. The *Virginia* had passed Long Branch on the New Jersey shore, and was steaming her way southward towards Atlantic City, which was to be her first port of call with the mail. The swell of the ocean was stronger now, and the steamer's decks sloped and tilted and rose and sank, which, along with the strong odour of poorly trimmed oil lamps, did very little to improve any of the passengers' appetites. They sat, unfamiliar and uncomfortable, facing each other in four pale-faced rows of twelve, with one at the end to pass down the gravy, and although most of them attempted to make amusing conversation about ocean voyages and *mal de mer*, it wasn't long after the first wafts of barley broth reached them that they began to excuse themselves from the dining-saloon, one and two at a time, to return with their hair standing on end because of the rising wind outside on the deck, their faces the colour of grubby bank-notes.

Collis ate a little soup, declined the meat-and-suet pudding, and finished up with rubbery orange cheese and dusty crackers, washed down with warm lager beer. He talked to a young student with a downy moustache and a linen coat that hung on him as gauntly as if it had been set over the back of a kitchen chair; and he passed a few words with a fat German woman who ate everything that was put in front of her, and wiped her mouth with the back of her wrist until it was shiny with grease. But there was no sign of the blonde girl he had seen on deck. She was probably in her cabin, lying down with a scent-soaked handkerchief pressed to her forehead. On steamers like the *Virginia*, the passengers were berthed fore and aft, since the paddles took up most of the space amidships, and that meant they were all tossed up and down, even in quite amiable seas, like queasy children on either end of a teeter-totter.

After dinner, Collis took a walk out on deck. His own stomach seemed to have settled down now, although he was still wishing he hadn't smoked that cigar. It was almost dark now, and across the glossy surface of the sea he could make out the occasional sparkle of light from New Jersey, or the dipping red lamps of inshore fishing boats. He looked upward at the thick smoke which blew into the night from the *Virginia*'s tall, thin funnel, and at the lights clustered on her masts. It was too cloudy to see the stars.

A little further along the deck, he saw the girl in the white dress. She was wrapped now in a dark-green plaid rug, against the chill of the evening, and she was accompanied by a woman in a brown coat who was so tiny as to be almost a midget. They were standing together watching the foam churned up by the paddles, not even talking. Collis walked up to them, took off his hat, and gave a slight bow.

'My compliments, ladies,' he said. 'Mr Collis Edmonds, of New York.'

The blonde girl turned to him and looked him up and down. Her eyes, even by the dim lights along the promenade deck, were remarkably blue; and close to, she had an irregularity of features that made her face not pretty but extraordinarily attractive, in the same way that a wild animal is attractive. Her eyes were set slightly too wide apart, and her teeth were a little uneven, yet her high cheekbones and her straight nose were classic. At her throat was a white silk ribbon, on which was pinned a cameo of blue and white. She did not smile.

It was the tiny woman who spoke first. She stepped forward until her little black boots were practically touching the toes of Collis's kid shoes, and she raised a tortoiseshell lorgnette to her black, beady eyes. Collis had the uncomfortable feeling that she was sizing him up for a sharp bite on the leg.

'Young man,' she shrilled, in a hard Baltimore accent, 'if you do not take yourself off at once, and stop bothering us, I shall call for the captain and have you thrown into the sea.'

Collis smiled, but his eyes were fixed on the blonde girl, his expression as warm and sincere as he could possibly make it. The girl tried hard not to smile back, but the corner of her mouth twitched very slightly, and she looked away in case he thought he was encouraging him.

'I mean it!' shrieked the midget woman. 'Off you go, or it's into the ocean for you!'

Collis leaned forward, so close to the tiny lady that he was peering through her lorgnette from the opposite side. 'To have met you, madam, even for such a short time, would be worth swimming ten oceans, not just one.'

'There aren't ten oceans,' said the midget woman crossly, although his flattery obviously softened her. 'There are only five, and two of those are far too cold to swim. In any case, we are married ladies, and I should hope that puts an end to the matter.'

'I wasn't aware that it was unseemly to present one's compliments to married ladies,' Collis told her. 'We are standing on the open deck of a steamer, after all, and I can scarcely think of anywhere else where our meeting would be less susceptible to misconstruction.'

'I would rather there were no misconstructions at all,' she retorted. 'Now, isn't there a bar where you could go, and seek some company of your own kind?'

'You're far too harsh,' said Collis. 'Although, come to think of it, I've always heard it said that beneath the harshest of exteriors, one invariably finds the softest of natures.'

'You're very impudent. I think you'd better be on your way.'

'Not until I know who has sent me.'

The midget woman gave a high-pitched sigh. 'You're very persistent, aren't you, as well as impudent? Very well, my name is Mrs John Edgeworth, and my companion is Mrs Walter West. I am travelling to Charleston, and Hannah – Mrs West – is continuing to San Francisco, to join her husband.'

'What about *your* husband, Mrs Edgeworth?'

The midget woman lowered her lorgnette. 'Mr Edgeworth is not well, I'm afraid. That is the purpose of my visit to Charleston.'

'I'm sorry to hear it,' Collis told her. 'I hope it's not serious.'

Mrs Edgeworth was silent. Mrs West laid a hand on her shoulder and said to Collis in a soft, hoarse voice, 'Mr Edgeworth was attacked and beaten by hooligans. He was on a business visit, selling imported rugs. He's – well, he's a small person, like his wife. The hospital telegraphed to say that he had very little chance of survival.'

'Then I'm even more sorry,' said Collis. 'If it isn't impertinent of me, I shall include him in my prayers.'

Mrs Edgeworth took out a small lace-trimmed handkerchief and blew her nose like a penny whistle. 'That's very kind of you, Mr Edmonds. I appreciate the thought.'

'Are you going far yourself?' asked Mrs West. The night wind blew her fine blonde hair in unravelling curls.

'As far as you,' Collis told her. 'I suppose it sounds very hackneyed, but I'm seeking my fortune out West.'

'You look as if you have done very comfortably for yourself in the East,' Mrs West remarked.

Collis shrugged. 'One is always striving to greater heights, I suppose. I hear that there are great fortunes to be made in California, given some luck, and plenty of hard work. May I ask what line of business your husband is in?'

'He's a retailer,' said Mrs West. 'He manages an emporium on Montgomery Street. Fancy goods, and notions, and such things.' She opened a small beaded purse and took out a calotype portrait, which she handed over to Collis with a shy, proud smile. He politely examined it by the light of the ship's lanterns, but all he could make out was a stiff, upright-looking man of about thirty, with a neat beard and a nervous stare. He handed it back without comment.

'He went out to San Francisco two and a half years ago,' said Mrs West. 'We've been writing to each other, of course, but a letter is nothing like a real, live embrace. I've missed poor Walter dreadfully, and he's missed me.'

'You must be very excited,' said Collis.

She smiled. 'I won't believe it until I see him. It's like a dream.'

'He's a very fortunate man.'

There was a difficult pause. Now he knew that Hannah West was married, and devoted to her husband, there didn't seem to be very much profit to be had out of continuing such a stilted and formal conversation. With the wife of a New York socialite, things might have been different, but he knew how doughty the morals of the merchant class were. Still, for all Mrs Edgeworth's shrill protestations, it was obvious that both women were lonely and apprehensive, and it seemed less than courteous to leave them to struggle on by themselves just because Mrs West was unavailable for a shipboard affair. He leaned on the rail, looking down at the frothed-up sea, and wondered if his stomach could stand another cigar, or if his nerves could possibly do without one.

'Walter built up the store from nothing,' said Hannah West. 'He said there were cows grazing on Montgomery Street when he first set up shop, but now it's becoming quite civilised. He started selling Brussels lace last year, and it caught on so well that he had to order five times as much for his next shipment.'

There was a further silence, and then Hannah West continued, 'I'm almost afraid to meet him, you know. It's been so long. I've tried and tried to remember what his voice sounds like, and how he looks, but it's been so difficult.'

Mrs Edgeworth reached up and patted her arm. 'You mustn't let yourself get wound up, Hannah. Winding up is for clocks.

111

Make sure she doesn't get herself wound up, Mr Edmonds.'

'Yes, I will,' said Collis.

Hannah looked away. The shadow of her hat fell across her face, but Collis could see a curved reflection of light on her lower lip as she spoke. 'I feel such a coward,' she said, in her throaty voice. 'Poor Walter has been so brave, going out there on his own and setting up a business, and here I am terrified to see him.'

'Why didn't you go out with him before?' asked Collis.

Hannah lowered her head a little. 'It was my mother. She was dying of consumption. I couldn't have left her.'

'I see. I'm sorry.'

'Oh, don't be, Mr Edmonds. It's kind of you to say so, but she went through dreadful agonies, and she's far better off in the cemetery. At least she's with God now, and peaceful.'

'Amelia was a saint,' declared Mrs Edgeworth. 'There was no question about that. And Hannah was more than a saint to take care of her for so long. It was a very dragged-out going, if you know what I mean.'

Collis looked up, and was suddenly and strangely aware that Hannah West was staring at him. He had the oddest sensation that all of this small talk about Walter West's store and the passing of Hannah's mother was nothing more than a whirl of windblown smoke that was blotting out what was really happening between them. They had said nothing of any intimacy or importance, and yet there was a tension and a disturbance between them. The deck rose and tilted beneath their feet. The paddles churned. But for a moment that was too prolonged to be accidental, they gazed at each other like people who are sure that they must have met before.

He looked away. In the distance, he could see the light that marked the inlet to Barnegat Bay. He said, almost too quietly for Hannah to hear him, 'Saints are very rare these days.'

They talked for a little while longer, about San Francisco and New York, about fashions and politics. It appeared from what Mrs West said that her husband was an enthusiastic supporter of John Frémont, the free-soiler, who had quite narrowly failed in last year's elections to become the first Republican President, and that he was almost religiously opposed to slavery. 'When Walter speaks of free soil,' said Hannah, 'he sounds as if he's speaking straight from heaven itself.'

Collis tried to smile. It was difficult enough to compete with an ordinary husband, he reflected, let alone a divine one. Still, at least

112

Walter West's politics were of Collis's preferred flavour, and he might make a good friend. With only $200 left to his name and with no prospect of employment, Collis was going to need all the friends he could muster. And getting to know Walter West would at least keep Collis within socialising distance of Hannah. A bird in the bush, even a bird in someone else's bush, was better than no bird at all.

At last, a few minutes after ten o'clock, Hannah and Mrs Edgeworth decided to retire to their cabin, and Collis raised his hat to them and wished them a good night's sleep. Before she turned to go, Hannah looked at him again with that odd, lingering magnetism, her eyes as blue as china plates, and he found himself still staring after her when she had closed the varnished saloon door behind her. Perhaps he reminded her of her husband. Perhaps, on the other hand, he didn't. He took out a cigar and clipped the end off it thoughtfully.

He didn't want to turn in straight away. He was tired, but he knew he wouldn't sleep. In any case, he was sharing his cabin with a huge bearded Latvian who had brought on board a catastrophic assortment of paper packages tied up with string and sealing wax, and Collis didn't particularly fancy lying awake in surroundings reminiscent of the parcel office at the New York & Harlem Railroad Depot. There were only twelve cabins on the *Virginia*, six for men and six for women, and all of them were shared. The passengers who couldn't afford cabins, or who had arrived too late to book one, were obliged to spend the night in the dining-saloon, or out on deck, huddled in blankets. Through the lamplit saloon window, at the far end of one of the dining tables, Collis could see that five or six of these passengers had a bottle of whisky open and a faro game going, and he decided that a couple of drinks and a few hands of cards might settle his mind. He would smoke his cigar and watch the coastline moving darkly past for a while, and then he would go inside and try his luck.

He thought of Delphine. He tried composing a letter in his mind. 'My dearest angel Delphine, now that I am being carried inexorably away from you . . .' 'My dearest darling Delphine, as this cruel steamer widens the distance between us . . .' 'My own dearest Delphine, I am staring out into the night wondering what to say to you . . .'

It was curious, but he simply didn't know what to tell her. He could say that he loved her, of course; but would that be really accurate? She had stirred up his lusts and provoked his passions, but somehow he didn't know enough about her to love her. He didn't know whether she would read a devoted letter from him with tears in her eyes or with girlish laughter. He didn't know whether she adored him or whether she was simply teasing him. He could picture her pretty face, if he closed his eyes, and he could still recall the galvanic sensations of their last moments together. But while she had appeared to give him everything of herself, even the most secret recesses of her body, it seemed to him now that she had kept in reserve whatever it was that made her Delphine.

In his mind, he crumpled the invisible letter he couldn't write and tossed it out on to the windy sea. Maybe after weeks and months and years had passed by, he would be able to think of Delphine in perspective. Maybe he would know what to say to her then. The problem was, the only news he had right now was that he had introduced himself to a married woman whose eyes had stimulated his imagination just as sensationally as Delphine's discreetly parted thighs had stirred his libido.

He threw his half-smoked cigar after his unwritten letter. Then he thrust his hand into his coat pocket, jingled his handful of dollars, and went inside to join the faro game. As he walked through the dining-saloon, through the blue haze of cigar and pipe smoke, the dealer, a lanky maudlin man in a tan coat and check breeches, pushed back a chair for him without even raising his eyes.

'C'mon in,' he said laconically. 'I reckoned you for a gambling man the second I first seed you.'

They stood side by side on the afterdeck under a sky creamy with clouds and waved goodbye to Mrs Edgeworth as she disembarked with her bevy of basswood trunks at Charleston harbour. A band was playing on the quay, all red jackets and gold frogging and shiny brass instruments, although not for Mrs Edgeworth. In the distance, flocks of birds rose from the rooftops of the white-painted colonial houses and wheeled out over the trees of James Island.

Hannah West was dressed in a simple grey-blue summer coat, with a blue bonnet She stood a few paces away from Collis, so that even a casual spectator could have told they were simply friends, and not man and wife. Collis, in his fawn day coat and dark-brown pants, was looking a little pale, with dark circles under his eyes. He had spent yet another night at faro, and when he had returned to his cabin just before dawn, his Latvian travelling companion had produced a bottle of home-distilled slivovitz and insisted on an endless series of toasts to the glorious Union, and to the glorious President, Old Buck, and to the glorious United States postal system, and to the glorious steamship *Virginia*. Collis had finally crept into his upper berth at seven in the morning, his head shattered like crushed marble, and he had slept an uneasy and fractured sleep until nine, when the *Virginia* had docked. He and Hannah West had said very little to each other, and he had stayed in the background while Hannah and Mrs Edgeworth clasped hands, and kissed, and promised to write. Collis had yawned.

Eventually, Mrs Edgeworth disappeared among the milling crowds of porters and carriages and longshoremen who clamoured around the quay, and Hannah turned away from the rail and stood for a moment sadly by herself. A photographer, his head draped in a black cloth, took an ambrotype of the scene from the back of a stationary wagon, and because Hannah was almost the only person not moving, she later appeared in the developed collodion print to be standing alone on the deck, accompanied only by faint ghosts.

Collis said, 'You are not alone, you know. Your husband is waiting for you.'

Hannah raised her head and smiled. 'You're a genuine gentleman, Mr Edmonds. When I first saw you, I supposed that perhaps you weren't. I'm sorry for that, because you've behaved most kindly.'

'I am only interested in making sure that you reach your destination safely,' said Collis. He wasn't entirely sure that it was true, but it was the right thing to say, because Hannah West smiled vaguely, and nodded, as if she had been suitably reassured. She paced up and down the planks of the deck for a while, taking the air, and he followed her at a respectful distance, but now that Mrs Edgeworth had gone he wasn't quite sure whether he should continue to accompany her quite so closely. If he wasn't going to succeed with any kind of romantic overture, then why should he spend so much time escorting her around the deck, and sitting beside her while she read *Uncle Tom's Cabin* for what she assured him was the fifth time, and while she crocheted complicated little spiderwebs for setting cups and planters and picture frames on? He told himself that it was mainly because there was nothing else to do on this tedious, threshing, nauseating steamer, except for gambling, and smoking, and drinking toasts to glorious but unlikely features of American life. But maybe it was something more than that Maybe, for some reason, he actually liked her.

'You know,' she said, 'this is the first time I have ever been further from Boston than Wakefield. This all seems so far away from home, and yet look at the people on the quayside. They seem quite unexcited by living so far away.'

'San Francisco is a good deal further,' said Collis.

Hannah nodded, and bit at her lips as if she were thinking hard. Then she said, 'Mr Edmonds – would it surprise you if I said that I am terribly frightened?'

He looked at her with that worried, sympathetic look of his, and slowly shook his head. 'Not at all. This is a big adventure for someone who's never been further than Wakefield. Especially a lady of delicacy, like yourself.'

'I don't mean that,' she said. It appeared that she was almost cross.

'Then what do you mean? I don't understand.'

'I thought you might. You seemed to be a man of – well, of sensitivity.'

'I might be sensitive, but I'm not psychic.'

'No, I suppose you're not,' she said. She lifted her wrists and unnecessarily unbuttoned and rebuttoned her gloves. 'I suppose it's too much to ask of you.'

'Mrs West, I'm a perfect stranger.'

She looked at him. Her blue eyes were piercing. Then they softened a little. 'You're not perfect,' she said. 'You're not really a stranger, either, not now. But your imperfections become you, and your familiarity is quite welcome.'

'Well,' he said, with a grunt of amusement, 'I'm pleased about that.'

'Mr Edmonds – ' she said.

'You must call me Collis, particularly since I'm no longer a stranger.'

She paused. 'Collis, then,' she said, and blushed. 'I was brought up in a very observant Boston Catholic home. We knew the priests and we knew the cardinal, and there wasn't a single Wednesday dinner went by without some priest joining us at the table. You must understand that it's taken me many years to come to my own personal understanding of God, and of the life that God wishes me to lead, and that I'm still afraid of the individual stand that my conscience led me to take.'

'What individual stand was that?'

'I married a Protestant. In spite of what my father said, in spite of how much my mother railed against me. In spite of the priests and everyone else. I loved Walter, and when he asked me to be his bride, I said yes.'

Collis remained silent for a moment, watching the way the shadows from the smoking funnel crossed her face. Then he said gently, 'Why are you telling me this?'

'I don't know. I have to tell someone, I suppose. I'm alone now, Mr Edmonds, and when a weight like this is upon one's mind, and one is alone, I think one must turn to whomever one can.'

'Please, call me Collis.'

'I'm sorry. Collis.'

She looked away, out across Charleston harbour to the distant, humped outline of Fort Sumter. The sea glittered in the morning sunlight. She said, as if she were reciting an article of law, an article which had been drafted and devised in the loneliest moments of her vigil over her mother's sickbed, 'I went against my church and my family and I married a Protestant. That's why, when Walter wanted to go to San Francisco, and mother was so sick, I had to stay. I stayed for two years, nursing her, feeding her, cleaning up her sputum, and changing her sheets. It was depressing and dreary, but I felt it was the penance which had to be done to make up for my disobedience. Every night I went on my knees and thanked Our Lady for sparing my mother for one more day, even though every day that my mother remained alive meant one more day away from Walter.'

She paused and licked her lips. She was quite pale now, and there were tears in her eyes, although Collis couldn't tell if they were tears of grief or tears from the ocean wind.

'When mother died,' she said huskily, 'I thought my penance was over at last. I had paid my debt to God and Our Lady for marrying Walter. But I don't think I had reckoned on the severity of the Lord's punishments.'

'What do you mean?'

She turned towards him, and it was obvious now that she was crying. She said, in a choked voice, 'I was separated from Walter for two years, Collis. Two years without the husband you love is an eternity. I'm afraid now that, during that eternity, I've changed. I've become a particular person who is different from the person I once was. I believe that I'm more self-reliant, less impetuous. I

117

believe that I'm stronger. Believe me, Collis, cleaning up the dying body of your own mother makes you strong. I believe that I have an inner courage that I once lacked altogether.'

'And? What difference does that make?'

She took out a handkerchief from her purse, but didn't wipe her eyes. 'A great deal,' she said. 'I believe that I can support Walter more, in his business, and that I can endure the hardships of a pioneer life much better than I could have done before.'

'But?' he asked her.

She lowered her head. Then she looked up again, but her mouth was pursed with grief, and she couldn't speak straight away. Collis waited for her, not moving, while the band on the quay played 'Queen of the Southlands'.

'I don't think I love him any more,' said Hannah. 'That was my true penance. To endure two years of separation, to work day and night to comfort my mother, all in the belief that when the end came, there would be happiness and mutual affection; and then to find that everything for which I had suffered so long had become ashes. Not in Walter's mind, because I think he still loves me. Only in my mind.'

She paused, then added, 'I take out his picture, and stare at it, and I think: Who on God's earth are you? Why am I travelling all this way for you? I don't even know who you are.'

Collis gave her a brief, twitchy smile. 'You'll get over it,' he said. 'If you ask me, you're just under the weather. You've got a bad attack of nerves, that's all.'

She shook her head. 'I know my own mind, Collis. I've been through enough wakeful hours holding my mother's hand in the dead of night to know my own mind. In the dead of night, you see the terrors of the day as they really are.'

Collis pulled a face. 'If you ask me, you're suffering from exhaustion and loneliness, not the wrath of God. Once you get to San Francisco, and once you get to know Walter again, you'll find it's all different. You must have loved him when you married him, and he can't have altered so much that you can't love him now. I don't suppose he's grown especially ugly in two years, or lost all his hair.'

Hannah shrugged. 'I don't suppose he has. But I don't mind about his face. Or his hair. It is he, himself, who worries me. I just don't think I love him any more.'

Collis took her hand. It was bold of him, but under the

118

circumstances she didn't resist. He held it closely and warmly, much more tightly than he would normally have held the hand of another man's wife, but then the man was still a goodish distance off, and the wife was plainly in need of more than the usual sympathy.

'You could always turn back,' he said gently. 'You could always disembark, here at Charleston, and take the next steamer for Boston. I would take a letter to Walter for you.'

She shook her head. 'You know I can't do that. Besides, the only family I have left in Boston is my brother, and we really don't get on too well.'

'Then you don't have any option but to wait and see, do you?'

'And if I still don't love him, when I see him? What can I do then?'

Collis released her hand. Her arm fell by her side, and hung limp. He said: 'I don't know. I really don't know. I wish I did.'

She looked out to sea, across the harbour. 'God moves in mysterious ways, his wonders to perform,' she said. There was the slightest trace of vitriol in her voice, but only the slightest trace. She sounded almost as if she sympathised with God's predicament, having to undertake even the simplest of tasks by the roundabout means of miracles, and visions, and holy puzzles.

'There is always divorce, if you really can't stand him,' Collis said.

'Not for me,' she answered. 'I'm a Catholic, remember. And apart from that, I don't hate him enough to hurt him. I don't hate him at all, to tell you the truth. I simply feel as if our marriage is a dull day. The sun's gone in.'

'Don't you think you might hurt him more by staying with him, not loving him, than by divorcing him?'

She thought about that for a while, and then shook her head again. 'It's impossible to tell. As you say, Collis, I think I shall just have to wait and see.'

She turned to him and said something else, but at that moment the ship's whistle blew, and all he caught was the word 'you'. The gangplank was dropped to the quayside with a crash, and the engines began to beat, and there was such a clamour of 'Goodbye' and 'Mind the ropes there' and 'See you next year', all mingled with shouting and whistling and a last chorus of 'I Wish I Was in Dixie' from the brass band, that he didn't get the chance to ask her what she had said. The mooring ropes were slipped from their capstans, the whistle blew again, a loud gooselike honk that echoed all across the estuary, and then the paddles began to froth and turn, and the *Virginia* was on her way to Panama.

As they passed Fort Sumter, with its Union flag flying from the battlements, Hannah said, 'I think I shall go lie down now. At least with Mrs Edgeworth gone I have a cabin to myself.'

'I only wish my pestilential Latvian friend had left with her,' said Collis. 'Perhaps I shall see you at lunch.'

'Not if it's hash again,' she said and smiled.

When she had gone, Collis sat on a deck chair to watch the *Virginia* putting out through Charleston sound to the sea. Beside him, in a well-tailored suit of light-coloured English twill, sat a man in his early thirties with a wide-brimmed hat and fraying moustache, a sharp-nosed, sharp-eyed fellow who could have been anything from a salesman to a gambler. A well-worn carpetbag sat at his feet like an obedient dog.

'You're bound for San Francisco?' the man asked, in a strong Tennessee accent.

'That's right.'

'And is that your good lady? The one who just went inside?'

Collis pulled a wry face. 'I only wish that it were.'

'Well, you don't seem to be doing so badly,' said the man in the wide-brimmed hat. 'The way she's been looking at you, I'd say you've won her affections, to say the least. That's why I thought she might have been your wife.'

'She's a wife, all right. But she's not mine. Her husband runs a store in San Francisco.'

'Is this your first time out?' asked the man.

Collis nodded, his eyes screwed up against the shimmering reflections from the sea.

'Well, allow me to introduce myself,' said the man. 'My name is Andrew Jackson Hunt. Named for General Andrew Jackson, of course. I'm off to San Francisco to start up a wholesale food business, and maybe open a restaurant, too.'

'Pleased to meet you,' said Collis. 'Edmonds, out of New York.'

Andrew Hunt, on closer inspection, had a sunburned look about his narrow, foxlike face that you never saw on New Yorkers. The fluffy hairs on his cheekbones had been bleached white by the sun, and there were creases around his eyes from squinting into bright skies. He didn't hold himself like a city man, either. He sat with his legs sprawled across the deck, and if anybody wanted to pass, he would withdraw them, and tip his hat, and say, 'Beg pardon

'You don't want to expect too much out of San Francisco,' he told Collis. 'You can make money there, sure enough, if you're sharp, and ready to work hard. But you have to remember that it ain't all that civilised. All that anybody ever does there is get drunk and run up and down the hills. Why, I remember the time when John Frémont built his first house there. It was wooden, and it came from China in pieces, and everyone sat around and laughed their butts off while he tried to figure out how it all went together.'

'I'm looking forward to meeting John Frémont,' said Collis. 'I've heard he's a very powerful personality.'

'Oh, he's not too bad a fellow,' observed Andrew Hunt. 'A mite peevish at times, and not so much of a great hero as everybody tried to make him out. But I guess he passes the Hunt humanity test, and that's good enough.'

'What's the Hunt humanity test?' asked Collis, amused.

'It's real simple. If a man makes two dumb mistakes for every one thing he gets right, and if he marries a pretty woman, and he don't hold with James Buchanan for President, then he's a human being, and that's all right by me. I guess John Frémont's managed all of those things, except he's probably made just a mite too many dumb mistakes.'

'He doesn't still live in his Chinese wooden house?'

'No, sir. He's got a grand place out on the Bay now, and Jessie put up a glass verandah around it, overlooking the ocean. You'd do yourself well to get in with John and Jessie. If you're able. In fact, if you're able, you'd do well to get yourself in with any of The San Francisco Chivalry, because that's the quickest way to make yourself influential.'

'What is the Chivalry?' asked Collis.

'Mary Bell Gwin is the chief buzzard. She's the wife of Senator Gwin, and if she says you're acceptable, then acceptable you are. But there's Eleanor Martin and Mrs Peter Donahue, too, they're twin sisters, and then there's the Parrotts and the Melfords and the Lathams and the Selbys. If you ain't on any of their invitation lists, then you ain't Chivalry.'

'How about you?' asked Collis. 'Are you on the invitation lists?'

'Me? You have to be joking. I wouldn't even turn up at their goddam breakfasts and balls and picnics and whatnot if you paid me to. They spend more time fretting about their oyster suppers

121

and their eggnog soirées than they do about the things that matter in life.'

'I see,' said Collis. 'And what do you think are the things that matter in life?'

'Work, and friendship, and outwitting the other fellow whenever you can, on top of all of which is sleeping peaceful.'

Collis laughed. But Andrew said seriously, 'What are yours?'

'I beg your pardon?'

'What are the things that matter to you?'

Collis looked at him for a moment, opened his mouth, but couldn't think of anything to say. 'I'm not sure,' he told him, after a while. 'I've never thought about it.'

Andrew crossed his legs and raised one bony, suntanned finger. 'In San Francisco,' he said, 'you'd better have your priorities sorted out real straight, because it ain't the venue for tenderfeet. If you spend so much as a half-minute sitting on your travelling trunk on the Embarcadero, trying to figure out what to do next, then the next thing you know you're going to be perched on air, because someone's whipped your trunk out from under you and sold it off as the latest import from the East. It's a city where dogs eat dogs, and cats eat mice, and merchants sell them all off for sausage meat before they've even quit squawking.'

'I was hoping for some sort of financial position, as a matter of fact,' said Collis, feeling very Eastern and very uncertain.

Andrew took out a silver snuffbox and flicked the lid with long, clawlike fingernails. 'The only financial position worth adopting is bent over double under the weight of a sack of gold dust. That's in my opinion, anyway. But you're a gentleman, ain't you, and you shouldn't have no trouble in making your way, not unless you're especially green. If you can get yourself introduced into society, and accepted as an aristocrat, whether you're genuine or fraudulent, then you should be able to pick whatever position you want.'

The *Virginia* was paddling out into open ocean now, and beginning to tilt and sway. Seagulls followed her into the Atlantic, circling silently around her wake. Andrew, shielding his snuffbox from the breeze, took out a pinch of snuff and dipped it into his sharp-pointed nose. He snorted once, and then took out a large clean white handkerchief and sneezed into it six or seven times.

'Confounded damned habit,' he complained, tucking the handkerchief away again, up his sleeve. 'Still, I guess it's more sociable than chewing tobacco. All that nyoing, nyoing, p-too.'

'Tell me more about the Chivalry,' Collis said. 'Who's the most influential man in town?'

Andrew grimaced. 'It might have changed since I was last there, but I guess the *richest* man in town is John Parrott, who owns the New Almaden Quicksilver Mine. He and Mrs Parrott live up on Rincon Hill in a place that looks like a bank vault that someone stuck a front porch on and decided to live in. But I guess that when it comes to influence, Laurence Melford's your man.'

'Laurence Melford? Don't I know that name?'

'You should do,' said Andrew. 'He's what you call your living legend.'

'Didn't he help General Kearny to form the first California government?'

'That's right.' Andrew nodded. 'And John Frémont has never forgiven him for it, although these days they're back on speaking terms. Still, you can't hardly blame a man for understanding which side his bread's buttered, now can you, and that's always been Laurence Melford's main talent.'

'Melford made his fortune in beef, didn't he?' Collis asked. 'I remember my father talking about him.'

'Beef, whisky, gold, you name it, he's made his fortune in it. He was only a raggedy-assed settler to start with, back in the '40s, but he was clever enough to make a friend out of General Vallejo, who was in charge of Northern California in those days, and Vallejo paid him back for his friendship by giving him land, and livestock, and enough sweet wine to drown a boatful of bishops. That was way back when San Francisco was still called Yerba Buena, and it wasn't no more than a row of adobe huts and a post stuck in the ground to tie up your donkey.'

Andrew paused, sneezed hard, and then turned back to Collis with an oddly surprised expression.

'I'll be damned if that stuff isn't overdoing itself.'

'It sounds like it,' said Collis. 'But what about Laurence Melford? Is he a hard man to get to know?'

'These days, sure,' said Andrew. 'He's one of the pioneers, you see, and that makes him first-class, tested-with-the-teeth Chivalry. One of the best lessons he learned from Mariano Vallejo was how to save his hide and hang on to his money, and he learned it good. When John Frémont marched into Sonoma in '46 to liberate it from the Mexicans, Melford was there with open arms and a ten-page speech of welcome. And when John Frémont was picked by the settlers to be the top dog of Yerba Buena, Melford was there too, clapping with the best of them. But, by golly, he was there again when General Kearny came marching along and kicked Frémont out, and the way I heard it, he gave General Kearny the same ten-page speech of welcome he'd given to Frémont with only the names changed. So when General Kearny went off home, and Frémont was packed off in irons because he'd refused to stand down, who was left on the top of the sandpile but Laurence Melford, and he made himself a whole heap of profit selling beef and provisions in San Francisco and all around, and even acquired himself the San Gabriel gold mine, by means that nobody ever did get around to making plain.'

'He sounds like a fascinating man,' said Collis. 'Is he a gambler?'

'Name me one man in San Francisco who isn't.'

'Where does he live? Have you ever been to his house?'

'I've seen the outside of it, sure. It's in South Park, which is up on Rincon Hill where the Parrotts live. There's some pretty fancy addresses up there, I can tell you. They've even got themselves a windmill up there, just to pump water for the lawns.'

'I'll have to pay it a visit.'

Andrew shrugged. 'I guess you could try. But I warn you they're standoffish folks, the Chivalry, even worse than any society you could find in New York or Memphis. When you're trying to show that you're class in New York or Memphis, it ain't so difficult, because you've got yourself a fine civilised city to do it in. But when you're trying to show that you're class in a shantytown like San Francisco, where any building that ain't made of wood is made of canvas, well, you tend to be three times as covetous of what you've got, and what you think you are.'

The gong struck for lunch, and a bearded steward banged open the door to the dining-saloon and shouted: 'Boiled rockfish, Swedish meatballs, and sharp Wisconsin cheese! Come and get it!'

'Oh, well,' said Collis, getting to his feet, 'I suppose we're in for another culinary adventure.'

Andrew Hunt grinned. 'It does me good to see you young society fellows come out here and cut your teeth on some rough-edged pioneer life,' he said. 'It'll make a man out of you, so long as it don't kill you first.'

'Come on, it can't be that bad,' Collis chided him.

'Oh, no? Well, there's plenty of fog and fever in San Francisco, apart from thieves, and rats, and Mexicans, and winter rain. And the Chivalry will do their darnedest to kill you off, if they don't like the look of you. And if you go sniffing around Laurence Melford's daughter, that'll be sudden death.'

'You didn't tell me he had a daughter.'

'Oh, sure he does,' said Andrew, tipping back his wide-brimmed hat and looking up at Collis with cynical amusement. 'Laurence Melford has the tallest, most toothsome young daughter you've ever seen in your life. She looks like her mother, you see, Althea Melford, and she's a rare beauty, only the general opinion is that Sarah Melford's even finer. But old man Laurence don't like the idea of anything but the cream of the cream for Sarah, as far as a husband's concerned, so the suitors get kicked out of the front door just about as fast as they try to get in. That's just a warning, if you ever get as far as meeting the Melfords.'

'I'll take it in the spirit it was given,' said Collis. 'Now, will you join me for lunch?'

Andrew Jackson Hunt shook his head and stretched out his legs even further. 'Round about noonish I'll have myself a measure of bourbon and a dry cookie,' he said. 'That's all that a man needs.'

'Please yourself,' said Collis, setting his hat straight.

Andrew nodded. 'I generally do. Be seeing you.'

In the week that followed, the *Virginia* steamed slowly down the coast of Georgia and Florida, with the sun hot and high overhead during the day and the passengers sleeping under awnings on the decks or fanning themselves in their cabins. Gradually, the coastline of Florida broke into fragmented keys, rafts of palms and grass on a remote, sapphire-blue sea, and then they were alone on the Gulf of Mexico, under a faultless sky, and an ocean that was marked only by the wide white wash of the *Virginia*'s paddles and the shadow of the smoke that trailed from her funnel.

Collis, after shaving in the confines of his shared cabin and breakfasting on oranges and fruit pasties taken aboard at Jacksonville, would walk the promenade deck with Hannah West until it was time for midmorning coffee. In her white and lemon-coloured summer dresses, under the shade of her white tasselled parasol, she looked even more desirable, and Collis found it increasingly difficult to talk to her in remote and gentlemanly terms. But since she had told him what she really felt about Walter West on the afterdeck at Charleston, she seemed to have become increasingly withdrawn, and now she spoke only of her childhood in Wakefield, and of what she had learned at school, and how she hoped to prosper in San Francisco. Collis found his attention wandering to a sluttish-looking half-breed girl who had come aboard with the oranges, or maybe the fruit pasties, and who had taken to sitting on the foredeck smoking thin cheroots, her long black hair blown in the wind, her toes brown and bare and her blouse loose and low.

Sometimes Hannah West would stand by the lifeboats and gaze out across the Gulf for an hour at a time, while Collis rested himself on a deck chair and drank tall tumblers of dry sherry with ice. At those times, they spoke very little, although Hannah would immediately come out of her reverie if Collis made any move to leave her, and she would smile at him so entreatingly that he would shrug and stay. The days grew hotter, and longer, and in the evenings they sat in the dining-saloon in the red feverish light of heated sunsets, their conversation murmured and polite, as their knives and forks clattered on their plates, as the day died in a flurry of moths and a bitter waft of coffee. At night, Collis would lie on his upper berth, feeling the sea breeze flowing through the open porthole close to his face, listening to the snores of his Latvian cabinmate, as yet another cord of slumbering firewood was sawn up, and he would think about Delphine, and her astonishing sensuality, and then about Hannah's strange and compelling profile, and her distracted way of talking, and then he would close his eyes and think for a moment about the big dusky breasts of the half-breed girl. He wasn't at all sure what it was that he felt for Hannah. She wasn't as blatantly provocative as the half-breed girl, and her sexual manners certainly weren't as forward as Delphine's. Yet she had an alluring way of standing, and looking, and talking; and when the wind blew her hair, it was all Collis could do not to reach out and curl its fine blondeness around his fingers. For some reason that he couldn't understand, he wanted very much to possess her, not simply sexually, but in every other way. He wanted to possess her childhood, all those images of cold winters in Wakefield, with the frost on the trees, and the sun dull and sullen behind the colonial houses. He wanted to possess her moments of happiness, the day she had married, the night she had lain in her lace-trimmed nightgown and first felt the heaviness of her husband on top of her, the squeezed-closed eyes, the breathing, the sighs of pleasure or of pain. He wanted to possess her now, on the deck of

126

this steamer in the dark wide warmth of the Gulf of Mexico, to touch her cheeks, her nose, her mouth, her ribboned underwear. More than any other woman he had ever met, he wanted to own her, to be as intimate with her as she was with herself. He wanted her as a mistress and as a friend, but even more than that, he seemed to want her as a means of escaping from his own past and his own memories, by taking on hers instead. She had married a Protestant and was stricken with guilt. She had suffered over her mother's deathbed. Now, she was uncertain of her love for the man she had sacrificed everything for. To take on this arcane, religious, and romantic guilt in place of his own remorse for Kathleen Mary and the sordid family squabbles that had led him to leave New York would be an intriguing relief. It would make his life mysterious and adventurous instead of cheap and embarrassing; and it would draw him into another world like a man drawn through a secret door. He almost relished the prospect of confronting Walter West, with Hannah swooning in the crook of his arm and declaring, 'She is mine now! You must set her free!'

He was thinking this way on a hot Thursday night, when they weren't more than a hundred miles from Cayos Miskito, off the coast of Nicaragua, and less than 350 miles from Aspinwall, on the isthmus of Panama. The ship's sails were up, because there was a light easterly wind, and they were rippling in the darkness, while beneath the decks the steam-powered engines were pumping and pounding as they turned the paddles around. Collis lay awake for a half-hour, and then he gradually eased himself off his bunk, dressed in nothing but his sweaty striped nightshirt, and climbed to the floor.

The Latvian was fast asleep, breathing out slivovitz fumes through his tousled beard. Collis stepped carefully over his parcels and packages and unbolted the cabin door. In the dining-saloon outside, the lamps had been turned low, so that they glowed dim and orange, and the passengers lay wrapped up in their blankets in different exaggerated postures of sleep, mouths open, hair tangled, necks at awkward angles. Collis passed by them all and padded down the saloon to the door which led out on to the deck. Someone snorted and turned over.

It was dark and windy outside. There was no moon yet. Collis's nightshirt flapped around his legs as he closed the saloon door behind him and stepped out on to the deck. The ship's paddles churned up an odd luminescence in the water, dark blue and shimmering, and there was a sharp smell of smoke on the breeze.

He made his way forward, along the promenade deck, until he reached the rail where the flag of the Atlantic Mail Line rumbled and snapped. He stood there for a while, breathing in the warm wind, and then he made his way back to the door that led to the women's cabins. There was nobody looking, and on the deck above him, in his wheelhouse, the helmsman was crouched over his lamp writing a letter; so Collis quickly opened the door and stepped into the shadowy passageway inside.

He paused for a moment. The passageway smelled of cologne and urine. He listened to hear if anyone was awake, and then he tiptoed along to the third door, and knocked.

There was no answer. He knocked again, harder this time, holding his breath. He heard a rustling of sheets, and then a whispered voice say, 'Who is it?'

'Hannah? It's me, Collis.'

'Collis? What do you want? What time is it?'

'I don't know, maybe two or three o'clock. I'm not wearing my watch.'

'What's the matter? Can't you sleep?'

'I was thinking of you, Hannah.'

'What do you mean?'

He paused. He wanted to be sure that he phrased this in just the right way. He said, 'I need to talk to you. It's important. I feel that something important is slipping away from us.'

'Collis, whatever it is, we could just as easily discuss it in the morning. You shouldn't be here. These are the ladies' quarters.'

'Hannah, if you would open the door for a moment, I could explain myself much more easily.'

'Open the door? Collis, it's out of the question. I'm in my night attire.'

'So am I,' he whispered back. 'So, well, that makes us equal.'

He heard her let out a short, testy sigh. 'Collis, I'm a married woman. It's bad enough that I should be *talking* to you at this hour, let alone contemplating opening the door for you.'

'Then you *are* contemplating it?'

'You have *obliged* me to contemplate it, by asking me.'

He paused again, and when he whispered again, there was a smile in his voice. 'And what is the outcome of your contemplations?' he asked her.

'I'm a married woman, Collis. It's out of the question. I may have mixed feelings about Walter, but it seems I shall just have to put a brave face on it, and make the best of what the Lord has seen fit to give me.'

'Hannah,' said Collis, 'you must understand that I have the strongest and strangest feelings for you.'

'Well, you must resist them. Any liaison between us would be a sin. I cannot think of it.'

'I'm not necessarily thinking of adultery,' said Collis. 'It's something else altogether. Something more. I feel I want to know you as a very close friend, as if I want to take responsibility for you. I want to know you so well that intimate relations between us *could* take place, but not as a first priority.'

'You don't *know* me. How can you say such a thing?'

'Of course I know you. We've been walking and talking on this damned boat for a week. There are dozens of people who are betrothed and married after only half the time that we've spent together.'

'But, Collis, *I* am married to someone else. I am not available for such a relationship. And however sad that may be, and whatever a waste of human lives you may think it is, it is the will of the Lord, and woe betide us if we ignore it.'

From one of the other cabins, a harsh woman's voice called out, 'Let him in, my dear, in the name of pity, and then we can all get some sleep!'

Collis giggled, but Hannah drew in her breath in embarrassment. 'Collis,' she whispered, 'you must go!'

'I'm not asking for anything improper, Hannah. I just want to talk about this feeling I have for you.'

'No, it's impossible. You'll have to go.'

'Hannah, please. I'm imploring you. I can't sleep for thinking about you.'

'And neither can anyone else!' the harsh voice put in.

'Please, Collis, you're humiliating me.'

Collis leaned his head against the door. 'Very well, if you want me to go, I'll go. But if you change your mind, well, you know that you only have to say the word.'

'All right,' said Hannah quickly. 'Now, please leave before one of the officers comes down and catches you here.'

'Good night, Hannah. Sweet dreams.'

'Good night, Collis.'

'I love you, Hannah.'

'*Please*, Collis, don't start again. You cannot love me, because I am not free to be loved.'

Collis pulled a face to himself in the darkness of the corridor. 'Who ever is?' he asked her. 'Freedom is only what you seize for yourself, after all. And look at us now. We're right in the middle of the Caribbean, in the middle of the night, with nobody to suspect or even care that we're together. What could be freer than that?'

'Collis, *God* knows that we're together.'

At that moment, a door further along the corridor cannoned open, and in the gloom Collis could make out a short barrel of a woman in a nightgown like a pink marquee, and a bristling forest of curl papers.

'God knows,' she barked, 'and everybody else in these cabins knows! And if you don't move your lecherous hide out of here this instant, I'll make sure the captain knows, too, and has you locked up in irons!'

'Madam,' said Collis hastily, 'I was on the verge of leaving.'

'Well, then, *move*!' demanded the woman. 'And make sure I don't catch you down here again, or I'll sit on your head, for impertinence!'

Collis called, 'Good night, Hannah!' and then quickly opened the door to the promenade deck and stepped back out into the breezy night. Scratching his head, he walked forward to the rail again and stood for a while by the flag. To starboard, along the dusky horizon, he could see the marking lamps of a night fishing fleet, and to port, the first barely distinguishable lightening of the sky before dawn. He wished he hadn't left his cigars in his cabin; he could have done with a smoke right now.

He looked behind him for a while, at the curtained portholes of the women's cabins. Hannah's must be the third one along. He debated with himself for a moment whether he ought to go tap at it, and ask her again to let him in, but he decided that enough was probably enough. It was going to be sufficiently difficult facing her on the promenade deck in the morning as it was.

He was still leaning against the rail in his nightshirt, thinking about this, when he felt a tug at his sleeve. He turned to see the half-breed girl standing there, a cheroot sloping out of the side of her mouth, her long black hair tangled and blown by the wind. Around her shoulders she wore a heavy red-and-blue Pueblo blanket, but beneath the blanket her blouse was so low over her heavy pendant breasts that Collis could make out the duskier, stippled skin of her areolas. She wore a wide, dark-blue skirt, but her feet were bare, and she had silver rings on every finger, including her thumbs, and on her toes. In the wind, Collis could smell an oily, exotic perfume, mingled with sweat.

'You want to smoke, señor?' the girl asked him.

He looked at her. She had the dark colouring and the accent of a Mexican, but there was something distinctly European about her face and her figure. She could have had French or German blood in her, or maybe even Slavic, because her eyes were deep-set and her cheekbones were angular and high. There was only a slight smile on her lips, and that was noticeably mocking.

'You're most kind,' Collis told her, with exaggerated courtesy. He watched her closely as she reached into the waistband of her skirt and produced a small wooden box with a decorated label. She opened it up and offered it to him: three dark hand-rolled cheroots of Cuban Tobaccos. He took one and put it between his lips, and she leaned forward so that he could touch the tip of it to the lighted cheroot she held in her own mouth and suck it into life. While he sucked, she stared at him, very close, with her deep, moist eyes.

'Are you going far?' he asked her, when his cheroot was properly alight.

'To San Francisco,' she told him.

'Do you know anyone there?'

She shrugged.

'So what are you going to do, if you don't know anyone?'

'I don't know,' she said. 'Work in a bar, maybe. Anywhere is better than Jacksonville.'

'You didn't like it there?'

She ran her hand through her thick, greasy hair. Washed and dressed properly, he reflected, she could have been almost beautiful.

'It wasn't the city,' she said.

'Was it your parents? A man?'

'A man? More like a dog who eats his own sick.'

Collis smiled wryly. 'Well, I suppose we all have our troubles.'

The girl blew smoke out of her nostrils, without taking the cheroot out of her mouth. 'This man, he was more than trouble. He was crazy. You never met nobody so crazy.'

'I'm sorry to hear it. Could I borrow your cheroot again? Mine's gone out.'

While Collis fed once more off the red tip of her cheroot, she held

131

his wrist to steady his hand, and looked at him fiercely. The fierceness was passionate, rather than aggressive, but all the same Collis found it more than a little disturbing, especially since he was dressed in nothing but his nightshirt. Once his cheroot was alight again, he stood well back from her and eyed her cautiously.

There was a long silence between them, while they both stood and looked at each other. The sky was gradually fading from indigo to pale blue, and the lights that hung from the *Virgina*'s masts began to pale. The girl turned to the ship's rail after a while and rested her elbows on it, smoking, her arms crossed under her breasts so that they were provocatively plumped up.

'I suppose it wasn't in my cards, that's all,' she said. 'A slave woman in Bryceville told my fortune in the tarot cards, and she said I was going to travel, and be lonesome.'

'You don't *have* to be lonesome,' said Collis, guardedly.

'Who would want me? A girl like me? And even if anyone *did* want me, I'm not so sure that I would want him.'

'What's your name?' Collis asked.

The girl half turned towards him. She tugged up her blouse a little, but there was a hint of a smile on her face when she did it. Behind her, the sea was a dull turquoise colour, laden with mist, and the darkness was draining away as rapidly as it had come. It must have been four in the morning by now, and it wouldn't be long before the crew and the earliest of the early-rising passengers would be up on deck.

'My uncle and aunt always called me Maria,' said the girl. 'But I heard that my father, before he went away, used to say I was Mamuska, after his grandmother in Poland. A place named Lwow.'

Collis held out his hand. 'Well – how do you do. I'm Collis Edmonds, out of New York.'

Maria-Mamuska declined to take his hand. 'We don't need to do that. You're in your nightshirt. I feel that I know you already.'

'You could get to know me better.'

'It's getting light,' Maria-Mamuska said. 'Maybe you ought to go dress. You don't want your lady friend to get the wrong ideas about us.'

Collis gave her a lopsided smile. 'Lady friend? I'm not sure if she's my lady friend at all. She's a lady, certainly. But that's half the trouble.'

Maria-Mamuska reached out and held Collis's hand. 'She won't let you play with her?'

132

Collis gave a grunt of amusement. 'If you want to put it like that, no.'

'Maybe you don't try hard enough.'

'How hard is hard?'

'Do you want to show me?'

Collis picked a shred of tobacco off the tip of his tongue. 'Is that a proposition?' he said.

Maria-Mamuska looked at him boldly. 'What do you think?'

'Well . . .' said Collis. 'I think it's dawn. And maybe dawn is too late for business that ought to be done at night-time.'

'Who cares what time it is?' said Maria-Mamuska.

Collis felt tempted. It was a long time now, almost three weeks, since he had been with a woman, paid or unpaid, and his encounters with Delphine and Hannah had only served to inflame him, rather than satisfy him. It was only four o'clock, after all, and the Latvian slept so drunkenly that not even the second coming of St Hilda would ever wake him before seven.

Maria-Mamuska stepped closer and held Collis's arm. 'You are a fine man,' she said. 'Good-looking, and rich. I never talked to a man like you before.'

'Rich?' said Collis. 'I'm hardly rich. Why do you think I'm going to San Francisco?'

'You tease me.' Maria-Mamuska grinned. 'Look at all the fine clothes you wear. Look at your fine hats.'

'Those are all I have, I'm afraid,' he told her. 'I left New York because my father's business went bankrupt, and because of gambling debts. If you want anything out of me, I'm afraid you'll have to put up with my being nothing more than good-looking.'

'You joke,' she said crossly.

'I wish I did. Unfortunately, it's true.'

She took away her hand. 'You're just trying to make a fool of me.'

'Why should I want to do that?'

'You're just trying to make me look stupid, that's all. You're just like Lucas. You're a crazy man!'

'Maria, listen – '

'No, I don't listen,' she said hotly. 'You strut around in all your wonderful clothes, you talk like a rich man, and it's all wind! All you want is to get into my bed! You're a crazy trickster, you understand that?'

133

'You don't *have* a bed,' he reminded her. 'You were trying to get into mine.'

'Same thing!' she snapped, tossing her oily black hair. 'And now who looks after my baby?'

'Your baby? What baby?'

'This one!' she pouted, slapping her stomach.

Collis couldn't keep himself from grinning. The sheer nerve of this girl was unbelievable. His luck, this morning, was patently with him. If she had continued to believe him rich, and if his carnal urgings had been overwhelming enough, they would have gone for a tussle on the top berth of his cabin, and afterwards, being the sort she was, she would have plainly blamed him for making her pregnant. He stood there in his nightshirt on the dawn-lit deck, his cheroot stuck in his mouth, his hands on his hips, and watched her righteous fury with the detached amusement of a spectator at a solo theatrical performance.

'You think you can *use* me!' she spat. 'You think I'm nothing but dirt! You think you can take my body and pay nothing for it! Well, mister, I was never a whore, not for money, and I won't be your whore for free!'

'I didn't actually ask you to be,' said Collis, puffing smoke.

She snatched the cheroot right out of his mouth, crushed it up in her fist, and tossed it over the side.

'That was regrettable,' he said. 'I was just beginning to enjoy the flavour.'

'You're mocking me,' she breathed.

'A little, yes. But you can't expect me to take you seriously when you're ranting and screaming so much. And you can't expect me to feel guilty because I don't want to look after some old fellow's illegitimate baby.'

Maria-Mamuska slapped her stomach again, so hard that Collis was sure her baby must have been wondering what it had done wrong, so early in its life, to come in for such a pasting. 'You men are all monsters!' she told him. 'You all make me pregnant! You all make me your slave! Well, I'll have revenge on you! You see!'

'For heaven's sake, calm down,' Collis said. 'You're making a damned exhibition of yourself.'

'*Hexhibition!*' she screamed. '*Hexhibition!*'

Collis, disconcerted, took a pace backwards, but Maria-Mamuska took another step nearer.

134

'Who cares about hexhibition! You want a hexhibition? You want one? Well, here's hexhibition!'

With her face stiff with anger, and her cheroot stuck firmly between her walnut-coloured teeth, Maria-Mamuska planted herself directly in front of Collis, seized the top of her blouse with both hands, and tugged it right down, baring a stunning expanse of womanly anatomy. 'Here!' she said. 'Is this what you mean? Is this what you mean when you say hexhibition?'

'Oh, God,' sighed Collis. He didn't know what else to say. He was frustrated, certainly, but this kind of one-woman circus was the last thing he wanted. He raised his eyes tiredly away from Maria-Mamuska's uninvited 'hexhibition' and, as he did so, found himself turning his head towards the cabins, as if something else were ineluctably drawing his attention. He heard bells jangle on the *Virginia*'s bridge, and he paused for a moment, but then his gaze travelled further, along the black-and-green-painted superstructure, further, past the bleached ropes and the lifeboats, along the rows of tarnished portholes, until it reached the third porthole of the women's quarters. There, framed in a circle of studded brass, like a horrified portrait on a drawing-room wall, was Hannah West's face, white, her eyes wide and her mouth so far open that she looked as if she had choked on a very dry piece of seedcake.

Almost simultaneously, as if by a prearranged signal, Hannah's drapes flew shut, and Collis clamped his hands over his eyes. He couldn't believe it. Of all the damned stupid despicable luck. He might have been able to save the situation with Hannah if he had met her in a gentlemanly fashion at breakfast, and buttered her muffins for her, and warmed her frostiness with his usual flattery. He could have assured her that it was lonesomeness, not lust, that had led him to tap on her cabin door, seeking comfort. He could have begged her forgiveness for his foolish behaviour, and bought her perfume in Panama to make up for it. Instead, what had happened? She had spied on him, the silly woman, and caught him standing on the deck at dawn in nothing but his nightshirt, apparently enjoying a one-man display of the largest and least respectable bosom on the entire boat.

'You may dress now,' he said to Maria-Mamuska, in a small, restrained voice.

He waited for what he considered to be a respectable time and then uncovered his eyes. She was still standing there bare-breasted, staring at him with that fierce look of hers, and the dawn breeze

135

made her nipples as stiff as charcoals. It made her eyes water, too, although Collis wasn't certain if she was crying or not.

He took hold of her Pueblo blanket and gently covered her with it. She stood where she was, not moving, although she lowered her head slightly, and some of the tension and anger seemed to filter out of her.

He said hesitantly, 'You mustn't blame every man you meet. I know you feel like it. But you must try to understand that what happened was the result of one old man's lechery, just one old man, and not every man in the world.'

'All men look at me the same,' she said, sullenly and softly.

'Well, they do,' Collis agreed, 'but that's because of the way you dress and the way you act. If you wear your blouse as low as that, and if you smoke that way, and talk so rough, then men are bound to think that you're easy pickings. I did myself.'

She lifted her head and stared at him defiantly. 'What do you know? You come from New York. You're a gentleman.'

'A *poor* gentleman.'

She gave him a half-forgiving smile. 'Not so poor. Not really so poor. And anyway, you'll make plenty of money in San Francisco.'

'I hope so.'

There was a short silence, during which the sky lightened surprisingly quickly. A door opened further down the promenade deck, and a sleepy-eyed man in crumpled broadcloth pants, an undershirt, and suspenders came out on deck, and systematically scratched his ribs and yawned at the distant coastline.

'I'd better get back to my cabin,' said Collis.

Maria-Mamuska nodded.

Collis waited a little while longer, and then said, 'What's going to happen to you? And what about your baby?'

She shrugged. 'You needn't worry. It isn't your problem. If you're poor, then you must have problems of your own.'

He bit at his thumbnail thoughtfully. 'I'll tell you what I'll do. I guess it's soft-headed, but who cares. Do you know any places in San Francisco?'

'I've never been there before.'

'Well, let's say Montgomery Street. That's a street that my lady friend mentioned. Her husband's name is Walter West – have you got that? – and he owns a general store.'

'Walter West,' Maria-Mamuska enunciated carefully. 'Who is Walter West?'

'That doesn't matter,' Collis told her. 'The important thing is that I'll meet you outside of Walter West's store on Montgomery Street three years and some weeks from now, on 18 September, my father's birthday, at noon. By then you'll have had your baby, and I'll know if I'm going to make any money or stay flat broke for the rest of my life. If it looks as though I've got some money to spare, well, I'll give you a little to help you bring up the child. If it doesn't, I'll say hello, and that'll have to be it.'

Maria-Mamuska brushed back her hair. 'Why should you do this?' she asked him.

He glanced back at the porthole, still with its drapes drawn, where Hannah had appeared. 'I don't know,' he said. 'Maybe it's an act of – I don't know, defiance.'

'Defiance? What do you mean? You don't talk straight.'

He shrugged. 'I'm not sure. I just get the feeling that once you're out of step with the world, once you're an outcast, it takes a hell of a lot of hard work and suffering to make your way back.'

'I still don't understand you. You're a funny man. A little crazy, as I said.'

'I'm only crazy because I'm not supposed to be here on the deck of this godforsaken ship at all. I should be waking up in my own bed on Twenty-first Street, in New York City, and I should be wealthy and organised and perfectly content. I should have gone out gambling last night, and had my supper at the Union Club, and maybe gone to a whorehouse to top off the evening properly. Instead of which I tried to seduce a married woman in a ship's cabin, and got myself thrown out by some hair-curlered Tartar I'd never seen before in my life, and then I spent the rest of the night arguing with a Mexican-Polish lady about whether I was morally responsible for her pregnancy or not.'

Maria-Mamuska grinned. 'You sure are crazy. But I'll come to that place. If you say Montgomery Street, 18 September, three years from now, then that's where I'll be.'

Collis clasped her hand, and then kissed her, very quickly, on the forehead. For some reason he couldn't begin to understand, he felt pleased, as if something quite happy had just taken place.

Right then, without any warning, Andrew Jackson Hunt appeared around the port side of the steamer, dressed in a tan suit, and tan-coloured cowhide shoes as wide and flat as cigar cases. He stared at the spectacle of Collis consoling Maria-Mamuska, with Collis in his nightshirt and nothing else, and Maria-Mamuska in her Pueblo blanket and a blouse that was obviously hanging loose, with undisguised pleasure. Collis couldn't do anything but look back at him, and give him the sort of turned-down smile which means 'Okay, you caught me, I give in'; but Andrew Hunt stepped forward and walked around them with both his hands clasped behind his back, as if he were admiring a new piece of statuary.

'Good morning, sir and madam,' he said with benevolence. 'And how are we enjoying our voyage?'

Only a few miles out of Limón Bay, on the isthmus of Panama, with the dark coastline already in sight, the *Virginia*'s steam engines blew a valve, and the ship wallowed offshore for most of the day, while the weather worsened, and the passengers were fed with stone-cold mutton and carrots. It was early evening before they eventually paddled into Aspinwall harbour, and it was raining out of a low sky the colour of dirty white bath towels. Aspinwall itself was built on a flat coral island in the middle of the bay, and as the *Virginia* approached it through the rain, it appeared to the passengers to be floating on the steamy water as if by enchantment, a clutter of wet red rooftops and peeling white stucco, like a town mysteriously set adrift from land. The passengers stood on deck with umbrellas, or sheltered underneath the sagging awnings, as they were slowly borne towards the United States Mail Steamship Company's jetty. There, silent and disinterested, a huddle of longshoremen waited in wet shirts and sodden straw hats, and a company official with whiskers and rows of gilt buttons held a dripping umbrella in one hand and a fizzled-out cigar in the other.

Collis, his trunk already packed for the journey across the isthmus, stood under one of the awnings on the afterdeck, crowded next to his Latvian cabin partner. There was no sign of Hannah, and he suspected she was still in her cabin. He hadn't seen her all day, and at lunchtime the steward had taken a tray along to the women's quarters, so he guessed she was feigning sickness. Maybe she wasn't feigning. The air was close enough and hot enough to make anyone feel sick. But the whole damned business made him feel unutterably depressed. As if life weren't galling enough already.

Maria-Mamuska, still wrapped in her Pueblo blanket, a bundle of belongings by her side, was standing in the rain by the forward rail, her hair wet and stuck to her face. Andrew Jackson Hunt had positioned himself not far away from her, and every now and then

Collis could see him turn and give her a cocky little smile. Well, thought Collis, if he's prepared to take on Maria-Mamuska's unborn infant, he's welcome to her. It was a pity she was so damned dirty.

Gradually, the *Virginia*'s engines slowed, and she turned and eddied sideways towards the jetty. Out of the mist, beyond the jetty, the white two-storey headquarters of the steamship company appeared, surrounded by spindly palms, and an assortment of warehouses and storage tanks and fenced enclosures. Further inland, through the rain, Collis could make out only a scattering of dilapidated tropical houses, and beyond, to the south, foothills that were so dark and moist that they looked as if they were forested with freshly steamed broccoli. Even before the ship berthed, he could smell the distinctive tropical odour of donkey dung and sewage and home-cured tobacco, and he could hear the screeching of parrots in the trees.

The gangplank was lowered, and the passengers filed off the *Virginia* and on to the jetty. The rain continued steadily, and hardly anyone spoke. The company official shook a few hands and then stepped up on to one of the jetty's bollards, holding up his umbrella as if he were going to attempt a leap into the sea.

'Ladies and gentlemen,' he said, in a congested Illinois accent, 'I very much regret to tell you that the rain has brought on a mudslide up at the Culebra cut, and that the railroad won't be running this evening. However, the company has arranged for you to stay here at Aspinwall for tonight, and we should be ready to roll by mid-morning tomorrow.'

There was a general murmur of dismay and disapproval. Even from where they were standing within the company's premises, it was clear that the town of Aspinwall wasn't as mysterious and magical as it had appeared from the bay. The heat was desperately oppressive, and every breath smelled of garbage and fever.

Andrew Jackson Hunt called out, 'What happens if the railroad isn't ready by the morning?'

The official shrugged. 'You're welcome to go by mule.'

'By mule? And how long would that take?'

'It's about five hours on the railroad. By mule, it could take you days. That's if you got there at all. The yellow fever's bad this year.'

'In that case, it looks as if we don't have much choice,' decided the woman who had chased Collis out of the ladies' quarters the previous night. 'Take us to the hotels.'

The company official led the way, while barefooted Jamaican porters took up the rear with the baggage. The *Virginia* was unloaded of her mail and her provisions, breathing and hissing and letting out an occasional *chuff* as her boilers were cooled off, and Collis turned back once and looked at her. She could return to New York and civilisation. God alone knew where *he* was going to end up.

Hannah was only a few paces ahead of him as they reached the wet railroad tracks of the company's terminal. Already a sorry collection of mule traps was gathered there to take the ladies, overlooked by six or seven Jamaican muleteers in ragged white shirts and soiled white pants, and only one complete mouthful of teeth between the lot of them. They chewed and spat and watched the soaking, pale-faced passengers treading delicately along the boardwalk towards them, and one of them made a coarse remark which set the others cackling like castanets. Collis quickened his pace a little so that by the time Hannah was lifting her skirts to step over the first railroad track, he was right by her side. He crooked his arm and offered it to her.

'Hannah?' he said.

She stopped and stared at him. There were plum-coloured circles under her eyes, as if she hadn't slept very well. Although she was carrying a small fringed parasol, her blue cape was stained with rainwater, and there were raindrops, or tears, clinging to her eyelashes.

She paused, and then turned away.

'I don't need any help, thank you. I'm quite capable of walking on my own two feet.'

'Hannah, you've misunderstood me.'

'I don't think so. Now, please, we're holding people up.'

She began to walk across the tracks, and Collis walked beside her. 'What you saw this morning, Hannah, that was nothing but a farcical mistake. The girl was half-witted. She was only trying to show off.'

Hannah pursed her lips. 'I see. She certainly succeeded, didn't she?'

'Hannah, this is a hot climate. All manner of odd things happen. But you mustn't read damning interpretations into every one.'

Hannah reached the far side of the tracks. The company official tipped his cap and gestured towards the mule traps. 'Madam, I am truly mortified to have you inconvenienced this way.' He grinned,

140

as if he were truly tickled to see this motley party of greenhorns having to spend the night in such a pestiferous place.

'Hannah?' Collis said.

'Yes, Collis, I hear you,' she said, in an expressionless voice. 'But I can only believe what I see with my own eyes, and my eyes have told me not to trust you.'

'What's that supposed to mean?' asked Collis. 'What does trust have to do with what happened this morning? We're not husband and wife, are we? We're not even lovers. How can I possibly be unfaithful to you if I've never made any promises to be faithful? Did you ever hear me give my oath never to look at another woman? Hannah, you're married to someone else – you can't *expect* it of me!'

'You're wriggling now, Collis,' she said, 'and it doesn't suit you.'

She reached the rickety mule trap with its dirty cushioned seats and its mildewed awning, and she reluctantly held out her hand to the muleteer to help her climb aboard it. She settled herself, and then she looked at Collis with self-possession and pride, but also with distinct regret.

'However much you protest,' she said, 'the fact remains that when we first met each other, we were both conscious of an affinity of spirit. It was possible that, in time, this affinity might have flowered. Instead, I looked out of my window this morning and saw the very first seedling being trampled underfoot.'

Collis wiped the rain from his face with his hand. 'Are you trying to tell me that we could have been lovers? In spite of everything you've said to the contrary?'

'It wasn't beyond the bounds of possibility,' she said with dignity. 'I have to confess, to my shame, that it did enter my mind more than once. I know I protested. But there were moments when it seemed like a sort of answer.'

'Then why did you turn me away?'

She lowered her eyes. 'I am not a New Yorker, Collis. I am not a woman of much intellect or experience. I know that I am attractive in your eyes, and in the eyes of many men to whom the sacraments of marriage are only there to be broken. I am attracted to you, too. There, I've said it. But I need to be handled with delicacy. I feel a great burden of guilt already, without having it aggravated. You came cantering up to me last night as if you were a steeplechaser, and I were just another hedge you wanted to jump. You were too

141

bold and too flippant. Collis – I need *reassurance* before I can ever consider becoming acquainted with you more closely.'

Collis reached out and took her hand. Her fingers were limp and yielding, but he still held on.

'You're as giddy and confused as any woman I've ever met,' he told her, as warmly as he could manage.

She kept her eyes down. 'Perhaps you're right,' she said. 'But I have my sensitivities, too. And what I saw this morning out on deck – well, it hurt my sensitivities considerably.'

'You mean you were considering taking me as a lover, and now you don't know?'

'Collis, it was that dreadful girl – '

'That girl was nothing! That was the most absurd thing that has ever happened to me! She just – popped herself out for no reason at all!'

'I see,' said Hannah disbelievingly.

Collis held her hand for a moment longer, then released it. It dropped by her side as if it were artificial. She really was the most frustrating woman. It was entirely in character for her to tell him *after* he had failed to seduce her that she had been willing at least to entertain the possibility of their becoming lovers, given the right approach. But why hadn't she told him *before*?

A muleteer came up, dragging behind him a wet, bedraggled mount with a worn leather saddle. 'This one is for you, señor,' he said. 'Better get up. We have to go now.'

'Is it far?'

'Just down Front Street, señor. A few hundred metres.'

'Then I'll walk.'

'No, señor, ride.'

'Just so that I'll have to pay you?'

'No, señor. The street.'

'The street? What's the matter with the street?'

The muleteer tried to think of the English words. Finally, with very careful enunciation, he said, 'Human doings, señor.'

Collis looked around the puddly railroad yard. Already most of the *Virginia*'s passengers had settled themselves in the traps or sat themselves astride single mules. In the mist of a rainy Aspinwall evening, they looked like refugees from some eccentric military campaign, the remnants of a disreputable regiment of cavalry. The *Virgina* let out a long hoot, and a mule, with great solemnity, dropped dung on the railroad tracks.

'Let's talk again later,' Collis said to Hannah. 'There's no need for us to be enemies, is there?'

'Who said we were enemies?'

'There's no need for us not to be friends. Even lovers, if that's what you will, and if that's what the Lord God wills.'

'The Lord God never wills immorality,' said Hannah.

'I don't believe He wills unhappiness, either.'

Hannah opened her purse and took out a handkerchief. It wasn't very clean, but then most of the *Virginia*'s passengers were running low on personal laundry. 'I'd rather you didn't take His name in vain,' she said.

'I wouldn't need to if you told me how you really felt.'

She patted the rain from her cape. 'I don't know how I feel, Collis. I believe that I've told you everything possible. I have thought about you as a lover, but it could never be a passing relationship, a brief affair. I would have to commit myself to you, and I would expect commitment in return.'

'Is that why you were so upset when you saw me with Maria? Because you'd already committed yourself, and you expected the same from me?'

She raised her head. The evening was very dusky now, and through the rain her face seemed to have the quality of a delicate luminescent painting.

'I suppose so,' she said.

Collis stood beside her trap for a while, and then went over without a word and took the rough rope rein of his own mount. Over in the far corner of the yard, sitting in the open doorway of a boxcar marked 'Specie & US Mails', were a dozen Jamaican porters, most of them half-naked. At a signal from the railroad official, they jumped down from the boxcar and gathered up all the hand baggage that couldn't be strapped to the mules and began to file out of the railroad yard and along the muddy road towards the town. One of them, the last, even carried a small boy on his back, on a wooden seat that was fastened around his shiny black head with a cloth band. The boy, in a sodden sailor suit, was pale-faced and fast asleep.

The chief muleteer, a fat man in a wide straw hat, now called, 'Hoi, hoi, hoi,' and waved his arm like a threshing flail, for everyone to follow. Unsteadily, everyone did so, shaken in their rickety traps, or with their bottoms swaying dangerously on the narrow wet backs of their mules.

143

Collis had never seen a town so dilapidated and discouraging as Aspinwall. Front Street, along which they followed the rusting tracks the of the trans-Panama railroad, faced out across the misty harbour, where small sailboats glided like ghosts. On the east side of the street, towards the town itself, there was a white stone freight depot, a couple of derelict wooden houses, one of which sported a fading sign that read 'Café du Chemin de Fer', an icehouse, two tired-looking saloons, a railroad office, and further along, the Hotel Colón, a run-down three-storey balconied building.

The street was unpaved, and thick with oozing, blue-black mud. It was littered with empty bottles, dead dogs, broken chairbacks, and garbage. On the front verandahs of the buildings opposite, idle Jamaicans watched the slow, slippery progress of the *Virginia*'s small cavalcade with glazed indifference. The population of Aspinwall was almost all black, and almost all poverty-stricken. They were the remnants of the Caribbean work force that the founders of the Panama Railroad Company had brought over, along with Chinese and Irish, to lay the tracks across the isthmus; and now they rotted, along with the town in which they lived, in a swampish miasma of disease, heat, and hopelessness. All that the founders had left behind of themselves was a red-granite memorial, streaked with rain, which was dedicated to the vision and fortitude of John Lloyd Stephens, Henry Chauncey, and William Henry Aspinwall.

Collis took a long look at the memorial as he rode past it. Then he raised his eyes upward, above the wet red rooftops, where huge black buzzards wheeled tirelessly around and around and around, as if the town itself were a corpse from which they could pick; and the rain fell as if it were going to fall for ever.

Chapter 4

It was still raining during the night as Collis lay in the Hotel Colón trying to sleep. He tossed around in his narrow iron-framed bed, tousled and sweating, and at last he sat up with the crumbly old mosquito netting draped around his head as if he were a new bride, or a man playing the ghost of himself. The heat seemed to be even worse at night, but he had heard that the night air carried fever, and so he had kept his shutters closed. He lifted the netting, groped to find his matches on the bedside table, and awkwardly lit his oil lamp. The yellowish light swelled to fill the room.

The Hotel Colón, when they had arrived, had turned out to possess a decaying French grandeur, with half-collapsed chandeliers and muddied carpets, although the rooms themselves were bare-boarded and rudimentary. Collis wouldn't have minded if they had been strewn with rushes. He had been so exhausted by the time a young pockmarked Spanish boy had shown him up to his balconied room on the second floor that he had closed the door and fallen back on his bed with a greater feeling of relief and luxury than he had ever been afforded by the St Nicholas Hotel or the Union Club or even one of the plushest bawdy houses on Mercer Street. After lying motionless for five minutes, he had kicked off his wet boots, stripped off his rain-darkened coat, and then lain back again and closed his eyes.

He had slept, he supposed, for about two hours. He picked up his watch from the table, but it had stopped at ten o'clock. He looked around the room. There was a cream-painted closet, a battered bureau with a china jug and a basin, and a reproduction of the *Madonna of the Rocks*. His trunk must have been brought up while he slept, because it lay upended next to the bureau. There was a close smell of tropical mould and camphor, and it made him sneeze, twice.

He got out of bed, squatted down by his trunk, and unlocked it. Underneath his linen coat, securely wrapped up in a towel, was a bottle of red burgundy, which he had purchased on the steamer. He took it out, sat on the bed, and dug the cork out of it with his penknife. He swilled out with wine the cloudy tumbler that the management had left by his bed, and then poured himself a large glassful. The water, Andrew Jackson Hunt had warned him, was as dangerous as the night air.

He was sitting there drinking and wiping the sweat from his forehead with the towel when he heard a hoarse whistling sound. He frowned and listened. There was another sound, too. A monotonous *pssshh-clank, pssshh-clank*, followed by a long sharp exhalation of steam. He got up and went across to the window that gave out on to the balcony. Through the slats of the shutters, he could see orange lights flickering and hear loud voices talking in Spanish, and laughter. Collis unfastened the latch, opened the balcony door, and stepped out into the hot night air.

Through the sparkling rain, only a hundred feet away across the muddy street, he saw a railroad train. It was obviously waiting for boxcars to be rolled out of the main yard before it went into the terminus itself. The locomotive was steely grey, with a tall bell-shaped smokestack, a green-painted cab with Gothic windows as elaborate as a gazebo, four huge driving wheels, and a red-painted cowcatcher. Behind it was a tender, piled with wood, as decorative and bright as a New York saloon on wheels. Behind that were four US Mail boxcars and six passenger cars with varnished sides and curtained windows.

In that dark, glittering night, with Limón Bay suffused in mist behind it, the locomotive and its train looked like a carnival. All its windows were alight, and from the lantern in front of the smokestack shone a wide beam that caught the falling rain in a whirl of gold. Showers of tiny red sparks flew into the night, while steam sizzled from the safety valve and dissolved around the wheels. An aroma of grease and woodsmoke mingled with the damp tropical putrefaction of Front Street.

Collis went back into his room to find a cigar, but he came back out again to light it, and to stare, while he smoked, at the shining train. He could see the engineer in his peaked calico cap and ticking-striped shirt, his back dark with sweat, and the fireman, stripped to the waist, tossing logs into the furnace. All along the length of the train, boxcar doors were being slid open and slammed shut, tappers were hammering and ringing at the wheels, and shunters stood in the rain waiting to marshal the train into the yard and disconnect it. They called and whooped in Jamaican patois and Spanish, and one of them blew persistently at a railroad whistle.

It was a carnival, but it was more. It was a carnival that rode through the jungle and the mountain passes, from one wide ocean to the other, and carried people of all kinds, people with ambitions and people with fears, cheap people and expensive people, liars and missionaries, to fresh and unknown destinies. It seemed to Collis like a strange decorated vehicle of human fate, a challenging and almost unmanageable apparatus which swept you out of your past and into your future whether you wanted to go or not. Right out there on Front Street, breathing and sniffling to itself in the equatorial heat, gilded and enamelled and enticingly bright, it was the sideshow that was going to bear Collis away to the rest of his life.

He left his hotel room and walked along the corridor until he came to the stairs. Although it was well past midnight, the bar down below was still open, and someone was playing a slow and sentimental tune on the piano. The hotel lobby must have been lavish once, in the days when the railroad was being constructed, but now it looked more like a barn that someone had perversely painted with dim murals of naked nymphs and Doric temples. Under the sagging chandelier, twenty or thirty men sat at scratched and drink-stained tables with their hats firmly on their heads, drinking bourbon and smoking pipes, talking too loudly and wishing to God they were someplace else. Three fans revolved uselessly, making no impression on the sodden heat or the dense tobacco smoke. By the desk was a black-framed list of the hotel rules – no smoking in the bath, no spitting off the balconies, no more than three to the bed. There were no palms in the hotel foyer, as in the hotels in New York; the management's policy was that if a guest wanted to look at a palm, he could step outside the door and see enough damned palms to last him for the rest of his life.

Collis went down the creaking stairs and across to the bar, where the Spanish barkeep was polishing glasses on the sleeve of his baggy shirt. Collis asked for a stone fence, but the barkeep only stared at him, so he made do with three fingers of Old Carstairs Authentic. Then he leaned back against the bar and looked around, still feeling tired, but somehow more excited with the way his life was turning out than he had been for days. Maybe now he was in Panama he'd begun to recognise that there was no turning back, and that whatever was going to come next, he was going to have to bite the bullet and make the best of it.

At the grand piano, by the light of a tarnished candelabrum, an elderly man in a soiled straw hat and whiskers as sparse as a tomcat was playing an emotional French tune, a tune of lost loves and

147

heartbreaks and Sunday walks on the banks of the Seine, with an unerring instinct for hitting the wrong note at the peak of each bar; meanwhile a tall man in a yellow vest was singing some other song altogether. Nobody seemed to mind, or care; here in Aspinwall on a rainy summer night, everybody had his mind on other things. There were occasional sallies of laughter, but they were short-lived and strained.

Collis had almost finished his whisky when Andrew Jackson Hunt came downstairs and walked across to the bar.

'How do you do?' he said, raising his hat.

'Much better, thank you for asking,' Collis told him. 'I managed to get in a couple of hours' sleep, at least.'

'Hmmm,' said Andrew Hunt, 'I wish I could. The problem is, my room is right next to the goddam water closet, and every time I'm right on the edge of nodding off, somebody decides to do their party imitation of Niagara Falls.'

'Have you seen the train outside?' said Collis. 'I was thinking of going across to take a closer look.'

'Haven't you ever seen a train before?'

'Of course. But not this close. I always kept away from the railroad tracks in New York to keep from frightening the horses.'

Andrew beckoned the barkeep over and asked for a bourbon and a refill for Collis. 'I'll tell you something,' he said, leaning his elbows on the bar and taking a good hard swig, which he swilled around his teeth. 'The railroad train is where the money is, and that's for sure. One day, somebody's going to be smart enough to lay down a railroad all the way from San Francisco to St Louis, and that somebody's going to make himself richer than Crease-ass.'

'Who?'

'What's the matter with you society people? Don't they give you a decent education? King Crease-ass, that's who I'm taking about, and that's who you and me could be like if we had the brains, and the backing. Look at this goddam Panama Railroad. How long does it take you to get to Panama? Six hours at the worst. And how much do the bastards charge for it? Twenty-five dollars in gold. By my reckoning, that's better than four dollars an hour, per person, in gold. Think what the hell you could charge for a straight railroad ride across to California, or back again, without ever having to set foot on a steamer, or come anywhere near this goddam jungle.'

The barkeep set down their drinks. 'I've already drunk half a bottle of wine,' Collis said. 'I don't want to get paralytic.'

'Drink it,' said Andrew. 'Bourbon is the best preventive for yellow fever there is, that and a little mustard. Barman, do you have some mustard? *Mootard*?'

The barkeep shook his head.

'They're all the damned same,' complained Andrew. 'They'd like to see you catch sick, and wind up with your legs sticking up in the air; that's what they'd like. And they get the pleasure of it often enough. There's consumption and smallpox and cholera and malaria and yellow jack around here, just about enough of it to wipe out half of Carolina, and a good piece of Virginia besides.'

'Don't they get sick themselves, living in this pesthole?'

'Sure they do. But you only get the yellow fever once. Usually, you die. But if you don't die, then you never get it again. Mind you, immunity to yellow fever don't protect you from cholera, or anything else.'

Collis drank his bourbon as if it were medicine. It made him feel more lightheaded than he wanted to be, and nauseated, but anything was better than catching some fatal tropical disease.

'They had so many labourers die when they were building this railroad, they didn't know what to do with all the bodies,' Andrew said cheerfully. 'So what they did in the end was, they pickled the dead men in barrels, and they sold them to hospitals and medical schools, for doctors to cut up. I heard the railroad company made a real decent profit out of that.'

'You're making it up,' said Collis.

'You think so? You ask anyone around here.'

Collis looked around the room again. A raddled man in a soiled velvet suit raised his glass to him and gave a gappy, suggestive grin.

'I think I'd rather go take a look at the train,' he told Andrew.

They stepped outside. The rain was so fine now that they could scarcely feel it. They made their way in silence across the muddy street, trying to dodge the thickest ooze and the widest puddles. Soon they were right up by the front of the locomotive, by the wide, splayed cowcatcher, and Collis looked up at the bright headlight as if it were the hypnotic eye of a huge Cyclopean monster.

They walked along beside the wheels, inhaling the smell of oil and steam, admiring the lavish giltwork and the shining brass. On the side of the cab was a scenic painting of Panama City, surrounded by cherubs and zephyrs and rosy clouds, as if it were a paradise on earth. The frames of the cab windows and the edging of the cab roof were picked out with gold Gothic patterns. Out of the rear window, his shirt-sleeved arms folded, a black cigar in his mouth, leaned the engineer.

'How do you do?' Collis called.

The engineer spat out into the night.

'Maybe,' Andrew said, after a lengthy silence, 'if you had to spend your life in a locomotive cab in Panama, then you wouldn't feel too happy about life, either.'

'Maybe he doesn't speak English,' suggested Collis.

They walked a little further along the length of the train, past the mail cars, until they reached the passenger cars. These were far less lavishly decorated than the locomotive, although they were built of solid heart pine, and two of them had ladies' apartments. Their seats were narrow and covered in plain broadcloth, but anything was better than the back of a mule. There were engraved-glass oil lamps burning at every seat.

After climbing up on the drop step and peering in at the windows, Collis and Andrew went slowly back to the Hotel Colón. Collis was feeling hungry now, and he could have done with a couple of thick chops and a tomato salad. Andrew took a couple of pinches of snuff, emitted two explosive bellows, and then blew his nose into his tobacco-stained handkerchief. The night was noisy with the rustle of rain on the rooftops, the gurgling of the sea by the harbour wall, the whirr of insects, and the ceaseless *pssshhh-clank* of the locomotive.

'What would it take to build a railroad from San Francisco to St Louis?' Collis asked.

Andrew folded away his handkerchief and looked at Collis sagely. 'Millions of dollars, to kick off with.'

'And what else?'

'Expertise, I guess. Although expertise can always be rented.'

'So where would we find millions of dollars?'

Andrew gave a northward sweep of his arm, encompassing the whole of the United States and its territories, somewhere out there in the rainy darkness. 'There's the government,' he said. 'They're willing to finance a railroad if someone comes up with a route to run it over, and they'll throw in more land than you could gallop across in a week.'

Collis nodded. 'That's right. And there's all those people you told

150

me abut earlier. All those people who live up on Rincon Hill in San Francisco. Wouldn't they be ready to put money into a railroad? Think how rich San Francisco would become, and how much richer *they* would become, if they were only connected to the East by a railroad.'

Andrew stopped walking and held Collis's arm. He frowned at him. 'Collis,' he said. 'You're not seriously thinking of building a railroad, are you?'

Collis smiled. 'I doubt if I could do it. But look back at that locomotive, and then tell me if you can think of anything more exciting than that.'

That night, when Collis returned to his room, something at least equally exciting to that was waiting for him. On his bed, in a wrinkled but clean pale-blue dress, with her hair washed and her skin shining, was Maria-Mamuska. Still wiping his mouth from a heavy meal of bacon and beans, he pressed the door closed behind him and leaned against it for a while, looking at her in the shadowy lamplight.

'I didn't expect you,' he said.

She smiled. 'When it's unexpected, it's better, huh?'

He pulled a face. 'I don't know. My mother always told me that predictability was a virtue.'

'You don't want to be virtuous, do you?'

'I don't know about that, either. It might make a change.'

She lay back on the bed and smiled at him. 'I can't trap you now. You know that I'm having a baby. So whatever we do, it can only be for love. Don't you think so?'

'Love? I don't love you. And I don't see how you can possibly love me.'

'By the morning I might.'

He grunted, amused. Then he walked across the room to the balcony and closed the shutters. It was stifling with the windows shut like that, but Collis preferred to sweat than be sent home pickled in a tub. Maria-Mamuska watched him, with the same provocative smile fixed on her face, as he approached the end of the bed and stood there unbuttoning his shirt.

'What happened to Andrew Hunt?' he asked her. 'I thought I saw him making eyes at you.'

'I don't like him,' she said. 'He looks too much like that crazy man.'

151

'I see. So you chose me instead. Well, I'm glad you cleaned yourself up.'

He sat down on the edge of the bed and pried off his boots. They were crusted with black mud, which he knocked off against the bed's iron leg. Then he loosened his cuffs and tugged his shirt over his head. Maria-Mamuska watched him, her eyes dark in the unsteady light from the frosted-glass oil lamp.

'You seem so unhappy,' she said.

'Unhappy?'

'Oh, I saw you joking with Andrew Hunt, and I know you like to tease people. But when I look at you, I think you look sad. I watched you when you were talking to Mrs West. Your face was very . . .' She pulled her mouth down into a glum expression so that he could see what she meant.

Collis stood up and unbuttoned his pants. He was quite glad he had put on fresh cotton combinations that morning, especially since Maria-Mamuska had taken the trouble to wash. He went over to the basin on the bureau, poured out a little water, and brushed his teeth with a gritty pink powdered dentifrice which he had bought at Jacksonville. He rinsed his mouth out, then came back to the bed.

'Is it a woman who makes you sad?' Maria-Mamuska asked. 'Some other woman? I don't mean Mrs West.'

He shook his head. 'No. It's more than that.'

'You don't want to talk about it?'

'There doesn't seem to be any point in talking about it. It's all behind me now, whether I want it that way or not. Talking about it isn't going to solve anything.'

He was silent for a long time, staring with unfocused eyes at the lamp. 'Do you want me to go?' she said.

'Why should I?'

'I don't want to stay here if you don't want me.'

Collis began to unbutton his combinations. 'You're very welcome to stay. I'd like you to. I'm just sorry I'm not rich. I'd buy you flowers, and diamonds, and whatever else this dump of a city had to offer.'

She sat up on the bed with a creak of springs. 'I'm sorry, too.' She smiled. 'But why don't we just say that we're doing this so that we'll have something to remember each other by? An old time that we can talk about when we meet on Montgomery Street three years from now.'

'Do you think I'd forget you?' he asked.

She shrugged. 'You might. If you get rich, and meet lots of beautiful girls.'

He looked at her. There was an unkempt, practical beauty about her which made him feel unexpectedly good-humoured. She was quite unlike Delphine, who played her erotic games as a teasing exploration. There were no ploys and counterploys and coquettish sidesteps. Maria-Mamuska saw love-making as a healthy recreation, like riding; and even if she fell a few times when she was out doing it, she accepted those falls as a legitimate (or, more strictly, an illegitimate) risk. She could be wildly theatrical, and impossibly illogical, but she was grown up enough to know what her body desired.

Collis, as he stood beside her in his stuffy tropical hotel room, decided he liked her.

She knelt on the bed and reached behind her to unbutton her dress. Outside, the rain had ceased falling, and there was no sound now but the insects and the endless clanking of the locomotive. She crossed her arms and pulled her dress over her head, and on the ceiling her shadow looked like a bird unfolding its wings and then settling again. She tossed her head once to throw back her long black hair.

Underneath her dress, she was wearing a ribboned bodice and bloomers. They were off-white from washing in the *Virginia*'s laundry room, and from the sweat of a night in Panama, but she had scented them with lavender powder, and hung a little muslin bag of pot-pourri around her waist. She let the ribbons of her bodice go, and her big brown breasts were bared again, wobbling heavily as she unlaced the bodice altogether, and as she rose on the iron bed to take down her bloomers.

Nude in the lamplight, she exuded muskiness and warmth; and although she was short when she stood up beside him, the fresh-washed crown of her hair barely reaching his chest, her body was full and well-proportioned. Her pregnant tummy was rounded and high, and Collis guessed she must have been carrying her baby for at least three months. But she was still sensual and provocative. He let his hand stray down her, appreciatively moulding itself around her every curve.

'I think the whole of America should be full of women like you,' he said.

She unfastened the last buttons of his combinations and pulled

153

them off his shoulders, baring his chest. She kissed his chest with selective kisses, as if certain spots on it were sweeter than others.

'You'd go crazy if it was,' she said. 'Even more crazy than you are now.'

She knelt down on the bare floor in front of him and took down his underwear. She stroked his hairy thighs as if she could hardly believe how white and lean he was: during the journey from New York he had lost ten pounds.

'The whole of America should be full of men like you,' she said, with a sly smile. 'But then, I'd be too jealous.'

She kissed him slowly, enough to make him shudder; then she lifted herself and turned around and fell back on to the bed, sinking into the cream coverlet. Collis dived after her, one swimmer after another, and they seemed to fall and fall through layer after layer of time and feeling, as if the bed could carry them down through years and months and mysterious hours, through memories of long-forgotten winters and summers, softly showered with ambrotypes of unremembered friends and faces, entranced by half-heard snatches of songs, tantalised by fleeting visions of lost loves. Collis even thought of Delphine, as he sank, and he might even have called her name out loud. He thought of Hannah, too, and glimpsed her for a moment in profile, with her blonde hair unfurled by the wind, a Renaissance heroine. But it was Maria-Mamuska with whom he fell. He saw a dark tangle of hair, a chestnut-brown eye that stared at nothing, a dark flushed cheek. He felt as if his sinking were almost over, as if the whole of Panama were pressing in on him, as if locomotives were rushing slowly towards his head from all sides. He felt the intense sensitivity of his own naked skin against hers. 'Maria-Mamuska . . .' he whispered, and then he was discharging everything he felt for her and for Hannah and for Delphine, and in one intense awesome flash it was over.

They lay side by side on the coverlet for a long time, until their panting had subsided, and until most of the night had passed them by. Collis guessed it would be dawn soon, but he felt too idle to get out of bed and go look at his pocket watch, which he had left on top of the bureau.

After a while, Maria-Mamuska kissed his shoulder. He turned and smiled at her, and she smiled back.

'Well,' she said, 'I guess it's the only way to tell.'

'The only way to tell what?'

She brushed back her hair. There were clear beads of sweat on her upper lip. 'How much you could love someone. It's the only way to find out for sure.'

He didn't say anything for a minute or so. He wasn't entirely certain what she meant. He looked up at the cracked, stained plaster on the ceiling, and at the twining column of black smoke that rose from the oil lamp. He could have done with a drink.

Maria-Mamuska propped herself up on one elbow. 'So many people must marry without knowing what their wife or their husband is like underneath. Look at you and me. I could have been the tattooed lady for all you knew, and you could have been the tattooed man.'

Collis frowned. 'Sure. But we're not thinking of getting married.' He paused. 'Are we?'

Maria-Mamuska shook her head. 'I wouldn't marry you even if we were.'

'I beg your pardon?'

She sat up and cradled her knees in her arms.

'What do you mean, you wouldn't marry me anyway?' he wanted to know.

'Just what I said. Why should I marry a man who couldn't make me happy?'

'You don't think I could make you happy? Why not?'

She gave him a smile. 'Now I've made you angry. You think I'm being bad to you.'

'I simply don't understand you, that's all,' he told her. But he admitted to himself inwardly that her words had made him feel more than usually sore. What kind of a gibe was that – that he couldn't make her happy? Damn it, he could make any woman happy. Hadn't he just this minute made her happy? What more did she want? Surely she didn't want *more*?

Maria-Mamuska kissed his hair. 'You mustn't look so sad. You're looking sad again. But you could never be right for me.'

'I don't know what makes you say that.'

'I say it because I don't like to be raped.'

He looked at her petulantly. 'You call that rape? How the hell do you work that out?'

'It was rape,' she affirmed, with a nod. 'If a man takes a woman to his bed, and yet his mind is someplace else, then that's rape. You weren't with me, Collis, you were far away, and all I could do was lie there and wait for you to come back to me.'

He sat up. He could hardly credit what he was hearing. 'What in heaven's name are you trying to say?' he said. 'What do you mean, you were waiting for me to come back to you? Where the hell do you think I was?'

'I don't know, Collis. Maybe with other women.'

He put his hand over his mouth. His eyes, framed by his thumb and his index finger, were both irritated and thoughtful.

'You mustn't blame yourself,' said Maria-Mamuska. 'Plenty of women would think you were wonderful. But wherever you went in your mind, and with your body, I would have liked to have come with you. I wanted us to get there together.'

There was a silence, and then Maria-Mamuska suddenly started to laugh. It was a hoarse, hilarious laugh, and Collis couldn't help smiling in response. But he said, as he watched her, 'I don't know what's so funny.'

She brushed tears away from her eyes. 'Nothing is funny, Collis. Nothing is funny except what men don't understand about women, and women don't understand about men. You're not funny. I'm not laughing at you. I think you're very good-looking, and very strong, but you're not the one for me. There is something else you have to do in your life before you think about staying with a woman. You must use some women first, as you used me tonight. That was all I should have expected.'

Collis reached out with his hand and gently touched her forehead with the tips of his fingers, almost as if he were giving her a blessing.

'I think you're quite amazing,' he said.

She took hold of his hand and kissed it. 'No, I'm not amazing. I'm one of those people who have to do everything the difficult way, and that's why I think like this. I'm not amazing. But *you* will be amazing. And this thing you have to do will also be amazing.'

'What thing?'

She bent forward and picked up her bodice from the floor. 'If you don't know, then I don't. But you will do something that will change the world, and people will say, there goes Mr Collis, he changed the world.'

Collis stood naked and silent. The flame in the oil lamp dipped and flickered, and all around, the Hotel Colón creaked like an old ship. His watch on the bureau said four-thirty, and he knew it would soon be light. Here, only about nine degrees north of the equator, the dawn came up as suddenly as a thrown-back curtain.

All through the long minutes of quiet, the locomotive on Front Street went *pssssshhh-clank, pssssshhh-clank*, patiently waiting, as a carnival waits, for the people to come and bring laughter and life to it.

The train pulled out of Aspinwall at eleven the next morning, chased by dogs and ragged children. The day was clear and brassily hot, and the mud of Front Street was already crusted like pastry. The *Virginia*'s passengers were pale and withdrawn on the whole, because none of them had slept very well, and although they had been served with cups and cups of fragrant Colombian coffee, their breakfast had consisted of not much more than dried-beef hash, beans, and potatoes fried in rancid oil.

Collis, however, was in a good mood. He felt that today's train journey was at last going to bring him face to face with the broad expanse of his future. Travelling through the jungle from the Caribbean to the Pacific was like disappearing down a rabbit hole, leaving behind his failures and his creditors, only to reappear in another world where his past errors were all forgotten. He was still irritated by Hannah's oblique approaches, and confused by Maria-Mamuska's self-reliance, but in this world of exotic trees and bright-blue skies, with parakeets shrilling and the locomotive broad-chestedly chuffing along ahead of them, it was hard for him to feel depressed.

Front Street, once they were past the hotel, deteriorated into ramshackle buildings and abandoned sheds. But then they were crossing the narrow Folks River, which separated the island of Aspinwall from the mainland, and after they had been treated to a vivid, clear view of the glittering bay of Limón, they were plunged almost immediately into the jungle. Here, the sunlight was filtered into a thousand different shades of green, emeralds and turquoises and glass greens, all sparkling with raindrops from the previous day's downpour. The air was musty with the scent of vegetation, and close with the damp decaying smell of the tropics. Collis watched in fascination as the train emerged from the undergrowth which grew around the tracks and the sleepers, and crossed a wide watery mangrove swamp, its wheels rolling only inches above the surface. All around, like the patterns in a kaleidoscope, the piercingly blue sky was reflected in the muddy brown water. Andrew took out a flask of bourbon, wiped the neck, and passed it over to Collis. 'That's Monkey Hill,' he said, pointing to a low mound to the east. 'That's where the railroad used to bury their dead before they got around to selling 'em.'

The train clattered and swayed on the uneven rails. The puffs of smoke from its bell-shaped stack sailed past Collis's window, then broke up and faded amongst the giant grey-trunked *cedro* trees. Collis lit a cigar and sat back to enjoy five or six hours of travelling through the most exotic landscape he had ever seen in his life. Andrew, on the other hand, bent over a chess problem with a stub of pencil from the Astor House Hotel in New York, took regular sips from his flask, and ignored the scenery.

Once across the mangrove swamp, the train made its way through crowded tangles of trees and plants, so dense that they sometimes formed a green, creeper-hung tunnel. Collis felt that if the train travelled slowly enough, the jungle would entwine itself around the wheels, and eventually overtake it completely. One day, an exploratory safari might find them, a party of cheerfully grinning skeletons, in a train from which scarlet hibiscus and pale orchids grew and trembled, with passionflowers and trailing vines twisted around the locomotive's smokestack and interlaced between the spokes of the motionless wheels.

Andrew evidently sensed what he was thinking, because he looked up and remarked, 'They have to cut back the jungle every year. Jungles don't like railroads. Not much more than brides like their husbands on their wedding night.'

Then he returned to his chess.

It wasn't long before the train reached the village of Gatun. Gatun station was a small white-frame building with green shutters, neatly fenced and meticulously kept. The village itself lay across a wide, muddy river, a sparse collection of grass huts; and from there the train was watched with disinterest by a ragged crowd of men in straw hats, women in sun-bleached cotton dresses, and naked children. Occasionally one of the more exuberant passengers would wave, or call out 'Halloo', but the heat, and the noisy lushness of the jungle, seemed to swallow their greetings up. More than that, the river kept up an oily sliding noise as it poured its way out to the Caribbean, a noise that put Collis in mind of flood and fever.

'That's the Chagres,' said Andrew. 'The first time I saw it, it was almost dry. But the way it rains around here, it gets real swollen at times. They reckon they average more than sixteen inches of rain in August, and that's if they're lucky.'

The train stopped for a short while at Gatun, hissing and steaming under the glaring sky. Some of the passengers alighted, and walked up and down the train, admiring the river and the distant hills, but Collis remained where he was. Andrew Hunt took some more snuff, and blew his nose, and then decided that his chess problem was impossible.

After twenty minutes, the train whistled, everybody clambered aboard again, and they slowly pulled out of Gatun and started to cross the swamps of Panama's Caribbean lowlands. The heat was building up, and several passengers drew down the window shades and sat fanning themselves with magazines and newspapers. The Hotel Colón had offered a limited number of *New Orleans Times-Picayunes*, two months old.

By noon, the day was so hot and steamy that it was like a dream. They rolled slowly over the Black Swamp, which was supposed to be bottomless, and where the railroad pilings sank year after year, and continually had to be built up. They passed the stations at Tiger Hill, Lion Hill, and Ahorca Lagarto – 'Hanging Lizard' – all as neat and white as the station at Gatun. As they crossed the swampy bottomlands, the Chagres twisted and wriggled beside them, on their right, disgorging last night's rain through the hectic jungle undergrowth. They passed Frijoles (literally, 'Beans'), and punctilious Jamaican stewards offered them quinine water with ice; however, several of the passengers had already drunk so much warm white wine and bourbon that they were sleeping, their heads vibrating against the panelled sides of the coaches. They crossed the Chagres River over the huge iron bridge at Barbacoas, the train wheels echoing over the metal supports, and the river foaming violently underneath. Then they were out in broad, green fields, under an intense blue sky, in which clouds floated like tethered balloons.

Collis, drowsy with heat and whisky, watched the meadows go by through half-closed eyelids. The train clattered on its rails, and yellow butterflies blew in and out of the windows. He thought about Maria-Mamuska, and what had happened last night at the Hotel Colón. He didn't know whether he was going to sleep with her again or not. That seemed to be up to her – a position that Collis found both novel and alarming. He didn't know, either, what Hannah would think of it if she ever found out. It would probably mean the end of what she had called their 'affinity of spirit'. But would it?

All that he could decide about his feelings at the moment was that his travels on the paddle steamer *Virginia*, and his first night in a tropical climate, had opened his eyes to his lack of experience with women. The morning after Maria-Mamuska's frank words of disappointment, he missed Delphine more than ever, and he would have gladly had her here on this train, as it rocked and swayed across the drowned meadows of Panama, across bridge after bridge, crossing all the twisting tributaries of the Chagres before it eventually began to slow, and apply its brakes, and steam slowly into the village of Matachín. It was at Matachín that the train would finally leave the course of the Chagres and begin to scale the valley of the Rio Obispo, the Chagres's largest tributary. It was at Matachín that the Chinese labourers who had worked on the Panama Railroad had given in to the terrible depression that follows bouts of malaria, and had committed mass suicide, by hanging or wrist-slashing or sticking themselves, like pigs, on pointed bamboo sticks.

The train whistled as it went through Matachín, but didn't stop. A scattering of Indians waved their hats at it as it passed, but few of the passengers felt inclined to wave back. The day was stifling now, even though the locomotive was beginning to rattle its way up the enclosed Rio Obispo valley towards the highest point of the crossing, the station at Culebra.

Andrew Hunt was asleep, his hat pulled over his eyes, his magazine slowly slipping off his lap. Next to him, a stove salesman from Pottstown, Pennsylvania, was sitting uncomfortably in his yellow linen suit, saying nothing, and almost certainly wishing he was back in Pottstown, Pennsylvania. Collis, his handkerchief long since sodden, wiped the sweat from his forehead with the back of his sleeve. He was so hot now that he didn't feel like doing anything, sitting, standing, drinking, or smoking. All he could do was sit still and perspire.

At last the train came around the long right-hand curve that took it into Culebra station. Its brakes squealed, and it gradually steamed and sniffed to a halt, the boxcars and passenger cars jerking and banging against each other as they came to rest. A Spanish voice shouted, 'Culebra! Culebra! Short stop!' and the train's passengers leaned out of the windows like chickens looking out of a row of coops, to see what was going on.

The village of Culebra, where the railroad cut through the mountains, was a collection of little more than a dozen palm-thatched huts, a small general store, and a three-storey frame building that proudly announced itself as the American Hotel. The air was cooler and fresher up here, and because the railroad engineers had hacked the forest back, there was even a light breeze blowing from the peaks of the mountains. Collis opened the door of his compartment and stepped down on to the hard-baked turf. Andrew Hunt, who had seen it all before, continued to snooze.

Compared to some of the stations they had passed on the way up to the summit, Culebra was busy. There were three or four trains of mules, heavily laden with baggage and provisions, waiting to continue their journey through the jungle to Colón. Even though the journey was far quicker and safer by rail, not everybody could afford the Panama Railroad Company's freight charges, and there was still a regular traffic along the muddy and treacherous mule trail. There were two or three dozen Indians here at Culebra, too, broad-faced and obliging, who would carry your bags for you, or sell you cheroots, or simply stand and stare at you with friendly, disconcerting intensity. The train whistled hoarsely, and the sound echoed across the clearing.

A Spanish railroad official in a sweaty uniform came hurrying along the length of the track. He said: 'Get back aboard, please, señor. We don't stop here long.'

'Is anything wrong?' asked Collis.

The official coughed and quickly crossed himself. 'Somebody sick, that's all. The hotel doctor look at her now. Then we go.'

'Her? Who is it? One of the ladies?'

'That's right, señor. Now, please, back in the train.'

Collis looked back along the train. He could see now that several of the women passengers had alighted, and were standing by the side of the track with their hand baggage. The conductor was helping them move into another car, while several Indians stood around and benignly watched. With relief, among the muslin-veiled hats and cream and yellow travelling skirts, Collis recognised Maria-Mamuska, in her blue dress, clutching her bundle and her blanket. He gave her a quick wave, and she waved back.

He couldn't, however, see Hannah.

'You must get back on board, señor,' the railroad official told him. 'You cannot help.'

'I can't see Mrs West,' said Collis.

'Mrs Vest?' asked the railroad official.

'No, I can't see her. She was in that compartment.'

'Señor, most of the ladies have found new seats already. Don't

161

worry about Mrs Vest. It's only one lady who is sick. Please now, back on the train.'

Collis shook his head. 'I want to make sure that Mrs West is well first. Come along.'

The official shrugged and closed the door of Collis's compartment. Then he followed Collis along the side of the track, still shrugging and having a quiet argument with himself under his breath. The conductor tipped his cap as Collis approached, under the mistaken impression that he was a railroad director, or someone important.

'What's happening here?' asked Collis.

The conductor, a lean pock-marked half-breed with a drooping waxed moustache, said, 'See for yourself, sir,' and indicated the open door of the ladies' compartment. Collis peered inside.

The blinds had been drawn so that the compartment was dim. He could see a portly man sitting with his back to him on the edge of one of the banquettes, and this was presumably the local doctor. On the banquette itself, a woman was lying, her face hidden from view; but Collis could see her small white kid shoes and her white stockings, and he knew with cold certainty that it was Hannah.

He climbed up on the step and entered the gloomy compartment. There was a smell of surgical alcohol and castor oil. Castor oil, for those who didn't have the stomach for bourbon and mustard, was another of those infallible preventives for yellow fever. Collis stepped cautiously forward and saw Hannah lying on a sweat-stained pillow, her face very pale, her blonde hair dark with perspiration, her eyes closed and swollen. She shuddered and twitched as if she were having a nightmare, and her hands kept clenching and unclenching. Collis stared at her for a long while, his throat dry and his heart beating in slow, taut bumps. It suddenly occurred to him that in the space of only a few weeks, he was standing witness for the second time at the tragedy of a woman caught up in the inevitable accident of her own sad life. He felt almost as if he had been chosen, as a terrible lesson, to watch these women struggle and fall and eventually succumb.

The doctor turned. He was French, with a tobacco-stained moustache and bad teeth. He looked as if he had been living out in the tropics for ever. 'What do you want?' he said thickly.

'I know this lady,' said Collis.

The doctor sniffed. 'Well, in that case, I'm sorry.'

'Is she seriously ill?'

162

'There are only two kinds of sicknesses ın Panama, my friend,' said the doctor, rising to his feet and tugging his coat straight. 'There are the sicknesses from which you recover, and the sicknesses from which you don't.'

'Will she recover?'

'I don't know. She doesn't have a very strong constitution.'

Collis looked down at Hannah, as white as the effigy on a saint's tomb. She seemed to have settled down now, but her lips were parted, and she was breathing with a small moaning sound, like someone in distress.

'What's wrong with her?' asked Collis. 'Can't you do something?'

'My friend, I've done everything. She has been dosed with castor oil. But if it's yellow fever, then there is no cure.'

'Do you think it is?'

The doctor glanced down at Hannah and pulled a face. 'Most probably. She has the fever and the shivers, and she is very thirsty. But she doesn't have any pains in the legs, which is one of the symptoms, nor does she have a headache. But these may come later.'

'What happens then? After the pains?'

The doctor laid a hand on his arm. 'Let me tell you outside, my friend. If it is yellow fever, then this is the last place you ought to be. I have seen the whole crew of a clipper die because one of their number caught this disease.'

Collis wiped the sweat from his face. 'Who's going to look after her, if it is yellow fever? Someone has to.'

'My friend,' insisted the doctor quietly, '*la fièvre jaune*, it does not distinguish between the young or the old, nor does it care if you are rich or poor. I suggest we step down.'

Collis reluctantly left the ladies' compartment and climbed down on to the track. Several more passengers had left their cars now and were standing around at a respectful distance. Collis found himself brushing down the lapels of his light-grey suit as if to brush off the odour of disease.

The doctor came after him and said something in Spanish to the railroad official. Collis couldn't understand it, but he caught the words *fiebre amarilla*, and *Panama*. The railroad official shrugged and went back towards the head of the train, still muttering to himself.

The doctor came up to Collis and said quietly, 'Since we're still not sure if it's yellow fever, they will keep her on the train until you reach Panama. There's a hospital there, not a very good one, but they can make her more comfortable than I can here.'

'But you said there's no cure.'

The doctor looked away towards the huts of Culebra, as if he was thinking about something else altogether – some stray lost memory of long ago. 'No,' he said, after a distracted pause. 'There isn't.'

He rested his hand on Collis's shoulder. Close up, Collis could see that his eyes were veined and bloodshot by malaria. 'First, there is pain, and fever. Then, after a few days, the patient seems to get better, although the face and the eyes take on a yellow hue. After that, as the patient begins to die, he will vomit up black blood in great gushes, what the Panamanians call *vómito negro*. That means the end is close. The patient will go cold, and die in nine or ten hours.

'I'm sorry,' the doctor added. 'It's not too pleasant. I wish I could tell you it was something like a fever, or a chill. But I really don't know.'

'Who's going to look after her, between here and the hospital?' Collis said shakily.

The doctor took out a small tin of blackcurrant pastilles and offered them around. Only the train conductor took one, but then he looked as if he'd suffered from every equatorial disease known to medical science, and survived them all. The doctor dropped a pastille into his mouth and said, 'There were some nuns here until last week, but now they've gone back to Panama. I don't know. I don't think you'll find anyone to stay with her if it's the yellow fever. She'll just have to take her own chances. They're slim enough anyway. If she dies now, or in a few days' time, well, I'm sorry, but it won't make any considerable difference.'

'There isn't any alternative, then, is there?'

'Je ne comprends pas.'

'I'll just have to stay with her myself.'

The doctor sucked his pastille carefully. 'I don't think you really understand what you're saying, my friend. Yellow fever comes here every two or three years, and wipes out hundreds of people, sometimes thousands. No one is spared. I have seen young railroad engineers, fit as you could wish, come out here from France. In a month they are wasted away, or dead. You think maybe you are strong enough to fight it off. Well, sometimes physical strength helps people to survive. But seventy-five per cent of the time, their strength is no use. They die.'

He sniffed. 'If you stay with that lady, and if that lady has yellow fever, then the chances are that you too will die. That is all I can tell you.'

Collis took a deep breath. He was frightened of disease. When his sister, Maude, had come down with influenza, he had studiously avoided her rooms; and while she had convalesced, sitting in the back parlour with her inhalers and her handkerchiefs, he had clamped his hand over his nose and mouth whenever he had gone in to say good night, although much of that had been done to tease her. Still, he found it almost impossible to think of leaving Hannah West alone and sick in a railroad compartment, even for the few short hours it would take to reach Panama City. Not after he had courted her so stubbornly, and promised her so much, and not after Mrs Edgeworth had adjured him so sternly to take care of her.

It could be, too, that he actually loved her, although he tried not to think of that. He knew he desired her, and wanted to possess her. But if that was all he felt about her, why did he feel the responsibility to look after her? Desire, as he knew from those favourite whores of his in New York City who had occasionally appeared with streaming colds or spots, was not a flower which flourished in the sick bay. Only love was hardly enough to withstand bad air and balsam, and the possibility of infection.

'I'll stay with her,' Collis said decisively.

'My friend, I urge you – '

'I'll stay.'

At that moment, Maria-Mamuska came hurrying along the track, holding her dress above her ankles so that she could run better. 'Collis,' she said. Her eyes were wide with shock. 'Collis, you must not do this.'

He gave her a small, tense smile. 'I believe I have to,' he told her quietly.

'She's not even your relative! Why do you want to stay with her?'

'I promised I'd look after her, that's all.'

Maria-Mamuska pouted. 'You're not telling me the truth,' she said. There was only a yard of railroad clinker between them, and yet it seemed like a mile. Heat rippled from the stones and from the roof of the train, and butterflies fluttered between the silent wheels. In the distance they could hear mules braying as they waited to be fed, and, nearer, the dribbling of steam from the locomotive.

Collis turned away. He didn't know how he could possibly explain what he felt to Maria-Mamuska. He could hardly understand it himself. But ever since Kathleen Mary had fallen from the parapet of the Monument Hotel, he had felt a growing sense of duty and responsibility towards himself, and towards other people, even strangers. He had tried to ignore it. After all, life was much happier without it. Yet it was there inside of him, whether he ignored it or not, and it was strong enough and demanding enough to make him say no to Maria-Mamuska, and yes to an act of duty.

'Will you fetch my bag?' he said to the conductor. 'It's in the third car back.'

'Yes, sir.'

'And would you be good enough to tell Mr Hunt what has happened? I believe he's still asleep.'

The conductor walked off, and Collis and Maria-Mamuska were left facing each other, with the French doctor placidly sucking blackcurrant pastilles a few feet away. The sky above them was blue and endless, although there were banks of heavy clouds forming over the mountains towards the south-east, on the wind that the people of Panama City called the fever wind.

'Have you lost your senses?' asked Maria-Mamuska. 'You will catch this horrible fever and – '

'You won't persuade me to change my mind,' Collis said. 'I don't know why, but you won't. This is one of those things that I have to do before I can go on living my life any further.'

'You love her?'

'I'm not sure.'

'Madam,' the French doctor said to Maria-Mamuska, 'If you can't persuade him to change his mind, with your looks, then I'm sure that none of the rest of us can. It seems to me that he is committed.'

Collis, in the back of his mind, saw Hannah sitting in the mule trap at Aspinwall, on the rainy night of their arrival in Panama, and he could almost hear her saying, '*I would have to commit myself to you, and I would expect commitment in return.*'

'Is there anything I can give her?' he said to the doctor. 'Anything to relieve the fever?'

The doctor shrugged. 'You can give her plenty to drink. There's some cold tea in a jug there. The Chinese used to drink tea when they were building the railroad up here, and since none of them got sick from the dysentery. I guessed that tea must be purer than plain water. Something to do with the effusion from the leaves, I think.'

166

'What about medicines?'

'I'm sorry, there's nothing. I'd be fooling you if I said there was. But I'll give you some smelling salts in case the pain and the fever are too bad. That's all I can do.'

Maria-Mamuska stood still, a little way away, holding her pregnant stomach and staring at Collis with black, tear-filled eyes. Collis took two small green bottles from the doctor, and then looked across at her, and knew that he could still change his mind. Nobody in the world was forcing him to stay by Hannah's side on the trip to Panama. He could have left her there, alone on the banquette, and her chances of survival would probably have been just as good, or just as bad. They way she was at the moment, she wouldn't even know he was there.

But now the conductor was coming back with his bag, and the Spanish railroad official was shrilling at his whistle and hurrying everybody back aboard, and Maria-Mamuska turned and walked away.

'I think you are mad,' said the doctor. 'But I wish you luck.'

Collis shook his hand. 'Luck is about all I need.'

The conductor gingerly tossed his bag into the train, and then stood back and saluted as if Collis were a war hero. Collis stepped aboard and closed the door behind him. The locomotive let out a blast of steam, and then released its brakes and began to move slowly out of Culebra, down from the summit of the Panama mountains, on the last stretch of its journey to the Pacific Ocean. It didn't whistle or ring its bell. Whistling and ringing were for celebrations.

Collis sat on the banquette opposite Hannah and watched her. She appeared to be peacefully asleep at the moment, although every now and then she gave a small shudder and turned over. He leaned over her and softly stroked her forehead, but that disturbed her, and so he sat back again, and crossed his legs, and looked out of the window.

The train passed between green forested mountains, and then through dark volcanic rocks, twisting and turning as it made its way down the valley of the Rio Grande. Soon, the mountains levelled into round hills, and then the hills gave way to miles of lowlands. The sun had moved around, and Collis leaned out of the window to catch the shadow of the train crossing the shrubs and the grass and the sodden turfs.

He smoked a couple of cigars, on the principle that smoking

167

would fumigate any fever that might be hanging in the air. But then he felt nauseated, and had to have a cup of cold tea to settle his stomach. He should have asked for a bottle of bourbon to help him while away the journey, and he thought enviously of Andrew Hunt. A half-hour had passed, and still Hannah hadn't stirred.

At last the train reached Ancón hill, overlooking Panama City itself, and the wide grey expanse of the Pacific Ocean. The engineer blew the whistle, and everybody clustered to the windows and leaned out. Looking back along the swaying train, Collis saw Maria-Mamuska, her long black hair streaming in the breeze. She didn't smile or wave, or give any indication at all that she had seen him. He withdrew his head and sat down in the compartment again, and there must have been cinders in his eyes, because they were watering.

He sat there for a while, feeling strangely bitter. But then he heard Hannah stir and moan, and he went over to her banquette. She had opened her eyes, and she was staring at him as if she didn't know who he was. She was still strikingly attractive, even though she was ill, and the fever had given her complexion an added brightness, like an ailing ice queen. She whispered, 'Is that you, Collis?'

He took her hand in his. 'Yes, it is,' he said. His throat felt unexpectedly tight with emotion. 'Would you like a drink?'

She nodded. He poured cold tea from the jug, and then supported her head while she drank. 'I'm so thirsty,' she said. 'I feel as if I'm burning and freezing, both at the same time.'

'Do you have any pain?' he asked her.

'A headache,' she said. 'And my legs seem to hurt. Do you have any powders for a headache?'

'Only smelling salts. The doctor up at Culebra wasn't exactly over equipped.'

'I couldn't face smelling salts,' she said. Collis smiled at her, and she gave him a wan smile in return.

'Did he say what I had?' she asked him.

Collis poured her some tea. 'Gastritis, I think he said. Something like that. A lot of people get it when they visit the tropics for the first time.'

'Then it's not too serious?'

He shook his head.

There was a short silence. She reached out and clasped his hand again. 'It's strange,' she said, 'but it *feels* more serious than that.'

168

Collis watched her for a while as her smile came and went, like the shadows on a summer afternoon. Her eyes closed, and as the train covered the remaining few miles into Panama City, she slept. Collis waited until she was breathing deeply, and then he went to the window and leaned out again, so that he could see the Pacific through the trees, and smell the damp cool mist that rose from the sea. He was quite sure now that Hannah had yellow fever; and worse than that, he was convinced that she was going to die.

The first he saw of Panama City was a blur of red rooftops through the flickering grey trunks of the palm trees. Then the train came out in the open, and he saw white crumbling buildings and brown cathedral spires, and a shallow bay of muddy turquoise in which steam tugs and sailing dinghies idly criss-crossed in each other's wakes.

The city itself was built on a curved spit of land which hooked into the Pacific, crowded and chaotic and hazy. Behind the city, in the grey sea, Collis could make out the misty shapes of several small forested islands, and the spare outline of a large steam vessel, the draught of which was obviously too deep for it to approach the shoreline. Up above, the sky was heaped with cumulus clouds, but they seemed to be rolling sedately north-west, back towards the mountains.

Within a few minutes, the train was joggling and rattling over switches and junctions and slowing down into the railroad depot. It whistled once, but it was a despondent whistle, without an echo. The afternoon was too dull and flat for the sound to carry. The brake shoes squealed like dismally-slaughtered piglets, and the trans-Panama railroad train came to a queasy, shuddering halt.

Collis opened the compartment door. Hannah was still sleeping, although she had mumbled something, and turned over on the banquette. Beside the train, three nuns were waiting, with white-winged coifs, attended by a Jamaican porter and a wheeled basket chair. Collis stepped down from the train and hailed them, and the nuns rustled towards him, starched and pale, their rosaries swinging at their waists.

Unaccountably, Collis felt embarrassed. The nuns were so young and waxen-faced, and the porter so black and emotionless, and they had actually hurried to help a complete stranger who was sick of the yellow fever. When he thought how heroic he had felt at Culebra, offering to stay with Hannah, he felt ashamed.

169

The depot was a large, arched building, with murky skylights and flaking white-painted walls. It was in a constant hubbub, but in a minor key; a depressing sound of escaping steam, arguing porters, angry passengers, and clamouring children. Over the noise, Collis said, 'She's in there. I believe she has the yellow fever. *La fièvre jaune.*'

One of the nuns, a thin girl with pale-blue eyes and translucent skin, gave him a nod of acknowledgment and directed the porter, in patois, to lift Hannah down from the train. The porter had a gold ring through one ear, and scabs on his legs. He stepped up into the ladies' compartment and carried Hannah down as if she were a small frail child. Collis could only watch.

'Does she have papers?' asked the nun with the pale-blue eyes.

'I guess so,' Collis said. 'They're in her bag, more than likely. Her name's Hannah West. She was going to join her husband in San Francisco.'

The nun nodded.

'You're going to take her into hospital?' asked Collis.

'Yes. It will ease her suffering.'

'You think she's going to die?'

The nun paused. Hannah was lifted carefully into the basket chair, her face white and fitful, her hands drawn up in front of her as if she were fending off some imagined animal. The drone of noise in the depot seemed to grow worse, and more irritating, and the locomotive let out a hideous bellow of steam.

'She has the yellow fever,' said the nun. She sounded French, or Belgian. 'With her constitution, there is no doubt what her fate must be. But the Lord will have mercy on her soul, and give her peace in heaven.'

For the first time, Collis understood that Hannah might actually be dead within a few days. He put his hand to his forehead, but his face felt frozen, incapable of any expression. He was detached from himself, someplace else altogether, listening to this strange nun in a building that was as close to Purgatory as he could imagine. He saw the Jamaican porter wheeling Hannah away, accompanied by two of the three nuns, and it was just as if a whole part of his own life were being carried off in front of his eyes, whole days and weeks of possibilities, of possible love and possible sympathy, of shared meals and shared laughter, of kisses and murmurs and tears.

Standing there, in the depot of Panama City, he abruptly burst into tears. It was partly the strain of staying with Hannah, and Maria-Mamuska's hostility. But it was also a desperate feeling of loss. To see Hannah taken away from him was like attending her funeral, and he didn't even have a flower to lay on her grave. He turned away from the nun who had remained behind, biting his lip with grief; but the nun touched his hand with her hand, cool and damp with perspiration, and he calmed himself and took a couple of deep breaths.

'It was brave of you to stay with her,' said the nun. 'Perhaps you had better come up to the hospital for a day or two, to make sure that you haven't contracted the disease yourself. It spreads so quickly.'

Collis wiped his eyes and nodded.

'I suppose you meant to sail on the *Pacifica*,' said the nun. 'It leaves this evening, so you will miss her. But the *California* is expected here shortly, and if you are well, you can take her.'

'Thank you,' said Collis.

Without another word, the nun led the way out of the depot. Collis followed behind her, watched by the curious eyes of his fellow passengers. He looked around for Maria-Mamuska, but she seemed to have left the railroad station already. Andrew Hunt was there, although he stayed well away, and gave Collis nothing more than a resigned shrug, as if to say, 'You put your neck in the noose, brother; don't expect me to do the same.'

The nun spoke briefly in Spanish to the train's conductor, instructing him to send Collis's trunk up to the Hospital of the Sacred Heart. The conductor nodded, eyeing Collis suspiciously. Then he called, 'Zambo!' to a black who was squatting beside the locomotive smoking a broken clay pipe, and passed the instructions on. The nun led Collis out through the depot to the Avenida Central, a wide street of peeling whitewashed houses which led away up to the cathedral plaza. Under a dull, cloudy sky, carriages and mule carts bustled backwards and forwards, porters carried steamer trunks and bags on their backs, hurrying this way and that like worker ants, and the usual collection of beggars rattled their tin cups and displayed their diseased and mutilated limbs. Not far way from the depot entrance, a plain black-painted donkey trap was waiting, with a young Spanish boy seated on the box, and the nun led Collis towards it. Collis helped her to climb aboard, and then stepped up himself, and seated himself on the narrow wooden bench. The Spanish boy clicked his tongue, and the donkey plodded across the rough unpaved street. Collis smiled at the nun uneasily, but in return she simply lowered her eyes.

Unlike Aspinwall, which resembled a decaying American frontier town, Panama City was entirely Spanish in character. It had a cathedral, and several churches, and it was crowded with white houses with red-tiled roofs and arched verandahs. The air was less fetid, although the roads were just as rutted and strewn with garbage, and most of the houses were cracked and flaking. Collis tried to look inside some of the open windows as he passed, but the interiors were too shadowy for him to make anything out. He had to cling to the brass rail around the donkey trap to keep himself from sliding about too much.

As they passed the Bóvedas, the old Spanish sea-wall, with its wide view of the misty bay, they saw a ghastly apparition. A handcart was being pushed along the promenade by a Jamaican in a tattered shirt. Sprawled across the boards of the cart was a naked dead man, half covered with a dirty sack. His ribs protruded and his skin was slack and yellow. Worst of all, his eye-sockets were empty, where his eyeballs had been picked out by buzzards. Collis had to turn away and hold his handkerchief to his mouth, and it wasn't until a few minutes later, when they were out in the fresher air of the ocean, that he was able to suppress his nausea.

'I'm afraid that's a common sight,' said the nun. 'The rains have been very heavy this year, and when the rains are heavy, the yellow fever is bad.'

'I don't know how you have the nerve to stay here.'

The nun smiled. 'God protects us from the fever until He is ready to take us into His arms.'

'Have many sisters died?'

She nodded. 'I have been blessed with a long stay here. I came here in 1855, when the railroad was finished. There were twelve other sisters with me, all from Antwerp. Only three of those twelve are still alive.'

'What's your name?' asked Collis. He could hardly believe her quiet resignation, and what, to him, seemed like suicidal folly.

'Sister Agnes,' she said simply. She kept her hands in her lap. They were small, heart-shaped hands, but they were rough from cleaning and working. Her face, in her wide-winged coif, was almost pretty; but it was sallow with tiredness and ill health. Collis watched her with sympathy, but he didn't know what else he could

172

say to her. He wasn't used to talking to women with whom it was impossible to flirt.

There was a small group of women sitting on the sea-wall, close to where it ended. They were smoking, and laughing among themselves. They wore flounced skirts of striped muslin, tied tight around their bare brown waists, and loose-fitting white muslin *quipil*, sparkling with gold and silver paillettes, over their bare breasts. Several of them wore crimson or yellow flowers in their hair.

As the black donkey trap passed, the women waved and called out greetings to Sister Agnes, who gave a modest wave in return. 'May the Lord bless you, señoras,' she called.

'You seem to know everybody,' Collis said.

Sister Agnes nodded. 'Two years is a long time to stay alive in Panama. After the first year, when they're sure you're going to survive for long enough to make it worth their while getting to know you, you'd be surprised how friendly they are. But so many die in the first month.'

They approached at last the grounds of the Hospital of the Sacred Heart, overlooking the bay, on a small hill. The hospital was surrounded by a high white wall with a tiled top, and its gardens were serene and quiet and shaded by trees and plants. The building itself had been converted from an old mission, with a wide porch, and a red-tiled verandah that ran around it on three sides. The windows were open to catch the sea winds, and inside Collis could see rows of iron beds where the sick lay dying, or hoping not to die, or gradually recovering.

Collis helped Sister Agnes down from the donkey trap. She led the way inside, through double oak doors into a gloomy tiled hallway. On the wall directly ahead of them hung a large crucifix, with a mahogany Christ suffering on the cross; and beneath it, on the dark Spanish-oak chest stood a brass jug filled with yellow tropical flowers. There was a smell of soap and boiling vegetables, as the nuns prepared the patients' evening meal.

'Your friend Mrs West will have been taken to the Gethsemane Ward, which is for white ladies,' Sister Agnes said. 'I expect that you will be able to visit her later. But meanwhile, I will have you shown to your own accommodation. We have a small cottage in the garden which we usually give to visiting priests, but it is empty at the moment. It is very plain, I regret.'

Collis reached out his hand, palm upwards. In the shadowy hall-way, Sister Agnes appeared younger, and he could see for a

173

moment what she must have looked like when she sailed from Antwerp, fresh and full of enthusiasm. She laid her hand gently in his, and her eyes, when she gazed at him, were lambent and understanding.

'I admire you very much,' he said. 'It is very kind of you to have me here.'

She answered, 'What you did, too, was admirable. You were the Good Samaritan.'

There was a moment's silence. He kept hold of her hand.

'I'm not really used to talking to women like this,' he said uncertainly. 'I usually flatter them, and tell them how pretty they are.'

'I am a bride of God,' said Sister Agnes quietly. 'Perhaps if you were to treat me as if I were married, that would make it more comfortable for you.'

He looked away. 'I don't think so.'

Sister Agnes asked, with great delicacy, 'Mrs West?'

He glanced back at her. 'You're very understanding.'

'It isn't all praying and burying the dead, being a sister here,' she told him.

Collis smeared the sweat from his forehead. It was cool inside the hospital hall-way, and his perspiration had turned unpleasantly chilly. 'Do you think a priest might help?' he asked. 'Do you think a priest would grant her absolution for what she's been thinking about me?'

'If she's truly penitent.'

'And do you think that might give her a little extra strength?'

'It's possible. It may have the opposite effect altogether. But mental strength is always an asset when someone is fighting *la fièvre jaune.*'

Collis coughed. 'I don't know. I think she'd be better off if she felt certain of what her future is going to be. At least, with her husband, she's going to have security. With me, well, anything could happen. She'd be divorced and disgraced, and apart from all that I'm almost flat broke.'

Sister Agnes nodded. 'You'd have to help,' she said plainly.

'What do you mean?'

'It's quite simple. If you have *both* been harbouring thoughts of adultery, then it is not enough to expect her to repent of her thoughts alone. You must do so, too, and tell her that you have done so.'

Collis bit at his nail.

'I know that it will be painful,' said Sister Agnes.

'Yes. But if you think it could help her to live . . . well then, it had better be done.'

'I'll send for Father Xavier.'

Collis attempted to look cheerful. 'That's that, then. Perhaps I'd better go to my cottage.'

Sister Agnes came across to him and raised her hands before him, without touching him, but as if she were blessing him, or bestowing on him some traditional and tender grace. Their eyes met, and there was a complicated exchange of feelings between them which neither of them could completely interpret. It had mainly to do with sympathy and with understanding, but it also involved apprehension, and affection, and with the mutual mysteries of a woman who could be pretty and yet celibate, and a man who could have a conscience and yet be adulterous.

Sister Agnes went to the wall and rang a small bell.

'Anthony will show you the cottage,' she said. 'I hope you will be comfortable. I hope, too, that the Lord will keep you safe.'

Collis had almost forgotten his exposure to yellow fever. He looked towards the double oak doors with their heavy Spanish locks and hinges, and it occurred to him that he might never walk through them again.

At about seven o'clock, when the evening air was a curious grainy blue, there was a rap at his door. He had been stretched out on his rigid bed, his hands under his head, thinking about Hannah and San Francisco and Sister Agnes, while the mosquitoes danced around his lamp, and painted statuettes of the Virgin Mary and the disciples regarded him silently from small wooden plinths on the whitewashed walls. Barefoot, but still dressed, he padded across the tiled floor, opened the cottage door, and said, 'It's time?'

'Si, señor,' replied Anthony, the Jamaican handy-man. 'Father Xavier, he come right now.'

Collis laced up his shoes, put on his light-grey coat, and followed Anthony through the garden. The sun had gone down only a few minutes ago, and the moon would soon be up. The garden, with its neat rows of plants and flower-beds, appeared in the twilight like a dream from the *Arabian Nights*. Each plant was set in a pottery bowl filled with water, to prevent the umbrella ants from devouring it, and around each bowl of water a small cloud of mosquitoes swarmed. One or two eccentric professors had tried to suggest that the mosquitoes themselves were carriers of disease, but experienced Panama hands knew that it was the warm south-east winds, and the damp, which spread the fever.

Father Xavier was waiting with Sister Agnes in the corridor outside Gethsemane Ward. He, too, was a Belgian – a small man with a spherical head, permanently astonished eyes, and eyebrows that seemed to be independently choreographed, so that when he expressed concern, or interest, they would each break into a little dance of their own. He was very clean, and his scalp was shaved so that it was prickly, and he wore a dove-grey cassock, with a plain silver cross. He spoke precise English, so precise that he must have learned it at an English theological college.

'Mrs West has exhibited a willingness to take confession,' said Father Xavier, shaking Collis by the hand. 'I understand that Sister Agnes spoke to her only a few minutes ago.'

'I see,' said Collis. He glanced into the open door of the ward, but all he could see was the corner of a bed draped in netting. 'What did she say? Is she feeling any better?'

Sister Agnes inclined her head a little. 'She is still feverish, and the headache is troubling her. It is quite certain now that she has yellow fever.'

'Does she know?'

'No,' said Sister Agnes. 'We find our yellow-fever patients are happier if they are unaware of the nature of their sickness.'

'What did she say about confession?' asked Collis.

'I asked her if she had anything on her mind which she would care to confess, and she indicated that she did.'

Collis swallowed. He had meant to say something, but he wasn't sure that he could keep his voice steady. Father Xavier's eyebrows undulated in sympathy.

'Do you want to talk to her now, Mr Edmonds?' asked Sister Agnes. 'I think it would be a good idea, while she is still awake. The illness is exhausting her, and as soon as this is over I think we shall probably give her a sleeping-draught.'

Another nun came to the door of the ward and whispered, 'Mrs West is still awake, Sister Agnes, but only just. It would be wise to hurry.'

'Very well,' said Sister Agnes. 'Do you want to go in, Mr Edmonds?'

Collis nodded. The nun beckoned him, and he entered the long dim ward, lit only by small orange lamps, where white-faced women lay in two rows of twelve, most of them too ill to sit up or stir. At the very end of the ward, isolated from the rest of the women by gauze-covered screens, lay Hannah, in a white cap and a white robe, her face drawn and her eyes dull.

'Please don't be long,' the nun whispered. 'She's very weak.'

Collis drew up a plain wooden chair and sat beside Hannah's bed, looking at her through the hazy material of the screens. She saw him and gave him a watery, welcoming smile.

'Collis,' she said softly.

There was a moment in which they looked at each other through the gauze, and in which they said nothing, nor had any need to say it. That spiritual affinity of which Hannah had spoken was truly there. They hadn't imagined it. Even now, as Hannah lay ill, Collis felt as natural with her, and as fond of her, as if she had been his wife for years.

'They asked me if I wanted to confess,' said Hannah.

'What did you tell them?'

'I said yes, I did.'

Collis nervously rubbed at his forehead with his fingertips. 'It's not too serious, this illness, you know. Least, that's what the nuns tell me.'

'I still want to confess,' she said. Hannah rested her head back on the pillow. 'It's strange,' she said, in a light voice, 'how clearly you can see your life when you're seriously ill. You wonder why you ever worried about anything. All those ridiculous little difficulties that you thought were terrible and impossible tangles. They can all be blown away by one breath of truth.'

'Hannah,' he said, 'I know what happened on the boat seemed serious at the time. I know we talked a lot about your marriage to Walter, and divorce, and all kinds of crazy things, but – well, I just want to say that for us to have any sort of intimate relationship – well, it could never work.'

She lay there for a while as if she hadn't heard him. Then she smiled and turned her head towards him, her eyes dim and misted through the gauze.

'I know what you're trying to do,' she told him. 'But you don't have to lie to me. I know that I'm going to die.'

'Hannah, that's ridiculous. You have a bad case of gastritis, that's all. You'll have to be here for two or three days, and then you'll probably be strong enough to leave.'

'No, Collis. I am not blind, nor deaf. I know what it is that I have. I know that there is very little hope. And I know, too, that you are trying to put my life in order for me.'

'Hannah,' insisted Collis, 'you're going to live. There is no question of fatality. None at all.'

She shook her head. 'When I was looking after my mother, I learned two languages, from books. Perhaps I don't pronounce them very well. But one of them was Spanish, and I know what *fiebre amarilla* means.'

Collis was silent.

'You mustn't think badly of yourself for having tried to deceive me,' Hannah said. 'I think I would have done the same, if I had been you. But I know that I will probably die, Collis, and so you don't have to pretend any more.'

Hoarsely, Collis answered, 'I didn't mean to deny what I felt for you. I only wanted to give you the strength to fight it off. I thought that if I was out of your life, you could concentrate all your energy on getting well, instead of worrying about me.'

She lifted her hand to the gauze, as if she were reaching out to him. He raised his own hand, and their fingertips touched through the thin fabric.

'If I thought that I had nobody in the world to turn to except for Walter, then I should be truly unhappy, and at my weakest,' she whispered. 'It is having you here that gives me strength. It is knowing that you could love me that gives me strength.'

He paused. 'How do you know that I could love you?' he said.

'Because I do, that's all. Dear Collis.'

Outside, in the corridor, he heard the echoing footsteps of a nun in clogs, coming back from the washrooms. And far away, hardly audible in the still equatorial evening, someone was playing a plaintive pipe. There was coughing from the next bed.

'I don't understand it,' said Collis. 'I hardly know you.'

'And I hardly know you. But it doesn't matter.'

Again, there was silence between them. Then Collis said, 'Father Xavier is outside. Shall I send him away?'

'No,' she said. 'I told you that I want to confess.'

'I thought you wanted to confess your adulterous desire for me.'

'Of course I do. But I can't repent of it. Most of all, I want to confess that I married a man to spite my parents, that I perversely flew in the face of the Holy Catholic Church, and that I made a mockery of the sacrament of holy marriage. I want to confess that I was self-willed, and hypocritical, and that I took the love of God and the love of Our Lady for granted.'

Hannah was weeping now. Through the blurry gauze, Collis could see the sparkling tears on her cheeks. He could only sit back and watch, and listen, and feel the deepest grief he had ever felt in his life. This woman, this wife, should have been nothing to him, a passing stranger, a face on a train; and yet he had accepted responsibility for her happiness and her future and, ultimately, for her death. He was stricken with sadness, and he could only sit on his cheap wooden chair, watched by nuns, and hear what she had to say.

'I want to confess that when I saw you, Collis, I fell in love with you. I had never known such a sensation. I was standing on the deck, and you raised your hat to me, and the feeling I had was so devastating that I couldn't speak. Then I saw you again, when you came to introduce yourself, and what I felt then was indescribable. Mrs Edgeworth kept telling me to control myself, that I was infatuated, but I couldn't think about anything or anybody else but you. Don't you understand how difficult it was for me to turn you away, the night you came to my cabin? Don't you understand how hurt I was when I saw you with that girl?'

She turned her face away from him. 'I love you,' she said miserably. 'I love you so much, and now I have to die. All I have to confess is my disappointment in the Lord, that He would not spare me long enough to know you.'

'Hannah,' Collis said softly.

She turned back towards him, her face wet with tears. 'Oh, God,' she sobbed. 'Oh, God, I could have loved you.'

He nodded, wiping the tears from his own eyes with his fingers. 'Hannah, I could have loved you, too.'

They both cried, separated by the gauze screens. Not for what they had lost, nor for the times they had spent together, but for what might have been, and now would probably not be. They cried silently, in the gloom of Gethsemane Ward, with the dusk gathering in the gardens outside, and the nuns fluttering to and fro in the way that had earned them the name of 'God's geese'.

Eventually, Sister Agnes approached and laid her hand on Collis's shoulder. 'You must leave now, Mr Edmonds,' she said. 'You don't want to risk infection any more than necessary. Gastritis can be very severe.'

'Mrs West knows that she has yellow fever,' Collis said You don't have to keep up the pretence any longer.'

'She knows?'

'She overheard the nuns talking, that's all.'

Sister Agnes looked towards Hannah, and Hannah nodded.

'I see,' said Sister Agnes. 'Then you know you are gravely at risk.'

Father Xavier came along the ward on his soft-soled shoes to stand a little way behind Sister Agnes, his eyebrows genuflecting towards the bridge of his nose, his beady eyes bright.

'Have you renounced your thoughts for each other?' he inquired.

Collis gave Hannah a last smile through the screens, and she managed a weak smile in return. He was pleased, for her sake, that she was religious, because at least she believed that when she left him she was going on to someplace better, where she would be cared for and contented. He couldn't imagine what Hannah's vision of heaven was like, but he was sure that it would, in some mystical way, include him.

'No,' Collis told Father Xavier. 'We haven't renounced them. Mrs West will tell you why.'

He waited at the Hospital of the Sacred Heart for three days. Most of the time he spent in his plain whitewashed cottage, writing letters to his father and his mother and his friends in New York on leaves of thin onion-skin paper which the sisters gave to him. He had a small desk with a view of the rear of the garden, and he would sit with his chin in his hand, staring out at the rows of plants as they nodded in the Pacific breeze, and at the grey clouds which rolled silently out of the south-east, day after day, and never broke.

He saw very little of Hannah. He understood she was worse, and that she was now suffering from the jaundice which had given yellow fever its name. Sometimes Sister Agnes would let him stand at the open door of the ward and look in, but all he could see through the isolation screens was the indistinct paleness of her face, and that told him nothing except that she was seriously ill.

On the morning of the fourth day, Sister Agnes came across the garden and knocked on his door. He was shaving with his hollow-ground razor and a cake of the hospital soap, which always smelled of cloves. Sister Agnes left the cottage door ajar because Collis was stripped to the waist, and she had no chaperone with her.

'I'm afraid Mrs West is considerably worse,' she said.

Collis set down his razor beside the china basin. He saw his face in the small rosewood-framed mirror on the wall, and his eyes were dark and worried. He saw his mouth say, 'How long do you think she has left?'

'I don't know. The *vómito negro* has not begun yet. There is still a little hope.'

'May I see her?'

'She is very ill, Mr Edmonds. It would serve no purpose, and it would increase your own chances of catching it.'

'I don't want her to die alone, Sister Agnes.'

Sister Agnes touched her pale forehead as if she had a headache. 'She isn't alone, Mr Edmonds. Our Lady the Queen of Heaven is with her.'

Collis wiped his face with the small rough towel that the nuns had given him and picked up his shirt from the back of his chair. At least his linen was all freshly cleaned and pressed, now that the hospital laundry was taking care of it. But in the watery sunlight which shone through the open window of his cottage, he still looked tired and thin, and he would have done almost anything for a New York steak and fried onions, and twelve hours' sleep in his own bed on Twenty-first Street.

'Do you think she'll last the week?' he said.

'She may,' said Sister Agnes. 'As I said, there's a little hope. But the fever is very high, and I have to warn you that anything could happen. She could die tonight.'

'I see. Does she know herself? Is she conscious?'

'No. She hasn't been conscious for almost eight hours now.'

Collis nodded. He couldn't think of anything else to say.

Sister Agnes waited for a moment, and then announced, 'I've come for another reason, too.'

Collis looked up.

'The *California* dropped anchor off the bay this morning. She's due to sail for San Francisco on Monday morning. I believe that you are probably free of the fever, and that you will be able to sail with her.'

'That's four days from now.'

'Yes.'

'Supposing – well, supposing Mrs West is still alive in four days?'

Sister Agnes was silent. Collis paced around the tiled floor of the cottage and then turned and looked at her straight.

'You don't think she will be, is that it?'

'The chances are not good, Mr Edmonds.'

He rubbed the back of his neck. He was so tired that he didn't know what he felt any more. The days were nothing but waiting in his cottage, writing and staring out of the window; and the nights were hot and sweaty and plagued with insects. Whole years could have passed, and he wouldn't have been able to tell the difference. The heat and the boredom of the equator seemed to drain away any will to do anything active or useful, and sometimes he stood for half an hour at a time, incapable of deciding whether he wanted to remain standing or whether he wanted to sit down again.

'I know you've done everything possible,' he said quietly. 'You've been very kind. Not just to Mrs West, but to me, too.'

He looked at her. Framed in the doorway, she was as fragile and delicate as a painting by Botticelli. He found it hard to grasp how someone so feminine and attractive could be so spiritual. If she stayed here in this hospital in Panama, she would almost certainly be dead within two or three years. She might not even survive as long as that.

'I was wondering if you'd ever consider leaving this place,' he said.

'Why should I do that? My life is here.'

'I know. And your death will be here, too.'

'You're concerned about my safety?' Sister Agnes smiled abstractedly. 'You're very thoughtful,' she said.

'But?'

'But I couldn't ever leave the hospital. This is where God needs me.'

'Even though you probably won't live to see twenty-five?'

'If that's what the Lord wills.'

Collis looked out over the garden behind her. He knew damned well that it was no use arguing. It was ridiculous even to suppose that he could have persuaded her to leave. What had it to do with him, anyway, whether she lived or died? What had any of these people's lives to do with him? A parakeet settled on the branch of a leafy plant outside, and whistled in the humid morning air. Collis looked back at Sister Agnes and shrugged.

'I'm beginning to grow very fond of you,' he said in his softest voice. 'And I'm not trying to flirt with you. I had a stupid crazy idea that I could somehow make you realise that there's a whole lot more to the world than what goes on here. You've already done more in two years than most people achieve in a lifetime. God can't be anything but grateful. Why don't you give it up while you're still young, and still alive?'

'You mustn't fear for me,' Sister Agnes replied. 'God and Our Lady look after me always.'

She paused, and then added, 'I'm an only daughter, you know. My father runs a small patisserie in Lokeren. They were so proud of me, my parents, when I joined the order. They tried to persuade me not to, of course, but once they knew that I was determined, they were proud.'

Collis took her hand. 'I'm proud, too,' he told her. 'I didn't really expect you to change your mind. But I hope you'll remember that I tried, and that you won't think too badly of me.'

'I have to go now,' said Sister Agnes. 'We have three new sisters from France here today. They came on the train from Aspinwall. They have to be greeted, and shown what they will have to do.'

She kept hold of Collis's hand, and she stood on tiptoes and kissed his cheek, her white starched coif touching his shoulder.

'I think you will be a very famous man one day,' she said, with great earnestness. 'My hope is that you won't forget me, and that you won't forget the reason I said I must stay.'

'I won't forget,' he said. He opened the door wider for her. 'Will you call by later and tell me how Hannah is?'

'Of course.'

He stood by the door and watched her walk through the garden. Her coif disappeared behind the plants like a low-flying seagull. Then he turned back to his bare white rooms, and he was frowning like a man who realises he has just failed to do something important, but isn't quite sure what. The bell on the hospital roof struck for morning prayers, and disturbed three huge black buzzards that had been perched on the terra-cotta coping. They circled, with rustling wings, and then settled again.

In the middle of the night, Anthony, the Jamaican porter, came to knock at his door and call Collis to the ward. Sister Agnes was there, and Sister Rosa, and Father Xavier. They were standing by Hannah's bed, exhausted and sweaty by the light of an oil lamp, and it was clear that Hannah's condition had deteriorated even further. She was a terrifying livid yellow, and she was shaking and mumbling in the throes of a freezing fever.

'She's conscious,' said Sister Rosa, a middle-aged nun with a vast bosom and a distinctive limp. 'That's why we called you. You may wish to say your goodbyes.'

'She's dying?' asked Collis, looking down at Hannah's drawn, waxy face. It hardly seemed like Hannah at all, but some grotesque death mask poured out of tallow. Only the flickering eyes and the softly gnashing teeth told him that she was still a real living being; and only the wedding band on her finger reminded him that she was Mrs West.

'She's very bad,' said Sister Agnes. 'Unless this fever breaks, she may go before morning.'

'It hardly ever breaks,' added Father Xavier. 'In a few lucky cases, perhaps. But you can see for yourself how sick she is.'

Collis looked around at their faces, and then knelt down beside Hannah's bed. She was murmuring and muttering, and throwing her head from side to side on the pillow, and she was glistening with sweat. Every now and then she coughed, and the coughing brought up dark spatters of blood, which Sister Rosa dabbed away with a muslin cloth.

'Hannah?' said Collis.

She moaned, and reached out as if she were trying to seize something out of the air, but she didn't answer.

'Hannah?' he repeated.

This time she simply tossed her head, and snarled and dribbled under her breath.

Collis waited for a moment, and then he stood up again.

'I think she's too – '

He couldn't say the words at all. He pressed his knuckles against his lips to try and regain his composure. In the darkness of Gethsemane Ward, in this hot and overwhelming equatorial night, he knew that Hannah was really lost. The nuns gently surrounded the bed, like settling doves, and patted the sweat from Hannah's face, but all the patting and the soothing and the selfless care in Christendom wasn't going to save her from the ravages of yellow jack.

'Thank you for calling me,' Collis said. 'I don't think there's much more I can do. Thank you.'

He left the ward and walked back across the garden. He paused at the door of his cottage, and looked up, and suddenly realised the stars were out. The humid clouds which had oppressed Panama City for the past week had at last passed over. He wondered whether it was a good omen, or whether it would simply make it easier for Hannah's spirit to rise and join the angels she had always been so unhappy without.

In the morning, at ten, she was no better. He waited in the corridor outside Gethsemane Ward for a while, but Sister Agnes wouldn't let him in. The fever was reaching crisis point. He went back to his cottage and drank the last of a bottle of Spanish wine which Anthony had brought up from the city for him. There wasn't even enough to get drunk on.

That afternoon, after a lunch of steamed fish and rice, he was driven in the donkey trap down to the offices of the United States Mail Steamship Company, where his ticket for sailing on to San Francisco was endorsed. The *California* was due to sail out of Panama City at seven on Monday morning, and make her way back up the coast, with stops at Tehuantepec, Guadaljara, Santa Barbara, and San Francisco. In the high-ceilinged office with its marble counters and clustered flypapers, Collis had to present a letter to the blue-uniformed Panamanian behind the desk, certifying that he had been kept in isolation after his exposure to *fiebre amarilla*, and that he was now considered by the sisters of the Hospital of the Sacred Heart to be free of infection. The Panamanian read the letter slowly, tracing each word with the tip of his pencil, and pausing every now and then to regard Collis, with deep mistrust. Finally, he stamped Collis's ticket, and returned the letter, folded, on the end of his letter opener, lest he catch some disease through touching it.

Collis left the office and climbed back into the donkey trap. The Spanish boy clicked his tongue, and they rattled off through the streets. They climbed the Avenida Central to the wide, rubbish-strewn Cathedral Plaza, under the shadow of the twin brownstone towers, where priests hurried as if Panama were about to sink into the sea, and old men sat and smoked cigars as if they didn't care if it did. The sun touched the spire of one of the towers and gave it a dazzling halo.

Collis said to the donkey-trap boy: 'Stop here for a moment, will you?'

The boy, without a word, obeyed, and the trap came to a halt. Collis his eyes still on the cathedral, climbed out and walked across the plaza He went up the steps and through the open doors into the musty interior.

185

It wasn't a grand cathedral, although it might have been once. There was a gaudy stained-glass window, some of its panes cracked and others missing, and by the Lady Chapel there was a glittering forest of devotional candles, most of them in memory of the dead, of which Panama City had more than its share. Several elderly women were kneeling in prayer, and, unaccountably, a man in a cream linen suit was sitting at a back pew, with a small mirror resting on the hymn-book rack of the seat in front, clipping the hairs in his ears with scissors.

Collis had never been into a Roman Catholic cathedral before, although he had an Irish friend who had once persuaded him to attend a Mass in New York. He shuffled uncomfortably into a pew and knelt down, glancing at the elderly women to see if Catholics prayed any differently from Protestants, and then he closed his eyes and said a prayer for Hannah.

It was a very plain prayer, but he addressed it to the Virgin Mary, because he knew that Hannah trusted and believed in Her. He didn't ask that Hannah should live. That seemed to be out of everybody's hands now. But he asked that she find happiness in heaven, and that she be reassured that she had been loved when on earth.

He bent his head forward and rested it on the hard wood of the pew. Under his breath, he whispered. 'Please give her peace. She deserves that much. Please.'

He knelt there in silence for a while, and then he realised that he had nothing more to ask for. He stood up and left the cathedral, leaving a dollar he could ill afford in the poor box. Across the plaza, under the glaring sun, its skeletal outlines etched away by the heat and the brilliant light, the donkey trap waited. Collis walked towards it, his head lowered, the sun on the back of his neck.

Sister Agnes was waiting for him at the hospital gate. He could see her from a long way off as they scaled the hill. When the donkey trap drew up, she hurried closer and held the brass rail around the seats. 'You must come quickly,' she said.

'What is it?' he asked her. 'Is it Hannah?'

She nodded, without answering, and led the way into the hospital, her habit flying out behind her. Collis swung himself down from the trap and followed, through the double oak doors, across the hallway, and down the bare tiled corridor to Gethsemane Ward. He knew that Hannah was dead. He was sure of it. While he

186

had been away fixing his ticket, the Lord God and the Virgin Mary had taken her away from him, and that was all there was to it. He turned into the doorway, and almost bumped into Father Xavier, who was on his way out to see where Collis was.

Collis looked down the length of the ward. At the far end, the gauze screens had been taken down from Hannah's bed. Three nuns were busying themselves with sheets and pillowcases, and Sister Agnes was walking quickly towards them, telling them to make haste, make haste, in Spanish.

Sister Agnes turned and beckoned to Collis, and it was only when she did so that Collis understood what was happening. As she stepped back, he could see that Hannah was still there in her bed, that Hannah was actually sitting up, propped by pillows, and that she was not only alive but awake. She was vividly white, and her eyes were smudged with exhaustion, but she was alive, and she was awake, and she was even smiling.

Collis walked along the ward, and the ward seemed endless. At last he stood beside Hannah's bed, while the nuns clustered around and watched him with smug benevolence, little fat-faced girls from Rheims.

'The fever has broken,' Sister Agnes said. 'We didn't expect it to; but the infection appears to have passed its worst. It seems that Mrs West has survived the disease, praise be to God.'

Neither Collis nor Hannah could speak at first. Collis took her hand, bony and thin after five days of debilitating sickness, and held it between his own hands as if it were the most precious possession he had ever owned. Sister Agnes, who had been cheerfully busy up until now, suddenly turned away and took a handkerchief out of her white habit, and the three young nuns from Rheims, who would probably die themselves within a few months, shed unashamed tears of delight.

'Hannah,' whispered Collis, his voice thick with emotion. 'Hannah, I prayed so hard for this.'

She smiled. Almost inaudibly, she whispered, 'Dear Collis, thank you.'

Collis looked up to Sister Agnes. 'When did this happen?' he asked her. 'Is she really better?'

Sister Agnes nodded through her tears. 'Early this morning was the worst time of all. Sister Rosa sat beside her from three until ten. She had a high fever, but she stopped coughing up blood and while you were out she cooled down. We don't know why. Sometimes, very occasionally, it happens this way. But she has almost certainly overcome the fever, and if she takes care she will soon be well again.'

She paused, and then she said, 'She is one of the few spared by God to serve Him longer on Earth. I am very happy.'

'How much longer will she have to stay here?' asked Collis.

'A week, probably two. We have to get her strength up if she is not to succumb to the fever again.'

'It's a miracle. I can hardly believe it.'

'Do you want to stay for a while?' asked Sister Agnes. 'There's a chair here. Sister Hilda, the chair, please. You can talk for five minutes, but please don't tax Mrs West too much.'

'Sister Agnes?' said Collis.

The nun half turned, but didn't look at him directly.

'I just wanted to say thank you, Sister Agnes,' Collis told her, trying to convey everything he felt for her in a few simple words. It wasn't enough, but it would have to do. Whatever he said, she had her own inner voice that was far more convincing than anything he could ever tell her. She stood there for a moment, still keeping her eyes averted, and then she gave a tiny nod to show that she had heard, before walking quickly along the ward and out through the door.

Collis sat down by Hannah's bed. He hardly knew what to say to her. She looked as if she had aged fifteen years in five days, and her profile was cut as sharp as white onyx. Her very cheekbones seemed to be translucent, and her blonde hair seemed to have been drained of its pigment by some strange effect of her disease, leaving it as dry and silvery as moonlight.

'I never believed this kind of thing could happen,' Collis said. 'I said a prayer for you in the cathedral on my way back here. It's like magic.'

Hannah turned to him. Her smile was wan but warm. She reached out for his hand with hers, and he took it again, and pressed his lips to it.

'God isn't magic, Collis,' she whispered. 'He must have a purpose in saving me. Perhaps He wanted me to know real happiness with you.'

'I don't know what His purpose is. I don't really care. I'm just overwhelmed that He spared you.'

They were silent for a time, and then Hannah said, 'You must go on without me, you know. To San Francisco. Sister Agnes told me

188

the *California* is here, and that you went down to book your passage on her.'

'That was before I knew you were going to be well,' said Collis. 'My God, Hannah, that was when I thought that I was going to be burying you by Sunday.'

'I know. But you must still go.'

'I won't hear of it,' Collis told her. 'I want to stay here until you get your strength back. From now on, I'm not going to leave you.'

She weakly shook her head. 'Collis, you'll have to. I have so much to work out in my mind before we can think of staying together.'

'What do you have to work out? Do you love me, or don't you?'

She smiled. 'I believe I do.'

'Then that's all you have to think about.'

'No,' she said, 'there's much more. I can't just arrive in San Francisco and tell Walter our marriage is over, and that I want to live with you. I have to prepare the ground properly, in a decent manner.'

'Walter's feelings are going to be hurt, Hannah, whether you do it decently or indecently.'

'I know. But Walter is my husband, and he has been sending me money every since he set up the business. He's been supporting me, and, in his way, caring for me. It wouldn't be kind or Christian to desert him so abruptly.'

'Christian? What does being a Christian have to do with it?'

'Being a Christian has to do with everything, Collis. You prayed today, remember? You can't appeal to God with one breath and dismiss Him with the next.'

'I didn't mean to be blasphemous, or anything like that,' Collis said. 'I just feel that it's more honest, and probably kinder in the end, if you tell Walter straight away.'

'Perhaps it is,' she said. There was a long pause while she swallowed, and regained her breath. 'But I still want time to think about it, and I still need time to recover.'

'I can stay here without worrying you, can't I?'

'You know you can't. In any case, you can't afford to stay in Panama much longer, can you? If you keep on missing boats, the steamship company may ask you to pay a surcharge, and what about making your fortune in San Francisco? The sooner you start the better.'

'You really don't want me around? Is this a gentle goodbye?'

'No,' she whispered, 'it isn't. But you must let me find my feet. I came very close to death last night. I knew that if I weakened, if I gave in, I would be drawn into the darkness, and that would be the end of me. It was an experience that brought me face to face with myself, Collis, with what I am; as if someone had set up a looking glass before me that showed me my soul as well as my body. I was frightened. I thought that I had actually died. And when I came around this afternoon, while you were away, I believed for a moment that I was in heaven, and not on earth at all.'

Collis stared at her for a while in silence. He understood what he was trying to tell him. She needed to feel more confident about herself and what she wanted out of life before she was prepared to make a final decision about Walter. And she needed something else, too, although she hadn't said so. She needed to *see* Walter, to make absolutely sure of her disappointment in him, to check if his whiskers were really as dreary as she had remembered them, and his conversation as dull.

If she didn't have the opportunity to do that on her arrival in San Francisco, she would be fretful until she did, and that would make any love affair between Collis and herself both irritating and unstable. That was why she wanted Collis to go to San Francisco ahead of her; so that when she came on a later ship, she would be able to go to the store on Montgomery Street at once, unruffled by arguments, and discover among the ribbons and the laces and the button hooks whether there was anything left of her once-rebellious marriage but a steady income, worthiness, and duty.

Collis turned away for a moment, looking down the lines of sick and dying women towards the afternoon sunlight.

'I don't know what we have between us, Hannah,' he said reflectively, 'but whatever it is, I don't want to lose it yet.'

'I don't, either,' said Hannah. 'But you will give me time, won't you?'

He nodded. 'Yes.'

Sister Rosa came limping into the ward then, with flowers she had picked from the hospital garden. 'Mrs West,' she ordered, 'you must take a sleep now. You are still very ill.'

'I must go,' Collis told Hannah. 'I've been overtaxing you.'

'No, no,' she whispered. 'You've been marvellous. You couldn't have been better. My mind will be at rest now.'

'If you're better tomorrow morning, we'll talk some more,' he

190

said, and gently squeezed her hand. He turned to Sister Rosa and asked, 'May I kiss her?'

Sister Rosa frowned. 'That is up to you, Mr Edmonds. The doctors would not disapprove, but I am not so sure about the Almighty.'

Collis bent over Hannah's bed and brushed his lips against hers. 'As long as the doctors are happy, I'll take my chances with the Almighty.'

Then he left the ward, and walked out into the garden, and stood with his hands on his hips, elated, and breathing as if he had run all the way up from the railroad depot.

He saw Hannah briefly at six on Monday morning, attended by Sister Rosa and Sister Hilda. The ward was still in the twilight of pre-dawn, and the nuns walked to and fro like ghosts. Hannah was weak and exhausted, but Sister Rosa told Collis grudgingly that she had eaten a bowl of gruel the night before, and that her condition was much improved.

'I shall leave my address at the post office when I get settled in San Francisco,' Collis said softly. 'In any case, if I don't hear from you in a month, I shall call around at the store.'

'I won't fail you,' whispered Hannah. 'I promise I won't fail you.'

Collis kissed her on her forehead, and then he stood up. He looked down at her for a moment, at her well-boned, animal-attractive face, as if he were taking a mental photograph of her. Then he turned and left the ward, his shoes clicking on the polished floor, and went through to the hallway where his trunk and his bag were waiting for him.

There was no sign of Sister Agnes as he left the hospital in the donkey trap and was taken down the rutted streets in the first light of the day. He looked back once or twice, but he couldn't even see her face at a window. It wasn't long before they went around a steep corner, and the Hospital of the Sacred Heart disappeared from sight.

He was rowed out to the Pacific mail steamer *California* by a toothless ferryman in a wildly fraying straw hat. The ship lay at anchor in the dull morning mist, the flag of the Union hanging from her stern, her two masts empty of sails, and a stain of black smoke rising from her funnel. Collis's skiff was brought under her lee, bobbing like a toy boat up against the side of a cast-iron bathtub, and a rope was thrown down, which the ferryman enthusiastically wound in.

Collis paid for the ferry, a quarter, and climbed the swaying ladder up the black-varnished side of the ship. His luggage was hoisted aboard, and he was directed by a steward with a face like an old walnut down towards his shared cabin. There were dozens more cabins and cots on the *California* than there had been on the *Virginia*, but she was still crowded, mostly with salesmen and fortune hunters and ladies in stained and crumpled dresses who looked as if they had suffered quite enough of steamships and railroads.

While he was still below, unpacking his shaving things, Collis heard the anchor rattle up, and the steam engines begin to turn over. He went to the porthole and looked out at Panama City, cluttered on its curved promontory, and he could just make out the roof of the hospital.

'Dear God,' he said, under his breath. Then he went back to his bag, and took out his nightshirt, his tortoise-shell comb, and his travelling clock.

Chapter 5

The paddlesteamer *California* passed through the Golden Gate on the morning of 21 September 1857, a month and a week after Collis had sailed out of New York harbour. The fog made the bay seem silvery and haunted, like the lake which dying Norse heroes had to pass across to reach Valhalla; and when the *California* started to protest mournfully with her foghorn, and when dozens of rotting and abandoned ships came mysteriously into view, still riding at anchor where their owners had left them years and years ago, rising and falling with ocean swell, Collis was almost convinced that they had reached the end of the world, the final graveyard of dreams and ambitions. For the first time since he had bought his ticket from the steamship office in New York, he felt a twinge of real apprehension. He knew from Andrew Hunt that San Francisco was less than comfortable; that it was populated by thieves, opportunists, and speculators; but at the very least he had expected to see a sunny, welcoming bay, with people waving and shouting. At the very least, he had expected some kind of rough-cut jollity. Instead, under this pall of pearly grey, ghostly and muffled, the *California* paddled her way past makeshift warehouses, tumbledown shacks, and half-collapsed jetties; and although the wharves and the landing stages were bustling with longshoremen and expressmen and men banging at crates with hammers and mallets, they seemed to be going about their daily business with a preoccupied grimness that was unmoved by the arrival of another steamship.

Eventually, with a last honk, the *California* slowed, and turned, and nudged her way into Broadway Wharf, the landing stage at the foot of Telegraph Hill. The engines were stilled and the steamer drifted gradually inshore, until her hull bumped against the wharf's wooden supports.

Collis stood straight and looked through the fog at the dim hills of San Francisco. They were patchworked with shanties, sheds, and tents, and the fog was made thicker still by the haze from hundreds of cooking fires. In what looked like the downtown district, he could make out a cluster of more respectable-looking frame buildings and adobes, and brick-built banks and hotels. But to a man from New York, who was accustomed to the sophisticated jostling of omnibuses and private carriages between tree-lined avenues and shady parks and rows of solid brownstones, San Francisco looked like a decorative rubbish dump, a higgledy-piggledy collection of iron, secondhand timber, and ship's canvas, in and out of which a population of extraordinary fierceness rushed and rampaged in oxcarts and on horses and on foot, shouting at the tops of their voices and wearing the sorriest display of hats that Collis had ever seen in his life.

To the west, towards the Presidio, the hills appeared to be more pleasantly wooded, but beyond the smoke and the fog and the shanties Collis could make out nothing more than bald sandy peaks and scrubby trees.

The wharf below him was tumultuously crowded with merchants and longshoremen and hotel agents, and the noise of shouting and hammering and whistling was deafening. Collis hadn't expected a hero's welcome. After all, those San Franciscans who hadn't struggled across the plains and mountains of America by horse or wagon train had made the same 5450-mile voyage and crossed the isthmus of Panama just as he had. But he would have thought a modest cheer and a handshake might have been fitting instead of this avaricious hubbub. Almost the entire population of San Francisco seemed to be swarming like a colony of termites, ready to overrun the ship as soon as the gangplank was down and pillage everything that wasn't firmly screwed to the deck.

He remembered Andrew Hunt's cautioning words, and he elbowed his way forward through the passengers lining the rail, and found his trunk. He stood by it, and even when a portly roofing salesman stepped backward on to his foot, he determined to remain by it at all costs.

At last, the gangplank was dropped to the wharf with a resonant bang, and before any of the passengers had the chance to step on to it, a feverish crowd of men in beaver hats and checkered vests and shapeless tailcoats came arguing and pushing and scrambling on to the steamer's deck and collared each of the passengers in turn to see if he had any cargo on board the *California* he wanted to part with – any dry goods, perfumes, haberdashery, digging tools, or liquor. Most of these men carried a small sack of gold dust, which they waved in front of the startled passengers' noses, or poured out into the palms of their hands, glittering and yellow, to tempt the unwary into making a quick sale. What most of the greenhorns hadn't had time to understand was that a case of beans out here was worth more than gold dust, and that any luxury items like soap or perfume could fetch a fortune among the ladies of South Park, or the prostitutes in the centre of town.

Dragging his trunk, and shouldering people out of his way, Collis eventually managed to disembark, and he found himself standing on the wharf among a crowd of curious bystanders, bearded sailors, Chinese in pigtails, Chileans in drooping sombreros, and scores of that particular variety of hardbitten, juice-spitting settler which San Francisco's shantytown sported in great abundance, and who could all have been brothers or cousins of the same man – a man with a sallow suntan, a prickly chin and moustache, a red washed-out shirt and baggy-assed breeches, a knocked-in hat, and an endless line in cussing. Collis was to run into this man again and again, in every saloon, on every upturned barrel, in every whorehouse, or standing in line at the post office for a letter that usually never showed up. He was the pioneer who had never quite made it, the forty-niner who hadn't come out to prospect for gold until '51, the storekeeper who had gambled away all his stores, the loser.

A short Mexican in a fringed sombrero and a soiled shirt led a sagging horse and a small wagon through the crowds, buttonholing anybody who looked like a passenger. Eventually he made his way through to Collis and asked: 'Hotel, señor? I take your trunk.'

'Not just now,' answered Collis. 'Listen – do you know of a man named Andrew Hunt? He runs a food business?'

The Mexican wiped his nose with the back of his hand, sniffed, and thought about that. 'I know Señor Munt, in the livery-stables business. How's he? Any good?'

'No, it's Hunt I want, not Munt.'

Another man standing nearby with a walrus moustache and a baggy black suit said: 'I know a fellow called Hunt. Fat fellow, with a stutter? Runs a store on Kearny, up by Market.'

'That's not him,' said Collis.

The man in the baggy black suit looked offended. 'What do you mean, it ain't him? His name's Hunt, ain't it? Goddam Easterners.' He stalked off, grumbling.

The Mexican went off, too, still leading his horse and cart. He spoke to one passenger after another, until Collis saw him cajoling the Pearsons, a pale-faced New England family to whom Collis had briefly spoken on the ship. There was a short discussion, and then the Mexican started to load the Pearsons' baggage on to his wagon

Collis heard him promise to meet them outside of the Yerba Hotel, 'in quick fandango time, huh?' Personally, Collis wouldn't have laid money on the Pearsons' chances of actually finding the Mexican or their baggage there when they arrived.

He pushed his way across to the father of the family, a onetime school teacher who wore wire-rimmed eyeglasses and grey suits of notable tiredness, and said, 'If I were you, Mr Pearson, I'd ride along with him, unless you want to lose your bags.'

Mrs Pearson, in a grey bonnet, her nose as unbecoming as a frigate bird's, blinked. 'Do you really think so?'

Collis nodded. 'That's what I think. It's the way these people make themselves a living, scavenging off people like you.'

Mr Pearson called, 'Hold on a minute, fellow!'

The Mexican was already climbing up on to the makeshift seat on the front of his cart. He waved reassuringly.

'Don't worry, señor. I see you double-quick at the Yerba Hotel. You don't worry about nothing.'

Collis jostled his way around to the front of the cart and held the horse's reins. 'You're not going anyplace, not without this gentleman.'

The Mexican looked at him suspiciously. 'What's it to you, señor?'

'It isn't anything,' said Collis. 'It's just that you're not leaving this wharf without this gentleman sitting alongside of you.'

The Mexican tugged at his untidy moustache. 'My horse, it's weak,' he said. 'You understand that? It's too weak for all this baggage, and me, and this gentleman.'

'It doesn't look weak to me,' retorted Collis. 'In any case, if you're concerned about your horse's health, why don't you lead it, and let the gentleman sit up on the seat?'

'That's not possible,' said the Mexican stubbornly.

'Give me a good reason why not.'

'I don't have to give you no reason. You get out of my way.'

Collis held the horse's reins tighter. The horse shied a little, but the Mexican was held fast until Collis decided to release him.

'You take your hands off my horse,' demanded the Mexican.

Collis shook his head. 'Just as soon as you let this gentleman ride alongside of you, but not before.'

'I don't do that. Nobody rides with me.'

'Then unload that baggage off that heap of a wagon right now, before I break your jaw.'

The Mexican waited for a moment, tense, chewing at his lip.
Already an interested crowd had begun to collect and they were
watching Collis and the Mexican with enormous amusement. Then
without warning, the Mexican shouted, 'Hi! Get up there! Hi! Hi!
Hi!' and snapped his whip across his horse's back.

Collis was ready for him. He dragged fiercely at the reins, and the
horse screamed and lost its balance on the boards of the wharf. As
the crowd scattered, the wagon overturned with a thunderous
crash, and the Pearsons' baggage was spilled everywhere. The
Mexican tried to jump for safety, but he caught his knee on the side
of the toppling wagon and was knocked backward. The crowd
cheered. They enjoyed a fight, whoever won.

The Pearsons, flustered and pink with embarrassment, collected
up their bags and their trunks. The Mexican climbed to his feet,
limping and hopping, and swearing in the names of St Catherine
and St Theresa and two dozen other saints. Each curse was
punctuated with a threatening gesture at Collis, but he stayed well
clear as he unharnessed his nag so that it could clamber awkwardly
to its feet, and righted his wagon with the noisy and enthusiastic
help of the crowd.

Mr Pearson came over and shook Collis's hand. 'That was most
courageous of you to do that for us,' he said. 'I guess we nearly had
ourselves taken for suckers. When we're settled, you must come
around for a Sunday dinner. Just leave your address at the post
office, and we'll get in touch.'

Collis dusted the sleeves of his coat. A boy from the crowd
handed him his hat. 'It wasn't anything to shout about. But I was
told that you have to watch your step while you're here. Just about
everything's in short supply, except for gold, and a family's
belongings could fetch a fair price.'

Mrs Pearson, all bonnet and beak, wrung her hands together
and exclaimed, 'You were extraordinary, that's the only word.
Extraordinary.'

Collis took her wrinkled glove, brushed it against his lips, and
smiled. 'My pleasure, Mrs Pearson.'

Mrs Pearson blushed and twittered and then went back to her
two plain pigtailed daughters, who had been standing watching the
whole proceedings with a relentless lack of interest.

He forced his way back through the crowd to where he had left
his own trunk. At first he couldn't see it, and for one dreadful
moment he thought that it had been hauled away by yet another of

the Broadway Wharf parasites. But a pimply youth with a pipe in his mouth said, 'Y'r baggage is over there, mister,' and indicated with a jerk of his head the side of a green-painted wooden office building which stood by the jetty.

Collis made his way over to the building; and right enough, there were his trunk and his bag, although sitting on his trunk with his legs crossed and his hat tipped over one eye was a short round-bellied man in a loud hound's-tooth suit of ginger and green and a glaring yellow vest, a man with bulging cheeks that were as sunburned as roasted pullets, and a ginger moustache, and a small bright nose. He took off his hat as Collis approached, and waved it, but he didn't make any effort to get up.

'Good morning!' he said.

'Good morning,' answered Collis. 'I guess I ought to thank you for keeping your eye on my trunk.'

'Not my eye, my ass.' The fat man smiled. 'Anybody can whip anything from under your eye, but from under your ass is a different matter.'

'Yes,' said Collis, slightly perplexed, 'I suppose you're right.'

The man stretched out a short arm, and they shook hands.

'I heard you talking on the wharf, asking after Andy Hunt,' he said. 'My name's Charles Tucker. I own a store out in Sacramento. Andy Hunt and me, we're good friends. I'm here buying foodstuffs today, and hardware. I must say I like your style, mister.'

'My name's Collis Edmonds, out of New York,' said Collis.

'That's right. Andy talked about you. Said you stayed with some lady who was sick of the yellow jack. Did she peg out?'

'No, no, she survived it,' Collis told him. 'I guess it couldn't have been too bad an attack. I didn't catch it myself, either.'

'Well, so I see,' said Charles Tucker, returning his brown derby hat to his gingery head. He suddenly looked somewhere over Collis's shoulder and yelled, in a high rasping voice: 'Wang-Pu! Make sure you collar all of that linen they've got aboard! I don't want no ifs and buts! The whole goddam shebang!'

Collis turned around. He couldn't see anyone in the scrum of the wharf that Charles Tucker could have been yelling to, but his voice had been so penetrating that Wang-Pu could have heard him from down in the *California*'s lower hold.

'You look to be a gentleman,' he remarked to Collis, turning back as if nothing had happened. 'How are you fixed for capital?'

'Very poorly, I'm afraid. My appearance is about all I have. My father's bank went down the drain last month, and I had a couple of gambling debts outstanding. Not to mention a rather awkward problem with a young lady of ill repute.'

'Well, don't you worry about none of that,' said Charles. 'Put all that behind you. There isn't a body in this whole city who hasn't left some embarrassing little heap of squat behind in the East. The main thing is that you're a gentleman; and as long as you're prepared to play on that fact, you'll get along fine.'

'That was about the meat of what Andrew told me on the ship,' said Collis.

'It was sound advice,' said Charles. 'Do you want a cigar? I'm just trying to think what you should do now, how you should get yourself started. Gambling, you said? Are you a gambling man?'

'I have been known to stake a bet or so.' Collis smiled.

'How much money do you actually have?'

Collis had never been asked a question like that before, so bluntly. He hesitated, almost stammered, and then said, 'Well – about a hundred and fifty. Maybe a few cents less. Why?'

'You're going to need stake money, that's why. A hundred and fifty will do you for beginners, but if you need to borrow some, I'll gladly oblige. I like your style, if you see what I mean. You're a gentleman. There aren't too many of those in San Francisco. There's those that *call* themselves gentlemen, like the Society of California Pioneers, which means everyone who came here before January 1, 1848. But not many of those are gentlemen in the sense that Eastern folk define it. Mind you, it's worth having a few friends among 'em, and I can introduce you here and there.'

'That's very generous of you,' said Collis.

'No, it's not generous at all,' retorted Charles. He took out his worn leather cigar case, offered a cigar to Collis, bit the end off his own cigar, and spat it out on to the wharf. He produced matches and they lit up.

'I'll tell you why it isn't generous,' added Charles. 'It isn't generous because I want something from you in return. Once you've gotten yourself settled here, I'd like you to work for me. I like your style. You'll give my business a bit of class, and you're tough, too.'

Collis suppressed a cough. Charles Tucker's cigars were exceedingly strong, and apart from that he hadn't eaten since dinner last night, a scrappy end-of-the-voyage meal of beef hash and potatoes. He was suddenly aware of how tired he was, too.

'Do you know of anyplace cheap I could stay?' he asked Charles. 'I think the first thing I could use is a bath and a couple of hours' sleep.'

'Of course, I was coming to that,' said Charles. He jumped down from Collis's trunk, tugged his vest straight, and stood beside him, at least six inches shorter, but straight-backed and perky, and looking as if he would gladly smack any man in the mouth as soon as say good morning.

'You can stay where I stay, whenever I'm in town,' he said. 'It's a fine hotel of sorts, and I'm friendly with the proprietor. Well, in actual fact, it's a whorehouse on Dupont Street, but they have five or six rooms that a visiting gentleman can use, and besides gambling they have some of the prettiest girls in the city. My wife thinks I stay at the Rassette House, which is more or less respectable as San Francisco goes, but they can't cook you an omelette that's good for anything else but patching your boots, and all their chambermaids are as ugly as paddle steamers. You're best off with Knickerbocker Jane, and that's experience talking.'

'Knickerbocker Jane?' asked Collis.

'You'll love her.' Charles grinned. 'Hold on a moment, and I'll have my carriage whistled up. Billy! Get the carriage around here, will you? Oh yes, Knickerbocker Jane is somebody special. She'll like you, too. She's fond of classy accents. They call her Knickerbocker because there was a fire at her place one day, and the fire company which came around to douse it was the Knickerbocker Number Five volunteer company. Jane rewarded each and every one of those firemen personally, and you know what I mean by that. Look now, here's the carriage now.'

Edging slowly through the wharfside crowd came a slightly shabby phaeton driven by a tall Negro in a cockeyed silk hat. It was reined up alongside, and the Negro climbed down, picked up Collis's trunk as if it weighed nothing at all, and slung it into the back. Then he bowed, gave an exaggerated grin, and opened the door for Collis to step aboard.

'This is Billy,' said Charles, by way of explanation. 'Billy will take you round to Knickerbocker Jane's, Collis. You tell her that Charlie Tucker sent you, and say you'd like a room for a week. Get yourself some victuals, and sleep off your journey, and I'll bring Andy Hunt around at seven, and we'll all step out for dinner at the International.'

*

It wasn't too far to Knickerbocker Jane's, but the streets were so clamorous and crowded that it took almost twenty minutes for Billy to nudge and push his horses as far as the junction of Dupont and Pine. Collis, sitting back on the sun-cracked leather of the phaeton's seats, was amazed by the rowdiness and the music and the boisterous laughter that went on all around him. The whole population of San Francisco seemed to be infected with the need to rush around at random from morning till night, only stopping for meals and beer.

At first, as they made their way along Broadway through the dock area, and the district he later learned to call Sydney Town, Collis was afraid that San Francisco might turn out to be even rougher than he had first imagined. Many of the buildings were not much more than shanties, or beached and abandoned ships that had been incongruously converted into warehouses, or hotels. Every other doorway proclaimed itself a saloon, with wooden signs reading 'Steam' or 'XX Stout', and a clientele inside who kept their hats on and their suspenders adjusted tight, and who spent all day arguing each other hoarse. There were plank boardwalks along the streets, but if they weren't crowded with people, they were obstructed by makeshift tents or lean-tos, in which you could gamble away six months of laborious gold-panning in an hour and a half, or have your hair cropped by an Italian barber and then glossed up with Taylor's Brilliantine, or even a tooth pulled.

The buildings that weren't saloons were dance halls, lunchrooms, dilapidated boarding houses, shipping offices, or gambling dens. The whole street was thronged with longshoremen and sailors, and Chinese carrying huge bundles of laundry and cumbersome boxes, and the air was vibrant with the strumming of guitars and the steady thunder of boot-heels on the boardwalk. Miners and drifters and casual gamblers sat in the sun, their black coats dusty and their necks red, drinking whisky and flipping cards on to upended barrels. And above it all, like the warbling of doves in a dovecot, the prostitutes called out sweet obscenities from their upstairs windows.

Further south, however, the buildings began to improve, and soon they were passing iron-frame hotels, red-brick banks, French restaurants, and fashionable drapery stores. Collis saw elegant ladies with parasols and gentlemen who were nobbily dressed even by New York standards. But the sidewalks were still teeming, and the street was a jingling clattering turmoil of carriages and wagons and horse-drawn omnibuses, and there was a bustling and buzzing of activity that would have made any Manhattan socialite feel quite ready to lie down after an hour, with a cold compress.

They were held up on the corner of Portsmouth Square by a jam of delivery wagons, which seemed to involve a great deal of shouting and picturesque cursing. Then they had to wait at Sacramento Street while a Chinese funeral went by, with tinkling cymbals, and a coffin the size of a small brigantine.

The speed of their progress wasn't much helped by an impassive-looking Chilean, either, who had chosen lunchtime to drive a herd of fifty or sixty oxen down towards the docks. Collis and Billy were trapped at Dupont and California for almost five minutes while the lowing, shambling, flybitten cattle went past.

At last, dusty and sweating, they drew up outside a three-storey building on Dupont Street, freshly painted a smart bottle green, with gold trim and two polished coach lamps outside the door. It was the best-kept building along the whole street, and it was sandwiched, both conveniently and respectably, between the surgery of Dr W. Carr and the offices of the Charitable Institute for Women. Opposite, their hats pulled over their eyes against the glare of the midday sun, a group of loafers sat at outdoor tables, drinking and playing cards and smoking pipes. They watched Collis with curiosity as he climbed out of the phaeton and crossed the boardwalk to ring at Knickerbocker Jane's bell. Billy swung Collis's trunk down and set it down on the ground.

'Looks a pretty trim place,' said Collis conversationally.

Billy, leaning on the trunk, simply raised an eyebrow.

The door remained closed, so Collis rang again. By now, the loafers across the street were regarding him fixedly, their hands of cards unplayed, their pipes clenched between their teeth, and even one or two passers-by turned to stare at Collis with unabashed interest. Whatever they did in San Francisco, they certainly didn't mind their own business.

'It doesn't seem they're answering,' Collis remarked un-comfortably.

'Maybe they all in bed,' said Billy.

'In bed? It's only lunchtime. It's the middle of the working day.'

'That's why they all in bed.' Billy cackled.

Collis rang for a third time, and quite abruptly the front door was opened, and a tall handsome woman with Titian hair tied up in black ribbons came stepping out on to the boardwalk. Her teeth were crooked, but in her lowcut black satin gown, which displayed a healthy acreage of soft and freckled bosom, you wouldn't have noticed, or even if you noticed, you wouldn't have minded. The loafers across the street all began to cheer and whistle and stamp their feet, and Collis found himself heatedly embarrassed.

'Hallo, Billy,' said the woman coolly to the coachman, and then she turned her green-eyed gaze on to Collis, her fingers playing absent-mindedly with the diamonds at her neck. She reminded Collis of the type of woman who would lustily introduce inexperienced boys into the arts and crafts of lovemaking, all low cooing cries of encouragement and white wobbling thighs.

The woman gave Collis an almost imperceptible curtsy. 'You must be a friend of Charles's,' she said, showing her crooked teeth in a smile. 'Well, any friend of Charles's is welcome here. Particularly such a gentlemanly one. We do have to cater to all sorts, you know, and it's pleasant sometimes to have a little style.'

'My name's Collis Edmonds, ma'am, out of New York,' said Collis. 'Mr Tucker suggested I might be able to stay here for a few days. If that's convenient, of course.'

He gave the woman one of his melting, hurt-looking smiles, and he knew damned well it was going to be convenient. It was probably such a rarity for her and her girls to have a properly dressed gentleman ringing at their door that they would have taken him in for his collar studs alone. She lifted her hand to be kissed and said, 'I'm Jane Spalding. Most people call me Knickerbocker Jane. Why don't you come on in? You look as if you could use a drink, and maybe some light luncheon.'

Knickerbocker Jane led the way into the house. The hallway set the tone for the whole building, and was probably the most elaborate and overdecorated hallway that Collis had ever come across in his life. The walls were hung with dark red watered silk, and clustered with gilded mirrors and silhouettes and atrocious oil paintings of sad-eyed Spanish women moping in weed-grown gardens. There were clocks, and whatnots crammed with cheap pottery ornaments, and Chinese vases filled with plumes of pampas grass, and cases of moths and butterflies. Above the doorway that led into the living-room was a polished brass plaque from the Knickerbocker Five Volunteer Fire Company, and underneath it the inscription *Exegi monumentum aere perennius*.

Billy carried in Collis's trunk, and Knickerbocker Jane gave

203

him an indulgent smile and said, 'Take it up to the third landing, will you, Billy? I'll have Henrietta pour a beer for you in the kitchen afterwards. Mr Edmonds, Collis, would you care to come this way?'

Collis handed Billy fifty cents for his time and his trouble. He was slightly offended when Billy bit both coins to see if they were sound before tucking them into his vest pocket. But Billy grinned at him and said, 'Don't trust nothing and nobody in this city, Mr Edmonds, not even yourself.'

Collis looked at him. 'What about Mr Tucker?' he asked.

Billy grinned even wider. 'Oh, you can trust Mr Tucker okay. You can trust Mr Tucker to skin a cat alive and sell the poor creature its own fur back as the latest style from France. That's what you can trust Mr Tucker to do.'

Collis thought about that and then said: 'I like that. I think I'm going to enjoy myself here.'

In the parlour, at a small table set with a white lace cloth, while Knickerbocker Jane watched him from the fastnesses of a purple plush daybed, Collis ate a light lunch of home-cured ham, California asparagus, cold potato salad, and fresh fruit. He smiled at her from time to time as he ate, and she smiled back, but they didn't speak much. He sipped chilled wine from a long-stemmed hock glass, but he wasn't altogether sure he liked it. It was much sweeter and mustier than anything he'd tasted in New York, and he reckoned that four or five glasses would probably give him a killing hangover.

The parlour was pleasantly cool and shaded from the sunlight, although it was just as overfurnished as the hallway. There were heavy velvet drapes tied up with gilt cords, marble statuettes of harassed nymphs, and a carved wooden fireplace that was encrusted with daguerreotypes, decorative seashells, lamps, doilies, and knickknacks. At least there were plenty of vases of flowers around, fresh-cut and sweet, and the brightness of the afternoon after the fog of the morning made him feel far more cheerful.

'Are you feeling refreshed?' asked Knickerbocker Jane.

He wiped his mouth with his napkin and nodded. 'I don't think I've had such a tasty meal in a month.'

'You don't like the wine, though.'

'It's – well, it's unusual. Is it local?'

'They make it up in Napa Valley. The Indians tread the grapes

204

with their bare feet, in a trough made from cowhide, and then they ferment it in skin bags.'

Collis held his glass rather anxiously up to the light. 'I thought I detected an unusual ambience,' he said politely.

Knickerbocker Jane laughed. 'I only served it because it's a curiosity. We have plenty of French wine here. When you're rested, I'll have the girls open a bottle of champagne.'

'Do you have many girls here?' asked Collis.

'Five at the moment. I used to have eight, but one was murdered about three months ago, when she was crossing the plaza after dark, and two of them just upped and left.'

'Good girls must be pretty hard to find.'

'*Any* girls are pretty hard to find. But the money's good. A girl could come out here from the East and make herself a fortune in three years, all in gold and silver. Years ago, I used to have an Armenian girl who could tie herself up in knots. You know, a contortionist. She charged twenty dollars in gold for a session, and she left this city richer than most of the bankers and merchants and miners you could ever meet.'

Collis got up from the table and crossed to the window. Outside, through the lace curtains, he could see a small scrubby yard, and bordering that, the backs of a row of clapboard stores and saloons. Beyond, there were the flat rooftops of the financial district and downtown San Francisco, and the naked summit of Fern Hill – a peak he would later learn to call Nob Hill. Nob Hill was too steep for a horse and carriage to reach the summit, and consequently nobody lived there.

'What made you come out here?' asked Collis. 'You sound to me as if you came from someplace like Baltimore originally.'

'Almost right.' Jane smiled. 'I was a Catonsville girl, to start off with. I married a sailor when I was sixteen, and I guess my mother and father thought that was good riddance. They'd never liked me. My father was a clerk in a bank, and my mother was half crazy.'

'Wholly crazy, I'd say, if she didn't like you.'

'I guess that's a compliment, but I wasn't much of a delight in those days. I was plain as a plank of pine, and the first thing that happened was the sailor ran off and left me. He was drowned off Assawoman Island four months later, so I guess that served him right. I went home to mother and father, but we argued so much that I ran off.'

'Do you mind if I smoke?' asked Collis.

'Go ahead. There's some good cigars in that mother-of-pearl box by the stuffed eagle.'

Collis took out a cigar and sat down on the daybed next to his hostess. The afternoon sunlight shone in shifting patterns through the smoke, and Knickerbocker Jane's face faded and reappeared like a memory.

'I made my first dishonest buck in back of a circus tent,' she said, 'one rainy night in Mousie, Kentucky. He was the man who took the money for the menagerie, and he gave me eighty-two cents, which was all he had in his overalls. He was old, maybe fifty, but he was kind, too, and I guess that was what made me feel that there wasn't any harm in that kind of work. I sold my body all the way to Omaha, Nebraska, and from Omaha I came all the way across country by wagon train, working whenever I needed to.'

Collis rubbed his eyes. He was beginning to feel very tired.

'I came here in '47,' Knickerbocker Jane was telling him. 'I used to work out of the old City Hotel in those days, on the corner of Clay and Kearny. That was a stew of debauchery and no mistake. The whole place was overflowing with gold, and you could make hundreds of dollars in one night, as long as you were willing to do anything with anybody.'

Collis looked at her wryly.

'Are you shocked?' she asked him. 'I have to warn you I'm a plain speaker, and I'm never ashamed of anything I've done.'

'I'm not shocked,' he told her. 'I'm just wondering how I'm going to compete with people like you and Charles Tucker.'

'Compete? You don't have to compete. We're your friends.'

'I know you are,' he said. 'You've proved it plainly enough. But I'm the next best thing to flat broke, and if I'm going to make myself any kind of a living, I'm going to have to compete, and do more than compete. I'm going to have to win.'

Knickerbocker Jane straightened her black dress. 'What's your particular line?' she asked.

'Nothing much. I gamble. But I lived off my parents until a month ago, and living off your parents doesn't do much to sharpen your skills. I'm quite reasonable at finance, but I'm not a genius. I ride. I smoke too many cigars. I get drunk.'

'What did Charles suggest?' asked Jane.

'He suggested I start off by gambling. But from what I've seen

206

this morning, it looks as though the whole population of San Francisco are whizees at gambling.'

Knickerbocker Jane stood up. She walked across the flower-patterned rug and stopped by the far window, the window that gave out on to Kearny Street. 'What you have to remember about San Francisco,' she said, 'is that everyone who lives here has given up everything they ever owned to try to make a fresh beginning. They are gamblers by nature, or they would never have come. I gambled when I came on that wagon train across the Sierras. You gambled when you came on your ship. If you want to compete and win in San Francisco you have to be prepared to lose all you've got. Your money, your reputation, your belongings.'

She turned and faced him. Her bosom bulged from her tight gown. 'Even your human dignity,' she said.

He slept until it was almost dark. When he woke up, he wasn't sure where he was, and he lay there staring at the china shepherdess on his mahogany bedside table with perplexity. He could hear people talking somewhere in the street below, and the rattling of carriages and carts, but he didn't recognise the faint aroma of perfume and cooking, and the blue flowered wallpaper was completely unfamiliar. He looked at the corner of his white embroidered pillowslip, at his sheet, and then across the room at the blue-painted door with its shiny brass knob.

He lay there for almost five minutes. Then he sat up and looked around him. Knickerbocker Jane had given him a quiet room at the back of her house, with a white-painted brass bed, a plain mahogany bureau, a washstand, and a brass-bound sea-chest. He climbed out from between the sheets, naked, and walked across to the yellow draped window. Spread out under the setting sun, its rooftops and chimneys and idly waving flags bright with that special clarity of San Francisco evenings, its hills sand-purple in the distance, was the city to which all his bad luck and his miscalculations had at last brought him, and in which he would have to learn to live. Not just live in, but lick. Because nobody was going to pay him for anything ever again, unless he earned it, won it, or stole it.

There was a knock at the door, and Knickerbocker Jane said, 'Collis? It's six o'clock. Didn't you say that Charles was coming around at seven?'

'I just woke up,' he called back. 'I'll be down in a little while.'

'Do you feel better?' she asked him. 'You looked awful pale at lunch time.'

'I'm fine.'

'Oh – would you like a girl for tonight? I'd appreciate knowing, then I can organise their evening.'

'I'm not sure I can afford it yet, Mrs Spalding.'

'Have it on the house. It's your first night in San Francisco. And don't call me Mrs Spalding. I'm Jane.'

'Well, then, I'm much obliged, Jane.'

He shaved in front of a small porcelain mirror by the fading light of the sun. Then he dressed in one of the white shirts that the nuns at the Hospital of the Sacred Heart had starched for him. He could still smell that peculiar odour of tropical mould on it, and for a moment he was taken back to Panama City, and Sister Agnes, and Hannah. He would have to take a walk along Montgomery Street tomorrow and take a look in at Walter West's store. He always liked to size up the competition; and in any case, there was a certain strangeness about meeting and talking to Walter West before Hannah arrived from Panama that appealed to him.

Since they were dining at a hotel, Collis put on his black tailcoat, his white starched vest, and his evening pants. He sat on the bed and pulled on his black patent pumps, then stood in front of the mirror again to tie up his black tie, with its pearl stickpin. He banged open his silk opera hat and put it on his head at an irreverent tilt. After all, this was San Francisco, in the exuberant West, and not Broadway on a Saturday night. He inspected himself as best he could in the mirror, and decided he looked tired, worldly-wise, and reasonably rakish.

He went downstairs. Halfway down, he glanced into the open door of one of the rooms. He saw the corner of a large oak bed, rich patterned rugs, and a small gilt chair. He also saw a girl's bare leg, poised on the chair like a ballet dancer's as she adjusted her garter. It looked as if life in San Francisco was not going to be too depressing after all.

Charles and Andrew had not arrived yet, but Knickerbocker Jane was waiting in the parlour, with French champagne in a bucket of ice, and strawberry wafers. Beside her, in a shiny cobalt-blue dress with a low, gathered bustline, was a petite Brazilian girl, with dark hair fashionably frizzed, and large, shy eyes. She wore a quite extraordinary amount of gold and diamonds – rings, necklaces, and studs – but then most of the prostitutes in San

208

Francisco did. They had a rare and sought-after commodity in one of the world's most profligate cities, and they charged dearly for it. There was a smell of expensive French perfume in the parlour, which Collis found unusually erotic.

'This is Ursula,' said Knickerbocker Jane, rising to her feet with a matriarchal rustle of skirts. 'Ursula, welcome Mr Edmonds. Ursula is one of our newer acquisitions, Collis. I'm sure you'll like her. She has a most ladylike manner.'

The champagne was dry, and cold; and although it didn't have quite the taste of champagne in New York, it was a welcome reminder of civilisation. Collis said to Ursula, 'Are you happy in San Francisco, my dear? You're looking well on it, I can say that.'

Ursula smiled, and nodded, but said nothing. Knickerbocker Jane, sitting magnificently on her purple plush settee, put in, 'You don't have to bother to talk to her. She speaks hardly any English at all. A ladylike manner, you see, but no English.'

'She's charming,' said Collis, and raised his glass to her.

Just then, the doorbell chimed, and Collis heard the front door open, and men's voices in the hallway. Into the parlour, smelling of whisky and full of exuberance, came Charles Tucker and Andrew Hunt, both dressed, unlike Collis, in day suits and derby hats.

Andrew Hunt clasped Collis by the hand as if he were a lost relative and slapped his shoulder several times. Charles Tucker was hardly less effusive himself, although he effused for the most part over Knickerbocker Jane's big soft cleavage. It was becoming clear to Collis that if Charles and Jane had never actually been lovers, commercially speaking or not, then Charles would certainly like them to be. Knickerbocker Jane poured more champagne, and everybody sat down in the best of spirits.

'I don't know whether this fellow is a hero or a nincompoop,' remarked Andrew, reaching out and resting his hand on Collis's shoulder. 'When I saw him go off with that West woman, and those nuns, I thought I was never going to see him again, and that's the truth. I thought, there goes another poor victim into the jaws of yellow jack.'

'God must have been smiling,' said Knickerbocker Jane, gently easing Charles Tucker's hand off her knee. 'God does that sometimes.'

'Whatever it was,' added Andrew, 'I'm most pleased to see you survived. Did the West woman get over it, too?'

209

'Hannah's all right, yes,' said Collis, a little more quietly than he'd meant to. 'She was recuperating when I left her.'

Andrew Hunt winked at Knickerbocker Jane. 'If you ask me, Collis had more than your usual soft spot for the West woman. What else would make a man risk yellow jack but love?'

'Love, or money,' said Charles.

'He could have both with the West woman,' said Andrew. 'I made a point of taking a look at her husband's fancy-goods store on Montgomery Street when I arrived here, and by the looks of it, it's turning out real prosperous.'

'Did you find out where Maria-Mamuska went?' Collis asked Andrew.

'The half-breed girl?' Andrew shrugged. 'She could be anyplace at all. But San Francisco ain't New York. You'll run into her, by and by, if you want to. Or even if you don't want to.'

Charles took out his watch and peered at it. 'We must be going soon. I'm hungry, for beginners, and we don't want to take all night eating if we're going to make Collis some money.'

Knickerbocker Jane came around, her skirts gracefully held in one hand, and refreshed their champagne glasses. 'You'll come back later, won't you? I'll have a faro game going in the smoking-parlour, and we may have Natalie on the piano if Mr Tibbett doesn't come around for her.'

'Well, we must teach you to sing,' Andrew told Collis, crossing his long spindly legs and sitting back with an expression of amusement and pleasure. 'You said you wanted to get into South Park society, didn't you? That would be an excellent way. Collis Edmonds, the baritone from New York. I suppose you're a baritone?'

'I can't sing a note,' Collis protested. 'If I tried to pose as an entertainer, I think they'd probably kick me out of South Park as fast as one of Sara Melford's suitors.'

Knickerbocker Jane raised an eyebrow. 'You know about Sara Melford?'

'Andrew told me about her on the ship. Is she really that difficult to pay court to?' asked Collis.

'Oh, yes. Laurence Melford keeps his eye on her twenty-five hours a day. Not that he has to. She's as cold as a shipload of cod She's very beautiful, mind you, but there isn't a man in San Francisco who can get anywhere near her. David Broderick told me she was waiting for a prince to visit San Francisco, or at least a count, and that nothing less would do.'

210

'David Broderick's our junior senator,' remarked Charles Tucker, taking out a cigar. 'He don't speak very fancy, but the miners and the storekeepers respect him. A good straightforward man, in his way. Laurence Melford hates him. Called him an ignorant labourer once, to his face.'

Collis accepted a cigar from Charles, and Ursula rose from her seat and came over to clip it and light it for him. When it was burning well, she knelt down beside him and put it gently into his mouth, stroking his cheek with her long fingers. Her blue silk dress had a slippery, exciting rustle to it, and her perfume was strong and exotic. Close to, he saw that she had a dark beauty spot on her cheek, and that her eyelashes were long and painted with kohl.

'This seems like the way to live,' he said, feeling suddenly very pampered and content. 'I do believe I'm almost pleased I left New York.'

Charles stood up and straightened his vest over his round stomach. 'In this town,' he said, 'you can be what you want to be, and do what you want to do. Now, I think it's time for some comestibles, and after that, we'll try our luck at gaming.'

The dining-room of the International Hotel on Jackson Street was a great deal noisier and more bustling than any hotel at which Collis had dined in New York, but the food was good, and just as fancified, and at least the diners took their hats off. Collis and Andrew and Charles took a table in the corner, and a waiter with big red ears and a long white apron brought them iced water, and a bottle of red wine with enough tannin in it to clean the family silver. They drank toasts to Collis's safe arrival, to San Francisco, and to themselves. Collis wouldn't propose a toast to luck. He was too unsure of his luck right now.

Charles pointed out some of San Francisco's celebrities and millionaires. In the far corner, half hidden by a potted fern, sat a short starry-eyed man with a bristly beard and short spiky hair. He was savaging a chop as if he had caught it trespassing on his plate, and waving a fork around to punctuate whatever he was saying to a plain, round lady with feathers in her hat. 'That's the treasurer of the Society of California Pioneers,' said Charles. 'He has no sense of humour whatever, so if you meet him socially, don't try to make him laugh. His name's William Tecumseh Sherman.'

While the waiter went to order their fish soup for them, Charles nudged Collis again and nodded towards a middle-aged man with a sharp-looking nose, grey hair, and a way of standing with his hands tucked up in his vest pockets, so that his elbows protruded. 'That's Hall McAllister, that one who looks like a turkey. He's a big-shot attorney these days. But he made his first pile selling beans and flour to the miners.'

'That's what's so damned galling about the pioneers,' said Andrew, tearing a piece of soda bread from the loaf in the centre of the table and pushing it into his mouth. 'They started off as poor and undistinguished as anybody else, and yet now you can't breathe the same air. I don't blame them for the way they live. I'd do the same if I was rich. But some of them ought to remember where their money came from.'

'There's a good example,' said Charles, pointing to a fat, red-faced man with his napkin tucked in at his neck. 'That's Sam Shields. He made his fortune by buying up a whole stretch of barren, useless land out towards Sacramento. He dumped cheap metal spelter in the streams, and it formed flakes in the water like gold. He sold that land for a hundred times what he paid for it, and there's a whole lot of broken-down prospectors in California that would give three months off of their life to see that man in prison.'

Their fish arrived. It was fresh and hot, with plenty of shrimp and sole and lumps of terrapin, and a good helping of cream and sherry added. Collis suddenly realised how starved he was for good food, and he ate in silence for almost five minutes, while Charles and Andrew talked about nails and wire and the price of sago. They were merchants in the plainest sense of the word, these men: they bought goods, and sold them for a profit, and anything they couldn't sell for a profit didn't interest them.

Collis looked around while he ate. The restaurant's walls were painted shiny cream, and hung with handsome mahogany-framed mirrors, which sparkled with reflected light from dozens of small glass chandeliers. There were perplexed-looking elks' and bears' heads on wooden shields, and paintings of California landscapes, most of them moderately crude, and even a gaudy portrait of the President, James Buchanan. The waiters moved between the tables and the potted palms and the laughing, chewing, gesticulating diners with the detachment of busy nurses, their hair glossy with pomade and their aprons stiff with starch. Across the aisle, a carver in a tall white hat and a black tailcoat was cutting pale bloody slices of rare beef from the largest joint that Collis had ever seen: in section, it was the size of a small oak tree.

Andrew and Charles had finished talking about raw sugar prices and how the hell was a man supposed to make a clear profit on long-grain rice, and now they turned their attention to politics. Like most of the merchant classes in San Francisco and Sacramento, they were Republicans, free-soil men, and their state of California had been declared free soil in the contentious Compromise of 1850. But even on their far Pacific shore, 2700 miles from Washington, they were roused and alarmed by the increasingly rancorous arguments on Negros' rights, or the lack of them, and whether the new Western territories should be slave states or guaranteed free. The arguments had split friendships, and even a few marriages. Among the Chivalry of South Park, up on Rincon Hill, the politeness between Northern and Southern pioneers was distinctly cool; and Andrew was telling Charles how young Willie Gwin, the senior Senator's son, had upset a luncheon party by declaring it was high time the South seceded and Washington was fired upon.

Charles dropped fragments of bread into his soup and noisily spooned them up. 'It goes from bad to worse, I'll agree,' he said, with drops of soup on his moustache. 'But there won't be war. I can't see that there'll be war.'

'What do you think, Collis?' asked Andrew. 'Your father used to have plenty of politicians for friends, didn't he?'

Collis set down his spoon. 'Yes, he did,' he said. 'But most of them were doughface Democrats, and if you want my opinion they're the worst kind. All compromisers and givers-in. If there is a war, it'll be their fault, even though they're the people who least want it. People like my father, who's always so worried about his plantation investments. People like *him*,' he said, nodding towards the portait of Old Buck.

'They only hang that portrait there for diners to throw their forks at,' remarked Andrew laconically.

Charles finished his soup. 'They can throw forks at him, but they have to admit he's kept us out of outright civil war. Well, he has, hasn't he? If he can keep the South from seceding, and hold the Union together for long enough, then it's ten to one that Congress can cobble together some sort of decent compromise on slavery before it comes to fighting.'

He blew his nose and added, 'I don't believe in wars. I believe in free soil, and I believe in setting the children of existing slaves free when they come of age. But a decent compromise is always preferable to war. That's my feeling.'

Collis shook his head. 'I think you're wrong. There is no such beast as a decent compromise, and especially not on slavery. It's like a houseowner coming to terms with a burglar, and agreeing that his guard dog will bark at the burglar, but won't bite. I think it's time for some biting. It's time we had men in Washington who stood up against the South.'

'I shouldn't say that very much more loudly, Collis,' Andrew said in a low voice. 'You have David Terry sitting a little way in back of you, and he's something of a Southern hothead. That's him, eating the salad. If he hears you malign the South, he'll shoot you as soon as look at you.'

Charles, oblivious to this aside, cut in. 'John Frémont tried to stand up against the South, or at least against the doughfaces, but look what happened to him. You couldn't have found a more ardent Frémont supporter than me. No, it's quite true. But Frémont lost, and we have to accept Buchanan for a while. The best we can do now is balance what we *want* against what we can reasonably *expect*.'

Collis leaned back while the waiter collected his empty soup plate. 'Frémont was inexperienced, that's all,' he said. 'He frightened Wall Street, too. I know he terrified my father. But he could do better next time.'

Charles shrugged. 'I don't think he'll try again. He's taken his defeat pretty hard, you know. He stays up in that house of his, moping, and Jessie says he's tired of politics, and life, and everything in general. He may go back to railroads.'

Andrew gave a sparse chuckle. 'Railroads? If you ask me, he'd be a damn sight better off moping.'

'What makes you say that?' asked Collis. 'He was quite a famous railroad surveyor once, wasn't he?'

'Whatever you've heard about John Frémont's magnificent exploits looking for a Pacific railroad route, the truth is that he didn't actually have a very happy time of it,' said Andrew.

'I thought he found quite a feasible railroad route,' said Collis. 'The Buffalo Route, or something like that.'

'The Buffalo Trail, so called, although I don't suppose you'd see many buffalo using it. They'd freeze their shaggy old butts off, and I understand, as a species, they're usually more sensible than that. No, it was back in '48, and Frémont was put in charge of finding a route from St Louis to San Francisco. He'd been a railroad surveyor in the army, you see, and everyone thought he'd be able to

214

locate a suitable path through the Rockies for a railroad to run, just about as easy as going for a stroll. They even used to call him the Pathfinder. That was a big joke. He got himself and his party lost up in the Sangre de Cristo mountains in a snowstorm, and ten of his men died from freezing. If it hadn't been for a band of Ute Indians he met up with, he would have frozen there, too. Mind you, he tells the story a little different himself. You ask him when you meet him. But that was the truth of what happened.'

'All the same, you don't think he'll have another try for the Presidency in 1860?' asked Collis.

'Not a chance,' put in Charles. 'He's a nice enough fellow, but he's a sore loser. And if you ask me, he finds it as difficult to find his way around the capital as he did finding his way through the Rockies.'

'Well, that's a pity,' said Collis. 'We need someone like him to stand up to men like Buchanan and Douglas, and show them up for what they are. It wouldn't surprise me if Douglas stands next time, for the Democrats, and by God we need someone who's got guts enough to come out and say that every compromise on slavery that men like Douglas make is just one more shackle on one more Negro's leg.'

'I wish you'd keep your voice lowered,' said Andrew. 'It's not that I don't agree with you, it's just that I don't want to be shot while I'm eating.'

'I think we'd be better off with a soft-shell Democrat for the time being,' put in Charles. 'I won't say I hold with them. I think they're the slugs and snails of the earth. But if we had a Republican President who spoke up and said what a Republican President would have to say, then he'd split the Union faster'n a fence rail.'

'A war's inevitable anyway, if we go on compromising,' Collis argued. 'And the longer we go on compromising, the worse it will be when it happens. It's like clamping the lid on a pan of boiling beans, and sitting on it, and hoping that it won't boil over.'

'Oh, I think you're exaggerating, kind of,' said Charles.

Collis looked at him. 'I don't think so,' he said. 'I met Senator Stephen Douglas once, a couple of years ago. He came to dinner at my parents' house on Twenty-first Street, in New York, quite soon after he'd gotten his Nebraska Bill through, setting up Kansas and Nebraska as new territories. My father thought he was the hero of the age. They toasted each other, and laughed at each other's jokes, and Douglas came out with all his purple spread-eagle oratory, and if you'd seen that little wing-collared toad it would have made you feel sick, I guarantee it.'

Collis leaned forward, his elbow on the table, the same way he'd done when the pompous little Senator from Illinois had sat opposite him at dinner. 'I asked him all about the Nebraska Bill, mainly because I didn't really understand what he was doing at the time. I asked him why he'd proposed that the new territories should be allowed to make up their own minds on whether they wanted to be slave territories or free soil, and he thought about that, and then he told me, very dignified, that he believed in the sovereignty of the common people, in their right to choose their own destiny. "Personally," he said, "I don't care if slavery is voted up or voted down."'

Andrew nodded. 'So *you* said, being the cussed young man you are, "The trouble with that, Senator, is that there isn't a dog's chance in hell of slavery's being voted down, and that's just as sure as every free-soiler who tries to cast his vote will get his hide whipped off by Southern bullies."'

Collis laughed. 'I almost said that. Not quite so impolitely. But Douglas said, well, he was sure that slavery *would* be voted up. Certain of it. But if it was the will of the people, he couldn't argue, no matter what he felt about it personally. And it was then that he turned to my father, who's a portly old buzzard, and said he was sure that most Wall Street bankers were in the same boat as he was, and had Southern business interests to keep sweet, so if slavery was voted up, his friends in the South wouldn't exactly hate him for it. And above all – and I can remember him saying this as if it were yesterday – he said that quite confidentially he'd wanted to see Kansas and Nebraska set up as territories without too much delay, without too much wrangling over slavery in Congress, because he was all tied up with some Chicago investors who wanted to build a railroad out of Chicago and westward through Council Bluffs, and they couldn't proceed until Kansas and Nebraska had their own territorial governments.'

'I heard stories about that, too,' said Andrew. 'You're right, Collis, it makes a fellow want to scratch himself, don't it? What's it coming to when one man can almost bring the Union to cracking apart just because he wants to line his pockets from some private railroad scheme?'

'Well, that's what I mean when I say the very people who don't want war will bring it on us by default,' said Collis. 'They'll go on giving sops to the South, and the South will go on bullying more and more out of them, until the time comes when we'll have to say, "That's enough, put 'em up, no damned more."'

'So you think there's going to be a war, do you?' asked Charles.

'Either war or something very much like it. It depends on who succeeds Old Buck.'

The waiter reappeared, wheeling in a trolley crowded with silver-covered dishes. He lifted the lids with all the style of a conjuror, broiled beefsteaks here, whole roast chicken here, brown fried potatoes here, corn, green beans, and broiled tomatoes here, grits here, abracadabra. Then he skimmed hot polished plates in front of them and began to serve out with a flourish.

Collis and Andrew both had steak. Each cut must have weighed almost two pounds on the slab, and they were black and crisp with charcoal on the outside and running with blood on the inside. Charles's chicken had been roasted with rosemary butter and gave off a rich, herby aroma.

Charles raised his glass of burgundy. 'Here's another toast. To the wholesale confusion of our appetites.' He watched with satisfaction as two plentiful helpings of fried crumbs were spooned next to his chicken.

They ate for a while without talking, except to ask for the gravy or the bread, or for more wine. All around them, the noise and the laughter of San Francisco society at dinner rose and fell. It was a strange sound, quite unlike New York when it ate out. Instead of the confidential scissoring of clipped Eastern accents, punctuated by occasional bursts of sardonic laughter, there was a constant repetitive quacking, as if an endless flock of migratory ducks were passing overhead. Collis glanced up a couple of times, and saw Charles cramming half a chicken breast into his mouth, and, at his far corner table, William Tecumseh Sherman with his head bent over his plate, spitting out a piece of gristle with the same ferocity with which he had eaten it. As he cut off yet another slice of steak, Collis realised he wasn't tired any more, and he certainly wasn't hungry, and that was why he was being so nitpickingly critical of San Francisco's comparative crudeness.

'It's business, not philosophy, that's going to bring us to war, what's what I think,' Andrew said.

'Well, business is very dear to our hearts,' answered Charles. 'Do you know something, I ordered a shipload of ice from Sitka in July, six hundred tons of it, and I unloaded it on San Francisco Bay and

217

sold some of it there, and transported the rest of it to Sacramento by steamboat and wagon. Four hundred tons of it melted, but I still made nine hundred dollars profit. I was very pleased with that little exploit.'

'Well, that's excellent,' said Collis, 'but the business of dry goods and the business of selling ice doesn't depend on slaves. As far as I can make out, it's not so much a question for most Southerners of whether Negros have any rights under the Constitution or not, as whether they can seriously afford to let their slaves go.'

'Chief Justice Taney doesn't seem to be able to let *his* go,' agreed Charles. He was referring, sardonically, to the Dred Scott decision, handed down in March. It was still being fiercely argued. The Supreme Court Chief Justice, with the President's open approval, had declared that the slave Dred Scott, who had sued for his freedom on the grounds that he had been living in a free state for four years, was still a slave and had 'no rights which the white man was bound to respect'. Free-soilers had been furious: they felt that slavery was being forced down their throats.

Andrew, steadily slicing up and devouring his steak as if his legs were hollow, said, 'Chief Justice Taney will be the death of us, one of these days.'

They set down their knives and forks at last, although Collis had left well over a pound of steak on his plate. Charles's chicken was nothing more than bones, a skeletal fishing boat beached on a shore of hominy grits, and Andrew relentlessly mopped his gravy with the last of the soda bread.

'Don't worry, Collis,' said Andrew. 'You'll get your appetite back when you've had a good sleep.'

Charles sat back and discreetly released the lower two buttons of his vest. 'Talking of Frémont and Douglas, you know, I was buttonholed by that railroad pest up at Sacramento last week.'

'What did he have to say?' asked Andrew.

'Oh, he was still going on about the Pacific railroad, and how he was sure he could take the Sacramento Valley Railroad right over the Sierra Nevada. If you ask me, he's probably crazy enough to be able to do it; but the fellow's such a goddam bore. All I know about trains is that they make steaming noises and they bring in my goods from the docks. This fellow's eternally on about cuts and grades and fills and tunnels. It's enough to make your damned head spin around.'

'Collis kept talking about a Pacific railroad when we were

218

crossing the isthmus,' said Andrew. 'I was afraid he was going to rush straight off the boat when he got here, and start laying track.'

'Everybody talks about Pacific railroads when they're crossing the isthmus,' said Charles. 'There's no doubt at all that if you *could* build one, you'd be richer than all hell. Especially if a civil war broke out, and you had control of the damned thing.'

'That's what I said to Collis,' Andrew assented. 'A man who could build a Pacific railroad would make himself rich as Crease-ass.'

'Who?' asked Charles.

'Never mind,' said Andrew.

'This fellow up at Sacramento – the railroad pest. Does he really believe he could build a railroad over the mountains?' asked Collis.

'He says so, but you have to remember he's a fanatic, and everything fanatics say you have to dilute with vinegar and lemon juice. I was talking to Colonel Charles Wilson – he's the president of the Sacramento Valley Railroad – and he says it took all his funds and all his energy just to build twenty-two miles of track up to the gold mines at Folsom. Maybe this railroad pest of his could do better, and you have to admit that he knows about railroads backwards, sideways, and forwards, but across the Sierra Nevada? Well, I don't think so. Do you know what the steepest grade is that a modern railroad locomotive can climb? One hundred sixteen feet to the mile, that's what Colonel Wilson told me, and that's so gradual you can't scarcely see it with the human eye.'

The waiter brought them another bottle of burgundy and poured a little into Charles's glass. 'Just dish it out,' Charles said testily. 'If it ain't the same as the last bottle, it can only be better.'

The waiter said placidly, 'Very good, Mr Tucker,' and filled their glasses.

'What I was saying,' went on Charles, angling his menu card to represent the steep western slopes of the Sierra Nevada, 'is that no modern locomotive can traverse the mountains because the grades are all too sharp. And even if you were lucky enough to find yourself a wiggly-waggly way through, all at the right kind of a grade, well, that probably wouldn't do you any good, because a railroad curve has to have a three-hundred-foot radius, so Colonel Wilson told me, otherwise the locomotive jumps off her tracks.'

'But the railroad pest still thinks there's a way?' asked Andrew. 'In spite of the fact that the menus in this restaurant are too steeply graded for the modern locomotive?'

'Why did John Frémont say there's a way?' Charles retorted. 'Listen, the Army Department sent out four parties of explorers to find ways across the Rockies and the Sierra Nevada, four, and why did *they* all say, each one of them, that they'd found a way? They all said there were ways because they were all supported by money and politics, that's why, just like Collis's friend Senator Douglas. The ones who found routes through the southlands were supported by Jeff Davis and the Southern hard-shell politicians, and the ones who found routes across the plains and the northlands were all paid off by Northerners.'

'Maybe they said they found ways because they *found* ways,' commented Andrew.

Charles smacked his hand on the table. 'If they found ways, smart-ass, why didn't they start to build a railroad? That was, what, three years ago, four years ago? I think the whole thing's impossible.'

'What's the name of this railroad pest of yours?' Collis asked.

'Theodore Jones,' Charles told him. 'He's a reasonable enough man in his way, unless you get him talking about railroads. His wife, Annie, often drops by the store for a talk with Clara. Nice people. But don't say anything that reminds him of railroads; don't say the words "grade", or "tie", or "brake", because that'll start him off for an hour.'

Collis smiled. 'I'd like to meet him.'

'You will. You're coming out to Sacramento, aren't you? But just be warned. Everybody says that Theodore Jones is Pacific railroad crazy.'

'Charles,' said Collis, with complete seriousness, 'when I crossed the isthmus of Panama, I nearly lost someone for whom I cared very dearly, because of the yellow fever. That's why I'm interested in the notion of a Pacific railroad, and if there's a fellow out at Sacramento who says he can find a way for trains to run through the Sierra Nevada, then I'd like to talk to him.'

Charles sighed. 'Well, to be frank, you won't have much choice, as soon as he hears that you're keen on railroads. But if you ask me, he's wasting his time, and he'll waste yours, too. I mean, supposing he does find a way through the Sierras – what then? He still has the Great Basin to cross, where there isn't water enough for a fly to wash his face, and no timber for hundreds of miles. How do you run a railroad across that? And after the Great Basin, there's the Rockies, and they're just as high as the Sierras. You've got yourself plains, and deserts, and mountains. You've got snow and you've got drought. How in hell can you humanly drive a railroad across all that?'

Over French cognac and Havana cigars, sitting well back in their chairs with faces flushed and polished with good eating and drinking, their conversation wandered from railroads to dancing, and from dancing to the theatre, and from the theatre, naturally enough, to women.

'It's clear to me that Collis favours a particular style of woman,' Andrew said. 'She may be dark, like that half-breed lady on the steamer; or she may be fair, like Mrs West. But she must have a substantial bust, not flat, and she must have a well-boned face. Above all,' he said, speaking louder to drown out Collis's protests, 'she must have mysterious eyes. Eyes that hint of repressed passions and exotic yet unfulfilled desires.'

Collis laughed. 'Exotic yet unfulfilled desires? You sound like a Turkish rug salesman.'

The waiter, with his shoelaces undone and a pencil stuck behind his ear, came around and asked them if they wanted more brandy. It was well past eleven o'clock now, and the restaurant had quietened.

Andrew raised his brandy glass and looked at Collis seriously, if not too steadily, his bright eyes blurred. 'The question is,' he said, 'what are you going to do about Mrs West? That's the question.'

'West is a good man from what I hear,' put in Charles. 'I don't think you'd be doing yourself any favours if you cuckolded him.'

'It depends on your definition of a favour,' said Andrew, drinking.

Collis tried to smile. 'I'm not sure what I'm going to do. She's a most captivating woman, and there's no mistake of that. While I was with her, I felt as if she had me under some kind of spell. I felt as if I was drawn to love her, whether I wanted to or not. But now – well, I'm not quite so certain. I have the strongest feelings of affection for her, and I expect that if she were sitting here now, she would only have to smile at me and I would swear that I loved her for ever. She has such a sweet, sad smile. Like a trembling orchid.

'Go on,' said Charles, amused.

'I wish I could,' Collis told him. 'But there are all kinds of problems. The main one, of course, is her marriage to Walter West. I haven't met the fellow yet. Haven't even glimpsed him. But it's only fair on everybody that she have the chance to be reunited with him. He did wait two years, poor fellow, after all, and if he was faithful that's a devil of a long time. He deserves a chance, doesn't he, after writing all those letters to her, and putting gunpowder in his coffee to make him feel less frisky? Wouldn't you say so?'

'I'd say that nobody gets any chances in love,' said Andrew, with a smile that wasn't quite a smile at all. 'I'd say they don't deserve them, neither. You see, nobody *deserves* to be loved. You either are or you ain't, and all the crying in China isn't going to change things.'

'You're very philosophical tonight,' remarked Charles.

'It seems to me that Collis is the one who's being philosophical,' said Andrew. 'Instead of being passionate, he's being philosophical. Could it be that absence has made his love for the lady less fond?'

'There's divorce, too,' explained Collis. 'That's a problem. She's a Boston Roman Catholic, and I think her marriage to Walter took all the religious fight right out of her. He was a Protestant, you see, and the family didn't approve. She suffered ten times over for that one act of disobedience, and to divorce him now might be more than she can bring herself to do.'

'So,' said Andrew, 'what are you going to do?'

Collis looked away and thought for a moment. 'I think I shall probably buy her roses.'

Charles laughed at that, and thumped the table in approval. Then he unwound his watch chain and inspected his gold half-hunter. 'I do believe it's time we moved on, gentlemen, if we're going to make any money for Collis tonight. Are you still up to a little gaming, Collis, or do you want to go back to Knickerbocker Jane's and fall into the arms of that Portuguese-speaking dove of yours?'

'I'm game for some gaming,' said Collis. 'At least I'll be sitting quiet when I'm playing cards. The slightest physical activity would give me chronic indigestion, right at this moment.'

'Huzzah,' replied Charles, 'then we're off.'

They left the International Hotel, bowed out by relieved waiters, and pushed their way through the glass-and-mahogany doors to the steps outside, where they saw Charles's phaeton waiting on the warm, breathless night.

'Just take us to the Eagle, will you, Billy?' ordered Charles, and so the coachman clicked his tongue and the phaeton clattered off on its way.

Although the restaurants and hotels were closing their doors, and sawdust from the floors of the better saloons was being swept out into the streets, San Francisco was still up, noisy and awake. The gaming resorts and gambling tents, illuminated from within by miner's lamps, were still crowded with shadows and alive with activity. Andrew remarked, as they passed, that the rent on one of those tents could go as high as $40,000 a year, and that a man could make himself a fortune in six months if he operated one.

From every open door came tinny piano music, wheezing accordion music, raucous barbershop singing, fandango guitars, and scraping violins. There were lights everywhere, in the city centre itself and sparkling all over the surrounding hills, lamps and cooking fires and torches, and it didn't surprise Collis at all that San Francisco suffered a major fire disaster every four or five years. In one of the worst of the recent fires, in 1851, the old City Hotel, where Knickerbocker Jane had first set herself up as a madam, had been burned to the ground.

Most of all, though, on the lighted and musical night air, at every corner, was the aroma of food. There was the hot, pungent smell of Mexican food, *enchiladas* and *frijoles refritos*; there was the waft of pioneer food, plain and filling, still cooked the same way it was cooked on the wagon trains that crossed the alkali deserts of Utah and the passes of the Humboldt Range, red-flannel hash and Indian-corn stew; there was seafood, breadcrumbed oysters and broiled lobster tails browned in butter; there was meaty South American food and Hawaiian food that was sweet and sharp with pineapples, and Australian beef and dumplings. And everywhere, like an exotic and persistent memory, from dilapidated upstairs rooms where dragon lanterns burned and where the shutters were open to the warm September night, from narrow alleyways and concealed doorways, came the spicy smell of Chinese food, wind-dried ducks and glazed fish, water chestnuts and crackling rice, and that particular invention of the San Francisco Chinese, chop suey.

'One evening, I'll take you to visit an opium den,' promised Charles. 'My servant Wang-Pu has a friend who runs a good place down near the dock. Mind you, I'm not so sure that there's very much difference between an opium den and the smoking-room at the Sacramento capitol, except that the Chinese tend to lie down when they smoke, and they don't talk so much claptrap.'

They reached the Eagle Saloon, on Kearny, north of Portsmouth

223

Square, and climbed down from the carriage. A sour-faced man in dusty black was leaning under the Eagle's gas-lamp, an ivory revolver handle prominently tucked outside of his coat tails, and Charles called to him, 'Keep your eye on the rig, will you? I want to send my man for some dinner.'

The sour-faced man nodded. This was the Eagle Saloon's 'minder', the man who made sure that befuddled customers weren't robbed and attacked on the saloon's doorstep. It was all right once they were out of sight and sound around the corner, but the management preferred to keep the street outside moderately quiet and respectable. It was better for business.

Billy crossed the road to the Barreltop Lunch for a plate of fried fish and pig's feet, topped with onions, while Charles led the way into the Eagle Saloon. He dropped a silver dollar into the minder's coat pocket as he passed, but the minder, thin and slitty-eyed and scarred by acne and probably only nineteen years old, didn't even blink.

As they went through the saloon doors, decorated with bottle-green glass and engraved with eagle motifs, Charles turned to Collis and said, 'All you can be absolutely sure of is that if some miner or mulewhacker tries to make off with my horses, then he's going to have his head blown off his shoulders and no questions asked.'

Inside, the Eagle Saloon was roaring with voices and laughter and piano music. The air was dense with cigar smoke, and through this haze, waitresses with plumed headdresses and long black dresses sewn with sequins passed with trays of whisky and steam beer. There was a long bar, at which a line of regulars leaned, their thumbs tucked in their vests and their hats tilted back on their heads, and behind the bar an unsmiling man with short-cropped hair and a walrus moustache poured the drinks with almost magical speed and skill.

The walls were all mirrored, at great expense, said Charles, because the mirrors came from Paris; and the mirrors gave the foggy, glittering illusion that the Eagle Saloon opened on to yet more Eagle Saloons, that the whole place was like an endless steamy railroad depot, through which a disconsolate passenger might wander for hours, and never find a train.

Collis tugged at his fingers through his evening gloves, so that the knuckles clicked. He was beginning to have a slight case of first night nerves, not because he wasn't sure of his skill at faro, but because of the loudness and the roughness and the unfamiliarity of the saloon.

A round-faced waitress with a large mole on the side of her nose came up to them and led them to a table. Collis took off his gloves, but not his hat, and ordered a straight bourbon. Then he flexed his fingers again and gave Andrew and Charles an uncomfortable smile.

'What do we do now?' he asked.

'It depends what you want to do,' said Andrew. 'If you want to play cards, or dice, we'll get you in on a game of cards or dice. If you want to suggest something else, then we'll see what we can do.'

Collis placed both of his hands flat on the table. Dimly seen through the cigar smoke, a fat pianist whose huge posterior overflowed his piano-stool like two bags of boiled pudding was banging out 'Bye and Bye You Will Forget Me', while one of the waitresses stood beside him and trilled the words in such a high soprano that nobody could make out what they were. 'I haven't played in a week or two,' Collis said. 'How about some practice, to unwind?'

'Sure,' said Andrew. He took out his leather purse and shook thirty or forty dollars in gold and silver coins on to the table. They spun, wobbled, and then lay flat.

'Okay,' said Collis. 'I'll give you ten dollars the next man to walk through the door will be wearing a checkered vest.'

'Ten dollars it is,' said Andrew.

'What kind of gambling is this?' demanded Charles. 'Ten dollars on a checkered vest?'

'Are you in?' asked Collis.

'Sure I am,' said Charles. 'I never heard anything so damned stupid.' He fumbled in his pocket and then put down two five-dollar gold pieces on the table. 'I'd still like to know what kind of gambling you call it.'

Collis paused, saying nothing, his eyes on the green glass panels of the Eagle Saloon's doors. He could see the silhouette of somebody outside; then the doors were opened a little way, hesitated, and closed again. Whoever was out there was talking to the minder, or saying goodbye to friends. The doors parted again, stayed half-open for a while, and then a middle-aged man in a brown suit and a yellow checkered vest walked in and crossed to the bar.

Andrew looked at Collis narrowly as he pushed ten silver dollars across the polished surface of the table. Collis counted them and stacked the coins into a neat castle. Charles pushed his over, too.

'That kind of gambling is called looking around the street before you walk into a place,' said Collis, without raising his eyes. 'There was another carriage waiting behind ours, and the fellow riding inside was the fellow you just saw.'

'You won't catch me like that again,' warned Andrew.

'I will,' said Collis, 'but next time don't say you weren't cautioned.'

Charles, tickled, looked from Collis to Andrew and back again, and then gave out one of his short, barking laughs. 'I think from now on we'd do better to skin other folks, instead of ourselves,' he said. 'I think you and us, we're going to get along fine together, Collis.'

With the silk fringes on her hips swaying and her plumes bobbing, the waitress came across the saloon with their drinks, and Collis winked at her as she set down his bourbon. He had to admit that he was feeling a hundred times improved in spirit.

'Shall we skin the house, then?' he asked, taking a sip of his whisky. 'I see some faro tables by the far wall there.'

'Faro it is,' agreed Andrew, and they left their seats and walked across to find themselves a game.

They joined a table where three grizzly-bearded miners were tossing the last of their drinks down their reddened throats, gathering up their winnings, and preparing to leave. They were horny-handed, these miners, and their faces were creased by years of squinting into brilliant sunlight, but their suits were cut from the best broadcloth, and they were all doused in enough French toilet water to fuel a bordello's bedroom lamps for months. One of them said to Collis, as he passed, 'Watch out for the dealer. He's a goddam unpleasant cuss, and he's got himself a Navy revolver under the table.'

Collis glanced across at Andrew and raised an eyebrow. But Andrew simply shrugged, as if it was quite usual for a card dealer to have a pistol at hand, and pulled out a chair for him.

The dealer was a humourless sort, with an off-white hat and a striped silk shirt. He had pale-blue eyes with needle-sharp pupils, and a moustache clipped as close as a currying brush. 'Good evening, gents,' he said in a marked New Orleans accent, and proceeded to shuffle the pack.

'I'll be casekeeper, unless there are any objections,' Collis said, sitting.

The dealer glanced at him acutely, shrugged, and passed over the abacus. On it were painted small pictures of all the cards in the suit of spades, and beside each painted card was a wire, holding a row of four beads. Whenever a card was played – any card in any suit, because the spades on the abacus had no special significance – Collis would record it by moving a bead. It was supposed to help players keep track of what was being dealt, and prevent arguments; although here, Collis reflected, it was probably necessary to save players from having their kidneys blown out.

'Are we all happy, gentlemen?' asked the dealer. 'Do you want a refill before we start?' He nodded to the waitress, who went to the bar to bring them more drinks.

On the green cloth table in front of them, stained by whisky and burned by abandoned cigars, the suit of spades was marked out again, full-size. The players could bet on any rank of card to win, or any rank of card to lose, simply by piling silver or gold dollars on the appropriate picture. If they were betting on a card to lose, they would top their pile of money with a small hexagonal copper token, stamped 'Eagle Saloon'.

Collis took out his purse, produced ninety dollars in silver coins, two-thirds of all the money he had left, and bet on aces to win, threes to win, and queens to lose, thirty dollars on each. Andrew, with an unlit cheroot in his mouth, watched him carefully and then placed his own bets. He, too, bet on queens to lose. Charles bet on aces to lose.

The dealer held the pack, face up, in the dealing box in front of him. He played the first card, soda, which didn't count in the game. Then he played the second card, the five of diamonds, and that was a loser. Collis recorded the play on his abacus without taking his eyes off the dealing box. Underneath the five of diamonds was the ace of clubs, and that was a winner.

'Nice one,' said Andrew, striking a match and lighting up his cheroot. The dealer, expressionless, paid Collis thirty dollars. All stakes, on winning or losing cards, were paid off at even odds. Collis placed thirty dollars on nines to lose.

The dealer took the winning card out of the box and placed it on the table to form a pile of winning cards. The next loser, the seven of hearts, he put down to form a losing pile. The next winner was the three of hearts. He paid Collis another thirty dollars, still, as

227

Andrew was later to remark, 'with a face like a brass doorplate'.

Collis, stimulated by the whisky and the noisy saloon, began to see the game in his mind with the brilliance of a kaleidoscopic picture show. This was his particular talent, and it had won him hundreds of dollars in New York faro games. He could imagine the whole pack of cards in his mind, like a brightly lit choir in their choirstall, and whenever one was played he could immediately picture it leaving the ranks, saying good night, and going off home. At any moment throughout the whole game he knew how many cards had been played and what they were, and so he knew which cards remained in the box. More than that, he could work out the odds on the order in which they were most likely to be played next.

It was impossible to predict which cards would be turned up as winning cards and which would come out as losing cards, and yet Collis believed he had a nose for that, too. Whether it was magic, or intuition, or self-delusion, he always felt that he could detect an underlying rhythm in the way the cards came out of the box, especially when he knew the dealer.

He had kept his bets down to thirty dollars on each card in the first game. As they came to the twenty-fourth winning card, three cards away from the end of the game, he had won two hundred and ten dollars and lost sixty.

'Do you want to name 'em?' asked the dealer, in a rusty voice, his eyes fixed unmovingly on Collis's necktie.

'Sure,' nodded Collis. 'One hundred fifty dollars says they're king, deuce, jack.'

Charles and Andrew placed their bets, too. The dealer dealt out the king of spades, the two of diamonds, the jack of hearts. The usual house odds on naming the order of the last three cards was four to one. The dealer sniffed, tugged at his moustache, and then pushed across a pile of gold five-dollar pieces.

They played for four hours at the same table. At three o'clock in the morning, the Eagle was still crowded, the blue cigar smoke hanging in dense and suffocating veils, and the noise and laughter was even louder than before. The piano player, revitalised by a supper of ham and eggs, was thumping out marches and stirring Republican songs, while an old hardware-store owner with a bald head tried to demonstrate to his friends how he used to dance the quadrille with his late wife's family. Outside in the street, there was the flat sound of pistol shots, but they were too far away for the Eagle's customers to be bothered.

228

Between Collis and the faro dealer a strange antagonism had grown up, a cold and uncomfortable atmosphere which both Charles and Andrew had obviously sensed as well. Collis had felt the man's dislike for him when he had first sat down at the table, and had ascribed it then to nothing more than the natural hostility that most pioneers felt for slickly dressed Easterners. But as Collis had amassed more and more money on the table, the dealer had grown increasingly rigid and chilly in his manner, and his eyes hardly ever moved from Collis's face.

The clock behind the bar mirror struck three-thirty. Collis took out his watch, checked the time, and turned the winder a few times.

'Are you playing, or what?' asked the dealer.

'I'm playing,' said Collis. 'Keep your shirt on.'

'I just dealt a card. Did you see it, or were you too busy with your timepiece?'

'You just dealt the nine of clubs. I have one hundred dollars on nines, to lose. Therefore you owe me one hundred dollars. Now, are *you* playing, or what?'

There was a tense silence. The dealer's eyes didn't blink, even through the thick cigar smoke, and his face might have been some failed bank robber's death mask.

'I'm playing,' he said, and dealt a six.

By four, Collis was beginning to feel the strain of his first day in San Francisco. His sleep during yesterday afternoon had eased the worst of his fatigue, but now he was ready for bed again. He asked for one more whisky all round and then said to the dealer, 'I'm set for one last game. You want to play?'

'I'll play,' said the dealer.

The girl brought more tumblers of bourbon and set them down. She glanced at the heap of silver and gold in front of Collis. 'If you get out of here with half of that, you can walk me home,' she said. 'You're pretty.'

The dealer said, without changing his expression, 'If he tries to get out of here with even a quarter of that, he won't be so pretty any more.'

Charles looked up, glared, and then snapped loudly, 'What kind of a dumb remark is that?'

But Collis reached across and restrained him. Feeling unnaturally unruffled, he gave the dealer one of his worried, sincere smiles 'You'll have to excuse my friend,' he said. 'Do you want to play

229

faro, or do you want to spend the rest of the night making cheap remarks?'

The dealer, for the first time that evening, gave a grin. Most of his front teeth were brown, and more than half were missing. Collis turned to Andrew and remarked, 'I wish I hadn't amused him now.'

They played. Collis lost steadily for the first part of the game, but then, as the odds narrowed, he began to win. He staked thirty dollars on queens to lose, and the next card was a losing queen. He staked forty on aces to lose, and the next card was a losing ace. By the time the dealer dealt the twenty-fourth winning card, Collis had nearly one thousand dollars in front of him.

'Do you want to name 'em?' asked the dealer coldly. 'I'll give you four to one.'

Collis puffed steadily at his cheroot. 'Not me,' he said amiably.

The dealer stared at him. 'You've bet every other game. You've bet big.'

'Sure. But there's nothing in the rules says I have to.'

'Supposing *I* say you have to?'

'You and that Navy revolver under your table?'

The dealer's eyes flickered, but his face stayed hard. 'That's right, mister. Me and that Navy revolver under my table.'

Collis took a sip of whisky, almost delicately. Then he set down his glass. 'Very well,' he said. 'I'll make you a bet. I'll name those cards, but for particular stakes. If I'm wrong, you can have all of this money here in front of me. If I'm right, I get your Navy revolver. No money, just your Navy revolver.'

'Come on now, Collis,' Charles said, 'if you're right at four to one you could walk out of here with a good grubstake.'

'There's always tomorrow night,' said Collis. 'Right now, that's all I want. This cardwhacker's Navy revolver.'

'Please yourself,' said Andrew. 'If you want to act crazy, act crazy. That dark girl on the steamer said you were crazy.'

The dealer was rubbing at his moustache, frowning and confused. At last he nodded agreement and reached below the green-cloth-covered table. He laid a long-barrelled blue-steel revolver on the table, and as he did so, the players at the next table abruptly went quiet and nudged their neighbours, and before anybody knew what was happening, the Eagle Saloon was hushed, and the tables all around them were cleared. Collis looked around and saw that almost the entire clientele was staring fixedly back at him, stiffly crowded in a circle as if they were posing for a group-photograph, hats on their heads, cigars in their mouths, coat pockets sagging. The piano player, the last to realise that there was anything unusual happening, went on pounding at 'The Green Hills of Virginia'; but then he sensed trouble, and turned around, and the music died on one clumsy chord.

'Are you ready?' asked Collis. 'Whatever all of this money adds up to, it says eight, five, king.'

The dealer coughed. Then, out of the box, he dealt the eight of hearts. Andrew glanced at Collis, gnawing uncertainly at his knuckle, but Collis, even though he saw him, did everything he could to stay straight-faced. It was one of the principles that Henry Browne had always taught him: stay calm, whatever happened; or try to. The odds were that everyone else was just as upset and wound up as you were.

Underneath the eight of hearts was the five of spades.

The tension was unrelieved. Collis blew out smoke, watching the dealer to see what he would do. Of course, there was nothing he could do. The Eagle Saloon may have been boisterous by New York standards, but it wasn't a hole-in-the-wall gambling hell. Collis reached across the table and picked up the Navy revolver. It was much heavier than he had expected it to be, and it smelled of oil.

'Give me your hat,' he said to the dealer.

The dealer blinked. *'Whut?'*

'Your hat. Hand it over.'

Uncertainly, the man took his white hat off and gave it to Charles, who passed it to Collis. Collis held it up by the brim and then looked across at the dealer, the pistol raised in his hand, as if he was sizing him up for one neat shot between the eyes. The dealer unconsciously wiped the back of his hand across his mouth.

Completely by surprise, Collis squeezed the revolver's trigger and fired through the top of the hat, upward into the ceiling. There was an ear-splitting bang, and the crown of the hat burst apart in black tatters. Almost everybody in the saloon, with the exception of the pianist, who was too fat, and one or two people who were too shocked to move, huddled in a rush under the tables.

Collis was trembling with tiredness and the strain of the game he was playing. But he handed the dealer's hat back to him with great control and calmness, and said, 'There. Put it on.'

The dealer examined the hat unhappily and then put it on his head. He looked like a hobo, or a giant firecracker that had failed

231

to light properly. There was a ripple of laughter around the saloon, and a sudden relaxation of fear.

'What's your name?' Collis asked the dealer.

'Dan McReady.'

'Where are you from, Dan?'

The man coughed. 'Vermont, originally. But I did time on the riverboats.'

Collis handed his revolver back to him. 'Well, Dan,' he said, so quietly that only Charles and Andrew could hear him, 'I guess we were all raw once, and all strangers to San Francisco, and I guess that we were all taken advantage of, now and again, because we were green. But I hope what I did to your hat is going to be a permanent reminder of something, and that is, just because you're green, it doesn't mean you're yellow.'

Dan McReady dropped his gaze.

'I'm going to take my money now, and I'm going off to get some sleep,' Collis said. 'But I hope you'll be here tomorrow, because I have an outstanding bet with you, four to one, and I want to make sure I get what's coming to me.'

There was a difficult silence. Then Dan McReady looked up again, and he was smiling, although he was plainly doing his best not to.

'You son of a bitch.' He grinned. 'You goddam son of a bitch.'

They shook hands, and the pianist suddenly burst into 'Dear Old Home of Mine', and Charles sat there shaking his head as if he'd just witnessed a tornado pick up a house and put it right down again without so much as disturbing the flowers in the front yard.

Collis woke up at ten. He could hear a clock chiming somewhere. He sat up in bed, his hair tousled, and blinked at the brightness of the primrose-draped windows. Then, his head beating with a hangover, he climbed out of bed and walked across to the washbasin. This must be civilisation, he thought to himself, examining his face in the mirror. Nothing else but civilisation could give anyone such a goddam terrible headache.

He dressed, slowly and carefully, with several pauses, in a plain light-brown suit and a white shirt, tied with a dark-brown necktie. While he was lacing up his shoes, he rested for a while and took a couple of breaths. He could recall the faro game quite clearly, and he certainly remembered firing through the dealer's hat. But he wasn't at all sure what had happened after that. They had drunk a few more whiskys with the dealer to celebrate, and then he had been introduced to some of the Eagle's regulars, and there had been drinks all around again, and at six o'clock, with the sky already light, Charles and Andrew had brought him back to Knickerbocker Jane's in the phaeton, with Billy grumbling and complaining all the way that all these late nights would give him dark rings under his eyes. It had been too late for any romps with Ursula, even if he had been able to raise the energy. Knickerbocker Jane had packed her off to bed just after midnight, with a grocer's assistant called Phelps. Guests were guests, but business was business.

Collis cleaned his teeth, then went downstairs to find himself some breakfast. On the landing, just coming out of her room, he met a small blonde girl in a décolleté day gown of white figured cotton, in which her breasts nestled like two soft-set puddings. She was blue-eyed, and snub-nosed, and couldn't have been much older than fifteen. Two diamond pendants hung from her earlobes, and in her cleavage was a gold-and-sapphire cluster which was certainly just as expensive as any piece of jewellery that Collis had seen on any woman at a New York society dance.

'Good morning,' he said.

The girl gave him a little curtsy. 'Good morning. I see you've recovered. Well, almost.'

'Recovered? Recovered from what?'

'Oh,' she said, pursing her lips. 'You must have been worse than I thought.'

'Worse than you thought? Why should you have thought I was bad at all?'

'Why,' she said, 'you had to be carried to bed this morning. A girl at each corner. And Knickerbocker Jane had to undress you and tuck you up. We all watched, of course.'

Collis looked at her warily. 'Are you pulling my leg?' he asked her. 'I'm sure I distinctly remember going up those stairs on my own, unaided.'

'You made it half-way,' she told him. 'But then you fell flat on your back and you lay there singing. You wouldn't open your eyes, and you wouldn't move, so there wasn't anything else for it.'

Collis cleared his throat and tried to stand straight in a dignified manner. 'I see,' he said. 'Well, er, how many were there?'

'How many what? I don't understand you.'

'How many were there, in the room? You know, watching.'

The girl closed her eyes and began to count on her fingers

whispering the numbers as she counted. Collis interrupted her by taking her hand in his and giving it a gentle squeeze. 'Never mind,' he said hoarsely. 'If there were that many, I'd rather not know.'

They began to descend the stairs together. Collis said, 'I don't suppose I need to introduce myself. You've probably seen all you require for the striking up of a fairly close relationship.'

The girl laughed. 'I'm only teasing you. It was Mr Hunt and Mr Tucker who put you to bed, really. But you were bad. If you'd had to make your own way back here, you would have been worked over for sure.'

The words of the street seemed strange, coming from the lips of such a young girl. 'Do you mind if I ask you your name?' Collis said.

'Why should I? Clara, they call me, although my real name is Clarabelle.'

'I think I prefer Clarabelle. It's prettier.'

She made a face. 'I hate it. I hate Clara, too.'

They reached the downstairs parlour. Collis opened the door for her, and she curtsied again and went in. Knickerbocker Jane was there, with her hair tied up in rags, in a lounging gown of layer upon layer of exquisite scalloped lace, with wide sleeves gathered at the cuffs, and a wide skirt. She was reading the *San Francisco Bulletin* on a long tasselled stick, with the aid of a pair of amber-tinted spectacles. Collis was sure he could see the rose-pink of her nipples through the lace.

'Ah, the dreamer awakes,' said Knickerbocker Jane. 'There's some black coffee here, fresh, if you'd like some. Charles tells me you created quite a stir last night, and it seems that you're richer, too.'

'It was only a game of faro,' said Collis. His face felt stiff, and he didn't seem to be able to pronounce his words properly. It would probably pass after a plate of ham and eggs and a quart of steamer beer.

'Only a game of faro? Well, it was the kind of faro that gets this city all stirred up. I wouldn't be surprised if the newspapers write about it. We'll have to buy this afternoon's editions to see if you're in them.'

Collis sat down. Clara went across to the rickety little occasional table and poured coffee. 'I didn't kill the man,' Collis said. 'I only shot a hole in his hat.'

'That's precisely the point,' Knickerbocker Jane told him. 'So many people get shot in San Francisco that it's not news any more.

234

But hats! How many hats get shot? They'll love you, you know. That's exactly the kind of extravagant behaviour that everybody in San Francisco adores.'

'In New York, it would be frowned on,' said Collis. 'If I did anything like that nobody would speak to me for at least a month.'

'In New York, there are more interesting things to do,' replied Knickerbocker Jane. 'Here, what is there? In the spring, you can go for a picnic on the seashore; in the summer, you can stay indoors and swelter. In the fall, it's so foggy you can never see where you are; and in the winter it rains all the time. Charles swears that Montgomery Street was so bad last year that an entire ox wagon sank into the mud and was never seen again.'

'You have your dance halls, and your theatre,' Collis said.

'Well, I suppose so,' said Jane unenthusiastically. 'And, incidentally, that reminds me. I have some tickets for the Empire this evening, to see Rodney Mulgrave perform. Would you like to come along?'

'I had planned on playing faro.'

'You can play later. You can play here, if you like. I should have a good crowd this evening.'

Collis sipped his coffee. 'Is it a big social event, this performance?'

'Of course. It's Mr Mulgrave's first night.'

'I see. Will Laurence Melford be there?'

'He's bound to be,' said Jane. 'And so is Sarah, if that's what really interests you.'

'I think I'm more interested in the father than the daughter. It seems to me from what Andrew said that he's the hardest nut in the whole social circle. Once you've cracked him, you've cracked every nob in San Francisco.'

'Does society mean that much to you?'

'It's where I belong.'

'You belong here too. You have friends here, which is more important.'

Collis bowed his head appreciatively, and finished his coffee. 'I'm going out for some breakfast now,' he told Jane. 'Then I'm going to take a walk around, to see what I can see. I should be back by lunchtime.'

'Don't be too late. Charles said he wanted to take you out to the Auction Lunch, on Sansome Street, and introduce you to some of his business friends.'

Clara gave him a little wave as he left the parlour and went to find

235

his hat. It had been hung in a closet in the hallway, along with dozens of other men's hats, opera hats and derbies and skimmers and beavers, all of which had presumably been left behind by forgetful customers. Collis pulled on his gloves and then stepped out into the dusty, sunny street, taking a left and making his way along to Stockton Street. As he walked north, he was surprised by the elegance of most of the wood-and-iron houses, and by the well-laid boardwalks.

It was a dry, bright day and he began to feel better after walking only a few blocks. He stopped at a reasonable-looking lunchroom called the Mission Eating House, where he sat alone at a wooden table which had one leg violently shorter than the other three, surrounded by clerks and storemen and carriers, but where he was able to eat a huge breakfast of venison steak, fried trout, hot rolls, toast, and brown bread, washed down with cold steam beer served in a pot the size of a flower vase. There was also a table of cheese and cold cuts, from which he picked honeyed ham and smoked pork, and pickled onions.

After eating, he lit a cheroot and walked across to Montgomery. He knew where he was headed, and it was no surprise to him at all when he arrived on the boardwalk between Bush and Sutter Streets, outside a wide brown adobe building on which there was a red-painted sign reading: 'Fancy Goods, Sewing Notions, Etc., Walter F. West, Prop.'

Collis stood outside the store, not moving, for three or four minutes. Passers-by jostled him, and mule wagons, struggling along the rutted street, ground past him in clouds of sunlit dust. But his thoughts, for those few minutes, were with Hannah, and in an equatorial garden under grey forbidding skies. His thoughts were with the kisses that might have to stay unkissed, with the hands that might never be held, with the moments of waking up next to Hannah that might never be. At last he tossed his cheroot into the road and entered the open door of the store.

It was dim inside the store, because the windows were small, and crowded with linens on display; but there was a circular skylight above the door which threw an elliptical pattern across the polished boarded floor, and on to the glass counter, where, with a tape measure around his shoulders and his hands clasped across the front of his dark-grey vest as if he were a preacher imminently about to sermonise, bearded and neat, rounded in appearance but not plump, his head slightly held to one side, stood Walter West.

236

He was so much like the picture that Hannah had shown him on the ship that Collis found the resemblance unnerving; as if Walter West would also recognise *him*.

Across the counter was spread a profusion of Valenciennes laces, silk soutaches braids, silk grenadine veils, point d'ésprit dress nets, grosgrain ribbons, pongee silks and Wamsutta cambrics. There was a smell of fabric dressing and mustiness, and a faint hint of lily-of-the-valley toilet water.

Collis walked across to the counter. Walter West smiled at him and nodded. 'Good morning. Can I help you?'

He was shorter than Collis had imagined him to be, and somehow plainer. He was, indeed, a very plain man. There were cuts on his fingers from handling threads and fabrics, and on the third finger of his left hand, a gold wedding band. It matched Hannah's.

'I was looking for a workbox,' Collis said. 'For a gift, you understand. A niece of mine. Very keen on sewing.'

Walter West pulled thoughtfully at his beard. 'I see. Well we have a variety. It depends how much you wish to spend.'

Collis didn't answer. He had been listening to Walter West's voice, which was kind, but rather reedy, instead of to what he had actually been saying. He looked up and said: 'Hm? I beg your pardon?'

'I said, it depends how much you wish to spend. You see, we have a fancy one here, with a picture on the lid, varnished, and the inside fully lined with sateen, and that comes out at one dollar and twenty-three cents. But if you didn't wish to lay out as much as that, this one here is plainer, but large, and it has a diamond-shaped mirror in the back, which is attractive.'

Collis cast his eyes over the two workboxes which Walter West had produced for him from beneath the counter. He had to admit that he didn't know a damned thing about workboxes, and it was almost embarrassing to meet a man who did. How could Hannah think of staying with a man like this, who spent all his hours surrounded by Newton suiting and washable buttons? He was probably worthy, and Christian, and an excellent husband, but a woman like Hannah deserved so much more. At least, he imagined she did.

'Are . . . either of these to your liking?' inquired Walter West, puzzled by Collis's silence.

'What? I'm sorry.'

237

'I have more in my store room. I could get them out for you.'

'No, no, don't trouble to do that. These are – well, these are very suitable.'

'Which one would you like?'

Collis reached into his pocket for his purse. 'The – er, varnished one. That one. Thank you.'

'Would you care for it gift-wrapped? That's three cents more.'

'Yes. That sounds like a good idea.'

Walter West tugged pink tissue from a roll beside the counter and began to wrap the workbox up. As he neatly creased the paper and folded it, he said, 'You're from the East, aren't you?'

'That's right,' said Collis. 'New York.'

'Recent arrival?'

'Very. I came on the *California* yesterday morning.'

'Come to look for your fortune, huh?' Walter West smiled.

'Something of that kind.'

There was a pause, while Walter West went to find ribbon to tie around the paper. Then, as he made a bow and pulled at the satin with the blade of his scissors so that it would curl, he said, 'My wife's on her way out here from New York.'

'Is that so?'

Walter West raised his eyes. To Collis's discomfiture, they were radiant with optimism and affection. Collis gave a quick, jerky smile and then looked away.

'She had to stay behind when I came out here. She had a sick mother, you see. But she's on her way out here now.'

'You must be looking forward to it very much,' said Collis.

'I can't tell you,' said Walter West. 'It's been real hard and lonesome, setting up this place on my own, without her. We wrote to each other, of course, but a letter isn't anything like having the woman you adore right by your side to help you.'

'No,' said Collis. He wished to God that Walter West would confine his remarks to the goods in hand, and stop making him feel so infernally guilty. The poor man seemed so vulnerably upright and well-meaning that to take Hannah away from him would be like shooting a wide-eyed, flop-eared rabbit from point-blank range.

'It's been two years,' said Walter West. 'I don't know whether you've ever been deprived of the company of the woman you love for two years, sir, but I can tell you that it's days of sadness and nights of real despair. I used to sit up in my bed some nights and look at the moon, and think to myself that same moon was shining over my Hannah even then, and that used to break my heart.'

'I'm sure both of you have borne it with tremendous fortitude,' Collis said.

'Thank you, sir. I think we did our best. It's been a trial right to the end, though. My wife got sick of the fever crossing the Panama isthmus, and she had to stay in the hospital for a couple of weeks. The captain of the *California* sent me a note yesterday afternoon that she was recovering, though, and I thank God for that.'

'She's lucky,' whispered Collis.

'I'm sorry?'

'I said, she's lucky.'

'Yes, I guess she is. But I'm luckier still. I'll have her here in a week, if all goes well, and then you can bet a gold mine to a hole in the ground that I'm going to be the happiest and the proudest man in the whole of this city.'

Walter West finished packing up the workbox and set it square on the top of the counter.

'There,' he said. 'I guess that'll make your young niece's day for her.'

'Yes,' said Collis. He shook two silver dollars out of his purse and laid them on the counter next to the parcel. Two sharp clicks of metal on glass. 'You won't think I'm impertinent if I ask you a question?' he said.

'I guess not. I guess it depends what the question is.'

'Well, it's this. When you said about your wife . . . well, being away so long . . .'

'Yes?'

Collis looked at him carefully. If there was any flinching, no matter how slight, he wanted to catch it. 'Did you ever, during those two years that you were without her, did you ever feel that perhaps you didn't love her any more?'

Walter West frowned. The sun was on his hand, and his wedding band, scored with thousands of scratches from hundreds of days of lonely work, gave off a dull, solid gleam.

'I'm not sure I get your drift,' he said, obviously a little upset. 'I've loved my wife from the day I met her, and if anything at all, I'm fonder of her now than I was when I had to leave her behind.'

Collis listened to this without changing his expression. It was all exactly as he feared it would be. Hannah would arrive in San Francisco, and this bearded haberdasher's dogged lonesomeness and patent need would make it impossible for her to break free from him. After all the strange conversations in Panama, after all the veiled promises and protestations of profane love, his affair with Hannah amounted to no more than this store, with its silks and its threads, and this dull man behind the glass counter. It all *weighed* too much, in the scales of Christianity and guilt, and all that Collis had to counterbalance it with was gossamer.

'I've changed my mind,' Collis said suddenly.

'I'm sorry,' Walter West asked him. 'What about?'

'About the workbox. I don't think my niece will really like it after all.'

'Well . . .' said Walter West, hesitantly.

'I have a marvellous idea,' put in Collis, before he could start objecting. 'Why don't you give it to your wife, when she arrives here?'

'My wife? Why should you want to give a workbox to my wife?'

'I don't, but now I've put you to all this trouble, gift-wrapping and so on, I don't like to walk out without buying the box. Let me buy it, and you can give it your wife.'

'That's very generous of you,' said Walter West, completely foxed. 'But who shall I say gave it? She'll know it wasn't me.'

Collis thought for a moment. Then he said, 'I know. Tell her it came from an anonymous but adoring admirer.'

Walter West gazed down at the workbox in its pink tissue paper, and then at Collis, and his face didn't look happy at all.

'Go on,' Collis said, 'it's just a joke. You can tell her what really happened later.'

Walter West, still frowning, opened up his cash register and counted out Collis's change. Collis slipped the coins into his purse, raised his hat, and walked back out into the street without another word. He turned once he was on the boardwalk and squinted back into the shadowy doorway. There, on the counter, was the pink-wrapped box, and there, standing behind it, his eyebrows dense with thought, was the husband of the woman he thought he loved.

He walked on to the post office on Washington Street. Since the *California* had come in yesterday with sacks of mail from the East, the street outside was crowded with lines of men waiting to collect their letters. Here there was a mixture of men of all kinds, miners and drifters shuffling in line with banker's clerks and auctioneers and servants from the big houses. Some of them talked and argued, and shook hands with acquaintances they may not have seen since the last mail steamer came in; others waited with their heads bowed, moving forward a step at a time to the pillared porch of the post office. A newsboy in a dirty shirt and bare feet walked along the lines selling copies of the *Tribune*. Collis joined the end of the line because he had nobody to wait for him.

It took him twenty minutes to get inside the post office, and it was a chaotic, disorganised, noisy scramble to reach the counter to collect his mail. The clerk, a blue pencil behind each prominent ear, quickly sorted through the E's and found two letters addressed to Collis.

He pushed his way back outside. For no reason that he could think of, he found that he was trembling. He walked next door, to a grocery store called Garret House, and found a spare wooden chair on the boardwalk, where he sat down. A man in faded blue dungarees leaned against the open door of the store smoking a pipe and watching him with unabashed interest.

One letter was from his mother. He recognised the spiky handwriting. The other handwriting he didn't know at all. It was loopy, slanting, and lean, and from all appearances, it was that of a woman. He tore open the letter from his mother first.

Collis,

It is with great sadness that I have to write to tell you that your dear father has passed away. He died of his heart ailment only three days after you set sail from New York, despite the best efforts of his doctors to save him. The strain of his business problems and the many personal difficulties he was having to face were all too much for him.

I suppose you will expect me to say that his passing was inevitable, and that I will forgive your conduct towards him in the last few days of his life. But I would not be true to my feelings if I said that. There was much that you did that was selfish and senseless, and which only served to aggravate your father's burden of ill health. It is possible that I will forgive you in time, but while I am in mourning I would prefer not to hear from you, or *of* you.

Your sister Maude and I are as well as might be expected. We are going to stay with friends in Sherman, Connecticut, who have a small cottage in their grounds. Your father's old friend Neiman Bennett is acting as executor, and he is being most generous with his time in settling the complications of your father's estate.

I am sure that you will join me in my prayers for the eternal rest of your dear father's soul; and I know that you will reflect for many years to come on how thoughtlessness towards others brings only sorrow, pain, and grief.

I am,
Your Mother

Collis read the letter twice, and then folded it up. He raised his eyes to the lines of men waiting outside the post office, and saw two or three men like himself, standing with torn-open letters in their hands, their faces saddened and numbed. He couldn't hold back a deep sob in his throat, and the man in the dungarees shifted his position and regarded him with even more obvious curiosity. He could hardly believe that his father was gone; his argumentative father with his broad black-vested abdomen that had always seemed to Collis like some permanent and enduring edifice, as solid and invincible as the bow of a man-of-war, or the buttresses of a church. He tried to imagine what his father had looked like, tried to picture the erratic eye and the grey moustache, but somehow he could only recall that childhood image of his father's vest, with its long gold watch chain.

So, Makepeace Edmonds was gone, and already interred, no doubt watched over by a white marble angel.

Collis opened the second letter. It was written on thin, flimsy paper, and he had to spread it across his knee with the side of his hand. On the head of the letter was written 'Orangeburg, South Carolina'. It was from Alice Stride.

My dear Collis,

You may be wondering why you are hearing from *me*, and not from Delphine. Well, the news may not have reached you yet, or you would understand. The Ohio Life and Mutual Trust Company, of which Mr Spooner is a vice-president and also a stockholder, has gone spectacularly bankrupt! It happened on 24 August, and many other Wall Street banks and brokers have been dragged to ruin. There is talk of specie payments being suspended at the banks, and thousands of men are out of work and roaming the streets. My father says that it

242

is one of the worst crises of our age, but that it is the inevitable result of worthless speculation in mining and railroad bonds.

'He should know,' Collis said to himself, under his breath. Then he went on to read:

The Spooners will probably have to leave their house and sell most of their valuables to pay their debts. Delphine, of course, is stricken and she begged me not to tell you, but I thought it only fair for you to know, rather than to wait for months in vain for the letter she will not send you. I know she loves you still. She talks of you all the time. But she will not hear of your marrying a pauper bride, and she knows she must give you up.

Please write if you have news of yourself. For myself, I am very well, and would much appreciate some correspondence.

I remain your affectionate friend,
Alice Stride

As if by coincidence, the barefooted newsboy came past waving copies of the *Tribune* and calling, 'New York banks suspend specie payment! New York banks suspend specie payment! Latest news by the Concord stage!'

Collis stood up and walked across the square. It was almost lunchtime, and he knew that he had to go back to Knickerbocker Jane's to meet Charles. But somehow he felt that he wanted just a moment or two to reflect, on his own, on the morning's losses. He began to walk up Sansome Street, past the shacks and the shanties and the cooking fires, watched by miners and loafers and gamblers, until eventually he came out on the sandy summit of Telegraph Hill, under the arms of the semaphore which signalled the arrival of incoming ships, with the wind whipping his hair, and the glittering bay spread beneath him.

He did not weep. But he stood there, with his hands in his pockets, his shoulders a little hunched, while across the rooftops of the business district a clock sonorously struck twelve, and seagulls turned and called above his head.

Chapter 6

Charles was already waiting for him at the Auction Lunch when he arrived, and waved to him over the crowd of stovepipe hats, which dipped and bobbed like the black funnels of a harbourful of steamships. The saloon was packed to the door, and almost deafeningly noisy with laughter and shouting and the earnest midday conversation of San Francisco's businessmen. A broad-faced whiskered man in a high silk hat and a formal suit gave Collis a nod of welcome as he came in; and as Collis elbowed his way towards the counter where Charles and his friends were waiting, he was surprised to see that another man in a high silk hat was serving the drinks and slicing up the corned beef and pickles behind the bar.

'Very nobby waiters they have here,' he remarked to Charles, as he shook his hand.

'Aha,' said Charles, 'there's a story behind that. But first meet my friends. This is Lloyd Wintle, the president of the Western Bank; and this is Arthur Teach, of Pacific Securities. Arthur claims he's a full-blooded descendant of Blackbeard the Pirate, which may or may not be.'

Collis extended his hand, first to Lloyd Wintle and then to Arthur Teach. Wintle was willowy and tall, with a nose that overhung his face like a flag overhanging a parade ground on a sultry day. His eyes were pale, and emphatically underlined with bags, and his hat appeared to lean at an unusual angle. But Collis had the impression from his handshake that he was determined, and competent to a degree, and rich, whereas Teach, who was far broader, and more whiskery, and who looked as if he could ravish somebody else's wife and chop logs at the same time, was poorer, and hungrier, and politically more radical.

'Nice to meet you, Mr Edmonds,' Lloyd Wintle said, with a noticeable Michigan accent, that particular articulation of flattened vowels from the back of the throat. 'Charles has been saying you're interested in railroads, and in cards. Understand you shot a dealer's hat to pieces last night, at the Eagle Saloon.'

Collis shrugged. 'I'm more interested in railroads than I am in shooting hats to pieces.'

'You sure you're not still suffering from isthmusitis?' said Arthur

Teach. 'Most of the railroad fanatics we meet around here are trying to redress a bad experience at Panama.'

The silk-hatted man behind the bar raised an eyebrow to Collis, as if to ask him what he wanted, and Collis asked, 'Can you mix a stone fence?'

The man nodded, and reached behind him to the shelves of liquor to bring down a bottle of bourbon and a jug of sweet cider.

'That's Jimmy Flood there, behind the bar,' said Charles. 'Billy O'Brien stands at the door, inviting folks in, and Jimmy mixes the drinks and cuts the bacon. They were friends from way back. They met in Poor Man's Gulch, and they both made up their minds to open shops here in San Francisco. Jimmy opened a livery store, and Billy opened a marine supply shop – or was it the other way about? But anyway, they both got wiped out by fire in '55. So they opened the Auction Lunch in the financial district here, and if you ask me they're going to make themselves rich one day, though not from selling lunches. But they keep their ears open to all the financial gossip, and they buy whatever stock their customers recommend, and that's how.'

Arthur Teach swallowed beer, leaving white foam clinging to his moustache, and he asked Collis, 'Do you think you've got that kind of a mind? The kind of a mind that can turn hard luck into hard cash?'

Jimmy Flood brought Collis's drink and set it on the battered and glass-ringed mahogany counter. Collis picked it up and then raised it as if to imply that he was drinking to Teach's health, and to Wintle's continuing good fortune, and to Charles's friendship. But he said nothing, and kept his face expressionless, and he could see that Wintle and Teach were more than a little unsettled. That was the way Collis preferred his new acquaintances to be, for the time being. He was a stranger around here, a tenderfoot, and he didn't know the fandango halls from the fish docks, and the only possible chance of keeping an edge was to act tight, and short on humour.

'Mr Wintle and me, we're always looking for investments, day and night,' explained Teach. 'Good sound mining projects. Commodities. Shipping. All that kind of thing. But the way we see it, any project needs two essential factors if it's going to work. It needs *vision*. You understand what I mean by vision? And it needs solid hard *workability*. Both those two. Because one won't get off its ass without the other, and the other won't pay back dividends without the one. You got me?'

Collis sipped his drink. He still didn't answer. Charles gave his friends a restless, jesting grin, as if to suggest that Collis wasn't always this way.

'That's why,' Teach added, 'I was impertinent enough to question you about your idea for a railroad. This dream that Charles tells me you have for spanning the continent. It's a pretty fancy dream. A big vision. Don't get me wrong. But it's going to need some pretty damned hard workability, too. You got me?'

Lloyd Wintle said lugubriously, 'I heard of a scheme for taking railroad locomotives over the High Sierras by hot-air balloon, with platforms hung beneath for the freight. I heard of another scheme for harnessing teams of moles, and digging right under the mountains altogether. Pretty crack-brained, huh? But those are the kind of schemes people come up with, and they come asking us for finance. Five thousand moles, all harnessed up, can you picture it?'

Collis took out a cheroot and lit it. 'You want a corned-beef sandwich?' Charles asked, but Collis shook his head.

Arthur Teach put down his empty bourbon glass. 'Charles gave you a pretty high recommendation, Mr Edmonds. I can call you Collis, can't I? But I just think you ought to know that some of the airy-fairy ideas you Easterners might have about the West, well, they're not strictly justified. We've learned to look after ourselves out here, and if we spend our money wildly on occasions, it's simply because we choose to, and not because we've been cajoled into supporting some hare-brained project or other.'

Lloyd Wintle nodded sadly. 'Some fellow came out here and said he'd thought up a way to send the human voice along a telegraph wire. Can you picture that? Thirty-five thousand dollars he wanted, for experiments. The human voice! By wire!'

Collis dropped his gaze. Beneath his grey frock coat, Lloyd Wintle's pants hung around his long legs in folds as elaborate and self-conscious as Leonardo da Vinci's drawings of drapery.

'We're interested in you,' Arthur Teach said, 'and whatever you do, because Charles says you're an interesting fellow. But I believe it's only fair to warn you that you're going to need more than dreams to make your fortune out here, and more than a couple of lucky games of faro. You're going to need substance. You look up on Rincon Hill, at South Park. Now there's substance. And substance comes from having what the people here really need, and what they'll pay for. Do you know something? There's a shipload of blankets coming in on Thursday next, on the *Aria*. Thousands and

246

thousands of pure wool blankets. And who do you think's going to be down on the dock, waiting for that ship, and waiting to buy up every single blanket she's carrying, even though it's still summer? Me. That's who. Because in a month it's going to be fall, and in another month it's going to be winter, and suddenly the folks of San Francisco are going to start feeling the cold and looking out for blankets. And who do you think is going to be the proud and profitable possessor of every blanket in town? Well, you guessed it, and that's what I mean by substance. Don't deal in dreams, Collis. Deal in substance. You got me?'

'You don't think a railroad's substantial?' Collis said.

'Not the dream of a railroad. No, sir.'

'So you wouldn't invest in a railroad?'

'Not unless I could see the surveys, and the projections of profit and loss.'

'You think Queen Isabella saw surveys and projections of profit and loss when she financed Columbus?'

'She had the latest information available. That's all I'm asking for.'

'Even though it's self-evident that a transcontinental railroad must be the most historic and dramatic project this country has ever known?'

'History and drama aren't the same as profits and dividends, Mr Edmonds,' Lloyd Wintle said softly. 'Not by a long chalk. And what Mr Teach is saying is that, in the end, it all comes down to profits and dividends.'

'Collis is just arrived, you know, Lloyd,' Charles put in uneasily. 'He hasn't even had the opportunity to look around town, and size up the possibilities. This railroad talk, well, it's only talk. Only a suggestion. For the first few months, Collis is going to come out to Sacramento and work for me.'

Teach raised a gingery eyebrow. 'What does Collis have to say about that?'

Collis smiled. 'What do you want me to say?'

'I don't know,' said Teach. 'You don't look like the kind of fellow who'd knuckle down to hardware and dry goods and really enjoy it. Not when your mind is buzzing with railroads.'

Collis thoughtfully drew smoke from his cheroot. 'I'm looking forward to working for Charles for a while, as a matter of fact. There are one or two important gaps in my education, particularly when it comes to business. I can play a tolerable game of faro, and ride a horse for sport. But if I'm ever going to lay a railroad line across those mountains, I'm going to require other abilities, too. Like working out the cost of timber, for railroad ties; and buying up spikes and rails. Like buying the right make of locomotive for the right reasons, and knowing how to work it. Like dealing with labourers and surveyors, and understanding how to lead them, and how to give them the same sense of purpose that I'm going to need.'

'You don't know any of that already?' asked Arthur Teach, gently gibing him. 'You make yourself sound uniquely unqualified, if you don't mind my saying so.'

'You can't be too hard there, Arthur,' Charles said. 'Nobody's ever done this before, right? It's not like asking a man if he's qualified to fix a barn.'

'Well, I don't know,' said Teach, throwing back a straight shot of whisky and coughing loudly. 'I'm not so sure that a cross-country railroad isn't anything more than a dream, and that it isn't going to stay that way, given the present state of railroad engineering. Maybe in twenty, thirty years' time. But who can afford to tie up good investment capital for twenty or thirty years?'

'I suppose you're making some sense,' said Wintle sadly.

Collis finished his drink and banged his glass on the bar. 'Gentlemen,' he said, 'I must be leaving you.'

'Collis – you can't go yet,' said Charles.

'I have to. I'm sorry. I need a new pair of evening shoes, and my white tie went missing last night. I wouldn't normally trouble, but I'm supposed to go out with Knickerbocker Jane tonight to see Rodney Mulgrave.'

'And quite apart from that, you don't like the way we're talking about your pet railroad scheme, do you?' asked Arthur Teach. He kept his eyes on Collis as he lit a small thin cigar, pinched out the match between finger and thumb, and blew smoke from his hairy nostrils.

Collis sighed. 'Mr Teach, Arthur, I'm not a railroad fanatic. I don't know a footplate from a funnel. But I do understand simple sense, and simple sense tells me it is well over five thousand miles from New York to San Francisco by sea, including an awkward crossing of the isthmus, while it is only three thousand miles from New York to San Francisco by land. Simple sense tells me many other things, too – such as the certain fact that every sod farmer and miner and cattle owner from Nebraska to California would go down on his knees and welcome a railroad across the breadth of this country as a godsend. A head of kale picked in Utah on Monday could be served up with butter in a New York restaurant by Friday; just as a plough blade cold-cast in Pennsylvania on Friday could be delivered to a Wyoming farmer within the week. You could move soldiers, too, and horses, and they would arrive fresh for battle in half the time. It's all simple sense, Mr Teach, whether the technical details have been worked out or not.'

Teach tugged at his moustache and then cleared his throat. But he didn't answer. 'You still don't think that it's feasible?' asked Collis.

Collis glanced over at Charles, but Charles was wearing a distinctly vacant face. From that, Collis surmised that Teach and Wintle were probably quite typical of San Francisco financiers, and that they were not entranced, as a rule, by daydreams. Too many innovators and too many eccentrics came to San Francisco with too many grandiose schemes, and too many thousands of dollars had already been lost in the financing of gas mantles that would never burn out, and automatic buttonhooks, and cargoes of unusual cheese. Until someone could show with surveys and graphs that a railroad *could* be laid through the Sierras, at least as far as Nevada, and that, once built, it would return some kind of sensible profit to its shareholders, finding support among San Francisco's business community was going to be more than sticky. Collis understood their reticence. He was a gambling man himself. And despite his idyllic mental picture of a shiny railroad locomotive puffing and whistling its way through seas of waving wheat, bringing the cheers and huzzahs and tossed-up hats of settlers and farmers and factory builders, despite his vision of American plains that would soon be ploughed and harrowed and bustling with broccoli, and American hills that would be crowded as poppy fields with red-roofed farmhouses and Dutch barns, he wasn't at all sure himself that a train could really make its way up and over the Sierras, up gradients as steep as slated church roofs, through snowdrifts that could bury a pioneers' parade, trumpets, hats, bunting, pioneers, and all, without a trace, and he wasn't at all sure that such a railroad could really make money, not *instinctively* sure. He didn't yet have the experience or the skill to judge profitability by eye.

'Do either of you gentlemen play cards?' he asked, in a tone of voice that made it sound as if he hadn't changed the subject at all.

'I'm afraid not,' said Wintle. 'My family's never held with gambling. We're plain church people, if you can picture it

249

'I'm not averse to a little gambling,' said Teach. He tapped the counter for another drink.

Collis smiled. 'That's good. Maybe I can make you a bet.'

Charles grinned uncomfortably. 'Collis has kind of a penchant for making wagers, don't you, Collis? He bet Andy Hunt last night that the first fellow to walk into the Eagle would be wearing a checkered vest, and by heck the fellow was.'

Teach watched Collis suspiciously. His eyes were bulbous and hooded, like a frog's. 'Name your wager,' he said in a quiet voice.

'All right,' said Collis. 'I bet you that I can have the Sierras surveyed for a railroad route by the spring, financed out of my own pocket, and that I can lay a line through to Nevada by the time five years is up. And if I win the bet, you'll have to buy me lunch at the International, and invest fifty per cent of whatever liquid assets you have in my railroad.'

Teach paused for a moment. Then he extended his hand, hard and short-fingered, with a single gold signet ring. 'It's done,' he said. 'And if *you* lose, I'll take fifty per cent of whatever liquid assets *you* might own at the time. But I'll forgo the lunch. This,' he said, raising his glass, 'is all I usually take at midday.'

There was a sudden lull in the saloon's laughter and conversation, and Collis had the disturbing feeling that the floor had moved under his feet.

'Earthquake,' Charles said, unconcerned.

Collis spent a long time dressing that evening. Out of his winnings from the Eagle Saloon, he had been down to Wills the tailor's and bought himself a new dress shirt, a new necktie, and a silk hat. He had also found a very reasonable shoemaker on Sacramento Street and had spent twenty dollars on a new pair of black kid pumps.

He had considered going into mourning for his father for a week or two, but after three stone fences he had decided it was really not worth it. His father was 3000 miles away, and buried, and they'd never been warm friends in any case. A prayer for his soul would have to be enough, and perhaps a very small private wish for forgiveness. Not that he'd ever tell his mother.

Outside his bedroom window, as he tied his tie, the sky was a pale grey-blue, and the lights in the houses opposite were smudged with fog. It was eight o'clock, dusk, and downstairs he could hear the bustling of full-flounced dresses and an occasional screech of annoyance as Knickerbocker Jane finished her gaudy and elaborate *toilette*. He leaned close to his mirror and snipped his sidewhiskers with a small pair of scissors.

At eight-fifteen, the doorbell rang downstairs and there was a commotion in the hall as the rest of the theatre party arrived. Knickerbocker Jane was fussing around them in a tiered dress of plum-coloured silk, a tiara of yellow ostrich plumes bobbing on top of her coiffure. Collis, as he came downstairs, thought she looked like an exotic bird. Apart from Collis and Knickerbocker Jane, the party included Charles Tucker, who was dressed in an old-fashioned evening coat with immensely wide sateen lapels, and who carried on his arm, almost as if she were a decorative umbrella, a short, angelic-faced girl with a ridiculously overdecorated bonnet and a gown of bottle-green silk; and there was Samuel Lewis, a Brobdingnagian man with wavy white hair and a crimson weather-corroded face that hung over every gathering of his more diminutive friends like a bloated harvest moon, portending things but never quite coming out with them. Sam Lewis was the president of the Bullion & Marine Bank, and the most influential member of the San Francisco Chamber of Commerce, but his aging bachelorhood and his habit of smoking particularly foul cigars had never endeared him to the South Park Chivalry. He was going to escort Knickerbocker Jane, and he stooped over to kiss her when he arrived as if he were bending over a plate of Italian noodles.

Collis was to go with the Brazilian girl, Ursula, who was dressed like the fifth prize in a South American church lottery, in shiny orange silk, her black frizzy hair covered by a cowl-shaped bonnet with ruffled white ribbons woven through the crown and a large floppy white bow at the neck. She bobbed a curtsy as she took Collis's arm, and afforded him a waft of thick patchouli perfume.

The girl on Charles Tucker's arm, Collis found out, was called Elsie, and she was the daughter of a joiner and carpenter called Billings, whose premises were on Market Street, and whose greatest claim to professional fame was that he had boarded over the ship *Niantic* after she had been dragged ashore from the Bay, so that her owners could open her up as one of San Francisco's first hotels. Elsie had a simpering, irritating voice, and Collis couldn't listen to her for very long, but Charles assured him that she knew a great deal about knurled prick punches, and adjustable spokeshaves, and ball-bearing breast drills, and anything and everything to do with a joiner's trade.

'It's not often you meet a girl who can tickle your fancy one day

and build you a combination bookcase the next,' Charles told
Collis, as they went outside on to the boardwalk to meet their
carriages.

Charles Tucker's down-at-heel phaeton was waiting at the
curbside, with Billy on the box in a heavy brown overcoat of marled
tweed. Charles helped Elsie aboard and then climbed aboard
himself. Billy tipped his tall silk hat and inquired, 'The Empire,
Mr Tucker?'

'That's right, Billy.'

Next, Sam Lewis's cabriolet pulled up, with an excessive amount
of jingling and bridle-shaking. It was a very nobby job indeed, this
carriage, with shining brasses, a black leather hood, and body
panels finished in shining Brewster green paint. The coachman
wore a grey brass-buttoned coat, and a black beaver hat, and
sported one of the reddest noses that Collis could ever remember,
and he could remember a few. He climbed down and assisted
Knickerbocker Jane and Ursula to mount up, and then he helped
Collis and Sam Lewis aboard.

Outside the white-porticoed theatre, with its flaring lamps, the
plaza was an impossible confusion of surreys and coaches and
shouting people. Collis, looking around, could see the black-and-
carmine carriages of the very rich, the South Park millionaires, and
the light yellow-and-beige runabouts of the young and debonair.
There was a smell of excitement and fog in the evening air, and
everywhere around there were men in evening dress with white ties
and curved white shirt fronts and silver-topped canes, and women
with velvet evening cloaks and sparkling jewellery. Perfume and
cigar smoke rose into the fog, and from the alley beside the theatre
came the spicy aroma of shrimp chop suey, stirred over a makeshift
charcoal fire by a pigtailed Chinese. It was impossible for Collis to
decide which of the handsome couples who were alighting from
their carriages and making their way through the wide-open doors
of the theatre were respectable, and socially elevated, and which
were not. After all, in a city where desk clerks wore diamonds and
prostitutes were dressed in the latest French fashions, it was often
the respectable who followed the styles of the sleazy, instead of the
other way about. Collis pointed to one gorgeous creature who wore
a glittering tiara and was arrayed in ostrich feathers dyed dark blue,
and was told by Knickerbocker Jane that this was Harriet
DeLancey, the most expensive prostitute in the whole city. But she
also pointed out the Thomas Selbys, looking absurdly pleased with

252

themselves as they were helped from their coach and the fat little Milton Lathams; and Senator William Gwin, dignified as a sailing yacht, with his wife Mary Bell. Someone let off some Chinese firecrackers, rattling and popping, and there was a good deal of laughter and shouting, and loud abuse from a coachman whose horses had been frightened.

'Can you see the Melfords here?' Collis asked in Knickerbocker Jane's ear.

She shook her head. 'They usually arrive late, so that everybody will notice them. They have a reserved box in the front.'

'Then I shan't miss seeing them?'

'Oh, no. You won't miss seeing the Melfords.'

Their cabriolet was able to push its way to the front of the theatre at last, and they were assisted on to the crowded boardwalk by Sam Lewis's coachman. Sam Lewis, head and shoulders above the throng of people, announced, 'We're going to walk to the Oriental for dinner when all this dangdratted thespianism is over. So meet us there at twelve, precise.'

The coachman touched his beaver hat, climbed up on to his seat again, and snapped his whip. Collis was left on the boardwalk with Ursula, trying desperately to push his way through the crowds of theatregoers and curious by-standers, and to follow Sam Lewis's enormous white head through the glass-and-pearwood doors of the Empire.

Inside, the foyer was more like the saloon of a sinking ship than a place of entertainment. The enthusiasm of the theatregoers verged on panic. Above them, a large chandelier sparkled, and there were red drapes hung all around, but they did very little to alter the impression that the Empire was simply a box into which a ridiculously large number of very excited people had jammed themselves. Collis kept his arm around Ursula's shoulder as they forced their way to the doors of the auditorium itself, and it took five minutes of struggling and jostling before, ruffled and slightly glassy-eyed, they finally found themselves in Sam Lewis's box.

Collis took out his handkerchief and dabbed at his forehead. Although it was chilly outside, the temperature inside the Empire was fierce. It was a theatre designed in the traditional manner, with a gilded proscenium over which two cherubs blew hunting horns, and with heavy red drapes; but there was nothing traditional about the way in which the audience behaved. They didn't arrive calmly and take their seats, the way an audience would have done in

New York, and await the performance in a murmur of polite conversation. Instead, they seemed determined to jump up and down, and argue, and shout to each other at the top of their voices, and wave, so that the main body of the stalls had the appearance of a squabbling flock of black-and-white gulls, all black evening coats and white shirts, bobbling and jostling, and the heat that was generated was enough to make Collis feel like fighting his way out into the plaza again and pressing his forehead against a cold store window.

Knickerbocker Jane opened her silver-link evening purse and took out a small engraved flask. 'Will this help?' she whispered to Collis. 'You look as if you're just about to shake off this mortal shackle.'

Collis gratefully took the flask, wrapped it in his handkerchief, and quickly tipped his head back to take a shot. It was cognac, VSOP, and it sank down inside him with a warmth and smoothness that slowed his pulse rate and brightened his eyes.

'Thank you,' he said, passing the flask back.

'I'd rather be in hell than here, how about you, Collis?' said Sam Lewis.

Collis coughed. 'I don't know. At least when you're here, you can leave when it's over.'

'Well, sure,' said Sam Lewis, 'but the virtue of hell is that they don't expect you to sit through some dangdratted thespianism, as well as roast.'

From the side of the auditorium, the orchestra began to troop in with their instruments. They sat in their pit, and shuffled their scores, and kept knocking over their music stands, and even when they were ready they took out a variety of handkerchiefs and blew their noses loudly as if they were retaliating against the audience. When they were quite finished, the conductor strutted in, a small Italian with curled-up whiskers and a shock of silver hair, and he stood in the limelight that illuminated his rostrum while everyone clapped, and a few of the less couth elements actually cheered. The next five minutes were spent in doleful tuning up.

Sam Lewis said to Collis, 'Charles tells me you're going out to Sacramento to work for him and Leland McCormick. Get yourself some business knowhow.'

'I was thinking of it,' said Collis.

'Well, you couldn't learn business under anybody tougher than Leland,' remarked Sam. He took out a black snakeskin cigar case and offered it around, but both Charles and Collis declined. He stuck one in his own mouth, and patted the pockets of his evening suit for matches, but nobody offered him a light. 'Charles tells me you're interested in railroads.'

'Railroads had crossed my mind.'

'Well, if I were you, son, I'd let them cross your mind and keep on going. Railroads are poison. And the reason they're poison is because you're investing your money in something that, once you've laid it, can't be moved. Look at that Theodore Jones fellow, the one out in Sacramento. Colonel Wilson brought him in to lay a line from Sacramento to Folsom, twenty-two miles of track, because Folsom was rich with gold. But what happened? The dangdratted gold mines gave out, and three-quarters of Folsom's population drifted away, and what was he left with? Twenty-two miles of roadbed and rails going absolutely noplace at all. And besides, no train could ever get over the Sierra Nevada unless you took it off its rails and hauled it over by mule.'

'I'll lay you a bet,' said Collis.

Charles raised a gingery eyebrow and tried to signal to Collis to behave more cautiously, but Collis felt determined. The more he heard from men like Teach and Wintle and Lewis that a transcontinental railroad was out of the question, the more certain he was that someone could build it. It *must* be possible. He couldn't believe that God could create a country so wealthy and free and fertile and leave it permanently divided by a range of impassable mountains; nor that He could allow so many people to suffer and die on their way through Panama without their lives at least having inspired others to find a way through the Rockies and the Sierra Nevada. It didn't make sense, to man or God. It had to be done, even if it couldn't be done.

'What will you bet, Mr Edmonds?' asked Sam Lewis. 'Will you bet you can drive a railroad locomotive right through the Sierra Nevada?'

'I'll bet I can find a pass, and prove it possible, within five years,' said Collis.

'And if you can? What do *I* have to do? Promise to give up cigars?'

'You have to invest one hundred thousand dollars in my railroad company, no questions asked.'

'But you don't have a railroad company.'

'At this rate, it looks as though I very shortly will.'

Sam Lewis let a dribble of cigar smoke escape from between his puckered lips. 'All right,' he said, 'it's a fair bet, and you're on. But what will you do for me if you can't prove that it's possible?'

'Mr Lewis,' said Collis. 'I'll buy you this theatre, so that you can have the express pleasure of burning it down.'

Sam Lewis gave a boiled, crimson, crinkly smile. Then he reached across and shook Collis's hand. 'You're definitely on. Definitely. It looks as though I can't lose either way, and by God, I've always wanted to burn down this dangdratted place.'

At that moment, Knickerbocker Jane reached over and touched Collis's shoulder. He turned towards her, and she nodded her head meaningfully towards the other side of the auditorium. He looked and saw that the curtains at the back of the Melfords' box were opening, and that the theatre manager himself was ushering the Melford family to their seats.

Knickerbocker Jane, without a word, passed over a pair of mother-of-pearl opera glasses, and Collis raised them to his eyes. The first to take her seat was Althea Melford, a tall, straight-backed woman in her middle forties, with coppery-brown hair drawn back from her face, and dangling ringlets. Her face was sharp, high-cheekboned, and Collis could almost imagine her as a queen of ancient Greece, or as Agrippina, tired of contemplating the ashes of Germanicus, and ready at last for a night of entertainment among hoi polloi. In her pale-blue silk evening gown and her diamonds and pearls, she stepped forward with a classic and haughty mien and sat down as if she were taking her throne.

Behind her, in a tizzy, came a woman who was obviously some relative or visitor, with a muddled hair-style and a black dress that would have been five years out of date in New York. She sat down abruptly and nervously next to Althea Melford, and dropped her purse. The orchestra played 'When the Moon on the Lake Is Beaming', but everybody's attention, surreptitiously or not, was on the Melfords' box. Someone in the stalls, for no reason at all, started to clap.

At last, the curtains parted again, and into the box came the girl for whom Collis had been waiting with such nervous anticipation – Sarah Melford. He knew it was she. She was taller than her mother, and just as straight-backed, but while her mother's hair was combed away from her forehead, Sarah's was curled in long glossy ringlets all around, and parted in the centre, shiny and brown as chestnuts. Her face was exquisite, with startlingly large brown eyes, and clearly defined cheekbones, and a nose that was thin but quite straight. Her lips may have been a little too full, but that could have been the effect of cosmetics. Her neck was long and white, and in her low-bodiced evening gown, as dark yellow as a Canada lily, her white breasts rose full and deeply cleft and decorated with diamonds and gold. She paused as she entered the family box. She was used to being stared at by all of San Francisco. In fact, she plainly expected it. Then, tall as she was, she took her place with unfaltering grace, and opened her yellow silk fan, as if to say, 'That's enough, you've seen all I feel like allowing you to see.'

Collis had been expecting a noticeable girl, even a beautiful girl. But Sarah Melford, from what he could see through his badly focused opera glasses, was a creature out on her own. She had inherited the classic, cold features of her mother; but they were softened somehow by whatever genes her father's family had passed ôn to her, and so she was fashionably pretty as well as perfect in bone structure and bearing. This had the effect of making her erotic, as well as aloof; of making it seem possible that she had earthy desires, as well as elegance. Collis could imagine sitting opposite such a girl at a society dinner, all solid-silver cutlery and sparkling candelabra, and taking off his shoe so that he could inveigle a bare foot up inside her petticoats, and have it gripped in between her hot bare thighs; while above the damascene cloth, feigning unawareness, they spoke of badminton, and riding, and the latest scandal from Washington. Sarah Melford was a rare and wondrous animal, and Collis found himself staring at her as if someone had stunned him with a club. She sat in her chair with utter composure, utter self-assurance, and the stainless confidence that comes from knowing that one is very rich, and very influential, and very beautiful.

Collis was so entranced with Sarah that at first he didn't notice the dark, imposing figure who came into the box and stood behind her. But then he perceived through his opera glasses that there was a broad tanned hand on the back of Sarah's chair, and he followed the hand to a wide white cuff, and then to an arm, and from the arm to a broad, immaculately tailored shoulder. He focused at last on a face, and it was the face of Laurence Melford, one of the most powerful of the California pioneers, a millionaire in gold, whisky, beef, silver, and real estate. A decider of destinies, and a political giant. From what he could make out, in the shadows of the Melfords' box, he was heavy-jowled, stern, bristling with grey eyebrows, like General Zachary Taylor, old Rough and Ready, except that his mouth was softer. He bore himself with the exaggerated dignity that all self-made men affect, as a substitute for illustrious ancestors and a wealthy childhood. Collis could see him turning his head from side to side, not so much as if he was scanning the theatre for anybody he might happen to know, but as if he was generously permitting the audience to admire the various aspects of his craggy and handsome face.

Sarah raised her hand and whispered something in her father's ear, and he bent over her chair. Collis could see Melford smile, and Sarah laugh, and he would have given fifty silver dollars to know what it was they were saying. He put down the opera glasses and looked across at Charles Tucker with an expression of appreciation, but of frustration, too.

'The princess on top of the glass mountain, I'm afraid,' said Knickerbocker Jane. 'The only man who's ever going to win *her* is going to have to be rich, and maybe titled, and at least as clever as Bret Harte.'

'She's right, Collis,' said Charles. 'That girl there is the living definition of the word "impregnable".'

'No girl is *impregnable*,' Collis told him, smiling.

'I think Charlie meant "inaccessible",' put in Sam Lewis. 'But I guess the one goes hand in glove with the other, so to speak.'

'They say she's never even kissed a man,' said Elsie, 'and never been alone in the same room with a boy, not in the whole of her twenty years.'

Collis raised his opera glasses again, but now, rapidly and unsteadily, the auditorium lights began to dim, and the occupants of the Melford box were lost in darkness, except for the occasional glitter of diamonds, or the shadowy flutter of a fan. The orchestra struck up with a scrapy version of 'The Dance of the Dryads', by August Müschler, and with a loud mechanical whirring the drapes across the stage began to open. The audience applauded and cheered and whistled, and Collis wearily peeled off his evening gloves and prepared himself for an evening of provincial entertainment.

Luckily, Rodney Mulgrave wasn't too dreadful, although Collis found his eyes drooping during an interminable scenario entitled 'The Highland Hero, Feared Dead, Returns to His Croft to Discover His Aged Mother Blind', in which Rodney Mulgrave, who was stout, with fiery ginger hair, played both the Highland hero and his aged mother, a double role which involved a great deal

258

of leaping from one side of the stage to the other, and an instant costume change which was effected by wrapping a plaid blanket around his waist (hero's kilt) and then quickly flinging it over his head (aged mother's shawl). Collis revived himself in time for the deeply emotional climax (in which the aged mother fondles her son's face and at last realises that he really has returned alive from the bloody sloughs of Culloden), although he found it hard to believe how the sight of a short fat man in a plaid blanket kneeling on a stage and palpating his own nose could draw such tears and sobs from so many people. Even Knickerbocker Jane was dabbing at her eyes with a handkerchief.

During the intermission, Collis sat where he was, preoccupied and quiet, and smoked a cheroot. Charles and Elsie went off to find champagne and chocolates, while Ursula sprayed herself with more perfume and fanned herself languorously.

Although his head was lowered, Collis had his eyes fixed on the Melford box opposite, where Sarah and her family were drinking iced white wine and laughing with the gaiety of those who know they are being admired. He stared first at Sarah, feeling the soles of his feet fizz with the sheer unusual beauty of her; and then he stared at her father, Laurence, because it was Laurence he was going to have to beat, or win over, if he wanted Sarah and if he wanted San Francisco. Laurence looked as hard and as uncompromising as a mountain in the Sierra Nevada.

At last, only a few minutes before the curtain was due to go up again, and the audience was about to be regaled first with Rodney Mulgrave's Shakespearean selections, and then his 'Soliloquy Spoken by a Marooned Mariner on the Occasion of Washington's Birthday', Collis excused himself, left the box, and walked quickly along the corridor that led around the back of the auditorium, pushing past languid young San Franciscan society dogs in cutaway coats and overdone neckties, and scented harlots in silk dresses who had gathered to make assignations for later in the evening.

He reached the curtains in back of the Melfords' box. They were guarded by a tall, hawk-nosed footman in a green frogged coat and white knee breeches. The footman's eyes swivelled down to look at Collis as a buzzard's eyes revolve to seek out a prairie dog. He said in a chiselled Connecticut accent, 'Yes, sir? Did you want something?'

Collis coughed. 'Well, er, yes. Yes, I did. I was hoping to present my compliments to Mr Melford. I happened to notice that he and his family were present tonight, and, well, I was hoping to present my compliments.'

'Your card, sir?'

'My card?'

The footman smiled a tight smile. 'How can I present your compliments without your card, sir?'

'I just arrived here. I mean, I just arrived in San Francisco. I haven't had occasion to have my cards printed up yet.'

'Then who shall I say is here, sir?'

Collis didn't know why he should feel so intimidated by this white-stockinged flunky. Perhaps it was the power and the wealth and the indomitable beauty that he represented. Perhaps it was the thought of Sarah Melford only two or three feet away from him, concealed by curtains but radiating the kind of magnetic attraction that makes iron filings form extraordinary curves and bars of metal cling to each other in scientific passion.

'Tell him Mr Collis Edmonds, out of New York,' said Collis, more hoarsely than he'd meant to. But then, on an inspiration, he added, 'Tell him it's the gentleman who shot a dealer's hat in the Eagle Saloon last night.'

'Sir?' said the footman, but Collis simply inclined his head persuasively to one side and said, 'Go ahead. You heard me.'

'Wait here,' the footman told him, and then pushed his way through the curtains. For a split second, Collis could see the back of Sarah Melford's gilt chair, her white shoulder, her dark-yellow dress; and he caught the warm perfume of wealth. Then the curtains closed again, and all he could do was wait in the corridor, his evening gloves clasped in his hand, feeling socially uncertain and gauche for almost the first time in his life.

He heard the orchestra begin the overture for the second half of Rodney Mulgrave's performance. He would have done almost anything for a swig from Knickerbocker Jane's flask. He coughed twice, although he didn't need to.

After a moment, the curtains opened again, and the footman reappeared.

'Well?' asked Collis.

The footman angled his head, in deliberate mockery of the way that Collis had nodded his. 'Mr Melford appreciates your compliments, sir, and hopes you enjoy the remainder of the performance.'

'Is that all?'

'Did you *want* more, sir?'

Collis pursed his lips. 'Does Mr Melford understand who I am? I am the son of Makepeace Edmonds, the late Makepeace Edmonds, of I. P. Woolmer's Bank, in New York. I am Collls Edmonds.'

'Yes, sir,' replied the footman. 'You are also the gentleman who shot a dealer's hat last night in the Eagle Saloon.'

'Did you tell him that?'

'Yes, sir.'

'And what did he say?'

The footman smiled archly. 'He said, sir, that I should send you away with the maximum dispatch. And that is what I have attempted to do.'

At that moment, the curtains swayed and parted again. Laurence Melford emerged himself, much taller and more powerfully built than Collis had imagined, with a shirt front that was piercingly white and a brow that was so shaggy and grey that he appeared to be looking at Collis through the severe confusion of a thorn-bush. He was rich with the smell of brandy, cigars, and French cologne.

'Will you keep this confounded noise down?' he asked, in a deep growl.

'I'm sorry, Mr Melford,' said the footman. 'But this gentleman here seems to think that you ought to know him.'

Laurence Melford examined Collis with slow deliberation and rubbed his chin with a broad, work-scarred, but perfectly manicured hand. There was a massive gold ring on his finger engraved with the Gothic initial M. He said, in the same rich *basso profundo*, 'Maybe I ought to know you. But I don't. And that's all there is to it.'

'You will,' replied Collis.

'I *will*? You mean you're going to take San Francisco by storm?'

Collis shook his head. His confidence was growing, now that he could see Laurence Melford for a man, and not for a legend. His father, in his greatest days at I. P. Woolmer's Bank, had made his underlings and most of his customers shudder with fear; but Collis had never been disturbed by him or by anybody, provided he could meet them face to face and talk to them man to man. As his friend Henry Browne had once laconically remarked, 'Never fear the other fellow for one moment. Always remember that he visits the watercloset, just as you do, and that his dignity, just like yours, has to be dropped around his ankles.'

'I intend to take the continent by storm,' Collis said. 'Not just San Francisco.'

Laurence Melford tugged at his ear. He looked extremely disinterested.

'I'm going to build a railroad, Mr Melford. A railroad that links up San Francisco with Nebraska, and Nebraska with New York. I'm going to turn this whole town upside down, and everybody in it.'

'I see,' answered Laurence Melford, unperturbed. 'And is that why you wanted to present your compliments? To warn me that this city isn't big enough for both of us, and that I ought to consider packing my trunks?'

'No, sir,' Collis told him. 'I came to present my compliments because I believe that, one day, you and I could be friends and associates, whether you can credit that now or not.'

Laurence Melford tugged his vest straight and lowered his chin so that it formed into impressive folds.

'Mr Edwards,' he said patiently, 'you will find when you have spent more time in our city that there are certain traditional, accepted notions of behaviour and class. We are divided here into what are vulgarly known as the Chivalry and the Shovelry. Not by prejudice, nor by intolerance, but by the simple fact that some of us were founders of California, and have acquired through time and experience and solid wealth the right to set the standards by which our city lives; and that others of us, the later arrivals, although we may be hard workers and opportunists of the finest kind, have to accept the guidance and direction which the founders provide. I am sure, Mr Edwards, that in New York City your credentials are excellent. You speak well; you dress well. I take you for a gentleman. But remember that this isn't New York City, this is San Francisco, and that life is different here. Whatever heights you are aspiring to reach, you will never reach mine, and it will save you both time and disappointment if you forgo trying.'

He cleared his throat, as if he were speaking at a public dinner. 'Now, you'll forgive me, won't you? I am a particular admirer of Mr Mulgrave's, and I would like to hear his soliloquy.'

'Mr Melford,' said Collis, as the millionaire turned back to the curtains of his box.

'Yes?'

'The day will come, Mr Melford, when you recognise me, as the aged mother recognised the Highland hero. You will squeeze my nose and say, "My God, it's you."'

Laurence Melford stared at Collis with glittering eyes. For some reason, Collis's words seemed to have troubled him.

'I was a hero once, Mr Edwards,' he said, in his deep, thick voice. 'I still am.'

'Yes,' said Collis, 'but you know what Emerson says – "Every hero becomes a bore at last."'

Laurence Melford frowned, and then gradually smiled. 'Maybe you're right, Mr Edwards. Maybe you're right. But if you're a hero, too, then the same fate will be waiting for you.'

The curtains suddenly parted, and Laurence Melford had to step back. It was Sarah, wide-eyed and surprised, her fan in her hand. 'Father?' she said. 'I was wondering why you were taking so long.'

Close to, Sarah Melford was even more disturbing than she was seventy feet away through opera glasses. There was a warmth about her, a heat as if her body and her personality were glowing with pride at all their attributes – their calm, and their beauty, and their composure. Collis saw that her eyes were very dark, but flecked with pale blue, and that there was a round mole on the side of her left breast, just before it disappeared into her cleavage. Her diamond necklace, in the shape of a wide five-pointed star, must have cost fifty or sixty thousand dollars.

Laurence Melford reached across and took his daughter's arm, consciously or unconsciously preventing her from stepping any nearer to Collis.

'We were having a brief philosophical discussion, my darling,' he told her. 'It's over now, and I'm coming back to join you.'

Sarah raised her head. She kept her eyes on Collis, as if he were an interesting sort of dog that had strayed into her parlour.

'Aren't you going to introduce me?' she asked her father. 'The poor fellow looks quite amusing.'

'There's no need for that,' said Laurence Melford. His soft mouth remained in a smile, although he glanced at Collis with eyes that warned, 'Keep off – don't ever think that this is for you.'

Collis, partly to needle Melford and partly because Sarah tantalised him so much, gave a polite bow from the waist. 'Collis Edmonds, Miss Melford, freshly arrived from New York. The man who shot a dealer's hat at the Eagle Saloon last night.'

Sarah smiled. 'I've heard all about you! Now, isn't that strange! I

263

heard Dezzie talking about you this morning, with the coachman. Dezzie's my maid, Desdemona. It seems you must be quite famous, Mr Edmonds! Fancy that!'

'We must be getting back, Sarah,' insisted Laurence Melford. 'I can hear that Mr Mulgrave has begun.'

'I suppose so,' said Sarah, fluttering her fan. She spoke in one of those high, breathy feminine voices that Collis had always found absurdly attractive. But it was what she was doing with her fan that intrigued him more than her voice. There were all kinds of secret code signals that young girls transmitted to their beaux by means of fans and handkerchiefs and even dance programmes, and if Collis's experience of New York balls was anything to go by, Sarah Melford was plainly signalling, 'I'd love to make your acquaintance.'

He gave her his finest seductive look, all melting and hurt and worried, as if he had loved once, and loved again, but his heart had been crushed by misfortune and cruelty. She looked back at him, and her eyes widened. He knew he had her attention, if nothing else.

'What do you do, Mr Edmonds?' she asked. 'Or are you a gentleman?'

Collis said, with soft regret in his voice, 'I *was* a gentleman, Miss Melford. I had all the breeding and the education that a gentleman requires. I lived in New York on independent means.'

'But?' asked Sarah Melford.

Collis dropped his gaze. She was sweet, and she might be making signals with her fan, but she was shrewd, too, like her father, and if he knew anything about twenty-year-old girls, she was even harder than her father understood possible.

'There was some unfortunate speculation. My family lost all their fortune. My father died as an indirect result.'

'I see. I'm sorry.'

'You don't have to be. My father enjoyed the better part of his life with the same intensity that he would have hated the worse part. But now I'm here in San Francisco to make a fortune of my own.'

Sarah raised her fan, spread it wide, and looked at Collis over the curved top of it. Two questioning eyes over a decorative picture of a Persian garden, with peacocks.

'Come on, now, Sarah,' said Laurence Melford. 'I'm sure Mr Edwards wants to see the show for himself. Don't you, Mr Edwards?'

264

'No, no,' said Sarah, fluttering her fan again. 'I wanted to ask him how he was going to make his fortune, in what kind of endeavour. I think he's terribly courageous.'

'Some nonsense about railroads,' grumbled Laurence Melford. 'Now, really, Sarah, we have to go in.'

'Railroads?' asked Sarah. 'But there are no railroads in San Francisco. At least, none to speak of.'

'There will be, Miss Melford,' said Collis. 'I'm going to build one.'

Laurence Melford interrupted, 'You *think* you're going to build one, sir. But take it from me that you will never succeed. Now, if you don't mind – '

'Mr Melford,' said Collis, in a much sharper tone, 'I will bet you anything you care to name that I will succeed.'

Laurence Melford pulled a testy face. 'I don't make bets, Mr Edwards. Especially not with artisans.'

'Father!' Sarah admonished him.

'I'm sorry,' said Laurence Melford. 'I should have remembered that you railroad people have special names, don't you? What are you, a switchman?'

Collis drew a breath. 'Mr Melford,' he said, 'I will bet you your daughter.'

There was a shocked silence. Sarah glanced at her father with an uneasy expression, and the footman took a couple of steps back. Then, without a word, Laurence Melford pushed his daughter away, back through the curtains, making her disappear like a stage conjuring trick. For a moment the strained, histrionic voice of Rodney Mulgrave wafted into the corridor: '. . . there is nothing in between but getting wenches with child, wronging the ancientry, stealing, fighting.'

'*The Winter's Tale*,' said Collis, surprised at his own knowledge.

Laurence Melford was angry, and unimpressed. He raised one solid finger to Collis, and when he spoke his voice was deep as a rumbling cistern.

'I don't know who you are,' he said. 'What's more, I have no desire to know. But I should warn you that I have dealt with opportunists and rapscallions of your sort before, and that I once had a man of your age hanged from the end beam of the Old Adobe, so that the birds could pick him. You have been forward, and impertinent, and if I ever see you near me or my family again, I'll have you run into jail as fast as you like. I can do that, you know, and you'd better understand it. Now, get out of here, before I have your arms broken.'

'The bet still stands,' said Collis. 'If you're going to insult me by calling me an artisan, then damn it I'll live up to your insult, and I'll work like an artisan, and I'll build that damned railroad just to show you that an artisan can do whatever a cowpoke can do, and have the cowpoke's daughter besides.'

'You infamous young jelly,' growled Laurence Melford. 'If you knew how many of your sort I've thrown out of my front door, you wouldn't even have the nerve to stand where you are.'

The footman stepped forward, unbuttoning the cuffs of his coat, and Collis glanced at him warily.

'I'm going anyway,' said Collis. 'But I'm sure we'll meet each other again, don't you, when I'm in better circumstances and you're in a better temper?'

Melford, stiff with anger, parted the curtains of his box. But before he returned to his family he raised his finger to Collis just once more.

'I warn you,' he said. 'By all the stars above, I warn you. Don't meddle with affairs that are far beyond you.'

'Warn away,' replied Collis. He bowed at Laurence Melford's disappearing back, and then he stepped smartly on to the footman's toe and continued quickly away down the corridor, turning only when he reached the corner by the auditorium doors to give the footman a wave. Then, stirred up, still trembling with nervousness and excitement, he returned to Sam Lewis's box on the other side of the theatre.

'Well?' asked Knickerbocker Jane. 'I could see a bit of flurry going on in their box. Did you get anywhere?'

Collis took out his handkerchief and mopped his forehead. 'I think so,' he said, pulling his chair forward. 'With Sarah Melford, anyway. I'm not so sure about Papa. I think he's one of these gentlemen who has to be your enemy before he can be your friend.'

'Not a good enemy to have in San Francisco,' commented Charles. 'Not a good friend, either. You'd have done better to leave well enough alone.'

Collis shook his head. 'I can't. Not a man as powerful and arrogant as that. Not when he's got a daughter that looks like Sarah.'

'Oh, well,' said Knickerbocker Jane and sighed. 'As the moth to the candle flame is drawn.'

That night, like a man revisiting a compulsive dream, he was back again in the smoky realms of the Eagle Saloon, at Dan McReady's faro table. Dan McReady had not acknowledged him when he sat down with anything more than a sideways flicker of the eyes, but both men knew why Collis was there, and what the terms of the game were. The atmosphere that they generated between them infected the rest of the saloon, too, and several other tables closed down as drinkers and gamblers came to stand around with cigars and whisky and watch Collis and McReady play.

Collis had brought with him, in a leather satchel he had borrowed from Knickerbocker Jane, the $1000 he had won the night before. He bet steadily, confidently, and evenly; but for the first part of the evening his luck didn't run very high. As the clock struck one, he was nearly $200 down.

He called for a stone fence, and this time the barman sent a boy to run out for a jug of cider. The stone fence was mixed strong, and served up in a thick glass tankard. Collis drank almost half of it, and then loosened his white tie.

They played until dawn began to shine through the engraved glass doors, throwing shadows in the shape of eagles on the dusty floorboards. Then they counted up what they had, and Collis found that he was $600 better off than the previous night. He stowed it all away in his satchel, and buckled it up, and as he did so, Dan McReady reached under his table and produced his white hat, with the crown still shot out. He placed it on his head without saying a word. Collis nodded in recognition of McReady's symbolic surrender, and swallowed down the last of his drink before he left.

He played at the Eagle Saloon every night for a week, except for Sunday. Sometimes Andy Hunt and Charles Tucker were there, sometimes he played with strangers. But every night Dan McReady was waiting for him, and every night they did nothing and said nothing, but played faro, hour after hour through the smoke-filled night, until the morning.

On Monday and Tuesday, Collis lost heavily. Those nights, Dan McReady finished up by shuffling his cards with a flourish, packing away the box, and leaving the table before Collis. But on the other nights, Collis bet more and won more than at almost any time in his life, and by dawn on Thursday he had pouches of gold dust worth almost $8000.

As he put them away, he said to McReady, 'I won't be back for a while. I've got a little work to do. But I won't forget you.'

McReady rubbed at his bristly moustache with his fingertips. His pale-blue eyes showed no expression at all.

'You're interested in business?' asked Collis. 'Big business? Plenty of financial rewards?'

McReady nodded. 'As long as it's nothing a man could get hanged for.'

'Do I look like a thief?'

'Does Parrott? Does McMullin?'

Collis smiled. 'There's thieving and thieving.'

McReady banged his pack of cards on the table to square them up. 'As long as you know which kind is smiled upon, and which ain't.'

'I guess I do,' said Collis. 'So, if you're interested, I'll give you a call, when the time's right, and maybe you'd like to size up what I'm planning to do.'

'All right,' said McReady.

The barman came across in his striped apron, his white shirtsleeves held up with armbands. The early-morning sunlight shone behind him, and he stood for a moment like a posed daguerreotype, his hands on his hips, his black cigarette hanging from his lips. In later years, in odd nostalgic moments, Collis would remember him standing there, one of the classic portraits of the old frontier.

'Would you gentlemen like to share a bottle of French champagne?' asked the barman.

Collis looked across at Dan McReady, then nodded. 'I guess we would. We may have something to celebrate here today.'

On Thursday afternoon, under a hazy sky, Collis rowed out into San Francisco Bay in a small whitehall boat, which he had rented for five dollars. He wore a white shirt, a beige vest, and his black silk opera hat. In the stern of the dinghy was the leather satchel he had borrowed from Knickerbocker Jane, and his folded coat.

The Bay was silent, and the waters calm. As he rowed, the oarlocks groaned and squeaked, one like Punch and the other like Judy. The wharves and the jetties were gradually opalised by fog, and at last the whole city disappeared, and Collis was left on his own, rowing out towards the Golden Gate as if he were the only man left alive in the whole world.

He had bought himself a compass and a chart of the Bay area from an overpriced marine store on California Street, but the price he had paid seemed to be worth it when he successfully reached the shelter of the Golden Gate's southern promontory, shipped his oars, and tossed overboard a small anchor on a long rope. The day was warm for the time of year, and there was only a faint breeze from the ocean, not even enough to disperse the fog, but he shrugged his coat around his shoulders and took a swallow of Knickerbocker Jane's brandy from a flask. It was better to be fortified than struck down by influenza. The water rippled and coursed around him, gentle and sibilant, and he lit himself a cheroot to pass the time. He checked his pocket watch, and saw that the time was two-fifty, a half-hour at least before the *Aria* was due to arrive. He began to hum to himself, one of the songs from Rodney Mulgrave's revue.

He was just thinking about taking another nip of brandy when he heard a long, low *moooottt*. He lifted his head and looked out towards the choppier waters of the Golden Gate. He couldn't see anything at first. But then, in utter silence, the prow of a ship appeared, followed by its hull, and its masts, and its rigging. Straining his eyes, Collis could make out the name *Aria*.

It was time to row, and row fast. He cut his anchor rope with a jack-knife, set his oars in their locks, and then heaved towards the grey, sliding shape of the *Aria* with every ounce of strength he could manage. After only a dozen strokes, he was gasping, but he kept going, pulling the oars through the broken waters of the Bay with the vicious determination of a man who knows he has enemies to beat, and a point to prove.

'Ahoy, *Aria*!' he screamed, turning his head as he rowed. 'Ahoy, *Aria*!'

There was no reply, no sign of life. The cargo vessel slid slowly past in the fog, her navigation lights dimly shining, as if she were crewless and deserted. But Collis kept pulling at the oars, because he knew from the shipping intelligence pages in the San Francisco newspaper that the *Aria* would drop anchor in the Bay only a short way off, and that he would reach her well before anyone on shore, even the lookouts on Telegraph Hill, had realised she was here.

He grunted and pulled, grunted and pulled, and his hands were already shredded with blisters. He began to curse every sleepless night and every cheroot, but he knew that he wasn't going to give in. At last he was pitching up and down on the rough water under the *Aria*'s port bow, and he heard the rattle and splash of her anchor going down.

'Ahoy, *Aria*!' he called, resting his oars. His dinghy rose and fell in the fog. 'Ahoy, there, *Aria*!'

'Ahoy yourself,' answered an irritable voice. Collis dipped his right oar in the sea and paddled himself around so that he could see who it was. He looked up, and there was a fat bearded sailor with his head shaved like a monk, leaning on the *Aria*'s ropes. Another sailor, thin and Latin, came up to join him.

'Is your master there?' asked Collis.

The fat sailor shrugged. 'If he ain't, we've lost him some way between here and Panama City.'

'Can I talk with him?'

'It depends who you be. It depends what you want.'

'Tell him I'm a merchant out of San Francisco, and that I'm carrying gold.'

'Well, that's of interest. Do you want to come aboard?'

Collis wiped sweat from his forehead with his sleeve. 'If I may. It's not much fun down here in a dinghy.'

The sailors disappeared for a while; then a rope ladder was dropped from the rail, and Collis was able to scull his dinghy close in to the *Aria*'s dark, crusted hull and tie up. Swaying from side to side to keep his balance, he slung his satchel over his shoulder and began to climb the awkward, crazily swinging ladder up to the deck. He was coughing as he swung his legs over the rail and jumped down on to the *Aria*'s cluttered foredeck, among tarry ropes and winching gear and frayed nets.

A small man with a fuzzy blond beard, a nautical cap, and a huge grey Norwegian sweater came walking along the deck to meet him. The man made no attempt to shake hands, but stood a few feet off, his hands in his pockets, his eyes as bright as an elf's. The fat sailor was bringing up the rope ladder with a great deal of clatter and whistling between his teeth.

'Are you the master?' Collis asked the small man, loudly.

The small man closed his eyes, as if that were a signal for 'yes.'

'Captain Heikefelt, isn't it? Captain Erik Heikefelt?'

The small man closed his eyes again.

Collis stepped forwards. 'I believe you're carrying some cargo that I might be interested in buying.'

270

Captain Heikefelt took off his cap and wiped around the inside of the headband with a green handkerchief. His hair was as blond and fuzzy as his beard, and it blew in the soft sea breeze like a dandelion.

'Coffee, I'm carrying,' he said, in a strong Swedish accent. 'Coffee and blankets and mining tools. That's all.'

'Do you want to discuss prices?' asked Collis.

Captain Heikefelt set his cap back on his head, as neat and straight as if he'd used a spirit level. 'Come to my quarters,' he said. 'I don't like to talk prices out on the deck.'

Collis followed him along the deck, up the companionway, and across to a varnished mahogany door with a fog-dulled brass plate which said *Kapitän*. Heikefelt nodded towards the plate and said, 'This came from Lower Saxony, this vessel, out of Bremerhaven. The first owner lost her when he divorced his wife.'

Collis followed him into a conspicuously neat cabin, with maps and shining brass lamps and a green-leather-topped desk. 'I shouldn't worry too much,' he said, as brightly as he could. 'I mean, think of all the fresh air you're getting.'

Heikefelt looked at Collis oddly. 'You want schnapps?' he asked. 'You look like maybe you've had too much fresh air yourself already.'

'That would be splendid,' said Collis.

The captain unlocked a tantalus that stood on a small oak table under the porthole and poured out two tiny glasses of pungent, oily schnapps. He handed one to Collis, said '*Skoal*,' and knocked back his own glass as if someone had punched him under the chin.

'*Skoal*,' Collis echoed hesitantly and did the same. The schnapps was surprisingly tasty, and very warming. In fact, Collis could feel the fumes rising out of his stomach like the fumes from a ship's boiler. His eyes watered, and he had to take off his silk hat and wipe them.

Captain Heikefelt pointed across to an upright wooden chair. 'Sit down,' he invited Collis. 'Then we can do some business.'

Collis pulled up the chair and sat down, while the captain sat in his revolving leather-backed chair in front of the desk. Collis noticed that there were no family portraits on the desk, no keepsakes or souvenirs. Only pens, pencils, dividers, compasses, and maps. Either Captain Heikefelt preferred to keep his home life out of his mind when he was at sea, or else he was married to the *Aria*, and no one else.

'I was surprised to hear that you were carrying blankets,' said

271

Collis, in an offhand way. 'I would have thought it much more profitable to carry nothing but coffee.'

Captain Heikefelt poured them both another schnapps.

'Of course,' he said, 'but the owners had to take blankets from a company in England, in payment of a bad debt. It was either blankets or nothing. So they took blankets. Thousands of blankets. You never saw so many.'

He tipped his head back again and swallowed his schnapps. '*Skoal*,' he said, wiping his mouth.

'*Skoal*,' said Collis, and tipped his own schnapps down. The second one was definitely better than the first. More warming, and less of a shock to the system. Given time, Collis felt that schnapps might even woo him away from stone fences, which were easily the worst drinks for hangovers in the entire liquid thesaurus.

'It seems to me that blankets, in this climate, are going to be something of a commercial liability,' said Collis.

Captain Heikefelt shrugged. 'It gets cold in San Francisco in the winter. I guess people will want blankets.'

'You try and tell them that now. You'll be lucky to sell them for fifty cents apiece. How many do you have?'

'Twenty-five short tons of five-pound blankets. That's ten thousand blankets.'

'Ten thousand?' said Collis. 'The whole population of San Francisco is only eighty or ninety thousand. You're going to sell ten thousand blankets to eighty thousand people in the middle of the warmest fall they've had for six years?'

'I have to,' said Captain Heikefelt. 'That's what the owners told me to do. Me, I'd rather sell coffee, and picks and shovels. How about one more schnapps?'

They said *Skoal* together this time, and tipped their drinks back simultaneously. Collis felt very warm indeed, and extraordinarily pleased with himself. It was remarkable how schnapps seemed to have the capacity to make him feel so pleased with himself.

'Usually,' Collis told Captain Heikefelt with great gravity, '*usually* I can only buy commodities that I can sell quickly. Coffee, salt, ice, those kinds of things.'

'Ice you have to sell quick,' agreed the captain.

'Yes,' said Collis, 'but usually I can only deal in commodities that I can unload within twenty-four hours. I don't have the storage space for goods that sell slowly. And nor does anyone else. There's a great shortage of space in San Francisco.'

272

'I know,' said Captain Heikefelt. 'I've been told that before.'

Collis stood up and went over to the porthole. It was still foggy outside, although he could just distinguish the dim outline of the distant wharves and warehouses.

'I'll tell you what I can do, though,' he said in a confidential tone. 'Because you're a splendid fellow, and you look like the kind of man who can do a little business on the side, on his own account, and keep it under his hat, I'll make you an offer for those blankets.'

The captain poured out two more schnapps. He downed his own glassful at once, and sniffed, but Collis paused before he drank any more. There appeared to be a point, with schnapps, when warmth faded rapidly into lightheadedness, and he didn't want to be incoherent when the time came for the deal to be clinched.

'I think I know of a storehouse, where I can put those blankets away, and sell them piecemeal,' Collis explained. 'The storehouse owner is a friend of mine, so he won't charge too much in the way of rental. Admittedly, I still won't make too much profit, but what's profit between friends, especially when we can make ourselves the price of a few good meals and a few good women for no trouble at all?'

Captain Heikefelt stared at him out of his fuzzy blond face, his eyes still bright but unfocused now, as if he were seeing Collis in triplicate.

'What do you want to do, then?' he asked. 'A little private deal?'

'You *could* call it that. I'll buy those blankets from you at seventy cents the blanket. Only you'll tell your owners that all you could get for them was sixty cents the blanket. Now, that leaves ten cents times ten thousand for your own private fee, and ten cents times ten thousand is one thousand dollars.'

Captain Heikefelt took off his cap again and laid it upside down on his desk. 'One thousand dollars, huh?' he asked. He leaned forward and peered into his cap as if he expected the money to be there. 'One thousand dollars?'

'That's right. All for yourself.'

'Drink your drink,' said Captain Heikefelt, nodding towards Collis's glass of schnapps. Collis picked it up, said, '*Skoal*,' and tossed it back. He was beginning to wonder if he really liked it or not. The movement of the *Aria* at anchor, combined with the stuffiness of Captain Heikefelt's cabin, was making him sweat, and feel distinctly bilious.

'What I want to know,' said Captain Heikefelt, 'is what you think

273

you will make out of it. Why do *you* want blankets, if they won't sell?'

Collis smiled his most reassuring smile. 'I made a little too much money out of a deal I was doing on behalf of a business partner. What I have to do now is lose some of that money by investing it, not disastrously, because that would be too suspicious, but *poorly*. I have to bury my extra profits under something that will keep them warm and quiet for a few months, and I can't think of anything more appropriate than blankets.'

Captain Heikefelt nodded. He seemed to accept that explanation. He poured out two more glasses of schnapps, with considerable unsteadiness, and then took a long swig from the neck of the bottle.

'One thousand dollars would do me very well,' he said, after a few minutes of rumination. 'One thousand dollars would do me fine.'

'Is it a deal, then?' asked Collis.

Captain Heikefelt took out his green handkerchief and blew his nose. 'You have time for one more schnapps?'

'You mean it's settled?' asked Collis.

Captain Heikefelt closed his eyes. 'I have the papers for the blankets right here, in my desk. Seven thousand dollars, is it, in gold?'

'That's right. I have it in thousand-dollar pouches. You shouldn't have any trouble transferring one thousand dollars into your own pocket.'

'I'll drink to that,' said the captain.

Collis picked up his brimming glass of schnapps. 'I was afraid you might.'

On Saturday morning, a bright sharp morning with the first snap of October in the air, Charles Tucker was expected to call for Collis at Knickerbocker Jane's at seven. They were going to Market Street wharf to board the steamboat *Wallace S. Martin* at eight, along with Billy, Charles's coachman, and Wang-Pu, his Chinese buyer. They were bound for Sacramento, for Collis to join Charles in his dry-goods and hardware business, and they wouldn't return to San Francisco until November. Charles had warned Collis to leave off his woollen underwear and stay with his summer cottons, because it was a good deal warmer inland at this time of year, and 'there can't be many things less comfortable than travelling to Sacramento in woollen long johns, when you should've worn cotton.'

A little after seven, Charles Tucker arrived, and Billy the

coachman was sent upstairs to Collis's room to bring down his trunk. As Collis came downstairs, with Billy behind him, Knickerbocker Jane came out into the hallway, in a white morning dress with pale-yellow embroidery flowers on it.

'Goodbye,' she said, with a curtsy. 'I hope you enjoy Sacramento. And do come back, whenever you wish. I'll always make you welcome.'

Collis leaned forwards and kissed her. She wore the same perfume as his mother used to wear, and for a moment he was overwhelmed with *déjà vu*. But then he stood straight, and smiled at her, and said quietly, 'Thank you, Jane. I may take you up on that, one day.'

Chapter 7

To any man who might have been disappointed on his first arrival in San Francisco that life on the brink of the world was not boisterous enough, nor eccentric enough, nor crowded with enough gambling and swearing and drinking and womanising, the paddle steamer *Wallace S. Martin* was a floating consolation prize.

It was a scabby, peeling boat, with its paintwork turned grey by the sun; but as it beat its way northwards between the reddish-brown hills that bordered San Paolo Bay, under a high clear sky, and then wound its way eastwards past Benicia, and through the marshy wind-ruffled approaches to the estuary of the Sacramento River, it was alive with singing, accordion music, laughing, and dancing on the decks. Men in wide-brimmed hats sat in the sloping saloons, betting on poker and faro any money that might have remained unspent after three weeks in San Francisco, and drinking cloudy whisky as if it were medicine. On the foredeck, under a flapping canvas awning, a band of six or seven Poles in red-flannel shirts, their faded pants tied up with string, played a fiddle and a squeezebox and sang ribald folk songs that seemed to have *dupa* in every other line. Around the galleried afterdeck, bright and tawdry as moths in the panels of sunlight that fell through the windows, girls paraded in dusty dresses, or sat on the knees of bearded and derby-hatted men, smoking and sipping port wine. You could have had any one of them, these girls, in a narrow bunk with varnished sides, for two dollars. They plied their trade up and down the Sacramento River and into San Francisco Bay as regular as pilots or stokers or barges.

Collis sat at a table in the upper saloon, on the starboard side where it was shaded from the midday sun. He was dressed in his light-grey suit, with a checkered hound's-tooth vest and a light-grey broad-brimmed hat. He was sharing a bottle of whisky with Charles, who was wearing a tight sandy-coloured suit and a ginger hat which matched his whiskers, and with Wang-Pu, the Chinese buyer, who was dressed most conservatively in a black morning coat, a black tie, and grey pinstripe pants. At the next table sat a card school of Sacramento merchants, shoulders hunched, playing their last few games before they returned home to their wives.

Charles was feeling breezy and expansive, and was looking forward to returning home. He had bought up some good-quality hardware and dry goods in San Francisco, all of which were being shipped inland by the steamer *Boroughmore*, and which would arrive in Sacramento in a day or two, in time for a grand sale. Charles confessed, too, that a couple of weeks in San Francisco was probably enough for any man's constitution, or at least for his, what with all those girls and all that rich food, and he was almost eager to return to Mrs Tucker's plain dietary regime, not to mention her plain looks.

Collis found Charles subtly changed from the first time he had met him, sitting on his trunk at Broadway Wharf. He was still forthright, still ebullient, but as he neared his home territory his forthrightness and ebullience became almost dictatorial. In San Francisco, when Charles made a humorous remark, you could laugh if you felt like it. But here, within thirty miles of Sacramento, it seemed as if an energetic appreciation of Charles Tucker's wit was mandatory.

'You see there,' said Charles, pointing northwards with his cigar to a small and sorry collection of wooden buildings among the trees and the hills. 'That's the town of Benicia. Used to be the capital of California, for one year, in '53. That was a big joke. General Vallejo, your friend Laurence Melford's buddy, bought all the land around here and established the town, hoping it was going to grow into a city, and that he'd make himself a fortune on land prices. He called the place Benicia after his wife, and if you'd ever seen Mrs Francisca Benicia Carillo Vallejo, you'd know why the whole project flopped. Homely isn't the word. What is the word, Wang-Pu?'

Wang-Pu sipped his whisky reflectively. 'The word, Mr Tucker, is hollendous.'

Charles let out one of his barking laughs, and Collis found his own face twisting into a smile. He didn't particularly want to smile, but until he had felt his way around Charles's home territory, and established the rules of the home game, he felt that a little sycophancy might take him a long way. It wasn't that he disliked Charles. Charles was direct, and aggressive, and emotionally honest. Collis couldn't yet vouch for his commercial integrity. But he felt that he could learn from Charles, and eventually use Charles's energy for his own particular ambition.

The *Wallace S. Martin* plied on, and music and pungent tobacco smoke and an occasional breeze-whipped playing card floated across the blue water. Charles, after a heavy breakfast of steak and coddled eggs and whisky, went to lie down for a while, ostensibly for the sake of his digestion, although Collis noticed him pause at the head of the companionway and nod his head to one of the dusty young moth-ladies who stalked the rear saloon. Collis turned away. It wasn't any of his business how Charles enjoyed himself, and Charles, after all, had been his first and most enthusiastic friend in San Francisco, after Andy Hunt. But Wang-Pu dryly remarked, 'I would say that Mr Tucker is about to make one of his grand but temporary farewells to the world and all its vices, wouldn't you, Mr Edmonds?'

Collis, drinking, looked across at Wang-Pu in surprise, almost alarm. It was nearly as startling as if somebody's pet lap dog had suddenly made an observation about the weather. Up until now, Collis had never really noticed the Chinaman at all. He had regarded him as nothing more important than Charles's servant and buyer, and he had certainly never heard him say anything remotely sardonic. But in the early-afternoon sunshine which irradiated the steamer's saloon, he suddenly saw Wang-Pu as a most individualistic person, a man with amusing brown eyes, a longish, northern Chinese face, and a smile which suggested a very secret camaraderie, a shared understanding of the world's weaknesses.

'How long have you worked for Mr Tucker?' asked Collis.

Wang-Pu smiled. 'Eight years, seven days a week, no vacation.'

'You have a family?'

'A wife, two sons, one daughter. I left them in Lianhuachi, near to the Changcheng.'

'The Changcheng?'

'The Great Wall. That which was built to keep barbarians like you away from civilised people like us.'

'Do you think that people like you and people like me are so very different?' Collis asked.

Wang-Pu shrugged. 'We both feel pain, if that's what you mean. I miss my family in China more than any white devil has been able to understand.'

'Why did you leave them?'

Wang-Pu looked away, out of the dust-bloomed window, at the flat waters of Suisun Bay. 'There was no opportunity for making money in China. My wife and family were well bred, but the harvests continually failed, and there was terrible flooding, followed by equally terrible drought, and in the end I decided to

278

leave China and seek my fortune elsewhere. It was almost impossible for me to bear the indignity of watching my wife trying to make herself new gowns from worn-out hangings, and see my children's arms so thin from underfeeding. I suppose you have no children, Mr Edmonds. But to hold your own child in your arms and to feel his bones through the skin, to see his eyes big and listless and hungry for food, that is a far greater pain than leaving him and working in a foreign land for money that will make him well.'

Collis didn't answer, but sat in silence for almost a minute, his elbow resting on the table.

'Have you ever told Charles any of this?' asked Collis.

Wang-Pu shook his head.

'I don't understand why you haven't,' said Collis. 'And most of all, I don't understand why you're telling me.'

'Your fortune is tied up with Charles, but your fortune is greater than Charles,' said Wang-Pu.

'What does that mean?' asked Collis.

'You are driven by something greater than yourself,' Wang-Pu told him. 'You also have sensitivities inside of yourself that are deep, although they are unresolved, and it is to those deep sensitivities that I have been addressing myself. You are a man who can understand the fears of others, as well as your own fears, and that is what will make you great.'

'What are you – some kind of a clairvoyant?' asked Collis.

Wang-Pu raised his hand in a quiet gesture of acknowledgment. 'Everybody in California is a clairvoyant. This is the territory from which there is no going back. Only forward. We have learned, over the years, to look only in that direction.'

'I still don't understand why you're talking to me this way. You don't talk to Andy Hunt this way, do you?'

'I tried. But he is not a responsive man, in that respect. In the end, I had to make a joke of what I had told him, and pretend that I had been quoting Confucius. What I have to tell *you*, though, is something different.'

Collis said nothing, but leaned back in his chair, waiting for Wang-Pu to speak. Wang-Pu poured the remaining four or five fingers of whisky into the glasses in front of them. 'If you really want to build a railroad, Mr Edmonds, then consider the Chinese for your labourers.'

Collis rubbed his chin with his hand. There was an odd pause, then he sat up a little, lacing his fingers together. 'Well,' he said, 'if you don't mind my saying so, and this is speaking theoretically, it seems to me that the Chinese aren't exactly heavyweights, as a race. I always thought the best railroad labourers were Irish, or Polish. Big muscular fellows.'

'Maybe it seems that way.' Wang-Pu smiled. 'But you must think of the numerous advantages of the Chinese character. The Chinese are industrious in a way which makes the hardest-working Occidental appear positively sluggardly. Their attitude to work is historical. They have a thousand-year heritage of cultivating rice fields of untold acreage, and of coping almost yearly with tragic and disastrous floods, on the Yangtze and the Hwang Ho. We may not be physical giants. But we have a persistence against which not even the Sierra Nevada can stand.'

'You seem pretty sure that I'm going to build this railroad,' said Collis. 'In fact, you seem a damned sight surer than I am.'

'You forget that I've already met Theodore Jones. I think I know what effect his technical expertise and your aura of destiny will have upon each other. Theodore Jones has the mechanical vision. You, from what I have observed, have the historical vision. Together, you will have both the competence and the inspiration to plan this railroad, and it is my humble suggestion that when that time comes, the Chinese people might be the ideal instrument for constructing it.'

'What's *your* interest?' asked Collis, a little too sharply.

Wang-Pu smiled again, as if to say that Collis was being predictably Western. 'My interest,' he said, 'is also in business. If you wish to summon Chinese labourers to this task, when it reaches fruitfulness, then I shall recruit them for you, and manage them for you. I am well known on Tong Yan Gai, which is what we call Sacramento Street. I will do it in exchange for reasonable moneys, and in exchange for being part of your destiny.'

Collis felt curiously disturbed. 'I'm not magic, you know,' he told Wang-Pu.

Wang-Pu sipped his drink. 'I know, Mr Edmonds. But you are one of those we call "fabled." One of those people who are selected by fate to fulfil a certain role in the history of the world. You are a hinge, if you understand me, upon which the future of this nation will hang.'

'I think you're flattering me. I'm broke. I'm an apprentice merchant, that's all.'

'Nevertheless, you are the perfect candidate.'

'You have an unnerving command of English, for a Chinese.'

'You have a very dull sense of your own importance, for an aristocrat.'

Collis abruptly laughed, and Wang-Pu laughed too, a high-pitched giggle that set Collis laughing even harder. It took them all of three or four minutes to recover, and then they sat there wiping their eyes with their handkerchiefs, and still letting out occasional chuckles.

'I never knew the Chinese had a sense of humour,' said Collis. 'You always struck me as dour.'

'It isn't a Western sense of humour,' Wang-Pu told him. 'But we take great pleasure in laughing.' He wiped his eyes again, and tucked away his handkerchief. Then he took out his gold pocket watch and examined it.

'Time for my medication,' he said. 'You'll excuse me a moment, won't you?'

'You're not suffering from anything serious, I hope?' asked Collis.

'An ulcer. I have to treat it three times a day.'

'You take kaolin?'

Wang-Pu smiled. 'I am Chinese, Mr Edmonds. I take the traditional Chinese cure.'

Wang-Pu opened a worn brown leather case that was lying propped against the legs of his chair. He bent over and reached inside, and produced a dark-red lacquered box, with gold paintings of Chinese trees on it. The box appeared to be ventilated with leaf-shaped air holes, and when Wang-Pu set it on the saloon table and opened the lid, Collis could see why.

Inside, the box was divided into compartments. In one compartment, there was a flat saucer of thin porcelain. In the second was a glass-stoppered bottle of dark liquid. And in the third, nestling in white cotton, were three baby mice, pink and hairless, but wriggling with life.

Collis looked at Wang-Pu uneasily. But Wang-Pu simply continued to smile, and set out the saucer on the table. He poured a little of the dark liquid into it, and then took up one of the baby mice by the tail, and dipped it into the liquid as if he were coating a quenelle with egg yolk.

'This is soya sauce,' explained Wang-Pu. 'It isn't medicinally necessary, but it gives the mouse some flavour.'

'Flavour?' asked Collis in disbelief; but before he could say anything else, Wang-Pu had tipped back his head, raised the squirming mouse to his open mouth, and dropped it down his throat The Chinaman gave a hefty swallow, and the little creature was evidently gone.

Collis, alarmed said, 'I don't *really* see what benefit that's supposed to afford you.'

Wang-Pu shrugged. 'The mouse bursts inside the stomach, and its warm blood bathes the ulcer. That is the theory, in any event.'

Collis waited for the Chinaman to say something else, but he didn't. Wang-Pu simple took anoher sip of whisky, put away his medicine case, and sat back to watch the shores of Solana pass them by, a dry-baked, desolate land, where birds turned and drifted like leaves on a still summer pond.

Collis was dozing in his chair as the steamer docked at Sacramento. It was early evening. He opened his eyes to see a tree-lined river-bank, and beyond, through a hallucinatory ripple of heat, a small town of flat-fronted houses and stores and saloons, neatly laid out in squares. The wood and adobe walls of the buildings were lit by sinking sunlight under a sky that was still stunningly blue. In the far distance, beyond the squarish outlines of the state capitol building and the cluttered rooftops downtown, across a wide purplish wilderness of trees and empty land, Collis could see the far, entrancing peaks of the Sierra Nevada. He straightened his hat, brushed his sleeves, and then stood up and went to the steamer's rail.

There were several steamers and small cutters docked along the river's edge, and the water was clustered with lighters taking goods and passengers ashore from the ships anchored out in midstream. Their oars dipped into the sun-gilded river and made criss-cross patterns of dazzling light.

Charles came up from astern, his face redder than usual, and hooked his thumbs into his vest. 'Well, Collis,' he said, 'I've brought you home, then.'

Collis nodded. There was a smell of dust and chaparral on the breeze. By the river's edge, a congregation of carts and Conestoga wagons had collected, and a group of men in plaid shirts and blue work pants were smoking pipes and watching the steamer tie up. On the foredeck, a man with a high, hoarse voice was playing the accordion, and singing, 'Oh, I remember well, the lies they used to tell, of gold so bright it hurt the sight, and made the miners yell.'

To the north, around a small promontory, and under a wide wooden bridge, lay the flooded land called Sutter's Slough. To the south, about a mile away, behind a stretch of trees, there was a plume of black smoke rising, slow and thick, and leaning slightly to the east.

'That's where the Sacramento Valley Railroad comes in from Folsom,' remarked Charles. 'I'll take you down to see Colonel Wilson in a day or so, unless he calls by the store beforehand.'

Collis eyed the distance between the plume of smoke and the faraway foothills. He had always known that the West was open, and almost endless, but to arrive here in Sacramento on a hot afternoon and see miles and miles of flat valley floor was almost enough to make him doubt his ability to build a branch line from one side of the city to the other, let alone a transcontinental railroad.

'I never guessed,' he said quietly.

'You never guessed what?' asked Charles, pleased to be back.

'I don't know,' said Collis. 'The distance, I suppose.'

'The distance?' said Charles, almost as if he had invented the whole idea of distance. 'Well, that's what California's all about. Valleys, and mountains, and wide-open spaces. It's a place you can breathe in.'

From the riverbank they heard a baritone voice come out with a loud 'Halloo,' and there on the roadway stood a tall, whiskery man in a buttoned-up morning coat; a man with a dark, Scottish-looking countenance, as if every angle of his face had been chipped out with a broken flint, and a chest that filled his coat as deeply as an oil barrel. He was standing by a small varnished surrey, in which two chestnut horses were harnessed, but it looked as if he were as capable of carrying them, the surrey and the horses, as they were of carrying him.

'That's my partner, Leland McCormick,' said Charles, and waved to the riverbank with both arms. McCormick waved back, and raised his hat.

'I got the barbed wire!' shouted Charles. 'Enough to fence off the whole of Northern California!'

'Did you get the stoveblack?' McCormick called back.

'Enough for everyone in the whole damned city to make up in blackface!' Charles told him.

McCormick guffawed. A few feet away, on deck, Billy the coachman gave a sour grin. But then the gangplank was let down to the riverbank with a hollow bang and a cloud of dry dust, and it was time to disembark.

They shook hands with Leland McCormick as they stepped on to the warm, hard-baked shore, and Collis was introduced.

'How's Andrew?' asked Leland. 'Still doing well with his food wholesale business?'

'Short on storage space, mostly,' replied Charles, as they climbed aboard the surrey. 'But he's lent me one of his rented warehouses for three hundred tons of Australian coal, provided I wash it out afterwards, and he's even found a corner for young Collis's first business venture.'

McCormick turned to make sure that all their trunks were aboard. Billy and Wang-Pu were making their own arrangements to ride to Charles's store on a hired wagon. There was probably enough room for them in the surrey, but Collis had the strong impression that neither Charles nor Leland was the kind of man, in Sacramento at least, to have servants riding along with him. Leland in particular. He seemed ponderous, and humourless, and permanently conscious of his dignity.

'Your first business venture?' he asked Collis, with a trace of a Scots accent. There was something his voice which made Collis feel that he was being patronised. Something, too, in the way Leland's dark, deep-set eyes never quite looked at Collis straight, but always appeared to be fixed on something more interesting, like his horses' ears, or a passing Chinaman in a coolie hat. They passed Wildmore & Glazier's store, and Stanton's Chop House, and then they rattled over the rutted thoroughfare to the end of K Street and turned east.

Collis took out a cheroot, bracing his feet against the floor of the surrey as he cupped his hands around the tip and lit it. He glanced as he did so at Leland's hands on the reins, with heavy, masculine gold rings on three fingers. Leland smelled of somebody's French cologne, but not offensively. Just enough to make anyone who had been travelling all day feel that he might smell of sweat.

'I had a tip that a cargo of blankets was due into San Francisco on the *Aria*,' Collis said, at length. 'I rowed out before she anchored and bought the lot.'

'Blankets?' queried Leland.

'I'll sell them readily enough when the winter begins to bite,' said Collis.

Charles laughed. 'It was all Arthur Teach's idea, originally,' he told Leland, with enormous good humour. 'But poor Teach made the mistake of telling Collis, and boasting about it, and before we knew it Collis had rowed out into the Bay and bought them right under Teach's nose. I would have given a five-dollar piece to have seen Teach's face when the *Aria*'s lighters came ashore and told him the blankets were all bought. I saw him later, at Barry & Patten's saloon, and he was ready to have Collis strung up from the Vigilance Committee's upstairs rooms like Casey and Cora.'

'Not seriously, I trust?' asked Leland.

'Not seriously,' said Collis.

Leland sniffed. 'I never know with San Francisco. The only way you can tell San Franciscans from savages is by their fancy clothes and their bread-crumbed oysters.'

Collis looked around K Street as they drove along. He could have remarked that it appeared, on first sight, to be a great deal more primitive than San Francisco, with the admitted exception of Sydney Town, between Kearny and Sansome north of Broadway, that fearsome collection of sheds and tents and rough saloons that greeted all those who disembarked for the first time in San Francisco. But San Francisco had its brick banks and its iron boardinghouses and its fireproof theatres, as well as its occasional marble frontage and its decorative offices and civic institutions; Sacramento appeared to be constructed very largely out of wood and brown mud.

The largest and most prosperous-looking row of buildings in sight were those along the north side of K Street. In particular, there was a hardware store, No. 54, with a front veranda, and handsome upstairs windows. It was only when they began to draw close, and Leland McCormick slowed the horses, that Collis could see the signs that were hung on the front of the store, in lavish serif script: 'Tucker & McCormick, Hardware,' and beneath that, 'Rubber Hose, Belting, Powder, Fuse, Rope, Blocks, Pitch, Tar & C.'

'Well,' said Collis, remaining in his seat in the surrey as Leland climbed down and tied the horses to one of the veranda posts, 'it seems that you have done great things for yourselves.'

Leland almost raised his eyes, but not quite far enough to look Collis straight in the face. 'We've built this up through good practice, prayer, and years of personal industry,' he said. Then he turned to Charles. 'You must come upstairs. Jane has been preparing a special dinner for you. She knows how much you like poultry.'

Collis felt as if he had been firmly put in his place. He paused for a moment, feeling the muscles in his cheeks tighten, but then he tossed his half-burned cheroot aside and stepped down to the street. If he wanted to make his fortune in California, then he was going to have to enlist the sympathies of men like Charles and Leland, and their friendship, no matter how they treated him. He followed them past barrels of tar and coils of rope into the shadows of the veranda, and then through the store itself, to the stairs at the back.

The store was gloomy and smelled of grease, hemp, and kerosene. There were stacks of rope, hairy and pungent, that reached almost to the cream-painted ceiling, and rolls of woven wire fencing, ten cents a rod. There were double-cap steel roofing, chain pump tubing, wagon scales, and force pumps. To Collis, who had never been into a hardware store before, the emporium of Tucker & McCormick seemed to be crowded with the most extraordinary and eccentric devices, mostly constructed of drop-forged iron or dull-polished steel, with hooks and springs and valves and odd attachments whose arcane purposes could only be guessed at. He began to wonder if he would be able to understand the hardware business at all, especially when Leland remarked to Charles as they filed their way past a stack of boxes, 'I'm running short on Hancock inspirators.'

They reached the door to the stairs, and Leland ushered them up. It was carpeted here, and there was an aroma of roasting chicken. They emerged in the hallway of a set of apartments, quite comfortably furnished with plain mahogany bureaus and upright chairs, and well equipped with jardinières and planters, from which ferns and aspidistras sprouted with all the clamourous health of a family of young children. They went through into a living-room, whose windows gave out on to a wide balcony and the dusty street below; and it was here, on a tapestry-covered davenport, that a small, big-nosed woman sat, in a gown of black watered silk with a white lace collar. Her hair was brushed flat and black on to her head, and two huge garnet earrings hung from her fleshy earlobes. Her eyes were bulbous and sorrowful. She stroked, or rather rubbed, as if it were a persistent stain on her skirts, a diminutive dachshund which sat in her lap.

Charles crossed the red-and-blue-patterned rug, took the woman's hand, and kissed it. 'Jane,' he said. 'You're looking more radiant than ever. The siren of Sacramento.'

Collis stood by he door, his hat in his hand, and gave the woman a pursed, aknowledging smile. She reminded him quite strongly of engravings he had seen in the New York magazines of Queen Victoria, and she seemed to behave with the same imperiousness. There was no question at all in Collis's mind that she was an unmitigated old boot. But he bowed slightly as Leland stepped forward, took her hand, and introduced Collis as 'our new junior assistant, my angel.'

'I'm pleased to make your acquaintance,' said Jane McCormick. 'You've come from the East, I presume?'

'New York, ma'am.'

'Hm,' said Jane McCormick, as if New York were a rural village that was only one stage more civilised than Chicken Thief Flat, or Gouge Eye, or any other of the ramshackle mining towns that surrounded Sacramento. 'You appear to be very *sartorial* for a junior assistant in a hardware store.'

'I was a gentleman who fell upon awkward times, ma'am,' replied Collis. It was as much as he could do to answer her courteously, considering that only a few months ago, in New York, he wouldn't have given half a breath to speak to a pompous middle-class matron like this.

Jane McCormick nodded in satisfaction. 'I see. I hope you know how to work hard.'

'I hope to learn, ma'am.'

'You're not too ambitious, I suppose? Ambition, in a junior person, is not really suitable, is it?'

Collis gave a little shake of his head. 'No, ma'am. Though one wonders, without ambition, how a junior person can ever aspire to become a senior person.'

Jane McCormick blinked at him with her protuberant eyes. 'If I had ever been blessed with a child of my own,' she said, 'I would have counselled him that hard work, and devotion to the catechisms, and consideration for others, would collectively have been quite sufficient to develop his character. Ambition is not the way to maturity, Mr Edmonds, any more than greed is the way to riches.'

Collis lifted his eyes and looked out of the window at the street. It was growing dark now, that soft periwinkle dusk that settles over Northern California at night, and the lights of Sacramento were beginning to twinkle and shine on the valley floor. He heard a wagon roll by, and someone calling out. A black maid in a white apron came into the living-room and lit four or five oil lamps, so that the room suddenly took on the appearance of a theatrical stage.

'You're right, of course, Mrs McCormick,' said Collis, looking back at her.

'Is Mary gong to be here soon?' asked Leland, unbuttoning his coat and sitting down in the largest smoking chair in the room. 'I was surprised she wasn't here already.'

'She said she would come over by seven,' Jane told him. 'She had to finish arrangements for tomorrow's social.'

Charles sat down, too, and nodded to Collis to make himself comfortable in a red brocade armchair. 'Mary,' he said, quiet affably, considering that Mary was his wife and that Mary had not been here to greet him after his trip to San Francisco, 'believes that the duties of a hostess are any woman's supreme priority. Husbands definitely come lower on the totem.'

'Charles and Mary have a marriage that was made in the *Elite Directory*, if not in heaven,' said Jane, which was a heavy attempt at a joke.

Collis managed a smirk in response, but it was clear that Leland neither understood his wife's humour nor appreciated it. He laced his big fingers together and said: 'I will have completed a year as a state senator in January. I'm thinking of running for governor again.'

'I think you should,' said Charles. 'Do you have a drink, though? I'm parched after that boat journey.'

'We have some Madeira,' put in Jane McCormick. She turned to Collis and said, in a tone that he could only think of as over-explanatory, 'We only use these apartments when business is very hectic. We have a house overlooking the river. A very fine house.'

At length, after twenty minutes of awkward conversation, they heard the downstairs door open, and the rustle of skirts as someone came up to the hallway. All the gentlemen stood up as a stern, white-haired woman appeared in the living-room doorway, in an evening cape of dark-blue merino wool, and a severe, dark-blue bonnet. Her eyes were as small as screwholes in her pale, square cheeks, and her mouth was straight as a slit-open envelope. She carried a forbidding black purse.

Charles stepped across and kissed her cheek. She was slightly taller than he was, or at least she appeared to be. She accepted the kiss in the same way that a statue accepts a bird perching

288

momentarily on its shoulder: I am here, I have to be here, and so I suppose I have to put up with such minor indignities.

'I don't suppose you managed to call on the Milton Lathams, Charles,' she said coldly.

Charles coughed.

'It doesn't matter. They're unbearably ostentatious anyway,' said Mary Tucker, and stepped into the centre of the room so that everybody could admire her extreme plainness. Collis could see why Charles took Knickerbocker Jane out to the theatre, and why he paid for young girls like Elsie. After a month or two with Mary, the sight of a pretty feminine face must have been as welcome as a cold beer would have been now, if only the dour McCormick had kept some on ice; and between Mary and Jane, Collis could only conclude that his two Sacramento business associates had netted the two homeliest wives in California.

Collis felt hungry, thirsty, and depressed. He wished now that he had stayed in San Francisco, and continued to make a modest living with cards. The memory of Knickerbocker Jane's whorehouse on Dupont Street, and his small but private room, with girls and bottles of champagne whenever he desired them, seemed now, in the presence of the Tuckers and the McCormicks, to be a Western paradise. If only the goddam High Sierras weren't out there in the darkness, challenging and strange. If only railroads had never been invented.

Mary Tucker had approached Collis now, and so he gave her a small bow and took her hand.

'Charles has told me so much about you,' he said. He tried to keep his voice as concerned and as serious as possible.

'I am the mainstay of Charles's life,' responded Mary. 'If it were not for me, Charles would have no notion whatsoever of his social duties. But I have always been one to believe that to uphold society, and the social round, is a sacred task. I hope I can expect your support for my glee club, Mr Edmonds.'

'I'm not sure at this moment,' Collis answered. 'Glee is a commodity of which I am a little short.'

Mary Tucker gave a brief, unamused smile, and then turned to Jane McCormick. 'Jane, my dear, you must ask your John for his recipe for that chicken stew. It would make a splendid Saturday luncheon for when the Reverend Spratt comes around.'

Eventually, the black maid summoned them all to the dining

room, and for the next two hours they sat under the wavering light of ten candles, eating onion soup, roasted chicken with hominy pudding and pickled yellow beans, bacon and tomato slices, and apple pandowdy. Outside, the night grew blacker, until their candlelit reflection in the windows appeared like a supper of ghosts. Collis, tired from the journey and the unfamiliarity of Sacramento, felt more like his reflection than his real self, and he ate his meal and stayed quiet while Charles and Leland talked of coal and pitch and saltpetre prices, and while Mary and Jane politely tried to claw each other's taste in Sunday hats to shreds of verbal millinery.

At last, however, it was all too much. Collis was either going to establish where he stood from the beginning, or else he was going to be drawn down into the maze of provincialism, from which he suspected much brighter men than he had been unable to find their way out. If he socialised with the Tuckers and the McCormicks, and the Reverend Spratt, and joined the Sacramento Valley Glee Club, he would only be filling his life with more confusions and complications, and he could see his vision of a Sierra railroad being gradually obscured behind a forest of screws, singing, swinging stanchions, and community suppers.

'I'm going to build a railroad,' he said suddenly. 'All the way from here to Nebraska.'

Charles looked across at him, displeased. Leland, wrestling with a slice of bacon, frowned at his plate with noticeable irritation. The two wives, who were well behind with their meal, because they had been trying to outdo each other in the fastidiousness of their nibbling, both sat back in their chairs and stared at Collis as if he had belched.

'Collis likes the idea of a transcontinental railroad,' Charles said with unconvincing cheer. 'In fact, he's wagered quite a few people in San Francisco that he can have it surveyed and ready to lay in not less than five or six years.'

Leland chewed his bacon, slow and deliberate. Then, swallowing, he raised his fork and pointed it across the table at Collis, waving it up and down to emphasise his words.

'We're Californians,' he said, in the tone of a man addressing the state finance committee. 'Whatever we do, whatever we invest, should have a direct benefit to the state of California and those who live here. You can't tell me that a transcontinental railroad would benefit anybody at all in California, not financially, and not socially. All it would do is drain our resources eastwards, and encourage an influx of tourists, scavengers, criminals, and adventurers.'

He paused, then added, 'I've heard this talk of a transcontinental railroad before, from Theodore Jones, and one or two other irresponsibles. Well, I don't want to hear any more of it, Mr Edmonds, not if you want to work here, because to my mind it's both reckless and fantastic.'

'It could be done, though, couldn't it?' said Charles, trying to defend Collis against Leland's sombre pronouncements.

Leland put down his fork. 'It could, Charles,' he said patiently. 'But those who invested in it would lose their shirts and I daresay their underclothing besides, asking the ladies' pardon. It would cost millions of dollars, and it would take years to construct, and it would rob California of her greatest political asset, which is her holy isolation from the East.'

'Don't tell me you're scared,' Collis said.

Leland looked at him with contempt. 'I've no need to fear the impossible, Mr Edmonds. Now, Charles, what were you saying about those pumps?'

Collis kept his eyes fixed on Leland's hard, straight profile. 'Changing the subject will not change my destiny, Mr McCormick.'

'Your destiny, Leland replied, 'tomorrow morning, and for a great many tomorrow mornings after that, is to make a complete inventory of all of our stock. I am perfectly aware that changing the subject will not alter that.'

Collis spent the next two weeks with a notebook and a pencil in his hand and a cheroot clenched between his teeth, pale-faced and irritable, counting valves and fuses and barrels of gunpowder, and noting them down, and then counting round-point shovels and screw dies of rubber belting, and noting *them* down. He was bored and he was angry, most of all at himself, for having to spend the whole day confined in this greasy hardware store, performing such menial work; and even at seven o'clock, when the store closed, his boredom and anger didn't abate much, because he would have to return then to Charles Tucker's red-and-green painted frame house not far from Sutter's Fort, and sit at Mary Tucker's dining table for mushy Brunswick stews and flavourless Indian puddings, while Mary talked monotonously of church socials and ladies' tea

291

parties, and Charles grunted in a variety of keys to suggest interest, surprise, sympathy, or disapproval, without actually saying a word. After dinner, Collis would have a smoke on the veranda, and then go to bed: brass, narrow, and abstinent.

Sitting on a keg of saddler's tallow on the store's veranda on his third Thursday in Sacramento, in shirtsleeves and a white wide-brimmed hat which he had bought for working outside, Collis wondered why he had come here at all. For all Charles's enthusiastic promises in San Francisco, he now seemed to have no intention of promoting Collis beyond the post of general help, and neither had Leland, whose interminable pomposity was leavened only by moments of dire moroseness, during which he would wander around the store bumping into things and complaining about God's plan.

None of this seemed to be bringing Collis any nearer to realising his vision, although he reluctantly had to admit that he now knew the price of sleepers and spikes and railroad ties, the price of English steel rails ($60 a ton, delivered on the East Coast), their length (15 feet) and their weight ($39\frac{1}{2}$ pounds to the yard). He had read through the heaps of hardware and engineering journals stacked at the back of the store, and learned to his surprise that the Union boasted 27,000 miles of railroad, costing over $920 million. He had found out something about locomotives, too, and how they worked. In his cream-painted bedroom on the third floor of Charles Tucker's house, while Charles and Mary softly snored in their separate bedrooms beneath him, he had frowned for hours over pictures of double-flue section engines, spread trucks, and wagon-top boilers.

In the early hours of this morning, while it was still dark outside, he had wakened up to find his lamp wick burned down, and a diagram of Bissell's new swivelling-truck patent still lying open on his worn patchwork comforter.

But as he sat outside the store just after ten o'clock, adding up bushels of staples, he was coming to the conclusion that he could have picked up all of this technical information just as easily in San Francisco, at the Mercantile Library or the Mechanics' Institute. The practical business experience for which he had agreed to come to Sacramento was being denied him, by both Charles and Leland. Charles, now that he was home, was not half so cheery and helpful as he had been in San Francisco, and Leland was openly obstructive. Maybe they were jealous, or plain unimaginative; who knew. It didn't really matter. What did matter was that Collis urgently needed to acquire the skills of a manager, and they were giving him nothing but the chores of a coolie.

He had just put down his pencil, with a mind to going inside the store and talking to Charles about his feelings, when a sulky came trotting along K Street, driven by a young bearded man in a long morning coat, and drew up not far away. The young man tied up his horse, straightened his hat, and then came across to 54 K with his eyes screwed up against the late-October sunlight.

'Can I help you?' asked Collis.

The young man gave a brief smile. He looked well bred, and quite self-assured, with pale and penetrating eyes. His beard had been meticulously clipped, and his moustache was brilliantined.

'I was looking for Mr Charles Tucker,' he said. The young man extended his hand. 'My name's Theodore Jones. You're new here, aren't you?'

Collis stood up and firmly put out his own hand. 'Collis Edmonds, out of New York. I've been looking forward to meeting you.'

'You have?' asked Theodore Jones. 'Has my reputation spread that wide?'

'Charles told me something about you. It seems that you and I have an interest in common.'

Theodore raised an eyebrow. 'You're not interested in a transcontinental railroad?'

Collis suddenly realised why Theodore was looking so sceptical. Here Collis was, sitting outside of a store on a tallow barrel, in a dusty hat, looking like nothing more than an underpaid clerk. He couldn't have appeared to the railroad pest like the stuff of which heavyweight investors are made.

'I'm helping out at the store,' Collis said. 'I'm a friend of Tucker's, you see. But I do have some finances of my own. Or at least I will have, when I get back to San Francisco and realise my assets.'

'You're *really* interested in a railroad?' asked Theodore cautiously, with one foot on the veranda step.

'Mr Jones,' Collis told him, 'I came across the isthmus, and nearly lost someone very dear to me from the yellow fever.'

'I'm sorry to hear it. She's recovered now, I hope?'

Collis glanced away. 'I guess so. Yes, she is.'

Theodore gently stroked his beard, looking at Collis with care. He had obviously been ribbed and teased in his time, and he seemed to want to make sure that Collis wasn't just another practical joker. Although he had a personality that struck Collis as warm and ingenuous, he didn't seem to have much in the way of a sense of humour. Collis could understand it, in a way. The vision of crossing the Sierra Nevada by rail didn't leave much room in anyone's brain for casual fun.

'Look,' Theodore said, 'my business with Charles isn't desperately urgent. Can you spare a half hour to talk?'

'Sure. I was about to down tools in any case.'

'That's good. If you want to go get your coat, I'll meet you across the street in the Sutter House.'

Collis went back into the soap-smelling shade of the store, where Charles was sitting at a stool, his sleeves held up with armbands, working on the month's accounts. He took his black morning coat down from the peg and said, 'I'm taking a half-hour break.'

Charles looked up, his eyes bright and fixed. But when he saw that Collis had already shrugged on his coat and was reaching for his hat, he said, 'Very well,' in a testy voice, and went back to his lines of figures and his metal spikes crowded with bills.

Across the street, the Sutter House was a boarding establishment and dining-room, with a high reputation for hash browns. It was run by a former wagon-train cook called Bilton, a hugely fat man with only one eye. The other eye, he claimed, had been lost when a spit-roasted pig, in a posthumous gesture of defiance, had spat hot lard at him. Bilton modestly announced that he could cook anything, from squirrel to horse, and make it fit for a hungry man.

Collis crossed the boardwalk and pushed his way in through the double doors. Inside, the dining-room was fragrant with meaty grease and the smell of freshly-brewed coffee. Theodore Jones was sitting in the corner against the light-green wooden dado, his legs neatly crossed, stirring a cup of chocolate.

'Coolish morning, Mr E,' said Bilton. 'What's it to be?' Collis, who hadn't yet eaten breakfast, looked up at the blackboard behind the counter and ordered a plateful of sausage and fried apples and a pint of black coffee. Then he went over to Theodore's table and pulled out a chair.

'You seem a little out of place here in Sacramento, if you don't mind my saying so,' said Theodore.

'I don't mind. You're an East Coast man yourself, aren't you?'

Theodore nodded. 'Raised in Bridgeport, Connecticut, as a

294

matter of fact. But when you're a railroad engineer, you don't ever have a place you can truly call home. Your home is where the tracks are.'

'I wouldn't have thought there was much work for a railroad engineer around these parts, not at the moment.'

'There isn't. After the gold mines at Folsom gave out, the directors of the Sacramento Valley suspended all their construction. But they're short-sighted, like everyone else in California. They don't understand the implications of building a road across the Sierras, or if they do, they're afraid of them.'

Collis picked up the salt cellar and looked at the tiny distorted reflection of his own face in the shiny top. 'You really believe it's possible?' he asked Theodore.

Theodore nodded. 'It's not only possible, it's urgent. Economically urgent, socially urgent, and politically urgent. Let me tell you something. Three years ago, the Secretary of War recommended to Congress that a transcontinental road should be built along the Southern Trail. It's madness, of course. The Southern Trail goes across country so desolate that Kit Carson says a wolf couldn't make his living off of it. Not only that, the Southern Trail actually dips below the Mexican border, and the Southern politicians had to cook up a scheme to buy land from Mexico to give the railroad a right of way. But it's what they desperately need, of course – a Southern-route railroad. The future of the South's economy depends on it. And that's why Jeff Davis, our unbiased and impartial Secretary of War, who also happens to have all his wealth tied up in his Mississippi plantation, has been so enthusiastic about supporting it.'

Collis sat back in his chair as Bilton laid a heaped-up plate of spicy sausage and apple in front of him, with sourdough bread, fresh creamery butter, and a chipped enamel mug brimming with black coffee. He dug in with his fork as Theodore watched him. Theodore looked like the kind of man who could admire food, even feel like eating it sometimes, but whose appetite was usually killed by what went on in his head.

'Davis has ordered a complete reconnaissance of the Southern Trail,' said Theodore. 'Flora, fauna, weather, natural resources, you name it. It will probably take years. But even if you leave aside the politics, even if you leave aside the fact that a Southern-route railroad will perpetuate slavery and give the South an economic bond with California that could isolate the North, Davis is completely wrong-headed. I'm a railroad surveyor and engineer, Mr Edmonds, and I *know* what's needed. I built the Niagara Gorge Railroad before I was twenty-eight years old, and I worked for years for the Erie Railroad at Buffalo. What's needed is a central, direct railroad that's comparatively cheap to construct, and that will cross the Rockies and the Sierras at susceptible points. What's needed is a railroad that will actually *work*.'

Collis wiped his mouth with his napkin and took a swallow of hot coffee. A fly settled on the rim of his plate, and he brushed it away. It twiddled around and then came back again. 'Can you find a way over the Sierra Nevada?'

Theodore Jones lowered his head and watched the bubbles on the surface of his chocolate slowly circling. Then he looked up again. 'I haven't found the ideal way yet. There's the Donner Pass, the old emigrant trace where all those poor people starved to death in 'forty-six, but that's pretty steep. Too steep, probably. There may be other ways. I'm *sure* there are other ways. But it takes months to survey those mountains, and you can take it from me that the conditions are pretty difficult.'

'You seem confident enough,' said Collis.

'Oh, I'm confident all right,' said Theodore. 'I'm not only confident, I'm sure. I know the people call me Pacific-railroad-crazy, and I know they've dubbed me the railroad pest. Even my wife says that nobody cares for what I say, and that I give my thunder away. But I say that this thing will happen as sure as next year is 1859, and that we must keep the ball rolling.'

Collis put down his fork. He looked across the table at this young energetic man with his neat beard and his grey but lambent eyes, and he couldn't help smiling with the pleasure of what he was hearing and what he was feeling.

'Let me tell *you* something,' he said, a little hoarsely. 'One night, in Aspinwall, on the Panama isthmus, I stepped outside my hotel and went to look at a locomotive that was standing on Front Street. It was raining, and that locomotive looked like some kind of great glistening monster that could sweep people away, willy-nilly, into all kinds of adventures and all kinds of unexpected futures.

'Well, that was the romantic side of it. I won't deny that my interest in the hardware of trains is more romantic than technical, although since I've been here in Sacramento, I've tried to make a reasonable study of the latest locomotives and passenger cars, and how they work. But I have a vision, too, that isn't romantic at all, but more to do with what this nation is, and how power and money can be harvested out of her, for the benefit of everybody, including me. And that vision is of great twelve-wheeler locomotives, drawing endless trains of freight and passenger cars, winding their way through the peaks of the High Sierras.'

Theodore licked his lips. 'You're not trying to make sport of me, are you, Mr Edmonds?'

'I daren't,' said Collis.

'You daren't? What do you mean?'

'I have thousands of dollars in bets riding on the certainty that I can survey and prepare a pass through the mountains for a transcontinental railroad. Half of San Francisco's banking community would scalp me if I failed. The less reputable half, I admit. But it looks as if you're the only person who can do it. So don't think I'm making sport.'

Theodore frowned. 'You made certain bets on this railroad even before you knew it was technically possible?'

'That's right.'

Theodore let out a long breath. 'Well,' he said, 'it seems you have even more faith in it than I do.'

'Not faith. Certainty. I'm certain, since I left New York, that God creates currents of history on which we all float. I'm not particularly religious, so don't question me too close about it. But I know that when I've offered up prayers to God, they've worked, after a fashion; and that when I've needed some kind of aim in my life, God has let me loose in one of his – what shall I call it? flows of destiny.'

Theodore finished his chocolate, watching Collis over the rim of his mug. Then, wiping his moustache, he said, 'Would you be prepared to support me? Have you seen my pamphlet?'

'Yes, I would, and no, I haven't.'

'My God, this is excellent!' said Theodore enthusiastically. 'My God, this is a real stroke of good fortune! You're right, God must have borne you here! That's the only way to account for it! You must come to dinner with Annie and me when you're settled! It won't be grand. Pot luck, probably, but I'm sure you won't mind.'

'Strictly *entre nous*,' Collis said, 'anything at all would be better than Mary Tucker's Brunswick stew. I think her John cooks with candlewax and iron filings, brushed out of the store.'

'Well, we don't have a John. Annie does all her own cooking.

She's a rare woman, you know. She's had to move twenty times in six years. She's followed me from New York State to California with scarcely a murmur of protest, and she's had to put up with all kinds of deprivations, not to mention my ceaseless talk about the great Pacific railroad. But she's always cheerful. We've only been back from Nevada Territory for a while. I was out surveying wagon roads for the silver miners. But she's managed to settle back here in Sacramento without any complaint, and make our home a picture. She's brought up our daughter, too, through all of this, as if everything else hadn't been quite enough for her.'

Collis forked up the last piece of apple and ate it. 'I suppose you know we'll have to go to Washington, if we're going to think about building a railroad with any seriousness. The first thing we're going to need is support from Congress, especially if Jeff Davis is promoting his southern route so strongly.'

'I know that,' said Theodore. 'I was planning to make a trip back East in February, and see what I could do to rouse some support among the Republicans.'

'I'll come with you,' said Collis. 'I think that I'm going to have to grow some political teeth as well as some business teeth, and I might just as well start right away.'

'Oh, you'll grow teeth all right.' Theodore smiled. 'And claws, too. Some of the strongest men in both houses are right behind Davis. And they're fighting for their lives, too. A central continental railroad would leave their plantations and their slave economy isolated and abandoned, to shrivel on the vine.'

'I know some of them already,' said Collis. 'Preston Brooks, of South Carolina. Stephen Douglas, of Illinois, who used to be a dinner guest of ours in New York. Alexander Stephens, of Georgia.'

'And don't forget William Stride, either,' put in Theodore. 'He's in so deep with the Southern Trail railroad that some people say they're going to name it the Stride & Pacific.'

'William Stride?' asked Collis intently. He had a vivid, momentary memory of the Astor Place Hotel, in New York, facing an aquiline man with side whiskers who kept his face in shadow. A man who had deliberately betrayed, and ultimately brought about the death of, his father, Makepeace.

'You know him?' asked Theodore.

Collis turned his face aside and squinted through the drifting smoke towards the dust-mealed window.

'Yes,' he said softly. 'I believe I do.'

Charles was annoyed when Collis returned an hour later. He had finished his accounts, and tidied the shelves, and now he was pacing the boarded floor of the hardware store, tugging at his stiff collar from time to time and working himself up into a state of proprietorial indignation.

'Ah,' he said, as Collis walked in, blowing his nose. 'You're back, at last.'

'Yes, I'm back,' said Collis, hanging up his hat.

Charles pulled at his whiskers. 'I suppose you know you were away from the store for more than an hour.'

'Was I? I was talking to your railroad pest, Theodore Jones.'

'What *is* it about you and railroads?' Charles snapped.

Collis took off his coat and hung that up, too. 'I'm not at all sure,' he said in a bland tone. 'I might just as well ask, what is it about you and hardware? What is it about you and rope? What is it about you and Hancock inspirators?'

Charles tilted his head on one side, angry and suspicious. 'Perhaps you need reminding that you arrived on Broadway Wharf without a single friend, apart from Andy Hunt, and that you carelessly left your trunk where any Sydney Duck could have walked off with it. Perhaps you need reminding that it was I who showed you around San Francisco, I who introduced you to all the palaces of pleasure, and I who brought you out here to Sacramento and gave you employment and lodging.'

Collis rolled up his sleeves. 'You're quite right, of course, Charles. You did all of those things, and I'm grateful.'

'But?'

'Did I say but?' asked Collis.

'No, you didn't. But you implied it.'

'Well,' said Collis, in a quiet voice, 'it does seem that you're expecting more than gratitude.'

'I'm expecting a full day's work, if that's what you mean.'

'Come on, Charles, this isn't like you. In San Francisco you were friendly and bluff and ready for amusement at any time of the day. Girls, drink, faro. And we were equals, too, wouldn't you say? Well, what's happened to all that now?'

Charles tugged uncomfortably at his whiskers. 'You have to remember that I'm a respected citizen here. One of the pillars of the whole community.'

'So you can't be friendly?'

'It isn't that,' said Charles. 'It isn't that at all. It's just that Leland thinks you ought to serve some kind of apprenticeship into the trade, and so does Mary.'

'Mary thinks I ought to spend my days counting up bushels of nails?'

Charles looked away, embarrassed. 'She's, well, she's right in a way. It takes years to learn this business. You can't find out all there is to know in two weeks.'

'Is that your opinion, or Mary's? Or Leland's? You haven't told me what Jane thinks I ought to be doing with my life.'

'We are all of a similar opinion,' said Charles. He was blushing.

'Then you're all wrong,' said Collis. 'And *you're* the wrongest of all, because you got to know me in San Francisco and you saw what kind of a fellow I can be. When I gamble, I win. When I live any part of my life, I try to come out of it with credit and success. That's how New York gentlemen are brought up, Charles. It's natural to them. And even though I hate to pull social rank on you, it's about time you and your dismal business partner, *and* your worthy wives, understood me for what I am.'

He finished rolling up his sleeves by giving each of them a sharp tug. 'If you gave me the opportunity, I could learn this business in a matter of weeks. I already know what a Hancock inspirator is actually for. Lifting water by steam pressure, so there.'

Charles gripped the edge of the wooden counter with both hands and pressed against it as if he were doing his daily exercises. 'I don't know what you *want*, Collis,' he said, in exasperation. 'I don't know what you could possibly *want*, other than this.'

He raised his head and looked along the rows of barrels of Peerless waterproofing compound, mineral barn paint, and carriage varnish. 'This is a prosperous business, Collis, with a good future, and it's founded on solid and respectable lines. In ten or twenty years, you could be a man of considerable means.'

'Ten or twenty years? You're fooling me, aren't you?'

Charles stared at him, perplexed. 'It took *me* that long.'

Collis stood close to Charles, and when he spoke his voice was very soft and conciliatory. His words, though, were the words of a New York society rake, still cutting and self-possessed, even if they had been tempered by bankruptcy, and Hannah West, and a hard crossing of the Panama isthmus. 'Charles,' he said, 'it took you that long because you are a natural-born member of the merchant classes, who revel in merchandise. It took you that long because you know your place in the world, and because ambition seems to you to be improper and alarming. But I am not like you, Charles, no matter how kind and sympathetic you have been to my present plight. I am one of the upper classes, and a capitalist by instinct, whether I actually own any capital or not, and as such I have talents of leadership which need only the minimum of training to assert themselves in full and glorious bloom.'

'What the hell are you saying?' demanded Charles.

Collis stuck his hands in his pockets and smiled. 'I'm saying, Charles, that unless you treat me as an associate, rather than a dogsbody, then I shall have to consider leaving you. I'm quite willing to knuckle under, and learn the business, but so far I haven't done anything but count the yardage of fuse, and the poundage of screws, and it really isn't going to help either of us if that's all I continue to do.'

Charles rubbed his face with the palm of his hand. He sniffed. 'I do sympathise,' he said. 'I do see what you mean, and I do sympathise.'

'You *sympathise*?'

'Well, you know what I mean.'

'I'm not at all sure that I do,' Collis told him.

Charles was about to say something, but then the brass bell over the store door jingled, and in walked Leland McCormick, his face contorted more than ever by the requirements of looking simultaneously dignified, disapproving, and heavily burdened by the retail hardware trade. He stood in the centre of the store, in his dark-grey tailcoat and his tall black hat, and he looked around it as if it were the most miserable discovery of his life.

'We are so low on endless belting that it is chronic,' he said, by way of greeting. 'Either that, or Mr Edmonds's latest inventory was not as thorough as it might have been.'

Collis gave a sharp, provoked smile. But Charles quickly put in, 'I let stocks of endless run down on purpose. We've had too many complaints. I'm recommending belts with laced joints now. At least they stretch when they're required to, instead of snap.'

'H'm,' said Leland as if he was unconvinced, and continued his slow walk around the store.

Collis took a cheroot out of his coat, where it was hanging on its peg, and then leaned over the counter to find a box of matches. He said evenly, 'My inventory was thorough to the point of absurdity, Mr McCormick, but I suppose that's just as well.'

Leland stopped and turned. He had a way of looking at people who surprised or irritated him which involved making one eye bulge and stare, and the other close into a disapproving slit.

'Why is that just as well, Mr Edmonds?' he asked, with heavy wariness.

'Collis put the cheroot between his lips. 'Because, Mr McCormick, it is the last I shall do.'

'I see. You're considering leaving us?'

'Not unless we're unable to come to some agreement about my position here.'

Leland continued to stare at Collis for a moment. Then he gave a brittle cough and looked away. He put his hands on his hips.

'An inventory is a task which anyone with the knack of counting up to one thousand can do with complete ease,' added Collis. 'I feel that my potential talents are being wasted. Perhaps deliberately.'

Leland plunged his hand into the open top of a keg of casing nails, sifting through them as if they were small silvery fish. 'I see you have that curious Eastern sense of your own importance,' he said, sifting and sifting again. 'Maybe you should understand that out here, a man is judged by what he does and what he's achieved, rather than where he came from or who his parents were.'

'You know just as well as I do that all that kind of talk is romantic claptrap,' said Collis genially. 'The West is ten times more sensitive about its social elevations than the East could ever be. Don't tell me you think Mr Bilton at the Sutter House is equal in social standing to you and your lovely lady – no matter how many fine meals he's cooked, and no matter how often he's proved himself worthy and honest.'

'Sophistry,' growled Leland, letting the last of the nails drop into the keg. 'And don't you light that damned smoke. There's enough black powder and fuse in this place to send us all to purgatory together without a moment's pause for prayer.'

Collis lit the end of his cheroot, drew at it deeply, and tossed the dead match on to the floor. 'At least if we go to purgatory together, we'll be doing *something* together. Right now, I feel as if you're making quite sure that I'll never rise above the station of errand boy and counter-upper-in-chief.'

Leland's cheeks twitched. 'You're ambitious,' he said slowly. 'That's why.'

'Of course I'm ambitious. But that should serve you well, instead of badly. Instead of crushing my ambition, why don't you use it to further your interests? I would, if I were you. If I were you, I'd take every ounce of my energy and every scrap of my zeal and turn them towards the making of money for Tucker & McCormick, and in particular for the making of money for McCormick.'

Leland was silent. Collis walked around the counter, smiling. On the dark wall behind him, beside the tiers of wooden drawers, was a calendar for 1857 with a fine steel engraving of the San Francisco fire of 3 May 1851, showing refugees running up Telegraph Hill like tiny beetles. 'Jane thinks – ' Leland began.

'That's exactly it,' said Collis. 'Jane thinks. Between them, Jane and Mary run this business as if they were puppeteers, and you two were their dancing-dollies.'

'That's absurd,' said Leland.

'Is it?' asked Collis. 'Ask Charles, then, what he really thinks about my taking a greater part in managing the store. Not what Mary thinks, or what he thinks you think, but his real feelings.'

Leland fixed his staring eye on Charles. 'Charles?' he demanded.

Charles cleared his throat and looked unhappy. 'I suppose what Collis says is true, Leland. Well, partly true, at least. It wasn't wrong of us to start him off right down at the bottom, and make him prove that he could tell one end of a nail from the other. But he's just as hardheaded as I am, and he's just as much of a society man as you; and if we don't let him make his way – well, I think we'll be holding back a good horse just because we don't like the sight of its ass as it goes past us.'

Leland pursed his lips. He said, in his most political tones, 'What worries Jane, Mr Edmonds, is that you will introduce gimcrackery into a business that has built its reputation on solidity. She isn't certain that you're stable enough, or that you have that particular doggedness which hardware selling asks of its managers.'

'In other words, I'm not dull enough.'

'I beg your pardon?'

'I might outshine her spouse, and if I did that, she might lose some of her control of the business, and what goes on there.'

'That is *not* what she meant,' said Leland stiffly.

'Well, maybe not,' said Collis. 'But I'm afraid the position remains the same. Either I have some promise of partnership, or J quit. That's all I can say.'

Leland looked at Charles, but Charles could only shrug. 'Very

303

well,' said Leland at length. 'Give us some time to discuss it. You can do that, surely?'

Collis nodded. He found, quite oddly, that he was beginning to like Leland. Of course Leland was boring and inflated, but any man who could live with a woman like Jane and still use words of three syllables had to have some virtues. Collis was certain that with a wife like that, his own mind would have turned to tapioca years ago.

Thinking of wives, he suddenly remembered the wife of Walter West, and both Charles and Leland looked across at him curiously as his face changed from amusement to unhappiness, quick and silent as a blind drawn down in a window across the street.

'You may come in,' said Jane McCormick.

He opened the door wider, and there she was on her davenport, her face as plain and bulbous as a garlic plant, and the same papery colour. Today, in the hazy light of an October morning, she wore a most unsuitable dress of yellow satin, with too many bows around it, fastened at the neck with a cameo brooch. The dachshund had eaten too much, and was sleeping in the corner of the room, exuding from time to time the most offensive smells. Still, Jane McCormick was well clouded in lavender.

'It was good of you to come up,' she said. 'Won't you please take a seat?'

Collis sat down in the large smoking chair, but found that the sun was in his eyes, and so he moved to a smaller chair right next to the end of the davenport. This seat had the added advantage of making it necessary for Jane McCormick to turn her head around awkwardly whenever she wanted to look at him. He gave her a little smile, although for the life of him he couldn't think why he had. It was about as enjoyable as smiling at a walrus.

'Will you have coffee?' she asked.

Collis nodded. 'One of your orange cookies wouldn't go down too badly, either, if you don't mind my suggesting it.'

'Of course not. I'm flattered. Now, where's that tiresome girl?'

Collis unbuttoned his morning coat and relaxed a little. He stayed quiet until the maid had come and gone, and then he said to Jane, quite bluntly, 'What a becoming dress. I haven't seen a dress so fine since I left New York.'

Jane blinked at him. 'Oh,' she said. Her hand came up and

304

touched the cameo at her neck. 'Oh, well, that's very civil of you to say so.'

'Not civil, Mrs McCormick. Truthful. There is a difference.'

Her cheeks coloured for a moment like the cheeks of a china doll, two round pink spots. But they faded again as she sat herself up more straight, and prepared the angle of her head for what she was going to say, slightly leaning to the left, one shoulder higher than the other.

'We had dinner here last night,' she said. 'Myself and Leland, Charles and Mary. Over the entrée, we discussed at some length what we were going to do about you.'

'Yes,' said Collis. He kept up a fixed, vacant expression in order to disconcert her as much as he possibly could. She smoothed her dress with square, unbecoming hands.

'I suppose it fell to me to tell you what we decided because of Leland's having to go to Auburn today,' said Jane. 'But, after a fashion, it also fell to me because I am the largest shareholder in the business, after Leland, and when Leland one day passes on to meet his Creator, I shall be in principal charge. So you can see that what happens to the business is of burning interest to me. It is my guarantee of a comfortable future. I want to see it managed sensibly and securely, and not gambled away on a whim.'

'Do you really think me whimsical?' asked Collis.

She looked up, blushing. 'Well – no. I mean *no*. I didn't mean it that way.'

'I don't mind,' said Collis. 'After all, I think *you* have a look of whimsy about you. And it's most attractive.'

She touched her brooch, her face, her flat brown hair. 'Whimsy? Me? Mr Edmonds, I do wish you'd stop this flattery. I have always been the most pragmatic of women.'

'Underneath the sensible exterior, there must be a young and whimsical heart. Don't tell me there isn't.'

'I – really, Mr Edmonds. You mustn't speak like this.'

'Is it wrong to express one's innermost feelings?'

She took a breath that was almost a gasp. 'Mr Edmonds, you know me for a married lady. Whatever your innermost feelings, you mustn't think that once we're alone you can throw proper social conduct out of the window.'

Collis would have liked to have thrown the dachshund out of the window. Its name was Urquhart, after the Scottish clan of which Jane fondly supposed she was a descendant. But he kept calm, and

305

half turned his face away from Jane, drooping his eyelashes in the sultry, wounded expression that Delphine had once called 'the petulant seraph'.

'It's not that your compliments are falling on stony ground, Mr Edmonds,' Jane said hurriedly. 'They are obviously sincere, and I'm sure that you mean well. It's just that I'm not at liberty to receive attentions of anything other than a courteous nature.'

Collis raised his head. He was acting so well that he thought he might even manage a few tears. Jane McCormick looked at him for a moment, her face sympathetic and sad, but excited, too, and she raised a hand towards him in that vague gesture that people use when they wave to a boat out to sea, not sure if the sailors have seen them or not.

'You won't think badly of me, will you, Mrs McCormick?' asked Collis, in a hoarse voice.

Jane was flustered. She bit at her knuckle, then turned and stared worriedly out of the window.

'The truth is,' she said, 'that we thought we might delay the matter of your partnership awhile.'

'Delay? For how long?'

'I don't know, Mr Edmonds. I'm really most confused. It was only a suggestion of Leland's, after all. He thought you might like to spend a little longer in Sacramento before you finally made up your mind that you wanted to join us permanently.'

'I see. And did you agree with him?'

'I – I thought I did.'

Collis stood up and crossed the room. He lifted aside the lace curtains and looked out westwards, towards the Sierras. He wasn't sure whether the white peaks he could see floating above a haze of golden mist were clouds or mountains. It didn't really matter. They were spectral and alluring, and he felt himslf drawn towards them. Up there were the high passes through which the emigrants had struggled with wagons and mules. Up there was a railroad trace to the East, crowned with snow and gilded with fame and potential profits.

Jane McCormick waited for Collis to say something, but when he didn't, she spoke meekly. 'Do you really want a partnership so very much? You don't seem like the kind of man who could be happy in hardware.'

Collis continued to stare at the Sierras. 'I've suffered a great deal of sorrow, Mrs McCormick. If I can find happiness of any description, I don't mind at all if it's in hardware. Nails and fuses and endless belting all have their own special magic, don't you think?'

Jane frowned. Collis let the lace curtain fall back. Then he came across and knelt on the rug beside the davenport, lacing his fingers together as if he were about to pray, or propose.

'I wanted a partnership because I thought it would give me a respectable way of staying close to you,' he said. 'But now you know the way I feel, now you know how much I admire and respect you, I quite understand that it's out of the question. It wouldn't be fair of me to stay here, expecting you to socialise with me, and dine with me, and work with me, all the time aware that – '

'Collis – Mr Edmonds – you mustn't. I'm sure we can find a way. I'm sure that for the sake of your happiness, and for the welfare of Tucker & McCormick, I can bear your closeness with fortitude.'

Collis could not believe what he was hearing.

'I'll talk toLeland,' she said quickly, fearful in case this enchanted moment should pass, and Collis should change his mind. 'I'll tell him that you ought to join the partnership straight away. Tomorrow, if the papers can be drawn up in time.'

Collis stood up. The maid came in with the coffee, on a black lacquered papier-mâché tray, and set it on a small wine table next to the davenport. She glanced at Mrs McCormick, then at Collis, pulled a face, and walked out again. Out of the rose-patterned Limoges coffee pot, a fragrant wisp of steam rose into the sunshine. There were orange and coconut cookies on a small dish.

'I'll have to invest money into it, won't I?' asked Collis. 'I don't have much ready cash at the moment.'

'You'll have the profits from those blankets soon, won't you? I can lend you a stake until the New Year. Perhaps Leland could even arrange to have shares transferred to you on loan.'

Collis took a cookie from the dish and bit into it.

'Well,' he said reluctantly.

'*Please* say yes,' she asked him.

He gave her his hand. She clutched it tight with both of her hands and looked up at him imploringly. Collis took a breath. 'Very well,' he told her. 'If you're sure that you want me to stay.'

Jane was so pleased that she clapped her hands like a schoolgirl. Then, sniffing with emotion, she poured out coffee, and they sat side by side on the davenport, sipping mocha and nibbling cookies, looking at each other from time to time with bright, exhilarated eyes, as if they had a wonderful new secret that nobody else could share.

Later, Collis went into the storeroom at the back of the shop and closed the door. He took down a half-empty bottle of bourbon from behind the kegs of flooring brads and poured himself three or four fingers into an enamel mug. He stood there swallowing the bourbon in large mouthfuls, quick and tense, like a man with a train to catch. He was beginning to understand how close he was to the richest and strangest adventure of his life. It frightened him. He frightened himself.

That evening, when Leland returned from Auburn, his coat soiled and his hat white with dust, he stopped on the store veranda by the hissing lamp where the moths flickered and flapped, and he looked a long time in silence at the sight of Collis relaxing in a basketwork chair with a glass of whisky and seltzer and a copy of the *Golden Era*. Not far away, in the darkness, sat Wang-Pu, himself just back from a sales trip to Placerville, smoking a small Chinese ivory pipe.

'What's this?' Leland said.

Collis folded over his magazine and replied calmly, 'Seven-fifteen. Store's been closed for a quarter hour.'

Leland removed his hat and struck it against the veranda post to knock the dust off. Collis took another swallow of whisky and continued to read. Wang-Pu said nothing.

'Did you speak to Mrs McCormick?' asked Leland.

'Uh-huh,' said Collis, without raising his eyes.

'And? What happened?'

'Nothing happened. We talked. She told me how you all felt.'

Leland put down his travelling case. 'So you know about the postponement in accepting you as a partner?'

'Yes.'

'And you're happy?'

'I'm happy that your lady wife has agreed to forget the postponement, and have me instated as a partner right away.'

There was a lengthy silence. The moths pattered and the lamp hissed. Leland lifted his head and stared upwards as if he could see clear through the veranda roof, right into Mrs McCormick's living-room, through the springs and stuffing of the davenport and into the workings of her brain. Then, without another word, he went to the store door, unlocked it with one of the keys on his jangling ring, and disappeared inside.

Wang-Pu sucked at his pipe. Both he and Collis sat quietly as doors banged upstairs, and voices were raised in argument. They heard Leland shouting, 'Are you mad, woman? Are you quite mad?' And they heard Jane shrilling, 'Your trouble is, you can't tell a talented man from a flea-bitten dog!' But then the living-room window was abruptly slammed shut, and all they could hear after that was heavy footsteps on the upstairs floors, creaks and squeaks, and indistinct wrangling that went on for nearly an hour.

'Surely the most terrible storm follows the greatest calm,' said Wang-Pu, with a wry grin.

Theodore Jones lived in a small square house on the southern edge of the city, among the scrubby trees on R Street, not far from where the Sacramento Valley Railroad ran into the streets on its arrival from Folsom. Collis had borrowed Jane McCormick's sulky to go visiting, much to Leland's displeasure, and he drove along by the river feeling easy and relaxed. He was looking forward to a good dinner.

It was the second day of November. The twilight sky was the soft colour of cornflowers, and the Sacramento River, as it eddied southwards, twisiting through the flats and mud bars of Solano County, was the same hue, but silvered. The paddle steamers moored along Front Street were strung with lights, and their tall chimneys and masts were silhouetted in black. Someone across on the west Sacramento shore was playing an accordion and singing 'Clear the Way'. A cool southwest wind was blowing.

As he trotted along beside the shade trees that lined the river, Collis heard the high whoop of a steam locomotive; and when he steered Mrs McCormick's grey towards the depot, and the street where Theodore Jones was staying, he saw a huge maroon-painted 4-4-0 with a bell-shaped smokestack backing along the road, with six or seven freight cars and a decorative green caboose. The locomotive rang its bell as it chuffed majestically on to the tracks that curved into Aspinwall's warehouse, and sparks tumbled out of its stack and into the evening sky like fireflies. Collis slowed his horse to a slow walk and watched with fascination as the shining train disappeared into the warehouse, its wheels grating and grinding on the steel rails and its cowcatcher wreathed in steam.

It took him only two or three minutes more to reach the Jones house. There was a warm light in the front window, and as he drove the sulky into the side yard and tied up the horse to a tree, he saw the drapes lifted back and Theodore Jones look out. He walked across the boarded veranda to the front door and knocked. He waited for a moment, listening to the clanking of the locomotive in the distance, and the soft rustle of the trees. He could smell pumpkin pie.

Theodore Jones opened the door and grasped his hand. 'Come in, we've been looking forward to this. Come in. Let me take your hat.'

Collis stepped inside. There was a small hall-way, hung with coats and hats, and a broken barometer. Then, through another door, a squarish living-room, with a wood fire burning to keep off the evening chill, and solid sawed-oak furniture of the kind that rented accommodations always used to sport in those days. There was yellowish wallpaper with sprays of roses, and a series of religious prints in dusty maple frames. In the far corner of the room there was a rolltop desk, where a bright oil lamp was burning, and this was strewn with maps and open books and bottles of ink. There were ten or twenty dog-eared copies of the *American Railroad Journal* scattered on the floor.

A door opened, and a young woman stepped into the room from the kitchen. She was flushed from cooking, and she had obviously just taken off her apron. She was not more than an inch taller than five feet, and she had a pretty, soft, oval face, and reddish-brown hair that was tied back in a knot. She looked as if she was practical, and straightforward, and not inclined to suffer any nonsense, because her face was freckled from the sun, and her hands were quite brown. Only women who worked to help their menfolk got suntanned. Collis, who was used to women shaded and sheltered by conservatories and parasols, found the sight of this speckly little girl quite intriguing, and when he bowed and took her hand, and kissed the back of her knuckles, he couldn't help lowering his eyes and glancing at the white circle that had been left on her third finger where she had taken off a ring while cooking.

'Annie, this is Collis Edmonds,' said Theodore, sticking his thumbs in his grey tweed vest and leaning back against the mantelpiece. 'Collis, this is my dear wife, Annie.'

'I'm honoured to know you,' said Collis.

Annie sat down on one of the grim armchairs and spread out her skirts. She was wearing a dark-brown cotton dress with an overlay

310

of white lace. It was simple, but it was special; and Collis, as he sat down opposite, made the ready observation that this was the sort of woman Annie was. Simple, but special. She wore no cosmetics, no perfume, and her nails were plain and unpainted. The only jewellery he could see was a small gold locket on a gold chain, which he guessed would contain pictures of Theodore and of their daughter Kate.

'I've been hearing all about you from my friends at the grocery store,' said Annie, with a smile that was polite, but strangely lacking in warmth. 'They say that you played Leland McCormick at his own game, and won, and still managed to stay friends.'

Collis crossed his legs. 'Oh, I didn't do anything. You know what gossip is. Leland and I have been the firmest of friends ever since I arrived in Sacramento.'

'I find that hard to credit.'

'Annie!' put in Theodore. 'You mustn't say such things!'

'I'm sorry,' said Annie, without sounding the least bit apologetic. 'It's a terrible habit of mine, to speak without considering the feelings of others.'

'It doesn't hurt my feelings if you suspect my friendship with Leland,' Collis said. 'As a matter of fact, I think he's a damned old fool. But Sacramento is a small community, and I'm a storekeeper here, and I have to behave myself according to the social rules.'

'You're either trying to play games with me, or else you're very cynical,' said Annie.

'You're making me sound that way,' said Collis. 'But I assure you that neither of those descriptions is accurate, or fair. I'm making my fortune, and to that extent I'm interested in my own welfare before the welfare of others. But I'm not cynical, and I'm certainly not playing games.'

Theodore took an old briar pipe down from the mantelpiece and blew down it to make sure it was clear. 'What I think is so marvellous is that you've been inspired about a transcontinental railroad for so long.'

'I suppose that's true?' asked Annie sharply. 'I mean, you really *are* interested, aren't you?'

Collis stared for a long time into her flecked hazel eyes. She didn't flinch, didn't blush, didn't turn away. 'You're very good at protecting your husband, aren't you?' he said carefully.

'Western women have to be. There isn't always the time or the opportunity for the niceties of feminine life.'

'You seem to have remained very feminine, in spite of that.'

Annie shrugged. 'Your reputation for flattery has preceded you, I'm sorry to say. My neighbour Martha Malone said that was the way you got yourself into Jane McCormick's good offices, by two hours of fluttering eyelashes and gushing compliments. I'm afraid flattery doesn't really work with me. I like to be praised, but I know what I am and what I'm not.'

Theodore, filling his pipe with shag, couldn't hold back a loud grunt of amusement. 'You'll find that Annie is her own woman, Collis.'

Collis sat back, regarding Annie with friendly interest. 'I believe I've found that already,' he said. 'It's remarkably refreshing.'

'Would you care for a whisky, or a glass of steam?' asked Annie.

'I think the whisky, please,' said Collis. 'My effete Eastern tastebuds haven't quite got themselves used to steam yet. But I'm persevering.'

'I *loathed* steam to begin with,' remarked Theodore. 'But here's an interesting thought: the San Francisco breweries are obliged to make beer by the krausening method – that is, by natural fermentation instead of added carbon dioxide – because they can't get sufficient ice on the West Coast for normal brewing. But if we were to build a railroad across the continent, the ice could be brought in boxcars, and we could set ourselves up in the lager business as a sideline. Now, how's that for foresight?'

Collis smiled at Annie as she handed him a glass of straight whisky. 'I think we'd better build the railroad first,' he said, in an even, steadfast tone. It was clear that Annie wasn't going to be impressed by anything except level-headedness and sincerity.

'That's what I keep telling Ted,' she said. 'Track first, fantasies later.'

Theodore, puffing good-humouredly at his pipe, his hands in his pockets, did nothing but smile. His railroad was too dear to him for gentle gibes like that to put him off.

Over dinner, sitting around a red gingham cloth laid with white dishes of potroast and prunes, hominy pudding, stuffed cabbage, and corn, the Joneses told Collis about their early married life together, about days in upstate New York and peaceful vacations in the Catskills, and about Theodore's work on the Niagara Gorge and the Erie railroads. Collis, in his turn, gave the young couple a rather romanticised version of his life in New York, and how the financial crash had ruined his father.

312

He thought about his mother, and his sister Maude, and wondered with an unexpected sense of guilt how they were.

Later still, by the fire, while Annie sat under the lamp and sewed, Collis and Theodore talked about railroads. Collis glanced over at Annie every now and then, and sometimes she returned his glances with a smile, but it was the look of a contented wife, a woman well cared for, and he knew that he could only treat her as a freind. Maybe it was time he made more friends, though, and fewer enemies.

Theodore said, 'There are some excellent surveys being undertaken in the East, for a railroad to the foot of the Rockies. The real man there to watch for is Thomas Durant, who's an executive for the Rock Island line. He's always been strong on the notion of a transcontinental road, very strong, and he's assigned one of his young engineers to survey the route from Council Bluffs westward, at least as far as Laramie.'

'Do you know the engineer?' asked Collis, holding his glass of whisky up to the firelight.

'Not personally, but by reputation. His name's Grenville Dodge, and he was trained under the Rock Island's chief engineer, Peter Dey. Thomas Durant sent Dodge out to survey the Platte River Valley – that was almost four years ago, and from what I hear he's been charting some pretty interesting maps.'

He relit his pipe and tossed the spent match into the fire.

'The problem is, of course, which railroad route will Congress eventually authorise? The Hannibal & St Joseph people have been pressing hard for a transcontinental line westward out of St Joe; and of course most of the Southern companies would like to see it come out of Memphis, or even New Orleans. The obvious choice to my mind is to take the track out of Council Bluffs, Nebraska, as an extension to the Rock Island line, because the route westwards from there is straight and flat, and I guess there must be two or three suitable railroad passes through the Rockies to Salt Lake City from Laramie. But it's going to take hard work in the political lobbies, as you said the other day. Hard work, and a great many powerful friends.'

'I have one friend in Washington,' said Collis. 'She's the daughter of William Stride.'

'Just how well do you know Stride?'

'I'm acquainted with him. I wouldn't count him as a friend. But then, I don't think we need to. As long as we can get some

313

introductions to Congressmen out of his daughter, then I think we'll have made a good start.'

'That sounds rather like hypocrisy to me,' Annie said. 'I wouldn't like anybody to use *my* friendship that way.'

Collis turned to her and nodded his head in recognition of what she was saying. 'In normal circumstances, Mrs Jones, I would agree with you. But this could be a small matter of personal revenge for me; and when I tell you one day what the good Senator Stride did to my family, then I'm sure that you'll understand.'

'Revenge is rather a low motivation for the building of a great transcontinental railroad, wouldn't you say?' asked Annie.

Collis remained expressionless. 'Many great achievements had their beginnings in base desires,' he remarked. 'Although I don't think this particular act of revenge is at all unworthy.'

'Well,' said Theodore, embarrassed, 'let's just say that we need to get to Washington as soon as we can, and start lobbying.' He started unrolling a large hand-drawn map of the Sacramento Valley. 'To begin with, we have to convince our investors, whoever they may be, that at every and any stage of its survey and construction, the railroad will return them profits. If they finance us to survey the Sacramento Valley and no further, then we will show them that we could use that short length of track to bring cordwood out of the forests into the city, and set up a thriving timber business. If they will finance us through to Nevada, then we will demonstrate that the line could economically be used to service the mines there. If they will pay us for survey alone, and not for construction, we will show them that our route can be used as a wagon road, if not a railroad.'

He sat back in his chair. 'The public has had railroad fever for years,' he said, 'but neither Congress nor private investors have the stomach to set the building of a transcontinental railroad in motion. Congress is hesitant because it is corrupt, and because it is being pulled one way by the North, and another way by the South, and a third by the Army Corps of Engineers, which is the most scandalous outfit of profiteers and double-dealers you ever came across. As for private investors, they won't put in a single dollar unless they believe they can have five dollars back by Friday, and they would rather put their money into land, or gold mines, or beef. Almost anything, rather than a railroad.'

'Well,' said Collis, 'we must do what we can to inspire their

314

generosity, as well as their support. It can be done, I think, if we can first show them that we can cross the Sierras.'

Theodore noisily rolled up the map. 'I'll find a way,' he told Collis, his eyes bright in the firelight. 'Now, would you like some more coffee?'

Over the next few days, Leland grudgingly began to accept that Collis was going to be an industrious and useful partner, and that his ambitions were not going to disturb the stability of Tucker & McCormick, nor shake the footing of its founder directors. He grumbled less to Jane about the way in which she had insisted on his transferring fifteen per cent of the store's assets into Collis's name, under the threat of not being spoken to for a month, and having to take his meals in the small study. And although he paced around the store as he always had, with a face as displeased as a horse with boils, he noticed with satisfaction that Collis was everywhere at once, checking through the selling and buying arrangements with Wang-Pu, ensuring that deliveries came on time from San Francisco, and training into the art of inventory a young pale-faced boy called Frederick Pugh, who wore a blue apron five sizes too large for him and always called Collis 'chief'.

Charles was guardedly pleased to have Collis as a partner. He was pleased because it took hours of work off his own shoulders, and because Collis's charming manners and nobby looks began to attract a noticeable number of new customers, particularly a certain type of blushing young lady who, once inside the store, seemed to forget altogether what it was she had come in there for. But he was guarded because his wife, Mary, disapproved of Collis, and the way in which Collis had hypnotised her friend Jane McCormick. 'Whenever that young devil is about, poor Jane's knees turn to water,' she snapped.

By the last week of November, Collis had straightened out the store so well that he decided to return to San Francisco for a week or two and see to his store of blankets. There were other things on his mind, too, like talking to Andrew Hunt about the possibility of setting up a railroad company, and maybe persuading Lloyd Wintle to change his mind about an investment. He decided it probably wouldn't be diplomatic to ask anything of Arthur Teach, but then Teach could eventually be compelled to invest in the railroad by the terms of his wager, which to Collis was a completely satisfactory twist altogether.

There was also Hannah. She must have reached San Francisco by now, and met up with her husband again, and he knew that he was going to have to see her again, and face up to what he felt about her. He had sat on the edge of his bed one evening and squeezed his eyes tight shut, trying to remember what she looked like. But all he could picture now was her blonde curls, and her delicate profile, and no matter how hard he tried to imagine her face, all he could see was a vague, haunting vision of the moment when he had first set eyes on her, on the windy deck of the steamship *Virginia*.

On a cool Thursday morning, he boarded the paddle steamer *Yuba*, of the California Steam Navigation Company, a fresh-painted vessel with shiny brass rails and holystoned decks, upon which a married lady might travel without upset or discomfort. He heard later that the *Wallace S. Martin* had gone aground on a mud bar and had been accidentally set ablaze, so that its complement of whores and gamblers had been obliged to wade to the Solano County shore with their dresses and their pants tucked up, carrying as many bottles of whisky as they could manage, while the ship crackled and exploded behind them.

He had booked himself a cabin, and he spent most of the journey on his bunk, reading the *Sacramento Union*, and staring at the white wooden ceiling above him and thinking about Hannah. He lunched in the ship's dining-room on smoked fish and sweet white California wine, and then he went out on deck for a walk and a smoke. He spoke to nobody, and was reading in his cabin when the *Yuba* docked at the Jackson Street Wharf in San Francisco, and he heard the now-familiar clamour of longshoremen, hotel agents, and Embarcadero riffraff.

As he walked down the landing ramp into the late-afternoon wind, he saw, of all people, Arthur Teach. The financier was standing by a smart black barouche, talking to two portly middle-aged men whom Collis recognised as partners in a freight corporation on Washington Street. Collis hoped for a moment that the press of people around the steamer's landing would block him from Teach's view; but then he decided that what he had done was free enterprise, not piracy, and that Teach would just have to accept him for what he was, as Leland McCormick had been obliged to do, too.

He crossed the wharf and raised his hat.

'Arthur. Gentlemen. My compliments.'

Arthur Teach stared at Collis in surprise. He was wearing a green

316

suit which was too tight under the arms, and made him look bilious. He looked at his two friends from the freight business, as if to judge from the expressions on their faces if Collis was really there at all, and then he stared back again.

'You've got yourself a damned barefaced nerve,' he said, in a throaty voice.

'I thought all was fair in love and market-cornering,' Collis smiled. 'And I did, after all, have a hell of a row to get out there.'

One of the portly freight men suddenly raised a hand. 'My word,' he said, 'you're Collis Edmonds, aren't you? The fellow who stole a march on poor Arthur here, over those blankets. Well now, let me shake your hand.'

They shook hands, and then the man led his partner forward, and they shook hands, too.

'If you can steal a march on Arthur, you're a good fellow,' said the freight man. 'Because Arthur's the best of his kind, aren't you, Arthur?'

'I suppose a few people might say that,' Arthur admitted, without very good grace.

'Then I think you two ought to show that you're still colleagues and friends,' said the freight man. 'Let's take ourselves along to the Bank Exchange Saloon, and have a drink on it, and maybe something to eat, too. Did you just alight from that steamer, Mr Edmonds?'

'Yes, sir, I did.'

'Then I'll have your trunk collected, and taken to wherever you're staying.'

'The International Hotel, sir.'

'Excellent. Are you coming, then, Arthur?'

Arthur Teach pulled a face; but then, despite himself, he smiled. 'All right,' he said. 'This town is too small for a man to bear grudges. But I warn you of one thing, Collis Edmonds. If I ever get the chance to pull the same kind of stunt on you, then by cracky I'll do it, and have a good laugh out of it besides.'

'That's a fair warning,' said Collis. 'Now, tell me how the weather's been here. Is it cold enough to start selling off those blankets yet?'

Arthur Teach laughed. 'What do you think of him, Garrett?' he asked the freight man. 'Doesn't he have the damnedest nerve?'

'A fellow needs nerve just to survive in the West,' remarked Garrett, as they climbed aboard Arthur Teach's carriage. 'To make money, he needs damned nerve. What the *damnedest* will bring him – well, only time can tell us that.'

He was beginning to know San Francisco better. From the window of his room on the fourth floor of the elegant five-storey International Hotel, which was one of the most fashionable addresses in town, he could look out over Jackson Street, and northwards to the sparkling lights of the Barbary Coast, that hive of groggeries, dance halls, whorehouses, dining-rooms, and sailors' cribs that sprawled between Pacific and Vallejo streets. To the east, if he leaned over the window-sill, he could see the solid red-brick banks and exchanges of the business district, and beyond to the waterfront. It hadn't been more than seven or eight years ago that the site of the International Hotel had been almost on the shore itself; but steady infilling of the bay with wooden pilings and sand from the southern valleys of San Francisco had taken the downtown area out as far as Davis Street, and further, engulfing abandoned ships and derelict jetties as it spread. In the old days, many of the businesses on Montgomery Street, which was now four blocks inland, had given their address as 'Montgomery Street on the Beach'.

These days, he knew how to get around on the coaches of the Yellow and Red lines, or the horsecars of the Sutter Street line, all at ten cents a trip. He knew where to eat, too, and during the first five days of his visit he dined at Gobey's Ladies and Gents Oyster Parlour on Sutter Street, which was celebrated for its boiled terrapin; at Delmonico's on O'Farrell Street, on broiled lobster; and at the Buon Gusto, where Charles had taken him one evening and introduced him to cioppino.

He did some business, buying belting and screws and hand pumps. He walked around a great deal, and bought himself two new suits, and some silk underwear. He bought an overcoat, too, because the days were growing colder and damper, and almost every morning a chilly fog would drift in from the grey Pacific. It was almost time to start selling his blankets.

But he stayed away from the places and the people who meant the most. He avoided Knickerbocker Jane's on Dupont Street, and he took trouble not to walk past William West's store on Montgomery. He didn't go to see Andy Hunt at his offices on Pine Street, by the California Market, because he didn't want to talk railroads until everything else for which he had come to San

Francisco had been settled. He was lonely and silent and he spent too long in the Bank Exchange Saloon, drinking sazeracs and stone fences. He returned to his hotel room almost every night with a thumping headache, and lay on his bed listening to the rattling and rumbling of carriages and wagons on Jackson and Montgomery, and the laughter of passing revelleers. He remembered it years later as a time that was as dark and self-engrossed as a mirror in a strange room, and its effect on him was so strong that he went to considerable pains never to drink alone again.

On the sixth day of his visit, he spent two hours dressing in a grey tailcoat and a grey silk hat. The morning was bitterly cold, and the office buildings and hotels outside his window were blurry with fog. He shaved carefully, combed his hair, and rubbed his hands with Lamot's Cologne. Then, after a pot of coffee in the hotel lobby, he put on his overcoat and went outside. His chest felt tight with anticipation.

He turned right at the corner of Jackson and Montgomery and walked south past the Monkey Block, the buildings which, apart from housing most of San Francisco's literary population, contained the Bank Exchange Saloon and Coppa's Italian restaurant. He was tempted to take a drink, but he didn't want to have whisky on his breath when he came face to face with Hannah again. He walked on, through the ghostly fog, and he felt as if he were walking through a dream.

He arrived at last at the corner of Montgomery and Bush, and only a few yards in front of him was the frontage of the store which announced itself as Fancy Goods, Sewing Notions, Etc., Walter F. West, Prop. He stood for a long time in the cold, his breath smoking and his eyelashes dewy with fog, before he continued along the boardwalk and stood outside the store.

She came out of the open door of the store and walked straight into him. The meeting was so abrupt, so unheralded, that neither of them could believe for a moment that it was really happening, and the first thing she said was 'Excuse me.'

'Hannah?' he said.

She looked up, startled. She was very small, much smaller than he remembered her, and she had lost twenty or thirty pounds in weight. Her blonde hair was drawn back under a plain charcoal-grey bonnet, with a lace trim, and she was wearing a severe grey cape. Her face was as grey and colourless as an ambrotype portrait, glass over dark paper, and her eyes, although they were as wide and full of feeling as before, seemed unnaturally and unhealthily large.

'Collis?' she answered. 'Is it really you?'

He glanced inside the open door of the store. 'Is Walter there?' he asked her.

'Of course. He's serving a customer.'

He took her arm. It was bony and frail through the sleeve of her dress. 'Can't we go some place to talk? We wouldn't want him to see us out here.'

'Collis, I can't. I'm on my way to buy bread.'

'But we have to talk. I've come all the way from Sacramento.'

She put her hand to her mouth and turned away from him. She had changed, illness and stress had changed her, but her profile was just as exquisite as it had been on that first afternoon on the *Virginia*, and if anything her suffering had sharpened it, and given it a quality of waiflike innocence.

'I arrived only two weeks ago, on the *Monterey*,' said Hannah. 'I've been resting a great deal, and I haven't even had the strength to write.'

'Did you get my message? The one I left at the post office?'

She glanced at him, and there was guilt in her eyes. 'I'm afraid I haven't yet discovered where the post office is.'

He held her arm tighter. 'Hannah,' he said, 'it was what we agreed. I left my address at the post office, and as soon as you arrived, you were going to get in touch.'

'I'm sorry, Collis. I haven't been well.'

'You're well enough to go for bread. The post office is only five blocks north and two blocks east.'

'Don't hold me,' she said. 'Please. Walter may see.'

He ignored her. 'We agreed that in Panama, didn't we? I would leave my address, and you would get in touch.'

'I don't know where the post office is,' she insisted.

He let her go. 'And you didn't want to find out, did you? You were hoping that I might have forgotten. Well, I haven't. I've been thinking about you constantly ever since I left you in Panama.'

'Collis,' she said faintly, 'I really don't think we ought to talk on the sidewalk. People are staring.'

He refused to look around, refused to look at anything but her. His heart was beating in great uncontrollable bumps. Somehow, he had known that his first meeting with her in San Francisco would be like this. But the dull predictability of it did nothing to lessen his pain. He felt as if he were suffering from the grippe, as if his body were trembling with sweats and sudden chills. She took a few steps along the boardwalk, north towards the corner of Bush Street, and he followed her mechanically, still staring at her, still stiff with the realisation that she didn't care for him after all. Why should she, now she was recovered, and back with her husband? Why should she, now she was safe and secure and respectable once more? Why should she, with God on her side?

'Hannah,' he said, in a tight voice.

She didn't answer, but turned her head away. From behind, in her severe bonnet and her cape, she could have been an elderly woman.

'Hannah, you have to tell me how you feel.'

She lifted her eyes. 'I feel unwell,' she said. 'The sisters did what they could to nurse me back to normal health, but my constitution was weakened by the yellow fever almost to the point of ruin. They told me that I would never be the same again. I am what you see me to be; and I shall never be any better.'

'Is that why you didn't get in touch? Because you didn't want me to see you this way?'

She shook her head. 'I wish I could say that it was. But I don't want to lie to you, Collis, no more now than I ever did.'

She looked over her shoulder at him and gave him a wan smile. 'By the time I reached San Francisco, after all those days on the *Monterey*, I wanted nothing from life but security and shelter. I didn't want romantic adventure. I didn't even want love. All I wanted was some place to lay down my head and rest; some place to be cared for and fed. I didn't want to be told that I was beautiful. I didn't want to be courted or impressed. I wanted ordinary days, and ordinary affection, and there was only one person I knew who could give me those things.'

'It was all a flight of fancy, then, what happened in Panama?' Collis said angrily. 'You used me to assay your love for Walter, and perhaps to put your religious convictions to some kind of test that wouldn't strain them too greatly? You used me to tickle your feminine sense of tragic drama?'

'Collis, please –'

'Please what? Please forget that I ever met you? Please forget that you ever stirred a passion within me that I never felt before, and which won't let me alone? Hannah, I've been here in San Francisco, I've been out in Sacramento, I've been working hard and working

321

fast. I've made money and I've made friends, all in the space of two months. But I've never been able to forget you, and I never will.'

She looked tired. 'I don't know what to tell you,' she said.

'Tell me what you told me in Panama. Tell me that you won't fail me.'

She gave a little 'hmph' of sad, amused resignation. 'I know I said that,' she said. 'And I regret it.'

'You don't mean that.'

'Oh, but I do mean it, Collis, most desperately.'

He tried to pull her towards him, but she twisted her arm free. 'How can you say that?' he demanded. 'After everything that happened in Panama, how can you say that?'

She was collected, and very cold. There was still something of the awkward, unrequited emotion in her that he had first sensed on the decks of the steamship *Virginia*; but it was certain that she had made up her mind about Collis, and that whatever he said, however much he pleaded or shouted or cajoled, he had lost her. He was beginning to wonder, now, why he had ever wanted her. She seemed so irritatingly dogmatic, so thin, so much like somebody else's wife.

And yet there was something inside her that disturbed him deeply; something that evoked the same kind of strange, faraway feelings of destiny that the High Sierras had aroused. It was as if Hannah and only Hannah could help him to live the life that was waiting for him in San Francisco, and Sacramento, and across the deserts and mountains of America.

'Was it really all a fake?' he asked. 'Everything you promised?'

'No,' she told him.

'Then why this? Why didn't you write? Even to tell me you didn't love me any longer?'

'I'm sorry,' she said.

He rubbed at his mouth with his hand.

'I don't know what else to say to you,' she said. 'I didn't know what to write. I suppose I was afraid of you. I don't know.'

They stood side by side on the foggy street corner for whole minutes, while passers-by nudged past them, businessmen and shoppers and Chilean dock-workers in blue wool coats, and wagons clattered across the rutted junction.

'Was, uh, Walter happy to see you?' asked Collis.

She nodded. Tears suddenly brimmed in her eyes and clung to her lashes.

'Well,' said Collis, 'I can guess that he was.'

322

He let out a tight breath and tried to smile. 'I guess I was just infatuated,' he told her. 'It shouldn't take me too long to get over you. I'm pretty busy right now. They made me partner in a hardware store out at Sacramento, fifteen per cent partner. There's more to do than any one man can cope with. Buying, selling. That kind of thing.'

'I'm sorry,' she repeated.

He reached out and gently touched her chin. 'You shouldn't be,' he said, in his softest voice. 'Whatever happened wasn't your fault. Whatever brought us together finishes here. It has to.'

He took her hand, held it between the palms of his own hands, and it was cold and thin, the hand of a woman whose love has almost died. She let out three or four muted noises of grief, and he felt his own eyes wet with desolation and disappointment.

The clock on the Mercantile Library Building struck eleven, sonorous and endless, and the chimes fell into the fog like the anchors of eleven abandoned ships.

'I think I'd better go,' Collis said.

She watched him cross Bush Street; and as he did so, a horse-drawn steamer from Engine Company Number Two on Kearny Street came jangling and clattering through the fog on its way to a fire on Market. Its three grey horses splattered through the mud, their nostrils fuming, and the highly polished brass steamer bounced after them, the fireman sitting upright and aloof in his cap and buttoned-up jacket.

By the time the steamer had passed by, Collis had disappeared into the crowds on the sidewalk, and Hannah could do nothing else but walk along Montgomery on her own, as far as the New Era German Bakery, where she waited in line at the marble-topped counter, amid the chatter of people taking tea and pumpernickel, and the crusty aroma of fresh-baked loaves, her eyes dry but vacant, and her hands clutched in front of her, holding her purse in a gesture that was both self-protective and pathetic.

The German girl behind the counter had to ask her what she wanted twice to get her attention.

Collis went after lunch to see Andy Hunt in his offices on Pine Street. Andy was right on the top floor of a narrow iron building with more curlicues on it than an Episcopalian christening cake. He was sitting at a battered desk that had once belonged to Joe Downey, one of the earliest of San Francisco's official clerks, whose

323

only claim to immortality was that he had gotten hopelessly drunk during the city's first municipal election, clumsily rigged the ballot, and announced himself mayor.

The desk somehow suited Andy Hunt's entrepreneurial abilities, which varied according to his mood, and also according to his intake of bourbon and crackers.

Andy was wearing a noisy green-and-orange plaid sport coat and a green wide-brimmed hat, and he was bent over a maelstrom of books and accounts and bills of lading. He was writing a business letter in an odd backward-sloping script and his long legs were wound around the rungs of his chair as if correspondence was a chore which demanded a great deal of twisting himself up into knots. Above his head, a gas-lamp glowed soft and white.

Collis, who was short on breath after four flights of wooden stairs, could do nothing at first but rap at the open door, and then step into the crowded office with his hat in his hand and wait for Andy to raise his head and see him. But Andy didn't have to look up.

'Collis,' he said, still scratching away at his letter. 'How the devil are you?'

'Winded,' said Collis.

'Everybody is when they first come up. It gives me a six-to-four advantage, right from the word go. Especially with debt collectors, or city officials. Have you tried asking for thirty dollars back rent when you don't even have breath enough to say "help"?'

Collis crossed the bare-board floor. The walls of the office were clustered with maps and timetables and orders, all of which riffled softly in the breeze from an open quarter-light.

'How did you know it was me?' he asked, setting his hat on top of a heap of papers. 'I didn't write to tell you I was coming down.'

Andy Hunt glanced up at him at last and gave a quick, foxy grin. 'I don't miss much that happens in or around the harbour,' he said. 'I've had to make it my business. And besides, Arthur Teach was grumbling about you last week in Captain Cropper's. He said you had the gall of a goat and the morals of a duck.'

Collis smiled. 'If I knew what he meant, I'd ask for satisfaction.'

Andy put down his pen, unwound his legs, and stood up. 'It's good to see you, anyway, looking so well. Charles wrote me they'd made you a partner.'

'Yes,' said Collis. 'And that's partly why I've come to see you.'

'I was surprised you didn't come earlier. Not prying, mind. But we could have had ourselves a roaring night out or two. There's a new house of assignation on Stockton Street, and I hear you can do whatever you care to do with three young beauties, all under the age of fifteen, all night, for less than the price of an oyster supper.'

Collis went to the window. It had a fan-shaped arch to it, and looked eastwards over towards Market Street and the Bay. The topmasts of clippers and schooners glided behind the foggy rooftops on silent errands of trade.

'I met Hannah,' he said.

Andy's face changed at once. He looked cautious, and a little unhappy. 'Ah,' he said.

'You sound as if you knew about her, too.'

'Well . . . Montgomery Street isn't far. My feet do direct themselves past the West emporium from time to time.'

'So you've seen that she's back with her husband?'

Andy nodded sympathetically. 'Back, and settled, by the looks of it. As a matter of fact, I did meet them on the street, her husband and her, and I did chew the fat for a minute or two. They were arm in arm, you know, as though they were very contented; although I must say that Hannah still appeared to be pretty sick.'

'She is,' said Collis.

Andy scratched the back of his neck. 'Maybe that's it, then,' he said. 'Maybe she went back to get herself nursed to rights by someone who wasn't going to give her too much bother.'

'She wasn't going to be bothered by me,' Collis told him. 'I could have cared for her just as well as Walter West. Didn't I care for her in Panama, when nobody else would?'

'Well, sure, you did that,' said Andy. 'But have you thought she may not want to start courting right now, because she don't feel her best? A woman likes to feel her best, you know, when she's out to win the man she fancies most. Maybe she wants to get better first; and then, when she's better, get in touch, and try again.'

Collis came away from the window and looked at Andy glumly. 'I don't think so. Not from what she told me this morning. It's a pretty idea. But I really believe I've lost her for good.'

'And is that so tragic?'

Collis shrugged. 'It depends what you mean by tragic. *She* doesn't seem to think it's tragic at all.'

Andy looked at Collis carefully. 'I'll bet you dinner at Delmonico's she does.'

'Then why did she say she didn't love me?'

'Because all women say that, when they're really smitten. It's their way of testing a fellow out. *They* may be deeper in love than a bug in a rug; but they want to know what *you* feel. And that's why they'll say that they never want to see you again, and all of that stuff, just to see what you'll do next.'

'All I'm going to do next is get drunk.'

Andy rejected that idea with an irritable wave of his hands. 'You don't get *drunk*. You keep your head. No woman is worth getting *drunk* over. The only things that are worth getting *drunk* over are horses, and heavy losses at faro.'

Collis took out a cheroot and offered one to Andy. Andy declined it.

'Listen here, Collis,' he said. 'You mustn't take this too damn bad. There's a kind of a soirée up at John Frémont's house tonight, and I've been invited to go along; so there wouldn't be any harm done if you came along too. You could meet John Frémont and Jessie, which is something I promised you way back on the ship; and from what I hear, Laurence Melford's going along too, with his family.'

'Laurence Melford?' asked Collis.

'That's right. Laurence himself, and Althea, and Sarah, and they do say Grant Melford, too. He's Sarah's younger brother, just come over from college in Massachusetts.'

Collis lit his cheroot. 'Really, Andy, my spirits aren't high enough for that kind of occasion. I think I'll probably take dinner on my own, and go to bed.'

'Nonsense! What are you, a hermit? You'll come along and like it.'

'Andy, I'm not in the mood.'

Andy looked at him slyly. 'You care for Sarah Melford, don't you?'

'Of course I care for Sarah Melford,' said Collis. He felt tired, and the thought of the Melfords, with all of their regal posturing and home-grown arrogance, was more than usually disagreeable.

Andy went back around his desk and sat down, with his heels firmly planted on his half-written letter.

'I think you should come whatever. It will do you good as far as San Francisco society is concerned, and what's more, Hannah will get to hear that you went, and might change her mind about telling you farewell. There isn't nothing at all like making a woman

326

jealous, especially when *you're* supposed to be jealous about *her*.'

'Are you really going to go on like this until I agree to come?' Collis said wearily.

'I surely am.'

'In that case, strictly against my better judgement, I shall. I'm staying at the International. Come around and pick me up whenever you like.'

'Well, that's fine,' said Andy. 'And now I guess you want to talk about your blankets.'

'I don't want to talk about them. All I want to do is sell them.'

Andy thoughtfully ran his tongue around the inside of his cheek. 'Is this an urgent sale? I mean, do you have to dispose of them while you're here, on this particular trip?'

'I must. Leland and Charles are both pressing me hard to pay for my share of Tucker & McCormick. They've already assigned me fifteen per cent of the stock, but on the strict condition that I pay them, in cash, before the end of the month.'

'Did they have any particular month in mind?'

'Of course they did. November. This month.'

'November '57?'

Collis stared at Andy sharply. 'What's the matter?' he asked him. 'Is there something wrong?'

'Not in particular,' said Andy.

'Well, what's all this hedging about? My blankets are still there, aren't they? They're still in the warehouse?'

'Oh, sure.'

'Then what?'

Andy took his feet off the desk and planted them firmly on the floor. Then he rested his hands on his knees and frowned somewhere in the middle distance in the classic posture of a man who does most of his constructive thinking in the outhouse.

'I want you to know that it wasn't my fault,' he said, by way of prelude.

'What wasn't your fault?'

'The fire. It wasn't my fault. It happens all the time in San Francisco. You know, what with the outdoor cooking and the oil lamps and the outlaws and all. I mean, half of San Francisco likes to watch things burn, and the other half spends most of its time setting light to them. So between the two you don't always stand too much of a chance.'

'My blankets are *burned*?' asked Collis. He felt almost as shocked

327

as if someone had told him his mother had died. 'All those blankets, all that investment – they're *burned*?'

'Oh, they're not a total loss,' said Andy. 'They're kind of brown around the edges, like overdone flapjacks, and most of the upper ones have holes, but, well, you could salvage a few. I lost five tons of oatmeal and two hundred gallons of turpentine in the same fire.'

Collis rubbed his eyes. he didn't know what to say. He could have cried, as a matter of fact, but he'd done enough crying for one day, for something else that had gotten burned. Something more fragile, and far less forgettable, than blankets.

'What the hell am I going to do now?' he asked Andy.

Andy pulled a face. 'Nothing you can do. None of the stuff was insured. You'll just have to get yourself back to the Eagle Saloon, and see what more you can take from the faro tables.'

Collis lowered his head. He bit at his thumbnail. If this wasn't the damnedest, most miserable day he'd ever had. It was like a punishment. First Hannah, and now this. And wouldn't that bristly bastard Teach have a good long laugh about it.

He frowned. Surely Teach should have known about it already. Yet when he'd talked to Teach on the wharf, and later at the Bank Exchange Saloon, he hadn't given Collis any indication at all that he'd heard what had happened. Collis looked up at Andy. 'Who knows about this fire?' he asked.

'Just about the whole of San Francisco. It was evening, see, and it was a pretty spectacular blaze while it lasted. Did you ever see two hundred gallons of turpentine go up in flames? The engine company thought they were going to lose the Maritime Hotel, and half the damned street.'

'Does Arthur Teach know about it?'

'Sure he does. Other people's misfortunes are every business-man's business around here.'

'But did he know my blankets were stored there?'

Andy was about to answer, but he paused, and squinted at Collis with slitted, suspicious eyes.

'I don't quite see which way you're aiming to piss,' he said cautiously.

'I just want to know if Arthur Teach was aware that the blankets got burned.'

'I don't know,' said Andy. 'I doubt if he did. I doubt if anybody did. Why should they?'

328

'That's just what I wanted to hear,' Collis told him. He stood up. 'Do you know where Arthur's office is?'

'Sure. It's on California, between Kearny and Montgomery, right opposite the Pacific Club. But I'd certainly like to know what you've got on your mind.'

Collis straightened his grey silk hat and tugged at his vest. 'I'll meet you tonight, at the International. That's all I'm going to say.'

Andy watched Collis walk across the office to the half-open door. He watched him raise his hat, bow sardonically, and leave. He stared for a long time at the empty landing. Then he sighed, shook his head, and went back to his crumpled business letter. Outside the window, the fog was gradually fading, and it looked as if the evening was going to be clear. The sky was high, hazy and pale, and there was a wind from the east that promised a warm weekend.

Chapter 8

As five o'clock chimed, Arthur Teach was finishing up his day's business at Pacific Securities. His office was a memorable example of San Francisco gothic, with high-vaulted ceilings and redwood-panelled walls. The same late daylight that had brightened Andy Hunt's loft was falling across his parquet floor in monastic shafts.

He autographed his letters with a quick, aggressive squiggle, and thought with growing ferocity of cold champagne and fried scallops.

There was a soft rapping at his door. Through the hammered-glass panel, like a drowned man lying beneath the ripples of a lake, stood Pudgett, his clerk, waiting with his hand on the doorknob for his master's reply. Arthur said to himself, 'Damn,' and then he called, 'Come in!'

Pudgett put his head around the door and smiled weakly. His hair was combed in five different directions at once, and he wore tiny eyeglasses on the end of his nose. 'I'm sorry to disturb you so late, Mr Teach, but you have a caller. He says it's a pressing matter, and won't wait, but is much to your advantage.'

'I suppose you forgot to ask his name,' said Arthur.

'No, sir, I didn't forget. McReady, sir. Mr Daniel McReady.'

Arthur signed another letter, sniffed, blotted it, and tossed it into his wooden Out tray. 'Where's he from? What's he want?'

'He declined to say, sir.'

'In that case, he will have to make his appointment in the usual fashion. I can't see people who decline to say why they've come. If they decline to say why they've come, then I can just as readily decline to be here to see them.'

Pudgett licked his lips. 'He said I should mention blankets, sir. A particular cargo of blankets.'

Arthur's hand remained poised over his last letter. The nib of his pen reflected a bright, wavering star. 'What?' he said softly.

'I don't know what he meant, sir. But he said I should mention blankets.'

Arthur looked down at the unsigned letter. He laid down his pen. Pudgett, from the doorway, watched him with uncertainty.

'All right,' said Arthur at last. 'You'd better show him in.'

Pudgett disappeared, and Arthur waited, without moving, his letter still unsigned and his pen spreading a black blot over the words 'Cordially yours'. The monastic shafts of light began to dim, one by one, as a screen of clouds passed across the sun.

'Mr McReady, sir,' announced Pudgett, and the door swung open as if someone had given it a sharp, bad-tempered push. Across the parquet, with metal-capped shoes that clicked as he walked, came a short, square man in a brown striped suit, a man whose eyes were as pale as opals, and by the look of him, twice as unlucky.

Arthur stood up and extended his hand. Dan McReady jerked his head forward and glared at the hand like a snappish dog. But he took it, and gave it a quick shake, and then he sat down in the studded leather guest chair with almost frightening abruptness.

'You told my clerk about blankets,' said Arthur.

'Yup.'

Arthur turned and looked at him. '"Yup"?' he repeated. His voice was the finest grade of sandpaper.

But Dan McReady was unabashed. 'Yup I told your clerk about blankets.'

'I see,' said Arthur, leaning on his desk. 'But are you going to tell *me* about blankets?'

'Sure. For a price.'

'What kind of a price?'

McReady stared at him with those pale, expressionless eyes. 'A fair price, Mr Teach. None other.'

'Of course,' said Arthur. 'As long as we both understand the meaning of "fair".'

Dan McReady didn't seem to be impressed by meanings, because he said nothing at all. Instead, he reached inside his coat and produced a well-folded piece of paper, which he tossed on to Arthur's desk. Arthur walked around and picked it up.

'That's a bill of lading from the *Aria*, sir,' said Dan McReady. 'If you can read, you'll see that it was issued for blankets, twenty-five short tons of five-pound blankets.'

'Yes,' said Arthur slowly, reading the bill with care. 'Yes, that's exactly what it is. But can I ask how it came into your possession? I thought I knew the owner of these blankets, and it certainly isn't you.'

Dan McReady shrugged, as if Arthur could think what he liked

'Did you buy them?' asked Arthur. 'How much did you pay?'

'They're temporarily mine, sir, as collateral against a heavy loss at cards. I'm a gambler, you see, by profession. You can ask around anywhere, and folks'll know me. As it happened, I was playing poker with the original owner of these blankets, and he went down by twelve thousand dollars.'

'I see. So he gave you the blankets in lieu of the debt?'

'That's right, sir. Although the arrangement is, if he can raise the cash by midnight tonight, he can have the blankets back. That's if I haven't sold them first.'

Arthur Teach rubbed his moustache. He didn't speak for more than a minute, and the silence in the office became tense and oppressive. From outside the hammered-glass door, there was the heavy slam of the Salamander safe being closed and locked for the night, and the clatter of inkstands being tidied up and nibs put away.

'Why did you come to me?' asked Arthur, at last.

Dan McReady's opaline gaze didn't falter. 'I know what goes on, sir, in the business district, and almost everybody got to hear of the way those blankets were bought from the *Aria*'s master before she docked.'

'Yes,' said Arthur, not particularly pleased. 'I suppose everybody did.'

There was another, shorter silence. Then Dan McReady said, 'Do you want the blankets, sir? They're not much use to me.'

Arthur cleared his throat. 'As I said before, it depends on the price.'

'The price depends on the weather, sir, wouldn't you say? Right now, the weather's warmish, and almost too pleasant for blankets, so I can't in all conscience ask for much. Say, two dollars the blanket, just to cover my outlay, and that includes commission, storage, and expenses.'

'Two dollars?' Arthur frowned. 'That's – what, ten thousand blankets in twenty-five short tons? – that's twenty thousand dollars.'

'Yup,' said Dan McReady. 'Your arithmetic's correct, sir.'

'Impossible,' said Arthur. 'Twenty thousand dollars is too much. Why, you got the blankets for twelve. Do you really believe I should pay you eight just for handing them over?'

Dan McReady's face didn't register the slightest hint of emotion. He could have been one of those bland, blank outlaws on a wanted poster; or a slightly simple second cousin peering out of the background of a family daguerreo-type.

332

'Handing them over is only a part of what you're paying for, sir,' he told Arthur, in a whispery, collusive voice. 'You're also paying, aren't you, for the privilege of having them offered you private, without the necessity to bid for them at auction; and the great satisfaction of having your revenge on the original owner.'

The gambler turned his eyes to the window. 'You know as well as I do, sir, that by January those blankets will be fetching four to five dollars the blanket, more if it's colder. Even at two dollars the blanket, if you decide you want to buy, you'll be depriving the original owner out of twenty to thirty thousand dollars, maybe more. And won't his teeth be gnashing then, by God, and won't you look the smartest dealer on Montgomery Street, bar none?'

'Two dollars is still too high,' said Arthur. 'Two dollars is out of the question.'

'It's up to you, sir,' replied Dan McReady. 'I won't lose nothing, whatever you decide to do. There's no skin off my nose, even if you let this chance for revenge slip by. Just remember that it's warmish now, while the sun's still up, but they say it's going to grow considerably chiller by midnight, and the price may have to rise, each hour you demur. It's two dollars now, at twenty after five, but it could be three dollars by ten o'clock, and three-fifty by eleven.'

He stood up and pushed back his chair. With two straight fingers, he retrieved the bill of lading from Arthur's desk and held it up.

'You can see this bill's authentic, sir, and not forged, and if you want to see the blankets themselves, they're at Parkinson's warehouse on Davis Street.'

Arthur Teach stood by the window. The temptation was very great. To have his own back on Collis Edmonds, and at the same time make himself more than half of the profit he had originally expected from the *Aria*'s blankets – well, it had the ring of justice about it, and it would work wonders for his reputation. It would silence those whispers of 'poor old Arthur' and those mock-sympathetic smiles whenever anybody mentioned blankets. It would do his spleen good, too.

He took a deep breath. 'Will you take a note?' he asked Dan McReady. 'Just until the banks open tomorrow.'

Dan McReady shook his head. Slightly, but emphatically.

'Well, that presents problems,' said Arthur. 'I'm not in the habit of carrying twenty thousand dollars in gold around my waist, and quite strictly I'm not permitted to take personal loans out of the office safe.'

Dan McReady's expression didn't alter. 'It's up to you, sir,' he repeated. 'Whatever you want to do, it's up to you.'

Arthur grimaced, and thought some more. 'These blankets,' he asked, 'they're pure wool, are they?'

'Finest money can buy, sir.'

'And they're in good order?'

'All things considered, sir, yes.'

Arthur hesitated a moment longer, but then he leaned across his desk and pinged a small brass bell. After a moment, Pudgett put his head around the door.

'Pudgett, is the safe locked?'

'Just this minute, sir.'

'Well, I want you to open it up again, and bring me twenty thousand dollars, exact, in gold dust. Then I want you to draw up a note for me, covering the company for that amount until the banks are open tomorrow.'

Pudgett blinked first at Arthur and then at Dan McReady, and then disappeared to do what he was told. Arthur hooked his thumbs into the pockets of his camel-coloured vest and gave Dan McReady a thin but quite triumphant smile.

Outside the Frémonts' white-pillared house overlooking the southern curve of San Francisco Bay, the carriages of the Chivalry and the richer members of the Shovelry were drawn up in gleaming, jingling ranks. Their horses snuffled from time to time and shook their heads, while their coachmen sat on the low stone wall that bordered the driveway, playing dice and smoking pipes. It was a cold evening, and the waters of the Bay were a dull lilac colour, flecked with spray.

Through the glass walls of Jessie's veranda, chandeliers sparkled and elegantly-dressed men and women could be seen talking and laughing. Bret Harte, who came along later, observed, 'There are more diamonds in this one house tonight than in the whole of South Africa, and enough silk to wrap up an elephant.'

It was one of those occasions which Jessie Frémont, as a hostess, enjoyed the most: an occasion when she brought together the wealthy, the socially graceful, the glib, the coquettish, and the pretty. She would mix them in ways in which they had rarely been mixed before, so that florid clerics would find themselves arguing with sallow-faced Sansome Street gamblers, and stiff-necked South Park ladies would find themselves provocatively entertained by

334

tousled young radical writers. As a Northerner, and the wife of the last Republican Presidential candidate, Jessie had been treated warily at first by the Southern aristocracy of Rincon Hill but her dinners and soirées had proved to be witty, glittering and bright, and were circled on the social calendar as emphatically as Mary Bell Gwin's costume balls, or Isaac Friedlander's monumental dinners.

Collis and Andy had arrived in a rented brougham at eight, after a couple of glasses of Pisco punch at the bar of the International Hotel. Collis, as he mounted the steps of the Frémont porch, looked unnaturally pale, and there were dark smudges under his eyes. But in his evening coat and his starched white collar, his pallor gave him the look of romantic dissolution, and from within the house there was a soft twittering among the fans and frills of South Park's pioneer daughters.

They entered the brightly-lit hallway and crossed the figured marble floor. A black footman in a powdered periwig was waiting to take their hats, their canes, and their cloaks, and then another footman led them through to the door of the main reception room to have their names announced. As Collis saw the sparkling mirrors and spangled lights, and as he heard the warbling of courteous conversation, he felt a sharp twinge of nostalgia for New York. He felt like a man in a foreign country who suddenly hears a traveller speaking English, or who catches the smell of codfish chowder after years of curried lamb. He hadn't attended a single society party since his arrival in San Francisco, and he had almost forgotten the pleasures of flirting with silly young girls, and of talking preposterous small talk with half-drunk gentlemen of wealth and position. After the way that Hannah had rejected him, and after his weeks among hardware-store managers and fussy middle-class women in Sacramento, his pride hungered for nothing more desperately than flattery from the opposite sex, and recognition from his social equals.

He stood tall, with his shoulders back and his chest well filled with air, as the footman called out: 'Mr Andrew Hunt, and Mr Collis Edmonds!'

Through the nearest throng of black-coated husbands and jewel-bedecked wives, a small, dark-haired woman appeared, dressed in a simple but expensive dress of soft white lawn, layer upon layer embroidered with pale-blue flowers. Her face was oval and gentle, with full lips and almost Egyptian eyes. She held out her hand to

Andy and said, 'Mr Hunt. We're so pleased that you could come. I see you've brought a friend.'

Andy bowed his head. 'I hope you don't object, Mrs Frémont. But I guessed you'd want to get to know him sooner or later, seeing as how he's going to make his mark on this city in any event. Mrs Frémont, this is Mr Collis Edmonds, from New York. Collis, this is Mrs Jessie Benton Frémont.'

'Well, well,' said Mrs Frémont, as Collis took her hand and brushed her diamond rings with a light kiss. 'I do warrant that I've heard of you already, Mr Edmonds. You've made yourself a small reputation for – what shall I call it? – *immediacy*.'

'Immediacy, ma'am?' asked Collis, amused. He was surprised to see how young Mrs Frémont was, considering that she had been married to John Frémont more than ten years ago, when he had explored the Oregon Trail and the Rocky Mountain passes with Kit Carson and Broken Hand Fitzpatrick, and that she had helped him in those days write a best-selling book about the West. She couldn't have been much older than thirty-one or thirty-two, and she was fresh and poised as a girl of twenty.

Mrs Frémont lowered her gaze, in a pretence of shyness. 'If blowing people's hats to bits, and rowing a Whitehall boat out into the Bay to corner the market in blankets, well, if those aren't examples of immediacy, I don't know what are.'

Collis put his hands stiffly to his sides and gave a mildly mocking bow. 'Personally, Mrs Frémont, I prefer to look on them as examples of contemporary humour.'

Mrs Frémont gave a high, light trill of laughter. Those of her guests who were standing nearest turned around suspiciously to see what it was that had delighted her so much. There were nudges and whispers, and more than one disapproving frown. San Francisco society was still sensitive to the point of mania about its rude Bear Flag beginnings and the shortness of its history, and it protected its golden circle by treating merchants, gate-crashers, and parvenus with elaborate disdain. What was disturbing them now, though, was that Collis had all the appearance and manners of an Eastern gentleman; and if he had managed to make Jessie Frémont laugh within one minute of meeting her, then perhaps he had all the necessary background and breeding to make him a social prize. It was all very disturbing, particularly to those covetous hostesses who didn't know who he was, or where he had come from, or if he might be the new 'catch' of the coming season. All around the room, the chatter of coversation changed tone, and became a whispery exchange of gossip.

'You must come over and meet my husband,' said Jessie Frémont. 'I'm not sure that he'll appreciate your sense of fun, but he always likes to meet newcomers to San Francisco, and hear what they think of it.'

'I thought at first that San Francisco was a gypsy carnival, held on a hill,' said Collis. 'But tonight I see that it has its beauties, its manners, and its graces, and that all three of these virtues have their queen.'

Mrs Frémont coloured. 'You're most flattering, Mr Edmonds. Perhaps you'd better come see my husband before you sweep me off my feet.'

She excused herself from her previous circle of friends and led Collis and Andy through the milling, curious guests as if they were visiting royalty from Europe (always a great social coup, even if they were only half-witted barons from Schleswig-Holstein). Collis played up to the general curiosity by nodding and smiling to everyone as they walked down the length of the reception room, with its palms and statues and rococo furniture.

Out in the glass-walled veranda it was cooler, and the conversation was more subdued. Collis recognized bank presidents and Montgomery Street financiers, and several other whiskery and respectable faces from Barry and Patten's and the Auction Lunch. In one corner, in a basketwork chair, a bearded man with concentrated eyes was talking with almost frightening intensity to a circle of enthralled young women. 'That's Herman Melville,' Jessie Frémont whispered, in passing. 'A very promising young talent. Have you read anything of his?'

Collis shook his head. 'I'm sorry to say that my recent reading has been confined to the labels of patent hangover cures. But I guess that's San Francisco for you. Libation first, luncheon second, and literature last of all.'

Jessie Frémont took them to the far end of the veranda, overlooking the Bay. It was dark outside now, except for a last mauvish swirl of clouds over the western hills behind them.

Collis recognized John Frémont from pictures in the San Francisco newspapers. He wasn't much more than medium height, with a faded suntan, and eyes that were hooded and sad. He was talking to a tall man who stood with his back to Collis; and while he talked, he stroked his beard as if he needed reassurance that he was still there, and that he wasn't out on some dust-blasted trail, or up to his waist in snow in the High Sierras. His evening coat hung on him as if he had lost weight since he was first measured up for it, and his necktie was floppy and carelessly tied. But he was good-looking, in a melancholy way, and when Jessie came up he gave her a look of welcome that would have charmed anyone.

Jessie took his arm. 'John, my dear. You must meet Mr Collis Edmonds, from New York. You already know Mr Andrew Hunt.'

John Frémont gave a brief nod, and shook hands absent-mindedly. 'I'm pleased to know you, Mr Edmonds. Welcome to San Francisco.'

It was then that the tall man to whom he had been talking turned around. It was Laurence Melford. He was looking tired, with that particular tiredness brought on by too many late-night dinners and too much champagne. He kept his hands by his sides, but he nodded to Andy, and then to Collis, and said, 'Gentlemen,' in a bass voice that was both dignified and warning.

'How do you like our city, Mr Edmonds?' asked John Frémont. 'Have you found a place to live yet? Our hotels are fine, well up to New York standards, but I'm afraid they're rather crowded. New people arriving by the minute.'

'It must have changed a great deal since the early days,' remarked Collis. He was talking to John Frémont, but he kept his eyes fixed on Laurence Melford. Melford, in his turn, was directing his attention towards the veranda's tiled floor, and listening to what was being said like a collage principal who has heard more trumped-up excuses than St Peter at the gates of heaven.

'Changed?' said Frémont. 'Yes, it's changed.' He sounded almost nostalgic. 'For instance, when Sam Upham first came here in the summer of '49, he set himself up in a ship's galley, which he'd bought himself for one hundred dollars, and all he had was a flour barrel for a table, and a nail keg for a chair. He was obliged to sleep crosswise, because the galley was eight inches shorter than he was. That was in Happy Valley, the wetlands south of Market Street ridge. And do you know something? He went away for a year, and came back to find the whole place burned down, and fine frame buildings standing right where his galley had been. That's how much it's changed.'

'You sound as if you miss the old days.'

'Do I?' said Frémont. 'I don't really think that I do. Maybe I miss the pioneering spirit. The roughness. The early people were honest, too. You could leave your stores for weeks, and nobody would touch them. It's not the same today.'

'It's a hive of cardsharps and villains these days, this city,' said Laurence Melford, as if he were talking to himself. 'And all the whores and crimps and raggle-taggle that go with them.'

John Frémont gave a quick, uneasy frown. 'But you haven't told us your business, Mr Edmonds, have you? *Are* you in business, or are you just touring?'

'I'm in hardware,' Collis told him. 'Do you know Leland McCormick and Charles Tucker? I'm their partner, out in Sacramento.'

'They're worthy men,' Frémont said. 'Both very worthy. You could have done a great deal worse than join up with them.'

'It's a beginning,' said Collis. 'Ultimately, though, I'm thinking of building a railroad.'

Laurence Melford stared at him sourly. Then he turned away and looked out across the veranda as if Collis's ideas about railroads were too tiresome to be listened to twice.

'A railroad?' echoed John Frémont. 'Well, that's most interesting. I undertook some survey work myself, for a railroad. Something a little more ambitious than anything that you're planning, I expect. A Pacific railroad across the Rockies. And it was rough, I can tell you. Blizzards such as you've never seen. We lost eleven men, frozen stiff. They said it was the worst snow for years.'

Frémont gave a vague smile. He seemed to be thinking about something else. 'I got most of my party out alive, thank God. And we did find a route for a railroad, the Buffalo Trail. But they were hard times. Very hard times.'

'Is the railroad going to be built?' asked Collis carefully.

'What?' asked Frémont. 'Built? Well, yes. All in good time. Congress has to budget money, and agree to apportion land. Then the way must be surveyed, and cleared, and the tracks laid. But I wouldn't be surprised if trains are running to and fro across America on the Buffalo Trail before I go to meet my Maker at last. And if they name one of those Rocky Mountain passes after me, well, I shan't be displeased.'

He stroked his beard some more, and nodded. Then he realized he wasn't being particularly attentive to his guests, and he looked up at Collis and asked, 'But how about *your* railroad? You must tell me something about it. Sacramento, you say. Is it connected with the Sacramento Valley line? What are you building? A branch of some kind?'

'No, sir,' said Collis. 'Nothing quite as modest as that.'

'Then let me guess. You're going to connect up Oakland and Sacramento by rail.'

Collis shook his head. 'Wrong direction. I want to build a road from Sacramento eastward, across the Sierras to Salt Lake City, and maybe further, to Laramie, and eastward on the Forty-first Parallel to Omaha, Nebraska.'

Laurence Melford gave a dismissive snort, and even John Frémont seemed wary. He looked at Collis with his head tilted to one side, as if to make certain that Collis was neither a crank, nor a joker, and it took him a long time to make his reply.

'Well, Mr Edmonds,' he said after a while, 'that's a very ambitious idea. But, if you don't think I'm being rude, where is your expertise? Are you an engineer, or a topographer?'

'No,' said Collis.

'Well, then, do you have friends in Congress? Do you have wealth?'

'Not much of the latter, Mr Frémont, and not very many of the former.'

'Then, my dear fellow,' said John Frémont, 'I regret to say that you can never succeed. I can understand your ambition. I sympathise with your motives. I don't necessarily agree with your route. But, all these things apart, you just don't have the wherewithal to get a railroad of thirty miles started, let alone three thousand.'

Frémont looked towards Laurence Melford for support, and he could see by Melford's indifference that Collis was probably nothing more than a talkative upstart, without funds or backers or friends in Washington. He was reassured by that. Pacific railroads were still a slightly tender subject in the Frémont household, in spite of John's boasts about the Buffalo Trail, and he privately preferred the idea of a transcontinental train to remain as a glorious unfulfilled national fantasy. It wasn't very comfortable for the Pathfinder's self-esteem to think that somebody else might lay tracks where he had met only frostbite and wretched failure. Particularly when that somebody was a jaded rake like Collis Edmonds, from out of the gambling clubs and drawing-rooms of upper-class New York.

'Take your very first obstacle,' Frémont said, with a twitchy smile. 'Not just a hill. The Sierra Nevada! Why, the Sierras are pretty well impassable for locomotives. The Donner Pass must be six thousand feet above sea level. And, er, the gradients are very steep. And in the places where they aren't, there are very few straight ways. So your railroad topographer is caught, as it were, between the grades and the curves.'

Collis stepped back as a footman brought a tray of champagne. They took a glass each, and then Collis said, quite gently, 'You're absolutely right about the Sierras. Or at least, I've been told they're almost impossible to cross. But why should *my* railroad not be able to negotiate them when *yours* apparently could?'

Frémont coughed. 'It's a question of expertise, Mr Edmonds. *My* railroad could find a way because it was expertly planned, and was not the devising of amateurs. Don't forget my nickname. The Pathfinder!'

'Yes,' said Collis, in a voice that bore just the slightest trace of sarcasm.

'*Yes*,' insisted Frémont. 'Because don't forget that when you were still at school, I was a railroad surveyor for the Army Topographical Corps, and I ran a line from Charleston to Cincinnati. And don't forget that I know about the ins and outs of drumming up political support in Congress. You can't just go around building Pacific railroads however you please. You have to have the backing and funding of Washington.'

'Of course,' said Collis. 'I forgot that your good wife's father is Senator Benton, of Missouri. He's a great supporter of Pacific railroads, isn't he?'

'Yes,' said Frémont. His tone was edgy. 'Yes, I guess you could say that.'

'You know something,' Collis went on, 'it always si __ me as remarkably good chance that you found the Buffalo Trail to be the most satisfactory route for a transcontinental railroad. Especially the way it runs west out of St Louis, and links up your father-in-law's state with the Pacific Coast. Remarkably good chance.'

Frémont looked at Collis with eyes as hard as pebbles. Collis, in return, gave him a friendly and guileless grin, and even turned to Andy and asked, 'Don't you agree with that, Andy? What remarkably good chance that was?'

'I hope you're not suggesting that Senator Benton and I were acting in self-interested collusion,' said John Frémont. 'Because if

341

you are, I must demand that you withdraw that implication at once.'

Collis blinked in surprise. 'My dear Mr Frémont, why should I ever suggest anything as low-minded as that?'

'I'm damned if I'm sure,' said Frémont.

'It wasn't a criticism,' said Collis. 'Far from it. It was a tribute to your surveying skill. Who else could have found a passable route along the Thirty-eighth Parallel but you? My railroad expert tells me that he'd no more think of surveying a track over the Sangre de Cristo mountains than he would up the side of City Hall. Yet you did it. You confounded everybody who didn't believe that a railroad route could be determined in advance by a politician and then confirmed by a surveyor, instead of the way these things are usually done, which is the other way about.'

'I hope you're not giving us another example of your rank impertinence, Mr Edmonds,' Laurence Melford said darkly.

'I don't think so, Mr Melford,' said Collis. 'I would rather be your friend, a hundred times more, than I would wish to be your enemy.'

'I have quite enough friends already, thank you,' said Melford. 'But if you wish at the very least to ensure my neutrality, I suggest you put any thoughts of a Pacific railroad well aside, and devote yourself to the hardware trade. I suggest, too that some kind of apology to Mr Frémont might well be in order.'

Collis stared at Melford and then at Frémont. Andy held his champagne glass in both hands and looked extremely uncomfortable.

'An apology?' Collis asked in a soft voice. 'An apology for what?'

'Your impertinence, whether it was intentional or not,' said Laurence Melford.

Collis looked at Laurence Melford steadily. 'If there's any impertinence here, and I'm sure you'll forgive me if I sound too serious, it comes from those who support the inhumane demands of the Southern slave economy, and all those who dance to its tune. *They* are the ones who ought to say that they're sorry, because they've put their own profits and political power before the pressing needs of the whole nation.'

John Frémont raised a hand. 'I think we're becoming too heated here, Mr Edmonds. Please, this is a party, not the floor of the Senate. I understand your sincerity, but you must also understand that Mr Melford and I are both just as sincere in what we believe. In any event, a Pacific railroad is still a dream, not a reality, and there are years and years of preparatory work to be done before it can be.'

'You're wrong,' said Collis. 'Given the backing, and the right surveyors, this railroad could be mapped out within five years, and laid within ten.'

'Not by you, sir,' growled Laurence Melford. 'And not along the Forty-first Parallel.'

'Forgive me,' Collins replied, 'but there speaks a man who owns a half interest in a cotton plantation in Virginia.'

'You're a damned devil, sir,' said Laurence Melford.

'Yes,' Collis told him, 'I am. And I think it's just as well. It's going to take a damned devil to build this railroad, if you ask me. It's going to take a damned devil to clear his way through all the bribery and the time-wasting and the political favouritism that's been holding this railroad back for so long. People are dying of yellow fever in Panama. Men, women, and children are dying of exhaustion on the emigrant trail. But what the hell does that matter, just so long as we don't lay the track to the North, or to the South, or in between, or wherever it doesn't happen to suit our unctuous members of Congress, and everybody else who's tugging at their coat tails?'

'I suppose your own interests are completely free of taint?' asked Laurence Melford sarcastically. 'You'll donate your services to the building of this railroad out of the goodness of your very romantic heart?'

Collis finished his champagne. It was too sweet, but cold and refreshingly effervescent. 'I'm going to build this railroad for lots of different reasons,' he told Melford. 'For money, of course. For power. For self-satisfaction, and pride. For a woman I once knew.'

'But, Mr Edmonds, what in the world makes you think that you can *do* it?' asked John Frémont. 'It would be the greatest project ever attempted in the whole history of civil engineering. It would shake this nation by the very roots. It would demand surveying skills far beyond the average, as well as new methods of tunnelling, and cutting, and bridge-building. It would tax the mind of a genius, to be quite frank. And you're not even an engineer!'

Collis rotated his empty champagne glass in his hand. 'I can do it, Mr Frémont, because nobody else can do it, and because nobody else will. They can dream of railroads. They can sing of railroads, and draw up optimistic maps. They can send parties of surveyors up into the passes of the Rocky Mountains, to get themselves buried in snow. But they can't build it. They're too frightened of splitting the nation. They're too frightened of losing money, and political power. But I don't give a damn about any of that. And if I don't do this with my life, then I'll go to my deathbed with nothing else to my credit but drink, and whores, and games of cards, and some loves that I might have had but let slip by.'

Laurence Melford, his eyes lowered, took the band off a large cigar and carefully tapped it to make sure it was sound.

'So the South is to be economically marooned because one New York elegantine is trying to make more of himself than a leg-jerking hound. Is that it?'

Collis shook his head. 'No, Mr Melford. That's not it. Although I'm not sure that I'd care if it were.'

'I don't think that kind of remark is really very constructive,' said John Frémont. 'You're well aware that I'm a Republican, but really . . .'

'But really what?' asked Collis. 'But really, we shouldn't mind turning a blind eye to slavery?'

'I didn't mean that,' said Frémont sharply. 'I meant that if some kind of political compromise could be worked out between the North and the South, the railroad could then be laid along a sensible mean. To my mind, the Thirty-eighth Parallel was such a mean.'

'Perhaps it might have been,' said Collis. 'But to *my* mind, the South will be marooned because she will never compromise. And more sadly than that, she will be marooned because of where she is. She can't make any compromises about her geographical location, no matter how much Secretary Davis and Senator Benton try to persuade us that the best routes run west out of St Louis, or Fort Smith, or Preston, Texas.'

Both John Frémont and Laurence Melford were silent. Laurence Melford clipped his cigar with a gold cutter, decorated wtih diamonds, but he was listening, and it was plain that he didn't like what he heard.

Collis continued. 'The man who can take the real credit for planning this railroad, my engineer, says there's only one obvious route. He knows Nebraska Territory, and the Rockies, and the Great Basin, and most of all he knows the Sierra Nevada, and in his opinion, the very first pioneers found the easiest trail, because they damned well had to. It lies, roughly, along the Forty-first Parallel, and Mr Frémont knows that as well as I do. What I'm saying is that no matter how much the South gripes at the North, the bitter facts are that God so created the geography of this nation that the natural highway from coast to coast, when we finally open it up, will leave the South and her slave economy beached, high and dry, and left to the fate that most of us Northerners think she deserves.'

Laurence Melford was silent. It was the same kind of silence that hangs in the air between a flash of lightning and the first heavy collision of thunder. When he spoke, his voice was a low, threatening grumble. 'I'm glad you believe you have God on your side, Mr Edmonds. You may well need Him, if you continue to press ahead with this foolhardy business.'

But John Frémont was more thoughtful. 'Who's this railroad expert of yours?' he asked Collis. 'It isn't Jack Dellman, is it? Or Theodore Jones?'

'It must be Jones,' said Laurence Melford. 'Dellman went to Europe to study engineering in London.'

John Frémont gave Collis a sympathetic smile. 'If your surveyor is Jones, Mr Edmonds, then I should take care, if I were you. He's a little fanatical, to say the least. You don't want to spend a great deal of money and invest a great deal of time, only to find that you're stuck up some snowbound mountain where even a goat couldn't go, let alone a ten-wheel locomotive.'

'I'll be careful,' Collis said. 'And, if you like, I'll even do for you what I've already done for three or four San Francisco financiers. I'll make you a bet that I can have my railroad surveyed and ready for laying track in five years.'

Laurence Melford pursed his lips in disgust. But John Frémont said, 'All right. You're arrogant enough. I'll bet you anything you like.'

'It isn't much to ask,' said Collis. 'It's nothing more than a celebration dinner, to be held here in this house, and hosted by you and your wife, on the night that my plans for a Pacific railroad are signed into law.'

John Frémont let out a sudden burst of laughter. 'My God,' he said, 'you have a natural talent for stirring people up. My God, you do. And you can't even help yourself from doing it, can you?'

'I only try to speak my mind,' said Collis.

John Frémont held out his hand. 'Well,' he said, 'I'm not yet sure that I like you, and it's plain that Laurence here believes you have the darkest motives for everything you do. But I'll take your bet, and if you succeed, I'll lay on your dinner. There's just something I

345

want in return, if you should fail. You'll be a witness to this, won't you, Mr Hunt?'

'Sure,' said Andy.

'If you fail to survey your railroad, Mr Edmonds,' said John Frémont, 'I want you to leave California and never return.'

Collis looked up. He could scarcely believe what John Frémont had said. 'That's kind of drastic, wouldn't you say?' said Andy Hunt.

Frémont gave a quick shake of his head. 'Just remember that California is *my* state, gentlemen, and has been since 1849. It was I who raised the flag at Sonoma, and it was I who made this city what it is today. All you have to do is ask who named the Golden Gate. It was I. Ask who brought civilisation and order. It was I.'

Collis was tempted to ask who had overstated his authority and refused to relinquish the governorship of San Francisco to General Kearny, thereby earning himself a short stretch in jail. But he decided he'd probably poked the bee's nest enough for one evening, and he gave John Frémont a nod of acceptance instead.

'If that's what you want, that's what you shall have. Life in this state won't be worth very much without a railroad in any case. Now, I'm sure this party isn't all railroading and political arguments, is it? Where can we go to eat, and perhaps to dance?'

'The buffet's in the back room,' said Frémont. 'You must try the smoked oysters. They're out of Mr Melford's own beds in the Bay, and they're quite delicious.'

'Excellent,' said Collis. 'And has Mr Melford brought his daughter, as well as his oysters?'

'Sarah is here, yes,' said Laurence Melford. 'But you'd be doing me a considerable favour if you stayed away from her.'

'You're a stern man, Mr Melford,' Collis replied.

'Yes,' said Laurence Melford. 'And you're even more of a devil than I first thought.'

'Well,' Collis told him, 'you know what Shelley said. Sometimes the devil is a gentleman.'

At the far end of the reception room, on a small dais, a string quartet struck up a quadrille, and a few of the prettier girls and some of the younger men began to dance. Collis paused for a while and watched them, his hands in his pockets, and he smiled at their stiffness and lack of grace. There were two things that obviously didn't travel well from the East Coast: wine, and stylish dancing.

'I've seen a troupe of Polish Army horses dance better than that,' Collis remarked to Andy.

Andy grimaced. 'There's a lack of good dancing teachers, that's the trouble. The best one was Ralph Durkee, and he went off to the diggings.'

'A dancing master, digging for gold?'

Andy nodded. 'There's no distinctions out at the diggings. It's every man for whatever he can get. You ought to get Charles to take you out to someplace like French Corral or Nigger's Hill. You've come all this way, you might as well see the elephant. You think this dancing's rough? You should see Saturday night out at Dutch Flat.'

After a while, when they'd had enough of watching the clockwork prancing of San Francisco's young socialites, Collis and Andy walked through to the buffet table, which was set up in John Frémont's back room, under a large dark oil painting of Sonoma in a thunderstorm. The table was magnificently decorated with flowers and shining silver tureens, and the buffet itself was arranged like the foothills and peaks of the High Sierras. Dish was stacked upon dish, garnished with oranges and limes and slices of avocado. There were clams, fried on the half shell; broiled lobsters, scarlet and singed at the edges; jellied shrimps; roast turkeys with crackly skins; hams; herrings; glazed pigs' heads with eyebrows of piped lard; headcheese; hot pork and beans; and a tumbling confusion of fruits, cheeses, nuts, and cookies.

Collis and Andy ate, and drank more champagne, and by the time nine-thirty chimed, Collis was brimming over with well-being, and more than ready to introduce himself to Sarah Melford. His conviviality was slightly strained, and he knew that he was mainly cheerful because he was drunk, but he didn't give a damn for Hannah, not a two-bit damn, and if she wanted to waste away the rest of her life with a haberdasher, then by God that was quite all right with him.

'Now, you're not going to cause another of your ruckuses, are you?' asked Andy.

'Certainly not,' said Collis, his cheeks flushed and his eyes dewy. 'Your trouble, Andy, is that you don't have enough faith in my New York courtesies and code of behaviour. I'm a gentleman. and besides, the plural of "ruckus" is "rucki". They taught me *that* much at school.'

'All you seem to have learned at school was how to make smart remarks,' Andy riposted.

'I learned geography, my friend, which was more than John Frémont seems to have done, for all his Army Topographical Corps. I learned that North was North, and South was South, and that West was west of East.'

Collis led Andy through into the main reception room again, excusing himself and smiling indulgently as he pushed his way past inquisitive society matrons in dresses like wedding cakes, and their starch-fronted, wax-whiskered husbands. He peered over the heads of the dancing couples, but he couldn't see Sarah Melford at all, and he was worried that she might have left. He asked Andy if he could spot her, but after craning his neck and looking all around, Andy shook his head. 'All I can see is a whole damn lot of heads bobbing up and down, like a pondful of pintail ducks.'

Quite suddenly, though, Sarah appeared at the door from the outside veranda, accompanied by a tall, broad-shouldered young man who could only have been her brother, Grant.

She was wearing a low-cut evening gown of gleaming dark blue. Her hair was pinned up, and her huge eyes were emphasised with cosmetics. She was even more beautiful than Collis had remembered, and she walked through the room with a sensual poise that turned everybody's head. He heard somebody say, 'That Melford girl is too pretty for her own good, if you ask me.'

Grant, on the other hand, was a rangy, big-boned boy, with all of his father's physique and not very much of his composure. It was only because he shared a striking sibling likeness with Sarah that they looked attractive together. He had thick, unruly hair and deep-set eyes, and his nose curved up like a gold panner's sluice. His collar was too tight for him, which made his neck bulge, and the sleeves of his tailcoat were too short. He probably hadn't worn it since his last vacation.

'Well,' said Andy, with resignation, 'there she is. You'd better go do your worst, and get it over with.'

The string quartet were bringing a cotillion to a scrapish sort of an ending, as if the music were a fish which they were required to fillet, and which had nothing left on it now but grey skin and untidy bones. Collis took the opportunity to cross the floor between the dancers, pardoning himself as he trod rather heavily on a small woman's toes, and to approach the younger Melfords from behind. They were talking politely to an elderly South Park duchess with a withered neck and strings of diamonds and pearls, and they didn't see Collis until he was right up next to them.

'Mr Melford,' said Collis, in his correctest tone. 'Would you permit me the pleasure of dancing with your sister?'

Grant Melford turned around, and so did Sarah. Grant was a good head taller than Collis, with black bushy eyebrows and cheeks that were ruddy with youthfulness, rather than drink.

'Do I know you, sir?' he asked, in a cautious voice.

Sarah, with an odd smile, said: 'No, Grant, you don't. But *I* do. You're the gentleman from the theatre, aren't you? The one who irritated Father so.'

'The same,' said Collis, bowing his head. 'Mr Collis Edmonds, at your command.'

'What's this about irritating Father?' said Grant.

'Only a jest,' said Collis. 'Now, about that dance?'

Grant put on a pouting, pugnacious face. 'Do you want to dance wtih him, Sarah?'

Sarah spread out her fan with a twist of her wrist and fluttered it. 'I'd be delighted,' she said. 'I've never had the pleasure of dancing with anyone so rude.'

Grant began to look very unhappy. He was plainly under instructions to supervise his sister's choice of dancing partners, and Collis had all the characteristics of that type his father had warned him to keep away, those 'smooth-talking, well-dressed reptiles that your sister likes so damned well.'

He said, 'I'm not sure that you can accept this dance, Sarah. I'd better ask Papa. It's Mr Edwards, is it?'

'Oh, don't be so silly, Grant,' said Sarah. 'I'm quite old enough to choose my own partners, and if I want to dance with Mr Edmonds, then I'm sure that I shall.'

The string quartet, after a few surreptitious swallows of steam beer from the glasses they kept under their chairs, began to strike up another dance. Already an awkward young man with a face as red as a newborn possum was struggling his way through the throng of guests towards Sarah, and Collis guessed that he was the next partner on Sarah's card, so he held out his hand to Sarah and said, 'Shall we dance, before it's too late?'

He led her out on to the polished parquet floor, and they joined with three other couples, two of them middle-aged and stiff as jointed marionettes, and the other young and awkward and inexperienced.

It didn't matter. As the quartet played 'Le Pantalon', the first part of the quadrille, in 6/8 time, Collis danced with an easy

349

perfection learned through good dancing lessons and years of practice at New York society balls, and Sarah danced with an elegance born of beauty, and balance, and supreme self-confidence.

Their partners hurried and stumbled, but neither Collis nor Sarah really saw them, except when they missed a step, or accidentally collided, and when that happened they simply danced their way around. They didn't take their eyes off each other, and the reception room sparkled and turned about them as if they were dancing on the axis of the world.

The quadrille changed to 2/4 time for its second part, 'L'Été,' and Collis felt intoxicated with champagne, music, light, and laughter. He had thought Sarah Melford provocative and beautiful before, but now she was infinitely desirable, and her face approached and retreated during the moves of the *contredanse* like a tantalising vision. They couldn't talk to each other as they danced, but her eyes were warm and expressive and bright with amusement.

Every now and then, as he spun around, Collis glimpsed Grant's glowering, unhappy face, as he stood there with his arms by his sides and his lower lip stuck out, waiting for the quadrille to end.

On the last chords of 'La Pastourelle', it eventually did. One of their partners, a small round Moravian woman in a diamond choker, was gasping and panting, and her husband had to support her. The younger couple gave a nervous smile and disappeared at once to find sherbets and lemonade. Collis was left alone on the floor with Sarah, and he reached out his hand to her and said gently, 'Will you take some refreshment? We've been dancing all this time and we haven't spoken a word.'

She came towards him, her silk skirts and underskirts rustling. 'Do you have to speak to let people know what you think?'

He gave a small shake of his head. 'Not with people like you.'

She held back her hand at the last moment and raised an eyebrow. 'I didn't know there were *any* people like me.'

'One or two. But none as beautiful.'

Suddenly Grant came up and stood right in front of Collis, with his hands on his hips and his face looking bigger and more boiled than ever.

'I've just spoken to my father about you, Mr Edmonds. He says you're to leave Sarah alone, please, with his compliments, and why don't you go dance with someone your own style.'

Collis raised his hand. 'There's no need to bark, Mr Melford. You can see that I haven't abducted your sister, nor seduced her. She's here, safe and sound, and smiling of her own free will. She's danced with me once with no apparent ill effects, and if she wants to dance with me again, then she will.'

'Not if I can help it.'

'You can't,' said Collis.

'What if I belt you in the nose?' demanded Grant.

Collis slowly let go of Sarah's hand. He felt suddenly cold, and he could feel the sweat of the dance under his armpits. If there was one thing that angered him beyond the point of coherence, it was the threat of assault. He wasn't particularly brave, and in most confrontations he would rather back down than risk a black eye. But young college greenhorns who thought they could frighten him with bluster and bunched-up fists were something else. They needed what his friend Henry Browne used to call 'the lesson that the rooster taught his eggs'.

Sarah sensed the change in Collis's demeanour. 'Grant,' she said, a little breathlessly, 'it's all right. We'll only have one dance more.'

'Father won't permit it. And neither will I.' He kept his eyes on Collis, and his lower lip firmly stuck out, like the bottom drawer of a bureau.

Collis looked at Sarah, and gave a weary shrug. 'Well,' he said, 'I suppose we must honour your dear brother's wishes. He seems to believe he has your best interests at heart, in a bovine fashion.'

'Bovine?' asked Grant. 'What's bovine?'

'I thought you were a college man,' said Collis, with overacted tiredness.

'I am, sir, and you'd better believe it. But what's bovine?'

He was talking so loudly now that people all around the room were turning their heads to see what was going on, and even the string quartet began to falter. His red-flushed cheeks had turned crimson, and there were clear droplets of sweat on his forehead. He didn't notice what an exhibition he was making of himself. He was concentrating too hard on doing what his father had told him to do, and that was to chase away hounds like Collis Edmonds.

Collis straightened his cuffs. 'Bovine,' he said, crisply, 'comes from a Latin word, *bos*, meaning ox. Roughly interpreted, it means that you're behaving as if you were solid dried beef from ear to ear.'

Behind Grant Melford's back, unseen by him, his father, Laurence, appeared in the veranda doorway, accompanied by John

Frémont. There was an embarrassed hush over the whole reception room, except for the thready strains of a popular song, and everybody's eyes went back from Collis, to Sarah, to Grant, to Laurence, and then back again. In the back room, a woman obliviously laughed a high scream of amusement.

Grant wiped the sweat from his forehead with the back of his hand. 'You'll take that back, sir,' he said shakily. 'You'll damn well take that back.'

Sarah stepped away. Collis glanced at her, but she gave him an almost imperceptible shake of her head. Even though Grant was her brother, this was man's business. The atmosphere was bristling with masculine anger and masculine pride.

'I'll do no such thing,' Collis said. 'It's absurd. You can't ask a man to take back an honest remark about an observable truth.'

Grant's voice was breaking with tension. He sounded as if he had a mouthful of smashed glass. 'Then, sir,' he said, 'you'll give me satisfaction.'

Collis stared at him, and then gave a *pfff* of hilarity. 'Satisfaction? How? By pouring gravy over your head and serving you up with beans?'

'I demand it!' roared Grant.

Collis tugged off his white evening gloves little by little, and then rolled them up. 'I don't think you know what you're asking,' he said in a very serious tone.

'I'm asking for an apology,' Grant blustered. 'Or, if I don't get that, satisfaction.'

There was silence. Laurence Melford, soft and deep, said, 'Grant.'

'This is my argument, Father,' he said loudly. 'I'm my own man now, and I'd appreciate it if you left it to me.'

'Grant,' said Laurence, 'I'm thinking of your safety as well as your pride. This man provokes people like you by nature. He even provokes me. But if we play the game by his rules, we'll only wind up defeated, and hurt.'

'He called me an ox,' said Grant.

Laurence Melford came down the steps from the veranda and crossed the reception-room floor. He didn't look at Collis once. Only at his son, who was now faced with the most dangerous decision of his twenty-year-old life.

'Of course he called you an ox,' Laurence Melford said warmly. 'He's good at choosing words that stir people up the most. He'll

352

probably be great, and rich, and successful, although I hate to admit it. But he'll only get that way because he can always find the words that shock people, and irritate people, and startle them out of their complacency. But why don't you be man enough to recognize what he's doing to you, and that you'd earn yourself far more respect if you refused to be goaded into behaving the way he wants you to?'

'Father,' said Grant, 'I'm asking for your support.'

'You know you always have it,' answered Laurence Melford, laying his hand on his son's shoulder. 'But not when you're risking your life for no sensible reason. Ignore this man. You're worth a hundred of him.'

Grant Melford wiped his forehead again. Staring at Collis, he said, 'What's it to be? You can choose your weapons, and the time, too.'

'Grant!' snapped his father.

Grant tugged his father's hand off his shoulder like a disillusioned infantryman ripping off one of his own epaulettes.

'I forbid it!' Laurence Melford told him loudly. 'I absolutely forbid it!'

'You forbid me to defend my good name?' shouted Grant.

'Your good name? He called you an ox, and by God, you *were* an ox to let him rile you!'

'Your father's right, Grant,' Collis said. 'You shouldn't have let it upset you.'

Laurence Melford gave him a quick, testy glance. 'There's only one thing I want to hear from you, sir, and that's an apology.'

'Ah. I was afraid you might say that,' Collis said.

'I suppose that means that you won't?'

'You called him an ox yourself, sir. I'm hardly likely to withdraw a remark that has such eminent endorsement.'

'There's no choice, you see, Father,' Grant put in. 'He's intractable. He's damned rude, and damned arrogant, and he needs to be whipped.'

'I don't care, Grant. I forbid you to duel.'

'Father, I shall do what my honour obliges me to do.'

Laurence Melford looked around. The quadrille music had faltered away altogether now, and the assembled guests were whispering and staring in embarrassment and confusion.

'Can we continue this discussion in some private place?' he asked John Frémont. Frémont nodded, and looked at them all sadly.

'This way, Laurence,' he said, and led them out of the main reception room, along the panelled corridor, and into a small study. Not far behind them, Jessie Frémont was taking Sarah Melford and her mother upstairs, to her private parlour. Sarah was looking strained and frightened.

Behind them, as they left, the gossip started up like a rising gust of wind through a field of dry wheat.

'Well, now,' said Laurence Melford, closing the study door behind him. 'How can we settle this quickly?'

'By tanning this insolent fellow's hide,' said Grant aggressively.

Laurence Melford turned to Collis. 'How much will you take?' he asked in a businesslike way. 'I'm really quite used to this kind of thing, so you don't have to skirt around the mountain to get to the mine.'

Collis lit a cheroot. He dropped the match into a china dish on the study desk, and it made a tiny tinkling sound.

'Believe it or not, Mr Melford, this has nothing whatever to do with money.'

'Come on, Mr Edmonds,' said Laurence Melford. 'You told me yourself you needed capital. How much do you want? A thousand dollars? Two thousand? How much will it take for you to go away and leave my family alone?'

Collis waved smoke away from his face. 'I think you've misunderstood this little argument, sir,' he said. His voice was very quiet. 'I did nothing worse than dance a quadrille with your daughter, and exchange a few polite words, and in the kind of society I come from, that kind of behaviour is considered not only normal but commendable.'

'I'm sure your social credentials are quite sound,' Laurence Melford told him. 'But whether they are or whether they aren't, that doesn't settle the problem that you've insulted my son, and he's demanding an apology, or satisfaction.'

'I suggest he put it down to experience, sir,' said Collis. 'Many more men will call him far worse names than I did, especially if he follows in his father's footsteps. And just like his father, he will have to learn to keep his temper and preserve his pride.'

'When I was a young man, Mr Edmonds, I would have been just as hot-headed as Grant about what you said, and I would have fought you, too, because I didn't have a father who loved me and cared whether I lived or died. As it is, I forbid Grant to fight you, and I don't expect an apology. But I want you to understand something else, Mr Edmonds. If you try to talk to me, or Sarah, or any other member of my family again, or if you pester us in any way, then I swear that I shall take the sternest measures I know.'

'What will they be?' asked Collis. 'Will you sell me off to the Barbary Coast crimps? Or will the Whitehall boatmen find me floating around and around your oyster beds, with my toes curled up?'

A muscle flinched in Laurence Melford's cheek. 'All you can do is try me,' he said. 'Try me, and find out for yourself.'

He straightened his coat, and looked significantly at both Grant and Collis to make sure that they understood how he felt. Then he turned around, opened the door, and left the study without saying another word.

Grant waited until his father had gone. He peered around the door to make sure. Then he said to Collis, in a heated whisper, 'What my father says doesn't alter anything. You called me an ox and you've got to take it back, or else I want satisfaction.'

Collis gave him a wry grin. 'Please, Grant, why don't you just let it lie? Your dear papa is determined to drop me into the Bay with an anchor around my neck, and you're hardly likely to get much more satisfaction than that.'

'I insist.'

'Don't be so goddam old-fashioned. Have you ever seen a duel? There's nothing heroic about it. A duel is either boring or tragic, sometimes both. What I said was a joke. If you didn't find it funny, then all you had to do was refuse to laugh. My God, if you'd made a fool of yourself like that in New York, you wouldn't have been invited back to the ratcatcher's ball.'

'Will you withdraw your insult?'

'No, Grant, I most certainly won't.'

'Then it's pistols,' said Grant.

'Pistols?' asked Collis, in disbelief. 'I never fired a pistol in my whole life.'

'It doesn't matter. You only have to fire once. I'll meet you at the northern tip of Lake Merced, tomorrow, at seven o'clock sharp. All you have to do is bring a second. I'll bring the guns, and arrange for a doctor.'

'You're out of your mind.'

'Perhaps I am. But I'm proud, too. And what will you be, if you don't show up to face me?'

'Alive,' said Collis. 'And just as much to the point, so will you.

It's not an easy matter being proud, especially when you're lying face down on the turf with a hole between your eyes.'

Grant wiped his perspiring face with a handkerchief. 'I would rather be dead than a yellow coward.'

Collis smoked his cheroot, and watched young Melford with his worried, dark-ringed eyes. Grant's fists opened and closed, opened and closed, in nervous anticipation. Eventually, Collis tapped the ash off the end of his cheroot and said, 'Very well. Seven o'clock tomorrow, sharp. Bring some champagne, and a couple of glasses. With any luck, we might both miss.'

He hardly spoke to Andy on the way back to the International Hotel. Andy didn't ask him much, either. Their rented brougham rattled and swayed over the ruts of Montgomery Street, and all around them the lights of San Francisco glittered and flared. Collis's head was thumping from too much champagne, and the night seemed to pass him by in a kaleidoscopic blur of piano music, laughter, fried shrimps, banging doors, and shouts. At the corner of Montgomery and California, a fandango guitarist in a wide-fringed hat was furiously strumming, and kicking at the planks of the boardwalk with his heel.

Collis looked the other way when they passed Walter West's store, between Sutter and Bush, but out of the corner of his eye he saw that the blinds of the second-floor windows were suffused with the orange glow of an oil lamp, and that shadows were flickering within. He pressed his lips together tight. He didn't want to imagine what was going on there. He didn't want to think about Hannah unbuttoning her dress, stepping out of her ribboned bloomers, and reaching out for someone else. He didn't want to picture Walter West's thread-scarred fingers caressing her face, or stroking her gleaming blonde hair. If he could have understood why he really loved her it might have been easier to bear. Instead, he had nothing to grasp but disjointed memories of Panama, and nothing to explain what he felt but fragments of half-forgotten conversation, and a grey vision of Hannah standing outside her husband's store with tears in her eyes.

'You sorted everything out with the Melfords, then?' said Andy.

'Kind of,' Collis told him.

'Well, you don't have to tell me if you don't want to. I don't mind. It was just that you came out of that study looking as if someone had put two spoonfuls of salt in your champagne.'

'It's sorted out,' said Collis. 'Or at least it will be.'

'Tell me about it when your hangover's gone,' Andy said and grinned. 'Come around to the office when you wake up, and we'll have ourselves a plateful of Caen tripe at the Poodle Dog.'

Collis pulled a face. 'Thanks, Andy. That's just what I feel like.'

They turned the corner of Jackson Street and drew up outside the International Hotel. The sidewalk outside was crowded with returning diners and theatregoers, elegant prostitutes in shining silks, small boys who were ready to run errands for two bits, shoe-shiners, horse holders, and laconic magazine sellers who leaned against the gas standards selling copies of *Varieties*. It was almost one o'clock in the morning, but San Francisco was still revelling in her perpetual carnival.

Collis got down from the carriage and reached out his hand. Andy shook it and said, 'Good night. Take some essence of peppermint before you go to sleep, and drink plenty of water. I'd hate to see you looking worse in the morning than you do now.'

'Thanks, Andy. I'll see you tomorrow.'

Collis stood on the sidewalk and watched the brougham turn and make its way back towards Montgomery. Andy raised his hat and gave him a foxy-faced grin, and it occured to Collis, with a feeling like lowering himself into a colder-than-tepid bathtub, that he might never see Andy again.

'Andy!' he called. But Andy simply waved and smiled and shook his head to show that he couldn't hear. The brougham paused for a moment to let a tarpaulined beer wagon rumble southwards on Montgomery, and then it was gone.

Inside the lobby, on a circular red-leather banquette, his face shadowed by the fronds of a palm, sat Dan McReady. He looked as if he had been waiting with stony patience for several hours. Collis walked across and stood beside him, his hat still in his hands.

Dan McReady's cold eyes remained fixed on the reception desk opposite. He was smoking a hand-rolled cigarette, and it waggled between his lips as he spoke. 'I talked to Teach,' he said, in his odd Vermont-Louisiana accent. 'In fact, we had ourselves quite a tête-à-tête.'

'And?'

'He bought them. That was the upshot. Twenty thousand in dust and small nuggets.'

'You put it in the hotel safe?'

'I weighed it first, and took out my ten per cent.'

Collis put his hat on again. 'I hope it was ten per cent precisely.'

'Don't you fear about that.'

Collis sat down beside him. 'What about the fire? Is that all arranged?'

Dan McReady nodded. 'I was just waiting to hear you say go ahead and do it. Then I was going to go ahead and do it. Do you want to watch?'

'Is it all ready to go?'

Dan McReady's cigarette had fizzled out, and he relit it. He sucked a few times until the tip was glowing. 'You've got the best in the business. Gordon Jarvis, from New South Wales. That man could set fire to a raincloud, if you paid him enough.'

'All right, then. Let's go watch.'

They stepped outside the hotel and hailed a shabby-looking cab that was waiting across the street. The girls came clustering up to them again, but Dan McReady pushed them aside and said something harsh under his breath that made them retreat. He opened the cab door for Collis and said to the driver, 'Davis at Sacramento. And make it as quick as you damn well can.'

It was a chilly night. Their breath smoked in the darkness of the cab's interior. Dan McReady sat upright, with his hands clasped together in his lap like a man on his way to a wedding reception. There was a smell of smoke and fog and Chinese satay in the air.

'You're sure Teach didn't suspect anything?' asked Collis.

'Nope. He wouldn't have paid over twenty thousand if he had. He was just bubbling over to get his revenge. Just bubbling over. You would've laughed.'

Collis stared out of the window. The cab was rattling south on Battery past the Merchant's Exchange. It was nearly one-thirty now In five and a half hours, he could be dead, lying in a pine box on the north shore of Lake Merced. He touched his closed eyelids with the tips of his fingers. He wondered if they would lay gold pieces on his eyes. Bits were in such short supply.

'Maybe you can do me a favour,' he said to Dan McReady.

'A favour?' The gambler turned his head and looked at him. His eyes registered nothing.

Collis swallowed. 'I, er, I'm fighting a duel. I wondered if you could come along and help me. Be my second.'

'A duel? Who the hell fights duels?'

'It looks as though I do. I didn't want to. But I guess things got out of hand.'

358

Dan McReady took a hand-rolled cigarette out of the breast pocket of his coat and put it between his lips.

'What's it over?' he asked Collis, searching for his matches. 'A woman?'

'It was Grant Melford,' Collis said. 'Laurence Melford's young whelp. All puffed up and indignant, and full of the family pride.'

Dan McReady grunted. 'In that case, I hope you blow his head off.'

'You'll come along?'

'If that's what you want. I could always bear to see a Southerner get his just deserts.'

Collis smiled uncertainly. 'You seem to be pretty sure that I'm going to win.'

'Sure you'll win. I fought a gunfight myself once, in a back street in Vicksburg. It wasn't exactly a duel, but it added up to the same kind of affray when you think about it. I stayed calm, and that was the reason I won. The other fellow was popping away, and all I did was walk right up to him and point my pistol at his forehead and say, "If you don't lay down your gun, it's St Peter for you, instanter".'

'I wish I had your confidence,' said Collis.

Dan McReady relit his cigarette. 'Just remember that a heavy-calibre pistol is not an accurate weapon. By no means. So the steadier you are, the better chance you have of hitting what you want to hit. Hold your pistol in both hands, take a good long aim, and don't fret about what the other fellow's doing. If he's as young and as burned up about things as you say he is, then the chances are that he'll miss you by continents.'

The cab had arrived at the corner of Davis and Sacramento. Dan McReady opened the door, climbed down to the street, and looked up at Collis like the prompter in a melodramatic play.

'It's those who don't want to die that usually do,' he said, with a hard smile. 'Those who don't care one way or the other, they're the ones who generally survive.'

Collis climbed down beside him and handed the cab driver a dollar. 'That's about the least reassuring thing that anybody ever told me,' he said. 'I just hope I don't take those words to my grave.'

'You're really scared?' Dan McReady pronounced it 'skeered'.

Collis looked at him. 'Yes,' he said. 'Wouldn't you be?'

The cab turned in the street with a grinding of iron-hooped

wheels and made its way uptown again, at a trot. Davis Street in the small hours of a winter morning was not a salubrious place to be, and the hazards to health weren't confined to the stinking pools of water that had collected in the sandy infill around the edge of the Bay. There were crimps, fleecers, and vicious ticket-of-leave men who didn't think very much about breaking a man's head with a bung starter to take his purse. Collis didn't know whether it was more frightening to stand on this bleak, fog-cold corner, waiting for Gordon Jarvis, or to face up to Grant Melford and his pistols-for-two. He felt chilled. His nose was running and he wished to God he was back in New York.

Eventually, a short, broad figure came limping along Sacramento Street from the direction of Battery. He walked straight up to Dan McReady and Collis and said gruffly, 'All's well. Who's this?'

'The client,' Dan McReady said. 'He's taking an active interest.'

'Doesn't trust us?'

Dan glanced at Collis and grinned. 'Maybe. Maybe not. Could be a fire bug, like you.'

Gordon Jarvis stepped into the light. He was wearing a seaman's jacket, with his hands jammed in the pockets, and his small round head was capped with a knitted fisherman's hat. His nose was twisted, his cheeks were folded with white scars, and his two front teeth were missing. He smelled strongly of Dutch gin. His eyes glittered in his face like chips of coal caught in a hearthside rug.

'How do you do, mister,' he said, in a strong Australian accent. He put out his hand, and Collis shook it. Unnervingly, Jarvis had only three fingers, no thumb, and it was all Collis could do not to tug his own hand away in repulsion.

'Dan tells me that everything's ready,' said Collis.

Jarvis nodded. 'All we need now is the match, and you can have your fire. It should be a good one, too. I've told the boys at Engine Company Five to give us a fair half hour before they turn out.'

'Nobody saw you move the blankets?'

Jarvis wiped his nose with his sleeve. 'We're not first-timers, mister. We moved all the blankets out of the old warehouse under tarpaulins, and if anybody asked, we said they were rotten hides. We had them into Parkinson's place by seven o'clock, and all locked up. Mr Stoddard gave us all the correct receipts, and he's more than happy to see the place burn down. It's overinsured, and overvalued, and he should be able to put himself up a decent new brick place instead.'

'Very nice, too,' said Collis wanly.

'Right then,' said Jarvis. 'Shall we go? The fun's all ready to start.'

They walked along the wet planks of Davis Street as far as California. The night was almost quiet now, except for the sounds of distant piano music and an occasional shout. The fog was precipitating cold moisture over the waterfront district like misery itself. Dan McReady let out one of his abrupt coughs – '*Ha!*' – and Collis glanced at him and hoped he wouldn't decide to let one out just at the moment he was going to fire at Grant Melford.

Parkinson's warehouse was a damp, sagging building that had been put together out of old timbers from Howison's Wharf. Its foundations had been shifting for five or six years, as the Bay infill slowly settled beneath it, and now the walls were leaning and the roof was shedding its shingles. 'If you want to watch, wait here,' Gordon Jarvis said, and he crossed the street with the gait of a determined gorilla.

Dan McReady's cigarette went out again, but he didn't try to light it. He stood there with his arms folded and his hat tilted back, sniffing with contented regularity and waiting for the first signs of Gordon Jarvis's success. Collis found himself whistling between his teeth. The buildings all around them were clotted with shadows.

At last, they heard a crackling sound. Collis looked across the street, straining his eyes in the darkness, and he saw skeins of grey woolly smoke pouring out the clapboarded sides of Parkinson's warehouse. Then he saw the first licks of flame, and in a few minutes the whole building was issuing smoke like the big black carcass of a dragon. There were pops and groans and creaks, and some of the joists fell inside the building, so that it staggered and leaned even further to the left.

Abruptly, there was a soft funnelling sound, and through the cracks in the timbers Collis could see that the inside of the warehouse had burst into dazzling, lascivious flame. Dan McReady sniffed and said, 'That's the whale oil. Gordon always likes to leave a barrel of whale oil around to hike up the heat. You watch her burn up now.'

The fire became ferocious, like a flaring disease from which no timber or rafter could escape. Thick, choking smoke was blown by the mild easterly wind across the city, and whatever Engine

Company Number Five had promised Gordon Jarvis about holding off, it wasn't long before Collis could hear fire bells ringing, and the rattling of horses and wagons.

It was too late now for the hook-and-ladder boys to do anything but keep the fire contained, but their steam pumpers arrived in a hissing, glittering, clattering cavalcade, and in a few minutes the intersection between Davis and California was crowded with tossing fire horses, volunteer firemen in shiny brass helmets and brass-buttoned tunics, hoses, pumpers, wagons, and all the inquisitive riffraff of the docks and market districts. The sound of bells and screaming steam valves was deafening, but it couldn't drown out the most terrible sound of all, which was the low breathy rumble of a building ablaze. Every now and then, as a main beam collapsed in a hail of sparks, the crowd would let out a curious moan of fright and pleasure, and the fire horses would stir restlessly in the harnesses. A fire in San Francisco appeared to Collis to be almost a ritual event, at which not only the engine companies and the spectators played out their parts according to what was expected of them, but the arsonists, too. Without fire-raisers, after all, there would be far fewer fires, and what would the splendid engine companies do then?

There were more crashes and creaks from the warehouse. Through the skeletal sides, Collis could see bundles of blankets burning, stack upon stack of finest English wool bedding. He looked up at the sky. The sparks were rushing up into the foggy night air and whirling around in a triumphant celebration of success. He just hoped he was going to stay around long enough to enjoy it.

'Pretty good, huh?' Dan McReady said.

'I guess so. I never saw a fire like this before. It's kind of depressing.'

'What's depressing about it? Nobody loses, and the firemen have a good time.'

'Arthur Teach loses.' Collis felt his face flush with heat, a consequence not only of the blazing fire nearby but of a sudden sharp remorse for what he was doing.

'Sure,' Dan McReady said, tugging at the brim of his hat. 'But Teach should have been more cautious. Revenge may be sweet, but it generally comes expensive.'

'Have you paid off Gordon Jarvis yet?' Collis asked.

'Not yet. He's supposed to be meeting us here.'

The steam pumpers were spraying the warehouse with veil after veil of water, and in ten minutes the fire had been reduced to a few sulky flickers. A party of volunteers had chopped their way in through the side gate, and were now happily tearing down a low shed which connected the warehouse to the shipping office next door. Collis asked Dan McReady, 'I suppose he's all right?'

Dan McReady gave a quick shake of his head. 'He's the best in the business. That's why I used him. He was transported to New South Wales in the first place for arson. He burned down a music hall in East London with seventy people in it, and they were goddam lucky they weren't all toasted in their seats.'

'That doesn't mean he hasn't made a mistake this time.'

'Listen,' said Dan McReady, sounding testy. 'You got what you wanted, didn't you? Twenty thousand dollars and your blankets burned for good?'

'Sure, but – '

'Gordon's all right,' Dan McReady put in. 'He probably had to get out the back way, and skirt around. He'll be here.'

They waited on the corner for nearly twenty minutes. Three o'clock struck. The engine company had doused the flames, and now the streets were thick with billowing, acrid smoke. There wasn't much left of Parkinson's warehouse but charred uprights and blackened ash. The firemen trod through the wreckage with their brass helmets dulled by heat and water, swinging their axes at anything that still smoked, and coughing. One of them was whistling Stephen Massett's railroad song, 'Clear the Way'.

'Men of thought be up and stirring, night and day!'

Dan McReady bit his lip. The warehouse was intermittently blotted out by smoke, and it came and went as if it were a magic lantern picture. The stench of wet burned wool was almost unbearable. One of the firemen was winding in the hoses across the muddy, ash-littered street.

'I can't understand it,' said McReady. 'He told me to wait right here. "Wait right here," he told me. He said he wouldn't be more than five minutes.'

Collis was too tired to wait any longer. 'If he's the best, as you said, then he'll come around for his money, even if he was to look you up at your office. He wouldn't give you a fire like that for free Not and keep his mouth shut about it, too. Now, let's go get a drink, for God's sake. My throat feels like a charcoal burner's chimney.'

'Maybe we ought to give him five minutes more ' McReady frowned.

363

'Dan,' said Collis, wearily, 'he's not coming. He'll be around tomorrow maybe, but it's pretty damned plain that he's not coming tonight.'

'Okay,' said McReady reluctantly. 'I guess you're right.'

They left the corner and crossed the street. A fireman called, 'Watch that hose, will ya?' and they had to sidestep as a wet canvas hose slithered past them like a glistening anaconda. The night disappeared in a rolling cloud of smoke, and then appeared again. Everybody's face was pale with tiredness and smudged with soot. They looked like clowns at a funeral.

As they passed the burned wall of the warehouse that fronted on California Street, they heard one of the firemen call, 'Captain! Come take a look at this!'

Collis walked on, but Dan McReady caught his arm. 'Wait. Just for a minute.' Collis sighed and paused. The fire captain was crossing the wreckage in his peaked cap and his shiny boots, his tunic strained in front by a mighty well-fed paunch, and his britches strained behind by an equally well-fed rump. Three or four more firemen joined him, and soon half the company were standing around in a circle, shaking their heads and talking. Collis couldn't hear what they were saying because of the constant hiss of steam from the pumpers.

'My God,' Dan McReady said suddenly and climbed over the charred boards which were all that remained of the building's south wall. He began to stumble across the black ruins, slipping twice and tearing the cuff of his pants. 'Dan – what the hell's the matter?' Collis asked. But then he glimpsed between the boots of the gathered firemen to what Dan McReady had already seen, and he hesitated for only a moment before he cautiously climbed over the boards after him, and walked towards the firemen with a feeling of unreality and fright. The firemen didn't even glance at him as he joined their circle and looked down at what they had found.

It was Gordon Jarvis. Collis knew it was Jarvis because of his three-fingered hand, and because it couldn't really have been anyone else. But there weren't any other ways of telling.

Maybe the cask of whale oil had flared up before he meant it to. Maybe he'd stumbled, or suffered a heart seizure, or twisted his ankle. Nobody would ever know what physical hell he had suffered, and Gordon Jarvis himself would never say.

Collis was almost back to the sidewalk before he realized he had turned away. The smell of burned wool now seemed like the ghastly fragrance of flesh. He stood there for two or three minutes, looking up California Street towards the Chinese quarter, where distant lanterns swung red and green in the early wind. He didn't know what to do or say. In less than four hours, the same ambition which had brought Gordon Jarvis to these ashes on Davis Street was going to take Collis to the north shore of Lake Merced. Collis couldn't deny that he was scared. Maybe Laurence Melford and John Frémont were right about the Pacific railroad, and he was all wrong. Maybe the dream of spanning America by rail was too grand, too arrogant, like building a tower of Babel on its side Hadn't John Frémont lost ten men, frozen in the mountains that were named for the blood of Christ?

Dan McReady came up at last and touched him on the arm. He was very white, and he had taken his hat off.

'I knew that fellow for years,' he said, in a whisper. 'A strange man, you know, and very violent. But he would have helped anyone who needed help, and set fire to anything at all if you'd asked him to.'

Collis didn't answer, but rubbed his smutty cheek with his fingertips.

Dan McReady said, 'It's not making you scared, is it? What happened to Jarvis?'

Collis gave him a long, serious look. 'In Panama,' he said huskily, 'I prayed in a cathedral for somebody's life, and that life was saved. But I've had a hand in two deaths now, a girl in New York, and now Gordon Jarvis, and I'm just wondering if God hasn't decided it's time I was judged.'

'Come on, you're just feeling tired, and upset. You didn't kill Gordon Jarvis. Gordon Jarvis wasn't anything more than a victim of his own life.'

'No, you're wrong. He was a victim of *my* life. The same way everybody else is. The same way I am, too.'

'I don't know what you're talking about,' said Dan McReady. He glanced back at the circle of firemen.

'I wish I could make it clearer. I wish I understood it myself.' The wind began to rise, and the fog listlessly stirred. Collis's dark curls were ruffled as if someone had run their fingers through his hair. 'I feel as if I were standing on the footplate of some kind of terrible train,' he said. 'It's running faster and faster, and no matter what I do I can't stop it, even when it knocks people down.'

Dan McReady took out a crumpled cigarette 'That, my friend, is

365

called fate. Everybody's riding one type of train or another. Some of them are slow, and rusty, and stop at every damned crossing on the way. Others are shiny and fly down the line like hot shit. But believe you me, and I've found this out for myself, they all wind up at the same old station. And whichever way they go, fast or slow, plain or fancy, most folks find the ride ain't hardly worth the price.'

Collis squeezed his eyes shut to try to restore some moisture under his lids. He said, 'You don't happen to want to fight this duel instead of me, do you?'

They parted on the corner of Montgomery and California. Dan McReady was going back to his boarding-house on Stockton, to change his shirt and shave. He promised to collect Collis outside the International Hotel a little after six o'clock, so that they could ride out to Lake Merced in good time for the duel. 'Don't drink anything,' he warned, 'and don't try to go to sleep. Just take yourself a quick, cold bath, and put on some fresh linen. It's easier to shoot straight in clean drawers. Don't ask me why.'

Collis watched him walk off into the darkness. An upstairs window across the street was still lit, and someone was playing the viola, so sadly and sweetly that you could have imagined the love of his or her life had just been lost. Collis waited on the corner for a while, then started walking doggedly north towards the International, and an early breakfast.

On the breezy shore of Lake Merced, under a November sky that was the colour of a Heermann's gull, the greyest and darkest of all the gulls, Grant Melford was already waiting with his seconds and his doctor when Collis arrived. The wind whistled through the pale grasses and made soft thundery noises in Collis's eardrums. He stood by the wheel of their hired carriage while Dan McReady gave the driver two dollars and asked him to wait. Fifty yards away, in his black cape and high silk hat, Grant Melford was watching him with a concentrated frown. Collis tried to smile, although he didn't know why.

At length, the carriage was driven away out of earshot, and Collis walked across the grass, closely followed by Dan, to say good morning. Collis was wearing his grey morning suit, freshly-pressed that morning by the hotel valet, and Dan McReady was dressed in a coat of brown herringbone tweed and a round white hat. He was smoking a cigarette.

Grant Melford's face was pale and oval as a sago pudding. He looked as if he hadn't slept. One of his seconds was a serious young college type, tanned, with a small moustache, who squinted out of clear blue eyes like a slightly maniacal badminton umpire. The other must have been a servant, because he stood a few paces back, and his morning suit was half a size too large for him. He was big-nosed, with curly coppery hair, and he said nothing at all, though Collis heard him grunt.

Even further away, on a small grassy embankment, the doctor waited like a buzzard on a branch. He was elderly, with fraying white hair and tiny spectacles. His old brown leather bag lay at his feet. He coughed a great deal as Collis inclined his head towards Grant, and towards his seconds, and as Collis said, 'Good morning, gentlemen. A dull day to die.'

Grant gave a jerky nod. 'Good morning, Mr Edmonds. Allow me to introduce Mr Snaith and Mr O'Rourke. Our medical prac-titioner is Dr Mince.'

Collis gave each of them a sloping smile. The doctor, unexpectedly, waved.

Grant took a deep, unsteady breath. 'I suppose you're not prepared to withdraw your remark of last night?' he asked Collis.

Collis glanced at Dan McReady, but all Dan McReady could do was give him a small shrug, as if to say, 'It's your duel – if you want to fight it, fight it.' The young college type, Mr Snaith, waited with a large mahogany box in his arms, his finger on the catch, keeping the lid closed until he had heard Collis's answer.

Collis cleared his throat. He felt as if he were someone else altogether. His chest was tight and he couldn't find a way to release the pressure. The wind blew fretfully all around him, and a flock of terns allowed themselves to be tossed out over the ruffled surface of the lake like the thrown-away pages of a tragic letter.

'No,' Collis said. 'I won't withdraw.'

'You're adamant?'

'I said no. Does no have any other meaning?'

Grant licked his lips. 'Very well. Then I must ask Mr Snaith to give you a choice of pistols.'

Mr Snaith unclipped the catch and raised the lid of the mahogany box. He walked across the grass towards Collis and presented its contents with a face that was almost too grim to be taken seriously. If Collis hadn't been so nervous, he probably would have laughed. He examined the box and wished the whole goddam business were over.

Nestling in green velvet were two long-barrelled pistols with varnished wooden handles. They were not at all decorative, and they smelled of thin oil. A brass plate on the side of the box said 'Lafoucheux'.

Mr Snaith said, 'Please choose one, Mr Edmonds. They are both loaded, and they both fire only one round each.'

Collis lifted the upper pistol out. He held it awkwardly, feeling the coldness and the weight of it. 'Very well,' he said, 'I'll take this one.'

Mr Snaith crossed back towards Grant Melford, and Grant took out the second pistol. The doctor, on his chilly embankment, started to cough again. It was two minutes after seven in the morning, and Collis was beginning to feel like going behind a hedge and relieving himself. It was bad enough fighting a duel without having a pain in the bladder as well.

Mr Snaith closed his box. 'Gentlemen,' he said in his clipped Boston accent, 'I crave your attention for one moment only. The rules are that you should each walk twenty paces away, turn, and fire whenever you wish. That is all. May God have mercy on you.'

Collis looked down at his pistol. 'I don't even know how to fire the damned thing,' he muttered to Dan McReady. 'What do I do?'

Dan McReady pinched the cigarette out from between his lips with his finger and thumb. 'That's a Lafoucheux,' he said. 'They're specially made for duelling, and they're bastards. You only have to tickle their triggers and they're off. So don't, whatever you do, put your finger anywhere near the trigger until you're aimed and ready to fire.'

'I'm terrified,' said Collis. 'You know that? I'm damn well terrified.'

'Of course you are,' Dan McReady told him. 'But don't be scared so shitless that you forget what I told you. Aim leisurely, holding the pistol with both hands. Pull back the hammer with your thumb until it's cocked. Then make sure your aim is true, and touch that trigger gently. That's all. Now go blow the bastard's brains out.'

Mr Snaith raised a red handkerchief. It snapped in the wind. 'Are you ready, gentlemen?'

Grant Melford called out loudly, 'Always ready, Mr Snaith, to defend my good name!'

Collis looked at Dan McReady and made a face. In return, he called out, 'Always ready, Mr Snaith, to compound one absurdity with another!'

Mr Snaith gave Collis a disapproving squint, but then he held his handkerchief up high, paused, and brought it down to signal that the duel had begun.

Collis turned his back and began to walk. The turf was sloping and uneven. Ahead of him, in the distance, he could see his rented carriage waiting, and it occurred to him that he could keep on walking, maybe breaking into a jog, and reach the carriage before anyone really understood that he was running away. Beyond the carriage were the peaks of Fern Hill, and beyond that, the city of San Francisco, hazy with the blue fires of breakfast. He coughed. He almost stumbled on a sandy hillock.

It suddenly occurred to him that he hadn't been counting. How many paces was this? Twelve, fifteen? Supposing Grant Melford got his first shot in before Collis had even turned around? Nervously, Collis looked over his shoulder and saw that Grant still had his back to him and was still pacing away. He was taking long strides, and in his black morning coat he looked like a big plump crow.

This must be it. Nineteen, twenty, stop. Turn. And Grant Melford was turning too. Forty paces wasn't nearly as far apart as Collis had imagined it would be. He could still see the pale frown on Grant's face, and the mole on his chin. Oh God, this seemed all so peculiar.

Grant Melford was raising his pistol. Collis had been so distracted by the ritual of the duel that he had almost forgotten what he had to do. But he saw Dan McReady standing there placidly in his brown tweed coat and his round hat, and he remembered his warning. *Don't put your finger anywhere near the trigger until you're aimed and ready to fire . . . Aim leisurely, holding the pistol with both hands.*

He had hardly brought his pistol up when there was a sharp snap, like somebody slamming a book shut. Collis winced, in spite of himself, and a surge of hot fear flooded right through his body. He waited to be hit, forgetting in his fright that any shot which struck him would have reached him and felled him before he heard it.

Nothing happened. Collis peered across the grass towards Grant Melford, and saw that he was standing there with an expression of almost comical horror, his thick eyebrows raised and his mouth open in a perfectly round O. A puff of white smoke was escaping across the grassy landscape behind him. He must have touched the sensitive trigger of his Lafoucheux before he had taken aim, and his shot had gone wide.

A slight echo came back from across the lake. A flurry of birds had risen in the distance, and now they were settling again. Mr Snaith and Mr O'Rourke turned their heads of one accord and looked at Collis with almost as much theatrical dread as Grant Melford. Collis stood where he was, straight-backed, with the long-barrelled pistol clasped in both hands, aiming directly at Grant Melford's head.

Collis, in that moment, had an insight into the meaning of real power. He didn't have the slightest intention of killing Grant Melford now. That would have been brutal and pointless. But Grant Melford didn't know that, and according to his own melodramatic code of conduct, Collis would have been quite justified in shooting him down at his leisure. He stood there, the poor boy, his arms down by his sides, his face caught in a spasm of honour. Collis made an elaborate show of taking a good long aim down the barrel of his pistol, and he could sense the terrible suspense, and the agony of each unfired moment.

What Grant Melford and his seconds didn't understand was that if Collis killed him, Collis would have accepted Grant's ridiculous premise that caustic remarks could be expunged only by shooting at people in fields; and, far worse, he would have thrown away the best opportunity he had yet had for coming to grips with the Melford family. An enraged Laurence Melford was one thing, but a Laurence Melford who would have to admit a grudging gratitude that his son's life had been spared – that would be something else altogether.

Mr Snaith said, in a strained voice, 'You may fire when ready, Mr Edmonds.'

Collis called back, 'Thank you, Mr Snaith.'

He could see Dan McReady smoking and watching him with mild interest as he raised the Lafoucheux high over his head and fired it straight up into the sky. It kicked his wrist and let out a stunning bang.

Mr O'Rourke suddenly began to clap, but he stopped as soon as Grant Melford glared at him. Suffused with outrage now, and crimson instead of white, Grant came stalking across the grass towards Collis and stood there with his fists on his hips.

'You didn't have to do that, you know,' he said loudly. 'There's no honour in shooting deliberately wide

Collis lowered his empty gun. He smiled. 'You're only annoyed because I made you look like an idiot. But I would have looked an even bigger idiot if I'd killed you. Now, can we consider this matter settled?'

Grant took a deep breath. 'I suppose that etiquette demands that we have to.'

'Well, that's very good,' said Collis. 'Did you remember to bring the champagne?'

Grant looked at him, and Collis realized with surprise that the boy's lower lip was trembling.

'I – I only brought – one glass,' Grant said.

Tears filled his eyes, and he quickly turned away, and hurried past Mr Snaith and Mr O'Rourke towards his carriage, which was waiting by the shore. The doctor coughed, picked up his bag, and walked slowly after him. Collis stood watching him go, and nobody else seemed to know what to do next.

Eventually, Mr Snaith came over to Collis and held out his hand for the pistol. Collis lifted the Lafoucheux, looked at it, and then gave Mr Snaith a small shake of the head.

'A souvenir,' he said. 'A small reminder that the pursuit of honour for its own sake can lead to sudden death at the hands of people you hardly know.'

Chapter 9

He returned to Sacramento the following Monday, tired, and almost glad to be back. It was much warmer inland, and he stood on the deck of the paddle-steamer with his coat unbuttoned. The steamer edged in towards the Front Street embankment, its paddles churning up the muddy river into brown foam, and the longshoremen and idlers watched it come in, leaning against trees and posts as if they were trying to form a human alphabet.

Collis saw Wang-Pu waiting for him in the shade of a red-berried elder, in a morning coat and hat. A few yards away, tethered to a rail, was Jane McCormick's horse and carriage, which Wang-Pu must have borrowed. The implications of that weren't lost on Collis, and he smiled to himself. The homely Mrs McCormick appeared to have missed him.

Before he disembarked, Collis talked to the steamer's mate, a man with a striped jersey and a head the colour and shape of a brass pot. He wanted his cargo of hardware unloaded as smartly as possible, and taken down to No. 54 K Street. He gave the mate two five-dollar gold pieces, which the mate pinched between his black-edged thumbnails, as a kind of impromptu assay, and then dropped into a chamois bag tied around his neck.

Collis walked down the plank, and Wang-Pu came forward and raised his hat. 'Good afternoon, Mr Edmonds. A pleasant journey?'

'The ship's piano was out of tune and the oysters were off, but apart from that, yes.'

'Mrs McCormick sends her compliments.'

'So I see.'

They walked across the dust of Front Street to the carriage and climbed aboard. Wang-Pu snapped the whip at the horse's ears, and they turned and trotted south towards K Street. The afternoon sun shone through the spokes of the wheels, and through the rustling leaves of the elders and bitter cherries.

'Mr Jones has been asking after you, too,' said Wang-Pu.

'Oh, yes?'

'He says he wants to go to Washington in February, and that he's booked your tickets on the *California* already.'

'That's presumptuous of him,' remarked Collis.

'Maybe,' said Wang-Pu.

Collis turned and looked at him. 'Why only maybe? What do you know about this that I don't?'

Wang-Pu looked back at him blandly. 'If you must know, I heard from a Chinese friend of mine in San Francisco. He wrote me about a certain warehouse fire on Davis Street, not so many days ago. I have the letter here, in my pocket. I wish you could read Pekingese, because the letter is full of very subtle implications. One of the characters has the unusual meaning: "that which was already consumed was consumed again".'

Collis pursed his lips, but then relaxed and smiled. 'It seems nobody can keep a secret from you.'

Wang-Pu snapped the whip. 'Secrets are the stock in trade of the Chinese people,' he said. 'We deal in secrets the way you deal in gunpowder and nails.'

'So you told Theodore Jones that I was probably back in business?'

Wang-Pu nodded. 'I gave him to understand that if you had been prepared to take advantage of Mr Teach by arranging to sell him your burned blankets, and then to burn them a second time, to conceal the fact of their first burning, then your interest in building the Pacific railroad must be almost as strong as his. If not stronger.'

'So he bought the tickets to Washington on your recommendation?' asked Collis.

'You could say that.'

Collis thought for a moment. 'What's your interest in this? Really?'

Wang-Pu was climbing down from the carriage and readjusting the slightly jaunty angle of his hat. 'My interest, Mr Edmonds? Only in fulfilling those things which have already been foretold.'

'What's been foretold? That Theodore Jones would drag me off to Washington because some interfering Chinaman told him it might be a good idea?'

'You mustn't take offence,' said Wang-Pu. 'Everything that happens is predicted. I consulted three fortune-tellers. All were in accord.'

'What did they tell you? To look out for a New York greenhorn in a silk hat?'

Wang-Pu was silhouetted against the setting sun. Its rays burned from his left shoulder like a dazzling epaulette. His figure was slight and lean, and his head was that almond-shaped oval of the northern Chinese.

'They spoke in symbols, as they always do,' Wang-Pu said. 'But they told me that I would be the first among my people to see the gate through the distant mountains, and that in the company of a white devil, I would lead hundreds of Chinese in the building of the greatest pathway this world has ever known. They said I would touch the robes of great glory.'

'Maybe they were good at making informed guesses. They must have known you were a friend of Theodore Jones.'

'No, Mr Edmonds. This was years ago, when I first arrived in San Francisco. This was long before I met you, or Mr Jones, or any of the people I know now.'

Collis looked at Wang-Pu and felt as if he had never seen him before. Suddenly, strangely, this amusing Chinese servant had appeared as somebody else altogether – a man whose destiny was mysteriously linked with Collis's own.

'We ought to talk about this some more,' Collis said.

'Yes,' said Wang-Pu, as if he knew what Collis had been thinking.

Collis looked up at the frontage of 54 K, the hardware store. 'I guess I'd better go tell Leland and Charles that I'm back. Can we meet tomorrow?'

'Of course. Why don't you come around to my apartments, and I will cook you a modest Chinese dinner. Eight-treasure tomatoes, lion's head casserole, and aromatic duck.'

'That sounds delicious.'

'It is the traditional cooking of Peking.'

They were standing next to each other now with unusual formality, as if they were strangers who had just been introduced. In a way, they were. They had just discovered why their utterly different lives had brought them to the same place, in the same year, and why the white of the High Sierra snow was in both of their eyes.

Collis and the McCormicks had dinner that evening at the Tuckers. They drank a toast of California Pinot Noir to their partnership, and then Charles fought with a gristly joint of beef and a blunt carving knife, while Mary passed around dishes of overcooked broccoli and watery squash. Collis told them about his visit to San Francisco, and about the hardware he'd bought, although he didn't mention *l'affaire des couvertures*, as Theodore

Jones was later to call the burning of the *Aria*'s blankets, nor did he tell them about his duel with Grant Melford. He knew now how calculating he was going to have to be to get his way with the railroad, and he wanted to keep their suspicions lulled until he was ready.

After a sad pineapple pudding, Collis at last produced the purse of gold which Dan McReady had left in the safe of the International Hotel. He held it up, shook it so that it gave that lumpy rattle peculiar to gold nuggets, and then passed it across the table to Leland.

'I still wish I knew how you made a profit out of burned blankets,' said Charles, peeling an apple with his penknife.

Collis smiled. 'Whatever you've got, there's always *somebody* willing to buy it. I was lucky, that's all.'

'How much is in here?' asked Leland, his eyebrows lowered with displeasure.

'Enough to cover those shares you made over, plus a little more, which you can take as an investment in new stock.'

Leland looked at the purse balefully and wiped his mouth with his napkin. 'You know something?' he said. 'I still find it difficult to believe that a man of your background should wish to become involved in a hardware business. I know what you've said about gaining experience. I know all of that. But it doesn't seem to ring authentic.'

Collis sipped his wine, and didn't answer at first.

Charles said, 'You've shown the enthusiasm, haven't you, Collis? That's all that counts.'

'I've shown the colour of my money,' said Collis, 'and that counts even more. If you don't like it, Leland, you know what you can do.'

'I wasn't doubting your integrity,' Leland said huffily.

Collis pushed back his chair and stood up. 'Mary,' he said, 'I want to thank you for your dinner. Jane, it was a pleasure to spend an evening in your company. Charles, thank you.'

There was a difficult pause. Then Collis turned to Leland and gave him a mock-respectful nod of the head.

'We'll be friends, Leland, I don't have any doubt of it.'

'Friends?' Leland said darkly. 'We shall see.'

The following morning, a boy with gingery hair and freckles arrived with a letter for Collis. It had come on the steamboat *Persephone*, which his own ship had actually passed on the way up to Sacramento. The *Persephone* had run aground on the mud flats, and had only been refloated in the early hours of Tuesday morning.

Collis was half-way through checking the stores that had been delivered from San Francisco. He was standing outside 54 K in his shirtsleeves, a cheroot between his teeth, directing three casual labourers as they rolled kegs of nails and gunpowder into the store There were always plenty of drifters and unlucky placers in Sacramento who were glad of a few hours' employment. It was a fresh, chilly day, with a southwest wind blowing in from the river.

Collis looked at both sides of the letter before he opened it. The boy stood and watched him. The envelope was cream vellum, and sealed with green wax. He couldn't make out the crest on the wax, but it looked as if it had been impressed with a heavy signet ring. The writing was lyrical and strong, in black ink.

He ripped open the envelope with his thumb. The boy was still there, so Collis delved into the pocket of his vest, brought out two bits, and handed them over. The boy hesitated for a moment and then ran off.

The letter was addressed 'Colusa, South Park, San Francisco,' and it read:

Dear Mr Edmonds,

I have heard, belatedly, the details of what happened between you and my son, Grant, out at Lake Merced. I wish simply to record that while I thought your provocative behaviour was in some ways contributory to the unfortunate events that followed, I am grateful for the restraint you showed during the duel, and for the manner in which you forbore to take a life which both etiquette and law had given you the opportunity to claim.

I am hopeful that if chance should ever bring us to meet again, we can exchange our respects as gentlemen, and put to rest all of the unpleasantness that has arisen between us.

If nothing else, sir, I am obliged to you for the life of my son.

The signature was large and dignified. Laurence S. Melford. Collis read the letter again, then folded it up and tucked it into his vest pocket. He wouldn't do anything for now. But the time would come when it might be just the lever he needed to loosen the grip that South Park's powerful hierarchy of shipowners, freight handlers, and stagecoach presidents still maintained on Northern California's commerce. When it came to building a railroad, they would be just as lofty an obstacle as the Sierra Nevada, and twice as harsh.

One of the casual labourers had stopped work to light his pipe. 'You!' Collis called. 'Go smoke your pipe some place else, on your own time. Collect half a morning's pay from Mr Tucker, inside, and then get going. I don't want to see you around here again.'

The man paused in his pipe-lighting, aggrieved. He wore the red-flannel shirt and the patched britches of an old-time prospector.

'Are you going,' Collis said, 'or do you want to make something of it?'

The man sucked at his pipe, then took it out of his mouth and spat. 'I'm going,' he said. 'But goddam your eyes.'

Collis looked away. 'Yes,' he said, as if he were talking about something else altogether.

He met Theodore Jones for lunch at Thomas's Restaurant on G Street. They sat in a straight-backed wooden booth and ordered plates of roast wild duck served very hot and very rare on wild rice, and glasses of cold steam. The place was crowded with state congressmen and local storekeepers, and waiters in long blue aprons hurried between the tables carrying trays of casseroled meat and beer.

'Well,' said Theodore, breaking off a piece of warm sourdough bread and buttering it, 'what happens now?'

'We go to Washington, I suppose,' said Collis. 'You seem to have it all mapped out.'

Collis cut the leg from his duck and picked it up in his fingers. 'There's only one thing that's still worrying me,' he said as he chewed, 'and that's the fact that we don't have a route over the Sierra Nevada. What happens if we go to Washington and all they do is ask us to show them the route?'

'Then we show them the route. We draw a red line across the Sierra Nevada and say that's it.'

'Just any red line, anywhere?'

Theodore nodded. 'That's one thing you'll learn when you get down to serious political infighting. Bluff is ninety-seven per cent of the battle. And anyway, most of the representatives are so ignorant they don't even know the topography of their own back yards, let alone the Sierra Nevada.'

'But we still have to find a route, don't we?'

'Oh, sure,' said Theodore. 'As soon as the winter snow starts to

377

thaw, I want to get up into the Sierras and make some preliminary surveys.'

Collis wiped his hands. 'Do you really think it's there?' he asked Theodore seriously.

'The pass? Of course it is.'

'I wish I had your faith.'

Theodore laughed. 'It's not a question of faith. It's a question of geographical probability, combined with engineering possibility.'

'A probability and a possibility don't make a certainty.'

'Listen,' said Theodore, 'why don't you come with me when I try to find a trace through the mountains next year? Maybe you'll see what I'm talking about then. You should have seen the railroad I built along the Niagara Gorge. Three experienced topographers said it wasn't humanly possible. I didn't worry about that. I just built it. It was only when it was finished that I realized they were probably quite right. It *wasn't* humanly possible.'

Collis smiled in amusement.

'You must come, anyway,' Theodore said. 'If you've never been up into the Sierras, you've got yourself a treat in store. The air's marvellous. Good for the respiratory system, and even better for the bowels.'

'All right,' said Collis, 'I'll come. Maybe we ought to take Wang-Pu with us, too.'

'Oh, sure. Then he could go back and tell all his would-be Chinese labourers what they'd be letting themselves in for.'

The waiter brought them two fresh glasses of steam. Collis raised his. 'Here's to Washington, then.'

Theodore nodded. 'To Washington. And to the day we can travel there by railroad.'

Collis spent a quiet winter in Sacramento. The days passed like slices of light falling through the spokes of a carriage wheel. Each morning he would be up at six, dressed in his clean collar and his grey coat, and walking down to the store. Each day would be spent in selling fuses and screws and gunpowder, in organising the stock, in compiling inventories and arranging for deliveries.

He lunched at the Merchants' Association Club, often sitting alone at a corner table. A week before Christmas, he moved out of the Tuckers' house and rented the second-storey rooms of a house on J Street, within sight of Sutter's Fort. Some evenings he spent alone, reading and smoking and drinking whisky; but two or three times a week he went to the Auburn Saloon on H Street or the Duffy House on I, where he played faro until two or three in the morning.

There was a passable whorehouse on the corner of Eighth and L Streets, Mrs Pangborn's, a four-storey frame building painted ochre-red, with green blinds that were always drawn. Collis went there once or twice a month, following along the musty corridors the firm buttocks of some girl dressed in nothing but a silk-panelled corset, and then lying in bed afterwards breathing in the smell of musk and sweat and listening to the distant repetitive banging of the house pianist's heel on the worn-out rugs downstairs.

He spent Christmas with Theodore and Annie Jones. It was a gentle, emotional day, and he found he was beginning to understand and love them both. Theodore carved the goose, and after their dinner they exchanged gifts. Collis had bought Theodore a bound monograph on the rolling of permanent way at Mount Savage, in Maryland, and a bottle of rose-scented toilet water for Annie. In return, the Joneses gave him a travelling-case with razor and scissors and hairbrushes, all engraved 'CE'. They stood in front of the fire and sang Christmas carols, unselfconsciously and with joy.

As 1858 began, Collis also began to deepen his friendship with Wang-Pu. They rarely dined out together, since a merchant of Collis's standing was considered eccentric and even anti-social if he ate with a Chinese, and both Collis and Wang-Pu decided that the interests of the Sierra Pacific railroad would be better served if Collis kept up his local respectability. But they spent many evenings in the calm simplicity of Wang-Pu's apartment, where Collis learned to sit on the floor crosslegged and eat with chopsticks, and where he learned the subtle pleasures of wind-dried ducks, kai-choy, and pig's-trotter jelly.

Wang-Pu talked about the summers in North China, and of outdoor feasts with his family, when they would eat so many river crabs that they would be sitting ankle-deep in empty shells. He talked of Buddhism, and of Chinese funerals and marriages. He tried to explain the visions in his mind.

These evenings always left Collis feeling peaceful and whole, and although he was still determined to press ahead with his railroad, as hard and as fast as he could, he began to see himself more clearly, and his ambition took on a shape that was as unmistakable as the distant peaks of the Sierra Nevada.

Wang-Pu said one evening, as they sat drinking rice wine, 'It is a rare thing, to have a dream for which one would happily give one's life. We are fortunate men.'

'You'd give your life for a railroad?' Collis said.

Wang-Pu nodded. 'Yes, and I believe you would, too.'

'I don't know,' said Collis. 'I think I'd rather stay alive, and go by boat.'

Wang-Pu put down his porcelain cup. 'Maybe. But what is a little death compared to a great fame?'

At last February came, and it was time for Collis and Theodore to pack. Charles in particular was irritated that Collis was going to go away for so long, but the store was in good order, and Collis promised that he wouldn't stay away for longer than three months, at least if he could help it. He borrowed a sea chest from Wang-Pu, and made sure that he packed his best evening coat and his white collars. Washington, after all, was a highly social place. On a fresh Wednesday morning, Wang-Pu drove Collis in the company's wagon down to the Sacramento River, where he met up with Theodore, and together they boarded the paddle-steamer *Occidental* and set sail.

The *California* took them to Panama City. The sky was overcast, and the weather after Sacramento was sultry and almost unbearable. There was a day before the train left for Aspinwall, and Collis went up to the Hospital of the Sacred Heart. In the dark hallway, under the crucifix, he asked a young Flemish nun for Sister Agnes. The hall smelled, as before, of soap and boiling vegetables. The nun shook her head and said, '*Je regrette . . .*'

He stood in the hospital cemetery with his hat in his hand while Theodore Jones waited with his arms folded, looking down at the grey curve of Panama harbour. The stone bore only her name, and didn't mention how young she was, or that her father had run a patisserie in Lokeren, or that she had once given courage in the hospital to a young American who had come through Panama with a woman, not his wife, who was suffering from yellow fever. It didn't mention that one month later, she had gone down with yellow fever herself, and had died in great pain.

Theodore came over after a few minutes and stood beside him. 'It's very said,' he said sympathetically.

Collis swallowed and nodded. 'She was so damned young. And pretty, too.'

'There's no point in getting yourself upset. She knew what the risks were, after all.'

'I'm still upset. My whole life seems to be spent standing over graves.'

'Everybody's life is.'

Collis lowered his eyes. 'I guess that's something about the West I haven't gotten used to yet.'

'You will, I'm afraid,' said Theodore, laying his hand on Collis's shoulder. 'Just count yourself lucky that you haven't gotten used to it the hard way. Two friends of mine died of cholera last year only one month after they got to San Francisco. It's the foul water, mainly, and the lack of good doctors. Someone worked out that one out of five people die within six weeks of arriving in California, and that three out of the remaining four get sick within three months.'

They left the hospital grounds, let out of the gate by an old bent Negro in a straw hat. They walked down by the seafront for a while, and then, after a muddy sunset, with the sea slopping against the harbour wall like tepid soup, they went back to the Grand Hotel for dinner, spiced meat and beans, which they washed down with bourbon, to keep away the fever and the dysentery.

That night, in his huge four-poster bed in the Grand Hotel, with the February wind blowing in from the Pacific through the open shutters, Collis sat up in his sweaty sheets and lit the oil-lamp. The wallpaper in his room was peeling and mildewed, and the hotel's plumbing shuddered like a man dying of disease. He poured himself a glass of whisky and stood looking at himself in the blotchy mirror. He looked older than he could ever remember. An old young man, with the tiredness of other people's deaths already on him.

They steamed into the Potomac late in the afternoon on the last Thursday of February. Collis and Theodore leaned on the starboard rail of the steamship *Charleston*, looking out over the wide herring-boned waters where the Eastern Branch flowed into the main stream, and beyond to the irregular skyline of Washington itself, with its bare trees and stately brick buildings. In the distance was the square pillared shape of the Capitol, still unfinished, and with its dome yet unbuilt. And there were the wide, muddy avenues, crowded with carriages and horse-drawn buses, and the criss-cross streets. Smoke from hundreds of household fires rose into the frosty air, and drifted away to the east. Over at the navy yards, a three-masted frigate was just putting to sea, drawn out on to the silvery river by three small steam tugs.

The *Charleston* was to tie up at Georgetown, where her owners' offices were. She paddled slowly upstream, rousing loose flocks of bufflehead ducks, and as she passed Mount Vernon, the captain tolled the ship's bell, and the gentlemen passengers all removed their hats as a tribute to George Washington. Soon, past the islands in midstream, the curve of Georgetown harbour came into view, thicketed with two- and three-masted schooners. High on a hill to the west, shadowed by the sinking February sun, were the buildings of Georgetown University, but the town itself was not much more than a waterfront lined with offices and wooden warehouses, and a hilly clutter of trees and private houses.

Collis stood straight, and held his cloak about him tightly. He was exhausted from the journey, and his face was unshaven and white. It had started to rain on their second day in Panama, and the isthmus train had been held up for two days by mudslides. Then the *Charleston* had jammed a paddle-wheel bearing off Cape Fear, and they had slopped around for half a day in an uneasy southeasterly wind. All Collis wanted now was a half pint of brandy and twelve hours' sleep.

The *Charleston* whistled hoarsely and began to nudge her way into the high wooden jetty. Soon she was tied up, and the gangplanks were raised to the walkway, and black porters came running on board to take the passenger trunks.

'Well,' said Collis, tiredly, 'this is where it all begins'.

Theodore stretched himself. 'This is where it continues. It all began a long time ago. It began when the first pioneer on the first wagon dreamed of riding across America on rails.'

'How do you know the first pioneer dreamed of riding on rails?'

'Have you ever travelled any distance by covered wagon?'

Collis shook his head.

'When you've crossed a desert by covered wagon, your backside dictates what your mind dreams about, and what your mind dreams about is parlourcar chairs, and a chance to put your feet up.'

They disembarked. It was almost dark now, and the jetty was lit only with flickering tallow torches. Their feet made a hollow sound on the walkway as they went ashore.

A smelly, closed-in cab took them into Washington itself. As it jolted over the unpaved streets, Collis found his eyes closing, and he had to sit rigidly upright to keep himself awake. It wasn't safe to fall asleep in a strange cab in an unfamiliar city. Too many travellers found themselves taken to the outskirts, robbed, and left in a ditch with nothing but their underwear, and sometimes not even that. It was a moonless night, and so the gas lights along Pennsylvania Avenue were lit. There was a smell of kerosene and horse dung in the air.

Eventually they drew up outside Willard's Hotel, a squarish red-brick building with its own gas lights, and their cab door was opened by a uniformed doorman with droopy grey whiskers and a green silk hat. They alighted, and Collis paid the cab driver six cents, and a penny tip.

As he conducted them through the mahogany swing-doors into the hotel lobby, the doorman muttered, 'Female companionship, sir?'

Collis laid a hand on the man's gold-braided epaulette. 'My friend, the next time you offer your procurative services, make sure that those to whom you offer it do not bear, as we do, the traces of three weeks' arduous travelling. We want a bath, a drink, a meal, and a bed. The female companionship can wait.'

They were sharing a suite of two rooms and a bathroom on the second floor. The suite was high-ceilinged, and carpeted in sombre brown. It smelled of must and stale cigars, a smell which reminded Collis of New York. On the wall was a 'A View of the President's House After the Conflagration of 24 August 1814', showing the derelict White House standing in open fields.

While Theodore bathed, Collis took off his shoes and rested in an armchair. A young black bellboy came up with a bottle of Old Tate whisky, a jug of iced water, and a copy of the *Evening Star*. He poked the log fires and stacked them up with wood, and then wished them good-night, and 'ex'lent dreams, sir'.

Collis looked through the paper. There was a great deal about the foulness of Washington's water, and Collis glanced across at the glass jug on his tray and decided he would probably take his Old Tate straight. The paper was also annoyed by a proposition to raise the steamer fare from Alexandria to Washington from twelve and a half cents to fifteen. The weather report 'from the Morse Telegraph line to the Smithsonian Institution' said that Friday would be drizzly, and the temperature no higher than forty-six.

Theodore came out of the bathroom in a pale-blue robe and slippers. His beard was wet and he looked like an otter emerging

383

from a stream. He poured two glasses of whisky and sat down by Collis to toast his toes by the fire.

'You seem depressed,' he remarked.

Collis dropped the paper on the floor. 'Maybe I'm just tired.'

'You don't have any doubts about what we're doing, do you?'

'No,' said Collis. 'No more than usual, anyway.'

They raised their glasses to each other, and drank. The straight whisky made Collis cough, and he had to take out his handkerchief.

'I can't pretend that it's going to be easy,' Theodore said, 'coaxing anyone in Congress to support us. Especially with all this talk of Southern secession, and the trouble in Nebraska Territory. But I guess we can try, can't we?'

'Sure,' said Collis. 'I should be getting used to hitting my head against stone walls by now.'

Theodore looked concerned. 'You're definitely out of sorts, aren't you? Why don't you take a bath? The water's good and hot.'

Collis rubbed his eyes with the back of his wrist. 'I think it's coming back to the East that's upset me. I'll get over it. But can't you smell this room? It's stuffy and stale, and you can just imagine all the fat old Congressmen who must have taken their fancy women up here, or sat here playing cards all night and talking about slavery and political corruption as if they were both games.'

'I know what you mean,' said Theodore quietly.

Collis loosened his necktie. 'I was frightened when I first came West, last year. I was lonesome, too, and I felt that I'd lost all of my friends. But now I'm back, the East suddenly looks old and haggard, and the air seems to stink of mistrust. I'm glad you're with me. I don't think I could have stood it on my own.'

Theodore eased off his slippers. 'Don't get yourself too worked up about it. It's something we're going to have to bear, whether we like it or not. Now, go take that bath, and I'll pour out another whisky for you.'

Collis finished his Old Tate and stood up. 'You're right,' he said. 'I'm just about done for.'

'Don't you want to eat?'

'Sure. But something light. Have them send up some steak and onions, and a bottle of champagne.'

Theodore went to the bell pull and tugged it. 'You wait until you see how small the steak is.' He smiled. 'Then you'll really know you're back East.'

*

Collis slept until one o'clock the following afternoon. When he got out of bed and opened the brown drapes of his room, the predicted drizzle had cleared, although the skies were still heavy and grey, and there was a damp wind from the east.

He poured himself a stiff whisky from the half-empty bottle left on the tray and swallowed it in one gulp. It made him gasp and shudder, but it got his circulation going, and washed out the taste of sleep and yesterday's tobacco. Then he went and knocked on Theodore's door, to find out if the railroad engineer was awake. There was no reply, and when he opened the door he found that Theodore was more than awake, he was up and gone.

Theodore was still downstairs in the dining-room, however, by the time Collis had washed and shaved and dressed in a brown morning coat with braided lapels. Collis ordered pickled oysters, veal Malakoff, and a lemon ice. Theodore had already eaten, but he asked for more beer and a pot of coffee. 'You don't know how good it is to taste lager after all these years.' He smiled. 'It's the nectar of the gods.'

'You can keep your lager,' Collis said. 'You can keep your Eastern food, too. I'd rather have a glass of steam and one of Bazzuro's bowls of cioppino.'

'Don't tell me you've become *that* much of a Westerner,' said Theodore.

The waiter brought Collis's oysters, and while he ate, Theodore sipped his beer and suggested a plan of campaign. First of all, in what remained of the afternoon, they should go see Alice Stride and ask if she could suggest some introductions to any Senators who might be remotely intrigued by railroads. Then, over the week-end, they should pay some social calls on congressmen staying at boarding-houses or hotels, most of whom were bored and homesick over Saturday and Sunday, and might well be receptive to roast beef, cheerful company, and a bottle of brandy – not forgetting some uplifting talk about crossing the continent by rail.

Sitting back over cigars and strong black coffee, Collis asked Theodore, 'Who's our major opposition? In the railroad business, I mean, not in Congress.'

'The Hannibal & St Joseph, no doubt at all,' said Theodore. 'They're quick, and they're aggressive, and the way they're building now they should have a line completed from the Mississippi to the Missouri by, what, the middle of next year. They're laying their railroad from each end of their surveyed route simultaneously, and that means they've already got track laid on the banks of the Missouri, before anybody else.'

Collis smoked quietly. Theodore sat up and drew a line across the tablecloth with his fingernail. 'If they get to build the railroad westward from St Joe, then we've got ourselves some real problems. Or at least we *could* have, depending on whether they plot their route through the Rockies at Pueblo, in which event we might still be able to join up with them in Utah, or whether they run the whole line south through Raton Pass and Albuquerque, and sneak into Southern California through New Mexico Territory, in which event we're left without a hope in the world.'

'As far as I can see,' Collis said, 'only one thing is going to guarantee a northern route, instead of a southern one.'

'Well, sure. It depends on who can give the most Congressmen the most money,' said Theodore.

'Yes, I agree with that,' Collis told him. 'But if the Southern states secede, then a northern route is a cast-iron certainty.'

'You really think they will? Secede, I mean? I know there's plenty of talk.'

'I don't know what they'll do. But did you hear Senator Badger just now? The South has been painted into a corner. If they don't declare themselves independent, then they'll have to accept the humiliation of being citizens of a nation the greater part of which they can't do business with, nor exploit for its natural wealth, nor even visit with their customary servants.'

Collis blew out a smoke ring, which shuddered and sloped across the table. 'I don't hold with slavery at all,' he said. 'But imagine what most Southern landowners and politicians must be feeling right now. Wouldn't you be thinking of secession, if you were them?'

Theodore quizzically put his head on one side. 'I think you'll do well in the lobbies. I just hope you don't wind up by starting a civil war.'

'I don't think there's much chance of that. In fact, I don't believe the South will secede for twenty or thirty years. Maybe more. Maybe never at all. But the threat of secession might be just enough to sway a few more Congressmen in favour of a northern route. After all, would *you* put million of dollars into a Pacific railroad if you thought that it might be taken over by secessionists at any moment? I wouldn't.'

'I didn't know you were so political. You surprise me.'

386

Collis smiled. 'It used to be a parlour game, to annoy my father. He was a Wall Street doughface of the worst kind, God rest his soul.'

'Is it really a parlour game? Or do you believe it?'

There was a pause. Outside the grimy windows of the hotel dining-room, the drizzle started again, and there was the wet, gritty sound of carriage wheels in thick mud. For all its grandiose designs, the width of its avenues, and the scale of its finest administrative buildings, the federal city was still mucky, unfinished, and unsanitary. Massachusetts Avenue, which was shown on the maps as a magnificent four-mile thoroughfare, degenerated after six or seven blocks into a rutted, muddy morass. Cows and goats wandered around Pennsylvania Avenue, and their droppings did little to improve the state of the streets.

'I've learned not to ask myself that question,' Collis said. 'I want certain things out of my life, and I believe certain things. They're very strong, these wants and these beliefs. Stronger than I ever thought possible. But I don't ask what they are, or why I have them, because if I start doing that, I might slip back into what I was before. Casual, devil-may-care, time-wasting, and no good to anyone at all. Least of all me.'

'This is recent, isn't it, this attitude? Something's changed you.'

Collis sucked at his cigar. He made a mouth like a pet fish, and let another smoke ring escape.

'Yes, you're right. I think I learned that I was more than the sum of my parents. I'd already found out that I was wiser and harder than my father. But there was still my mother, and I guess I had to fight her by proxy. You probably don't understand what I mean.'

'I think so,' said Theodore. 'You found a woman who reminded you of your mother, and you tested your wits against her, and won.'

Collis nodded.

Theodore didn't say anything for a while, but then he stretched and yawned in his chair. 'I think we'd better go see your friend Alice Stride,' he suggested. 'Because if we don't, I'm going to fall asleep right here and now.'

When he was in Washington, Senator Stride occupied a four-storey brick house a block south of Pennsylvania Avenue on Eighteenth Street, which he had bought in 1854 for $4200 cash. He liked to take his family with him in the winter months, because there was entertaining to do, and both his wife, Margaret, and his daughter,

Alice, were pleasing to his guests. They would flutter their eyelashes and whisper flattery behind their fans, and the Southern democrats, who liked their ladies flirtatious and feminine, adored them. Congressman William Aiken of South Carolina, who owned more than a thousand slaves, called Margaret Stride 'the Star of G Street'; and Alice was a particular favourite of Georgia's 'Little Wizard', Alexander Stephens.

It was raining in wet, persistent curtains as Collis and Theodore climbed down from their cab outside Senator Stride's black-painted railings. On a gas standard nearby, a sodden poster offered a one-cent reward for the return of a runaway cabinet-maker's apprentice, Ezekiel O'Toole, and solemnly threatened that anyone 'employing or harbouring said boy will have the law enforced against them'.

Collis paused in the rain to read the poster, and then turned away from it, shaking his head. 'And that's in our federal city,' he said.

Theodore shrugged philosophically. 'There's a weekly slave auction just two blocks from the White House, every Thursday. We ought to go along next week, and then you'll see what slavery's all about.'

'I don't think I care to,' Collis told him.

They went up the steps of Senator Stride's house and pulled the rain-dewed bell handle. Then they waited, while wagons and carriages clattered along Eighteenth Street, and the rain gurgled in the lead gutters. At last the blue-painted door of Senator Stride's house was opened, and a black servant in a white starched shirt and a scarlet tailcoat stood in front of them. 'Yes, gentlemen? Are you expected?' he said.

Collis handed over his card, the one he'd had printed after Laurence Melford's servant had admonished him at the Empire Theatre. It read: 'Collis T. Edmonds, 54 K Street, Sacramento, California'. The servant took it in a white-gloved hand, but didn't read it. He probably couldn't read. Senator Stride had been foremost in declaring in the House that 'the giving of book-learning to niggers would be a crueller deed than teaching a horse to sing opera; for while a horse would not hanker to take the stage of the Ford's Theatre, a nigger would believe he could converse equally with white; and that would be laughable.'

'That's for Miss Alice, if she's at home,' Collis said.

The black servant nodded his head. 'I'll see, sir. Please wait for a moment.'

Theodore stood patiently while the rain from the porch drummed on the top of his hat. He gave Collis a quick, reassuring smile. After a minute or two, the black servant came back and said, 'Miss Alice says she won't be more than a moment. Please come in.'

They stepped inside the hall-way. It was dark, and fitfully lit by candles. On one side there was a heavy oak dresser, with brass handles; on the other, a hall-stand hung with wet capes. A wide staircase curved upwards into the gloom.

'Rather tomblike,' remarked Theodore, as the servant took their hats and capes.

Collis tugged at his cuffs. 'From what I remember of Senator Stride, he's a pretty tomb-like man.'

The servant said, 'This way, please,' and led them through to an ante-room. 'Miss Alice asked that you make yourselves at home.'

They paced around the ante-room for a while, and then they sat facing each other on two claw-footed armchairs, silenced and stilled by their sombre surroundings. Behind Collis's back, the windows were hung not only with almost impenetrable lace, but with brown velvet drapes, fringed with dusty tassels; and these seemed to have the effect of strangling even the coppery green light that came in from the drizzle outside. It would have been an unpleasant strain on the eyes to have read a Bible in there, or a newspaper of any quality. There was a grotesque fireplace, with fluted uprights, and carved bunches of grapes, and this was surmounted by one of those blotchy mirrors into which newcomers glance and then surreptitiously touch their cheeks, to see if they have somehow contracted leprosy.

A black marble-and-gilt clock stood on the centre of the mantlepiece, which was otherwise bare. Collis took out his own watch to check the time, and the clock was depressingly accurate.

Theodore looked up at an oil painting on the wall beside him. The paint was crazed, and it had been varnished so heavily that it was almost impossible to distinguish what the subject was. But he leaned back a little and said, 'It's a portrait. An old man in a powdered wig. He must be one of Senator Stride's ancestors.'

Collis got up to inspect the picture more closely. 'Yes,' he said. 'He reminds me of Stride. He has the same look of a bald eagle, with his eyes fixed on some suitably plump and defenceless prey.'

Theodore smiled. 'I can see what you mean. But you're not still sore about your father, are you? We shouldn't have come here if

389

you are. It wasn't really Senator Stride's fault, any more than it was yours.'

'I think it was very largely *my* fault,' said Collis, looking down at Theodore seriously.

'And Senator Stride's, too?'

Collis gave an affirmative nod.

Theodore let out a long, anxious breath and then covered his mouth with his hand.

'You're not going to start questioning my morality again, are you?' Collis said. 'About seeking help from a man I despise?'

'No,' said Theodore, 'I'm not going to do that. But I do believe you ought to start considering some of your principles more closely.'

'I see. You're still thinking about Arthur Teach, are you, and *l'affaire des couvertures*?'

'I'm thinking about *you*, as a matter of fact. You seem to be less compromising lately. Both with other people and with yourself.'

'Other people are uncompromising with me,' said Collis.

'Well, I know,' answered Theodore. 'But even Annie noticed, and remarked that you were harder in your criticisms these days, and more determined in the way you talked.'

'Aren't you pleased? We won't be able to build this railroad without determination.'

Theodore lifted his eyebrows in a subtle facial shrug. 'Maybe you're right. But I hope your determination won't ride roughshod over other people's feelings.'

Collis looked at him. 'You think that what I did to Arthur Teach I might do to you, too?'

'I guess it's possible.'

'But the railroad is *your* scheme, Theo. The plans and the engineering are all yours.'

'I know,' said Theodore. 'But plans and engineering don't come to life without vision, do they? And the vision is yours. And who do people remember? The visionaries, or the engineers? Do they remember Hannibal, or the man who guided him over the Alps?'

Collis was silent for a moment, his arms folded, his thin face engraved by shadows. 'I'll make you one promise, Theodore Jones, and as God is my witness I will never go back on it. Your name will be marked on our railroad, when it's built, as proud and prominent as the name of the railroad company itself.'

Just then the doors opened, and a breathy voice said, 'Collis!'

Collis turned, and there was Alice Stride, her face bright, her hands held up like a child at a Christmas party, in a grey velvet dress with a cream lace collar, and lace cuffs. She came tiptoeing into the room on tiny laced-up day shoes, and kissed him on both cheeks, pip-pop, and then laughed a little high trill of delight.

Collis held her hands and squeezed them. She hadn't changed, except that her hair was now tied up in ribbons. She was still vivacious, still poised, but her nose wasn't any smaller, and her eyebrows were still heavy, and Collis still had the impression that she was the kind of girl who teased and mocked her men friends, rather than flirted with them, trying to attract with clever banter the attention that her looks rarely brought her.

'You've lost weight,' Alice told Collis. 'And you're so brown! If you stay out in California any longer, you'll be the first Black Republican who's actually black!'

'You haven't changed at all, Alice,' Collis said. 'You're still the way I remember you. Charming.'

'You didn't answer my letter.' She pouted, with feigned – or maybe not-so-feigned – hurt.

'I know,' said Collis, 'and it's been worrying me for weeks. But how could I find the words to answer?'

Alice put her head on one side. 'I'm not quite sure what you mean by that. But since you're usually so glib, I'll give you the benefit of the doubt. Anyway, you're being very bad-mannered. You haven't introduced me to your handsome friend.'

Theodore gave a restrained bow. 'I'm honoured to make your acquaintance, Miss Stride. I'm Theodore Jones, a railroad engineer, from California.'

'He describes himself very modestly,' said Collis. 'He is, in fact, the finest railroad engineer and surveyor on the continent.'

'Well, that's very nice,' said Alice.

'It's more than nice,' Collis told her, 'it's the whole reason we're here. Except, of course, for me to renew our delightful friendship.'

'I'm pleased you added that,' Alice remarked, with a tart little smile.

'I'm teasing,' said Collis. 'I've thought about you many a night in Sacramento, when the coyotes were howling at the moon, and the cool winds were blowing in from gold-mine country.'

'Which reminded you most of me?' asked Alice sharply. 'The coyotes or the gold mines?'

'The moon, of course,' said Collis. 'So serene and lofty that the dogs could never reach it, no matter how they howled, and the gold miners could never afford it, no matter how much gold they dug up.'

There was a taut silence, and then Alice suddenly laughed out loud, a long peal of soprano joy. Theodore had to cover his mouth with his hand again, but this time to smother his mirth. Collis stood smiling with pleasure until Alice had recovered herself. She looked at him with dewy eyes, her hands clasped together, her diamond rings bright.

'You're quite shameless,' she said. 'Mr Jones – don't you think he's shameless? He could flatter a donkey into thinking it was a palomino. Thank goodness Delphine isn't here. She would have fainted in a vapour, from sheer excess of compliments.'

'How is Delphine?' asked Collis. 'Is she still in New York?'

Alice shook her head. 'She's here in Washington now. There was tragedy in her family after the financial crash last year. Her father – well, her father is in a hospital. He made an attempt on his own life, by eating broken glass. They fear he may never recover his sanity. Her mother took it badly and went to stay with Delphine's aunt in Boston. Delphine, because we are friends, and because my father is her godparent, came here.'

'Is she staying here now? In this house?' Collis enquired.

'She did for a while. But I told you in my letter how determined she was not to be a burden on her family and friends. We argued with her, of course, and told her that she was always welcome, as long as she wanted to stay. There was no persuading her, though. After six or seven weeks, she found a position.'

'I can't believe it,' Collis said. 'Delphine, in a position?'

'You mustn't underestimate her strength of character,' said Alice. 'She may be very pretty, and flirtatious, but she is also a girl of great courage.'

'But what position has she taken? She's not in a store, is she?'

Alice smiled. 'No, nothing like that. She's working as a governess for Senator Carslake's children. I saw her only last week, taking the three little mites for an afternoon walk in the park. She's very well, though subdued, of course.'

Theodore cleared his throat. 'Is this a lady friend of yours, Collis?'

'Yes. Or she was, before I had to leave New York.'

'She still is, Collis, rest assured,' put in Alice. 'Although I fear that what I said in my letter is also still true. She has no wish to meet you again, not in her present circumstances.'

'That's absurd,' said Collis. 'She may have no money and no family, but what difference does that make? After I left New York, I was down to a few hundred dollars, and I had nothing to my name but disgrace.'

'It's different for a woman,' Alice told him. 'A woman needs a family of means behind her so that she does not feel obligated to accept proposals of marriage for the sake of domestic security, and so that the man she marries never has cause to say that she wed him for his money, or for his house. She also expects to offer her new husband a respectable dowry, and to be married in a ceremony of circumstance for which her father has paid.'

'But isn't your father acting as her legal parent? And aren't you all the family she could wish for?'

Alice smiled sadly. 'We are. But Delphine is quite determined that she must accept what fate has brought her. She comes here for luncheon and dinner from time to time, and we always invite her to parties. Yet she won't change her mind, and stay.'

There was a short, regretful silence. Then Alice said, 'You must take some tea, in any case. Why don't you come through to the conservatory, and Hubert can bring us a tray. Do you like great cake, Mr Jones? It used to be baked by Martha Washington, for special days at Mount Vernon, and she passed the recipe to my grandmother.'

Alice rang the bell, and the black footman, Hubert, reappeared. He led them through the gloomy hallway to the back of the house and opened the conservatory door for them. Then he arranged white-painted cast-iron garden chairs around a table for them, and they sat down, rather stiffly, while tea was prepared.

With the afternoon so dark and the drizzle so persistent, the conservatory was like a chamber in Neptune's palace. All around them, dark-leafed plants crowded and twined, and even the decorative iron pillars were sprouting leaves. On the glass roof over their heads, the rain ran down in endless scallops and then trickled into the gutters.

'The truth is,' said Theodore, 'we are looking for your help.'

Alice smiled at him cautiously. 'I don't see what *I* could possibly do to help *you*.'

393

'You could do a great deal,' put in Collis. 'You see, we need to talk to as many Senators and Congressmen as we can about the possibility of building a Pacific railroad.'

'Ah. You've come to Washington to lobby.'

'Mostly, yes. And to sound out opinion, too, about what we're proposing to do.'

'That's strange,' Alice said. 'I wouldn't have thought of you for one moment as a railroad man, Collis. Or even a businessman. I always saw you as careless, fancy-free, and answerable to no one at all. Especially to politicians, or stockholders.'

'I've changed in the past five months,' said Collis.

She looked at him. Her eyes were deep, and they glittered in the subaqueous light like faceted jet. There was something about her expression that reminded Collis disturbingly of her father; as if behind her grace and politeness there was a personality of utter coldness and reserve.

'I've noticed,' she said. 'You would never have come to me for help before, not for anything. I know how difficult you found it to ask my father for money.'

'So what do you conclude from that?' asked Collis.

'It's simple,' said Alice. 'I conclude that whatever this Pacific railroad business is all about, it's more important to you than anything has ever been before.'

Theodore gave Collis a quick, uncertain glance. But Collis sat back in his chair and smiled. 'What if it is? Is it so terrible for a man to find a vocation?'

'Not at all,' teased Alice. 'In fact, I think that railroads are quite romantic. But if you feel so earnestly about it, and place so much value on my assistance, then I must be able to ask for something in return.'

Collis looked at her suspiciously.

'I don't want anything arduous from you, nor at all unpleasant,' she reassured him coquettishly. 'I would simply like you to escort me to the White House next week. Harriet Lane is holding a dance for some of her younger friends in Washington, and although Congressman Taylor has already asked me, I should prefer to go with you.'

Theodore, amused, said, 'That doesn't sound like too demanding a deal, Collis. In fact, I envy you.'

'Of course it isn't demanding,' said Alice lightly. 'Quite apart from the pleasure of having Washington's most distinguished young hostess on your arm, you'll be able to meet lots of young congressmen, and harangue them about railroads all night.'

'Theodore must come, too,' said Collis. 'After all, he knows the hard facts about the engineering.'

'Theodore is most welcome to come,' Alice told them. 'I have the partner for him. A young lady who thinks that beards were devised by the Lord for the sole purpose of tickling her cheeks.'

'I'm married, I regret,' said Theodore.

'I don't think that will present any difficulties,' said Alice. 'So is she. Her husband's Senator Fredericks, and he's in Minnesota this month, caring for his sick father.'

Theodore was about to protest, but Collis gave him a frown which meant, 'Not now – wait until we've gotten what we came for'. And so Theodore tried to look pleased, and folded his arms, and bent forward in his chair as if he was suffering from indigestion. Just then Hubert came in with the tea-tray, which bore a Georgian silver teapot left behind by the British at Bladensburg, and fine Sèvres cups. There was a fresh cake, too, sliced and still warm.

'Now,' Alice said as she poured the tea, 'let me think of some likely Congressmen for you. And some lawyers and bankers, too, who might be interested.'

She passed Collis his cup and added, 'I could give you an excellent tailor, if you're thinking of wearing anything special next week.'

Collis said, 'You're very kind. But the Congressmen and the lawyers will suit me well enough.'

After a night of boisterous winds, the morning was dry and crisp, and when Collis walked to Senator Carslake's house, the muddy streets were already forming a crust. Wastepaper and rubbish had been blown everywhere, and the wooden sidewalks, where there were any, were swirled with the chaff from dried horse manure. Collis smoked a cheroot and walked with his hands in his pockets.

Senator Carslake's house wasn't far from Senator Stride's. It was one of the Seven Buildings on Nineteenth Street at Pennsylvania Avenue, next door to the corner house where President James Madison had lived with his wife, Dolley. Collis went straight up to the front door and rang the bell.

He had to wait for two or three minutes before a coffee-coloured Negro came to the door and opened it. 'Yes, sir? You expected, sir?' he said.

'I want to see the governess, Miss Spooner,' replied Collis.

'I'm sorry, sir. The rule is, the staff don't have no callers.'

'Then I want to see the Senator.'

'I'm sorry, sir. The Senator, he ain't here. The Senator, he's in Baltimore.'

'Then Mrs Carslake.'

'She's got herself a headache, sir. I'm sorry.'

Collis took a card out of his breast pocket. 'In that case, would you be good enough to leave this on the hall-stand for Miss Spooner, and ensure that she gets it?'

'I can't do that, sir. The rule is, staff don't get no calling cards, no more than callers.'

Collis let out an exasperated sigh. 'What do you suggest I do, then? Slit my throat and write a message on the front steps in blood?'

The Negro peered at him warily. 'The front steps, they get cleaned at ten, sir, so there ain't no point in that.'

Collis took off his hat and carefully wiped around the band with his handkerchief. The Negro stood by the door, watching him patiently. The wind tossed some loose straw against the railings in front of the house. At last Collis looked up and said, 'It's all right. You've got me beat, whatever I ask for. You can close the door now.'

Collis left the house and walked south on Nineteenth Street. He felt empty and depressed. He had been thinking about Delphine all night, until his bedsheets had been twisted up like a rope, and he had been obliged to take a large tumbler of Old Tate to get himself to sleep. It had never occurred to him that he might see her again so soon. After he had left New York, he had imagined that he would spend years and years in California, impoverished and aimless, and he had let himself forget her. Even when Alice had written him and said that Ohio Life and Mutual had crashed, and that Delphine was a pauper, he had consciously let his memories of her fade away, like a calotype clouded by too much silver nitrate.

But now she was close, and her name had taken on life again, and warmth, and all night long he had been tempted by a ghostly image of that last day in the Spooners' front parlour. He had dozed once, and heard her whisper, 'Collis, my lover'. The whisper had seemed so loud that he had sat up in bed and looked around his room to see if she was really there.

As he crossed F Street, taking two or three quick steps to avoid a farmer's wagon laden with winter vegetables, he saw the children.

He didn't realise at first that they were *the* children, Senator Carslake's children, gathering at the side of F Street on their way back from a walk. There was a pale-faced boy of nine, in a brown tweed overcoat; a girl of seven, with chestnut ringlets and a white fur muffler; and a boy of four, still dressed in skirts, who was holding the hand of his governess.

Collis had already raised his hat before he fully understood that she was Delphine. She was even more petite than he remembered, and her hair was drawn up and pinned under a severe blue bonnet. Her dress was pale blue, with an overdress of black, and there was no mistaking at all that she was employed to look after these three children, and was not their mother. Mothers rarely took their own children out, and when they did, they rode in carriages.

He called hoarsely, 'Delphine?'

She was busy ushering her little cavalcade across the ruts of F Street. She looked up, and her eyes were as dreamy and huge as ever. Her full pink lips were slightly parted, her cheeks were flushed with the February cold, and she was so pretty that he wondered why he had ever left her in New York, only to meet her here, now, under these sad and strange circumstances, on a windy street in Washington.

Delphine reached out and held the older boy back. The girl looked up at her and said, 'What is it, Spooner? What are we waiting for?'

But Delphine said, 'Hush, Amelia. This is a gentleman.'

'I didn't know staff were acquainted with gentlemen,' the older boy piped up. 'I thought staff weren't supposed to.'

'Delphine?' Collis repeated.

She dropped her gaze. Instead of looking at his face, she looked at the white flower in his buttonhole. 'Collis. Is it really you?' she said, in a haunted voice.

'Yes,' he told her. 'It's really me.'

'I thought you'd gone to California,' she said. 'I didn't think – '

'No,' said Collis, 'neither did I. But I've gotten involved in a plan to build a railroad, and I had to come back to lobby Congress.'

'A railroad?' she asked, with an uncomprehending frown.

The older boy said, 'Oh, Spooner, you know what a railroad is. Even you. Now, can we get back? Cook said there's fried chicken for lunch, and I'm starving.'

'Ernest,' said Delphine, abstractedly. 'Your manners.'

'I beg your pardon,' Ernest retorted. 'I'm "ready for lunch", not "starving".'

'That's better,' said Delphine.

'Can I see you?' asked Collis. 'I'll be here for at least a month.'

'That's really impossible. I'm sorry, it's quite impossible.'

'Do they train you staff to say that around at Senator Carslake's? "I'm sorry, but it's quite impossible"?'

'Collis, I can't, that's all. I'm not a lady any more. I'm a working woman. I'm a governess.'

Collis reached out and held her arm. She didn't make any attempt to push him away. 'You're being ridiculous,' he said gently. 'You're not a working woman now and you never will be. Look at you. You're beautiful.'

'Staff are not allowed to be beautiful,' she said, turning away. Her eyes suddenly filled with tears. 'It's no good, Collis. I thought you'd be gone for ever.'

'Alice told me you wouldn't stay with the Strides, even though they begged you,' said Collis.

'My father never took charity. I didn't want to let his memory down.'

'He's not dead yet, is he?'

She took out her handkerchief and dabbed at her eyes. 'No. But nearly. The doctors don't expect him to live out the year.'

'And Winifred? Your mother?'

'She won't talk to anyone. When father goes, she'll probably go too. She's so thin now, you'd never recognise her. Remember how well she used to be?'

'Yes.'

They stood for a while without talking. A Conestoga wagon ground past them, and Ernest fidgeted from one foot to the other. Amelia complained, 'I'm cold.'

'Do you have some free time?' Collis asked. 'Do they give you an afternoon off?'

'Tuesdays, between two and six.'

Collis cleared his throat. 'Can I see you then? We could go take some lunch. Or walk in the park, if you haven't had too much of it lately.'

'No.' She looked so pretty and sad that Collis could hardly bear it.

'Delphine,' he insisted, 'it doesn't matter to me that you've lost your money and your family. I don't think any the less of you. In

398

fact, I admire your courage and your pride. I think you're wonderful. Don't you understand how much we have in common? We've both lost everything, and now we're both fighting back. Couldn't we do that together?'

She shook her head. The tears were running freely down her cheeks, and she couldn't speak for unhappiness.

'Couldn't we just talk?' asked Collis. 'Couldn't we just sip over a cup of coffee and a plateful of cookies and talk about old times?'

'Spooner,' Ernest said nasally, 'this is absurd. It's time we went back for lunch. Come along, now, or I shall tell Father you've been courting a man.'

Collis turned on the boy and snapped, 'If you don't stop whining, I'll pull down your britches and tan the skin off your – '

'That's enough, Collis. I really have to go.'

'I'm sorry,' Collis told her. 'I didn't mean to be rude.'

'It's not that, my darling,' she replied. 'It's not that at all. You can swear in five languages, and I'll still love you. I loved you the moment I first met you.'

'Then what are we doing, arguing about going out for tea? If you love me, then go back and tell Mrs Carslake she can go look for someone else. Come back with me to California.'

Delphine touched a stray dark curl that had come free from her bonnet. 'It's too late now, Collis,' she said softly. 'I'm sorry.'

'I don't understand what you're trying to tell me. Why is it too late?'

'You didn't write,' she said. 'I thought I'd lost you for good.'

'But I'm back now. I'm asking you to come away with me. What further proof of my feelings do you want?'

She looked at him, misty-eyed, and then she reached out and touched his cheek with great gentleness. 'It's just too late,' she whispered. 'When the New Year came, and I still hadn't heard from you, I . . .'

She lowered her head. The ribbons of her bonnet were stirred by the wind. F Street was grey and chilly, and a red-faced man with a wicker basket on his head walked slowly past, tolling a handbell and calling, 'Rockfish! Rockfish! Thirty-six cents the bunch!'

'When the New Year came – what? Tell me!'

She didn't raise her head. 'I gave in to a gentleman who had been persistent in his attentions.'

'Gentleman? What gentleman? What are you saying?'

She raised her face to him, as she had raised it that first day in

Taylor's restaurant on Broadway. Her eyelashes were wet with tears. 'I cannot say it loud in front of the children,' she said, so quiet that he could scarcely hear her. 'It was their father.'

'Senator Carslake?'

She nodded.

'But, for God's sake, you're living and working in the same house as his wife!'

'Yes, and she knows what's happening.'

Collis bit his lip. He couldn't think of anything to say. He felt as if he'd just awoken with an unbelievable hangover, to find that he'd been robbed of everything he'd ever owned. It had been lazy and thoughtless of him not to write to Delphine, and ridiculously conceited to think that she might have kept herself for him in case he ever returned. He felt he could be excused that omission, though, and that sin, because he'd never thought he would return, especially so soon. What really hurt was that his freshly revived dream of courting Delphine had been besmirched so abruptly, and in such an ugly way. He had seen Senator Carslake once, in New York, and from what he remembered he was paunchy, irritable, and coarse as a bear.

Delphine went on, 'I cannot tell you much. But after Michael was born, Mrs Carslake was unable to be a wife to the Senator any longer. There was some infection, I don't know what. So she tolerates the arrangement in order to keep him content, and to maintain her place in Washington society.'

'What are you whispering about, Spooner?' Ernest said sharply. 'We have to go!'

Collis ignored him. 'But you,' he asked Delphine. 'What about you? Surely you can't love him?'

'I don't.'

'Then why do you go through with it? Delphine – it's hair-raising!'

'I go through with it because I do. There isn't anything else.' Delphine's eyes welled with tears again. 'If I could have come to you as I was when I met you in Taylor's, with my father and mother beside me and my dowry untouched – if I could have stood before the minister as a virgin, on your arm – then I would have. But it's too late now. Those days are gone. I cannot come to you penni-less, without a family, and I cannot come to you spoiled by a man upon whom you would not even deign to waste your spittle. I cannot.'

400

'I'll come by the house on Tuesday afternoon,' Collis said.

'No, Collis. Not on Tuesday, nor ever.'

'Delphine – '

'I have to go. The children will be late for their luncheon.'

Without another word, Delphine took Michael's hand, and then ushered Amelia and Ernest across the street in front of her. Collis followed close behind, but she wouldn't turn around, wouldn't slacken her step, and when they reached the north corner of F Street, he stopped and let her walk on towards Pennsylvania Avenue without him. Ernest turned around half-way up the block and stuck his tongue out.

Collis stood there watching her, feeling breathless, helpless, with his arms by his sides, his back slightly bent, his fists clenched. She and the children became smaller in the perspective of Nineteenth Street. A governess in a blue bonnet, with three charges in their winter coats, under a sky that was almost white with cold. A puff of vapour came out of Collis's mouth as he breathed. Another puff. Delphine went up the steps of Senator Carslake's house, and disappeared.

Harriet Lane was President Buchanan's niece; but because Old Buck had lost the only love of his life in a ridiculous lovers' tiff when he was young, she did duty as his official hostess, and in that role she was much admired, particularly by Washington's Southern elite. She did everything she could to nurture the spirit of Southern gentility in her soirées and dinners, and her closest friends were the political families from Georgia, Alabama, and the Carolinas. The Strides, of course, were closer than most.

Harriet was blonde, and more than moderately handsome, with eyes that were violet by legend but muddy blue when you looked at her near. She carried herself with an *hauteur* that was a little too *haut* to be taken seriously, but Alice had always found her loyal, and witty, and devoted to her Uncle Jem. The President may have been a doughface, and a soft-shelled compromiser, but he was charming in company, and the most considerate of hosts. Harriet's 'drawing-rooms' reflected that charm and consideration with merry conversation, elegant music, and tables of fussy food.

'You won't be fierce tonight, or sarcastic?' asked Alice, as they drew up in Senator Stride's carriage at the South Front of the White House. It was nearly a week later, the first Friday in March, and the weather had begun to soften. A warm south wind, freshened by the

Potomac, was blowing gently in through their open carriage window.

'We struck a bargain, didn't we?' Collis said. 'You provided the introductions, and now we're providing the escort.'

'You needn't make it sound as if you're escorting me under duress.'

'I'm sorry. That wasn't my intention. I value your company just as much as I value your help.'

Alice lifted her large nose and fanned herself a little with her pierced-ivory fan. 'Sometimes, Collis Edmonds, I'm not at all sure how to take you.'

Theodore sat opposite, in the darkness of the leather seating, and said nothing. He was saving his own talk for later, for any Senator or Congressman who might be persuaded to give them support for the Sierra Pacific railroad. Over the weekend, and during the early days of the week, he and Collis had already cut their lobbying teeth on ten members of the House of Representatives, both Democrats and Free-Soil Republicans, and on six members of the Senate. Both of them had been frustrated and depressed by their experience, and they saw tonight as their last effort to rouse some support. For all the money they had spent on dinners at Balzer's Restaurant on I Street, and for all the hours they had sat and watched Congressmen devouring huge platefuls of veal, roast beef, and smoked ham, washing everything down with French wine and brandy, they had succeeded in arousing only the sketchiest interest in a Pacific railroad, and they had learned only one important thing about influencing Congress. Senator Salmon Chase of Ohio had put it best, when they dined with him at their own hotel. He had sat for an hour eating their food, and all they had seen of him until eight o'clock was the top of his bald, liver-spotted scalp, and his bushy eyebrows. Then, as he wiped his mouth with his napkin, he had looked up and told them, 'An excellent dinner. And a very interesting discourse on trains. However, it won't be enough.'

'Not enough?' Collis had asked him.

The Senator had smiled and shaken his head. 'To navigate your way through the cloakrooms, and to net the support you want, you have to be furnished with the best of baits.'

'What did he mean by "the best of baits"?' Theodore had said later. 'What more can we give them, apart from meals, and wines, and promises of shares in the railroad?'

Collis, sitting back in his hotel armchair with his shoes off, had

402

answered, 'The best of baits is money. These Congressmen are the hungriest group of men who ever got together, and we're going to have to bribe them until they burst.'

Theodore had sat down too, defeated. 'What with? We won't have any money until we have their support, and we won't have their support until we can buy it. It's a vicious circle.'

'It's a circle we'll have to break.'

As the Stride carriage waited its turn among the clutter of broughams and barouches outside the White House, Collis was thinking about something else which had made the week unhappy, apart from the avaricious Congressmen and Senators who were prepared to eat but not to listen. He was thinking about his three afternoon visits to Senator Carslake's house, in an attempt to see Delphine. On Monday, Tuesday, and Wednesday, he had waited around the corner from Nineteenth Street on Pennsylvania Avenue, his face wrapped in a scarf in case she recognized him and tried to avoid him, and he had paced the boardwalk until it was dusk. Even on Tuesday, her afternoon off, she hadn't appeared; and it was only on Wednesday evening, when he had finally called at the house to ask for her, that he learned what had happened.

The coffee-coloured Negro had told him, 'Miss Spooner? She took the children down to Richmond for a while. Mrs Carslake's instructions.'

Collis had stood for a while on the corner, where years ago children had gathered to watch Dolley Madison at her window, feeding her pet parrot. So this was how it ended. The romantic arrangement that his mother had made with Winifred Spooner, the flirtatious conversation in Taylor's Restaurant, the ride in Central Park. He remembered Delphine saying, *'I suppose it's a punishment for both of us. Most of these terrible things are. I've been too forward and you've been too reckless, and the Lord has seen fit to separate us.'*

The Lord's punishment, he thought. Exact, painful, and just to the point of cruelty.

'I wish the footmen would hurry,' said Alice. 'This is quite ridiculous.'

Collis leaned out of the carriage window. The curving stairs that led up to the south porch of the White House were twinkling with hand-held links as Harriet Lane's guests were taken inside. There was a bustle of conversation and laughter. He could see young ladies in silk and velvet dresses, and men in red and green tailcoats, with showy neckties and fancy vests. A tall young man who walked

403

past their carriage even had his whiskers and his eyebrows dyed pale blue to match his coat. The evening wind was fragrant with perfume.

At last their carriage shifted forward, and the door was hastily opened by a black footman in a frogged coat and a white-powdered wig. Collis and Theodore both stepped down, looking very New York in their black tailcoats and starched shirts, and helped Alice to alight. Alice was far more Washington, in a scarlet velvet gown trimmed with long white silk ribbons, and a scarlet cape with an overlay of Nottingham lace. The footman guided them towards the stone staircase, while another black boy led their carriage away. The footman's torch made a flaring sound in the wind.

The tall South Front windows glittered with light, and the entrance was crowded with chattering guests. Collis patiently ushered Alice through the throng, feeling uncomfortable and out of place, and wishing very much that he hadn't been obliged to come. Theodore, right behind them, looked hot and miserable, and before they managed to push their way through to the drawing-room, he had to take out his large white handkerchief and wipe the perspiration from his face. All around them, the hall-way and ante-rooms were jostling with dandified young Southern men, all curled hair and contrived poses, and by young Southern women, as pretty and white as porcelain shepherdesses, with bare shoulders and daringly low dresses, their laughter so high and precious that it sounded like the resonance of fine crystal. These were the sons and daughters of some of the wealthiest and most influential slave-owners of Virginia, Georgia, Louisiana, and Mississippi. They represented huge wealth in cotton, fruit, livestock, and Negroes. They represented the South, in all her pride, her courtesy, her culture, and her disdain. None of them had heard of Antietam.

They came at last into the East Room, where Harriet Lane was receiving her guests. The chandeliers were dazzling, and the heat of the candles and the press of perfumed human bodies was almost enough, as Collis said afterwards, to roast a grouse before it could run across the room. The walls were pale egg-shell blue, and hung with gilt-framed pictures of George and Martha Washington, and Thomas Jefferson, and serene views of Harper's Ferry and the Great Potomac Falls. There was a small orchestra playing cotillion music on the far side of the room, by the windows, but the noise of the guests almost swallowed them up.

Alice introduced Collis to Harriet Lane, who was sitting in a rococo chair fanning herself furiously and offering her hand to anyone who cared to come and kiss it. She was wearing a silvery silk dress, and a necklace of rubies and diamonds, and her auburn hair was decorated with silver and diamond combs. She could have been pretty, but she was pink and bothered, and Alice whispered later that she was *not* looking her best. She had probably argued with the caterers, or with the orchestra, or with her dressmaker. In any case, she looked Collis up and down and spoke quite sharply to him, as if he had done something wrong by simply walking into the room.

'You're very sombre, Mr Edmonds,' she said, looking away from him. 'I trust nobody close to you has passed on.'

'It's my usual evening dress, Miss Lane,' said Collis, bowing. 'I'm sorry if you find it funereal.'

'I find it snobbish, as a matter of fact,' retorted Harriet Lane. 'Only a Yankee could arrive at a Washington party dressed so plain, and looking so superior about it.'

'My apologies,' said Collis. 'But only another Yankee could be so sensitive about it.'

Harriet Lane turned back towards him and stared. 'I may have been raised in Pennsylvania, Mr Edmonds, but my heart is here.'

Collis smiled. 'I suppose one's heart would rather be any place than Pennsylvania.'

Alice took hold of Collis's arm. 'Come on, Collis,' she insisted. 'I think we should see what good things Miss Lane has provided to eat. And then perhaps a dance.'

They retreated out of range of Harriet Lane's displeasure with Alice Stride so flushed across the breastbone from heat and embarrassment that she clashed with her gown. 'Really, Collis!' she kept saying. 'I can't understand you! You seem determined to upset everybody!'

Collis held her arm and piloted her towards the buffet table, which was laid out under a long mirror on the east side of the room. There were great silver bowls of ice, misted with condensation, in which freshly-opened Potomac oysters lay glistening in the light of the chandeliers; there were joints of rare beef as pink as roses; and chicken and lobster salads so decorative that chefs must have twiddled and breathed over them for hours. Collis took a plate for Alice, and had one of the servers heap it with ham and oysters and jellied tongue before she could protest. He took a whole smoked grouse for himself, while Theodore less impetuously picked a lobster salad, and then they went to sit down at the tables that were set out in the corner.

'I shall never know how to speak to Harriet again,' said Alice. 'This is a fine return for all those introductions I gave you.'

'You asked me to escort you,' said Collis, with his mouth full. 'You didn't say that I had to kow-tow to your doughface friends.'

'How can you call Harriet a doughface? She's a lovely woman! She's sensitive, and beautiful, and she's worth twenty-five of you!'

Collis sliced off another piece of grouse. 'I shouldn't worry about it, Alice. Old Buck will be out of office in two years, and then it won't matter if you're friendly with Harriet or not.'

'I don't know how you can say such things,' said Alice.

Collis took a sip of chilled white wine. 'I can say such things, my dear, because I've discovered at last what kind of a place Washington is, and what kind of people it harbours. This is the seat of government, yes; but it's also the seat of corruption, greed, trickery, and every variety of swindle known to man.'

'I didn't know you were such an evangelist,' Alice told him.

'I'm not. I'll tell you something, Alice. When I was gambling and whoring in New York, and spending my nights in Green Street brothels, I thought I was one hell of a terrible devil. But since I've come here, and seen Congress like a nest of cuckoos, with their beaks all stretched open for bribes and favours and everything they can get, I've realized what an amateur I am. I'm not evangelising about them, I'm simply expressing my admiration that they have managed to sink so low without actually penetrating the earth's crust.'

'I hope you're not including my father,' said Alice, putting down her fork.

Collis looked at her fork, and then at her. 'Would it upset you if I were?'

She thought about that. Then she picked up her fork again. 'No, I suppose it wouldn't. I know what he has to do to survive.'

'All right, then,' said Collis. 'We'll grant him the right to survive, even when it means watering railroad stock, and selling off land that only exists on maps.'

'That wasn't his fault, that land sale in Oregon. He bought the land himself from somebody's map.'

Collis raised his hands. 'I'm not saying it *was* his fault. I'm simply saying that the games they play in this city are very dirty games, and that if I'm going to get what I want, I'm going to have to learn to play them, too.'

Theodore picked flesh out of a lobster claw. 'What Collis is trying to tell you is that we've lost our political virginity on this trip,' he remarked blandly.

Alice tugged at her necklace. 'I see. Well, I suppose I should congratulate you, after a fashion.'

'You think I've changed, don't you?' said Collis.

Alice looked at him. 'Yes,' she said, in a steady voice, 'you have.'

'Are you sorry you asked me to escort you?'

'Not entirely. A little.'

'Because of Harriet Lane?' asked Collis. 'Or for some other reason? Something personal, perhaps?'

She was silent. Her eyes clouded like breathed-on garnets.

'The truth is always slightly painful, isn't it?' she asked him.

'Yes.'

She smiled. A hurt smile. 'Well, then,' she said, 'if the truth is painful, we shall tell each other lies.'

'All right,' said Collis. 'You've bargained well for this evening out. Let's lie, if we must, but let's enjoy it, for all of our lies.'

Alice looked close to tears. But Collis pushed back his chair, and stood up, and offered his hand. 'Would you care to dance, Miss Stride?' he asked her. 'I would consider it an honour.'

'Thank you,' Alice whispered with a catch in her throat, and stood up too. Theodore was left to finish off his wine and his lobster salad in earnest solitude, with flecks of shellfish in his beard, while Collis and Alice joined the dancing. He raised his head from time to time to see where they were, and he couldn't help noticing how calm Collis looked, how self-contained, as if he had emptied himself of any regret for Hannah, or any pain for Delphine. He couldn't help noticing, either, how Alice danced as if she were dreaming and how the glittering White House chandeliers found reflections in her eyes.

It was a few minutes after midnight when Senator Stride's carriage rolled up to the door of the house on Eighteenth Street, and Collis and Theodore and Alice alighted. A kerosene lamp was flickering above the porch, but there were no lights along the street. The carriage rolled around the block to the stables, while Collis escorted Alice up the steps to the door, and knocked. Theodore had drunk half a bottle of wine too many, and stood on the sidewalk trying to fasten his evening cape with careful and incapable dignity.

Hubert, the manservant, opened the door. But as Alice stepped inside, and Collis took off his hat to bid her good night, a tall figure appeared in the hall-way behind him. It was Senator Stride, in a dressing-gown and fez, and he looked as if he was just about to retire to bed.

'Is that Mr Edmonds I see there?' the Senator asked loudly.

'Yes, Father,' said Alice. 'We've had a very pleasant evening.'

'Well, now, Mr Edmonds,' said the Senator, crossing the hall and coming up to the front door. 'The last time I heard anyone talk of you, you'd gone to California with your washbowl on your knee. Didn't you care for it there, or wouldn't they have you?'

He gave a deep, genial laugh. He hadn't changed. He was as saturnine and craggy as ever, and his eyes were still shadowed and dark.

'I went to California to rebuild the fortune that my father had unhappily lost in New York,' Collis said coldly. 'No thanks to you, I might say.'

'Oh, you shouldn't take it so personal,' said Senator Stride. 'Politics and finance, well, they're both battles of a kind, running battles, and folks tend to get hurt in battles. It's the way of the world.'

'Getting hurt is one thing,' said Collis. 'Getting killed is another. My father died when I. P. Woolmer's went down, and you could have saved him. Worse than that, I. P. Woolmer's brought down Ohio Mutual, too, and that drove poor George Spooner to madness, which is worse than death, in its way.'

'Well, you *are* in a grave mood,' said Senator Stride. 'But won't you come in and take a drink? A brandy, to warm you up? I don't drink myself, as you know, but I'll sip a fruit cup with you.'

Collis hesitated, but Alice took his arm and smiled. 'Of course you'll have a drink, won't you? It would be so nice if you and father could make everything up.'

'Very well,' said Collis. 'I have a friend with me, too, Mr Theodore Jones.'

Senator Stride gave a warm smile. 'I know.'

'You know?'

'I don't stay alive and well in Washington by going around with my eyes closed and my fingers in my ears,' said the Senator 'I know what you've been up to, and why you're here, and I've been waiting for this opportunity to chew the fat with you.'

'Theodore?' Collis called.

Theodore blinked up at him from the street. 'Damned cape won't work,' he said. 'Tried to fix it every damned way.'

Collis went down and took Theodore's arm, and led him up to the porch. 'The Senator wants to talk about railroads,' Collis explained. 'Do you think you're sober enough to remember your finance, and your engineering, and your topographical surveys?'

'Off by heart,' assented Theodore. 'Every nitpicking detail. Off by heart.'

'All right, then,' said Senator Stride. 'You'd better come in.'

Alice said good night in the gloomy hallway. She kissed Collis's cheek like a little beaky bird, and ran upstairs. Senator Stride led Collis and Theodore through to his library, where the sullen remains of a log fire burned in a marble fireplace as impersonal and impressive as the Parthenon, and where bald-eyed busts of Socrates and Tertullian stood on shelves lined with books on politics, history, horse breeding, and music. There was a worn leather settee by the fire, and an unruly collection of armchairs, and a ginger tomcat lay on the rug with an expression of disgruntled hedonism, as it tried to bask in the dying warmth of the logs. A piano stood in the far corner, scattered with sheet music. Senator Stride went across, raised the lid, and played a few bars of music that Collis didn't recognize.

'The opening of Anton Eberl's symphony in E-flat,' said the Senator, with a dry smile. 'Eberl was a close pal of Mozart, and if you ask me he could have been a damned sight better. But that's the way things go, isn't it, Mr Edmonds? The people with the real talent are always overshadowed by the people with the style.'

Theodore sat down in one of the armchairs and tried to focus his eyes by stretching them sideways with his fingertips, like a Chinese.

'You mean the good people always get themselves trodden under,' said Collis.

'Not at all,' replied the Senator. He closed the piano. 'Socrates said that nothing can harm a good man, either in life or in death, and if you apply that thought to your dear father, you have to admit that it holds true. Your father was lost way before you ever came to ask for money. He was lost because he tried to play a straight game in a crooked way, whereas if he'd played a crooked game a straight way, nobody could have touched him, not even me.'

Hubert came in with a tray of glasses. He poured a large Napoleon brandy for Collis, and a freshly-squeezed orange juice for the Senator. Theodore declined a drink with a weak wave of his hand.

When the servant had gone, Collis said, 'I hadn't heard you were any straighter than most, Senator, if you'll pardon my candour. There was the Oregon land swindle, for example, and then the Milwaukee railroad fraud. Your name was hanging around both of those like rotten shad.'

The Senator kept on smiling. 'You're missing my point, Mr Edmonds. I know that both of those episodes were shameful, and that a great many innocent investors lost their money. I regret that. But in the same breath, I have to say that if you look at my personal involvement, it was entirely straightforward, entirely honest, and at no time was I ever aware that non-existent land was being sold, nor that railroad stock was being watered.'

He sat down on the settee, and set his half-finished glass of juice in the hearth. 'What do you want me to do, Mr Edmonds? Give up business altogether? Because that's what I'd have to do, to keep out of swindles and double-dealing altogether. I don't have any doubt that there'll be hundreds of more swindles in American business as time goes by, and I don't have any doubt that my name will be hanging around any number of them. But if I washed my hands of anything that looked slightly shady, like Pontius Pilate, my place would simply be taken by characters twice as disreputable as me, twice as greedy, and twice as ready to cut the throats of people like your father and George Spooner. I have to admit that I'm motivated by profit – both in business and in Congress. But I like to think that my particular brand of greed is honest, and above-board, and that while I may cram my mouth with as much of my fellow diner's food as I can get, I won't bite his ankle under the tablecloth.'

Collis sat down too, and slowly swirled the brandy around in his glass. 'I'm not sure why you've invited me in,' he said. 'I thought you were heavily involved with the Hannibal & St Joseph, and with Jeff Davis, and all the southern-route lobby.'

'That's right,' said Senator Stride. 'The first Pacific railroad has to be built south of the Thirty-eighth Parallel, in my view, unless this nation wants to see itself politically and economically torn apart.'

'So you want to stop me?'

Senator Stride frowned. 'Stop you? Why should I want to stop you? From what I've been hearing, you're determined, and raring to go, and you've got the best engineer for the job.' He glanced at Theodore. 'When he's sober, at least.'

'He only got drunk because he was disappointed,' said Collis. 'It didn't seem there was anybody in Washington willing to listen.'

'That doesn't surprise me. But *I'm* willing to listen. In fact, I'm willing to go further than that. I'm willing to put up money to help you form a railroad company.'

Collis peered at the Senator narrowly. 'I'm not sure that I can believe what I'm hearing.'

The Senator looked amused. 'What you're hearing is good sense. I can't pretend that I wouldn't prefer to see the first transcontinental railroad run westwards out of St Joseph, or Memphis, or even Vicksburg. But there's heavy industrial money in the North, and they're going to need a Pacific railroad some day, even if it's not the first. I'd rather have a share of that railroad than not.'

Collis stared at the Senator for a long, silent moment. Then he turned to Theodore. 'Did you hear that? The Senator wants to back us.'

Theodore lifted his head.

'That's right,' said Collis, 'you heard me correctly. The Senator wants to back us.'

'What does he want in return?' asked Theodore slurrily.

Senator Stride reached out and tickled his ginger tomcat under the chin. 'A share,' he said. 'That's all.'

There was silence. The logs stirred and suddenly collapsed in the grate, sending a shower of sparks up the chimney.

'I'll lay out ten thousand dollars to start with,' the Senator went on. 'That should cover the expense of this trip, and give you enough to go back to California and form a company.'

'What about a survey?' Theodore wanted to know. He was very much the worse for drink, but he hadn't lost his engineer's sense of priorities. 'It's going to cost us thirty-five thousand dollars just to map our trace through the Sierra Nevada.'

'You should raise that yourselves,' said Senator Stride. 'It would be far too blatant if I financed that for you. But your company stockholders should be able to lay out most of it.'

He stood up and walked slowly back to the piano. He raised the lid once more and began to play with one hand, a lyrical, mellifluous melody. 'Once you've surveyed the route through the Sierra Nevada,' he continued, 'I can put the squeeze on quite a number of Congressmen and Senators to support you. Democrats and Republicans, both. You'd be surprised how many of them owe me favours, of one sort or another.'

He played, and Collis listened. Theodore was beginning to sober up, and he kept looking at Collis anxiously. Collis lifted a finger as a warning to Theodore to hold his peace. This was bear country, where a man who made the wrong move too quickly could get himself nastily gnawed.

'Of course, you'll need money of your own,' Senator Stride explained. 'There are one or two less scrupulous Representatives who will only cast a vote for gold. But once you've established with surveys that you can lay down a railroad where you claim you can lay down a railroad, then I can start to get things moving. I can get you Congressional letters of support, and you can take the letters back to California and raise more money on the strength of them, and then you can bring the money back here to Washington and buy more support, and so on. Congress is like a fountain of money. The more money you pour into it, the more pours out.'

'It could take years to survey the route properly,' said Theodore.

'That doesn't matter to me. In fact, as far as I'm concerned, the longer you take, the better. I want to see the Southern route laid first, because I've already invested a sizable amount of money in it, and I believe that it's going to keep the South strong. Jeff Davis tells me they should have the first topographical reports ready in two years. So take three or four years, if you need them. Take five.'

Theodore bit his lip. 'Two years isn't long,' he said worriedly.

'No, it isn't, as these things go,' said Senator Stride. 'And that's partly why I've made you the offer I have. I know the southern railroad will be laid down first, because it's way ahead already; but unlike some of my colleagues in the Senate, I recognise that a northern route will eventually have to come.'

He played a trickly little coda, and then looked up at them, his eyes dark. 'There are some who say this country will go to war. Well, I think that's bull. I hate the way the damned Yankees have milked the South as much as anyone. But business is business, and this country has to learn to get along with itself. I think that building a southern-route railroad first and then a northern-route railroad about five or six years later – well, that should help to even up the political balance.'

'And your personal bank balance, of course,' said Collis.

The Senator paused. Then he said, 'Yes,' and chuckled.

Theodore beckoned Collis to bend his head nearer as the Senator began to play more of Eberl's symphony in E-flat. 'Two years,' he whispered. 'How can we get our surveys together in two years? We don't even know if we can find a suitable pass!'

Collis sat up straight again. 'We'll find it,' he said, under his breath. 'You've always believed it's there, and so it must be.'

'You've never seen those mountains! It could take us *years*!'

'Yes, it could,' said Collis. 'So we'll just have to start looking straight away, won't we? The day we get back to Sacramento.'

Senator Stride stopped playing. He looked at Collis for a while, as if he was thinking deeply. 'Do you still believe I killed your father?' he asked.

Collis finished his brandy. He set down the glass on the small wine table beside him.

'I'd like to reserve judgement on that,' he said quietly.

Senator Stride stood still for a while, saying nothing. Then he gave a little nod. 'You're beginning to learn, aren't you, Mr Edmonds? You're really beginning to learn.'

Chapter 10

They reached Sacramento on 21 April 1858. They were both ill with the grippe, and with intestinal influenza, and for the first week back they were nursed by Annie Jones at Theodore's house on R Street. She brought them chicken broth, and hot sourdough bread, and as many eggs as she could possibly afford, and by the following Sunday they were beginning to lose their Panama isthmus pallor, and to stay around to talk for whole hours at a time without suddenly shuffling off to the privy at the back of the yard. The sun was warm, and the days were long, and they sat outside the house under the shade of the trees, Collis whittling a whitewood stick and Theodore smoking his pipe, and you could have mistaken them for two old contented men in retirement. The only difference was, they talked between themselves of the Sierra Nevada, and how they were going to find their way through. They spoke of Johnson's Pass, and Slippery Ford, and Steam Boat Springs. They scratched maps in the dust at their feet, and went over and over the valleys and the passes that Theodore had explored when he was surveying wagon roads to the silver mines in Nevada.

Collis called in at the store on K Street every morning, and had dinner with Charles and Mary two or three times a week. Charles was blustery and irritable at first, because he thought that Collis had been taking advantage of his friendship by going off to Washington so soon after buying himself in. But one evening Collis walked around to the Tuckers' house and rang the bell, and when Charles answered the door Collis had that particular look on his face that meant he wanted to talk.

Charles was in his vest and shirtsleeves, and smoking a cigar. He was looking gingery and hot. He closed the door behind him and stepped out on to the veranda. A couple of puffs of cigar smoke chased each other across the yard. He sat on the veranda rail, his eyes half-closed against the brightness of the sinking sun. 'You look as if you've got something on your mind,' he said.

'It's you, Charles, as a matter of fact. You and Leland.'

'No problems, are there? Business is going good.'

'Well, let's put it this way – you've got what you wanted out of my

414

coming out here to Sacramento. Fresh blood, new ideas. That kind of thing.'

Charles inclined his head to show that he certainly conceded that. 'As long as you don't make a habit of taking a vacation back East every two or three months, I'd say we're getting along fine.'

Collis took out a cheroot. 'As a matter of fact, it's that "vacation" I want to talk about. I found out a whole lot of hard realities about life on that trip, and I got a measure of just how difficult it would be to get a Pacific railroad built across the Sierras. Politically, I mean, quite apart from actually laying down the track.'

'Does that mean you've gone off the idea?'

'Are you hoping I have?'

Charles inspected the wet end of his cigar and stuck a piece of stray leaf down with spit. 'In a way. I'm not saying it wouldn't do something for Sacramento, as far as business goes. But I don't really believe that it's possible, not in our lifetime. I think you're wasting your time, and your money, on something that ain't going to happen for twenty years.'

'Good,' said Collis.

'Good?'

'I'm glad you admit that it *might* be possible, even if we don't live to see it. That's better than damning the whole notion outright. You see, what I want us to do, you and me and Leland, and maybe a couple of other Sacramento merchants, is form a railroad company, and have a pass surveyed through the Sierras.'

Charles looked at him narrowly. 'You want me to put money into a railroad? That's like asking me to burn it.'

'That's where you're wrong. This survey can't lose money, even if the railroad never gets built. If we can't whip up enough political and financial support from Congress, then we simply clear a wagon road through to Nevada Territory, and charge a toll on that.'

Charles sucked at his cigar two or three times before he realised it was dead. Collis handed him a match, which he struck on the veranda post. He cupped his hands and lit up again before he answered.

'How much do you need for this survey?'

'Thirty, maybe thirty-five thousand. If seven of us put in five thousand each, that should see it through.'

There was another long silence. Then Charles said, 'You've done something to me. Do you know that?'

'I don't understand.'

'Well,' said Charles, trying to find the words, 'before you came here, I was one of the kings of this city, me and Leland both. But ever since I met you, I get the feeling that I've been pushed into the background. Don't think I don't like you. I do. I like what you are, and I like the way you work. The moment I saw you on the wharf that first day you came to San Francisco, well, I knew we'd get along then.'

'But?' asked Collis gently.

Charles shrugged. 'I don't know how to say it. But the store's running your way now, and even Mary's not so disapproving of you these days. Wang-Pu put it the best. He said to me last month, when you were away in Washington, "That Mr Edmonds, he's going to have us all riding trains across America whether we like it or not."'

Collis lowered his eyes. The shadow of the trees was silently swaying on the boarded veranda floor.

'Maybe Wang-Pu's right,' he said, and his voice was slightly hoarse. 'But maybe something's happening to this nation and we're all just a part of it. Maybe we don't have any choice. Not you, nor Leland, nor me.'

Charles didn't answer. He smoked for a while, and then he stood up and opened his screen door. 'Mary's expecting some folks around later to sing some psalms. I'd better go in and wash up.'

'What about the railroad company? Do you want to think about it?'

Charles shook his head. 'No. I'll have a note for the five thousand drawn up tomorrow.'

'Then you'll do it?'

'For some reason I can't explain, Collis, I will.'

'How about Leland? Will you talk to him?'

'Sure. He'll do it if I do.'

Collis brushed his hair back from his forehead with his hand. 'Well,' he said, and he felt strangely unsteady, 'thanks.'

Three days later, in the sombre mahogany offices of Leland McCormick's attorneys on H Street, eleven men gathered for the drawing up of the articles of the Sierra Pacific Railroad Company. Behind a large desk with a green leather top, on which were spread the company's papers, sat Mr Frederick Drew, the attorney, in a high starched collar and pince-nez, while beside him sat a scruffy clerk who kept bending forward and scratching his ankle.

In a variety of chairs, in a rough semicircle, sat Collis, Charles, Leland, Theodore, and a young lawyer from San Francisco with peeling sunburn, who represented Andrew Jackson Hunt. There were also five other Sacramento traders in dark frock coats – Edward Willard, Jr., Stanley Montrose, Bryan W. Meadows, Percival Giddings, and John Dunthorpe. There was a great deal of coughing, and taking of snuff, and scratching of nibs. On the window-sill were stacks of sun-yellowed legal papers.

Leland McCormick was appointed president of the Sierra Pacific, while Charles Tucker was named construction chief, Collis Edmonds was treasurer, and Andrew Hunt was secretary. Theodore Jones was formally hired as the new company's official engineer and surveyor.

Afterwards, the assembled men went across the street to Murphy's Hotel, where they drank a solemn toast to their enterprise, and Leland made a ponderous speech about the pioneering spirit of those who lived and worked in Northern California. Collis stayed at the end of the bar with a glass of whisky, which he hardly touched. Theodore, his cheeks flushed with success, looked across the room at him and raised his eyebrows in an expression which meant: 'What's wrong?'

Collis gave him a quick smile which meant that everything was fine. He couldn't have told him how much he was thinking of Hannah and Delphine, a few last glimpses of scented memory before the Sierra Pacific Railroad overwhelmed them altogether.

'Sacramento,' Leland was saying, 'as its just reward for this day's work, will soon be likened to the fabled marketplaces of the Orient, thronged with the busy denizens of two hemispheres, brought here by the great highway of nations upon which we have so confidently embarked.'

He said nothing about his unshakable conviction that, though it might be profitable, the Pacific railroad would never reach any further than Nevada.

Collis looked down at his whisky. Then he picked up the glass and swallowed the drink in one gulp.

Collis was shaving in the bedroom of his apartments on J Street when there was a frantic knocking at the downstairs door. He heard Watkins, the black cleaner, shuffling along the corridor to answer it. The knocking came again, louder and more insistent. Collis pulled down his cheek with his fingertips and carefully shaved his side whiskers. The outside door was opened, and he heard voices. He rinsed his hollow-ground razor.

It was early October, nearly seven months since the Sierra Pacific Railroad Company had been formed, and the summer had passed uneventfully. The political news from Washington was that Congress was still in a furious ferment over slavery, but Senator Stride, in a short letter to Collis and Theodore, had dismissed most of the talk of civil war as 'hysterical nonsense'. He had asked how the railroad survey was progressing, and whether there was any sign of a negotiable trace through the High Sierras. Collis had yet to reply. The truth was that Theodore was still preparing his equipment for the survey, and was still relying on topographical probability rather than hard rock. The Sierras glittered in the late sunlight every afternoon, as impassable by steam locomotives as ever.

Collis emptied his floral-patterned washbasin and wiped it out with his towel. Then he walked through into his sitting-room, where his clean white shirt was hanging up on the window valance. As he put in on and buttoned it up, there was another knock, this time at his own door.

'Who is it?' he called. 'I'm dressing.'

'It's me, Theodore!' He sounded breathless, and unusually excited. 'You must open the door! It's wonderful news!'

Collis went to the door and unlocked it. Theodore came bursting in like a bear, his coat collar folded back the wrong way, his necktie still untied, and his eyes wide with enthusiasm. He was holding up a letter and waving it around. 'The most marvellous thing! You'd hardly believe it! The most marvellous thing has happened!'

Collis closed the door and walked back across the room tucking his shirt-tail into his pants. 'Well?' he said dryly. 'You'd better tell me what it is.'

'I had this letter this morning. It's from Dutch Flat, in the Sierra foothills. You must read it. Read it, please.'

Collis took the letter and opened it out. It was written on cream-coloured paper with the printed heading: 'Dutch Flat Drugstore. Daniel F. Kates, Proprietor. Pharmaceuticals, Toilet Articles, Notions.' Beneath the heading, in sepia ink, a firm and literate hand had written:

Dear Mr Jones,

I am acquainted with your articles and pamphlets on the subject of a Pacific railroad, and I am impressed by your ideas of a locomotive highway to link California with the Eastern plains. There is no question in my mind that our commercial fortunes would be much enhanced by such a link.

With the intention of trying to find a wagon route eastwards out of Dutch Flat, to connect my small town with Nevada Territory over the Sierra crest, I recently came upon a corridor through the rock which to my inexperienced eye is considerably less demanding in gradient than the old emigrant trace.

It occurred to me that you might be interested in making a preliminary survey of the corridor, which runs south of the Donner Lake but north of the peaks above Lake Bigler. I am here at my pharmacy at most times, since I am doctor, drugstore proprietor, and general servant of this small community; and I would be honoured to guide you up into the Sierras at your earliest pleasure.

I remain your servant, sir,
Daniel F. Kates.

Collis put the letter down. 'Well?' he asked Theodore. 'Do you believe there's anything in it?'

'It's a chance, that's all that counts. And a chance that actually pans out could save us years and years of surveying. If this is genuine, we could draw up a route in a matter of twelve months, maybe sooner.'

'Don't get yourself too excited,' warned Collis. 'He's only a pharmacist, not a railroad surveyor. What looks like a good railroad route to him may look like nothing more than a donkey track to you. I mean, what does he know about curves and grades? What does he know about anything?'

Theodore took the letter back and carefully reread it. 'He seems like a sobre enough man to me. And if he's read my pamphlet, he must have some kind of idea what I'm looking for.'

'All right,' said Collis, 'I'll admit that. But there's only one way to tell for sure, isn't there? Go take a look for ourselves.'

'You'll come?' asked Theodore.

'Sure I'll come. I'm the treasurer of the Sierra Pacific Railroad, aren't I? And I want Wang-Pu along, too. I want him to tell me if his

Chinese workers can cope with the kind of country we're going to have to face up there.'

Theodore pulled nervously at his beard. 'This is really extraordinary,' he said. 'This is really wonderful. You'll need a heavy coat, of course, and stout boots. And a hat, with flaps to cover your ears. I'm sure that Percival Giddings can supply all that. I can scarcely believe it. Oh, and don't forget your warm underwear. It's very cold up there, even this early in the winter. Collis, this marvellous!'

Collis buttoned up his pants. 'Do you want to join me for breakfast?' he asked. 'I was thinking of ham and scrambled eggs at the Western Rooms.'

'No, no,' said Theodore. 'I must make some preparations. I must tell Annie what clothes I'm going to need. I must get out my good theodolite.'

'All right,' said Collis. 'When do you want to leave?'

'It's, what, Thursday today. We should set out on Monday morning. Don't forget gloves, either.'

'No,' said Collis. 'I won't forget gloves.'

Theodore opened the door. Then he paused. 'Oh, and one more thing. I know it sounds morbid, but I think it's better to be well prepared for the worst. It can be dangerous up there, especially if it snows. So if there's anyone you want to write to – well, it's worth thinking about.'

Collis looked at him with a patient, indulgent smile. 'You sure you don't want me to take a shroud in my knapsack?'

'It's not a joke, Collis. Remember what happened to John Frémont's expedition.'

'Very well, Theo. I'll write to my mother and sister, make a will, and order my headstone from Grosser and Buch. And in the meantime, I'll go talk to Wang-Pu, and see what he thinks about coming along.'

Monday morning was bright, dusty, and windy. They drove out of Sacramento on a buckboard with 'Tucker & McCormick' painted on the side in faded black lettering. They had two fresh chestnut horses from the K Street stables, and enough blankets and coats and changes of clothes to last them for two weeks. Collis wore a wide-brimmed, low-crowned hat and a brown wool coat, while Theodore was dressed in a blue cotton jacket he used to wear on the railroads and a straw Panama. Wang-Pu, who sat in the back amid all the bedding, looked as if he were going to his uncle's wedding, in a black tailcoat and a tall black hat.

They didn't say much as they travelled. They passed stubbled wheatfields and stands of rusting deciduous trees. Then, as the road climbed through Folsom and Rocklin, up the valley of the American River, it became winding and uneven and strewn with stones, and they jolted through the midday dust with aching backs and pained expressions of acceptance. Collis smoked, and wiped the sweat from his face, and occasionally took a swallow of sherry and whisky mixed, from a bottle he kept under the buckboard's seat.

This was gold-mining country. As they followed the trail upwards, past sloping fields of dried grass, they came at last through groves of widespreading oaks, under which the sunlight winked in heliographic spangles, and out into a raw landscape of canyons and ridges that had been laid bare by hydraulic mining. There was nothing but wind, glare, and silence. All around, the ochre soil had been sluiced away from the foothills by thousands of gallons of high-pressure water, until the rocks were exposed like the jagged teeth of an old-time pioneer, and the bones of the Sierras showed through.

Alongside the trail, for mile after mile, wooden flumes carried fast water down out of the mountains to the mines below, leaving the silted bed of the American River, which appeared and reappeared below them at turn after turn in the trail, as a winding yellow ribbon of mud. It was this mud that was seeping westwards into the Sacramento River, and down into San Francisco Bay, staining the water and polluting the oyster beds. 'There used to be trout in that river,' Theodore remarked. 'These days, I wouldn't give a catfish any chances.'

Collis squinted out over whole fields that were nothing but picked-over boulders, shimmering with winter sunlight. He saw abandoned arroyos, with derelict mining huts and collapsed flumes that still spouted cascades of white water. And for hour after hour, there was nothing but hollows and spines of rock that had been scratched at and scraped at until every fragment of loose topsoil had been worried free. There were hillsides that had been blasted with huge charges of powder, twelve or fifteen hundred kegs, until they collapsed and could be washed over with nozzles for the tiniest specks of gold.

Collis felt as if he were travelling across the surface of some desolate prehistoric world, with only the grating of the buckboard's wheels and the hot low whistle of the wind to disturb the silence. Up above them, red-tailed hawks turned and turned in the blatant sky.

But they were making their way up into the mountain now, and the mining valleys were more deeply clefted. The steep sides of the road were bristling with Shasta firs, mountain hemlock, and pines. It grew cooler, and more fragrant, and through the dark trunks of the trees they could make out the peaks of the High Sierras, as white as sugared almonds.

The mining communities through which they drove were generally no more than a cluster of makeshift cabins, a general store, and a cookhouse-cum-saloon. Bearded men in dusty hats watched them pass. Sometimes they called 'How d'you do?' but more often they stayed silent.

They spent the first night by the side of the road, sleeping on blankets in a stand of Digger pines, with a small fire burning to keep away the wildlife, human or animal. The next morning they led the horses down to a broken flume to drink, and then Collis and Theodore shaved with ice-cold water and soap. Wang-Pu kept his chin clean the Chinese way, by plucking out each hair individually.

They reached Gold Run, sixty-four miles out of Sacramento, a little before noon. It was sharp and clear up here, and the mountain wind was snapping a flag on a tall flagstaff. The settlement of Gold Run itself was a cosy collection of shacks and cabins in a clearing of pines and sequoias. A wide flume curved in from the mountains and down beyond the trees to the slopes that were Gold Run's whole reason for being there. Theodore halted the buckboard alongside a rough boundary fence, and they all climbed down.

A toothless man with a grey beard was leaning against the door of the cookhouse. Thick smoke issued from the tin chimney, and there was a rich, greasy smell of stew. The old man was whistling between his gums and spitting from time to time on to the pine needles.

'Sharp morning,' he remarked, as they tied up their horses and walked over towards him.

'Good for the lungs, after the valley,' said Theodore. 'How far is it to Dutch Flat?'

'In a hurry, or dawdling?'

'Shortest time possible.'

The old man looked over his shoulder into the cookhouse to

make sure the food wasn't bubbling over. Then he said, 'Not more'n two hours. Lookin' for anyone special?'

'Daniel Kates, as a matter of fact,' said Theodore.

'Doc Kates? You ain't sick, are you?'

'No, no. This is just business.'

'That's okay then. But you can't be too careful. Had a whole bout of cholera last year. Fellows was dropping like fir cones.'

Collis looked into the smokey interior of the cookhouse. There were rows of cleavers hanging up, and a large smoke-blackened cauldron boiling over a brick range. He sniffed in the aroma of the stew.

'Smells good,' he told the old man. 'What's in it?'

'The usual.'

'What's the usual?'

'Well, I got twenty-two men to feed, barring myself. That works out at eleven squirrels, two jays, a couple of nutcrackers, and eight pounds of greens.'

Collis nodded. He suddenly didn't feel so hungry any more. 'You take the tails and the beaks off before you start cooking, I hope?'

The old man spat. 'Sometimes. Did today. Want some?'

'No, thanks. Thanks all the same.'

They did accept the old man's offer of hot coffee, however. They took their chipped enamel mugs to the edge of the treeline and looked down while they sipped the black, bitter brew at the gold miners working on the slopes. At the top of the slope, the water from the wooden flume was directed into a tall slatted box, and from the bottom of the box came a long canvas hose, which looped its way down the rocks to a man standing at the foot of the hill. He was gripping a brass nozzle at the end of the hose, and spraying the gold-bearing gravel away from the rock face.

'You see that jet of water?' said the old man, coming up behind them. 'That's so goddam powerful that if a fellow stood in front of that, it could cut him in half.'

'Thanks for the warning,' said Collis.

After they'd emptied the dregs of their coffee on the ground and tipped the old man a dollar, they untied the horses and climbed aboard their wagon again. They clattered out of Gold Run and continued to climb through the pine forests towards Dutch Flat. A chilly breeze began to blow, and Collis buttoned up his coat

'Did you ever do any surveying up this way before?' Collis asked Theodore.

423

Theodore shook his head. 'A little. Not much. I've been along the Carson River, and down along the south shore of Lake Bigler, and back to Sacramento through Carson Pass, but I must admit I gave this whole area up. I kind of assumed that the Donner Pass was the best corridor there was, north of the Lake, and when you've seen it for yourself you'll understand why I wasn't too hopeful. It's even worse in the middle of winter, of course.'

They came through a small stand of pines, and there was Dutch Flat – a small dusty community with one wide street, and a flagpole, and that abandoned silence that always characterised a mining town whose veins had given out. The sound of their buckboard wheels seemed unnaturally loud and intrusive, although as they came closer they could hear a baby crying somewhere, and the uneven tinkling of an upright piano.

It wasn't difficult to locate Daniel Kates's drugstore. It was one of the few two-storey buildings along the street, and there were five or six men sitting on the stoop outside, a couple of white-bearded old-timers, and a man with a drooping moustache who had his scruffy shoes propped up against one of the veranda's white-painted uprights. Two or three children in leggings and long dresses were playing hopscotch in the dust. From the top of the veranda, a makeshift pole stuck out over the street, and suspended from this was a large apothecary's pestle, painted gold. On the store windows, gold lettering announced, 'Drugs, Toilet Articles, Notions', and there were enamelled advertisements for Star Tobacco around the door.

Wang-Pu tethered the horses while Theodore and Collis went into the drugstore. It was cool and dim inside, with glass-fronted counters and cabinets, and it smelled of barley sugar and peppermint and oil of cloves. Each cabinet was crowded with patent preparations, like Dr Griffith's Toothache Remedy, and Hard Water Cocoa Soap, and Eastman's Camphor Ice; and along the back shelves were glass jars of rock candy, green and orange and red, and preparations for the ladies, like White Lily Face Wash (contains no lead, arsenic, or bismuth). Behind the counter was a short, ruddy-faced man with eyeglasses and a white apron. He had full whiskers, once fair but now almost white, and bulging blue eyes. He looked like the kind of man who would take no nonsense, and listen to no slander, and who would always be ready to pack his medical bag and come out to help you, even in the coldest of winters.

'Mr Kates?' Collis said.

'Doc Kates to most people,' said the drugstore proprietor. 'How can I help you?'

'I'm Collis Edmonds, of the Sierra Pacific Railroad Company. This is Theodore Jones, the railroad engineer. And this is Wang-Pu, our assistant.'

Doc Kates came around the counter and grasped Collis by the hand. Then he shook Theodore's hand, and Wang-Pu's, and his whiskers bristled with confidence and pleasure.

'Am I glad you gentlemen came! I was beginning to doubt you would. After all, we're pretty small beer up here in Dutch Flat. Not much of a mining town any more. Not much of anything, to tell you the truth. How would you like a fruit soda? Or maybe something stronger?'

'I could use a beer,' said Collis.

'I have a keg of North Beach steam out in back. Listen, why don't I get my boy to mind the store while we talk? I can't tell you how glad I am that you came.'

Doc Kates's 'boy' turned out to be his thirty-year-old son, taller and darker than he was, but with the same style of whiskers, and the same straightforward friendliness. He tied on a striped apron while Doc Kates led them into a small parlour in the back, and invited them to sit down at a kitchen table laid with a green gingham cloth. Through the windows, Collis could see a long sloping garden where pieces of white cloth fluttered to keep the birds away from the vegetables, and beyond that, the beginnings of a dense pine wood. Doc Kates drew them each a glass mug of steam, and then sat down himself.

'I didn't know whether you'd credit my story or not, that was the trouble,' he told Theodore. 'You can ask any of the old miners around here about ways through the High Sierras, and sure, they know hundreds of ways. They know passes you could stroll through in your shirtsleeves, pushing a baby in a perambulator. But you ask them where to locate these passes, and suddenly they get a little vague. Oh, it was a long time ago. Or, oh, it must've been snowed under by now. Or, oh, there was a heavy rock fall, and I guess the pass is blocked.'

'Most of the experts in the East say there isn't any way for a railroad track to come through the Sierra Nevada at all,' Collis said.

Doc Kates drank some beer, which left foam on his whiskers.

'Well, that's what I thought. But a year back, I took to going out on foot and exploring. I did it because I enjoyed it. The folks around here are pretty much dependent on having me around, in case someone needs a tooth pulled, or a broken ankle set, or a baby delivered. So now and again it's good to get out on your own, where you don't have to worry about measles and sore throats and labour pains. It's real peaceful when you're walking across the mountains. You'll see for yourself. Nothing but you and all those peaks, and maybe the North Fork rushing through the valley beneath you.'

'You sound like a man of inner tranquillity,' said Wang-Pu.

Doc Kates smiled. 'Well, I guess you could say that. But I'm a man who cares for his town, too, and apart from taking walks for the pleasure of it, I made a real effort to look for a better pass across the Sierras. I thought to myself, if Dutch Flat is going to die out because she's running short on gold, then there's only one way to revive her, and that's to link her up with Nevada Territory, and make her a staging post between the silver mines and Sacramento.'

'So you looked,' said Theodore. 'And what did you find?'

'Just what I said in my letter. A pass through the mountains that's level, and not too winding, and certainly wide enough for a wagon road.'

'You can negotiate gradients and bends in a wagon that a locomotive could never cope with,' said Theodore.

'Well, I know that,' replied Doc Kates. 'And that's why I asked you to come up here and give me a professional opinion. I'd like to think a railroad could run through here. It would do a hell of a lot for Dutch Flat. But I don't have any expertise as far as surveying goes, none at all, and what looks to me like a railroad bed might not look like anything to you.'

'Can you spare the time to guide us?' asked Collis. 'The railroad company will offset your costs.'

'You don't have to pay me,' Doc Kates told him. 'If the pass that I've discovered is suitable for running a railroad through, that's reward enough for me. When do you want to leave?'

'Tomorrow morning,' said Collis.

'Well, that's pretty short notice. I'll have to see if Nathan can look after the store. But I guess it's okay in principle. Yes, I guess so.'

'What's the weather like up there?' asked Theodore.

'Patchy. There's been some early snow. It's over seven thousand feet above sea level when you get to the top, so I hope you've brought yourselves some warm clothes. It might be fall down in Sacramento, but it's already winter up here.'

'We're prepared,' said Collis.

'The Donner party were prepared in 'forty-six,' Doc Kates reminded him. 'One of our old-timers here found the bodies, and it was pitiful.'

Wang-Pu said quietly, 'There is a saying in Peking that if your path takes you into the mouth of a tiger, then all you can do is pray that he does not close his jaws.'

Doc Kates let them use two of his upstairs rooms to unload their blankets and their supplies. There were two narrow beds up there, and a sagging sofa, and out of the windows they could see the forests and the distant snow-capped summit of Mount Rose.

They took off their shoes and relaxed for an hour, and then Doc Kates came up and knocked on their door and invited them out to meet some of the citizens of Dutch Flat. It was an idle, social afternoon. They called in on Mrs Fitzpatrick, who had come to California six years ago, and lived for a while in Yankee Jims before Mr Fitzpatrick had been unjustly accused of stealing another man's gold, and had had his ears cut off, and then been shot down. She gave them coffee and sugar cakes, and the crumbs that were left on the table she gathered in her apron and shook out in the yard for her chickens.

They sat on a log under the shade of the pines and talked to old Wallis, a forty-niner whose face was as soft and brown and wrinkled as an overripe pear; and he talked of the days when Auburn used to be called Rich Dry Diggings, and when men had been disembowelled with shovels in a fight over who should pan gold from a dry creek bed. 'Them were rough days,' said old Wallis, 'but they won't come back no more.'

At evening, they gathered on the veranda of the drugstore and listened to one of the old-timers reading from a Book of Wonders about the camel, which the author proclaimed 'the ugliest animal I ever saw'. The wind blew through the pines, and Doc Kates rocked himself backwards and forwards in a rocking-chair, until it was too dusky to read any more, and everybody went back to his home for supper, and bed.

It was overcast the next morning when they set off. The mountains were deep green, and crowned with clouds. They wore their knapsacks strapped to their backs, and they were all dressed in warm coats, gloves, and walking-boots. Only Wang-Pu insisted on retaining his tall hat. 'I am a gentleman at all times,' he said. 'Even in the mountains.'

From Dutch Flat, the trail rose steadily. The north fork of the American River glittered through the trees to their right, and the South Yuba River lay somewhere off to their left, so they were climbing a natural granite ramp between the two, all that remained of a prehistoric peneplain. As they walked, the cloud cover gradually thinned, and, by noon, when they were nearly fifteen hundred feet above the valley of the American River, they were red-faced and sweating and almost ready to give in. They stopped on a high rocky bluff, and took off their knapsacks, and passed around a bottle of water, and a flask of whisky.

'From here on, it starts getting harder,' said Doc Kates, unwrapping a loaf of sourdough bread and a piece of bright-yellow cheese. 'If you look down there, you can see where we've come from, up from the Flat, and if you look over your shoulder, you can see where we're going to, right up to the crest at the old emigrant pass.'

Collis shielded his eyes from the grey glare of the sun. Ahead of them, mantled in pines, the Sierra Nevada waited in imperious silence. They were so high, so massive, so dark, that as the clouds drifted past their peaks, it seemed as if the whole world was turning under Collis's feet.

Neither Collis nor Theodore talked much as they rested. They drank, and ate their bread, and then they gathered up their baggage and set out again. Throughout the afternoon they climbed higher and higher, until they began to see mountain peaks topped with snow, and the wind began to blow uncomfortably cold. Collis pulled on his gloves and turned up the collar of his coat.

'It's been real cold this year,' said Doc Kates. His breath was smoking in the dusky evening air. 'I got myself caught in a snowstorm already, and damned near froze to death. If you're going to build a railroad through here, you're going to have to keep the line clear with snowsheds, especially in the valleys, where it drifts.'

Theodore had lagged behind as they climbed towards Lake Valley and into the forests, but every twenty minutes or so he'd been jotting notes into a small dog-eared pad, and pausing to read the temperature and the altitude. 'It looks pretty good so far,' he

428

said, peering up towards the summit. The crests of the mountains were sparkling in the light of the dying day, as if they'd been sifted with frosting. The sky behind them, though, was sullen and grey, and the wind was rising.

They spent the first night at Bradley Hay Camp, a motley collection of pine huts which had long been abandoned to squirrels, decay, and curious bears. Collis swallowed a cupful of warmed-over broth, ham and split-pea, which Doc Kates had cooked up the evening before; and then he folded together a makeshift bed out of blankets in the corner of a hut and went to sleep. Doc Kates slept over on the other side of the hut, snoring deeply.

In the middle of the night, Collis was woken up by a door banging. He lay on his back for almost an hour, listening to the wind and the sounds of the forest. He felt closer to God up here in the mountains, for some reason he couldn't explain to himself. It wasn't just the altitude, or the silence. Perhaps he was getting closer to what God had always wanted him to do.

They left Bradley Hay Camp the next morning a few minutes before eight. Theodore wrote that down in pencil in his logbook. '7.56, Hay Camp, Therm 39, Aneroid 24.00.' It was even colder than the previous day, and for the first two or three hours of their walk, they were soaked by fine, persistent rain. They trudged miserably up the muddy, uneven trail, through fir trees that were beaded with silvery wet, up slippery outcroppings of rock, and all around them the mountains were hidden behind pearl-grey curtains of drifting mist.

The rain cleared towards lunchtime, and at 12.23, with the thermometer at 43 and the barometer at 23.77, they stopped on a windy ridge overlooking the deep valley of the American River and ate sausage and bread. Doc Kates, with his mouth full, said, 'Fine view from here, what d'you think?'

'I wish my feet were as pleased as my eyes,' said Wang-Pu.

They climbed slowly for the next two hours, leaving the American River behind them and crossing the ridge northwards to the valley of the South Yuba River, which busily foamed and splashed between the granite mountains. It was penetratingly cold up here, and as they approached the cleft where the South Yuba cut through the summit of the Sierra Nevada, more than seven thousand feet above sea level, the first few whirls of snow danced around them and clung to their clothes.

They stumbled across the summit at 4.17. The snow was thicker now, flying over the dark ridges like clouds of frosty locusts, and Collis could hardly make out the high peaks of the Sierra Nevada all around him. But he paused for a while, his collar turned up against the wind, and breathed in the freezing air in painful satisfaction. These were the mysterious mountains that had been beckoning him for so long. This was the place where his whole life was going to change. He wished he could shout out loud that he'd shown them all at last – his father, his mother, his miserable sister; Knickerbocker Jane and Charles Tucker, Leland McCormick and his plain-faced wife. All those people who had patronised him, or nagged him, or treated him as nothing more than a ridiculous rake. All those people who had loved him, or who had claimed to love him, and then denied him love. All those people who had died, because of him. And most of all, himself.

'Come on, Collis,' Theodore called. 'We don't want to get caught up here in the dark. Doc says this snow could get worse.'

Collis brushed the snow from his hair. 'We've beaten them, Theodore. Do you know that?'

'Not yet we haven't. We still have to find a negotiable way through to Nevada.'

'You think that there's really a way?'

'I hope so. Doc seems confident enough.'

Wang-Pu was waiting for them beside the trail. He was wiping the inside of his hatband with a clean white handkerchief. It was sweaty work, climbing mountains, even in the snow. 'We should leave the last word to the mountains themselves,' the Chinaman said. 'Only the mountains will show us if they wish to be conquered or not.'

'You think mountains have a will of their own?' asked Collis. 'Like women?'

Wang-Pu replaced his hat and tugged the straps of his knapsack tighter. 'These mountains have,' he said quietly.

They were walking downhill now, beside the tumbling gorge of the South Yuba River, but they were protected from the worst of the wind and the snow by the crest they had just crossed. Towards nightfall, the snow died down, and they came through a silent skirt of pines to Donner Lake, where Doc Kates loosened his knapsack and dropped it to the ground.

'We can spend the night here,' he said. 'In the morning, we'll make our way down to the Truckee River.'

The lake was still, an amber mirror under a slate-coloured sky. It was edged all around with a sawtooth pattern of pines, through which the cold wind whistled a remote, selfish song. They seemed like the loneliest men in all of America. On the far side of the lake, two snow-crested mountains gradually faded into the darkness and the mist.

Wang-Pu, still in his tall hat, gathered chips and kindling and started a fire. They sat by the edge of the lake, and Doc Kates stirred up a mess of beans in a billy can, and brewed some coffee, and by the time they'd finished eating and drinking it was completely dark. While the fire flickered and died down, they settled back in their blankets and lit up pipes and cigars, smelling the clear ice-cold water of the lake, and the scent of pines, and the smoky aroma of an outdoor camp. They talked for over an hour about the way they'd walked during the day, and the way they'd walk in the morning; and then they wrapped themselves up as warm as they could and went to sleep.

During the night, a gust of freezing wind blew out their fire, and scattered its embers along the shoreline.

By noon the next day the sky was the colour of tattered rags, and the wind had veered so sharply that it was blowing from the northwest, from Alaska, down the Coast Mountains of Canada, and the Cascades, until it complained and worried over the high peaks of the Sierra Nevada like a mangy hound with teeth of ice. There were more flecks of snow in the wind, and Theodore's thermometer showed the temperature was way below freezing.

The four of them walked eastward, climbing and sliding down the rocky slopes, their shoulders hunched against the wind, their mouths muffled with scarfs. Collis had never been so damned cold in his whole life, and the excitement of crossing the summit had been spoiled already by painful blisters, aching calf muscles, and tiredness. Doc Kates might have been used to striding over the granite terrain of the Sierras, but Collis wasn't, and neither was Theodore, who was hobbling twenty yards behind the rest of them with an expression that reminded Collis of St Sebastian. Wang-Pu's feet probably hurt, too, but he had his Buddhism to help him through, and he walked tirelessly and quietly, as if he were doing nothing more strenuous than strolling out to Mission Dolores on a Sunday afternoon.

Doc Kates paused from time to time on rocky outcroppings to let

431

them all catch up; but as soon as they had, he was off again, scrambling along the valleys like a white-bearded goat.

Collis kept up with him for a while, and they talked. 'I guess my life would've turned out wholly different if my wife hadn't passed on,' said Doc Kates. 'It was our third child, and I tried to save her, and the child, too, but all the doctors in California couldn't have done nothing more than I did, and they both died. I buried them out back. A big grave, and a tiny grave, and the words "Joined in Motherly Love". But once I'd gotten over my grief, I knew that she would have liked me to carry on, and live my life peaceful and helpful, and so that's what I did. I guess in a way that it was Wilhelmina's dying that led me to find my way through the mountains, because I never would have gone exploring if she'd been alive.'

'I get the feeling that your Wilhelmina won't have been the last person to lay down his life for this railroad, one way or another,' Collis told him.

Doc Kates rubbed the filaments of ice from his beard. 'Well,' he said, 'that's the way a country's made, ain't it? Not out of houses or bridges or railroads, but out of people. Still, I'd sure be pleased if you could name one of these passes for her, or maybe a railroad crossing or something.'

Collis looked at him. 'I'll try,' he said, in a gentle voice.

They were walled in by forests and high granite peaks as they made their way along the South Yuba valley, but the gradient was still gradual enough for a twelve-wheeled locomotive. Once the loose boulders had been cleared away, and the most awkward outcroppings of rock had been penetrated with picks and brought down with high explosives, there wasn't any doubt at all that a full twelve-car train of passengers and freight could steam its way from Sacramento, up the natural ramp between the American and the South Yuba rivers, through the crest of the Sierra Nevada where the South Yuba had etched its own valley, along by the Donner Lake, and as far as Collis and Theodore and Doc Kates and Wang-Pu had already managed to walk.

Theodore, in spite of his blisters, was growing more and more excited. He kept tugging at Collis's sleeve and nodding his frost-whitened beard in glee. 'It's fine so far,' he said. 'It's really fine.'

'You can really run a railroad through this valley?'

'No doubt about it. No doubt at all. We don't have to follow the riverbed – that twists and turns too much. We can cut a railroad bed into the slopes at the side. I did the same kind of thing at Niagara. It's not technically difficult. There's only one curve that I'm not too sure about, just above the lake, but we can always fill the side of the mountain, and that won't cost too much.'

'Are you sure about that?' asked Collis. 'That looks like solid granite to me.'

'Oh, I'm sure it's loose, most of it,' Theodore told him. 'Weathered down, and easy to shift. It won't take more than a few weeks to clear it away.'

'If you say so,' said Collis. 'I hope you're not being wildly optimistic.'

Theodore stopped walking and stared at him. His eyes were red-rimmed with cold, and his hair and beard were a thicket of sparkling icicles. 'I want to tell you something, Collis,' he said, in a hoarse, intent voice. 'A railroad is going to run through here, even if these mountains are made of solid iron.'

Collis stared back at him. Then he looked across at Wang-Pu, who was waiting a few feet away with silent patience, his coat tails blown by the wind. Wang-Pu gave him a look which meant, 'Time will tell'.

'Okay, Theodore,' Collis said and walked on.

The most dramatic moment of all came quietly. They were struggling down a slope of loose granite boulders when they came at last to a deep, sheltered valley. Behind them was the high crest of the Sierra Nevada; ahead of them was yet another crest, steep and forested and dark, and drifted with snow. From their right, from the south, splashing and bubbling over the black rocks of its granite bed, they saw a river, making its way down the valley until it forked, only a few hundred feet below them.

Doc Kates stopped. He made a sweeping gesture with his arm. 'This is it,' he said, in a voice congested by cold. 'This is the key to the whole thing. That river flows down from Lake Bigler, until it reaches here, and then it divides. This fork to your left is the South Yuba, which flows back the way we came, and into the Donner Lake, and then down through the mountains into California. But the other fork, ahead of us, that's the Truckee River, and that flows northeast, right around the base of these mountains, into Nevada.'

Theodore shaded his eyes and peered ahead, into the course of the Truckee. To the east, the river valley was wide, and far gentler than the twisting gorge of the South Yuba. A few gusts of snow made it difficult to see for very far, but Doc Kates said, 'It doesn't

433

get any worse than what you can make out from here. It's pretty well straight all the way.'

'It's incredible,' Theodore whispered. 'Look at it, Collis. It's incredible.'

Doc Kates added, 'If you walk straight ahead from here, you can cross into Nevada Territory in two, maybe three hours. Then the river crosses Steamboat Valley, and runs into the Washoe Mountains. From the Washoes, it bends northwest, but that doesn't matter, because you're out on to the Great Basin by then, and I shouldn't think you'd have any more need of it.'

Collis wiped snow from his face with the back of his glove. 'Well, professor,' he said to Theodore. 'It looks as if we're in the railroad business.'

Theodore looked across at him, and he was smiling irrepressibly. 'I believe you may be right.'

'It seems as if the mountains have given us their answer,' put in Wang-Pu with a smile.

'Very poetically put,' said Collis. 'But do you think your Chinese people could tackle this rock?'

'The Chinese are masters of persistence,' answered Wang-Pu. 'They will tackle this rock for you, no question at all. If you ask them to cut it, they will cut it, no matter what it takes.'

'What did I tell you?' Doc Kates said proudly. 'Didn't I tell you I'd found a trail?'

'Gentlemen,' said Theodore, 'I think this moment calls for a celebration.'

Doc Kates opened his knapsack and produced a bottle of home-distilled whisky. He wiped off the neck and passed it around, and each of them lifted it in turn, and then took a large swallow. The snow hurtled around them as they toasted the new railroad route, and on that dim slope of the Sierra Nevada they looked as tiny and faint as smudges on a frosty window.

'Here's to the Sierra Pacific,' Collis said and drank a mouthful. He coughed, and for a moment he could scarcely breathe. 'What's in this stuff?' he asked Doc Kates. 'Kerosene?'

'That's the finest sour-mash whisky,' protested Doc Kates. 'I always add a little surgical alcohol to give it pep.'

'I was damned lucky I wasn't smoking,' said Collis, passing the bottle back. 'I could have blown myself up like a keg of powder.'

It was nearly three o'clock now, and the snow was falling thicker. The clouds had turned a threatening shade of weathered lead, and

434

the wind was getting up again. 'Unless you want to make camp in the Truckee valley, I'd say we'd do well to beat the retreat,' Doc Kates said.

'It's only October,' said Theodore. 'This snow can't last too long.'

'You want to bet?' asked Doc Kates. 'Up at this height, I've been caught in snowstorms in late September. It depends on the wind, see. If the wind's from the northwest, you're in trouble.'

They tightened up their knapsacks, put away their whisky, and began to make their way back along the South Yuba valley, leaving the Truckee behind them, with its promise of Nevada, and the Great Basin, and the Rockies beyond. The wind was blowing so fiercely now that the snow flew horizontally, and they could hardly see which way they were going. Collis slipped twice into soft, knee-deep drifts, and he had to claw at the rough granite slopes to save himself. Ahead of him, as he struggled along, he could see Theodore's dark, bent figure; and a little way in front of Theodore, so blurred by the snow that he was hardly visible, except as a tantalising phantom, was Doc Kates. Collis turned once or twice, and there was Wang-Pu, his head lowered, coming up behind him.

It seemed as if they had been walking for days. The cold was unbearable. Collis lost his hat in the wind, and soon his hair and his eyebrows were thick with snow. His nose and his ears seemed to have swollen to three times their usual size, and he couldn't feel his hands at all. There was nothing ahead of him but flurrying white, and Theodore, and nothing behind him but Wang-Pu, and more flurrying white. If it hadn't been for Doc Kates, stolidly pushing forward in front of them, they would have been lost in minutes. Collis felt as if he were dreaming some exhausting, ridiculous dream, in which the whole world had burst open like a pillow fight, whirling with goose feathers, and smothered in impossible softness.

When they reached the crest of the Sierras, the snowstorm hit them with its full force. The wind was so devastating that Collis could hardly breathe. Doc Kates had waited for them, his face ghastly with cold, and he shouted, 'Keep going! It's mostly downhill from here! Just keep going!' Theodore raised one snow-gloved hand to show that he understood.

The next hour was an agony of white. Collis' eyelashes were crusted with ice, so that even blinking against the wind was painful. And although it was past six o'clock now, and the sky was a grim, impenetrable grey, he still had to keep his face screwed up against the brilliance of the snow, and his cheek muscles felt as if they were frozen into a hideous grimace. The Yuba valley was deep with drifts, and so they had to lift each leg up out of the snow as they walked, like exhausted performing horses. Collis saw Theodore stumble and fall twice, and even Doc Kates was slowing up.

Collis closed his eyes and concentrated on walking. The snow pelted against his eyelids. He knew that he was going to have to collapse soon, and give up this insanity for good. What was the point of walking when it didn't get you any place at all, except a few yards further in the same shrieking wind, and the same numbing snow? What was the point of struggling when there was no hope of winning anyway?

Collis opened his eyes. In front of him, Theodore had fallen into the snow. Collis pranced forward as quickly as he could, panting with effort. He took hold of Theodore under the arms of his frozen coat and tried to pull him upright. Theodore raised himself a little, but then fell sideways, and lay in the deep snow with his face coated white.

'Theodore!' yelled Collis. He glanced up desperately, and he could see Doc Kates gradually vanishing into the blizzard.

'Theodore, get up, for Christ's sake!'

Theodore's eyes were open, but he didn't appear to see Collis at all. He gave a weak shake of his head and mumbled, 'Can't. Too cold.'

'You have to! If we lose Doc Kates, then we're finished! Get up off your ass and move!'

The wind was whistling and whooping all around them, and Collis had to lean forward to hear what Theodore was saying.

'Go on,' whispered Theodore. 'Go on without me. Take my maps, notebook.'

'Don't be so damned stupid! Get up, and walk!'

'I can't, Collis. I've had it. I'm too cold.'

Collis stood up, peering ahead for any sign of Doc Kates. But the ferocious whiteness enclosed them on every side, and Doc Kates was gone.

'Theodore!' he shouted. 'Get up, you dumb bastard! Think about Annie!'

Theodore closed his eyes. 'I can't.'

Collis looked back the way they'd come, to see if he could make out any sign of Wang-Pu. But the snow was so thick that Wang-Pu

436

could have walked straight past them only seven or eight feet away, and they wouldn't even have seen him.

Collis leaned close to Theodore's ear. 'Listen, you railroading idiot,' he said tersely, 'if you don't get your carcass out of this snow and start walking, then none of this railroad is ever going to be named after you. Not one grade, not one curve, not one damned whistlestop. We won't even have a Theodore Jones latrine.'

Theodore raised his head. 'Damn you, Edmonds,' he said.

Collis reached out his hand. Theodore stared at it for a long moment, blinking the snowflakes from his eyes. Then he slowly lifted his own hand and let Collis clasp it, and with numb, wooden movements, he climbed to his feet. Collis held him for a while, held him close, until he regained his balance against the wind; then Theodore nodded, to show that he was going to try to make it on his own, and he shuffled forwards, pausing now and again to rest. Collis stayed close, supporting him, pushing him, and keeping him upright when the wind was gusting its worst.

They were protected for a while by pine trees growing along the ridge that overlooked the South Yuba River. The blizzard sounded strangely ghostly and hollow here, as if the mountains were haunted, and the pines waved at them like desperate people trapped in a nightmare.

Then they were out in the open again. They were making their way downwards, they knew that much. But any other sense of direction was smothered by snow, and a wind that shrieked across the slopes was as cold and overwhelming as a torrential wave of seawater. Collis slid and fell, and rolled for twenty feet down a steep embankment, choked with snow. But he was unhurt, and he managed to pick himself up again and wait for Theodore to come staggering slowly down the slope and catch up.

'How are you feeling?' Collis shouted at Theodore.

Theodore shook his head. 'I can't go on much longer.'

'We're going down the mountain all the time,' Collis told him, pointing with his gloved hand so that Theodore understood. 'We should get out of this snowstorm soon.'

Theodore didn't answer, but stared at him with reddened eyes.

'Let's go!' yelled Collis, pushing him forward.

Collis remembered afterwards how the tiredness in his legs and the stupefying cold had almost brought him down. He remembered stumbling across stinging slopes of wind-whipped drifts, ready to collapse, and yet kept upright by the drifts themselves, two and

437

three feet deep. He remembered heaving Theodore out of the snow again and again, getting him on his feet, shoving him bodily forward, even when he had hardly any strength to carry on himself. He remembered cursing Theodore with every curse he could think of, just to get him moving; and he remembered cursing God, and the snow, and Doc Kates, and life itself.

But the snow eased as they lost altitude, and in an hour or two they found themselves making their way through the forests in nothing worse than a heavy sleet. It was still cold, but the blizzard was behind them, and they barged through the darkness with the jerky, uncontrolled energy of exhausted men who know that they have made it through the worst. They didn't speak now, not even to swear at each other. They were utterly tired, and quaking with cold.

Theodore reached out and held Collis's shoulder to slow him down.

'Do you know where we are?' he asked him thickly.

Collis took out a handkerchief that was already soaked through and wiped the rain from his face. 'I haven't a clue. But we can't be far off the trail. We haven't crossed the American River, or the South Yuba, so we must be going west.'

'I hope to God you're right. I think I could have crossed the Rio Grande in that snow, and not even noticed.'

They kept on until they were deep among the trees. There was a fragrance of wet pine needles, and their footsteps were muffled. It was so dark that Theodore kept bumping into tree-trunks, and swearing under his breath. They let gravity guide them; let their own tiredness draw them downhill. They lost their footing on loose rocks from time to time, and Collis wrenched his ankle on a tangled pine root. But they could listen to that devouring wind blowing high above them, and the way the rain rattled through the branches, and know that they were safe.

The fire at Bradley Hay camp only had to wink at them once through the swaying lodgepole pines. Collis stopped, resting against the rough bark of the trees. 'Did you see that?' he asked Theodore.

'It's Bradley Hay Camp. It must be,' Theodore said.

'Thank Christ.'

It took them another five minutes to climb down the steep, sodden slope that enclosed the camp on the south side. But then they were crossing the trail, and there were the cabins, and outside them was a high fire of dry pine logs, stacked like a tepee, flaring and spitting in the rain. Collis supported Theodore with his shoulder for the final few yards, but they reached the cabin door at last, and inside was Doc Kates, sitting by a woodburning stove, with his coffee-pot boiling, and his mountain-climbing boots set out to dry.

The old man stood up. There were holes in his socks and his toes showed through. His eyes brimmed with tears. 'Thank merciful God you've made it. Thank merciful God. I believed I'd lost you.'

He helped Theodore to sit by the stove. Collis sat down beside him, unlacing his boots. Doc Kates brought out mugs and poured them both coffee.

'Did Wang-Pu get here yet?' asked Collis. 'We thought he might have passed us in the snow.'

Doc Kates frowned. 'I kind of guessed you three would all be together.'

Collis looked at Theodore. It hadn't occurred to him that Wang-Pu might have been left behind in the blizzard. He'd assumed that the Chinaman's natural wit and instinct for survival would have brought him safely down from the Sierras without any need for help from the stumbling white devils. He thought of the quiet, sarcastic man from the Great Wall of China and bit at his lip in anxiety.

'Maybe we should go back and try finding him,' he said, without conviction. He knew he was too tired to stand, let alone walk for miles up the mountains in the dark.

'It won't do any good,' Doc Kates said. 'You'd never find him now, not unless he was heading dead this way. Let's just hope he had enough sense to keep on going downhill, and didn't slip and break his leg.'

Theodore stared at his steaming mug of coffee. 'My God,' he said. 'I hope he's all right.'

They sat in silence for a while. The wind whistled over the moss-covered cabin roof. 'We can go first thing in the morning, if the snow's died down,' Doc Kates said. 'You should have your strength back then.'

'Can a man survive out there, in that snow?' asked Collis. 'Have you ever known it to happen?'

Doc Kates rubbed at his beard. 'Not in walking-clothes, as he was. He wouldn't stand a chance. He'd get tired, and he'd lie down, and that would be the end of it.'

'We can only pray that he managed to get down below the snowline,' Theodore said.

'Yes,' answered Doc Kates. 'I'm afraid that's all we can do.'

The next morning was bright, and the sky was so blue it was almost violet. They ate sausages and beans on the stoop outside the cabin, and then they packed up their knapsacks to go look for Wang-Pu. Collis felt as if he'd been pummelled all over by playful bears, and his legs were stiff and patched with bruises. But the wind was fresh and mild, and the smell of the pine forests was curiously refreshing, and after he'd eaten he was ready to go back up the mountains and face the snow.

They climbed for an hour, skirting the woods, because Doc Kates reckoned that Wang-Pu's likeliest descent would have been close to the way that Theodore and Collis had come down. They hardly talked at all. Theodore coughed now and again, and blew his nose, and it looked to Collis as if he was coming down with the grippe. The day was very warm and serene, and the only sounds were the trickling of melting snow and the chirping of kinglets. Above the forests, whenever they came out on bare granite escarpments, they could see the peaks of the Sierra Nevada stretching majestically for fifty miles. The mountains were still surrounded with clouds, still as forbidding, but the wind had changed again during the night, and Doc Kates guessed that any threat of a snowstorm was well past.

They crossed and recrossed the trail seven or eight times. They scrambled down rocky gullies and trudged up long drifts of soft snow. The sun passed over their heads at noon and they were still looking, their eyes crinkled against the glare, their shadows on the snow around their knees.

Collis never forgot the moment when they found him. It was past five o'clock, and the sun was low, but still hot. The deeper violet skies of the morning and early afternoon had faded into a silvery lilac, and the snow was tinged with the same delicate colour. They passed an outcropping of black rocks and came to a triangular field of snow, smooth and unmarked with footprints. Theodore was coughing.

Doc Kates shaded his eyes with his hand. 'What's that?' he said.

Collis looked. He couldn't see anything at all. But Doc Kates pointed. 'There. Just to the left of those rocks.'

Collis screwed up his eyes. He was almost blinded by the sunlight. By the side of a small angular boulder, perched on the snow as if someone had just dropped it there, was Wang-Pu's tall silk hat.

They didn't have the strength to run. They crossed the triangular slope doggedly, churning up the snow as they went. They reached the hat, and Theodore picked it up. The label read, 'Weingott & Son, Hatters, San Francisco,' and Theodore said, 'Yes. This is Wang-Pu's.'

They split up, and searched the slope until they had patterned the smooth wind-blown surface like a white maze. It didn't look as if there was anything there at all, rabbit, bird, or raccoon, let alone a lost Chinaman. But then Collis climbed the rocks to see if he could make out any signs of Wang-Pu from higher up, and he found him.

The rocks had formed a roughly rectangular depression, and in this depression Wang-Pu rested, on a bed of snow, as if he were lying in state on a bier. His face was grey, and his lips were rimed with frost, where his last breaths had been frozen by the wind. One arm lay crookedly across his chest.

Collis turned and called, 'Theodore!'

Theodore, half-way across the snowy slope, looked up. So did Doc Kates. Collis said, more quietly, 'He's here.'

They shipped Wang-Pu's body on the paddle-steamer *Ulysses* back to his Chinese friends in San Francisco. It was a soft, sunny October morning, and they stood on the banks of the Sacramento River watching the steamer turn its wheels and slowly make its way downstream. A few yards away, dressed in white costumes with sleeves that billowed in the wind, stood five or six members of the Yeong Wo family, the Chinese fruit farmers of the Sacramento Valley whom Wang-Pu had befriended.

Charles put his hat back on his head. 'Well,' he said, 'there isn't anything more to be done.'

Leland, who was looking hot, said, 'That's as may be. But it doesn't bode well for the railroad, does it, if a man can die of frostbite in the middle of October on the very route which we're proposing to use for the conveyance of mothers and children?'

Jane was holding on to Leland's arm, her face shaded by a primrose parasol, which lent her pale face a bright and bilious hue of yellow. She was making it obvious these days that Collis was no longer her favourite, and that she mistrusted his intentions.

'That blizzard was a freak,' Collis said. 'Doc Kates said so, anyway. It doesn't usually blow as bad as that in October; and even if it does, we can keep the railroad track protected with snowsheds.'

'Don't you feel any sorrow for Wang-Pu?' demanded Leland.

'He was our trusted servant for years. How can you go on with this, after the way he died?'

Collis took out a cheroot. 'You may have been acquainted with Wang-Pu for years, Leland, but you never knew him. Not as I did. So don't talk to me about sorrow, or grieving. I've said my own prayers for Wang-Pu, and when we build this railroad he'll be remembered.'

Charles cleared his throat. 'Talking of railroads, Collis, I think it's time we sat down and had a serious discussion about the Sierra Pacific.'

'You've got cold feet? Because of Wang-Pu?'

'It's not so much Wang-Pu. It's the whole enterprise. Leland and I have been talking about it a great deal since you've been away.'

They were walking along the riverfront now, towards their carriages. Collis paused to light his cheroot. 'What have you decided?' he asked them, puffing smoke. 'That a railroad can't really be built, and that the Sierra Pacific Company ought to become the rubber-hose and tallow-candle subsidiary of Tucker & McCormick?'

'It's a question of profitability,' growled Leland. 'There isn't any evidence to show that a transcontinental railroad will ever be adequately used. The people who live in the East want to stay in the East; and the people who live in the West don't want the Easterners to-ing and fro-ing through the lands they've come to call their own.'

Collis smiled at Leland indulgently. 'You're frightened, aren't you?' he said. 'You're frightened of financial risk, frightened of the outside world, frightened of competition. Well – all I can say is that a grown man like you should pluck up his courage and face whatever the world has to bring.'

'Your damned insolence never improves, does it?' said Leland.

'Personal criticisms apart, Collis, are you sure that Theodore knows what he's doing?' asked Charles. 'He's always been called Pacific-railroad-crazy. Maybe he's so enthusiastic about taking a train over the Sierras that he's seen that pass through rosy-tinted glasses.'

Collis climbed up into the carriage, sat back, and took off his hat. 'I saw the pass for myself,' he told his partners. 'And more than that, I damned nearly died up there, and so did Theodore. But when we run the railroad through the Donner Pass, and the Truckee River, all our passengers are going to be safe and snug, and they'll be able to look out of the windows at the slopes where Wang-Pu died, and sip their coffee, and not know a damned thing about it. You ought to go talk to Doc Kates sometime, up at Dutch Flat. He says that America was built out of people, and he's right.'

Leland tugged at his collar. 'You may be right,' he said stiffly. 'Your pass may be just the trace we've been looking for. But Charles and I have decided absolutely that the railroad doesn't have to go further than Nevada. We can make an excellent annual profit by supplying the towns and mining camps there, and all along the way, and we certainly don't need to waste money on airy-fairy dreams of going all the way through to Salt Lake City. For God's sake, man, who wants to travel across the Humboldt Desert?'

Collis didn't feel in the mood for pushing Leland any further. When Leland was feeling pontifical, all a reasonable man could do was nod, and say yes, and move anything combustible out of range. What was worse, Leland had his wife's support today, although it was more out of spite for Collis than love of her husband, and with Jane holding on to his arm and saying 'That's right, Leland,' and 'Of course, Leland,' the president of the Sierra Pacific Railroad felt that every word he spoke was of Biblical moment.

'We didn't build up the hardware business on risk, Collis,' Charles put in. 'So there isn't any reason to start now.'

Collis nodded. 'Very well. Let's talk about it later. Right now, I'm going back to the store to see what's happened to those cases of fuse that were supposed to come up from San Francisco this morning.'

Mary Tucker, in a pale print frock and a bonnet that made her face look like the moon, said, 'We haven't talked about a replacement for poor Wang-Pu.'

'I'm going to San Francisco in a couple of months,' Collis told her. 'I know some of Wang-Pu's friends. Maybe I can find somebody suitable.'

Leland raised his chin and pouted. 'Just make sure you pick somebody honest, with references, and make sure you bring them back here for us to vet.'

'I don't trust the Chinks,' said Jane. 'Not the usual run-of-the-mill Chinks. They burn all their old newspapers and think it's magic. They steal, too, and sell young girls for slaves.'

'Yes,' said Collis, 'they do all of those things. They're nearly as corrupt and superstitious as we are.'

Jane looked at Collis with eyes like boot buttons, trying to convey in one plain glare all that she felt about the way he had led her on, and excited her, and then let her down. Collis had what he wanted, and so he simply nodded his head in a gesture that anyone else would have taken for respect.

Back at 54 K Street, Collis found a portly man in a gravy-stained vest and whiskers waiting for him, sitting on the steps with a rolled-up newspaper tucked in his coat pocket. It was George P. Kemp, of the *Sacramento Record*, and he'd come to talk about the new railroad pass over the Sierra Nevada. He stood up as Collis climbed down from his carriage and brushed dust from the seat of his pants.

'Are you Collis Edmonds?' he called.

'That's right.'

'Well, sir,' said George Kemp, extending his hand, 'allow me to congratulate you. You're now famous.'

'Thank you,' said Collis. 'Won't you come inside? We were about to open a bottle of sherry.'

Meanwhile, the *Ulysses* carried Wang-Pu's body in its plain pine coffin around the second wide bend in the Sacramento River, and the city where Wang-Pu had lived and worked disappeared from view.

That night, late, Collis walked down to the river on his own. The trees whispered among themselves in the evening wind. In his hand, Collis carried an envelope. It contained the ashes of a short letter he had written to Wang-Pu, wishing him peace and happiness, wherever he was going. Collis didn't know if what he was doing was the right thing, according to Wang-Pu's religion, but he guessed it didn't matter too much if Wang-Pu's spirit got to hear what he had written.

He stood for a while by the steep riverbank, watching the Sacramento slide by. A black labourer was sitting against a tree not far away, humming an endless sad melody that he was obviously making up as he went along.

Eventually, Collis lifted the envelope and spun it out over the river. It fell flat on the water, and turned around, and then the current carried it away. Collis, under his breath, said, 'Goodbye'.

He waited a little longer, and then he walked back along K Street, and it seemed that night as if the whole of California was warm and silent for the last memory of Wang-Pu.

As it turned out, it was nearly a year before Collis next took the steamer down to San Francisco. It was a dull year, a year of consolidating the hardware partnership, a year of trying to drum up interest from disinterested investors in the railroad route over the Sierras, a year of smoking too much, drinking too much, and staring out over the Sacramento Valley and thinking of Hannah. Young Frederick Pugh did most of Wang-Pu's work, and did it smartly and well, although Collis was still anxious to hire a Chinese to help with those wharfside deals that called for subtlety and oriental skill.

But in the early fall of 1859, tired and tanned from a long Sacramento summer, Collis boarded the *Excelsior* and sailed for the coast. He knew that there was a strong possibility of buying up a cargo of rope from the Far East. He wanted to talk to Andy Hunt, too, whose interest in the railroad had been slipping, and persuade him that the route they'd discovered over the Sierra Nevada was ideal for a transcontinental line. Andy was determined when he wanted to be, and Collis badly needed his support against Leland's ponderous doubts and Charles's impossible bluster.

He lunched at Gobey's Ladies and Gents Oyster Parlour on Sutter Street before he went to talk to Andy. He wanted to think out the best way to win Andy over, and apart from that, it was cheaper to eat on his own, since Andy had a knack of excusing himself and going to the men's room whenever the waiter brought the check. He sat at the worn, scratched table, supping crab stew out of a deep white bowl and breaking fresh sourdough bread. Just opposite, a fat man with red cheeks and a green tailcoat was sitting in the yellow sunlight that fell through the stained-glass windows, talking loudly about Ah Toy, San Francisco's first Chinese madam, and how elegant she used to be.

'A soiled dove of the finest feather,' the fat man remarked, and laughed.

Collis left the restaurant a little after two o'clock and walked to Andy's office to help digest his food. The afternoon was cloudy and close, and he had to take off his hat from time to time and wipe his forehead. He wondered if he ought to pay a visit to the Kong Chow Temple and light a candle for Wang-Pu. He'd drunk too much champagne with his meal and he felt light-headed.

Just as he was turning the corner of Stockton Street, a dark-blue carriage drew up beside him, its horses shaking their bridles, and the coachman called, 'Sir! Mr Edmonds, sir!'

Collis stopped and looked up first at the silk-hatted coachman and then inside the carriage itself. It was a small enclosed brougham, with dark-blue drapes at the windows to match the paintwork, and so it was difficult to make out who was inside. Only when he saw the gilded initial M on the door did he realise who it was. Somebody unlatched the door from inside, and half-opened it, and from the way the coachman conscientiously turned his head the other way, Collis gathered that he was expected to climb aboard.

It was shadowy inside, and perfumed. And sitting back on the blue velvet cushions like a single white lily in a garden of lilies of the Nile was Sarah Melford. She wore a bonnet decorated with white petals and carried a white fan. Her wide-apart eyes stared at Collis unblinkingly as he took off his hat and sat down awkwardly on the opposite seat.

'Mr Edmonds,' she said in her breathy voice. 'I was so surprised when I saw it was you. I haven't seen you for such a long time. I had to ask Martin to stop.'

She lifted her hand, and Collis took it. 'I'm honoured to meet you again,' he said in a cautious voice.

'Are you here for long?' asked Sarah. 'I thought your business usually kept you in Sacramento.'

Collis released her hand. 'I'm in town to drum up some support for my railroad. Among other things.'

'Ah, yes. Your railroad. Father mentioned it only yesterday. There was quite a long article in the *Bulletin* about it.'

'What did they say?'

Sarah Melford smiled vaguely. 'They said you were very heroic, as a matter of fact, the way you found a pass over the Sierra Nevada. But they didn't believe the tracks would ever be laid.'

She paused. Collis said nothing.

'Is it true that you nearly died?' she asked. 'Or was that just some newspaper reporter's imagination?'

'It's true,' he told her.

'Well, then,' she said, 'I have to say that I'm glad you survived.'

'What did your father think?'

'Father? Not much. I think he was impressed, though. He said you might even have the damned nerve to carry it off. The railroad, he meant.'

Collis looked down at his hat. 'I'm not sure if I can,' he said quietly. 'We lost one of our friends up there, in the mountains And I don't think my fellow investors are exactly lion-hearted, to say the least.'

'I'm sorry,' she said.

'You don't have to be.'

She turned her profile towards the opposite window. The daylight was diffuse and pale. Through the fine material of her dress he could make out her deep shadowy cleavage, and the firm shape of her breasts. She was a very desirable girl. He wondered what it was that cautioned him to keep his distance from her.

'I don't want to detain you,' he said. 'Where were you going?'

'Only to my dressmaker's. I have a fitting this afternoon, for a ballgown.'

'Wouldn't your father be annoyed if he knew we'd met?'

'Of course. But Martin won't tell him. Martin's very practised at keeping his mouth closed.'

Collis waited for a while, but Sarah Melford didn't appear to have anything more to say. 'Was that all you wanted?' he asked. 'Just to say hello?'

'Is there anything wrong in that?' she asked him.

He shook his head. 'I don't think so. It depends why you wanted to do it. Elegant young ladies don't usually invite strange men into their carriages unless they have something particular in mind.'

'Is that how they think in New York?' Sarah wanted to know.

'They did the last time I was there.'

'Well, in that case, they must have very prurient imaginations.'

'If you say so.'

Sarah Melford coloured. 'I do. I don't even know what you're trying to suggest.'

'I wasn't trying to suggest anything,' Collis told her with a smile. 'I was just wondering if you found me interesting because I spared your brother's life, or because your father finds me eminently suspicious, or because I have rather more life in me than most of the plump young Californian drones that your parents seem to invite to their parties.'

Sarah brushed her skirt straight. 'You're being very insulting. There are plenty of young men in California worth fifty of you.'

'Well, I know that,' said Collis, 'but the way your father sees it, the problem with Californian men is that the virile ones are far too uncouth, while the couth ones have about as much masculinity as a ripe cantaloupe.'

Sarah stared at him. Her eyes were fascinating. They were liquid, deep, and dark. She looked shocked for a moment by what he had said, but then suddenly she pursed her lips and let out a burst of laughter.

447

'I can't believe it,' she said. 'You're quite as terrible as everybody says you are.'

Collis reached across the carriage and took her hand between his. 'Shall we meet again sometime?'

'We may,' said Sarah. She spread her fan. 'Now you'd better go, before Martin is tempted to jump to conclusions.'

'I thought he could keep a secret.'

'He can. But some conclusions are harder to keep secret than others.'

Collis lifted Sarah's hand, kissed it gently, and then reached for his hat. 'It's been a pleasure,' he said, and opened the brougham's door.

He climbed down to the street again and stood on the corner watching as the carriage wheeled around and went on its way along Sutter. Then he continued his walk to Andy Hunt's office. He felt a little unreal, as if what had happened was the kind of dream you can have between sleeping and waking, bright with unexpected images, warm with imaginary smiles.

Collis didn't spend a very satisfactory afternoon with Andy Hunt. Andy was tied up with a business problem involving a Chinese shrimp camp, and he had only half an ear for Collis's difficulties with Leland and Charles over the railroad.

'As long as we make a profit, what's the difference?' he kept asking, as he shuffled the heaps of paper on his desk, in search of a dried-abalone contract. 'That's what we're in it for, aren't we? Profit?'

'Of course we are,' said Collis. 'But we're not going to net the greatest profits unless we take the greatest risk.'

Andy looked up at him. 'I've already handed over five thousand dollars. What more do you want me to do?'

'I want you to have faith,' said Collis.

Andy found the contract he was looking for. 'I have faith on Sundays,' he said. 'The rest of the week I have judgement.'

'I see.' Collis tiredly rubbed his face. 'Well – can I count on your favourable judgement, even if I can't count on anything else?'

Andy frowned, as if he hadn't understood a word they'd been talking about. 'Do you know that abalone is a Spanish word?' he said. 'I always used to think it was Chinese.'

Collis never knew why he tried again. He used to think about it, years later, and all that he could remember was that he had an hour to spare before he was due to go to the Western Mercantile Bank and discuss the raising of loans for survey equipment, and that he was walking south on Montgomery looking into store windows and wondering what expensive little treat might mollify Jane McCormick when he got back to Sacramento. He saw some spermwhale teeth, carved into the shape of clowns, and some of Shreve & Company's delicate European china, but he couldn't imagine Jane's being particularly pleased with whale's teeth or hand-painted plates. He paused in front of a cosmetic-store window, shading his eyes against the reflections on the glass, and examined some of their soaps and spices. Then he moved next door to a bric-à-brac store, and inspected their Chinese ivory and their French fans.

It was only then that he raised his eyes and looked at the image in the dusty window. There, reversed was Montgomery Street, with a covered wagon shaking its way past, and there reversed, was the store across the way. Over the shopfront were the words TSEW RETLAW, and standing on the boardwalk outside, his hands behind his back, was Walter West himself, enjoying the hazy afternoon sunshine.

Collis stayed where he was, watching the reflection. A woman in a wide bustling dress had to push past him, all fuss and flounces, and he raised his hat to her, but wouldn't move. He took out his watch and saw that he had forty minutes left before his appointment at four o'clock.

Walter West paced along the front of his store, as if he were waiting for somebody. He paced back again. Five minutes passed. The clouds cleared away from the sun, and the street was brighter again.

Quite suddenly, Walter West disappeared into his store. A moment later, he reappeared, with his hat. Collis saw him turn and say something to somebody inside, and then walk quickly northwards on Montgomery Street, as far as California, and turn right, out of sight.

Collis licked his lips. He waited for one minute more, just to make certain that Walter West wasn't going to come back, and then he turned and crossed the street. He stopped at the store door, his chest feeling tight and his heart beating uncomfortably quickly. Then he stepped inside, into the shade that smelled of linen dressing and lint, and approached the counter.

She was there, her head bent over a box of small white buttons, which she was sorting into sizes. Her blonde hair was pinned up with mother-of-pearl combs, and she was wearing a plain blue-grey dress. Collis stood at the counter watching her, and it seemed compellingly clear why he wanted her so much, and what she had done to attract him in Panama. He couldn't put the clarity of his thought into words. It was a revelation more than an idea. He just knew that he loved her.

'I won't be a moment, sir,' she said, as she picked out buttons.

Collis didn't answer at first. He was looking at the perfect curve of her forehead, and the straightness of her nose. She had more colour now, and she didn't seem so emaciated. Sarah Melford might be dark and captivating, an aristocratic young beauty with poise and *hauteur*, but Hannah had something that reminded Collis of the brightness of sun behind trees, the dazzling reflection from a lake, the tremble of fuchsia in San Francisco's afternoon gardens.

'I'd like a workbox, please,' Collis said quietly. 'Something for my niece.'

Hannah raised her head. The buttons she was sorting spilled across the counter. Some of the larger ones wobbled and wobbled and at last lay flat. '*Collis*,' she whispered.

He tried to give her a smile, but she couldn't quite manage it. 'I thought I'd call by to see how you were.'

She touched her hair, as if suddenly conscious that she looked untidy. 'I'm well,' she said, breathlessly. 'At least, I'm much better. But how are you? I read about your expedition in the mountains last year, but I haven't heard anything since.'

'I'm all right. Three of us got out of it with nothing more than frostbite. I lost a good friend, though, frozen to death. A Chinaman.'

'That's terrible. They said you were looking for a railroad route?'

'We found one,' Collis told her.

'He didn't die in vain, then. Your Chinaman.'

'I guess not.'

She lowered her eyes. 'You're still going ahead with your railroad? I didn't know if you were or not.'

'Women and children are still having to cross the Panama isthmus.'

She didn't look up. 'I suppose you're talking about me '

Collis picked up one of the buttons and twiddled it between his fingers. 'In a way,' he told her.

450

She gave a quick, understanding smile. A mahogany wall clock chimed half past four.

'You remember that first night in Aspinwall?' he asked. 'I saw the train standing outside the hotel, in the street, and that was when I first began to think that a Pacific railroad was possible. If a train could cross an isthmus, why not a continent?'

He paused, and then added in his gentlest voice, 'The point is, knowing that something's possible isn't the same as having the inspiration to make it come true. I didn't get that inspiration until I fell in love with you.'

'You mustn't say that,' she said softly. 'I don't know how you can.'

'Why not? Because you said you didn't want to see me again? Because of Walter?'

'I don't know. Because of everything.'

'You think I don't mean it?'

She lifted her head and gazed at him. 'Yes,' she said, 'I think you mean it. But I can't think why.'

Collis gave her a wry grin. 'I can't think why, either. But what does it matter?'

'It matters a great deal. You're not supposed to love me. You shouldn't have come here.'

'I was just walking past. I thought I'd like to see you again.'

'Even after everything I said?'

He nodded.

'You must have thought I was a righteous shrew,' she said, with a soft self-chastisement that startled him.

'I don't know what I thought,' he told her in a puzzled voice.

She laid her hands flat on the counter and spread the buttons across the glass. 'You thought everything I wanted you to think. You thought that I was a plain, sickly woman, with more than a touch of religious hysteria. You thought that all I wanted to be was Walter's faithful companion, and that I was happy to spend the rest of my life sorting buttons and cutting lengths of lisle. You thought that everything we lived through, and said, in Panama was nothing more than the silly intoxicated daydream of a woman who didn't have the courage of her convictions, or of her own feelings.'

Collis frowned. 'I don't understand what you're trying to say.

Hannah looked up at him proudly, a little defiantly. 'I won't pretend that I didn't try to purge my affection for you out of my soul. I prayed with the nuns in Panama City. I talked especially with

451

Sister Agnes, and confessed what I was feeling for you. She said I should seek help from the Holy Mother, who would guide me back into the sanctity of marriage, and she said that I should forget you.'

'Sister Agnes said that?'

'Yes,' Hannah whispered. 'And I believed that she was right. I came to San Francisco, and I was determined to make my marriage with Walter work. If I saw you, I was going to say that whatever had passed between us was understandable, and forgivable, but nothing more than infatuation.'

'You did it, too, didn't you?'

'Yes.' She nodded. 'But you have to remember that I was sick. Maybe it doesn't sound like a very good excuse, now that I'm better. But I was weaker than a baby, and I didn't have the strength to do anything but survive from day to day. As long as I stayed alive, I didn't care about love. And poor Walter was so kind. He nursed me, and fed me, and cared for me as nobody else could have done. No, Collis, not even you.'

Collis cleared his throat. 'I guess Walter *is* the motherly type.'

She smiled sadly. 'You mustn't be unkind about him.'

'I don't mean to be. I guess I'm just confused. I don't know what I expected when I came in here, but this isn't it.'

'*I* expected never to see you again, ever,' Hannah said. 'Not to talk to, anyway.'

'You're trying to tell me that everything you said was untrue? Hannah – you're trying to tell me you still *love* me?'

She didn't answer. Collis shook his head in disbelief. 'What about Walter?'

'I told him everything that happened. Everything about us. I had to.'

'What for? You could have made out that we were nothing more than travelling companions.'

'I know. But I didn't tell him for *his* sake. I told him for mine. I thought that if I confessed everything that I'd felt about you – well, I thought I wouldn't feel it any longer.'

There was a moment of intense quiet between them. People passed on the boardwalk outside, and carriages clattered along Montgomery Street, but all their attention was focused on themselves, and what they had come to mean to each other. Looking back, Collis wasn't at all sure how it had happened. It hadn't started with flirting, or stolen kisses, as his affairs usually did. There hadn't been any coquettish loveplay, of the kind that

452

Delphine had once enjoyed; but then Delphine's affection had shown itself for what it really was. There wasn't any of Sarah Melford's aristocratic suggestiveness, either.

Yet there was a natural closeness, a feeling of peace, and a warmth that Collis could only interpret as his first experience of a mature and complex love. He realised, with respect and amazement, that none of their arguments had done anything to spoil it. He said, intently, 'Hannah.'

She looked at him, and her eyes were glistening with tears. 'You'll never know how much I've missed you,' she said. 'I fought and fought, and I prayed every night, and I still couldn't forget you. These past two years, I've thought about you and nobody else.'

Collis moved aside a stack of hat boxes and came around the glass-topped counter. He held out his hand, and she took it. 'You mustn't stay too long,' she said. 'Walter's only gone as far as the Wells Fargo office.'

'What if he comes back?' said Collis. 'If you still love me, and if you want me, then he's got to find out some time.'

'I can't hurt him, Collis. He's a very gentle man.'

'So what are you going to do? Stay with him for the rest of your life, masquerading as his affectionate spouse?'

She gave a nervous shake of her head. 'I don't know. Oh, Collis, I'm very muddled. I was all ready to believe that I'd never see you again.'

Collis squeezed her hand tight. he could feel her wedding band. She seemed so slight and small that he felt he could have picked her up in his arms, like a child. He said, almost as if it were a question, 'Kiss me?'

She stared at him. 'I can't. Walter will be back at any moment.'

'Then the quicker you do it, the less danger there is.'

'Collis, I can't.'

He drew her close. She tried to pull herself away, but he wasn't going to let her. He bent forward and touched his lips against her cheek, and then against her lips, and then there was nothing that she wanted to do to stop him. She could feel the roughness of his dark-shaved chin, and smell the blend of spicy cologne and tobacco that would always remind her of the days they had spent on the *Virginia*. She parted her lips just a little.

They stood away from each other. They were still holding hands. They could have been an engaged couple in a photographer's studio, posing to celebrate their betrothal. Her hair shone around her head like a halo, and her face was vivid with excitement and relief, and with fear too, of what she would have to do next.

'I won't push you, Hannah,' Collis said. 'I don't think either of us could stand it. You have to be sure.'

She looked at him as if she wanted him to tell her, here and now, that everything was changed, that her life with Walter was over, and that he would take her away this afternoon. But then she gently took her hand away, and dropped her gaze, and tried to accept what he had to say.

'I have to stay in San Francisco until Monday,' he told her. 'Why don't you think, during the week, what you really want to do, and then let me know what you've decided before I leave.'

'Collis,' she said, 'I'm not at all sure that's the best way. I mean what if Walter – '

Collis pressed his forehead with his fingertips. 'Hannah, there isn't any other way, not for us, not now. If you're going to leave Walter, you'll have to leave him openly, and with dignity, and for good.'

'It would mean divorce,' she said.

'Yes,' Collis told her, 'I know. That's why I think you have to spend a few days making up your mind.'

She looked across the store, at the bolts of fabric, at the windows, at the plaster girl in her party dress. 'I believe God meant us to be happy, Collis. I believe that now.'

'If I hadn't come here today, what would you have done? Would you have stayed with Walter?'

She gave him a wry smile. 'Yes, I expect so. But life is made out of accidents, isn't it? It was an accident us meeting in the first place. If it hadn't been for Mrs Edgeworth, I would have sailed to California by a later ship. As it was . . .'

She paused. She shrugged. Collis reached out and touched a stray curl of blonde hair.

'I'll tell you what I'll do,' he said quietly. 'On Sunday afternoon, I'll take a ride out to Mission Dolores. I'll be there by three o'clock. I'll wait by the flagpole in front of the porch for an hour. If you really want to give up Walter, and if you really want to stay with me, then take a Yellow Line coach out there and meet me. If you don't, well, I'll wait until four, and then I'll go home.'

At the Eagle Saloon on Thursday evening, Collis met Dan McReady, who took him down to a Chinese restaurant on

Sacramento Street called Dear's. There were red-lacquered lanterns swinging outside in the summer wind, and the fragrance of five-spice powder and honey was wafting from the back.

They pushed their way through a beaded curtain into a low-ceilinged room, where Chinese sat at low tables, eating with chopsticks from dishes of prawns and bamboo shoots and stir-fried vegetables. There were one or two white devils there, too, eating with knives and forks. Dear's was a favourite among Western businessmen from the financial district, mainly because the proprietor spoke broken English, and the proprietor's daughter was delicately pretty and would greet each white devil with a courteous smile.

Miss Dear, in a shiny red dress, with ribbons in her straight black hair, tottered in front of them to the rear of the restaurant, where there were three or four private booths, enclosed with pierced and decorated screens. She bowed to Collis and Dan as she ushered them into the nearest booth on the left.

Drinking green tea, and smoking a pipe that smelled like burning flowers, was a small Chinese in a black mandarin skullcap and a black silk shirt decorated with embroidered birds. 'Collis, this is Mr Yee,' said Dan McReady. 'Mr Yee, this is Mr Collis Edmonds, of the Sierra Pacific Railroad Company.'

The Chinaman indicated that Dan and Collis should sit down. 'I am very honoured to meet you,' he said. 'I have read about you last year in the *Golden Hills News*.'

'I guess they mentioned Wang-Pu,' said Collis.

'Yes,' said Mr Yee. 'There are many Chinese in San Francisco who mourned for Wang-Pu.'

Miss Dear came in with a fresh pot of tea, and more cups. 'Have you eaten yet?' Mr Yee asked. 'The specialty here is wind-dried duck. I can recommend it. The red-cooked pork with squid is also good.'

'The tea will do fine, thanks,' said Collis.

They sat for a while sipping the scalding tea, and then Mr Yee put down his cup. 'You were a friend of Wang-Pu's, Mr Edmonds.' It wasn't a question.

Collis nodded.

'Wang-Pu talked about you often. He said that the future of the Chinese people in San Francisco was in your breath. That is a Chinese expression which means that your life is tied up with their fate.'

455

'I'm flattered,' said Collis.

'You have no need to be,' replied Mr Yee. 'None of us chooses the path he treads.'

'I believe in destiny,' Collis told him, 'but I'm not a fatalist. I could pack my bags now and go back to Sacramento, and spend the rest of my life being a middling-to-average hardware dealer.'

Mr Yee shook his head and smiled. 'You could no more do that than I could. What you have to do has been written in your future for centuries past, and it will be written as your history in centuries yet to come.'

'Perhaps.'

Dan McReady took out a red rag and blew his nose. 'What Mr Edmonds really wants to talk about is labour, Mr Yee. Chinese workers to build his railroad for him.'

Mr Yee poured out more tea and looked down at the leaves as they settled in the cup. 'I know that, Mr McReady. We have already discussed it among the members of my tong.'

Collis said nothing. He had learned from Wang-Pu that a respectful silence is considered a thousand times more valuable than even the most worshipful words.

'Whenever you want labour, Mr Edmonds, we can supply it,' Mr Yee said. 'Hundreds, if you need them, or thousands. They come in from China every week, and we can organise them for you. All you have to do is say the word.'

'What will you want in return?' asked Collis.

Mr Yee raised his hand. 'Nothing. What you are planning to do is just as much our destiny as yours. We do not expect to be paid for fulfilling our future.'

Collis took a notepad out of his tailcoat pocket and scribbled three or four words in it, in pencil. 'I've written myself a reminder,' he told Mr Yee. 'When we finish the railroad, the Sierra Pacific will make a financial contribution to the Chinese companies, one dollar for every man who worked on the track. What the companies do with the money – well, that's up to them. But I hope they use it for better housing and better schools.'

Mr Yee looked at Collis without blinking. Then he said, 'I believe there is no question. You are, indeed, the man.'

Dan McReady sniffed. 'What do you mean by that? What man?'

Mr Yee smiled at him. 'Mr Edmonds knows what I mean. True, Mr Edmonds?'

'I think I'll try some of that wind-dried duck, if there's any going,' Collis said. 'How about you, Dan?'

Mission Dolores had been proudly established in 1776 as Spain's northernmost outpost on the West Coast of America. Now it stood peeling and decrepit among the barren hills of southwest San Francisco, its cemetery overgrown with pampas grass, juniper bushes, ferns, and poinsettias. Birds settled on the clay-tiled roof, watching for bread and oranges discarded by the Sunday visitors who came out to promenade, and picnic, and canter their horses.

Collis walked around the mission, waving his hat to keep himself cool. Then he stood beside one of the whitewashed adobe walls for a while and had a smoke. He could see the flagstaff from where he was standing, but he wanted to stay in the shadow. There was no cloud, no breeze. Just the glaring sun, and the afternoon dust.

At about ten after three, he went inside and looked at the church. It was darker there, and cool, because the heat of the day was kept out by mud walls that were four feet thick. There were decorative altars, nearly ninety years old, carved in Mexico and brought to San Francisco by ship, and statues of the saints that had been crudely fashioned by the local Indians. The ceiling was painted in blues and reds and pale greens.

Collis stood there for a while, in the shadows, and then in a halting, embarrassed voice, he began a prayer. 'Dear Lord,' he said, as if he were starting a letter to a friend in a foreign country, 'I don't know what it is that You want of me; or even if You want anything from me at all. But I guess it's You behind all this, because it's all too big to be anybody else.'

He paused. He felt like a fool. But he knew, somehow, that God was really there. He knew that God was waiting for him to continue, that God expected more.

'A lot of people have died,' Collis said in a husky voice. 'There was Kathleen Mary, at the Monument Hotel, and there was my father, and then there was Wang-Pu. A lot of people have suffered, too, and I'm sorry about that. Hannah suffered, and Delphine suffered, and I guess my mother suffered, as well. I just hope that You're guiding me, Lord. I just hope that whatever it is I'm doing, You're still there, holding my hand, because if it all came to nothing, if we never built the railroad, well, I don't know what the hell it would all have been for. I'm sorry. I didn't mean to say "hell".'

He waited for a few minutes longer. He could hear excursionists laughing outside, and somebody blowing a slide whistle.

'Stay with me, Lord,' he whispered at last. 'If that isn't too impertinent; after everything I've done. So many people seem to depend on me. So many people seem to be waiting for what I'm going to do. It's a hell of a lot to carry, all on your own.'

He looked up at the crucifix on the adobe wall. 'I'm sorry,' he said. He didn't know what else God expected to hear. He lowered his eyes to the wooden floor. The pampas grass rustled outside the open door.

He left the church and walked for a while among the gravestones. He stood for almost five minutes in front of a marker which read: *'Ici reposent Athalie Baudichon avec Charles et Blanche ses deux Enfants trois victimes de l'horrible explosion du Steamboat Jenny Lind le 11 Avril 1853. Priez pour eux.'* He felt saddened, and suddenly tired. He went and sat for a while at the front of the Mission, on a rough stone wall, only a few feet away from the flagstaff.

Four o'clock came. A few high cirrus clouds shadowed the sun. Collis reached in his pocket and found that he was out of cheroots. Four crushed-out butts lay in the white dust at his feet. He leaned forward, resting his elbows on his knees, and whistled tunelessly between his teeth. He knew she wasn't coming. Not this late. Not at five after four. If she'd really wanted to come, she would have been here at three.

Some of the day-trippers began to gather up their bags and their picnic baskets and make their way towards the Yellow Line coaches. A breeze whipped up the dust and set the flag pulleys clanking dolefully against the flagstaff. A Spanish priest walked across the courtyard, his head bent, and Collis watched him until he was out of sight.

Well, he thought, this is how it ends. He stood up, brushed down his tailcoat, and put on his hat. He had a return stagecoach ticket into San Francisco, and he reckoned on going back to the International Hotel, changing, and then having dinner at Delmonico's with Dan McReady. Perhaps he would get drunk, with toast after toast to Walter West, for his persistence and his worthiness, and his commonplace luck. Damn all haberdashers, he thought. Damn all haberdashers to hell.

He crossed the rough, stony courtyard towards the place where the Yellow Line coaches turned around. One of them had just arrived from downtown, and the conductor was holding the horses while the passengers disembarked. The wind sizzled across the dusty ground.

A man in a brown tailcoat and thick whiskers stepped down from the coach and turned to help a small blonde woman in a grey dress. Collis was confused at first, because the man seemed to treat the woman with too much familiarity, as if she was his wife, or his niece. But as Collis came nearer, he saw that the conductor had left the horses and had walked across to help the woman with two large carpetbags, and a small leather trunk, and he realized that she must be Hannah. She had to be.

'Hannah!' he said, with a dry throat.

She didn't even hear him; she was too busy looking in her purse for a tip for the conductor. But he was walking towards her, almost running, and a scenic photographer caught them both at that moment, tiny figures under a wide afternoon sky, he with his hat in his hand, she with her head just lifted, and the photograph was later exhibited at the Merchants' Hall in San Francisco, although the caption never said who they were.

Chapter 11

He booked her a separate room at the International – not because
the management was fussy about ladies and gentlemen of quality
sharing rooms for what they discreetly called 'private conversations', but because San Francisco was too small and Collis was
already too well known for a double booking to go unremarked in
the scandal papers.

Neither of them wanted to humiliate Walter any more than they
had already, and Hannah that evening was still very shy, and
unsettled, and frightened by what she had done.

Over a fish dinner in the downstairs restaurant, Collis held her
hand and told her, 'I was sure you wouldn't come. It's like a
miracle.'

'A miracle?'

He shrugged. 'Well, a minor miracle. Not quite the raising of
Lazarus, but the raising of my spirits.'

'Yes,' she said. 'Mine are raised too. I feel like a silly young girl
again. You won't fail me, will you?'

'Do you really think you have to ask?'

She gently stroked the back of his hand, touching the whorls of
his knuckles. 'No,' she said, and the tear that hovered on her
eyelash sparkled like the single diamond in her ring.

'Did you tell Walter you were leaving for good?'

She nodded. 'He wouldn't have accepted my going at all if I
hadn't. He would have told me to hang on, to give him a second
chance, to wait and see if my feelings could change.'

She paused, and added, 'He was very sad. I think he cried more
than I did. But he did say that he would try and understand, and
that if I really didn't love him he wouldn't stand in my way.'

'He won't contest a divorce?'

Hannah turned away. Her pale profile was framed by a panel of
fluted oak, and she was so still and melancholy that she could have
been posing for a portrait of Rapunzel, waiting for her lost prince.

'Hannah?' Collis pressed her.

She lowered her eyes. 'We didn't discuss a divorce.'

'Why not? Surely a divorce is the whole heart of the matter.'

'It's too early,' she said. 'I've left him, yes, but I haven't even unpacked my bag yet. I can't think of the future until I've learned to cope with the present.'

'I see. So you would rather we lived in sin than cut off your last ties to Walter?'

She lifted her head again. 'We won't be living in sin, Collis. Don't think the idea hasn't tormented me for hours. But I've come to believe that seeking my own happiness, even if it hurts Walter, is not a sin. Being with you makes me happy. I love your energy and I love your determination. And I promise you, my darling, that I will discuss a divorce with Walter, one day soon when the time is right.'

Collis laid down his forkful of shad. He took up his glass of champagne and raised it to her.

'Well, then,' he said, 'here's to us. Here's to our folly, and here's to our future, and here's to our love.'

Hannah didn't hesitate. She raised her glass and drank. Then the tears glittered in her eyes again, and she said: 'Oh, Collis. Don't fail me. Please don't fail me.'

At ten o'clock, they retired to their separate rooms – Collis on the fourth floor and Hannah on the third. Collis took a bath, and shaved, and drank a small glass of bourbon while he sat wrapped in a towel reading the evening's paper and cooling off. He wasn't entirely sure that Hannah wanted him to come to her room tonight; or, if she did, when. She had kissed him very firmly and lovingly on the lips as he left her outside her door, and said good night to him in a way that had seemed to suggest she was expecting a later assignation. But the more Collis thought about it, the more he began to doubt whether it had.

He sprayed himself with lavender cologne, combed his hair, and began to dress in a freshly boiled shirt and evening clothes. Of course she wanted him to come down to her room and make love, he reassured himself. Why else had she left Walter? Yet Hannah's affections confused him, and he still had disturbing recollections of that night aboard the *Virginia*, when she had refused to let him into her cabin. He didn't relish the idea of a repeat performance in the august corridors of the International.

He went to the door, opened it, and stepped outside. Then he changed his mind and came back in again. He could see himself in the mirror over the fireplace, biting his lip. If only he were sure. But then he heard the high laughter of a girl in the corridor outside, and he thought, to hell with it. I've upset her before, and if I upset her again, it's too bad. I actually love the woman.

Downstairs, outside of room 304, he tugged his coat-tails straight, ran his hand through his hair, and knocked. A stately woman with silver hair and ropes of silvery pearls came gliding past him with all the magnificence of a China clipper, and he gave her a quick and uneasy good evening.

At last, he heard the latch on Hannah's door unfastened. The door opened two or three inches, as if the wind had blown it, and Collis hesitated for a moment. Then he heard Hannah's soft, Boston-accented voice say, 'Come in, my darling.'

He stepped in and closed the door behind him. Hannah's room was smaller than his, lit by a single frosted-glass lamp. Hannah herself was sitting on the edge of the veneered bed, her long blonde hair brushed and brushed, her eyes bright. She wore a long white nightdress of layered lace, with wide sleeves and decorated cuffs, and she looked as pretty and sad as a seraph.

'I, er – I came down,' said Collis, uncertainly.

She smiled and held out her hand. 'I was waiting for you,' she said.

He came across the room and took her hand between his. 'You're not feeling any regrets, are you?' he asked her.

'I regret having to hurt Walter,' she told him. 'And as the days go by, I will probably have other regrets. But as long as you understand what I am feeling – as long as you don't expect me to go through the rest of my life without a single backward look – then I am sure everything will be perfect.'

Collis bent forward and kissed the gleaming parting of her hair. 'I love you,' he said. 'But don't expect perfection of me. I have never been perfect, and I never shall be.'

She raised her face to him, and he kissed her forehead, her closed eyelids, and then her lips. 'I don't really want perfection,' she whispered. 'I want you . . .' Then she touched him with her left hand, tentatively, cautiously, like a blind girl reaching up to touch someone she thought she recognised from years and years gone by.

He sat down on the bed beside her and held her in his arms, feeling the warmth and softness of her body through tiers of lace. They were posed like lovers in an illustrated romance, and all they needed was cherubs, with ribbons and posies, and a frame of summer flowers.

462

'You frighten me,' she said softly into his ear. 'I have dreams about you that I can't understand. And yet in the hour I first saw you I knew somehow that I would be compelled to love you.'

He kissed her on the lips, again and again, so that she couldn't tell him any more. He didn't want to hear her doubts, or how she felt about the nature of their love affair. At first he kissed her gently, but as his feelings were aroused, he kissed her more deeply, and more hungrily.

'Hannah,' he said, winding her blonde hair around his fingers. 'Why the hell did you ever marry?'

'Sshh,' she told him.

'Why didn't you keep yourself wrapped up in tissue paper?' he persisted. 'Why did you ever feel the need to walk up the aisle with a man like Walter?'

Hannah pressed her finger against his lips. 'Walter's a good man. Kind, and considerate. And we can't turn the clock around backwards. If it hadn't been for Walter, I never would have met you, and so you have that to be thankful for.'

'I would have met you somehow. I'd lay money on it.'

She smiled. 'Don't let's bet on love.'

He kissed her again – a long, lingering kiss that neither of them could bear to finish. But when their lips did part, and they stared at each other so close that the pupils of their eyes were dark and unfocused, they knew what would happen next. Collis stood up, went to the door, and turned the brass key in the lock. Then, standing with his back to the lamp, he took off his evening coat and unfastened his cufflinks. In the subdued light, in his spotless white shirt and his white evening vest, he looked more handsome than Hannah could ever remember. Something had changed him since he had been in California – experience, maybe; or the discovery of what he really wanted out of his life. But whatever it was, it had given him far more poise and maturity than before, and she knew she could love him now as a man of character, and not just as a good-looking adventurer. She had recognised this subtle and attractive new quality in him at the store yesterday, and perhaps if Collis had known how much it had tipped the balance against Walter, he would have thought about Hannah more cautiously.

Hannah could scent more than lavender cologne when she came near to Collis. She could scent that he had ambition, and a hunger for success. Unlike poor Walter, who would have walked a hundred yards on hot bricks just to keep her; and yet who had sat in his shop while she told him she had to leave, and wept, unable to say even a single word which might have persuaded her to stay, or even delayed her for five more minutes at the door.

Collis sat on the end of the bed and prised off his glossy black evening pumps. Then, as he stood up to unbutton his shirt, Hannah leaned over to the lamp, turned the wick down, and blew into the glass bowl to extinguish it. The room was crowded with darkness, perfume, and the rustle of clothes.

Naked, Collis climbed on to the bed. The faintest smudge of light penetrated the heavy brown drapes, and he could just distinguish her blonde hair spread across the pillow, and her face, although it was too dark for him to make out her expression.

He lay next to her, and kissed her, and this time she responded to him with an urgency that startled him and aroused him even more.

'You're like a dream,' he breathed. 'You're like somebody sent from somewhere mythical to tempt me.'

She said nothing, but kissed and nipped at his lips.

His hand traced the warmth of her body through her nightdress, downwards, until he reached her thigh. Then, as if he were slowly crumpling up a love letter, he gathered up the lace tiers of her nightdress in his fingers and lifted them, above her knees, above her thighs, above her waist. She shivered, not so much from cold, but from being exposed to him, her thighs slightly parted.

'Hannah . . .' Collis whispered, and his fingertips traced a pattern around her bare stomach, galvanising her nerve endings. Involuntarily, she opened her thighs a little more, longing with uncontrollable immodesty for him to touch her there, to trespass with his fingers on the very last preserve that her marriage had kept for Walter and for nobody else.

It would take her months before she could tell Collis about Walter's fumbling in bed, about his awkward and untimely attempts at sex. Perhaps she never would. But right now she wanted what by holy or unholy intention was hers by right.

She could feel Collis arched above her now, a crossbow of muscle and desire. She held one hand against his firm muscular chest. With her other hand she caressed his side, the ridges of his ribs, the muscles around his hips and back. And with a daring that almost frightened her, she reached into the hollow inside his thigh, and caressed him without a bit of shyness.

She heard him mumble something. She felt his kisses on her

464

cheeks and eyes. Then, with a sharp inhalation of breath, he began to fall towards her, surrendering to his desire no less than she to hers.

She squeezed her eyes tight shut. The sin of adultery was already committed. This wasn't going to make it any worse. Yet to refuse Collis now – right on the very point of penetration – wouldn't that at least show God that she earnestly repented, that she was truly sorry for what she was doing? Wouldn't it show that she could be strong at the moment of greatest temptation?'

But she heard herself breathing, 'Now . . . oh, please, Collis, now . . .' and she felt him slide inside her, so deeply it seemed as if gravity had turned itself inside out, as if the whole room had swayed and tipped in an earth tremor.

She clutched him, for balance as well as for passion. He half withdrew from her, and then pushed himself inside her again, even deeper this time, into the secrecy of her body. And he didn't stop. He didn't suddenly shudder and roll off her, as Walter had always done. He kept pushing into her, rhythmic and forceful, again and again and again, until she began to wonder if she was going to be able to stand it. Her senses seemed to jumble up. She heard him panting. She heard the odd crunching sound of the horse-hair mattress. She thought she heard laughter, too, but it wasn't his, it came from a faraway world of propriety and trifling flirtations.

Most of all, though, she felt the tingling in her body, as effervescent as soda, as fresh as snow. And Collis kept on pushing and pushing and pushing, arousing her far beyond anything she had imagined possible, so that she no longer cared about adultery or decorum or God, or even who she was, or why, and so that she no longer knew where she was or what was happening to her.

She might have screamed. She might have imagined screaming. She could feel a miraculous pressure building up, and she didn't know whether she wanted it to break or not, for it would surely overwhelm her, and even bury her like a violent earthquake. Yet how could she hold it back, with that taut, tight touching that wouldn't stop?

But it wasn't an earthquake that overwhelmed her at the end. It was an abrupt awareness of reality, that what was happening wasn't an earthquake at all. It was the vivid understanding that she was in a dark and unfamiliar hotel room, and that she was making love with a man who wasn't her husband. A young, virile man who was already deep inside her, and whom she craved to have even deeper inside her, so much that she was lifting her hips towards him in a way that was outrageous for a woman of any decency.

Finally her fears and inhibitions began to teeter around her like a building on the verge of collapse, swaying on the uncertain foundations of guilt, and duty, and wifely fortitude, dropping cornices and window ledges and showers of roof tiles, until Collis gasped, and she felt a sudden bulge and pulse, and the whole edifice of Hannah's life seemed to come thundering down in a tumult of days and years and months, of smashed photographs and broken friendships, of ripped-away responsibilities and torn hearts.

'At last you're mine,' said Collis softly, and kissed her.

She opened her eyes, trying to see him in the darkness. He smelled of cologne, and bourbon, and tobacco; but of soap, too, a clean smell. She felt very warm and languid, and she stretched. 'Perhaps it would be better to arrange for a divorce sooner, rather than later, after all,' she said.

She felt him turn towards her, interrogatively.

'Well,' she said, as if to justify her change of heart, 'you want to take me back to Sacramento with you, don't you? And your Jane McCormick wouldn't really approve if we were living in sin.'

'That's true,' Collis said carefully.

There was another pause, and then she said, 'You sound as if you're not sure you want me to get divorced. Do you?'

'Of course I do. As long as it's something you've considered with care. I don't want you to do anything you're going to feel sorry about afterwards.'

She kissed him, so lightly that he scarcely felt it.

'Do you feel sorry about what we did just now?'

'No. Of course not.'

'Well, then. That's the way I feel about divorcing Walter.'

There was a rap at the door. A woman's voice drawled, 'Can I turn your sheets down, ma'am?'

Hannah kissed Collis again. Then she called back, 'Later, please, if you don't mind. I'm occupied at the moment.'

Collis gave an amused snort and sat up. 'When will you talk to Walter?' he asked her.

She reached out and touched his bare back, tracing invisible tattooes. 'I was hoping that you would,' she said.

'Me?'

'Well, man-to-man. You know the kind of thing.'

Collis peered at her through the gloom. 'I'm not entirely sure that I do.'

He decided to stay in San Francisco until the weekend. The weather was clear, but bitingly cold. Hannah spent most of her time at the International, in her room, or taking tea in the lounge, but on those afternoons when Collis wasn't organising shipments of guncotton and screws for Tucker, McCormick & Edmonds, he took her for walks along the grey Pacific shore, or into Chinatown, to look at the shops and the restaurants.

He found that, almost mysteriously, he was widely known along Sacramento Street, and Chinese silversmiths and shoe menders would nod to him as he went past. He was unsettled, in a way, by the strange trust which the Chinese people seemed to have invested in him, as if they saw his future far more clearly than he did.

On Wednesday, he talked to Mr Yee again, who recommended that he should approach the leader of the On Leong Tong, a certain Mr Kwang, who had staying in his house a nineteen-year-old cousin whose entrepreneurial abilities might make him a suitable replacement for Wang-Pu. Although the name, in English, meant 'Chamber of Tranquil Conscientiousness', the On Leong Tong was Chinatown's principal trafficker in slave girls, and Mr Kwang was said to be concerned at the amount of attention his young cousin was lavishing on the merchandise. He might agree to let him go.

Collis and Mr Kwang met on the second-floor balcony of Mr Kwang's lavish house on Jackson Street, overlooking a private garden of fountains and palms. Brilliantly coloured parrots squawked and chirped in bamboo cages all around them, and as they sat over musky-smelling tea and platefuls of tiny Chinese savouries, girls as pretty and brilliant as the parrots brought them fresh napkins, and sweetmeats, and tobacco.

Mr Kwang must have been all of seventy, but his face was unnaturally smooth, and his hair was still black. He had no teeth at all, but ate his food by pursuing it around his mouth with his tongue. He wore a robe of pure silk and gold thread that must have cost thousands of dollars. A few feet behind him, staying respectfully quiet, sat his young cousin, Kwang Lee, and an alluring half-breed girl in a tight peacock-coloured silk dress. Collis guessed her age at eleven or twelve, even when Mr Kwang told him that she was the finest hummingbird he had ever known. A hummingbird,

467

Wang-Pu had once told him, was a girl who was proficient in oral sex, a *fellatrice*.

'Well,' said Mr Kwang, after they had finished eating, 'I hear that you seek an assistant at your store.'

'A buyer, to be more accurate,' Collis told him. 'Someone to come down to San Francisco on a regular basis and keep our supplies flowing through.' He tapped his head with his forefinger. 'Someone with his head screwed on, who won't get gypped.'

Mr Kwang nodded and smiled. 'Kwang Lee is such a fellow. He is not trustworthy when there are girls around, but in every other way he is most hardworking and shrewd. Perhaps a year or two with you and your colleagues in Sacramento might be good for him.'

'From what Mr Yee told me, he sounds ideal.'

'You wish to employ him on trial, then?' asked Mr Kwang.

'Twenty-five dollars a month, with board and food provided in Sacramento, and all expenses paid when he's away.'

Without even looking over his shoulder, Mr Kwang said to Kwang Lee, 'That's settled, then. You'll pack your belongings, Kwang Lee, and go to Sacramento with Mr Edmonds when he leaves on Saturday.'

Kwang Lee inclined his head.

'You won't regret it, Kwang Lee,' Collis told him loudly. 'Mr McCormick and Mr Tucker and I, we're all going places. If you get into the business now, you'll be a big shot in a few years' time.'

Kwang Lee nodded again, but said nothing.

Mr Kwang raised his hand, and a girl shuffled in from the house to bring him two carved-ivory pipes, and tobacco.

'These are opium pipes from the T'ang dynasty,' said Mr Kwang. 'But I myself never smoke opium. Only fools need dreams.'

'I have a dream,' said Collis carefully.

'I know,' Mr Kwang replied. 'But your dream will one day become a commonplace reality, unlike the dreams that come with opium. Your dream will one day seem so ordinary that people will not even remark on it.'

'I wish I had your confidence,' said Collis.

'No,' said Mr Kwang. 'You wish you had my tranquillity.'

Collis frowned. He wasn't at all sure what the Chinaman meant.

'You allow obstacles to stand in your way,' continued Mr Kwang, carefully thumbing tobacco into the tiny bowl of his pipe. 'You do not look at them the way I do, and simply say, "Begone".'

'I see your philosophical point,' said Collis. 'But there isn't any

468

hope the Sierra Nevada is going to vanish, just because I want it to.'

'The Sierra Nevada isn't your only obstacle,' said Mr Kwang expressionlessly.

Collis looked at him closely. 'What do you mean?'

'You are a well-known personality in San Francisco, Mr Edmonds. Your comings and goings are noted. I understand that a certain storekeeper is an obstacle for you these days.'

'You mean – ?'

Mr Kwang raised his hand. 'It is best not to say too much, even in the privacy of one's own house. Servants, like parrots, can learn to talk – and not always in the most discreet of places.'

'The lady in question is going to seek a divorce,' said Collis. He took a melon seed from the small porcelain dish in front of him, split it with his teeth the way Wang-Pu had taught him, and ate the kernel.

Mr Kwang lit a match and sucked gently at the long stem of his pipe. 'Divorce is not always the most honourable way, is it? And to marry a lady who is divorced, well, that is not always good for face, is it?'

'Face?'

'You understand, Mr Edmonds. You were a friend of Wang-Pu's.'

Collis felt uncomfortable. 'I'm not sure what you want me to do, Mr Kwang.'

'Do?' asked Mr Kwang, his face as smooth as a blanched almond. 'I don't want you to do anything. That is the whole point of what I have been telling you. Be tranquil, do nothing, and your obstacle will disappear.'

On Friday, Collis and Hannah ate lunch at the California Market, at Darbee & Immel's, a huge mound of shellfish, a small rump steak each, and a pot of hot coffee. Collis had spent most of the morning with Andy Hunt, arguing about the railroad, and he was going to talk in the afternoon to Horace Johnson, one of the directors of Pacific Mail, in an attempt to soften up the steamship line's adamant opposition to transcontinental trains. Johnson had once said in public that California's economy and security depended almost entirely on her isolation, and that to build a railroad link with the east would destroy 'at a stroke' her political integrity and her financial strength.

Johnson had failed to add, of course, that a railroad link would also destroy the hugely profitable monopolies of the stage-line owners and the steamship companies.

Hannah ate very little lunch, and looked pale. It was plain to Collis that the strain of staying in San Francisco, only a few blocks away from Walter, was beginning to take its toll. He was sure that she loved him far more than Walter, if love was what it was; and that she was still prepared to ask Walter for a divorce. But the effervescence of their first night together had been flattened by days of waiting alone in her room at the International, of watching the afternoon light sink gradually across the floral wallpaper to the floor. She was beginning to doubt herself again, to worry that her infatuation might not be worth the loss of her respectability, her cosy marriage, and her peace of mind with God.

Collis realised that she was faltering. Her lovemaking on Thursday night had been distant, distracted. He knew that if he didn't take quick, positive steps to re-establish her social position, he could well lose her.

He said, over the coffee, 'When I've spoken to Horace Johnson, I'll go down to the store and see Walter.'

She looked up, her eyes widening. 'Do you mean that?'

Collis nodded. Around them, the lunchroom was noisy and jostling, and the clatter of empty clamshells being cleared off plates sounded like castanets. 'I want to keep you, Hannah,' Collis added, and reached out to take her wrist.

'Yes,' she said, lovingly but somehow vaguely. 'But you won't be cruel to him, will you? You won't – '

'I'll treat him as gently as china,' Collis assured her.

Hannah picked up her coffee cup, realised it was empty, and put it down again. 'I shall wait for you then, at the hotel,' she said. 'You won't be too late, will you? You won't keep me in suspense for too long?'

Collis didn't answer. There was nothing he could say until he'd talked to Walter. The waiter came up with his white towel slung over his shoulder and demanded laconically, 'Through?' and Collis gave him a shrug which probably meant yes.

An hour later, in the oak-panelled offices of Pacific Mail, he stood by the window of the waiting-room, gazing out over a triangular view of Montgomery Street, and waiting, as Hannah was waiting for him, for his appointment with Horace Johnson. He had already smoked two cheroots, to the annoyance of the stiff-bosomed receptionist, and he was thinking about a third.

As three o'clock struck, however, Horace Johnson's door opened, and Horace himself appeared, a big, broad example of San Francisco's most robust eaters and drinkers. He was ruddy, white-whiskered, with a pair of mean pince-nez clipped into the fruity flesh of his nose. He waved Collis inside as if he were directing traffic.

'I know why you're here,' he said, in a deep, rich voice.

'Only to further our acquaintance, and our understanding,' said Collis guardedly. 'I don't really expect to win your support.'

Johnson sat down in a huge leather library chair and stuffed his fat fingers together. 'You expect right, Mr Edmonds, I've already spoken to that flash partner of yours, the one with the checkered suit. And the only reason I've taken you up on your suggestion that we meet today is that I want to make my views emphatically clear to all of you, individually – as clear as I damned well can.'

Collis remained standing, his hat in his hand. 'I appreciate your directness,' he replied with a sour smile. 'I've heard you're a blunt man, as well as a big one.'

Johnson stared at him for a moment, and then chuckled. 'I like your impertinence, Mr Edmonds. I always enjoyed a little impertinence. But mark my words – by the time you've lived in this fair city of ours for as long as I have, you too will have a profile to be proud of.' He patted his stomach as if it were a small boy who had done well at school.

'I'm going to build a transcontinental railroad, Mr Johnson, and I want it to terminate right here in San Francisco. Will Pacific Mail stand in my way, no matter what?'

Johnson brushed his whiskers. 'It isn't just the Pacific Mail Steamship Company that's going to stand in your way, Mr Edmonds. Nor is it just the California Steam Navigation Company, nor any one of the ferry lines, nor Wells Fargo. It's the whole of the San Francisco business community, which is already alert to what you and your little band of Sacramento storekeepers is up to. If you were to terminate a transcontinental road in San Francisco, on the waterfront, then you would effectively control all the shipping that goes in and out of here, and through the shipping, you would effectively control the city itself.'

'I know that,' said Collis. 'But how can you stand in the way of progress? The Sierras will be crossed by rail one day, and what are you going to do? Lay your belly across the tracks and refuse to let the locomotives pass?'

471

'I'm going to say one thing only,' Horace Johnson growled. 'Any attempt by you or your cronies to bring the railroad into San Francisco will be resisted by the full strength of my steamship company, and by all of those companies that make up the business life of this city. You'll fail, I warn you, so don't think you'll ever collect on any of those bets you made with Arthur Teach and Laurence Melford and all those other fellows.'

'You know about those?'

Horace Johnson nodded, as if to say, 'Who doesn't?' Then he said, 'I'll lay you a bet myself. For every yard of waterfront you ever gain for your railroad, I'll buy you a bottle of brandy.'

Collis put his hat back on his head and tapped it. 'Mr Johnson,' he said, extending his hand, 'I am about to embark on a very drunken decade.'

Afterwards, closeted with Hannah in the darkness of her hotel room, he tried to think who to blame. Was it Horace Johnson's fault, for keeping him so long at the steamship office? Was it his own fault, for talking so freely to Mr Kwang? Or was it the fault of the railroad itself, that glittering and apocalyptic vision which demanded so much human life and so much human suffering?

The railroad seemed rapacious. Collis could understand why men like Horace Johnson were afraid of it. He was afraid of it himself. He felt as if he and his partners in the Sierra Pacific were custodians of some dark steel sword, as magical and mythical as Excalibur, which, unsheathed, could cut America's ties with the traditions of her past in one slice. It depressed him, this thought, but it also excited him. He knew that they were going to wield it one day, and that life in America would never be the same again.

He had left Horace Johnson's office at a quarter after three. The afternoon had been growing snappish, and he had buttoned up his gloves. He had stopped at a cigar store to replenish his cheroot case, and then walked on to Walter West's notions emporium. His heart had been beating steadily but distinctly. In his long grey coat he had felt like an apprentice mortician, attending on the decease of a marriage.

The bell above the door had jangled as he had pushed his way inside. The store had been oddly silent. He had paused, then crossed the boarded floor and called, 'Mr West? Anyone there?'

The stiff shop dummies with their bright-pink faces had smiled back at him sightlessly The dust of thread and cotton cloth had

472

fallen through the sunlight. There had been that sharp smell of dressing, and of linseed. In a back yard somewhere, a woman was calling, 'William! William! Here, kitty!'

'Mr West?' Collis had called again. Again, there had been no answer. He had waited a few seconds more, and then walked up to the counter and pinged at the brass bell with the flat of his hand.

The ping had died away. Collis had turned around, his back to the counter, and taken a deep breath. It had been bad enough trying to screw up the courage to talk to Walter West about divorcing Hannah in the first place. To be obliged to wait in this dim and silent store was fifty times worse.

He had heard a shuffling noise, and turned around again. He had listened, alert, his pulse rushing in his eardrums. Nothing for a few moments, but then another shuffling noise, and something which could have been a whisper. It had appeared to come from behind the counter.

Collis had cautiously made his way around a stack of gingham to the end of the counter, and peered over. What he had seen had made his scalp freeze and prickle. On the buff-coloured bolts of calico behind the serving area had been dark splashes and squiggles which were unmistakably blood.

'Oh, my God,' he had breathed. He had pushed the gingham out of the way and stepped right around the counter. And there, lying amid bloodstained receipt books and unravelled tape measures, his hair and his beard clotted with gore as black and sticky as molasses, had been Walter West.

Collis had been stiff with fright and horror. He had seen men killed before, men crushed by carriages, children left floating and bloated in the East River, but the sheer quantity of blood that had plastered the body of Walter West had been hideous to the point of unbelievability. How could anyone have so much blood?

Dragging over a bolt of linen to kneel on, Collis had crouched, shaking, beside the haberdasher's body. He had coaxed, hoarsely, 'Mr West? Walter?' But Walter West's eyes had remained puffy and closed, and when Collis had placed his fingertips close to his open mouth, he had felt no breath. Maybe the whispers and scratchings that Collis had heard earlier had been Walter West's final twitches of death.

Collis had felt very sick. This near to the body, he had been able to see what had happened. Walter West had been attacked with knives or hatchets, so sharp that many of his facial wounds appeared to be nothing more than thin red hairlines. His forearms and his hands had been savagely cut, which must have meant that he had tried to protect himself against his attackers.

His tweed vest had been slashed into bloodstained tatters, and only his watch chain had been holding in a soft bulge of pale-pink intestine.

Collis had stood up. The store had suddenly become oppressively stuffy and hot. He had been sweating, and trembling like a man with chronic pneumonia. He had walked to the door, and stood there for a time looking out at the curious reality of the street outside.

He had known that there was no question of calling the police. He was living with Walter West's wife in a situation which even the most broad-minded of investigators would regard as improper, and a first-class motive for murder. He had to leave, discreetly and unnoticed.

He had tilted the brow of his hat down so that it covered his forehead. Then, quickly, he had stepped out on to the sidewalk and closed the store behind him. He had heard the bell jangling loudly. Loud, yes. But not loud enough to rouse the dead, Collis had thought.

The sweat on his forehead had chilled as he walked north on Montgomery as far as Clay. Then he had turned right and gone mechanically downhill towards the waterfront. He had followed the waterfront as far as the old Pacific Street Wharf, oblivious to the wagons and carriages and noisy jostling of merchants and lightermen and stevedores. Then he had turned down a side alley and pushed his way into a notorious crimps' bar called the So Cheerful. It had been stinking and crowded in there, full of sailors and drunks and cheap whores, but Collis had badly needed a drink. He had elbowed his way up to the bar, where a bald-headed negro with gold earrings had been filling up pots of steam beer, and he had asked harshly for a bourbon. The negro had set down a whole bottle of Kentucky Eagle and a glass. The men who drank at the So Cheerful didn't generally seek their oblivion in small measures.

He had knocked back one shot, then poured himself another. A young girl with dyed black hair and cheeks rouged into bright crimson spots had pushed up close to him. She had smelled of sweat and lily of the valley. Her pale-brown Spanish-style dress had been left unlaced so that her nipples were bare. She had saucily squeezed Collis's thigh and said: 'Got a drink for a good girl, lover?'

Collis had stared at her. Walter West was lying cut to slivers on the floor of his store, and Collis himself, not a week ago, had damned the poor man to hell. Sweet Jesus Christ, he had thought, how little we really want those things which we pray for.

He had walked all the way to Knickerbocker Jane's. He hadn't known why he had felt the urge to go there, but he had headed that way, directly, and without any thought of first going to see Hannah at the International. He hadn't yet worked out how he was going to cope with Hannah, and he had needed to talk to somebody sympathetic about his own shock at discovering Walter West's body before trying to deal with hers. Knickerbocker Jane could give him an alibi, too, and that wasn't an unimportant consideration, especially with the law so watchful these days.

Knickerbocker Jane had received him in her parlour. She had been dressed in black, ironically, for the death of a favourite client. He had died on Tuesday – an elderly banker who for nine years had lavished on her his thick bankroll and his thin seed, and had always called her 'my lamb'. Jane hadn't been particularly pleased to see Collis, and she had turned her cheek away when he had attempted to kiss her. Like the queen of the whores; which she was. Or like his own mother.

'Do you want a drink?' she had asked him. 'You look as if you could use one.'

'I've had enough, thanks. Down on the waterfront.'

She had watched him silently for a while, her back straight, her freckled cleavage swelling over her tight black ruched bodice. 'Something's happened,' she had said, and her voice had been a touch softer. 'Have you had a spat with your Hannah?'

He had had trouble speaking. Whisky and delayed shock seemed to have swollen his lips, and made it difficult for him to enunciate. 'I went around this afternoon to see her husband, to talk about their divorce. We thought it was best if I faced him directly. More honourable. But when I got there, he was dead.'

'Dead? What do you mean?'

'Exactly that. Murdered. Cut to pieces like meat. There was so much blood I don't know how I kept my lunch down.'

'Did anybody see you there?' asked Knickerbocker Jane. She was immediately alert to the danger of the law.

'I don't think so. I left right away.'

'Well, that's one blessing at least. If anyone asks, you spent the afternoon here, with my new girl Laura from Denver. Brunette, she is, with a birthmark inside of her thigh the shape of Rhode Island.'

'Rhode Island?' Collis had asked incredulously.

Knickerbocker Jane had stood up, with a rustle of black skirts. 'Do you know who might have killed him, or why?'

'I don't have any idea. He was only a shopkeeper. I mean, miners get killed, gamblers get killed. But shopkeepers?'

Knickerbocker Jane had laid a hand on his arm. 'Did anybody know you were going to see him, apart from your Hannah? Did anybody know you were in the vicinity?'

'I saw Horace Johnson at the Pacific Mail Steamship Company directly beforehand. But I don't think he knows about Hannah. He wouldn't connect me with her husband's death.'

'You have to be careful of Horace. He's fat, but he's sly.'

'You know him?'

Knickerbocker Jane had smiled. 'Horace Johnson has appetites far beyond food and drink, my love. He's one of my regulars.'

Collis had looked at Knickerbocker Jane with his head on one side. 'You, er, you wouldn't – tell me what those particular appetites are? By any chance?'

'I shouldn't.'

'But supposing he's heard about Hannah? If he doesn't know about her now, he's bound to hear about it sooner or later, when we marry. Or, if we marry. Wouldn't it be safer if I knew just a little about him? Something to protect me?'

Knickerbocker Jane had nodded. Then, with a flourish, she had sat down again, and set her glass on the wine table beside her.

'Horace Johnson,' she said, without any preamble, 'is a devotee of that very special kind of sport we call "discipline". He likes to be manacled to the bed, and abused by two or three girls at once.'

'Horace Johnson?' Collis had asked, raising his eyebrows.

'It isn't uncommon for powerful men, men who inspire fear in everyone they meet, to need an occasional moment when they are completely at the mercy of someone else. I have state senators come here from Sacramento for "discipline". Even a Congressman once.'

Collis had rubbed his chin thoughtfully. 'Wouldn't Mrs Johnson give him the treatment he needs?'

Knickerbocker Jane had laughed. A laugh as dry as her sherry. 'You still need to know a little bit more about San Francisco society, my love. Mrs Esther Harris Johnson is the daughter of Milward Harris, the chief executive of the state harbour commission. A strict, upright, churchgoing lady, not to Horace's taste if you're talking about sex, but one whose family connections have given Pacific Mail a tight, tight grip on the waterfront. Horace Johnson didn't marry for love, or even for "discipline". He comes here for that. Horace Johnson married for commerce.'

'Well, well,' Collis had said. Knickerbocker Jane's worldly wisdom and complete equanimity had begun to calm him down. And for the first time since he had knelt down beside Walter West's butchered body, he had allowed himself the callous but irresistible thought that Hannah was now a widow, respectably free, and that no divorce would be necessary.

'Do you think I should tell Hannah?' he had said quietly. 'Tell her myself? About finding the body, I mean.'

Knickerbocker Jane had shrugged. 'It's up to you. I would have thought it more prudent to wait for someone else to bring her the bad news.'

'Yes,' Collis had said. The gilt clock on the mantelpiece had struck five. He had stood where he was for a moment, and then he had leaned over and kissed Knickerbocker Jane full on the mouth.

'I'm sorry about your banker,' he had said.

She had looked away. 'Thank you. I'm sorry about your shopkeeper. But life goes on for the rest of us, doesn't it?'

Collis had visited one more person before going back to Hannah at the International. Dan McReady, at the Eagle Saloon. Dan had been busy at the faro tables, relieving two bearded gold miners of seven months' hard-earned profits, but he had asked one of the other dealers to sit in for him while he came across to the bar and talked to Collis.

'Dan,' Collis had said, in a quiet, confidential voice, 'what do you know about Mr Kwang?'

Dan had knocked back a shot of whisky, coughed, and pulled a face. 'No more than anyone, I guess. A tough son of a bitch. But a man of his word. The kind of man who knows which way the world's going to turn.'

'Meaning?'

'Meaning he'll do you a favour today, but he'll expect a much bigger favour in return from you tomorrow.'

Collis had stirred his stone fence with his finger. 'That was what I was afraid of.'

'I don't follow.'

'It's very easy. I should have thought of it before. When I went around to talk to Mr Kwang, I happened to mention Walter West.

You know, Hannah's husband. I told him that Walter West was an obstacle, just like the High Sierras.'

'So what did he say?'

'He said not to worry, to be tranquil, and my obstacle would disappear.'

'And?'

'Walter West has been murdered. This afternoon, in his own shop.'

Dan McReady's eyes widened, and then he pulled a long, long face. An exaggeration of dolour and disapproval. 'That's real bad news. How did he die?'

'Choppers, I guess, or knives. Whatever they were, they were sharp as all hell. They cut his guts out without even taking the buttons off of his vest.'

'That's Chinky business, all right,' Dan had said. 'They kill people the same way they cut up their food. A white man would've used a gun, and just blown his head off.'

Collis had tipped back his drink. He had paused for a moment, and then held out his glass for another one. 'It seems to me that Mr Kwang has done me a favour. Very friendly of him, wouldn't you say? All I'm worried about now is what he expects in return.'

Dan McReady had puffed out his cheeks. 'He'll tell you, when the time comes. Meanwhile, if I were you, I'd count your blessings, and hope that the good Mrs West doesn't take the intelligence too hard.'

'I'm afraid of that, too,' Collis had said. 'But I'm sure she will.'

And that was why he was sitting in Hannah's room, with the lamps unlit, while Hannah herself paced around, a handkerchief twisted between her hands, her eyes reddened from crying, and why his throat was dry from too much bourbon and too many hours of talking in a low, sympathetic voice. He was tired now, and his mind was swimming in whisky, and all he really wanted to do was to go to bed and sleep it all off. But Hannah was alive with nervous energy, questioning, questioning, and clenching her fists, and trying with frustrating and useless persistence to understand why, why, *why* Walter should have been sacrificed this way, and whether it was her fault, or whether it was nothing more than one of the horrors of fate – that fate which always strikes down the unlucky, and leaves the lucky unscathed.

The news had reached her before Collis. A small boy had been sent to the International with a message, and he had waited for his bit tip while she read with blurry eyes that her husband was mortally injured. She had stared at the boy after she had finished reading, and for some reason she had believed that he was the son that she and Walter had always talked about having. She had whispered, 'Christopher,' but the boy had simply frowned back at her through the jiggling prisms of her tears.

Her face had been white as a menu when Collis had knocked at her door.

'You didn't go to see Walter,' she had said. Her voice had sounded odd, like somebody talking into an empty cup.

'I, er, no. No, I didn't, I wanted to talk to you first. I mean, talk to you some more. I wasn't quite sure what I was going to – '

Her look had silenced him. 'A boy came, with a note. He's been murdered.'

Collis hadn't tried to act. He had been too tired for that. Instead, he had simply stood in Hannah's room while she poured out her guilt, and her grief, and her grief at not feeling more grief than she did. It was only when she had utterly exhausted herself, when she had cried her eyes dry, and when she was simply talking for the sake of not having to think, that he reminded her of the simplest and most telling fact of all.

'Hannah,' he said, 'you're a widow.'

She stared at him. It was so gloomy in the room now that they could scarcely make each other out.

'Perhaps if you'd gone there, you might have saved his life,' she said.

Collis made a face. 'I might have. But then again, I might have been killed along with him.'

'Don't say that. I can't bear it.'

'Hannah – I can't bring him back. I can't change the course of history. I didn't go to see him today, and that's all. I don't know why he was murdered. Maybe he had some business enemies you never even knew about. Maybe he owed people money.'

She went to the corner of the room, with her back to him.

'I shall have to mourn,' she said in a small voice.

'For how long?'

'In Boston, it would have been a year. But, under the circumstances, I think six months should be sufficien*

'These are modern times, Hannah. Fast times. Six months can see a whole lot of changes.'

'I know, Collis. But my husband is dead, whether I loved him truly or not, and I shall mourn him.'

They buried Walter West four days later, on a Tuesday, at the Lone Mountain Cemetery. From the Presidio, coincidentally, came the sound of a bugler practising taps. It was a cold, brisk day, and the mourners walked along the neat cultivated lanes of the cemetery with their breath escaping in intermittent puffs. There were some friends of Walter's there, mostly storekeeprs, and a portly representative from the merchants' association, who kept taking out his heavy gold watch and staring at it. Collis stood bareheaded by the grave for a while, with Dan McReady a little way off, and Kwang Lee, in a shiny black top hat, remaining politely beside a newly planted cypress.

Andy Hunt was looking for Collis at the cemetery gate, in a vivid heather-coloured tweed coat. His cheeks were red and he was out of breath.

'Andy,' said Collis, taking him aside. 'What's the matter?'

'I've just been down on the Embarcadero,' Andy told him. 'There's news from the East, just come in on the *Sonora*. John Brown attacked Harper's Ferry in Virginia, with a band of twenty men, and held the United States armoury for a while, trying to set off a rebellion of slaves.'

'What happened?' Collis wanted to know. 'Did any of them rise up?'

Andy shook his head. 'Brown was surrounded by marines, and captured, and two of his sons killed. Looks like they'll hang him, too. Just a case of trying to take the whole slavery issue into his own hands, and not having the wherewithal to carry it off. But the way it's set the South afire, it looks as though we might have secession at last.'

Hannah was waiting for Collis a few yards away, on the arm of a tall homely woman called Freda McPherson. Collis put his hand on Andy's shoulder to calm his excitement. 'I'll talk to you later. Right now, I have a funeral breakfast to attend.'

'But you know what this means,' hissed Andy. 'If the South secedes, and there's a war, then they'll *have* to build the railroad, and build it on our route, too!'

'You're very pepped up about the railroad all of a sudden,' said Collis. 'The last time we spoke, you were all shrimp camps and imported lumber.'

480

'Collis,' said Andy, grinning, 'never let it be said that Andrew Jackson Hunt, with a name like Andrew Jackson Hunt, is too blind to read the writing on the wall.'

'You know what the writing on the wall actually said,' put in Collis. 'It said, *"Mene, mene, tekel upharsin."* Which means, "You have been weighed in the scales and found to be wanting."'

Andy's grin only widened. 'There's only one thing I'm wanting, Collis, my friend, and that's the profit we're going to reap from this railroad.'

Collis hesitated for a second. Then he saw how impatient Hannah was growing, and he simply shook Andy's hand in a formal way, as if Andy had been doing nothing more than offering his sympathies. He walked over to Hannah and held out his arm to her. There were tears in her eyes which may have been caused by nothing more than the cold wind.

Hannah's arrival in Sacramento, white-faced and dressed in black, was the final indignity for Jane McCormick. True, Hannah was discreet enough to rent rooms at the Wallis House on H Street, a quiet and respectable hotel run by a one-time Baptist preacher who had been thrown down a flume out at Rich Bar by miners who had taken exception to his sermons, and broken his back. And true, Hannah hardly saw Collis at all, apart from their taking lunch together from time to time, and spent most of her days reading, or pushing her landlord in his wicker wheelchair. But it seemed clear enough to Jane that she had been superseded in Collis's affections by this pretty, demure blonde in black, and that Collis had been toying with her feelings from the very start.

Leland, who had never been particularly fond of Collis in any case, soon sensed his wife's freshened hostility and took it as tacit permission to be as awkward and objectionable to Collis as he knew how.

Only Charles Tucker's enthusiasm for the railroad kept Collis's spirits up. Charles had been increasingly difficult and morose over the last year. Mary had kept him at home in Sacramento, and he was missing Knickerbocker Jane 'like a bagful of fleas'. But with the news of John Brown's attack on Harper's Ferry, and with the mounting expectations that the South was going to secede, Charles began to believe that the railroad might actually be started, and that even if they drove it no farther than the silver mines of Nevada

Territory, it would bring him prestige, profit and better still, a means of putting Mary in her place.

Railroads weren't hardware stores, and railroad camps weren't ladies' front parlours. Railroads were men's business. Railroads were Milholland locomotives with seven-foot drive wheels, grease, steam, and anthracite. Railroads were blasting and cursing and digging and laying track.

With a railroad to build, Charles would be free to express his appetite for bluster, hard work, whisky, oyster loaves, and girls with fat bottoms. Not just on occasional trips to San Francisco, either, but all the time. Whenever they talked of railroads, Charles would wink at Collis, and Collis, secretly amused, would wink back, and between the two of them they'd know what Charles had in mind. Their friendship improved with every political bulletin from the East – the more alarming the better.

Theodore kept in touch with Washington by letter, writing almost every week to the allies they'd made among Republican Congressmen – the men they'd fed, or paid, or actually befriended. The news was that the Democrats were severely split between 'hard-shell' pro-slavery supporters, led by John Breckinridge of Kentucky, and 'soft-shell' moderates, led by Stephen Douglas. On the other hand, the Republicans were still being treated warily by the Northern business establishment. They were, after all, outrageously radical. Yet Northern workers were gathering around to support the Republicans in encouraging numbers, and something else had happened, too.

The Dred Scott decision had roused into political action a young attorney and ex-Congressman named Abraham Lincoln. Infuriated by Chief Justice Taney's opinion that the black people had no rights to speak of, Lincoln had taken up the leadership of the Illinois Republicans, and was campaigning hard for the Presidential nomination for 1860.

Theodore had been involved in a brief flurry of correspondence with Lincoln in 1857, after one of Lincoln's most-publicised hearings. The owners of the Mississippi paddle-steamer *Effie Afton* had been taken to court for ramming the bridge which carried the Rock Island railroad over the river at Davenport, and Lincoln had appeared for the railroad. The deeper implications of the case hadn't been lost on those who had heard it. It had been tne first naked struggle between the economy of the South, whose prosperity depended on river traffic bringing down the Mississippi to St Louis and Memphis and New Orleans all the food and timber and livestock of the Midwest, and the economy of the North, whose expansion depended on railroads running goods across the continent through Chicago and New York.

Lincoln had argued in court that railroads had as much right to cross rivers as steamboats had to paddle up and down them, and that it was the manifest destiny of the American people to forge their way west. Theodore had dug out his own notes of his hearing when it first looked likely that Lincoln might win the Republican nomination, and he had put it under Collis's nose with a meaningful tap of his finger.

'There's our man, Collis,' he had said. 'If Abraham Lincoln's nominated, and elected, then we'll take ourselves off to Washington right away, and by God we'll get our railroad.'

Collis had been sitting in the Jones's living-room, after one of Annie's best meat-pie meals. 'Lincoln?' he had asked. 'What's our benefactor William Stride going to say if we court Lincoln?'

'I don't think that Senator Stride's opinion is going to matter,' Theodore had said, sitting down in his rocking chair and crossing his legs. 'Because if Lincoln's elected on his anti-slavery platform, it's a railroad to a red cent that Jeff Davis and the rest of the South will secede in weeks rather than months. And where, I might ask, will that leave Senator Stride, with his substantial interest in a northern-route railroad?'

As 1859 turned, as the Sierra snows thawed, and as spring began, Collis began to see more of Hannah. He took her out to a merchants' hall dance, where amid laughing and clapping and furious fiddling, they showed off their fancy Eastern dance steps to the stiff-legged storekeepers of Sacramento. Hannah still wore a black ribbon on her arm, but Collis had been right. Modern life moved too fast for a widow woman to keep up her mourning for the full year, especially if she was young and energetic, and had a suitor as popular as Collis.

The news came at last that John Brown had been hanged. And the same afternoon, Collis and Hannah were taking a drive out of town in Collis's new wagon, northeastward as far as the old Vallejo farm, to deliver a load of pitch and guttering.

It was the last day of January, 1860. The sky was clear and sharp, and the wagon wheels ground noisily over the rutted track. Collis was wearing a flecked tweed suit in grey and white, and Hannah was dressed in a dark-brown cape, and a brown bonnet. Her pale hands lay in her lap like two birds.

'How is the railroad?' she asked. 'Any news?'

Collis shook his head. 'Not since last week. Mind you, John Brown's execution might help us.'

'You don't really want the North and the South to go to war?'

'It's not a question of what I want. It's inevitable. If it was just a moral issue about slavery, it wouldn't happen. If it was just a political issue about who controls Congress, it wouldn't happen either. But it's a financial issue, an issue about money, and when men find their gold is threatened, they will go to war.'

'And war will help you?'

'War will be the making of us.'

Hannah looked out over the flat landscape of the valley. The distant mountains appeared strangely close, as if they were a model. 'I have decided to come out of mourning,' she said.

Collis glanced at her. 'You mean it? When?'

'Today. Now.'

She turned to him, her eyes liquid and wide. Then she tugged off her black armband and threw it away. One of the wagon wheels ran over it, and left it on the trail, crushed and dusty.

Collis reined back the horses, and the wagon clattered to a halt. The only sound was a faint northwesterly breeze, and the occasional stirring of a horse's hoof. Collis stared at Hannah for a long time, unsure of what he should say.

'You don't think of Walter anymore?'

She shrugged. 'Sometimes. But when I do find myself thinking of him, I try to remember how it felt in that notions store on Montgomery Street, with nothing ahead of me but years of measuring percale, and of Walter's unceasing humility. I realised when I met you, Collis, that I am not a woman who can care for humble men.'

'Hm,' said Collis.

There was a very long silence. The wind whistled between the spokes of the wagon wheels. Then Collis snapped his whip and released the brake, and the horses started off again. Hannah, surprised, had to hold on to the seat tightly to prevent herself from falling.

'Is that all?' she demanded. 'Is that all you're going to say?'

He looked at her, but didn't answer.

They rattled on for half a mile or so, and then Hannah suddenly reached over and seized the reins. The horses reared and jostled, and the harness jangled, and the wagon came to a stop.

'Is that all you're going to say?' Hannah wanted to know, her cheeks flushed with anger and embarrassment.

Collis shook his head. He was enjoying this. At last, with Walter dead and with Hannah's mourning over, he could treat her the way that she really ought to be treated: as a spirited, pretty woman, with a mind of her own. He loved her. He loved her so much that he hadn't slept with her since he had brought her back to Sacramento. He had been saving himself for this very moment, the moment when Hannah herself had been obliged to wait for so long for more of the passion she had tasted at the International Hotel that she couldn't wait any longer.

'What should I say?' he teased her.

'Anything!' she snapped. 'Anything, apart from "Hm"!'

Collis reached into his coat pocket and took out his silver brandy flask. 'How about "Have a drink"?' he asked her.

She pouted and refused to answer.

'You can just drive on,' she said.

Collis took up the reins again. 'Okay,' he said. 'How about "Will you marry me?"'

There was a second in which he wondered if he hadn't played her along too far. She stared at him, her eyes glistening, and he couldn't read her expression at all. But then she swallowed back her tears, and gave him a nod, and he knew that everything was fine. He suddenly found that his own eyes were ridiculously watery.

'That's it, then,' he said. 'That's that business concluded. Now, what do you say we go deliver these gutters?'

There were many times, before they were married, when he sat and wondered about the mystery of his relationship with Hannah. He would sit on the porch of Theodore's house, while Theodore pored over his charts and his logs and drew endless maps of the Sierra foothills, and he would smoke a cigar and think to himself: Why?

Why had they been brought together, and why had destiny turned itself inside out to accommodate their selfish desires? Their love for each other had been oblique from the beginning, a love that was felt in sympathetic nuance rather than open and hungry passions. Yet because of that it was all the stronger, and all the more disturbing.

He even asked Theodore one evening what he thought about

them, but Theodore had simply unwound his wire-rimmed spectacles from his ears, laid down his compasses, and given Collis nothing but a friendly and baffled smile.

Collis and Hannah had announced their engagement a week after their ride out to the Vallejo farm, and they had set their wedding date for mid-March, 1860. As far as Theodore was concerned, they were going to be man and wife because they'd taken a liking to each other and that was all there was to it. He didn't share Collis's feelings of fate and destiny. Man made his own destiny, as far as Theodore was concerned, by hours of hard work and by bribing as many Congressmen as possible.

In the first week of March, Theodore called around at the hardware store and laid a roll of charts out on the counter. Leland and Charles were both there, and Collis, too, and they gathered around the drawings like men who have paid out good money for oil paintings, sight unseen, and now were going to get the chance to see what their investment had brought them.

'There isn't any doubt that the trace is gradual enough, and straight enough, and sufficiently workable to take a railroad,' Theodore told them. 'There will be very little bridge-building, although I suspect I might have to span the Little Bear River, and there will be very little tunnelling, too. The most difficult tunnel will have to be at the summit of the mountains, just below the Donner Pass, where the road will have to be cut through fifteen hundred feet of solid rock.'

'Fifteen hundred feet doesn't sound like too much of an obstacle,' Leland remarked.

Theodore shrugged. 'It depends on the consistency of the rock. I haven't surveyed it in any detail yet, of course, but from what I saw when we first climbed up there, it looks like flawless granite.'

'What happens once we're past the summit?' asked Collis.

Theodore stood up straight. 'Once we're past the summit, there will be six or seven more tunnels to cut at the very least. We'll have to cut into the sides of the mountains, too, so that we don't have to follow the emigrant trail around every wiggle and every waggle along the way. But the summit tunnel will be the crucial achievement. Once that's complete, we'll be able to take all our workers and all our heavy equipment up into the High Sierras by rail, and the building of the road into Nevada should go forward at speed.'

'How soon can we file this route with the government?' asked

Leland. 'It seems to me that we've had our money invested for quite a while, without much prospect of any returns.'

'I'll have to carry out a completely detailed survey before I can file,' Theodore told him. 'That means weeks, even months, up in the mountains.'

'And how much will it cost?' Leland enquired.

'Another twenty thousand dollars at least. That's on top of what all of you have already invested.'

Charles pushed his hands into his vest pockets. 'Twenty thousand dollars? Where are you going to find that?'

'Gentlemen,' said Theodore, 'we are all partners in this railroad. The question is, where are *we* going to find all that?'

'Senator Stride?' asked Collis.

Leland puffed out his cheeks and slowly shook his head. 'I doubt if your Senator friend will want to commit himself much further. Not with things the way they are in Washington.'

'The trouble is,' Theodore said, 'that I'm not getting much financial support from anyone around here, nor in San Francisco. The local traders want to wait until we've got full approval from the government, and a few miles of track laid, and the San Francisco business establishment is about as hostile as it could be. Sam Lewis promised me money when we found a route, but even he's backed out.'

'You can't simply file these maps?' asked Charles.

Theodore shook his head. 'They're not sufficient. I haven't even measured the grades, or costed the construction.'

'Well,' said Leland, clearing his throat, 'what are we going to do? We can't stretch our own credit any further.'

Collis sat back on the edge of the counter thoughtfully. 'I have an idea,' he said.

'A twenty-thousand-dollar idea?' Charles asked him.

'Maybe a thirty-thousand-dollar idea. Or even more.'

'Where are you going to get that kind of money?' Leland scoffed. 'You hardly make enough in the store to cover the cost of your keep.'

'Just listen,' said Collis. 'It seems to me that there are two key men who can help us, individually, or even jointly. The first is Senator Stride, who's already been prepared to put ten thousand dollars of his own money into the railroad, and under the right circumstances might be persuaded to put in more. The second is Laurence Melford.'

'Laurence Melford would gladly see us, *and* our proposed railroad, toasting in hell,' said Charles. 'Surely you don't expect any support from him?'

'He's the key, though, isn't he?' Collis put in. 'He's the richest man in San Francisco, after Parrott, and he's the social leader bar none. If he can at least be pressed into giving the railroad the nod, then there's no question at all that the business community will advance us whatever we need.'

'You're talking rot,' said Leland, with a dismissive wave of his hand. 'You could no more press Laurence Melford into approving a transcontinental railroad than you could catch fleas with a butterknife.'

Theodore, however, knew the workings of Collis's mind better than Leland and quietly said, 'All right – supposing it's possible to win Melford over. Not his support, perhaps, but at least a withdrawal of his out-and-out hostility. What about Stride?'

'Stride's in a delicate political position right now, but he offered to help us before, and there's no reason why we shouldn't ask him for more help now.'

'What if he refuses?' asked Leland.

'Then the Washington newspapers get to hear a most unpleasant story about him – about how he took in the destitute daughter of an old friend whose business had been ruined by the crash of '57, and how he sold that poor innocent girl to another Senator, as a slave, and a drudge, and for his carnal amusement.'

Theodore stared at Collis. He knew that Collis was talking about Delphine, and he could scarcely believe what he was hearing.

'What stuff and nonsense,' Leland said. 'You can't – '

But Theodore interrupted, 'You wouldn't. Would you? Think what such a story would do to Delphine. It would ruin her. And it's not even true.'

'It's mostly true,' said Collis. 'It's true enough to show Stride up as the venal character he really is.'

'But Delphine's reputation?'

'She's sleeping with Carslake, isn't she? Half of Washington must know about it already. And she's nothing more than a governess, and general help about the house. What kind of a reputation is that?'

'I'm talking about her moral reputation!' shouted Theodore, shocked. 'Did she drag *you* down in the dirt, when *you* were destitute, and she was still wealthy?'

'I offered to take her away,' said Collis edgily. 'I offered her everything.'

'And because she said no, you're quite happy to use her however you will? Even if it means destroying the poor girl's life?'

Collis took a breath. 'Theodore,' he said, 'it won't be the first life this railroad's taken, and by God you know as well as I do that it won't be the last.'

'The railroad! The railroad! All I ever hear from you is the railroad! You're obsessed! You talk about it as if it were some kind of God! You talk about conquering the High Sierras as if it were more important than humanity itself – your own humanity, or anybody else's!'

Theodore stood facing Collis, and he was breathing hard.

'Collis, I believe in the railroad more than anything,' he went on, his voice quieter, but still shaking. 'I've lived and breathed the railroad for year upon year, even when I've been mocked and ridiculed. The railroad pest, that's me. And proud of it. But, sweet Jesus, Collis, I can't match what you feel about it. You feel something about it that I can't even begin to understand.'

Collis looked around at his partners. Leland was standing with his hands clasped in front of him, stiff and curious. Charles was open-mouthed, as if he were waiting patiently for a fly to buzz past. Theodore was still staring at him, with sweat on his forehead, his eyes dark from hours of drawing and reading.

'The railroad will make us great,' said Collis, in a very soft voice. 'It will make this country great, too; and no greatness is achieved without sacrifice.'

'Voluntary or involuntary, I suppose?' asked Theodore bitterly.

'We may not have to resort to such measures,' said Collis. 'But if this railroad isn't going to die of starvation, and of neglect, and of general obstinacy, then we're going to have to fight for whatever we can get by whatever means necessary.'

Theodore angrily gathered up his drawings and his maps. 'You can contact me when you've raised the twenty thousand,' he said. 'But please don't tell me how you managed it, because I just might feel constrained to abandon this project once and for all.'

Collis lit up a cigar. 'You'll have one consolation, Theo,' he said, as the engineer turned his back and walked towards the store door. 'When the railroad's finished, and you're riding along its tracks, you'll be able to reflect that however it was built, whatever it cost you alone were guiltless and lily-white.'

Theodore paused, without turning around.

Collis puffed smoke and added, 'Are you sure you still want that station named after you?'

There were three clouds in the sky on the day Collis and Hannah were married. It was a simple, direct ceremony, carried out by Justice Boardman in his front yard on I Street. An unseasonably hot wind blew from the south, and ruffled Hannah's pale-blue silk dress. She looked pretty but tired as she walked on Collis's arm from the white-picketed yard to the varnished carriage which was to take them around to 54 K for their wedding breakfast.

A photograph showed them about to mount the carriage, with Charles holding Hannah's elbow, and Collis, bareheaded, frowning against the sunlight. Leland was posed with his thumbs behind the lapels of his morning coat. Mary was as rigid and white as the angel on a badly-sculpted tombstone. Jane McCormick was not there. A sick-headache had obliged her to remain in her drawing-room with the blinds drawn, her pet dog snuffling and letting off wind in the corner.

Kwang Lee set off firecrackers as the wedding carriage rolled away, as well he might have done. Charles called for nine cheers, and found himself cheering the last five of them on his own. It wasn't that Collis and Hannah weren't popular. It was simply that the plain folk of Sacramento found Collis too intense these days, too highly-charged, and Hannah too withdrawn.

The three clouds stayed motionless in the sky. Annie Jones waved her hat from the roadside as the wedding carriage went past, but Theodore kept his eyes on the ground. 'Is he still mad at you?' asked Hannah, holding tight on to Collis's arm.

Collis nodded. 'He won't be for long. Wait until I rustle up the money he needs to finish his survey.'

The wedding breakfast had been prepared by Zeitman's, the bakers, under Mary Tucker's supervision. Thus although it was excellently cooked, it was good solid food with very little of the fancy about it. Twenty of them sat around the table in the upstairs dining-room at 54 K while three Chinese boys served stuffed cabbage, veal birds, lamb shanks, and rutabaga pudding. They drank steam beer, sweet white Napa Valley wine, and sherry, and drank more toasts than they could count. Leland made a speech which lasted nearly twenty minutes, and referred to Collis several times as 'our esteemed expeditioner to distant summits'.

Collis, rising to reply to their toasts, said, 'I wish to thank all of you who have had faith in me, here in Sacramento, and even those who haven't. You all know that my colleagues and I have embarked on a difficult and controversial enterprise which, if it succeeds, will bring fresh prosperity to this town of ours, and momentous changes to the whole of the nation. We need all the support and encouragement we can get, and I'm happy to say that, today, I have acquired one of the finest supporters and encouragers that any man could hope for.'

Everyone applauded and cheered. Even Theodore tapped his spoon handle on the table and smiled across at Annie. As Collis sat down, however, it was to Hannah he looked first, and he was struck by the expression on her face. She was so calm, so self-possessed, and she was smiling with such obvious certainty about her new position as Mrs Collis Edmonds of Sacramento that Collis found himself wondering for a moment just who had married whom.

Charles stood up, swayed a little, and raised his glass. 'For myself,' he said, 'I would like to say that Collis and Hannah Edmonds have both brought new life and new hope to Sacramento, and that I shall look forward eagerly to the birth of their first two progeny. The child, first, of course, but quickly afterwards the infant railroad! And when these arrive, all in the fullness of time, the Edmondses will be the only couple in Sutter County who have one baby which cries at night, and another which whistles!'

Collis, smiling, glanced at Hannah again and took her hand. She looked prettier than ever in the reflected sunlight of noon, proud and elegant and strong. He thought to himself as he caressed her fingers, and the new gold band which he had given her only an hour ago: I don't know you yet, Mrs Edmonds. I don't know you at all. But I feel sure that I'm going to find out.

He looked across the table, across the silverware and candles and decanters of wine, and caught Theodore's eye. Theodore held his gaze for a moment, and then deliberately turned away.

His rooms on J Street he had never really thought of as home, until tonight. His landlord's wife, an impossibly talkative woman who always wore an old-style Shaker bonnet, year in, year out, inside the house or out, had 'prettified' the sitting-room and the bedroom for him and his bride, with fresh flowers and wax polish, and put up a rather depressing print of Daniel Boone leading settlers through the

491

Cumberland Gap, which she and her husband had given to Collis as a wedding gift.

Collis carried Hannah over the threshold, and set her down, a little short of breath, on the sofa. She smiled and reached up her arms for him, and he leaned forward and kissed her on the lips.

'Well, Mrs Collis Edmonds,' he said.

'Well, Mr Collis Edmonds,' she answered him.

He sat down beside her. 'Would you care for a sherry? Or I could ask Mrs Hawkins to bring up some tea.'

Hannah shook her head. 'Right now, my darling, the only refreshment I need is you.'

He kissed her again. 'If all your talk for all the years of our marriage is going to be as pretty as that, then I think I'm going to be happy.'

'You *think*?'

He grinned. 'I know for certain.'

He stood up and walked across to the window. Outside, on the dusty sidewalks of J Street, a group of children were playing hop-and-jump, and laughing.

'We didn't talk about progeny, did we?' he asked. He turned so that she could see he was only half-serious. 'I mean, before we decided to marry, we didn't even give them a thought.'

She stood up, too, and walked across the patterned rug to stand beside him. She linked her arm with his, gently, as if she had been doing it for years.

'They'll come in time, if the Lord wills it,' she said.

'I was kind of surprised that you didn't – well, that you and Walter didn't have any. You were together for nearly two years, after all.'

She lowered her eyes. Her eyelashes shone blonde in the late sunlight. On the figured walnut table beside her, a vase of spring flowers cast a shadow like an old woman's silhouette.

'Walter – wasn't very good at that kind of thing,' she said, in a tone as soft as the sunlight.

Collis cleared his throat. 'I see. Well, let's not speak of it anymore. I didn't mean to embarrass you.'

She lifted her face to his. 'You didn't,' she said. 'I can't pretend that I haven't been married before, and lain with another man, any more than you can pretend to me that you haven't lain with other women. We're old enough, aren't we, to talk of such things freely? We're husband and wife, as well as lovers.'

492

'Well, yes,' Collis answered uncomfortably.

She smiled. 'If you want to talk of progeny, then of course we shall. But my feeling is that Charles was right. We shall have two children – our natural son, and our railroad. And if you want to know which of those is most important to me now, then I am bound to say the railroad.'

Collis released his arm from hers and walked over to the chiffonier. He unstoppered the sherry decanter, poured himself a large glass, and then stood looking at Hannah while he sipped, his eyes questioning, but without saying a word.

'You fell out with Theodore because you told him the railroad would make you great,' she said huskily, 'and that the goal of greatness justifies any and all means which may be necessary to achieve it.'

'Yes,' said Collis.

'Well, I agree with you, fiercely,' she said, turning towards him. 'Because the railroad will make you rich, and celebrated, and powerful, and I know that is what you want to be. You will fulfill yourself, if you build this railroad. You will be able to live any way you want, and in any company you desire. Men like Laurence Melford will seem like cheap storekeepers in comparison: and when they talk of California in years to come, they won't talk first of Vallejo or of Frémont. They will talk of you, of Collis Edmonds, who laid the first transcontinental railroad across the High Sierras.'

Collis said nothing. But Hannah came towards him with a sweep of her skirts and held his hand.

'Whatever we have to do, you and I, to make this railroad possible, we shall,' she said. 'I have learned a bitter lesson about life from my marriage to Walter – that conventional morality and godliness are not necessarily one. For is it godly to be unhappy and unfulfilled? If Walter had not been killed, I still would have divorced him, in the face of the church and of polite society; and whatever you need to do to find your heart's desire, your railroad, whether it is respectable or not, I will be there to help you.'

She hesitated, then said, 'I know what kind of a man you are, Collis. Even more than you do yourself, perhaps. I have taken you on as my husband because I love you, but also because I want to see your dream become real, and to be part of your dream myself.'

There was a long silence, two or three minutes or even more. At last Hannah said, 'Do you understand me?'

Collis kissed her. 'I do. And I love you, too.'

They made love that night more lingeringly than they had ever done before. They let each kiss last for whole minutes, and each caress stretch out across the moonlit bedroom like the fading echoes of a song. When Collis first embraced Hannah as her husband, she slowly dug her long fingernails into the muscles of his back, deep, and held him against her as if she wanted him to suffocate her; and as their lovemaking moved to its exquisite culmination, she moaned and sniffed with pleasure, and with disappointment that it was over.

Collis sat up in bed afterwards, propped up on his feather pillow, watching the bald light of the moon fall across the rug, and shine on the backs of his silver hairbrushes. Hannah snuggled up close to him, and gradually fell asleep.

He wondered if he would ever be able to tell Hannah about Mr Kwang, and the favour that the On Leong Tong had done for him. Somehow the thought of having to conceal his complicity in Walter's death for the rest of his married life seemed to be too complicated to bear. It would be like trying to speak to Hannah with a fishbone in his throat.

He looked across at his cigar case, and considered lighting one up. But then he remembered that Hannah was not his mistress anymore, she was his wife, and she would probably object to stale cigar smoke in the bedroom. He watched her sleeping for a while, and touched her eyelids and the tip of her nose with his finger. She looked older when she was asleep, but still beautiful. He wondered if she was dreaming of the High Sierras.

Kwang Lee had a silent and sometimes mocking manner about him, but in time he became as attached to Collis as Wang-Pu had been and served him as efficiently and as loyally. Unlike Wang-Pu, he did not believe in dressing formally, and his usual get-up was a linen cap with the peak turned backwards; a very clean blue shirt, and a hardware apron with dozens of pockets. He lived in a room at the back of the store, and cooked his own food in a wok, and brewed endless cups of Dragon Well tea.

Sometimes Collis joined him for a small bowl of tung-po pork, or bacon and bamboo-shoot soup, and Kwang Lee would tell stories and jokes about his childhood in Hangchow. But there was no sentimentality about them, as there had been with Wang-Pu.

Kwang Lee was a smart cookie, a wisecracker, and it was impossible to tell if any of his stories were true.

Once Collis asked him if Mr Kwang was a man who believed in having favours returned, even favours which hadn't been asked for.

Kwang Lee was stirring bean sprouts in his wok, and the room was hazy with blue smoke. 'You mean Mr West?' he asked directly.

Collis raised his eyebrows. 'Then it *was* Mr Kwang?'

'Of course. You did not suspect it to be anyone else, did you?'

'I guess not.'

Kwang Lee added shrimps and fish gravy to his lunch, and quickly stirred them in. 'You have to be on your guard with Mr Kwang,' he said. 'He has said himself that there is no finer way of influencing those around you than to do them good turns. Mr Kwang has changed your whole life, has he not, with that one good turn?'

'Yes,' said Collis uncertainly.

Kwang Lee looked up from his cooking and grinned. 'In that case, one day Mr Kwang will expect you to return the compliment.'

Collis picked up a pair of chopsticks and dipped into Kwang Lee's wok, taking out a sample of bean sprouts and shrimp. He ate it slowly, and then said, 'More soy sauce.'

Kwang Lee smiled and reached for the blue earthenware bottle.

Collis and Hannah left J Street in August, and rented a large white house a little further out of town, on I Street. Hannah began to furnish it and decorate it in a style which she considered suitable for the treasurer of the Sierra Pacific Railroad and his spouse, with plush sofas and heavy armchairs and marquetry tables. She preferred soft colours, like dove greys and pale blues, and the inside of the house, at certain times of the day, had the quality of a smoky dream, a cloudiness about it.

They lived together peaceably, and gently, although they were both quite aware that the time would have to come when their real mettle was tested, and their personal strengths would have to clash. But that would come with the railroad, when the three store-keepers of Sacramento were ready to turn the whole world inside out.

In early September, Theodore travelled to Washington again, in another dogged attempt to raise funds for his detailed survey of the Sierras. He wrote back to his partners that 'the prospect of starting the railroad seems further away than ever, for although many agreed it is a *good idea*, they are not prepared to back their enthusiasm with money.'

Leland, who had been toying with the idea for more than a year, had made up his mind at last to run for the governorship of California. He hadn't really wanted to run until the next elections, but Jane was becoming irritable about the amount of money and credit they had already tied up in the railroad, and it seemed to her that if Leland was in the governor's mansion, his influence over state's expenditure on railroads would at least protect the money they had risked so far.

Collis, smiling, said it smacked of corruption. Leland said testily that it smacked of nothing but good sound sense.

During the year, tension between Southerners and Northerners became increasingly open. One evening, there was a fierce argument in the drawing-room of the Willard Mannings, up on Rincon Hill, between Willard Manning himself, a Virginian, and a young man from Illinois called Sturgeon. A knife was drawn, and Sturgeon was stabbed in the face and chest. For the next two weeks, San Francisco society fumed and bubbled with suppressed fear.

Hannah was sitting in their light, spacious front parlour, embroidering a firescreen, when Collis returned home from the store the Tuesday after the Sturgeon stabbing. He came across and kissed her, and then went to the pearwood cabinet for a drink.

'Did you hear the news from South Park?' asked Hannah.

'About the Willard Mannings? Yes. Kwang Lee told me.'

'What do you think about it?'

Collis turned. 'What do I think about it? I don't think anything about it. The North and the South are steaming themselves up into a condition of civil war, and incidents like this are all part of it.'

Hannah laid her embroidery in her lap. Her blonde hair was tied up in plaits and pinned with combs, making her look rather cold and Nordic.

'Don't you think it's time you went to San Francisco and talked to Mr Laurence Melford?'

'Melford? You mean about the railroad?'

'Of course about the railroad. What else? The time is just ripe, with all this uncertainty about the coming elections. Even Laurence Melford isn't going to be fool enough to ignore the possibility of war, and of Lincoln's being elected.'

Collis finished mixing himself a stone fence, and then walked thoughtfully across the room. 'I was going to wait to see the outcome of the elections themselves. But I guess you could be right.'

Hannah reached out her hand for him. 'If the election goes to Douglas or to Breckinridge, then Melford will ignore you. If it goes to Lincoln, then everyone will be panicking too much to think clearly about railroads at all. Now is an ideal moment, don't you think? It is far easier to trade on fears than it is on certainties.'

Collis squeezed her hand. 'Hannah, my darling,' he said, 'I do believe you'll make a fine businesswoman yet.'

She smiled. 'I know my own weaknesses, Collis. That's why I can see those in other people.'

'Even in me?' he asked her.

She nodded, happily. 'A man without weaknesses is like a garden wall without a gate.'

Collis sipped his drink and thought about the plan he had devised for Laurence Melford. He hoped to God it would work; but, even more, he hoped to God that Hannah wouldn't get to hear of it.

Collis did everything he could to persuade Hannah to stay at home in Sacramento while he went to San Francisco to deal with Laurence Melford, but she refused to hear of it. She had friends in San Francisco she wanted to visit, and shopping to do, and she also wanted to tend Walter's grave. Collis, who before their marriage would have found it comparatively easy to insist that he should go alone, now found Hannah's gentle obstinacy to be more than he could handle. So their maid, Lilah, packed Hannah's trunk with nightdresses and frocks and bottles of cosmetics, and Hannah joined Collis on the deck of the steamer *Renown* in her most elegant cream cap and parasol.

They stayed at the International, mostly for the sake of sentiment. The manager shook Collis by the hand and welcomed him back, and gave Hannah a distinctly uneasy look.

'Mrs Edmonds,' explained Collis, without looking up from the register book.

The manager clasped his hands together and said, 'Of course.'

'The *real* Mrs Edmonds,' said Collis, putting down the pen. 'We were married in Sacramento in March.'

'Of course,' said the manager. 'Congratulations.'

Hannah maintained a face of stony disapproval until they were shown up to their suite. Then, when the porter had gone, she burst out laughing. 'The poor man,' she said. 'Did you see his face? He couldn't believe that the terrible Collis Edmonds was actually married.'

Collis took his pocket watch out of his vest and checked the time. 'No,' he said, trying to smile. 'No, he couldn't, could he?'

Hannah sat up. 'You don't seem very amused. Didn't it amuse you?'

'Sure it amused me.'

'You're not laughing.'

Collis shrugged. 'I was thinking of Laurence Melford.'

She took off her bonnet and tossed it on to the bed. 'Of course you were. I'm sorry. I shouldn't have been so frivolous.'

'No, no. I like you when you're frivolous. It lets me know when you're happy. Before, you were always so serious. So worried.' Collis came over and gave her an unconvincing kiss. He tried to smile, but he knew she wasn't fooled. He hesitated for a moment, but then he opened his trunk and took a clean white shirt out of its tissue-paper wrapping.

'You're not going out right away?' Hannah asked him.

'I have to. I want to let Andy Hunt know that we're here, and Dan McReady, and then I want to go down to Laurence Melford's attorneys and fix up an appointment to meet him.'

'Very well,' said Hannah, as if disappointed that he was going out so soon, but trying to show that she didn't care. 'Then you won't mind if I go down to Liebes and try on some new dresses?'

'Of course not. And tonight we'll go have dinner at the Poodle Dog. How would you like that?'

'That would be nice,' Hannah said, a little airily, and went towards the bathroom.

Collis caught her arm. She didn't turn to face him, but stopped where she was, her head slightly lowered.

'Everything's all right, you know,' said Collis. 'It's all completely taken care of.'

'Yes,' said Hannah.

'I have the feeling you don't trust me,' Collis told her.

'Why shouldn't I?'

'No reason. But when I said I had to go see Andy and Dan – '

Hannah turned her head and kissed him, slowly and lovingly, on the lips.

'Whatever you think is best for the railroad, my darling, is best for us,' she said.

*

'I think you're crazy,' Andy Hunt said. 'Overplaying your hand.'

'I don't think there's any other way,' Collis told him. 'Not unless we pull out a gun on him, and say that's the way it's going to be, whether you like it or not.'

'It's sure tricky,' put in Dan McReady.

Collis sat down. They were gathered in Andy's cluttered office on Pine Street, a little after five in the afternoon, and outside it had begun to rain. Fat, wet drops that dribbled down the windows like the tears of saints.

Andy, in a peppery-coloured suit, was chewing a bulky cud of tobacco. Dan McReady looked more formal than usual, in a striped serge suit. He picked at his cuticles nervously and cleared his throat from time to time. It was plain that neither he nor Andy was particularly enthusiastic about Collis's plan.

'We're talking about pressure,' Collis said. 'Laurence Melford will only react if it looks as though his family's being threatened, or his livelihood. And since there isn't any possible way we can threaten his livelihood, we have to go for his daughter.'

'I hope you realize he's going to nail your heart to the front doors of the Melford Building if anything goes wrong,' said Andy. 'And mine too, if he finds out I've been helping you.'

'I'm lucky,' said Dan McReady. 'I don't have a heart.'

'Listen,' Collis explained, 'the single most important factor is that whatever he thinks of me, Laurence Melford trusts me with his children's welfare. After that duel with Grant, he sent me a letter thanking me for firing into the air. I could have blown Grant's head off, and the law would have supported me. He knows that. But he thinks I'm a humanitarian, and that I wouldn't harm anybody unless it was in self-defence.'

'Is that true?' asked Andy sharply.

'True enough,' said Collis. 'True enough to carry us through this particular ploy, in any case.'

Andy spat brown tobacco juice into the brass spittoon beside his desk.

Dan McReady said, 'I still think he's bound to find out it's us. I mean, who else would do it – and for what motive?'

'Anybody would do it,' said Collis. 'And for the same reason, too. For money.'

'Well, I think it's a hell of a risk,' said Andy. 'And I for one don't fancy hanging by my neck from any second-storey balconies just for the sake of a railroad.'

499

Collis stood up. 'You don't want any part of it, then?' he asked Andy.

'I didn't say that,' said Andy. 'I just said it's crazy.'

Collis smiled. 'That's all right, then. Welcome to the gang.'

Dan McReady let out a short, dry laugh.

Chapter 12

During the afternoon, while Hannah was resting, Collis took a cab south on Kearny, across Market, and then south again on Third Street and up the lower slope of Rincon Hill to South Park. He was nervous, and he constantly drummed his fingers on the sill of the carriage's window. The afternoon was cloudy, and it looked as if it could rain.

South Park was an elegant ellipse of London-style brick houses, standing nearly a hundred feet above the level of the city on its own airy hill. It was here that San Francisco's millionaires and socialites had clustered themselves, around an immaculate garden, well away from the crowds and the smells of the docks and the markets. The garden was surrounded by wrought-iron railings and locked gates, to which only the residents had keys.

It wasn't surprising that South Park was unsettled these days. Most of the families who lived here were Southerners, and most of their money came from plantations in the South, and slave labour. In a few years' time, many of them would be ruined; and even sooner than they could have suspected, the cable-car companies would excavate Second Street, cut right through Rincon Hill itself, and destroy their charmed way of life forever. Rincon Hill today is irrevocably buried under the approaches to the Bay Bridge.

Collis alighted from the cab outside No. 12 South Park, and told the driver to wait. The house was flat-fronted, with fresh-painted railings and gleaming brass door handles. The nameplate announced that it was called Colusa. The net curtains were drawn back in fancy flounces and tied with white silk ribbons. Inside one of the front windows, Collis could see a white parrot in a white cage. He rang.

The door was opened promptly by a Negro footman. 'Sir?' he asked.

'I have a letter for Miss Melford,' said Collis. 'I'd be obliged if you'd make sure she gets it.'

The footman held out his white-gloved hand. Collis made as if he was going to give him the letter, but then suddenly whipped it back out of his reach.

'Miss Melford, you understand?' he said. 'Not Papa or Mama. Not brother Grant. Miss Sarah Melford herself.'

The footman said, 'Yes, sir. I understand you, sir.'

'Good fellow,' Collis told him, and handed him the letter and fifty cents. Without any sign of acknowledgement, the footman closed the door and left Collis standing in the damp afternoon wind.

Well, that was that. The first part of his plan was accomplished. Now he had to go make arrangements for the rest of it. He turned away from the door and beckoned his cab driver.

As the cab circled around the private gardens, around the breeze-blown flowers and the neat green grass, Collis sat up straight in his seat so that he could look back at the Melford House. For a moment he thought he could see one of the decorative net curtains drawn aside, by the hand of an unseen watcher, and then let fall again. He tried to smile to himself. If there was one weakness which everybody shared, rich or poor, it was curiosity; and it was curiosity which would win him the alliance of Laurence Melford.

'Where now, sir?' the driver enquired as they rattled over the planks of Third Street.

'Jackson Street,' said Collis. 'Mr Kwang's, if you know it.'

'Oh, yes, sir,' the driver told him, clicking encouragement to his horse. 'I know it all right.'

Mr Kwang was working on his accounts. He was sitting cross-legged in a dim room, lit only by a Chinese oil lamp with a blue-and-white shade of the thinnest frosted glass. He was writing on sheets of rice paper with a bamboo brush, and every now and then his fingers would fly at a large ebony-and-ivory abacus which stood beside him, making the beads rattle across the wires like a volley of musketry.

Collis was shown in, and he stood without speaking for a while as Mr Kwang completed a column of figures. Then Mr Kwang looked up at him and said, 'Mr Edmonds. Please make yourself comfortable.'

'I hope I'm not interrupting,' said Collis. 'I didn't have time to make an appointment.'

Mr Kwang set his brush down in a small porcelain dish of ink. 'You are a friend of the Chinese, Mr Edmonds. You are welcome at any time.'

Collis took off his hat and sat down on the floor. 'You've already done me one favour, Mr Kwang.'

Mr Kwang's face was expressionless. 'Investment in the future of the Chinese people is not a favour, Mr Edmonds. By helping you in your personal difficulties, I hope I have assured the employment of Chinese labour on the transcontinental railroad.'

'Yes,' he said solemnly, 'I believe you have.'

'You would like tea?' asked Mr Kwang.

'No, thanks. I don't have the time. I came for something quite specific.'

'Ah,' said Mr Kwang, nodding. 'Is it money you want? I regret I can't help you there. All of my money is tied up in property, and in girls.'

'No, not money,' said Collis. 'Opium.'

'Opium? You surprise me. You don't mean to take it yourself?'

Collis shook his head. 'Oh, no. Nothing like that. I just want enough to put someone to sleep for an hour or two. Enough so the person doesn't really realize what's going on.'

Mr Kwang looked down at his accounts. 'You have something very devious in mind, Mr Edmonds. Something that involves the participation of somebody who, under normal circumstances, would not be willing to help you.'

'You're an astute man, Mr Kwang.'

'I am the leader of the On Leong Tong, Mr Edmonds.'

Collis cleared his throat. 'Then you can help me?'

'Possibly. But the opium will have to be taken as a tincture. You can't persuade anybody to smoke it against his will.'

'I'll pay for it,' said Collis. 'I didn't come here expecting something for nothing.'

Mr Kwang regarded him for a moment with that smooth, impenetrable face. Then he clapped his hands, once, and his young hummingbird appeared, in a dress of turquoise silk. He spoke to her, quickly, in Hokkien. She nodded and went shuffling off.

'I hear you were married,' said Mr Kwang, as they waited. 'I should offer you my congratulations.'

'Kwang Lee told you?'

'I don't recall. My informants are too numerous. I know everything that happens in Sacramento, in Napa, in Sonoma, in Oakland, almost as soon as the ferries dock. I deal in girls, Mr Edmonds, just as you deal in hardware, and I need all the intelligence I can get.'

The girl came back and handed Mr Kwang a small white bottle with a sealing-wax stopper. Mr Kwang passed it to Collis.

'In that bottle is a strong tincture of opium,' he said. 'Be careful with it. Too much, and you may arrest the heart.'

Collis looked at the bottle for a moment and then slipped it into his coat pocket. 'I'll be careful.'

Mr Kwang smiled faintly. 'You need not pay me now. But when you have successfully accomplished whatever you intend to do with that tincture, you may present me with a railroad flag as a souvenir.'

'How do you know this has anything to do with the railroad?'

Mr Kwang picked up his brush. 'You are getting yourself a reputation, Mr Edmonds. Everything you involve yourself in, no matter what it is, has something to do with the railroad.'

Collis looked steadily at Mr Kwang. A gong reverberated somewhere in the house, like a reminder of a far country and a long-lost life. Collis stood up, paused, bowed, and then turned to leave.

Mr Kwang said: 'There is a Chinese saying, Mr Edmonds, which is almost impossible to translate. But the meaning of the words is that he who tries to buy the future can only do so at the expense of the past.'

Collis stopped for a moment by the bamboo curtain. 'You're a hard man, Mr Kwang,' he replied. 'Harder than I am, without a doubt. But give me time.'

He waited for an answer, but all he heard was the sudden rattle of the abacus. He pushed through the bamboo curtain, walked along the narrow balcony, and then went down the stone steps to the street.

His last call of the afternoon was on Pine Street, at the corner studio of W. P. Naylor, Ambrotypist & Photographer. It was a small, dusty place, crowded with tripods and rolls of background paper and smelling strongly of sodium hyposulphite. In the window, faded by the sun, were gilt-framed photographic portraits of W. L. Winn, one of the pioneers of the fashionable San Francisco soda fountain; and of a homely lady in a white dress who plainly fancied nerself as Ophelia.

Collis went into the studio and pinged the brass bell on the counter. He waited for a while and then pinged it again. At length, there was a flurry of shuffling and cursing from the back of the premises, and a thin young man emerged, in rolled-up shirtsleeves

504

and acid-stained vest, his spectacles perched amid his wild prematurely grey hair.

'Yes?' he snapped.

Collis handed him the letter of introduction which Andy Hunt had written out for him. The young man peered at the front of it, then at the back of it, and then ripped it open with an orange-stained thumb. He read it quickly, sniffed, and then crammed it back into its envelope.

'You know the consequences of what you're asking, I suppose?' the young man said twitchily.

Collis nodded. 'That's why Mr Hunt sent me to you. Apparently you know the value of keeping your mouth closed tight.'

'I know the value of not trusting Mr Andrew Jackson Hunt as far as I can toss him.'

He took the letter out of the envelope again and re-read it. 'Photography is a great art, you know,' he said biting his lip. 'Don't you think it's sacrilege to put it to such purposes?'

'Let's just call it progress,' said Collis.

'Progress? Well, I suppose so. If the recruitment of scientific methods for the more efficient extortion of money can be called progress – then, yes, I suppose it's progress.'

'I gather you're not usually above taking a few sportive pictures,' said Collis with a tight smile. 'Mr Hunt said, "Naylor's your man, for that kind of thing."'

The young man extricated his spectacles from his hair and put them on. He stared at Collis with eyes as pale and cold as a Sacramento salmon. 'Mr Naylor's dead,' he said. 'Died years ago, of pneumonia. My name's Figgis. But everybody still calls me Mr Naylor in any case, on account of the name of the business.'

'You can help me?' asked Collis.

'I suppose so. When, and where?'

'In two days' time, most likely at Knickerbocker Jane's.'

'I see. Well. I've done some work there before.'

Collis rolled off one of his leather gloves, took out a cheroot, and lit it. 'Sportive work?' he asked Mr Figgis.

'You needn't be so patronising,' the photographer retorted. 'What you're asking for here is just as bad. Worse, in fact.'

Collis nodded. 'That's why I came to see you in person. To make sure that you were a good, trustworthy fellow.'

Mr Figgis hesitated for a moment, still chewing at his lips. Then, quite suddenly, he reached under his counter and produced a lavish red-morocco album, embossed with gold leaf. He laid it flat and opened the first page so that Collis could see it. Framed in a soft oval halo of sepia was a portrait of a plump naked girl with her hair tied up in plaits and a necklace of wild flowers.

'You see?' said Mr Figgis. 'You can call it "sportive" until you're black in the face, but it's art, too.'

Collis leafed through the album. There were daguerreotypes and ambrotypes of girls sitting dreamily in artificial sylvan settings, of girls kissing each other on rustic bridges, of girls fondling naked gentlemen with moustaches, narrow chests, and stocking garters.

'Fifty dollars the whole album,' remarked Mr Figgis, as if that were an extra credential for its artistic merit.

Collis closed it. 'Do this job well – give me half a dozen pictures that are half as good – and I'll come back and pay you twice that much for it.'

Mr Figgis looked down at the album and frowned. 'This is not going to be dangerous, is it?' he asked. 'I don't ususally take on anything dangerous.'

'Dangerous?' asked Collis. He shook his head. Then, without another word, he left the studio and stepped out on to Pine Street again to call his cab.

Mr Figgis watched him through the dusty glass of his window, and the late sunlight cast the shadow of the gilded letter N across his face, like warpaint.

Collis and Hannah dined that night at the Poodle Dog, in one of the private rooms upstairs. These rooms were furnished with parlours, bathrooms, and even bedrooms, and were mostly used by ladies and gentlemen who wished to dine and then dally together without being seen in public. There was even a separate entrance at the side of the restaurant, where ladies could alight from their carriages, veiled or disguised, and make their way directly to the upper three floors.

Collis ate there because the surroundings were silent and sumptuous, all velvet and brocade drapes, and because the food was good. Hannah was a little uneasy about it, but then Hannah seemed uneasy about their whole trip to San Francisco.

'Have you arranged to meet Laurence Melford yet?' she asked Collis, as they ate a concoction of San Francisco Bay shrimps, cream, and brandy.

'I've contacted his attorneys,' Collis said, without looking up.

'But what are you going to say to him, even if he condescends to meet you? You keep saying you've got it all worked out. You keep saying you've got a plan. But you won't tell me what it is.'

'It's complicated, that's all,' said Collis, taking a swallow of champagne. 'And I didn't want you to trouble yourself about it until I'd gotten it all arranged.'

'Collis,' she said, 'that's what I'm here for. That's why I married you. I *want* to trouble myself with your business, and with all of your plans, whether you've finished arranging them or not. I don't want you to think that you can't involve me in any of your ventures until they're satisfactorily settled. You're not a cat, you know, bringing in dead mice to please its mistress.'

Collis smiled. 'You're a perfect wife, Hannah. Do you know that?'

'I wish I were. But I can't be, unless you allow me to be.'

'How am I preventing you?'

She set down her fork. 'You're preventing me by refusing to tell me how you're going to persuade Laurence Melford to approve the railroad. For goodness sake, Collis, it was my idea to come to San Francisco in the first place. The least you can do is tell me what you have in mind. I might be able to improve on it.'

Collis paused, and then he said, 'I doubt it.'

'How can you doubt it until I've had the opportunity of trying?'

Collis wiped his mouth with his napkin. 'Hannah, my dearest, I don't think you completely understand. Laurence Melford is more than a rival – more than a Southern businessman with an antiquated point of view about railroads. He's a rich, ruthless, and very powerful enemy. He wouldn't stop at anything to keep the transcontinental railroad from crossing the Sierras, not just because he believes it threatens his wealth and his influence, but because he knows that it will wreck the whole world as he knows it. He's frightened, as well as angry, and that's what makes him so formidable.'

'I appreciate all of that,' said Hannah. 'But isn't that all the more reason why you should seek from me all the assistance you can? If he's so formidable, if he's so ruthless, surely it makes sense for you to confide in me?'

Collis pushed aside his plate of shrimp. He had a fragment stuck between his teeth, and it took him a moment to worry it out. Then he said, 'Under normal circumstances, Hannah, I'd agree with you.'

'But these circumstances aren't normal?'

'My plan isn't – altogether normal.'

'You mean it's illegal?' she wanted to know.

He gave her a quick, embarrassed smile. 'Let's just say that it skirts around the law as it's generally understood.'

'Like the blanket affair?'

Collis nodded. 'A little like that, yes.'

She reached across the table and held his hand, her fingertips touching his wedding band.

'I think you believe me to be far more sensitive and shockable than I really am,' she said. 'I'm a Catholic believer, and I try to live my life by the Good Book, but the Lord is as practical and sensible as anyone here on earth. He knows that men have to trade and do business to better the life of the community; and unless what you're planning to do is harmful or hurtful, I'm sure He's capable of forgiving. Or at least of understanding.'

Collis laid his hand over hers.

'It's for the railroad, Collis,' she said. 'Think of the days when I was on the brink of death from the yellow fever. Think of all the people you'll save in the future from the pestilence in Panama. Your plan may not be legal, but if it harms no one, how can anyone complain that it hasn't been undertaken for the greatest of goods?'

Collis looked at Hannah for a long while. At her clear blue eyes, her high cheekbones, her hair as blonde as fresh-cut pine. He thought of their nights together, for some reason of which he wasn't quite sure – of making love to her, of feeling her soft breasts in the hollows of his hands. He touched his cheek and remembered how he had woken on the morning after their wedding, with the imprint of an embroidered pillowcase on his skin.

'Hannah,' he said in a quiet voice, 'I married you because I loved you, with a passion that was real but which I was unable to understand. Now I've found out what excited that passion, apart from your beauty. You're a railroad builder's wife, that's what you are. You're full of strength, and determination, and of tireless cunning, too. I married you because I couldn't possibly have married anyone else.'

Hannah blushed and smiled. 'I feel the same way about you '

There was a discreet rapping at the door. Collis called, 'Come on in, it's unlocked,' and a waiter appeared to clear their dishes and set out the next course. He kept his eyes studiously averted as he served

508

them, and even when Hannah said, 'It's all right, you know, we're very respectably married,' he kept his head lowered and backed out of the door as quickly as possible.

Collis took the lid off his lamb pot pie, and for a moment he was wreathed in fragrant steam.

'I never know how anyone manages to dally in this place, after the food they serve,' he said, picking up his fork. 'There's still the boned capon to come, and the ham in champagne sauce, and the saddle of venison, and you mustn't miss the *bouchée à la Palermitaine*.'

'Collis,' said Hannah, 'my corset is beginning to feel distinctly too small.'

He glanced up at her. It was the raciest thing that she had ever said to him in normal conversation. He knew why she'd said it, too: to let him know that she was 'one of the fellows', and that whatever his plan was for dealing with Laurence Melford, he could safely tell her about it.

He put down his fork again. 'Hannah,' he said, 'I simply can't tell you what my plan is. Not yet. Don't think badly of me, will you, for keeping it a secret just for now?'

The smile left her face like a reluctant guest. Then it came back again, but forced this time. 'All right,' she said. 'If you feel you really can't, then I respect your judgement. You're my husband, and I accept what you say.'

Their conversation during the remainder of the meal was stilted and uncomfortable. Hannah didn't eat much, and left her peach pie untouched. As he cleared away the last dishes, the waiter caught Collis's eye and pulled a mournful face, as if Collis's chances of a vigorous evening's entertainment were looking more than poor.

After the waiter had left, Collis said, 'That fellow doesn't think much of my prospects tonight.'

'What fellow?'

'The waiter. He just gave me a nod of deep commiseration.'

Hannah loftily looked away. 'Well,' she said. 'He may be quite right.'

He was writing at his escritoire in their suite at the International Hotel the following morning when he realized the significance of the day's date. 18 September 1860. His father's birthday. The day on which three years ago he had promised to meet Maria-Mamuska outside of Walter West's store on Montgomery Street, at noon.

He sat up straight in his chair and wrapped his green silk dressing-gown tighter around his chest. In the bedroom next door, he could hear the occasional chink of Hannah's teacup, as she took her breakfast in bed. He had been writing a letter to Leland, to be taken up by ferry to Sacramento. His pen had paused over the unfinished sentence '. . . and seventy-five short tons of iron pit supports,' and had dropped a blob of ink in the shape of a duck.

He rubbed his forehead with his fingertips. Did he really want to see Maria-Mamuska again – always supposing she was still alive? She would have been lucky to survive for so long, what with San Francisco's bad drinking water and contagious diseases, not to mention the risks of childbirth. For all Collis knew, she was lying under the gritty clay of Lone Mountain Cemetery, sightless and skeletal; or thirty feet under the waters of San Francisco Bay, raped and robbed, with her throat laid open.

He didn't owe her anything, after all. She had ignored him at Panama City station. And even if she was alive, and free of gonorrhea, she had probably forgotten their rendezvous completely. She wasn't the kind of girl that Leland would call 'attentive'.

Yet, Collis stood up, and went slowly into the bedroom, and stood watching Hannah in her white lace bed jacket. And, after a minute or two, he said, 'I'm going to have to keep a luncheon appointment today.'

'Oh, yes?' she answered, deliberately busy with her toast.

'It's, er . . . well, it's all to do with the plan. A business contact.'

'I see.'

He crossed the room and sat down on the edge of the bed. 'Hannah,' he pleaded. 'Do you really have to treat me so hard?'

She looked at him as she ate. 'Do you think that I treat you hard? All the circumstances considered?'

'Hannah – you know perfectly well that I'm going to tell you everything about this plan, just as soon as it's been successfully accomplished. The moment I can come back to you and say, "It's all over, it's all wrapped up," I'll explain the whole thing to you from beginning to end.'

'I'm your wife, Collis. I have a right to know now.'

He took a breath, as if he was going to say something sharp, but then he let it out again. 'I'll be back by three o'clock,' he told her, getting up from the bed. 'Why don't you ask one of your lady friends to come around and take luncheon with you?'

She set aside her breakfast tray. 'I'll do whatever I consider fit,' she said, and when he started to open his mouth again, she said, 'Just as you do,' and smiled.

'Hannah,' he said. Coaxing her.

'Collis,' she replied. Resisting him.

He put on one of his most appealing expressions, but all she did was slowly shake her head.

'Oh, dammit!' he shouted at last. 'Won't you understand that I *can't* tell you?'

Walter West's store on Montgomery Street was already looking derelict. The blinds were drawn, and pine planks had been nailed across the front door to protect the premises from looters. A tattered poster said: 'Closed, Due to Sudden Bereavement. Store & Stock to Be Sold by Auction.' Collis went up to one of the side windows where the blinds had sagged, and rubbed away the dust in an effort to see inside. He could just make out an overturned chair, and a bolt of cloth.

The deputy sheriff had investigated Walter's murder 'with all the necessary zeal', but after questioning numerous tong leaders and drinking numerous bottles of warm rice wine, he had concluded that Walter had been murdered 'in a fit of pique, by an oriental person unknown,' and that the culprit was probably 'well away by now'. The truth was that San Francisco's few law-enforcement officers were not only mystified by the Chinese, but afraid of them, too. It was better to accept their hospitality and their chop suey without comment, and leave them to deal with their own affairs.

Collis leaned against the horse-hitching rail outside Walter West's store, tilted the brim of his hat against the hazy noon sunlight, and waited. Several people turned and stared at him as they walked by, since his likeness had appeared five or six times in the papers, and it was unusual to see such a well-dressed man loafing on a street corner. Collis smiled once or twice at some of the prettier girls who passed, and took out his pocket watch to check the time. He'd give her ten minutes, and then go.

A small blue-painted carriage drew up in front of him. He moved aside to let the coachman climb down, open the door, and extend the steps. He was damned if he was going to wait very much longer. Perhaps he'd take Hannah for an excellent lunch someplace, and see if he couldn't calm her down. He'd *like* to be able to tell her his plan. In fact, he'd prefer to. But how could he possibly explain it without embarrassing her? How could he possibly explain it without embarrassing himself?

He wasn't even looking towards the blue-painted carriage as the coachman helped his passenger to step down. He was conscious of a lady in a blue cape and feathered bonnet, and he took a further step backwards to let her pass; but his eyes were on the sidewalk, for the first glimpse of that long black hair, of that low Spanish-style blouse.

But then she said, 'Collis?' and he turned.

He stared. He didn't even recognise her at first. She seemed to be taller, and far more attractive, and her embroidered cape was well cut, well styled, and obviously expensive. Her hair was pinned up with diamond-studded combs, and she wore sparkling diamond earrings. She carried a parasol with self-confident grace.

She was still Maria-Mamuska, though – with those same dark slanted eyes, and that soft, sensual, slightly parted mouth. She was smiling at him in pleasure and amusement, and as he stepped forward she gave him a mocking little bob. He took her hand and held it between his, and he did nothing at all but stare at her.

'There!' she told him. 'I never forgot the day. 18 September, your father's birthday, at noon. I often used to pass by this store, and wonder if you would remember it, too.'

'You look quite beautiful,' he told her. 'I've thought of meeting you here from time to time, and I've thought of what you might look like. But I never imagined this.'

She leaned forward and kissed his cheek. She smelled of Eau de l'Isle, the season's most fashionable fragrance. 'When you come to San Francisco,' she said, 'you do one of three things. You die, you stay as you are, or you get rich.'

'And you got rich.' Collis grinned.

'You, too, from what I hear. My maid reads the newspapers for me. I like to hear what's going on.'

'Your child?' he asked her. 'Did you have your child?'

'A boy,' she said. 'He's almost three now. He looks like his father, but that doesn't matter. I will teach him to grow up like a gentleman.'

Disregarding the stares of passers-by, Collis suddenly reached out and held Maria-Mamuska close, and kissed her. 'I m so happy

512

to see you,' he said. 'And I'm especially happy to see you looking so well.'

'Would you like to take lunch with me?' she asked. 'My house is on Bush Street. You must tell me all about yourself and your railroad.'

'I'd love to.'

They climbed into the carriage and the coachman closed the door. He was a short, impassive Mexican with a moustache as droopy as seaweed. 'The house, Miss Paradise?' he asked and Maria-Mamuska nodded.

'Miss Paradise?' asked Collis, as they joggled off along Montgomery Street. 'Is that what you call yourself these days?'

'It was the wine merchant's idea. He said that all ladies of pleasure should have professional names.'

'I don't quite understand.'

She held his arm and kissed his ear. The carriage was bright with sunlight, and flickering reflections from second-storey windows. 'When I first arrived in San Francisco,' she said, 'I worked in Mr Gordon's sugar refinery, packing bags of brown sugar. Well – I was pregnant, what choice did I have? But when George was born, and I was well again, I made up my mind to do something better. Something to make me lots of money. Mr Gordon had always told me to make the best of my natural assets, and that's what I did. I named George after Mr Gordon, you know.'

'How did you start?' asked Collis.

Maria-Mamuska snuggled up closer. Collis hoped that Eau de l'Isle wasn't too strong and too recognisable. He'd meant to buy some for Hannah but he hadn't gotten around to it yet.

'It was Mr Gordon himself who helped me,' said Maria-Mamuska. 'He knew a lady called Mary Miller on Geary Street. She runs a very respectable house, you know. Very genteel, with well-dressed girls, and tea and cakes for the clientele. They even have signs on the wall saying, "No Vulgarity Allowed."'

'So you took up the oldest of all professions?' asked Collis.

Maria-Mamuska raised her head proudly. 'I've enjoyed every minute of it, and every man. Perhaps if I'd had to work in a four-bit crib on Meigg's Wharf I wouldn't have liked it. But Mary Miller taught me how to look after myself, how to please my clientele, and she gave me the name of a good doctor, too.'

Collis sat back on the carriage's dark-blue velvet seat. 'When did you decide to set up business on your own?'

'When I was taken to the opera for the first time, and saw Belle Cora and some of the other madams, in all their pearls and their jewels and their beautiful dresses. I realized they were rich! And I thought to myself, I'm at least as pretty as Belle Cora, so why shouldn't *I* be rich, too?'

'You mentioned a wine merchant,' said Collis. 'Where did he come into it?'

'Well,' said Maria-Mamuska confidentially. 'It's not generally known, but several of the bigger wine importers help to finance the parlour houses where their champagne is sold. They can make so much profit, you see; and so they pay for leases, and for furniture, and some of them even bail out the girls when they're arrested as common prostitutes.

'Myself, I went to Dunglas & Company, because I'd heard they were more respectable than most, and I talked to young Mr Dunglas himself. Very accommodating, he was. He bought me my house, he paid for the furnishings, and as long as I sell fifteen cases of French champagne every week, he'll give me anything and everything I want.'

Collis couldn't help grinning. 'I always thought you were a remarkable young lady,' he said. 'That night in Panama, when you told me right to my face that I hadn't satisfied you, that was proof enough for me. I was just hoping against hope that you were still alive, and that your child had been born safe.'

'Even though you're married?' asked Maria-Mamuska, with a touch of slyness in her voice.

'Your maid read that to you, too?'

'Oh, yes. And I'm pleased for you. She's your kind of woman, isn't she? Strong, and sure of what she wants.'

'Is that how she struck you, when you first saw her?'

Maria-Mamuska kissed him again. 'You thought she was so pitiable, didn't you? The poor lady, travelling all the way to San Francisco by herself, going out to join a husband she'd forgotten how to love! But you mark what I say, she knew what she wanted all along, from the moment she set eyes on you! *There's* a handsome young man with his head fixed on the right way around, she thought. And didn't she get you, in the end? She's a clever lady.'

Collis held Maria-Mamuska's hand. Her nails had grown now, and were finely manicured. Every finger was decorated with a gold ring, each one set with diamonds or sapphires or South American emeralds.

'I think you're misjudging Hannah more than a little,' Collis said. 'She didn't find it easy to leave her husband.'

'She must have found it easier once he was dead.'

Collis didn't want to talk about that. 'That was a tragedy,' he said, and turned away.

Maria-Mamuska reached out and touched his cheek. 'I'm sorry,' she told him. 'I didn't mean to offend you. Please forget what I said. Why don't you tell me about your railroad instead, and what you're doing in San Francisco?'

Her house on Bush Street was a narrow four-storey gingerbread building with railings and balconies, one of a terrace of six. It was discreetly painted in grey and white, but the shine of its brasswork and the over-elaborate way in which its lace curtains were arranged somehow gave it away as a house of entertainment, rather than a residence, or a boarding-house.

Stepping down on to the boarded sidewalk, Collis tugged on his gloves and said, 'It's very handsome. I must congratulate young Mr Dunglas, if ever I have the pleasure of making his acquaintance.'

'Don't you dare,' said Maria-Mamuska, as she gathered up her dress to step down.

She dismissed her coachman and led Collis inside. The house was less lushly decorated than Knickerbocker Jane's, and the colours were more muted, creams, and tobacco browns, and bottle greens. On the walls were oil paintings of plump and contented nudes, their flesh white and luminous, their eyes as vacant as sheep's. There were spittoons in every corner, and ashtrays, so that the house had the atmosphere of a gentleman's smoking parlour rather than a dolled-up whorehouse.

A pretty Chinese girl in a maid's apron was waiting to take off Maria-Mamuska's cape. Collis gave the girl his gloves and his stick, and she bowed her head to him respectfully.

'I wanted my clientele to feel at ease,' said Maria-Mamuska, taking Collis through to the living-room. 'In so many parlour houses, the poor fellows feel as if they daren't cuss, or smoke, or tell stories. I still expect good behaviour, but I don't have the gentlemen gathered around the piano singing hymns, as Mrs Kahn does. And I do serve liquor.'

'A glass of champagne would go down very well,' said Collis.

Maria-Mamuska pulled a brown velvet bell rope. 'You must

have some of our dim sum, too, while you're here. Do you like Chinese food?'

'I've been obliged to. The Chinese community seems to have elected me its unofficial hero of the decade. I've promised them work on the railroad, you see, laying the tracks and digging the tunnels.'

'Is it the railroad that's brought you down here this time?'

Collis stood with his back to the fireplace. Maria-Mamuska, spreading her shiny blue skirts, sat down on a davenport opposite. In the pale light of the early afternoon, she looked like the coy erotic fantasy of a popular painter – a wild woman dressed up in silks and lace, with a lace-and-pearl choker around her neck, diamonds in her hair, and her full breasts cradled in nothing but a bodice of sheer embroidered lawn.

'I've come down here to see if I can't persuade San Francisco's business community to lay out some capital,' he said. 'We have a full survey to undertake, up in the mountains, before we can convince Congress that we've really found a feasible route, and that's going to take money. More money than we've actually got.'

'You don't believe they'll actually advance you anything, do you?' asked Maria-Mamuska. 'It says in the newspapers they hate the railroad.'

'They'll lend me the money if Laurence Melford says it's a good idea to lend me the money.'

'Laurence Melford? But he's the worst of them. I've seen him at the opera. A real pioneer bigwig, and a Southerner, too. When Laurence Melford says hop, everybody hops.'

'That's exactly why I have to get his support,' said Collis.

Maria-Mamuska pulled a face. 'I think you're crazy. He wouldn't support you if you held a gun to his nose.'

'Supposing I held one to his daughter's nose? Metaphorically speaking. Don't you think he'd change his mind then?'

'*What* speaking?'

'Metaphorically. That means I don't actually intend to hold a gun against her nose for real, but I do intend to do something that will have the same kind of result.'

The Chinese girl came in with champagne. They each took a glass, and toasted each other in silence. Collis walked over to the window and then turned around. Maria-Mamuska could only see a silhouette of his face, half obscured by the sunlight.

'I intend to put pressure on Laurence Melford in the one place where he's really vulnerable. If he thinks that Sarah's at risk, he'll do anything, and say anything, to get her out of trouble.'

'You're going to threaten her life? How can you do that? Melford will have you hanged.'

'I'm not going to threaten her life at all. I'm going to threaten something which Laurence Melford, as a Southern gentleman and an overprotective father, holds even dearer than life. Her reputation.'

Maria-Mamuska sipped champagne. Her eyes, above the sparkling rim of her glass, were frowning with an unspoken question.

'Maria, the very first thing I ever learned about the Melford family was that Laurence Melford was the kind of man who wouldn't tolerate anything but the best for his daughter. He kicked would-be suitors out of his front door like mongrels out of a butcher shop, only harder. He's obsessed with the idea of Sarah as a Southern flower, untouched, unsullied, beautiful and courteous. Well, I thought, supposing someone showed him that she wasn't that way at all, and supposing someone threatened to show the whole world that she wasn't that way at all, unless he agreed to some measure of gentlemanly co-operation?'

Maria-Mamuska fanned herself slowly with her hand. 'I think I'm beginning to see what you mean. You mean blackmail on his daughter's reputation? But how are you going to do it?'

'I shouldn't be telling you this,' said Collis.

Maria-Mamuska laughed, in a friendly way. 'You shouldn't, but you probably will. Most men tell me most things, which is what makes me good at my profession. I always say that even the most anxious man finds it easier to talk to a prostitute than he does to anybody else, including his wife. *Especially* his wife, sometimes.'

'You've changed a great deal in three years, haven't you? You've learned a lot.'

'Yes.' She smiled. 'About myself I've learned a lot, and about men. Most parlour houses only take care of men's physical lusts. But here, I take care of everything.'

Collis took a cigar from a humidor on the mantelpiece. He crackled it close to his ear, then slipped off the band, clipped it, and lit it. Maria-Mamuska watched him appreciatively.

'You have style, you know,' she told him, gratuitously

He smiled at her. 'You have style, too. More style than any madam I know. I was going to ask Knickerbocker Jane to help me,

517

but maybe you ought to hear what I've got in mind, just in case you can help me instead.'

'Before you start,' Maria-Mamuska said 'have you told Hannah about any of this?'

He looked at her, with cigar smoke dribbling out of his pursed lips. He shook his head.

'All right,' she said and nodded, as if she understood why. 'Now, tell me what you plan to do.'

'There's a letter for you,' Hannah said. 'It came at three o'clock, by hand. The crest on the back says "M". For Melford, I suppose.'

'You're not still angry with me?' he asked her, taking the envelope and peering at it closely.

She was dressed in an oyster-coloured satin dress, with white frills at the bodice and cuffs. Her blonde hair was curled and styled, and she looked classically beautiful. She looked at him and shrugged, and then reached out and gripped the cloth of his sleeve. 'No. Of course I'm not. I love you.'

He kissed her. He held her close, and kissed her again. She was warm and she smelled of soap, as well as some perfume that he recognised. He stood straight, and put his head on one side, the way his father always used to when he asked a question. 'Eau de l'Isle?' he queried. 'When did you buy that?'

She pretended to look offended. 'Why should you care?'

'I care because you're my wife,' he told her. 'And, most of all, I care because I love you.'

'Quite a good reason,' she said, pretending to relent a little.

He sat down at his escritoire and began to tear open his letter with the paperknife. A long silence. Eventually, he raised his eyes.

'What does Laurence Melford say?' Hannah asked.

'It's not from Laurence Melford, as a matter of fact. It's from his secretary. It says that Mr Melford sees no possible point in our meeting, and that his opposition to the transcontinental railroad remains as firm as always.'

'Oh. What are you going to do?'

Collis rolled the letter into a ball between the palms of his hands. 'Do? I shall do what I was always going to do. I shall stick to my plan.'

'The plan you won't tell me about.'

'That's correct. The plan I won't tell you about.'

She let out a short, exasperated breath. 'Very well. If you won't tell me, you won't. But I think I shall dress for dinner now, and if I were you I wouldn't expect me for at least two hours.'

'Hannah,' he said.

But she slammed the door to the bedroom and left him appealing to empty air. He sighed, and sat down at his escritoire. He supposed there was no use letting Hannah upset him. Carefully he uncrumpled the letter and spread it out on the tooled-leather top with the side of his hand. He read it again, whispering the words out loud, by the failing light from the window.

> My dear Mr Edmonds,
> You were fortunate to give your invitation to my best friend among all of our servants, since he passed it directly to me as you bade him. I shall be delighted to meet you on the 20th at W. L. Winn's, at three and I look forward to a most sociable reunion. I hear that you have married. Should I congratulate you? And should I ask if that makes a difference?
>
> Regards,
> Sarah Melford

Collis took out his matches and struck one. Within a minute, the letter was curling up into black flakes in his ashtray. He waved the smell of smoke away with the San Francisco paper.

Although it was a simple plan, it was both innovative and chancy. Nobody had ever attempted blackmail with risqué calotypes before – not as far as Collis was aware – and he knew that the success of what he was about to do depended as much on Laurence Melford's temper as it did on his own timing and efficiency.

If Laurence Melford stayed perfectly calm, and thought the situation out logically, he would soon come to realise that in practical terms the means whereby his daughter's reputation could be sullied on a wide scale were simply not at hand. It was possible, of course, that postcards could be printed up and sent to some of San Francisco's most respectable homes. It was possible that J. Walter Walsh, the scandal-sheet publisher, would reproduce a woodcut of one of the pictures in his *Illustrated Varieties*, or that the *California Police Gazette*, whose main interests were sex and prizefighting, would mention the existence of unseemly photographs of Sarah Melford in their gossip column. It was even possible that the *Bulletin* would find a space for a respectable news item about 'scientific extortion'.

But Laurence Melford was rich enough and powerful enough to make even Walsh think twice – despite the fact that Walsh was the man who had nonchalantly told his readers one week that only *five* libel suits were pending against the *Varieties*. And if Melford was quick, he could make sure that anybody who was liable to be shown a calotype, or to hear about it, was convincingly assured that the whole business was nothing but a scandalous fake.

What Collis was counting on was that Laurence Melford would *not* stay perfectly calm, and that he would *not* think the situation out logically. Like a gamble on the last three cards in faro, Collis was making a half-educated, half-intuitive guess that Laurence Melford would react with nothing but irrational rage. In Collis's opinion, he would be just as furious if one man had possession of intimate calotypes of Sarah as if pictures had been freely distributed to every miner, winer, and manjack in the whole of northern California. He considered himself a Southern gentleman, and Sarah was his only daughter. The family reputation was paramount.

The plan depended on one thing more: complete anonymity. Not just now, but forever; because if Laurence Melford ever found out that Collis had played such a trick as this, Collis's life would be in constant danger from every stray opportunist and bounty hunter who wanted to find an easy way to please San Francisco's most influential man, and to make a few dollars besides. That was why Collis had felt dubious about asking Knickerbocker Jane for help. She had too many customers who were friends of Laurence Melford's and she entertained too many enemies of the railroad, and she talked too much. She had told him about Horace Johnson's liking for 'discipline' – all well and good. But what had she told Horace Johnson about him?

In Andy Hunt's office, on the afternoon of 19 September, Collis talked to Andy, Dan McReady, and Mr Figgis, the calotypist. He drew a map on a large sheet of brown wrapping paper which he had pinned to the wall, and he explained the plan in detail.

'Sarah's agreed to meet me at W. L. Winn's Fountain Head of Luxuries at three o'clock. I shall be there, waiting for her, as conspicuously as possible; and I shall keep asking the waiters what the time is, so they won't fail to remember me.

'Any time after five minutes of three, but probably later, Sarah's carriage will draw up in the street outside. Now – here's where the crucial timing comes into it. Andy has arranged for a wide wagonload of fish crates to turn into the street directly after Sarah's carriage, and to stay so close behind that Sarah's coachman has no option but to let Sarah alight outside the café alone, so that he can move on directly, and not obstruct the way.

'The coachman won't suspect anything, of course, because he'll believe that she's being helped down by one of Winn's flunkies – who in actual fact will be *you*, Dan in a brass-buttoned tunic, and a cap.'

'Not to forget my false moustache,' said Dan.

'That's right,' said Collis. 'Nor your Navy revolver, either.'

'What happens then?' asked Mr Figgis dubiously.

'A little brute force,' said Collis. 'Dan will take Sarah's arm, as tight as he can, and propel her past W. L. Winn's door and into the alley at the side, where a cab will be waiting. He'll tell her to come along quietly, and that she won't be harmed as long as she's quiet and agreeable, and doesn't struggle. The cab will take her as quick as possible to Bush Street, while Dan covers her eyes with a handkerchief. That's essential. She mustn't ever find out where she's going, or where she's been.'

Collis reached across to the corner of Andy's desk and picked up the small wax-sealed bottle which Mr Kwang had given him. 'As soon as Dan brings her in through the door of Maria's house, Andy and Dan will hold her down and administer the opium tincture. I don't know how long it takes to have any effect, but Sarah's coachman won't raise the alarm for an hour or more, and that should give us plenty of time. When Mr Figgis is through with his pictures, Dan will take Sarah back to Harrison and Third Street, release her, and then make his getaway.'

Andy leaned back in his chair, his feet planted on his desk, and picked his teeth. 'It all sounds very fancy,' he said. 'But I can think of at least three moments when the whole thing could go horribly and disastrously wrong. Supposing she ignores Dan's warning and calls for help? Supposing she gets away? And I'm still not convinced that you need to go to such complicated lengths to raise money. Surely we can knock on a few doors, talk to one or two banks. All we need is twenty thousand, after all.'

Collis tossed down his pencil. 'You'll never understand, will you? It's not just twenty thousand we need. That's only for Theodore's detailed survey. We need the promise of ten or twelve years of

521

continuing support. We need long-term investment. How do you think we're going to make sure that Congress approves our route, rather than anybody else's? How do you think we're going to pay for our first track, and our first locomotives? By knocking on doors? By going around to two-bit San Francisco banks with our caps in our hands? We're talking about a project that's going to cost us millions of dollars. *Millions.* And that means we need all the most influential San Francisco businessmen behind us, or at the very least not against us.'

'All right,' said Andy, raising his hands in a gesture of surrender. 'I just think the whole scheme's pretty bizarre, that's all. Who ever heard of blackmailing anyone with calotypes?'

Collis coughed. He had been smoking too much lately, and drinking too much. 'It'll catch on,' he told Andy. 'One day, everybody will be at it. You wait and see.'

'What happens if something *does* go wrong, and we get ourselves caught in the act?' asked Mr Figgis.

'We deny everything,' replied Collis. 'We insist that someone must have made a ridiculous mistake, and that we're all perfectly innocent.'

'And if that doesn't wash?'

'Then we ride for Nevada as hard as we can,' Collis told him, with a lopsided grin.

Andy stood up. 'There's only one thing I don't yet understand,' he said. 'How are you going to explain to Laurence Melford that you had a clandestine meeting arranged with his daughter? She's going to tell him, you know, and so is her coachman. Don't you think he's going to suspect your involvement right away?'

'That's where you're wrong,' said Collis. 'If I go to Laurence Melford and explain that I wanted to see Sarah secretly, just for one last romantic farewell, then he's more likely to believe that I didn't have anything to do with her abduction than if I feign innocence. If you plead guilty to a small sin, then people usually believe you when you swear to God that you didn't commit a big one.'

'I don't know,' said Andy. 'I'm not at all sure this is going to work. Laurence Melford's a pretty hard nut.'

'What can we lose?' asked Collis. 'Even if Melford doesn't agree to help us, he still won't know that we did it. He won't have any proof at all. And we'll have the finest collection of calotypes of Sarah Melford that anybody ever owned. They'll fetch a fortune as postcards.'

'Well . . .' grumbled Andy, unhappily.

Collis put out his hand. 'Let's make a pact,' he said. 'Let's agree to try this plan, and let's agree to carry it off as best we can. If it fails, well, I'll openly admit that I'm wrong, and that we should try more conventional methods. But I personally believe that it's going to succeed, and that by next week we're going to have this stuffy provincial city and its boondock business right where we want them.'

Andy stared at Collis's outstretched hand for a moment, and then shook it. Dan McReady stood up and shook hands, too. Mr Figgis stayed where he was, on his bentwood chair, but he said, 'All right. I'll go along with that. As long as you pay my bail when I'm caught.'

That night, at the International Hotel, Collis couldn't sleep. The plumbing was rattling, someone was singing off-key immigrant songs in an upstairs room, and it sounded as if there was a fight going on in the street outside. After an hour or so, he sat up and walked quietly out of the bedroom into the parlour, closing the door behind him. He lit the lamp on his escritoire and sat down with a sheet of hotel notepaper and a pen.

'My dearest Hannah,' he wrote, and then hesitated for two or three minutes, his pen in the inkstand, his forehead creased with a frown.

'I have been unusually difficult and hard to live with for the past few days,' he continued. He crossed out 'difficult' and substituted 'quick-tempered'.

'I want you to know, however, that I love you dearly, and without reservation, and that I shall never do *anything* to harm you. You are the light of my life. My friend, my wife, and my inspiration. When we cross the Sierras at last I shall be thinking of you, just as I am thinking of you now, and saying a humble prayer to my Maker for bringing us so luckily and so accidentally together.'

He sat reading and re-reading what he had written for a while, and then he sprinkled sand across the paper to dry the ink. He didn't really know why he had felt the need to write Hannah a note. He could have woken her up and told her to her face how much he loved her. But somehow he felt that she would find a few written words more reassuring. She could take a letter out of her pocketbook and read it when he was out.

He realised he probably felt guilty, too, about keeping the

523

calotype plan such a secret from her. He remembered his mother saying, 'If there were no such an animal as guilt, then many a family duty would go undone.' He wondered briefly how his mother was keeping, and whether Maude had gotten herself married. To walk down the aisle with Maude – now *there* was a penance.

He wrote a short letter to Charles, to be taken up to Sacramento in the morning. A Dutch vessel had docked at San Francisco with surveying equipment and machine tools, and the captain could probably be persuaded to do a better deal on the price if Charles sent down a consignment of fresh fruit from the Sacramento Market.

Upstairs, the immigrant singer was bawling 'Sweet Betsy from Pike':

'Oh, don't you remember sweet Betsy from Pike,
Who crossed the big mountains with her lover Ike,
With two yoke of cattle, a large yellow dog,
A tall Shanghai rooster and one spotted hog.'

Collis considered having a sharp word with the management in the morning.

In the morning, it was raining. Collis went to the window and stared through the rain-dribbled glass at the muddy streets, the struggling wagons, the umbrellas, and the glistening rooftops. He hoped that the street outside of Winn's wasn't too rutted; and he hoped, too, that the weather wouldn't put Sarah off their rendezvous altogether. He'd known many girls in New York who never ventured out when it was wet, for fear of muddying their petticoats and spotting their silks.

Hannah was sitting up in bed. 'You were late last night, my darling,' she remarked.

'I couldn't sleep.'

'You're not worried, are you?'

He turned and crossed the room in his billowing nightshirt. 'Worried? Why should I be? They're late with the coffee this morning, don't you think?'

'It's this plan, isn't it?' she asked him. 'You're not at all sure if it's going to work.'

'It'll work,' he insisted, opening the bureau drawer to take out his clean underwear. 'I don't have the slightest doubt of it.'

She was silent, and then she said, 'I do love you, you know

He stood up straight, holding his combinations up as if they were a pale and shrunken ghost, with buttons.

'I love you, too,' he said, and he knew that he meant it.

They breakfasted downstairs in the hotel restaurant on smoked fish and scrambled eggs. Then Collis asked the doorman to hail them a cab, and he took Hannah up to the top of Telegraph Hill, where they walked for almost an hour under Collis's big black umbrella, holding hands and saying nothing at all, while the rain fell in white misty sheets through the Golden Gate, and the hills of San Francisco rose all around them like islands in a mysterious oriental sea. All the houses on Telegraph Hill were closed and shuttered. There was no sound but the gurgle of rain in their gutters, and the occasional grating echo of a handbrake as a wagon was driven awkwardly downhill past their disapproving frontages.

As Collis and Hannah made their way down the southern slopes of the hill towards Washington Street, however, the wet day livened up. They walked through Little Chile, where music played, and the sharp aroma of Chilean stews reached their noses from half-open kitchen doors. The rain drummed on their umbrella like a Latin dance, and children ran after them, muddy and brown, and begged for bits.

They lunched at a German restaurant on Montgomery, facing each other over a circular tablecloth of migraine whiteness. The rest of the room was dim, and darkly panelled as a bank; and if it hadn't been for the loud laughter of a party from the Deutsches Club on the other side of the room, and the waiters bringing them white wine and *Haxe* on heavily-laden trays, Collis felt that he could have been back at I. P. Woolmer's, in New York, before any of this had ever happened.

As he sliced his pork knuckle, he said quietly, 'The plan is going to be carried out this afternoon.'

Hannah stared at him. 'So soon? You're sure you're ready?'

'I've been arranging it ever since we arrived here. I'm as ready as I can ever be.'

'Will it take long?' she asked, and she was really anxious now

'I hope not. But you can do me a great service by staying calm, and not mentioning my whereabouts to anybody, and waiting at the International until I come home.'

'Are you going to be late?'

He swallowed and raised his glass of wine. 'I may be. But don't fret. There's no danger, and if everything goes well, we should be several thousand dollars richer by the time we return to Sacramento.'

She raised her glass in a discreet toast. 'I wish I could kiss you,' she said.

He raised his glass in return. 'I wish I could make love to you,' he whispered, and he enjoyed her sudden blushing as much as the wine.

He arrived at W. L. Winn's at ten minutes of three. The gilt-lettered windows were steamed up because of the wet weather, and it was difficult to see inside. He paused under the front awning, took down his umbrella, and shook it vigorously. The doorman watched him from the shelter of the entrance, like a gopher in a dry burrow, and made no move at all to come out and assist him. That was one advantage of the rain, thought Collis. The real doorman was far less likely to come out and collide with the fake doorman, and cause unnecessary scuffles.

Collis had already walked past the fish-crate wagon, which was waiting around the corner. Its two six-year-old oxen were dripping with rain, and its Chilean driver was hunched under a wet sack. Collis had to admit that Andy Hunt had done his bit. The fish crates were stacked precariously high, and there were baling hooks and stray pieces of timber sticking out in all directions. There was no chance that Sarah's carriage would be able to draw to one side of the street to let the wagon go by – not unless the coachman wanted to lose half of his varnish. Collis took out his pocket watch, checked the time, and then stepped inside the fountain.

It was crowded and bright inside, and chirpy with the talk of young ladies taking tea. There were cream-painted iron pillars and frondy palm trees, and the furniture was elegant wrought iron. Collis stood for a moment in the doorway, looking out over the strawberry ices and the cream cakes and all the fluffy and feathery bonnets, trying to see if Sarah had arrived already. But she hadn't, of course. She was too well mannered to be punctual. One of the waiters came forward and asked him if he wished to take tea.

'I want a table for two,' he said, still looking around for Sarah. 'I'm expecting a young lady guest in a short while.'

'Of course, sir. I have one here at the back, if you'll follow me.'

'There's a table free by the window,' said Collis.

'I'm sorry, sir. Reserved. Now – please come this way.'

Collis reached out and discreetly seized the waiter's wrist. He

526

twisted it around, hard, just to make his point, and then he pressed a dollar into the man's palm and forcibly closed his fingers over it.

'I said, there's a table free by the window,' he repeated.

The waiter winced. 'Yes, sir. For a moment I didn't see.'

Collis sat down, flicked out his coat-tails, and picked up the menu. There was a mahogany clock on the wall behind the cash register, and it already said two minutes of three. Underneath it, the lady cashier was lancing her iron-grey bun with hairpins. Collis inspected the menu quickly, and when the waiter came back, he ordered 'Coffee, black; and a pastry.'

'Lemon pastry? Or vanilla pastry? Or bilberry pastry? Or – '

'Anything. As long as it's not stale.'

'All of our pastries are fresh-baked today, sir,' said the waiter indignantly.

'Just bring it, will you?'

When the waiter had gone, Collis wiped the steam from the window with his grey morning glove. There was no sign of Sarah Melford's carriage yet. Nothing but rain and passers-by, and wagons rolling through the mud. He prayed that none of the wet-hooded carriages which were bumping along the street would get themselves bogged down in front of Sarah's carriage, and prevent her coachman from moving on. He looked at the clock again, and with a hesitant shudder, the minute hand moved to twelve.

The waiter brought his coffee and a lemon pastry, and banged them down on the table in front of him. He spent a restless minute cutting the pastry with his cake fork, until his plate was strewn with flaky fragments; and then he sat looking at it with no appetite at all. He took two or three sips of hot coffee, but it didn't seem to taste like anything. He could see the waiter watching him balefully from the opposite side of the fountain, and even though it annoyed him, it was just what he needed. An independent witness who would remember his face.

The clock shuddered around to five after three. At the next table, two young girls had succumbed to an uncontrollable fit of giggles, and Collis glanced at them in irritation. He finished his coffee and swallowed a gritty mouthful of grounds by mistake. Outside in the street, like undersea divers in a strange dream, shoppers and clerks and messenger boys struggled through the mud and the fierce gusts of rain.

At eight after three, Collis looked up and the Melford carriage was suddenly there. Dark-blue, its varnish beaded with rain, with

Martin the coachman sitting stiffly up front in his waterproof cape and his tall hat. Collis's heart began to beat at a fast, regular rate, and he quickly wiped the window again so that he could see what was happening.

The fish-crate wagon –where the hell was the fish-crate wagon? It was time –where was it? Martin was already reining in the horses and tugging at the brake, and Collis could see the mud being scraped from the iron rims of the wheels. He looked towards the fountain entrance to reassure himself that the doorman was still sheltering from the rain, but a large woman in a black cape was obstructing his view. He turned back to the window again.

At last – there it was. The fish-crate wagon. Grinding its way along the street like Krishna's Jagannath, an unsteady tumbril of wet crates and broken lumber. Its wheels were almost hub-deep in the mud, and the oxen were dragging it rather than pulling it, but the Chilean driver was standing up on his seat, cracking his whip again and again, and cursing so loudly that Collis could hear him from inside Winn's, and somehow the wagon was slowly creeping forward.

Collis saw the door of Sarah's carriage open, and Sarah herself begin to step down. He saw Martin turn in his seat and wave to the Chilean driver to wait.

'*I don't wait!*' screamed the Chilean. '*I stop, and I don't never get moving no more! You shift your ass! You move!*'

Martin said something in reply which Collis couldn't hear. But the Chilean shook his head fiercely and cracked his whip again, so that his huge disastrous load continued to bear down on the Melford's brougham at the same relentless pace. Collis was sitting rigidly in his chair his fists clenched in apprehension. Now, for God's sake. Now!

With the orchestrated timing of one of those elaborate clockwork toys, everything happened at once. Dan McReady rushed forward from the alley, in his blue doorman's jacket and his bushy false whiskers, and took Sarah's hand as if he were claiming first prize in a raffle. Nodding and bowing, he busily assisted her to step down on to the wooden sidewalk, and at the same time jostled his large green Winn's umbrella around so that Martin found it impossible to see his face.

Dan smartly slammed the carriage door, whistled a piercing whistle between his teeth, and shouted, 'Off you go now, driver!'

Martin hesitated, but the Chilean was screaming at him again, '*Move out! Move out!*' and so he tipped his hat to Sarah, released his handbrake, and drove the Melford carriage away. Collis caught a momentary glimpse of Sarah standing on the sidewalk under Dan's umbrella, modestly but elegantly dressed in a grey overcoat, and he could see that she was smiling at the chaos in the street. But then a Chinese laundryman passed in front of Winn's window, with a bundle of washing on his head, and when Collis looked again she was gone.

That was all. He didn't even hear the cab in the alley pull away. He could hardly believe it was over, and he sat back on his wrought-iron chair feeling peculiarly deflated. What was worse, he would have to wait here for at least ten minutes more, to make sure that his alibi was conclusive. He called the waiter and ordered another cup of coffee.

'Is that clock correct?' he asked. 'My visitor was supposed to be here by three.'

'The correctest clock in the city, sir,' the waiter said sarcastically.

Collis drank more coffee, and the minutes passed by so slowly that he felt as if he'd been sitting in Winn's all day. At last, at twenty past three, the waiter came across and flicked his tablecloth with a napkin. 'It seems as if your lady friend has been unavoidably detained, doesn't it, sir?' he said.

Collis glared at him. 'Yes,' he snapped, with as much self-control as he could muster.

'I don't mean to offend, sir,' said the waiter.

Collis tossed two bits on to the table. 'I know you don't *mean* to,' he said. 'The trouble is that you do.'

He paid for his coffee at the desk, shrugged on his coat, and stepped out into the rainy daylight. At the next corner, he flagged a cab down and asked to be taken to Sacramento Street. He sat back on the wet leather seats, smoking and impatiently watching the raindrops trickle and jerk their way down the window. When they reached the firehouse on Sacramento and Kearny, he rapped on the hood for the driver to stop, and he climbed out. The rain was easing off now, and there was a wash of glittering yellow sunlight on the sidewalks. He was pleased about that, because to complete his alibi he was going to have to walk three blocks to Bush Street, right down to the next firehouse, and hope that he didn't run into anybody who might recognise him.

529

He reached Maria-Mamuska's house with his shoes spattered in mud. The Chinese girl let him in, took his coat and his umbrella, and gave him a pair of oriental silk slippers in vivid green. Andy Hunt, in a loud brown herring-bone suit, was waiting impatiently for him in the front parlour.

'Well?' asked Collis. 'What's happening?'

'This had better not backfire,' said Andy. 'By God, I tell you, Collis, if this backfires –'

'It's not going to backfire,' Collis told him sharply. 'Now, what's happening? Did she get here all right?'

'Sure. Dan had her blindfolded and everything. We took her upstairs to Maria's back bedroom and she's there now.'

'Did she take the opium?'

Andy nodded. 'She struggled at first, and wouldn't drink it. But Maria had the answer. She told her it wasn't poison, and that if she wouldn't swallow it, she'd have all her hair cut off. Well, that did the trick. She drank it right down without any more fuss.'

Collis took out his watch. 'How long ago was that?'

'Not long. Ten minutes or so.'

'Is Figgis here?'

'Oh, yes. He's been here since two.'

Collis thought for a moment, and then said, 'All right. Let's go up and take a look.'

They climbed the narrow, soft-carpeted staircase to the landing. There Andy opened the first door on the right-hand side and led Collis into a small front room, wallpapered in dark purple, with a purple velvet daybed and two plushy purple armchairs. Andy went over to the wall and beckoned Collis to come closer. Then he lifted a small wooden flap on the wall and peered through a spyhole which gave out on to the larger back bedroom where Sarah was being held.

'Let me see,' said Collis. Andy put his finger to his lips.

Through the spyhole, Collis could see only part of the room. He could make out the foot of Mr Figgis's tripod, and a part of Maria-Mamuska's gown, but for the moment he couldn't see Sarah at all. Perhaps she was already alseep, and Maria-Mamuska's maid was undressing her. He turned back to Andy and whispered, 'I don't see her. It looks as though the opium's worked.'

But Andy was just about to take another peek when a clear, distinctive voice said, 'I really don't know why you're keeping me here. My father will make sure that every one of you is hanged.'

Andy looked at Collis and made a face. 'Doesn't sound as though she's very sleepy, does it?'

Collis put his eye to the spyhole again. He saw Sarah this time, as she stalked haughtily across the room with her arms folded. She was still wearing her grey overcoat and her bonnet. Then he saw Dan McReady, flushed and sweating, his false moustache hanging loose from one side of his cheek. Then Sarah appeared again, as awake and as intractable as before.

'You sure Mr Kwang didn't sell you a pup?' asked Andy.

'I don't know,' said Collis. 'What do I know about opium?'

'Well, if she doesn't zizz off soon, we're sunk,' said Andy. 'She may take a drink if we threaten to cut her hair off, but you can bet your boot buttons she ain't going to take off her clothes.'

'Damn,' said Collis, to nobody in particular, as he saw Sarah walk across the room again.

A door opened and closed, and then Dan McReady and Maria-Mamuska appeared in the back bedroom, perspiring and dispirited. Maria had disguised herself with a black lace-edged mask, but when she saw Collis she pulled it off and threw it aside.

'That lady may be everything you say she is,' Maria-Mamuska told Collis. 'But one thing she isn't, and that's sleepy.'

'She's not even yawning,' said Dan.

Collis sat down on the daybed and looked at them without saying a word. If they didn't get their calotypes, Sarah's abduction would be nothing more than a ridiculous charade. Apart from the sheer absurdity of returning Sarah to the bosom of her family completely unharmed and untouched, at the cost of two cabs, one Chilean fish-crate wagon driver, two cups of coffee, and a lemon pastry he hadn't eaten, there was the painful prospect of having to go back to Hannah and admit that his wonderful secret plan, the plan which had led to so many arguments, had dismally failed.

'It's that Chinese bastard, Kwang,' Andy said. 'He probably gave you a bottle of rice wine, or pig's piss, or whatever it is those Chinks use to cook with.'

Collis shrugged. 'He said it was opium tincture, and strong, too. How much did you give her?'

'Four spoonfuls, just as you said.'

'Well, I don't understand it,' said Collis. 'He specifically said that if she had anything more than a few drops, she'd fall flat on her back. He warned me not to give her too much, in case it killed her.'

531

'Aah, you know what these Chinese are like,' said Andy. 'All noodles and shrimps and hocus-pocus.'

'What are we going to do?' asked Maria-Mamuska softly. 'If she doesn't sleep, then we can't take the pictures.'

'I'm thinking,' said Collis. 'There has to be a way out of this somehow.'

'I could punch her,' suggested Dan McReady helpfully.

'Don't be so damned stupid,' said Collis. 'The whole point of this plan is that she doesn't get harmed. Not physically, anyway.'

'We could keep her here until she drops to sleep naturally.'

'And then what? You can't take calotypes at night. It's going to be difficult enough as it is unless the sun comes out.'

'Maybe we have to let her go,' said Maria-Mamuska.

'And maybe we have to tell her what's going on,' said another voice, cultured and sharp.

They looked up, in complete shock. Standing in the open doorway in her grey overcoat was Sarah Melford, straight-backed, composed, and not drugged in the slightest. Just behind her, Mr Figgis was trying to communicate with a variety of shrugs and facial contortions that he had tried to stop her, without success.

'Is this a kidnapping?' asked Sarah, stepping into the room. 'Is it serious, or is it a joke? Collis – seeing you here, I must conclude that it's a joke.'

Collis pressed his fingers against his eyelids as if he could make the whole scene vanish. Then he opened his eyes again, and found it was all still real, and sighed.

'Well?' demanded Sarah. 'Aren't you going to tell me what's up? Aren't you going to tell me who are these peculiar people, and why they've brought me here?'

Collis stood up and bowed his head. 'I'm sorry, Sarah. In the surprise of the moment, I forgot my manners. This is Maria, whose house this is. This is Mr Dan McReady, of the Eagle Saloon. And this is Mr Andrew Jackson Hunt, one of my partners in the Sierra Pacific Railroad. Oh – and the gentleman behind you is Mr Figgis, the calotypist.'

'I still don't understand,' said Sarah. 'Are you keeping me here for a ransom? Are you going to sell me off to white slavers? And why were you going to take calotypes of me?'

Collis turned to Maria-Mamuska. 'I believe we could all use a drink,' he told her. Maria-Mamuska nodded, said, 'Sure,' and went to arrange it, dropping a curtsey to Sarah as she passed her by.

'Andy, Dan,' said Collis indicating that he would rather be left alone with Sarah. They left, both of them sheepish. Dan peeled off his false moustache as he walked out, grimacing with the pain of it.

'Perhaps you'd care to sit down,' Collis told Sarah.

'Very well,' Sarah replied, walking across the room and arranging herself on the purple daybed. 'And perhaps *you'd* care to explain.'

'You don't mind if I smoke?'

'You look as if you need something to settle your nerves.'

'Yes,' said Collis. 'I believe I do.'

'This is serious, isn't it?' asked Sarah. 'It's not just some kind of a practical joke against my father?'

'Well, it is and it isn't,' Collis admitted. 'It's a joke in the sense that we never had any intention of harming you. And it's a joke in the sense that it's new-fangled, and nobody's ever tried it before. But, well, it didn't quite work out the way we planned it.'

Sarah leaned forward on the daybed. In the gloomy afternoon light, her eyes glistened brightly, and her diamond choker sparked off curved rainbows and winking stars. Collis could smell her perfume, and he knew that he'd forgotten how beautiful she was, and how sensual.

'I didn't really want to involve you in this at all,' Collis said. 'More than anything, I didn't want to take advantage of your friendship. But there are other considerations, far more pressing. I'm afraid you were perfect for what I wanted to do.'

'But what *did* you want to do?' she asked him. 'You still haven't told me.'

Collis stood up and paced across to the spyhole. He lifted the flap, and a dusty ray of sunlight pierced the room. The rain must be clearing outside, he thought. He wished to God he'd never been headstrong enough to believe that his preposterous plan would work.

'Your father and I, when it comes to business, are mortal enemies,' he said. 'For me to make my fortune, I desperately need to build my railroad. For him to preserve his fortune, he desperately requires that I shouldn't. So we're at total odds; and there is no way the conflict can be resolved unless one of us resorts to unfair pressure.'

He turned to her, with a resigned smile. 'That's why you're here. You're my unfair pressure. I was going to have you drugged with tincture of opium; then undressed, with Maria-Mamuska as a

533

chaperone, and photographed by Mr Figgis. I was then going to have a sample calotype sent to your father, with a threat for money. Signed anonymously, of course, by the Calotype Gang, or whatever came into my mind.'

Sarah looked back at him with an expression of disbelief. 'He wouldn't have paid,' she said. 'He would have turned San Francisco upside down, looking for the culprits, with the express intention of having them hanged.'

'Precisely,' said Collis. 'Except he never would have found them.'

'No,' she said. 'I don't suppose he would. Even I don't know where we are.'

Collis sat down again, breathing out smoke. 'We would have sent a second calotype, maybe even a third, with more demands. Your father would have gone berserk with rage. Then, at the right moment, I would have approached him at his office, very discreetly, and told him I had been given to understand that he was being put under pressure from blackmailers. He would have been angry with me at first, and even suspected I had something to do with it. But my alibis would have been seamless, and after a while he would have had to listen. I would have offered to act as a middleman – to retrieve the calotype negatives, all of them, provided he did me a favour in return. I wouldn't have asked for much. Just that he should withdraw from all active resistance to the Sierra Pacific Railroad, and announce in the *Evening Bulletin* that he considered the railroad inevitable, desirable, and profitable to all who might care to invest in it.'

There was a pause. Then Sarah said, 'That was all you wanted? You were prepared to go through all of this performance, all of this kidnapping and photography and false blackmail, just to have my father say that?'

'Your father's word is San Francisco's law. You should know that by now. The whole of the business community takes its cue from Laurence Melford, and so do the pioneers. He's a solid-gold, one hundred per cent, rich, influential, irresistible Bear Flagger.'

'Yes,' she said, frowning. 'I think I'm cross with you, Collis.'

'Well,' Collis told her, 'I'm not surprised. The most I can ask of you now is that you accept my apologies, and my explanation, and forget about the whole thing. I won't try it again.'

'You won't have to,' she said.

'I'm sorry?'

'I said, you won't have to. I know what your railroad means to you. I've read about you in the newspapers. I also have the wit and the intelligence to know what it's going to mean to San Francisco. It's going to help San Francisco to grow up – to grow more educated, more aware of the world around it, and more fashionable. How do you think it feels to wear dresses that have travelled for two hundred days around Cape Horn, knowing that even before you've set eyes on them, they're nine months out of date? What do you think it's like going to operas and concerts and theatrical plays that are eons behind New York? For the sake of their absurd monopolies, my father and all his cronies are doing everything they can to keep us isolated, and stifled, like a bunch of country simpletons on a hill.'

Collis put his head on one side quizzically. 'Are you trying to tell me that you *agree* with the railroad?'

'Agree with it? Are you mad? It would change my whole life. I could travel to Washington whenever I wanted. I could go to New York. I could order clothes and books and expect them within the month. My father's mistake, Collis, was to bring me up as an educated and fashionable and self-opinionated young lady, and I'm not the only one. There are plenty of wealthy young men and women in South Park who feel just the same as I do. We're bright, social, and cut off from civilization, and we don't like it.'

'Oh,' remarked Collis. He didn't know what else to say.

Sarah stood up, and came across to him, and took his hand. 'Listen,' she said, 'we can make your plan work, but we'll do it my way.'

He couldn't believe what he was hearing. 'You want us to go ahead? You want us to – you actually want us to take the calotypes and blackmail your own father?'

Sarah beamed and nodded. 'Not completely undressed, mind,' she said, raising her finger. 'A few pictures in my corsets. But we can always imply in our blackmail letter that we have something more intimate.'

'We?' asked Collis, stunned.

'Yes, we. We're the conspirators, aren't we? I just as much as you, if I let you take these pictures of my own free will.'

'Well, yes,' said Collis, still unsure of her. 'But how can you blackmail your own father? He's – well, he's your father.'

Sarah leaned forward and kissed Collis on the forehead. 'It won't do him any harm, my dear. He won't lose any money, or any prestige, or anything. Everyone around him is so sycophantic that

535

when he says he's in favour of railroads, the whole business community will probably nod, and say how farsighted he is, and how adventurous, and why didn't *we* think of that.'

She smiled at Collis for a moment, and then added, 'I wouldn't hurt him, Collis, not for anything. I love him. But he's made me into my own woman, for better or for worse, and this woman he's made believes that the railroad will change this city into the most exciting place on earth.'

There was a hesitant knock at the door. 'Come in,' Collis said, and Maria-Mamuska came in with an anxious expression and two flutes of champagne on a tray.

Collis said, 'Bring more champagne, Maria, and join us. And tell Andy and Dan and Mr Figgis to come in, too, I think we have something to celebrate after all.'

He learned during the course of that afternoon a lesson that, in time, was to change his view of women radically; a lesson that over the coming years would deepen and strengthen his marriage to Hannah, as well as his friendship with Sarah Melford. While Mr Figgis took ten or twelve calotypes of Sarah, lying sprawled on the bed in her pink-ribboned corsets with her eyes closed, as if drugged, she and Collis talked about her father, and about San Francisco society, and about the new breed of California debutantes.

'I don't know how our parents expected us to turn out,' said Sarah. 'They were made of tough pioneering stuff themselves, which most of us inherited; and on top of our fine genetic inheritance they gave us money, and influence, and a thorough education. Did they expect us to be meek, and subservient – polite little ladies who desired nothing more out of life than to flatter their daddies and go to tea parties?'

'Your father means well, though, surely?' asked Collis.

'Meaning well and doing well are not the same thing,' said Sarah. 'He can be very understanding and lovable on occasions, but he's bull-headed, and reactionary, and he doesn't give me any freedom with boys. I was walking out with that delicious Francis Bret Harte until recently, until my father got to hear about it. Bret's so witty – and you couldn't find anyone more respectable than the secretary to the director of the mint. But no, father said he scribbles, and so he wasn't fit company.'

'Can you keep still, please?' complained Mr Figgis from beneath the musty depths of his calotypist's cape.

'Is that why you're helping me?' asked Collis. 'To make your father realise that you're not such a pristine princess after all?'

'I have my honour,' said Sarah. 'But I have my life to lead, too, and my own politics to follow.'

Collis stood up and strolled across the room with his hands in his pockets. Mr Figgis clucked loudly at the disturbance, but Collis ignored him.

'You know something?' said Collis. 'When I first saw you at the theatre, arriving in your box with your family, I think I fell in love with you instantly.'

'Most men do,' said Sarah, in a matter-of-fact way.

'Andrew Hunt had told me on the ship from New York that you were incomparably beautiful, but unassailable, too. Nobody could get past your father, he said. Not unless they were a baron, or a prince. Or John Frémont's father-in-law's best friend.'

Sarah smiled. In her corsets and her garters, with her big soft breasts pushed together into a tight cleavage, and her long legs revealed in nothing but silk stockings, she looked infinitely desirable to Collis, and even Maria-Mamuska was watching the proceedings with appreciation.

'Are you *still* in love with me?' Sarah asked.

'Of course,' said Collis, 'and I always shall be. But I would rather love you as a friend than as a lover. If I seduced you, if I managed to clamber up to the top of that glass mountain you sit on, I don't think our association would last longer than a week. I would have conquered that pinnacle that every able-bodied man in San Francisco dreams of, but what would I have to show for it? No -- you've shown me today that you have intelligence, and wisdom, as well as beauty, and I value those more.'

'Apart from which, you're married now,' said Sarah. 'And don't tell me you don't love your wife madly.'

Collis grinned. 'Well, there's that point, too.'

They both started laughing, and Mr Figgis struggled his way out of his cape in annoyance.

'Do you want these pictures or not?' he demanded.

Collis put his arm around Mr Figgis's shoulders. 'Of course we do, my dear fellow. We promise to be still as statues from now on. Just tell me one thing, Sarah, before you pose again. What are you going to tell your father when you get home?'

He was back at the International Hotel by six. The rain had cleared.

and it was a bright, clear evening, with a dazzling sunset over the bald peak of Fern Hill. In their suite, Hannah was dressing for dinner, in the hope that Collis would be back in time. He came in, walked quickly across the room, and kissed her as she sat at her dressing table.

'How did it go?' her reflection asked him in the mirror.

He kissed her again. 'It went completely wrong, but completely right. I shall tell you everything about it over dinner. How do you fancy Delmonico's?'

She turned on her stool and looked up at him. 'I'd love Delmonico's,' she told him, with an abstracted smile. 'Did it really go so well?'

He peeled off his coat, loosened his necktie, and began to unbutton his shirt. 'I hope you're feeling broad-minded,' he said. 'But I'm sure you are. You're a very bright, broad-minded wife.'

'You flatter me.'

'No, I don't. I'm telling you the truth. And I should have told you the truth before. Now this is all over, I promise you one thing, and I promise it solemnly. I shall never keep anything from you again, the way I did with this plan. Because, my God, if Sarah Melford can see the sense in what I'm doing, after all I put her through, then I know full well that you can.'

Hannah blinked at him. 'Sarah Melford?' she asked.

He approached Laurence Melford a week later in the dining-room of the Hotel du Commerce. It was a noisy, high-ceilinged place, with polished carving trolleys being speedily wheeled from table to table, and waiters hurrying in and out of the service doors with lobster, and brant, and hare chops in salmi; and above it all there was the raucous sound of businessmen who had taken one cocktail too many, talking one octave too high.

Laurence Melford must have seen him coming, because his head sank a little, as if he didn't wish to be recognised. But Collis came smartly up to his table, bowed, and said, 'Perhaps you have a moment, sir?'

Laurence Melford was lunching with Andrew Crawford, the wealthy ships' supplier. Crawford sat back in his seat, a little perplexed at Collis's interruption, but Laurence Melford didn't even raise his eyes.

'I'm having a private lunch, Mr Edmonds,' he said, in a low and

538

testy voice. 'If you wish to see me, you may make an appointment through my staff.'

'I really think it better if I see you now,' said Collis. 'Begging Mr Crawford's pardon for the inconvenience, that is. How are you, Mr Crawford?'

'I was well, thank you, Mr Edmonds, until I saw you,' said Crawford, wiping his mouth with his napkin and pushing away his plate of broiled venison.

Laurence Melford pulled a sour smile. 'I think you'd better leave, Mr Edmonds,' he suggested. 'My servants are waiting outside, and they could always be summoned to have you expelled.'

The Maître d' had seen out of the corner of his eye that Laurence Melford was disturbed by Collis's presence, and he came across with his plum-coloured nose and his curled-up shirt front to find out what was wrong.

'You want a table, sir?' he asked Collis, trying to nudge him away from Laurence Melford's side.

'No, thank you,' said Collis, without looking at him. 'And if you push me once more, I shall punch you very hard in the belly.'

Laurence Melford raised a hand. 'It's all right, Carlo. I can deal with this. Mr Edmonds and I go through this kind of performance with tiresome regularity.'

'I didn't want to bother you for long,' Collis said. 'Just long enough to say "Calotypes".'

Laurence Melford's cheeks tightened, and his eyes suddenly looked very dark. Andrew Crawford noticed the change in him and frowned uncertainly. 'Larry?' he asked. 'Do you want me to leave? I don't mind if it's really important.'

Laurence Melford hesitated, and then nodded. 'Just for a minute or two, please, Andrew. Carlo – would you take Mr Crawford's lunch to that table over there for him, please? And would you bring a drink for Mr Edmonds?'

Andrew Crawford stood up, and Collis sat down in his place. Before the waiter arrived to take the plate away, Collis forked up one of Andrew Crawford's slices of venison, and he chewed it placidly while he waited for his drink. Laurence Melford watched him with the patronising coldness of a god on Mount Olympus.

'Well?' he asked, after Carlo had set down a stone fence and left them alone.

'Well,' said Collis, running his fingertip around the rim of his glass, 'I hear you're having some embarrassing trouble. I also hear that the trouble isn't completely unconnected with photographic reproductions of a member of your family.'

'How did you hear that?' he said harshly.

'Mr Melford, I was a tenderfoot in San Francisco when you first met me, but these days I'm a little more *au fait*.'

'I suppose you set up this dirty little business yourself?'

'Mr Melford, I'm a respectable hardware dealer from a respectable city. I'm also a partner in the Sierra Pacific Railroad Company. You don't seriously think that I'd get myself involved in a nasty affair like this, do you?'

'Yes, if you want my candid opinion,' said Laurence Melford. 'But I don't suppose I'll ever be able to prove it.'

Collis swilled his drink around his mouth before swallowing it. 'I happen to be friends with the leaders of several Chinese tongs, Mr Melford. If you hadn't been so racially prejudiced, you would have had the good sense to cultivate a friendship with them yourself. They are the wisest and the best-informed men in the whole of this city.'

'They're a collection of crooks,' remarked Laurence Melford.

'Yes,' agreed Collis. 'But it takes a crook to know what crooks are up to; and they tell me on excellent authority that Sarah was temporarily abducted last week for the purposes of a very novel and ingenious crime.'

Laurence Melford toyed with his fork. His suppressed anger made the glasses and plates tremble.

'I won't beat around the bush,' said Collis. 'I happen to know, by a fortuitous stroke of luck, the identity of the perpetrators of this crime. They were unscrupulous, vicious, unprincipled, and mean; Sarah was fortunate to escape unharmed. But I must warn you that they won't stop at anything if they're not humoured.'

'You sound as if you're acting as their collecting agent,' said Laurence Melford.

'Not at all. I've come here to see you today because I'm in the happy position of being able to make a deal. It so happens that these rogues owe me a sizable favour – a favour which only just kept them out of jail. Now, if I were to go to them on your behalf, and insist that this favour should be returned at once, in the shape of all their calotype negatives of Sarah, they would hardly be in any kind of position to resist my demands.'

Laurence Melford's eyes were as narrow as musket slits in a

stockade. 'You'd do that? And what would you expect for your trouble?'

Collis smiled. 'I'm an opportunist, Mr Melford. I can't deny that. As soon as I heard about this lamentable business, I thought to myself, *aha*, here's another opportunity to help the cause of the Sierra Pacific Railroad.'

'Yes?' growled Laurence Melford. 'How, exactly?'

'I'll get those negatives for you if you stop blocking my plans for the railroad,' said Collis. 'That includes saying or doing anything to discourage any of your fellow businessmen from investing in it, and any attempts to manipulate the state administration into voting against public funds for it. I shall also expect you to write a letter to the principal San Francisco newspapers, saying that, on reflection, you now regard the arrival of a transcontinental railroad link to be historically inevitable.'

Laurence Melford sat quiet and hunched for a long time. The only sign of the fury that was grumbling and boiling within him was the way in which he was slowly digging his fork into the table, again and again and again.

Finally, he spoke. '*You* arranged this, didn't you, Edmonds? Not some anonymous gang. *You* had my daughter abducted, *you* had her female sanctity despoiled, and *you* had all those calotypes taken. *You* wrote the threats for money, and didn't you know, right from the goddam start, that it wasn't money you were after at all. You bastard.'

Collis blandly finished his drink and wiped his mouth on the edge of the tablecloth. 'You can think what you like. But as you said yourself not five minutes ago, how are you going to prove it? I've offered you an easy way out of it; a way that doesn't harm Sarah or impugn your dignity; and it seems to me that you don't have much alternative but to take it.'

'I should have known what kind of a reptile you were the first day I saw you,' said Laurence Melford. 'I should have trusted my nose.'

Collis said nothing. He didn't trust himself, right at that moment, to keep Sarah's collusion a secret. It would have silenced Laurence Melford completely – but at the risk of ruining the plan. The maître d' came past, giving Collis a slanted glance of disapproval, and Collis lifted his empty glass for another stone fence. The maître d' paused, but when Laurence Melford gave him a barely perceptible flicker of his eyes, he grudgingly took the glass and went to refill it.

'What you're asking from me is more than I can reasonably give

541

you,' Laurence Melford told Collis. 'My whole livelihood depends on keeping Northern California isolated from the East; and apart from that, I am a Southerner, and I know what a transcontinental railroad route will do to the South's economy.

'But I will make a bargain with you, Edmonds. You're looking for investment in your railroad. Well, I'll make that investment myself, up to fifty thousand dollars, but on the strict condition that it's kept a secret. And on the condition that I don't have to write any letters of support to the newspapers.'

Collis sat back in his chair. 'Fifty thousand dollars? In negotiable bonds? Or what?'

'Fifty thousand dollars in gold. Payable over six months.'

'That sounds fair. But if you can't bring yourself to support the railroad in public, why give me money in private?'

'Because I happen to know how much railroads cost,' said Laurence Melford. 'I happen to know the price of rail, the price of locomotives, the price of timber, and the price of labour. Fifty thousand dollars, if you're lucky, might buy you one trestle over one river. It won't be anything more than a drop in an ocean, and if you'll return those calotypes for that amount, then you're welcome to it.

'What I will not do, ever,' he continued, 'is endorse your railroad to my friends. For if I do so, I will be publicly denying my most deeply held principles. I will be publicly denying the South, and I will be publicly denying my belief in Northern California as a haven from the machinations of North-eastern industrialists. Even my daughter's reputation is not worth that much.'

Collis got to his feet. Carlo, the maître d', was just arriving with his second drink, but when he saw Collis's face, he stood a little way off and waited, chewing his lip. Collis looked at Laurence Melford for a moment or two, and then he buttoned up his gloves.

'I admire your integrity, Mr Melford,' he said. 'I only wish I could admire those prejudiced and self-serving interests which you so mistakenly believe are "principles" – the subjugation of the Negro against all humanitarian credenda, and the deliberate isolation of a whole people from the benefits of modern progress for the sake of two or three profiteering monopolies.'

Laurence Melford's self-control almost broke. He held up his fork in his white-clenched fist, and he bent it as if it were made of the cheapest zinc, instead of steel. The maître d' turned away, and with one deft tilt of his head, drank Collis's second stone fence himself.

542

'Mr Melford,' Collis said, 'you can make up the fifty thousand dollars in five ten-thousand-dollar sacks, and have them delivered once a month by messenger to myself at 54 K Street, Sacramento. Do you know how many calotypes there are?'

'The letter said ten,' said Laurence Melford tightly.

'Very well.' Collis nodded. 'When each sack of gold is delivered, two of the calotype negatives will be returned to you in a sealed envelope. I expect you can understand my reasons for delivering them up so parsimoniously.'

'I will have you hanged for this one day,' Laurence Melford said. 'You just remember that.'

'And you just remember that I could have blown your son's head off, and that you thanked me for saving him, in writing; and that your daughter is safe and well, whether it was I who arranged her abduction or not. And one thing more. These fifty thousand dollars will go towards railroad bonds, which will be made up in your name, and sent to you along with the negatives, so that when the railroad eventually prospers, you will prosper too, even though you don't deserve to.'

Collis leaned forward and put his head very close to Laurence Melford's. 'I have destiny on my side, Mr Melford. It's sweeping me along, and everybody who comes near me gets swept along too. It's not your fault if you've failed, so why don't you finish your lunch with Mr Crawford and thank the Lord for small favours.'

Collis didn't give Laurence Melford the chance to reply. He nodded to the maître d', to Andrew Crawford, and walked quickly out.

Back in Sacramento, a month later, he received a long letter from Theodore. Theodore's tone was unusually warm and friendly, and he told in detail of his moderate success in stirring up political support from Congressmen and Senators, and how it now looked likely that he was going to be appointed clerk of both House and Senate committees investigating railroad routes to the Pacific.

'I have talked for an hour to Mr Lincoln,' Theodore wrote.

He is very enthusiastic about the route we discovered with Doc Kates, and he has privately promised me that, if elected, he will push ahead with a bill for a transcontinental railroad as soon as possible. The only thing that worries me is that if Lincoln believes the railroad to be so urgent, he must seriously be anticipating the secession of the South and even war. The Southern politicians certainly hate him here. They call him an African gorilla and a slang-whanging lawyer.

There was a long postscript. Collis took the letter to the window and read it by the last light of the sun. Hannah, who was sitting reading a book, looked up at him and saw by his expression that he was both moved and disturbed.

> I met Sen. Stride twice. He said adamantly that he had invested enough in the railroad and that these were difficult times for a hard-shell Southern politician to be putting money into Northern industrial projects. However (spontaneously, and much to my regret) I reminded him of his responsibilities to Miss Delphine Spooner, and what had befallen her. Whereupon he agreed to subscribe twenty thousand dollars more to the railroad, sufficient for a *full survey* of the Sierras, and I am sorry to say that I accepted. I believe I owe you an extensive apology, and I only hope that I have done nothing to harm Miss Spooner.

Collis threw the letter down on the white lace tablecloth. He looked down at the scattered pages, his hand over his mouth, and said nothing.

Hannah stood up. 'Is there something the matter?' she asked him.

'What?' he said distractedly.

'I said, is there anything the matter?'

'Oh. No, there isn't. Just a letter from Theo.'

'You look upset.'

He shrugged. 'Yes, I suppose I am. It's funny how your own way of working, when other people try it, always seems so tawdry.'

Hannah didn't pick up the letter, but came instead to stand beside him and lay a hand on his shoulder.

'Go to the back of the house,' she said. 'There's still light enough to see the Sierras.'

Chapter 13

What happened during the fall and winter of 1860 and the early spring of the following year – the election of Abraham Lincoln as President and the subsequent breakaway from the Union by South Carolina and six other cotton states – all of these events seemed peculiarly remote and unreal to the people of San Francisco and Sacramento. They were part of a distant political nightmare which they could only hear about secondhand, either from weeks-old dispatches carried by the Pacific Mail steamers, or from the riders of the Pony Express. Suddenly the self-satisfied isolation of northern California became a source of champing frustration, and in the drawing-rooms of South Park and the lobby of the San Francisco Stock Exchange, rumour and feverish fear were both heightened out of all proportion by the latest news reports from the East.

David Terry, out loud, called Lincoln 'a nigger's lackey', and John Frémont, at an eggnog party, referred to Jefferson Davis as 'the lowest form of treacherous pond life'.

But it was all so far away that it seemed like a theatrical performance, rather than a real political crisis. Even Collis, who was desperately anxious to hear that the nation's wrangles over slavery had taken a decisive turn one way or the other, so that he could plan ahead for the Sierra Pacific Railroad – even Collis found that the bulletins from Washington had a sense of melodramatic dread that was all heavy piano music and vibrato violins, and it was hard for him to believe that secession had come at last.

He felt as if he were sitting in the upper balcony of a theatre, peering through the wrong end of his opera glasses while a stage musician ostentatiously sawed a pretty young lady in half. It was all too distant to be able to make out if the pretty young lady was really being dismembered; and even if she were, he was too far away to be able to do anything about it.

All the same, there was a great deal of what Andy Hunt called 'secesh madness' in San Francisco, and a lot of rash talk about war. The Southerners in particular could think of almost nothing else but fighting, and several dinner parties became positively bellicose, with bread rolls being thrown, and even knives. On the night that

San Francisco heard that Texas had seceded, the wintry streets were electric with fright, and bristling with joyous aggression. Shots were fired into the sky, and even on Sacramento Street, in Chinatown, there was a ringing of gongs

America was on the brink of the grimmest and most glorious military spectacle of the century. More than 2,250,000 men were to fight in the coming war; and more than one out of every four of them were to die. Between them, the secessionist states formed a Confederacy which covered 750,000 square miles, a greater empire than Napoleon had been able to subdue with his armies in fifteen years. What was more, the statesmen and soldiers and ordinary people of that Confederacy shared a love of the South which was fierce, and deep, and enduring; and from the day that it was announced that Abraham Lincoln had carried the electoral college, they knew that their love was on the line. It was time at last to put up, or bow down. It was time for Bull Run, and Shiloh, and Antietam, and Gettysburg. It was also time for the railroads.

Theodore, freshly excited by Lincoln's success, had travelled to Washington yet again, and two days after the inauguration, on 4 March 1861, Lincoln had told him at a private meeting that 'there must be war, no matter how conciliatory I am; the South has the need of it'. Lincoln had repeated to Theodore his support for a transcontinental railroad, and had given him a tortoiseshell pen as a souvenir.

The very next day, as Theodore packed his steamer trunk to return to California, the news came from Richmond that Jefferson Davis, who had reluctantly agreed to accept the Presidency of the Confederated States the previous month, had already called for 100,000 military volunteers.

Theodore wrote to Collis; 'I do not doubt for a moment that we have now arrived at that great crossroads in history for which we have been waiting for so long. It is a *tragedy*, and there is considerable sorrow and bewilderment here in Washington, both personal and national. But now (at last!) they may "Clear the Way" for the railroad.'

He enclosed a cutting from the *Petersburg Express*, which read; 'The election of Lincoln is truly a national calamity. May God avert the storm which is now impending.'

Collis showed the letter to Leland and Charles. Leland was not so sure about the prospect of civil war; and in any case he was too

546

preoccupied these days with his Republican candidacy for the governorship of California to worry about very much else except his long-winded political speeches, which he practised nightly in front of his cheval-glass, his hand thrust into his coat in unconscious imitation of Daniel Webster. Charles, on the other hand, firmly believed that there would be war, that there *must* be war, since he saw no other way of getting a few months' respite from Mary. Whatever any of them felt about it, however, there was little doubt in their minds that the events of the winter had given the Sierra Pacific the best chance it had ever had of going ahead. Jefferson Davis and most of the fiercest supporters of a southern railroad route had now abandoned Washington for Richmond, and that left the Sierra Pacific and the Union Pacific with what Collis believed to be the only feasible route for the federal government to adopt. Theodore's surveys of the Dutch Flat-Donner Pass-Truckee River trace were at last on the verge of acceptance. They had been so generously financed by Senator Stride's 'conscience money' that Theodore had even been able to take Annie along with him on several of his expeditions, and she had illustrated his statistics with pages of alluring watercolours of California flowers.

Laurence Melford, too, had been as good as his word, and had delivered fifty thousand dollars for the return of Collis's calotypes of Sarah. Collis had already used the money to place an order for the Sierra Pacific's first lengths of rail, at fifty-five dollars a ton, and for their first locomotive, a small tank engine from Zerah Colburn's works at Paterson, New Jersey. Collis had told Leland that he would christen the locomotive *Jane McCormick*, and although Leland had been unimpressed, Jane had softened considerably towards Collis, and had even sent Hannah a basket of preserves.

Collis himself had been quiet, and industrious, but Hannah had sensed that he was unsettled. Several times during the winter she had walked into his study on the second floor of their handsome, comfortable house and found him standing by the window, staring sightlessly down at the street below, with his hands in his pockets and his forehead pressed against the glass.

He was looking older. There were wisps of grey hair on the right side of his head, and his cheeks were becoming angular, and lined. He found that he was increasingly forgetful. He would leave a half-finished drink on a table and go pour himself a fresh one. He forgot Hannah's birthday, and had to make up for it by buying her a diamond-and-sapphire ring which cost him nearly two thousand dollars.

The truth was that he was beginning to feel that his dream would never happen. And far from exciting him, as they had Theodore, the political events of the year had disappointed and depressed him. Why hadn't Lincoln called for a railroad right away? Now that the South had gone secesh, what was everyone waiting for? Collis was stretched to the limit on credit, and beyond, and unless the new administration gave them the go-ahead within the next few months, he could see the glorious Sierra Pacific Railroad announcing itself bankrupt without a single inch of track laid.

One evening in April, when the warm winds of early summer were blowing across the Sacramento Valley, Hannah stepped out on to the back veranda and found Collis sitting in the rocker, his legs straight out, his hands in his pockets, and a cheroot clenched between his teeth. She stood beside him silently for long minutes, her face gentle, her hair drawn back in combs, her pink dress turned lilac by the dusk.

'You're unhappy, aren't you?' she asked him at last.

He took the cheroot out of his mouth. 'Unhappy?'

'You're expecting something from life that life won't give you. What is it? Is it fame? Or is it just affection?'

He looked at her. 'You give me all the affection I could wish for.'

'I can't give you fame.'

'I'm not sure that I want it. I just want to be fulfilled.'

'You will be,' Hannah assured him, resting her hand on his shoulder.

He reached up and laid his hand over hers. 'I wish I could be as confident as you are. Every letter I get from Theo is full of hope and reassurance, and yet what have we actually done? We've found a railroad route over the Sierras, we've surveyed it, and we've filed the papers. All at our own expense. So now what happens? Do we have to wait for war? Do we have to dig our way through the mountains with our own bare hands?'

'Collis,' said Hannah, 'you mustn't lose faith.'

'I know,' he told her. 'But it's damned difficult not to, sometimes. I used to have visions of that railroad. I could see the rails themselves, stretching all the way towards the horizon. But now, whenever I think about it, the rails just melt away in front of my eyes, as if they were cast out of nothing but ice.'

'Collis   ' said Hannah. 'God will find a way.

'God?' he asked her. 'Don't you think you and I have called on God a few too many times already?'

'You don't think that He would help us again?'

Collis released her hand, stood up, and walked across to the rail of the veranda. There was a row of apple trees in the small, dusty yard, and their leaves had caught the last of the daylight, so that they flamed like torches against the lavender-coloured sky.

'I don't want to take His generosity in vain, that's all,' Collis said quietly. 'I prayed that your life should be saved, when you were dying in Panama, and it was. I prayed that we should be able to marry, and we were. But miracles don't come free. Even if you don't have to pay for them, someone else does, and that's what I'm afraid of. This railroad has already cost more than I care to think about. Only God knows what would happen if I asked for divine intervention.'

'There's no harm in trying, Collis,' Hannah said intently. 'There's no harm in prayer.'

'Isn't there?' he said, glancing at her sideways.

She reached for his hand again. 'Prayer brought us together, and kept us together. Where's the harm in that?'

'You'd never understand.'

Hannah frowned. 'What's come over you, Collis? You talk as if I've done something terrible.'

He stared at her. 'Maybe you have. Maybe you've convinced me that as long as I believe the Lord is on my side, I can do anything I want. Build railroads over impossible mountains, ruin women's reputations, blackmail respectable businessmen, even take innocent people's lives.'

'You've never taken anybody's life.'

'Haven't I?'

'Of course not. And all those other things. You haven't done anything like that. You're just feeling depressed, that's all. Wait until Theo comes back from Washington. Then you'll feel better. God does understand, you know, and forgive us our trespasses.'

'That's just as well. I'd be burning in eternal hell fire by now if He didn't.'

'Collis,' she said. 'Don't talk that way.'

He was tempted for one irrational moment to tell her about Walter, and the On Leong Tong. He even began to say, 'You're going to find this difficult to believe, Hannah . . .' But somehow the

549

words came out into the soft evening air like a profuse and empty apology, written in decorative scrollwork on shreds of finest silk, and the wind blew them away in front of his eyes.

She wouldn't want to know. Even if she had already guessed at it, she would prefer the truth to remain as it was, unspoken.

'Your God,' he said, shaking his head. 'Your wonderfully convenient God.'

Hannah looked at him, tight-lipped. Then she turned and stalked back across the veranda to the screen door, her skirts lifted to keep them clear of splinters.

'You try me sometimes, Collis,' she said. 'I pray to God that your railroad gets built, just to put an end to your irritability, and your moods, and your eternal dissatisfaction.'

The screen door banged shut behind her. Collis hesitated for a moment, then sprang after her. He caught up with her at the foot of the back staircase, in a dark corner of the downstairs passage. He seized her arm and turned her around. Her face was bright, and defiant, and she looked up at him challengingly.

'Well?' she demanded. 'What are you going to do, strike me?'

'What do you think I am?' he snapped.

She hesitated. Her face was pale and beautiful in the shadows, as if she, too, were a dream. 'You're a man with a single idea,' she said, in a gentle voice. 'You've clung on to that idea because you believe you have nothing else. Now, because your credit's spread so thin, and because Mr Lincoln still hasn't made up his mind, you're worried you're going to lose your one idea for good. And then what will you do? Run a hardware business with Leland and Charles for the rest of your life? Sit in the parlour smoking your cheroots in the evening, watching me crochet? Swap tales with Theo of the days that might have been, like two old dotards, on the back porch?'

Collis gripped the lace collar of her pink dress, and the embroidered cotton of the bodice she wore beneath it, and tore them roughly sideways, baring Hannah's right breast. She gasped, partly out of genuine surprise, and partly as a theatrical reaction to a theatrical gesture.

'I'm going to build this railroad,' he whispered, and she could see his eyes glittering in the darkness. 'I'm going to build this railroad, and by the time this decade's out, you're going to go riding on it like a queen. You just remember that.'

He held her bare breast in his warm, dry, masculine hand, the ball

550

of his thumb rotating softly and provocatively. She tilted her head back, as if she was expecting him to kiss her neck. He leaned forwrd, his lips slightly parted. He hesitated; then he kissed her with great tenderness and controlled passion on her mouth.

'I believe you,' she said. 'I'm sorry.'

He said nothing at all. The house was quiet in the dusky warmth of the evening. The servants had left at noon for the market, and then for a few hours off, and they wouldn't return until dinnertime. Hannah kept a pet cockatoo in the front parlour, in a white cage, and they could hear it rattling and scratching.

Collis took Hannah by the wrist, opened the door to the back stairs, and led her up. The stairs came out by the door to their bedroom, and Collis pushed it open, so that the last reflected light of the day was diffused across the landing. Then he bent down and picked Hannah up in his arms, holding her like a new bride, except that one of her breasts was exposed, and that she was very much more attractive and magnetic to him now than a new bride ever could have been. Her pink skirts hung down like the petals of a rose mallow, and her blonde hair was shining.

He laid her down on their wide, quilted bed and quickly stripped off his vest, his shirt, and his trousers. She watched him without a smile, although she was already feeling breathless for him. The room around them was decorative and warm, and the pink glass perfume bottles on her dressing-table sparked like magical potions.

Naked, his body thicker now, but still muscular, Collis climbed on to the bed. He whispered, 'Hannah . . .' and the way he whispered it carried a host of implications. An implication of desire; an implication of deep and fulfilled emotion; and also an implication of determination. Hannah reached down and lifted up her skirts for him, revealing her white bloomers with their tiered flounces.

He made love to her slowly. The enamelled clock on the mantelpiece seemed to jump whole hours. She opened her eyes every now and then, and felt as if she had been dozing, and dreaming, and dozing again. There were moments of languorous pleasure, when she lay back on the bed while Collis caressed her and touched her. There were moments of intense exertion, when they were both panting and sweating and clutching each other. Collis made her do things that she had never done before, and had never thought possible, and the sensations of that evening, as they passed, were like the charcoal-grey leaves of one of Mr Figgis' private albums, illustrated with potent and erotic memories. She would treasure them for years to come.

At last it appeared to be over. His anger and his passion were both subdued. He went to the chair by the window and sat there naked for nearly ten minutes, watching her in silence. Sometimes she looked back at him, and sometimes she didn't. Sometimes she closed her eyes and felt nothing but the kisses he had given her, and the contented, spent feeling between her thighs. For some reason which amused her, she thought she was probably pregnant. She laughed out loud, without really knowing why.

Collis said, 'What's so funny?'

'Nothing,' she told him. 'I'm just laughing.'

'Good.' He smiled, and stayed where he was, while the moon suddenly appeared at the edge of the window behind him.

On 12 April, Confederate mortars opened fire on Fort Sumter. Three days later, after Fort Sumter had surrendered, President Lincoln called for troops. It was war at last.

The call to arms took days to reach San Francisco, but when it did, the response was aggressive and immediate. From the same city, and sometimes from the same street, men packed their trunks and went off to fight for the Union or for the Rebels. In the Bank Exchange Saloon, two young men from South Park, friends since school, toasted each other in champagne and wished each other well. The next day, they both boarded the same steamer for Panama City, and they played cards on the train together all the way to Aspinwall. They shook hands for the last time on the quay, in the soft tropical rain, before one embarked on a ship headed for Charleston, and the other for New York. Both died – one at Chancellorsville and the other at Fredericksburg. Both were twenty years old.

John Frémont and William Tecumseh Sherman both sailed east from San Francisco to join the Union Army; and the Frémonts' house was requisitioned for the defence of San Francisco Bay, so Jessie had to pack her bags, too. The glass veranda on which Collis had argued with John Frémont and Laurence Melford was demolished, and brick cannon emplacements were put up in its place.

David Terry sailed to the Southern states to join the Confederates. The volatile young William Gwin, son of Senator Gwin, was already in the Confederate Army, along with Grant

Melford. Senator Gwin himself, after being temporarily imprisoned on suspicion of enlisting young men for the South, took
his wife Mary Bell and his family and sailed into exile in France.

Even Dan McReady went off to join up with the Connecticut
volunteers. In Sacramento, Collis waited with almost un-
controllable impatience for news that the 'Act to Aid in the
Construction of a Railroad and Telegraph Line from the Missouri
River to the Pacific Ocean' was at last going to be drafted, and that
Congress had finally decided on the route. Theo had written to say
that although Congress was looking favourably on the Sierra
Pacific surveys, their old adversaries the Hannibal & St Joseph
Railroad were still pressing hard for a line out of St Joe; and that
James C. Stone, the president of the Leavenworth, Pawnee &
Western Railroad, had now employed a professional lobbyist to
pursue *his* route out of Missouri. Collis was seething for days, and
refused to eat, even though Hannah did everything she could to
calm him.

In July, the Army of the Potomac, the greatest army ever seen on
American soil, was routed at Bull Run by the Rebels, and its
soldiers were still running when they reached the rutted streets of
Washington. For the next three years, the war would rage
backwards and forwards between the two capitals, only 110 miles
apart, and out over the surrounding countryside. Collis read the
reports from the East and felt as if he were being slowly consumed
by fire from the inside out.

Another winter passed. Another spring. At last, in April 1862,
Collis decided to travel to Washington himself. He took Kwang
Lee with him and sailed from Sacramento's Front Street levee on
the morning of 6 April. Hannah remained in their carriage, under
her lemon-yellow parasol, and waved him goodbye with her
handkerchief. He stood by the steamer's rail and blew her a kiss.

He had left her a letter under the pillows of their bed. Part of it
read: 'I know that my temper has tried you very hard over the years
we have been together, but I wish you to know that I love you more
dearly than my own life, and that your support and understanding
have been more valuable to me than gold. When the railroad is
built, many people will take credit for it, but I alone shall know that
you were the inspiration for it, and the strength which ensured its
creation.'

He had to wait in San Francisco for two days for a steamer. He
visited Andy Hunt, who had been making himself a healthy profit

by selling supplies to the army, and 'services', too, with the help of Maria-Mamuska. Maria-Mamuska herself was prettier than ever, and thicketed with diamonds and pearls, and almost every gentleman in San Francisco who had a taste for high-class ladies' boarding-houses had visited her four-storey gingerbread house on Bush Street for 'cakes, champagne and *l'amour.*'

Collis even had a drink with Arthur Teach, who had grudgingly forgiven him for *l'affaire des couvertures* and was even quite eager to talk about railroad investment. The news had arrived in San Francisco that the Rebels were playing havoc with the Missouri railroads. They had dynamited bridges, torn up tracks, wrecked trains, and captured engineers. They had even kidnapped the president of the Hannibal & St Joseph and threatened to blow off his head unless train services were halted. The Leavenworth railroad was just as vulnerable to the Confederate cavalry, and for all James C. Stone's political weight, it was becoming increasingly plain that the only safe route was going to be westward from Omaha.

'I think you have it in the bag,' said Arthur Teach. 'And once you have it, you might look to Pacific Securities for some finance.'

'Considering the blankets, that's very generous of you,' Collis told him. He raised his glass.

'Considering the blankets, that's the only way I'm likely to get my money back,' Arthur said and snorted.

The morning on which Collis and Kwang Lee were due to sail for Panama City on the *Gulf of California* something odd and unsettling occurred. Collis was shaving in the bathroom of his suite at the Oriental Hotel when there was a knock at the door. He slung his towel over his shoulder and went with foam on his face to see who was there. It was Kwang Lee, already dressed in his grey tweed travelling suit and grey derby.

'Come in,' said Collis, 'I won't be ready for a while yet.'

'No hurry, sir,' Kwang Lee told him, closing the door. 'While you shave, let me tell you some interesting news.'

'What's that?' asked Collis, lifting his nose so that he could shave his moustache. He rinsed his razor and peered at himself in the mirror. Every morning he looked older, he thought. Every day the railroad was delayed, another hair turned grey. 'There are more damned lines on my face than there are over the Sierra Nevada,' he muttered.

'I was talking to friends of mine in Chinatown,' said Kwang Lee, taking off his hat and sitting down in Collis's armchair. 'They told me interesting news of Sarah Melford.'

'Sarah Melford? What on earth can anyone in Chinatown have to do with Sarah Melford?'

'Plenty, sir, these days. Every two or three weeks, Sarah Melford calls at the house of Hang Far, of the Kwong Dak Tong, although she wears a cloak and hood so that nobody might recognise her.'

Collis turned and frowned at Kwang Lee through the bath-room door. In the next suite, somebody was having a shouting match with his wife; the Oriental Hotel was notorious for its paper-thin walls.

'What does she go there for?' Collis asked.

'Hang Far was not eager to say at first,' said Kwang Lee. 'But I told him you would give his cousin Hang Ching a position in your railroad company in due time, and so he agreed to tell me what he knew.'

'I hope Hang Ching doesn't expect to be anything more exalted than tea boy in chief,' said Collis. 'But anyway, what did Hang Far say about Miss Melford?'

'Sarah Melford has been visiting him for more than one year – ever since her father found out she was still meeting Mr Francis Bret Harte secretly. There was a great argument between father and daughter. Her father forbade her to see Mr Harte again, or any men at all without his permission. Hang Far did not know all the details of the argument, but he said that Sarah Melford was greatly distressed. She was in love with Mr Harte, you see. She went to Hang Far for something which would ease her sorrow. Hang Far did not want to give it to her, but she offered him much money, and Hang Far is a businessman, after all.'

Collis stepped out of the bathroom and stared at Kwang Lee intently. 'What?' he demanded. 'What was it she wanted? What do you mean, "something to ease her sorrow"?'

Kwang Lee raised his hands helplessly. 'You cannot deflect a person who is bent on self-destruction,' he said.

'You mean opium?' asked Collis. 'Sarah Melford goes to the Kwong Dak Tong for opium?'

Kwang Lee nodded.

Collis pressed his hand against his cheek. He walked across to the bureau, and then back again. My God, he thought, it's all my fault. If I hadn't given her that tincture of opium, she never would have known what it could do. She must have been affected by it after all.

Maybe the whole reason she agreed to pose for those calotypes was that she was affected by it. And now, because of me and my railroad, she's become an addict.

'Listen,' Collis told Kwang Lee. 'I want you to go to Hang Far this morning and find out when Sarah Melford is next expected to visit him. Then I want you to postpone our sailing. I'm not leaving San Francisco until I've seen her.'

Hang Far was round, and plump, and dressed in formal black tailcoat and white wing collar. Unlike Mr Kwang's, his house was built and decorated in Western style, with oak dadoes and traditional furniture, and oil paintings of English foxhunts in gilt frames. He was smoking a cigar and reading a copy of the San Francisco newspaper when his servant showed Collis and Kwang Lee into his library. It was a dark room, lined with leather-bound books, and dominated by a huge partner's desk of carved mahogany. It smelled of ink, and books, and Chinese tea. On the wall over the fireplace was the only Chinese picture Collis saw in the whole house – a view of the Yangtze gorge in Szechuan.

'What time are you expecting Miss Melford?' Collis asked.

'At three,' said Hang Far. 'Would you care for some tea while you wait? I have some Cloud Mist tea from the Lu Mountains, which I am sure you will enjoy.'

Collis sat down in one of Hang Far's club-style armchairs. 'I'll just have one of your cigars, thank you,' he said.

The three of them waited in silence. A large brass clock on the desk ticked away the minutes as if it had a speech impediment. Collis sat with his hands in his lap and looked unrelentingly at Hang Far, who smiled from time to time as if he was enjoying a mild private joke.

It was two days since Kwang Lee had told Collis about Sarah. They had postponed their sailing on the *Gulf of California*, and now they were booked to leave on the *Halethorpe* on Wednesday next week. Hang Far had assured Kwang Lee that Sarah would be calling by on Thursday for her supply of laudanum. For a hundred dollars, he had agreed to let Collis come, too.

At three-twenty, the library door opened, and Hang Far's servant came in. 'The lady is here,' he said, looking sideways at Collis. Hang Far said something quiet and quick in Chinese, and the servant turned and went out again.

Collis stood up, and almost at the same moment, Sarah walked in

556

through the door. She stayed where she was, her white-gloved hand on the polished doorknob, her back straight, her face expressionless. She was wearing a striking blue overdress of turquoise silk, embroidered and decorated with braid, and a veiled hat in which three turquoise feathers bobbed; but her face, compared with the last time that Collis had seen her, was ghastly. Her cheeks were so white that she had rouged them, and now she had the appearance of a tragic clown. Her eyes were circled with livid purple, and they stared at Collis without surprise or apparent emotion.

'Sarah,' said Collis huskily.

'It's you,' she said. 'Why . . . what are you doing here?'

'What do you think I'm doing here? I heard about you from Mr Hang.'

'Ah,' she said. 'I forgot you were so friendly with the Chinese. Well, how are you?'

'I'm well. I'm off to Washington next week. But what about you?'

'Me?' asked Sarah vaguely. 'Well, my dear, I'm all right. I'm very well. I shall be better later, of course, when Mr Hang has given me his little treat.'

Collis took her arm. 'Sarah,' he said, 'this has got to stop.'

'Stop? Why should it have to stop? Don't you think I look better now than ever? Don't you think I'm the Princess of San Francisco?'

'I don't know what's happened to you,' said Collis, and his voice was uneven with emotion. 'You look desperately sick.'

'Sick?' she said, tugging her arm away. 'Of course I'm sick. I'm always sick until I visit Mr Hang. Aren't I, Mr Hang?'

Hang Far shrugged non-committally.

'Sarah,' said Collis, 'the first time I ever saw you, you were coming out on to the balcony of the theatre, in your yellow dress, and you looked like the kind of woman that men could go mad for. You were beautiful. You were graceful. You were everything a young woman should be.'

Sarah reached out for an armchair and unsteadily sat down. 'Yes,' she said, with an odd little-girl sigh. 'Yes, I suppose I was. Francis always used to tell me that. "Sarah," he used to say, "you are the dictionary definition of ecstasy, made flesh."'

'You loved him very much, didn't you?'

Sarah absent-mindedly reached up and touched the feathers in her hat. 'I loved him totally. But that was all a long time ago.'

'What would he say if he could see you now?'

'Oh – I expect that he'd be very annoyed. He doesn't like the Chinese, you know. He was always complaining about their heathen ways. But what does it matter? He's off with someone else now. It's all past history.'

'So why do you persist in taking these tinctures?' asked Collis. 'Can't you see what they've done to you?'

'They make me feel well,' said Sarah. 'I feel cold, and they keep me warm.'

Collis knelt down on the German rug and took her hand. He could feel the bones of her fingers through the white cotton. And in spite of her overdress and her petticoats, he could see that she was savagely thin, and that her figure had been reduced to that of a starving seamstress.

'I want you to leave with me, now,' said Collis. 'I'm going to take you to Dr Cooper, and together we're going to get you well again.'

'I want my tincture first,' said Sarah stiffly.

'No,' said Collis. 'From now on, you're going to survive without it.'

'What's making you so concerned?' Sarah asked him. 'You weren't so concerned when you took those pictures of me, were you? You weren't so concerned when you drugged me with tinctures then?'

'I'm concerned now because I wasn't concerned then,' said Collis. 'I didn't realise what effect that tincture would have – I didn't know about you and Mr Harte.'

Mr Hang walked over to his desk, opened it, and took out a small glass bottle. 'Would you like this?' he asked Sarah.

'Mr Hang,' Collis said with ire, 'I want you to put that away.'

'Mr Edmonds,' said Hang Far, 'I allowed you to come here unwillingly, and only for observation. You were not to come here to interfere in my legitimate business.'

Collis stood up. 'You call that stuff legitimate business? Have you seen what you've done to her?'

'It is her own choice,' said Hang Far.

Collis snatched the bottle from Hang Far's hand, unstoppered it, and turned it upside down. The laudanum splashed on to the desk and the rug and left spots of wet on Hang Far's discarded newspaper.

'Well, you white people are certainly fond of dramatic gestures,' said Hang Far equably. 'But there is plenty more tincture where that bottle came from.'

'Miss Melford's not having any of it,' said Collis. 'Come on, Sarah – we're leaving.'

'No,' said Sarah. 'Don't you think you've interfered in my life enough already?'

Collis seized Sarah by the wrist, pulled her out of her chair, and swung her around so that she was facing the mirror on the library wall.

'Look at yourself!' he shouted. 'Look at what you've done!'

Sarah looked, and then turned towards Collis. 'You have many talents, my dear,' she said calmly. 'You have determination, and you have style. But you will never be a saviour of souls. Your ambition is too destructive. Now, I'd appreciate it if you left. What I do here with Mr Hang is my own business.'

'I shall tell your father,' said Collis.

'I doubt if my father will believe you. I doubt if he will even listen to you, after you blackmailed him with those pictures.'

'Sarah,' said Collis, 'for the love of God.'

Sarah lifted her veil. Her face had the whiteness and the texture of chalk.

'You may kiss me, Collis,' she said, with arid dignity.

Collis stayed where he was. On the other side of the desk, Hang Far smiled at him like a friendly restaurant proprietor. After a moment or two, Collis turned and said: 'Come on, Kwang Lee, we have to go.'

Outside, on Jackson Street, he tugged on his gloves and looked up at the sky as the first few spots of a spring rainshower spattered on to the sidewalk.

'You are going to leave Miss Melford like that? You are going to do nothing?' asked Kwang Lee.

'There's nothing I can do,' he said bitterly.

They arrived in Washington on the last day of May, 1862. They had seen very little evidence of the war on their journey, since the Union Navy was far stronger at sea than the Confederacy; the paddle-steamer *Ulysses*, on which they travelled from Aspinwall, was cautiously approached off the Florida coast by an armour-plated Rebel ship, which eventually did nothing but signal them bon voyage. They also approached close enough to Charleston harbour for Collis and Kwang Lee to see the Union blockage ships on the horizon.

Washington itself had become a teeming military encampment.

559

It was still as mucky and untidy and unfinished as before; and the Washington Monument was still an unhappy stump in the middle of a patch of waste ground. But these days the city had 150,000 soldiers to house, as well as its politicians, and most of the parks had been taken over for camps and temporary barracks, and trees had been chopped down to build huts and fences. Locomotives and railroad cars were shunted along Maryland Avenue, and ordnance carriages churned up the muddy streets even more deeply than the hansoms and broughams of prewar days.

Not that the city's social life had abated. Although public transportation was almost non-existent, and most of the streets were only occasionally lit, there was still a furious round of parties and soirées every night, and the *Washington Star* complained that many of the gambling houses were crowded during the day by officers in uniform. The President had cut down on his social calendar after the death of his son in February, but White House receptions were still popular, and always so crowded that local pickpockets made a very respectable living.

Collis had been unable to book a hotel room, but Theo found him a suite of rooms on Connecticut Avenue, on the second floor of the abandoned home of Senator Irwin Teasdale, of Arkansas. The first floor was occupied by Colonel Merritt 'Bones' Bonham, of the newly-formed Army Balloon Corps, although from what Collis could hear going on downstairs, Bones did very little ballooning and a very great deal of drinking, not to mention the horseplay that went on with a number of fat women with loud voices. Kwang Lee occupied a small room at the back of Collis's apartments, where he set up his wok and his tea kettle, and where he unaccountably pinned up a theatre poster for *Uncle Tom's Cabin*.

Theo had put on weight, and had acquired the pallor of men who spend all their days in the cloakrooms of Congress and in the coffee-houses of Pennsylvania Avenue. He seemed to have ambivalent feelings about Collis's arrival -- relieved, because he needed the support of someone enthusiastic and hard-headed; but wary, too, because he had learned to play the political game the Washington way, and he was afraid that Collis might trample on his carefully-nurtured connections.

He came around to visit Collis the afternoon after their arrival. His eyes were puffy from lack of sleep, and his beard was tangled. He paced around the upstairs drawing-room in his dishevelled, soup-stained suit, and seemed to be vague and preoccupied.

Collis, dressed in severe grey, sat still in his armchair and watched him.

'We seem so near to a charter, and yet there are so many sticking points,' said Theo. 'Just when the committee appears to be ready to approve the Sierra Pacific, somebody comes up with an objection, or a question, or an alternative.'

'Are you sure you're pushing them hard enough?' asked Collis.

'I'm not *pushing* them. If I pushed them, they'd dig in their heels even deeper. I'm trying to *cajole* them.

'Our best hope is Lincoln,' Theo continued. 'He's very much in favour of the Sierra Pacific-Union Pacific route. The only trouble is, he's so involved with the war these days, it's almost impossible to get near him.'

Collis stood up. 'Would you like a drink?' he asked Theo. 'You look as if you could use one.'

Theo rubbed his eyes. 'Yes,' he said. 'I believe I could.'

Collis was just about to ring the bell for Kwang Lee when he heard a sharp knocking at the downstairs door. It was repeated almost immediately, and he heard Kwang Lee's slippers shuffling on the staircase as he went down to answer it. A moment later, Kwang Lee came back, opened the sitting-room door, and handed Collis a visiting card.

Collis held the card up to the light. It read: 'Please see me. Alice.' He glanced at Theo, and then passed the card over so that he could read it, too.

'Show the lady up,' Collis said.

Alice Stride appeared in a long dark-blue cloak, with a hood. She was pale, and wide-eyed, as if she had recently suffered a fever. She came across the room slowly, with one hand clasped over the other and her elbows drawn in like an old woman feeling the cold.

'Collis,' she whispered.

Collis reached his hand out and took her arm. 'My dear Alice,' he said. 'What's happened? What are you doing here? You look so unwell.'

'It was only the grippe,' she said. 'The winter was bad here, and medication was short, and it went around the whole city.'

'Sit down – please,' said Collis, and gently led her over to his armchair. 'You must tell me what's been going on. Kwang Lee – bring us some fresh tea.'

Alice loosened the cord of her cloak and brushed back her hair with her hand. 'It's father,' she said. 'He's in desperate danger, and I

561

don't know what I can do to help him. When I heard that you'd arrived here on a visit -- well, of course I came to see you.'

'What's wrong?' asked Collis.

Alice said, 'It was the war. We left Washington and moved to Richmond when Lincoln was elected. Father was one of the people who persuaded Alexander Stephens to stand as Vice-President of the Confederacy. Everything was fine, and we were all well, until November, when father insisted on going back to our house at Culpeper to rescue some of the paintings and the silverware. He said we would need them if the war became worse, and he didn't want the bluebellies to have them.'

Collis drew up another chair and sat down. 'Go on,' he encouraged her.

'It was inevitable, I suppose,' said Alice. 'Father was on his way back with a wagonload of valuables when a Union raiding party ambushed him and took him prisoner. When he told them who he was, and produced papers to prove it, they brought him back here to Washington and locked him up. They held him without trial for four months, although they were always threatening to charge him with conspiracy and espionage and all manner of trumped-up crimes.'

'Where is he now?' Collis asked.

'He escaped. I came here to Washington myself in January, with the help of Senator Harris, of Philadelphia. I tried several times to have my father released legitimately, but I was told that he was an important hostage, and they would never let him go. But one day last month, without my knowledge, father persuaded the army to let him visit an old friend in Georgetown. They sent him with two armed men as an escort; but once in his friend's house, he and his friend disarmed his escort, and shot them both. My father escaped, and now he's hiding in Washington with a family of Southern sympathisers.'

Collis looked at Alice carefully. 'What can I do?' he asked. 'I'm only a visiting railroad lobbyist, from California.'

'You're more than that,' said Alice. 'You're clever, and you're imaginative, and I'm sure you can think of a way to get my father out of Washington and back into Virginia.'

'You're asking a lot,' said Collis. 'Your father's face is so well known, I don't suppose there's a single boy in the whole Union Army who wouldn't recognise him on sight, and bayonet him, too. If he's killed two of his guards, then that makes him a

562

murderer, and you know what the penalty for assisting a murderer can be.'

'Collis,' said Alice. Her eyes glistened with tears. 'I wouldn't ask if you weren't my last and my only hope.'

Collis thought for a while. Theo, who was agitated by Alice's presence, stood by the window and drummed his fingertips on the pane. It was like the sound of rain, or distant horses.

Eventually, Collis said, 'All right, Alice,' and Theo at once stopped drumming, so that the silence in the sitting-room was quite complete.

'Oh, Collis,' said Alice. 'Oh, Collis, thank you.'

'Don't thank me yet,' said Collis. 'It won't be cheap, and it won't be guaranteed.'

'My father has plenty of money. I've managed to release most of his assets while I've been here. Just tell me how much you need.'

'Collis,' said Theo sharply. 'Don't you think we've bled Senator Stride enough?'

Collis lowered his head impatiently. 'I'm not talking about bleeding, Theodore. I'm talking about helping. And in a time of war, helping the enemy, especially an enemy as wanted as Senator Stride – well, that can't come at a bargain price.'

'For God's sake,' said Theo.

'For anybody's sake you like,' Collis retorted. 'The fact remains that the man is a murderer, and an escaped prisoner of war, and that to spirit him out of Washington and back to the South can't possibly be effected for nothing.'

'You wouldn't even have the first idea how to do it,' said Theo. 'You've only been back in Washington for a day.'

Collis reached over and held both of Alice's hands. 'I'm going to get your father out, don't you worry. All he has to do is wait for my instructions. If you pass this house again, and there's a red-white-and-blue rosette nailed to the front door, then knock, and I'll tell you everything you need to know.'

Kwang Lee came in with a tray of fragrant tea and set it down on the table. Theo looked at it, and then at Collis, and then stalked angrily out of the room.

In his gambling days in New York, Collis had learned that if a trick works once, it will invariably work again. That was why he paid two hundred dollars to the proprietors of the Columbia Hotel on Pennsylvania Avenue for two hours' use of a south-facing sitting-room; and that was why he talked during the next two days to Representative Harold Watkins, of Minnesota, and to a reticent gentleman who ran a small specialist store on Ninth Street. Then, the following Monday, he nailed a rosette to the door of Senator Teasdale's house, and waited for Alice to call back.

The meeting at the Columbia Hotel was arranged for two-thirty on Wednesday afternoon. It was then, as only Collis and the reticent gentleman from Ninth Street knew, that the natural sunlight in the sitting-room was at its brightest, so that anyone who sat by the window in one of two carefully-positioned armchairs was ideally lighted for a wet-plate collodion photograph. Representative Harold Watkins certainly didn't know, as he stumped heftily up the hotel stairs in his green broadcloth suit, his face as purple as a blueberry. Neither did the man who stepped quickly down from a black private carriage outside, and crossed the sidewalk to the hotel entrance with his hand raised to shield his face and his hat tugged down over his eyes.

Collis was waiting by the door to greet Representative Watkins as he came puffing in. 'You won't be sorry you came,' he said with a warm smile. 'This is what I call the opportunity of a lifetime.'

Watkins circled the suite like a gasping hippopotamus, wiping his neck with a pocket handkerchief and saying over and over again: 'Stairs. You didn't tell me there were going to be stairs. I wouldn't have come at all if I'd known about the stairs.'

He was just beginning to cool off when there was a quiet knock at the door and Senator Stride stepped in.

Considering how long Senator Stride had been imprisoned, and how much he had aged since Collis had last seen him, he was surprisingly fit, and composed. Only his deep-set eyes, already dark, seemed darker. He shook Collis by the hand, and then Representative Watkins, and at last Collis had his two subjects sitting in their allotted chairs by the window. Only Collis noticed the lens that protruded from the curtained-off doorway at the back of the room, and only Collis heard the click of the mechanism as the reticent gentleman from Ninth Street took his first picture.

'Well, Senator,' said Watkins. 'I never thought I'd live to see *you* in such a difficult hole.'

'I never thought I'd live to see this nation of ours torn in half by civil war,' said Senator Stride. His voice was hoarser than before, from all of his months in prison, but it was still commanding, and deep.

'Mr Edmonds tells me you need assistance to leave Washington undetected,' said Representative Watkins.

'That is just about the case,' Senator Stride said and nodded. 'I'm willing to pay, of course, as much as is necessary.'

Representative Watkins pulled at his nose with his finger and thumb, and sniffed. 'I'd have to ask twenty thousand. There are all kinds of palms to be oiled; all kinds of arrangements to make.'

'If that's what it takes,' said Senator Stride. 'If I don't get out of Washington soon, I'm going to be captured again, and shot.'

Representative Watkins raised an eyebrow. He had a head that reminded Collis of a large plum pudding, steaming on a plate. Even the freckles on top of his bald pate looked like a frosting of Demerara sugar. The camera mechanism clicked again, and Collis grimaced at the loudness of it.

'There will, of course, be expenses,' said Representative Watkins. 'I'll have to pay for a carriage, and a boat, and for someone to row you across the Potomac.'

'How much?' asked Senator Stride.

Representative Watkins puffed out of his cheeks. 'In all,' he said, 'about ten thousand dollars.'

'So you're asking for thirty?'

'With five for personal expenses, yes. Thirty-five thousand.'

Senator Stride looked at Collis darkly, but all Collis could do was shrug. Collis was only acting as entrepreneur, and Senator Stride himself was in no position to haggle. Either he relied on Representative Watkins, and paid Representative Watkins's price, or he would eventually swing from the gallows in Washington's jailyard.

'Very well,' he said, and unbuttoned his vest just far enough to expose a canvas moneybelt wrapped around his waist. Representative Watkins sat back in his chair and licked his lips with unconcealed relish as Senator Stride counted out twelve thousand dollars in gold coins, and set it out on the table between them in seven neat stacks. The afternoon sun shone through the bare windows and sparkled on the coins as if it could give its attention to nothing else, as if it were obsessed by them. Collis had previously taken down the lace curtains to improve the quality of the light, but now the light itself was enhanced by Senator Stride's gold.

Representative Watkins leaned forward, and spots of golden reflected light lit up his jowls.

'I believe we can do business, Senator,' he said.

565

From behind the curtains, there was another loud mechanical click.

Collis said nothing as Representative Watkins gathered up the money and scooped it into a leather portmanteau. But as the Congressman started to rise from his chair, Collis said, in a gentle but arresting voice, 'There's one bit of business we haven't quite finished with yet.'

'Yes?' asked Representative Watkins cautiously. 'What can that be?'

'*My* business,' said Collis. 'The business of the Sierra Pacific Railroad, and its charter from Congress. The business of the Railroad Act. That's what we haven't quite finished yet.'

'I don't see the relevance,' said Watkins, standing up and supporting himself on the table. 'Fugitive Senators and transcontinental railroads are birds of a very different species, and I don't care to discuss them both at the same meeting. I'll have to bid you good-day.'

'I'm afraid you're mistaken,' Collis told him, stepping between Watkins's green broadcloth belly and the door of the suite. 'Fugitive Senators and transcontinental railroads are all part and parcel of the same arrangement, by courtesy of the camera.'

'Camera? I don't understand you.'

Collis reached behind him and drew back the curtain. Blinking in the light, like a gopher discovered in its burrow, was the reticent gentleman from Ninth Street, with his waxed moustache and his tinted spectacles, and his large box camera.

'You have just been photographed, Representative Watkins. Not once, but several times, in the act of accepting money from a Southern Senator whom you know to be a wanted fugitive. It seems to me that the only way in which you can prevent those photographs from falling into the hands of those who might wish to damage your career, or even those who might wish to throw you into prison for collusion with an enemy – it seems to me that the only possible way you can do that is to withdraw your objections to the route of the Sierra Pacific Railroad, and to advise your cronies to do likewise.'

'Get out of my way,' said Watkins haughtily. 'You don't alarm me one bit.'

'And why's that? Because you don't mind solitary confinement? Or don't you tremble at the prospect of political disgrace?'

Watkins came very close to Collis, so that Collis could smell the lunchtime brandy on his breath. He lifted one pudgy hand and prodded Collis hard on the breastbone.

'You don't alarm me because if you show those photographs to anybody at all, they'll ask *you*, too, what you were doing in the company of a wanted murderer and escaped prisoner of war, without making any effort to detain him. *You* will be liable to arrest and disgrace, just as much as I.'

Collis smiled. 'You don't understand, Congressman Watkins. I have already sent my Chinese assistant to bring the military here.'

Senator Stride, who had been sitting silently in his chair, now suddenly turned towards Collis and stared at him in shock.

'You've betrayed me?' he demanded. 'You've betrayed my daughter's confidence?'

Collis thought, and then nodded. 'You could call it betrayal. But perhaps a better word for it would be revenge.'

'My God, you're unscrupulous,' said Senator Stride. He stood up, his face concentrated with indecision, and then he reached into his coat and tugged out a short-barrelled revolver. He aimed it at Collis without saying a word. Representative Watkins stepped back in alarm, and behind him Collis heard the breaking of glass as the Ninth Street photographer dropped one of his plates.

'So, you're going to shoot me,' said Collis. He was trying to speak in a normal voice, but somehow his words came out high and unbalanced, as if he were being strangled with rawhide. He became abruptly and uncomfortably aware of the details of the hotel room all around him – the damp-stained wallpaper, the dusty plants, the unpolished coal scuttle in the fireplace – and he thought, I shall die here.

Senator Stride held his revolver steady for almost a minute. Then he lowered it. Collis still watched him warily in case he changed his mind and lifted it again.

'I should shoot you,' Senator Stride told him, in a regretful tone. 'This is war, after all, and I would be quite within my rights. But I won't. There doesn't seem to be much honour in it.'

'Honour?' asked Collis.

'That's right,' said Senator Stride. 'It was a quality on which the Confederacy was founded, and which I hope it will always retain. Courtesy, bravery, and honour. The marks of a gentleman.'

There was a tight little pause, and then Senator Stride walked past both Collis and Representative Watkins, opened the door, and went out on to the landing. Before either of them could prevent it, he stopped at the top of the stairs, aimed the pistol at his own face, and fired. There was a deafening bang, which made Collis's ears sing. Then the Senator turned, collapsed, and tumbled ignominiously head over heels all the way down to the second-storey landing. A cloud of blue smoke hung above the upstairs bannister, and the wallpaper was sprayed with a feathery pattern of blood.

Representative Watkins's teeth were chattering. 'I must leave,' he said. 'Good God, they mustn't find me here.'

Collis gripped his arm, so savagely tight that he squeaked. 'You won't forget the Railroad Act, will you, Congressman?'

Representative Watkins took a deep breath, and then said, 'Very well. You can take it that my objections have been withdrawn. Yes, and those of my friends. And may your soul rot in hell.'

He was about to dash off when Collis gripped his arm again. 'The gold, Congressman? Since you don't have any expenses anymore, with Senator Stride dead, you don't need the gold.'

The Congressman looked down at his portmanteau. Grudgingly, he handed it over. 'When you've taken the money out, send the portmanteau back to my office,' he said. 'It was a present from my late wife.'

'I'm sure she would have been proud of you,' said Collis. 'This money is going back to Senator Stride's daughter. It won't bring her father back, but then it won't bring mine back, either.'

'I've got to go,' said Representative Watkins.

Collis watched the fat man hurrying down the stairs. Hotel guests were already coming out of their rooms to see what had happened, and Watkins had to push his way past them with his hat raised so that nobody would recognise him. Washington was a small city, and its politicians were well known.

Senator Stride lay where he had fallen. His bloody face was pressed against the baseboard, and he was not quite dead. His breath came in long, quivering sighs. A woman brought him a piece of torn sheet soaked in brandy, and pushed it carefully into his mouth. It was impossible to tell if it brought him any relief or not, for in two or three minutes, he died.

Collis closed the door of the hotel room and looked across at the photographer, who was hastily packing up his camera and his plates. The photographer gave him a nervous, unhappy glance, and then went on fastening up his polished oak boxes.

Collis went to the window and shielded his eyes against the

568

sunlight as he looked down into the street. He felt exhausted, as if he had been running hard for hours.

'I'll be going now, Mr Edmonds,' the photographer said. 'I'll send you the prints in the morning.'

'Very well,' replied Collis. Then, more softly, 'Very well.'

Theodore, when he discovered what had happened, was furious. He met Collis at the bar of the Emmett House Hotel, on Pennsylvania Avenue between Seventh and Eighth, and he appeared more harassed than ever, with his necktie hanging loose, and his lapel inside out.

'Theo,' said Collis, with exaggerated concern, 'you're allowing this railroad to get you down. Have a drink. You'll feel much better.'

'I don't want your drinks and I don't want your sympathy,' hissed Theo. 'I want to disassociate myself from you and all the rest of this company's motley collection of directors as soon as I can. You're nothing but a gang of small-minded thieves and twisters.'

Collis raised his hand to attract the barman's attention. Then he turned to look at Theo; and, as he did so, the sun waxed strong and bright through the yellow glass of the hotel windows, and the curls of tobacco smoke around Collis's head shone like a Satanic wreath.

'I've heard a lot of talk about honour and moral rectitude since I first got involved in the Sierra Pacific,' Collis said gently. 'But without pushing, without pressuring, without using whatever means we have at our disposal, this fabulous railroad of ours will never be built. Just you remember that.'

The barman set a whisky down on the counter in front of Theodore. Theodore looked at it, tossed a dollar down beside it, and then walked stiffly out of the bar.

Through the weeks of bargaining that followed, Collis and Theodore were seldom apart. In committee rooms, in hotel suites, in restaurants, and even on board a naval ship moored on the Potomac, they sat side by side and argued for their railroad with compelling accord. It was only when the day's business was over – when the cigars were crushed out in the smoke-filled rooms and the papers were gathered up from the tables – that Theodore would coldly and immediately leave for his hotel, while Collis went off to have dinner with one Congressman or another, or off to his rooms on Connecticut Avenue.

For both of them a government charter for the Sierra Pacific was their most pressing consideration. But once they were sure of that, both of them were quite aware that Theodore would do everything he could to buy Collis and his partners out. Theodore had seen the railroad as a vision of pure technology. As far as he was concerned, Collis's and Leland's motives were muddied with greed, with self-interest, and with a ruthless disregard for human sensitivity.

By June, with the Army of the Potomac still trying to force its way deeper into Virginia, the terms of the railroad charters were at last agreed. All of the Congressmen involved in the drawing up and ratification of the act were now well provided for, with promises of railroad stocks and bonds, and Thaddeus Stevens, the Representative from Pennsylvania, had insisted that all the iron used in the construction of the railroad should be made in America – which, since he was one of the country's largest iron manufacturers, suited him fine.

The Pacific Railroad Act granted to the Sierra Pacific Railroad ten miles of land in alternative sections on either side of its right of way for each mile of track laid down. In addition – and Collis had fought hard for this – the company would be given loans of $16,000 a mile on the plains, $32,000 through the Great Basin, and $48,000 through the Sierra.

On 1 July 1862, a humid and unpleasant day, with thunderclouds hanging over the western horizon, the Army of the Potomac began to retreat from Virginia after the battle of Malvern Hill. That afternoon, in his rooms, Collis heard that President Lincoln had signed the Pacific Railroad Act.

Once the messenger had left, Collis called for Kwang Lee to bring him a drink. Kwang Lee came in with a whisky on a small tray. He was dressed in a smart grey tailcoat, and a clean white shirt.

'You're all smartened up,' said Collis, taking his drink.

'Yes, sir. I heard about the railroad. Good news, huh? Allow me to offer my congratulations.'

'Thank you, Lee,' said Collis. He took a mouthful of whisky. Then he stayed where he was, sitting in his chair, for almost an hour. A thundershower came and went. He heard army gun carriages in the street outside. It was only at five o'clock that the sky began to brighten, and the raindrops clinging on to the window began to sparkle the way they had on the window of the Monument Hotel, longer ago than Collis could recall.

*

Two days later, in Sacramento, Hannah left the house shortly after sunset and walked down to the front gate, where their black houseboy, Juno, was waiting patiently with the carriage. The evening had that soft, dusty quality that is particularly Western, and the horses fidgeted in their harness.

Hannah mounted the carriage and took the reins. 'I won't be long, Juno,' she told him. 'No more than an hour or two. I'm visiting Mrs Weiss for supper.'

'Yes, ma'am,' said Juno. 'Please take care, now.'

Hannah clicked her tongue, and the horses trotted ahead. She drove quite briskly towards downtown Sacramento, in the direction of Mrs Weiss's house on J Street; but once she was out of sight in the twilight, she turned the carriage and headed for the intersection of Eighth and L.

She felt as breathless now as she had on the first occasion when she had visited Mrs Pangborn's. She felt just as resolved, though, in spite of all the agonies of conscience she had gone through; in spite of the fact that she knew now that she had abandoned her religion forever.

She wondered as she drove along L Street whether her religion had at any time amounted to anything more than a substitute for real love. Had it really all been false? Had all those prayers to the Virgin been hollow? And how did God regard her now? As a lost sheep, whom He would search out and gather in His forgiving arms? Or as a damned soul, guilty of breaking both the sixth and the seventh commandments, and duly earmarked for eternal punishment?

She looked up over the rooftops of the clustered wooden houses, and the sight of the stars made her shiver. Maybe it was growing colder. Maybe she was frightened by the thought of Mrs Pangborn's shining instruments. Maybe she was disturbed by the way the stars hung all around her like haughty witnesses to her sin.

'Forgive me,' she whispered, knowing how false it sounded. One of the horses twitched its ears.

She had made Collis a promise on their wedding day – that his firstborn child would be the railroad. It had to be that way, for Collis ate, drank, breathed, and slept the railroad. Everything he did in the hardware store was directed towards making more money for the railroad. Every book and pamphlet he read was concerned with iron and steel and bridges and railroad locomotives. If they had a child before the Railroad Act was signed, then that child would be nothing to Collis but an interference in his midwifery of a child far more precious. At least, Hannah believed it would, and she couldn't bear the idea of it. When she and Collis had their first child, their first real child, she wanted that child to be everything.

Last year, she had fallen pregnant in April, the month that war had broken out. She had decided at first that she wanted to keep the baby, but by July Collis's angry moods about the slow progress of the Railroad Act had at last turned her mind against it. While Collis had spent his time writing furious letters to Theodore in Washington, and fretting about finance, Hannah had been going through a silent self-crucifixion. I am going to have to kill my child, she had thought, one sunny morning in mid-July. It is better for it to return to heaven, and to spend the rest of eternity in innocent happiness, than to be born into a world in which it will be second-best in its father's affections to a railroad company.

She had talked to the tough, stringy little woman who cleaned the church every Monday. They had stood among the wooden grave markers, under a hot sun. The woman had suggested Mrs Pangborn, who was often having to perform 'little operations' for her working girls. The next evening, when Collis had been staying late at 54 K Street to talk to Leland, Hannah had taken the carriage and driven herself to Eighth and L, just as she was tonight.

Collis had never known. Nor, she thought, would he ever know.

It was dark by the time she reached Mrs Pangborn's house. She tethered the horses around the corner on Ninth, so that the carriage wouldn't be seen outside the whorehouse. Then she walked across the street, her face veiled, her black coat swishing on the dusty road. Very faintly – so faintly that she could scarcely hear it – a piano was playing 'Roses Red and Roses White'. She stepped up to Mrs Pangborn's door and knocked.

One of Mrs Pangborn's girls let her in – a frizzy-haired blonde with pink cheeks and a chubby bottom. Hannah was sure she had seen the girl working during the day at Oppenheimer's Pastry Parlour. To serve cakes by day and fornicate at night – that was a strange way to make a living. There were red chrysanthemums on the wallpaper, and the hallway smelled of perfume and tobacco. The smell brought back her fear.

Mrs Pangborn herself was waiting in her back parlour. It was a small, stuffy room, with a heavy sideboard, a bookcase crowded with dog-eared editions of pornographic books, and a tall china Dalmatian with one of its ears chipped off. The leaves of the mahogany table had been extended, and Mrs Pangborn had draped it with a white sheet. On the sideboard, her instruments were laid out, with towels, bandages, and a china basin of water.

'Well, my love,' said Mrs Pangborn. 'You're back again, then.'

The statement was neither accusing nor surprised. Mrs Pangborn was as forgiving and as tolerant as twenty priests, and apart from that she had seen between more legs than most people could count. She was small, and well rouged, with a face as intense as a beaver's, and her gingery hair was piled into tight curls, out of which her diamond earrings swung alarmingly. While Hannah stood in the doorway, she tied a floral apron around herself and gave Hannah a reassuring grin.

'All right last time, wasn't it?' she said. 'No problems, no complications? Well, it's going to be just the same tonight.'

Hannah felt faint, as if she were dreaming. But she took Mrs Pangborn's words as the cue to take off her coat and lay it over the arm of the sofa. Then she turned around, so that Mrs Pangborn could unbutton her dress.

In a few minutes, Hannah was lying awkwardly on the table, her head propped up by a pillow, her underskirts raised up, and her thighs spread so that Mrs Pangborn could get to work. Mrs Pangborn washed her hands, and then brought the oil lamp closer, so that she could see what she was doing.

'Would you care for a drink?' she asked Hannah. 'I've got a bottle of brandy in the cupboard.'

Hannah shook her head, 'No, no. Just – do what you have to do.'

She lay back on the pillow as Mrs Pangborn reached for her instruments, and closed her eyes. This is the second and last time, dear God. I promise you that. Next time, the Railroad Act will have been passed, and Collis will have his charter, and the child can live. Next time, when I get pregnant, it will be the most important event in Collis's life.

She let out an 'Ah!' of pain as Mrs Pangborn thrust two fingers deep inside to feel the neck of her womb.

'Well, that looks dandy to me,' she heard Mrs Pangborn saying. 'That all looks dandy to me.'

Then she leaned over Hannah and said loudly, 'You won't even know what's happened.'

573

Hannah looked across at a cheap etching on Mrs Pangborn's parlour wall. It showed a dour Indian overlooking the Mariposa Trail in Yosemite. She thought that she had never seen an Indian. How curious, to come to the West, and never to see an Indian.

She thought of Collis, too, and tried to imagine his face in her mind. My dear Collis, she thought, and for some reason her eyes filled with tears.

Mrs Pangborn said, 'Am I hurting you, my love?'

But Hannah whispered, 'No. You're not hurting me at all.'

The letters crossed at Panama City. Collis's letter had just reached the Pacific after being carried across the isthmus by train; and Jane McCormick's letter had just reached Panama on the Pacific Mail steamer *Icarus*.

Collis's letter read:

Great and wonderful news! Today, President Lincoln at last signed the Railroad Act, and we have been granted nearly all the money I wanted. I am so pleased that I cannot describe my feelings, although somehow after all these years of trial and struggle the final Presidential signature has come as something of an anti-climax. Theodore and I are proceeding instanter to New York, where we are going to order up all the rails we will need, and all the railroad equipment. We will also establish the Sierra Pacific Railroad as a New York company and try to raise extra money. I expect to be back in Sacramento by September at the latest, so do take heart.

Jane McCormick's letter read:

I write with tragic intelligence. Late today, Mrs Edmonds was found expired in her carriage on the outskirts of the city, after a search by deputies and by friends for the greater part of the morning and afternoon. She had not returned home last night after taking the carriage and telling Juno that she would be spending the evening with Mrs Weiss. At midnight, Juno alerted the neighbours, who immediately initiated a search. Mrs Weiss had not seen Mrs Edmonds, nor did she have any arrangement to meet her. Dr Gizzard has already inspected Mrs Edmonds's remains, and is of the opinion that she passed

574

away as a result of blood loss following the miscarriage of a child.

To return to New York after all the years he had spent in California was, for Collis, a moving but also an unexpectedly depressing experience. As the steamer *Ariadne* paddled her way slowly in through the misty reaches of New York harbour, and he saw once more the rooftops and spires around Battery Park, he had to turn away, and walk the length of the deck, with Kwang Lee following a little distance behind him.

He came across Theodore leaning on the railings and staring out towards Governors Island.

'Are you pleased to be back?' he asked Theodore.

Theodore shrugged. '*You* don't look as if you are.'

'It was about here, about this far out of the harbour, that I first saw Hannah,' Collis said. 'Before that moment, there was nothing worth having in my life at all. No purpose, no merit, nothing.'

'Is there now?' asked Theodore sharply.

Collis stood beside him, looking at him with an expression of regret. 'Do you really have to hate me?' he asked. 'After all, we've got everything we wanted. You've certainly got everything *you* wanted. As soon as we've collected enough iron and steel together, we can start to build a railroad.'

'It wasn't worth the price.'

After they had docked, and collected their baggage, they took a cab to the St Nicholas Hotel. Collis said nothing as they were driven to the corner of Spring Street and Broadway, but simply stared out of the window at passing streets.

Time, and the war, had changed New York more than he could have imagined. Maybe his memory was playing him tricks, but the streets seemed to be far more crowded than they had ever been before, and the gutters were piled even higher with rotting garbage. The buildings seemed meaner, and closer, and in worse repair than before; although several new hotels and bars had materialised from nowhere, and there was a magnificent new store not far from the St Nicholas Hotel.

If Collis had driven uptown he would have seen more change. House-building on the East Side had reached as far as Fifty-ninth street, where he had ridden his horses with Delphine and Alice Stride; and the potter's field on Park Avenue between Forty-ninth and Fiftieth streets had been broken up for the building of the

575

Women's Hospital. It would later become the site for the Waldorf-Astoria

The only suite of rooms free at the St Nicholas was the bridal suite, on the second floor. Collis liked the irony of that, and he took it, although it cost more than they could really afford. 'Isn't that fitting, Theo?' he asked as they were shown upstairs. 'Here we are, on the brink of a divorce, and we're sharing the bridal apartment!'

Theo gave him a quick grimace and said nothing.

The bellman opened the doors of the suite for them and let them in. The suite was justly famous. *Putnam's Monthly* had called it 'scandalously splendid' and reported that 'timid brides are said to shrink aghast at its marvels.'

There was a massive rosewood bed, covered with white lace and satin, heaped with white satin cushions, and topped by a white satin canopy. Even the walls of the suite were covered in white satin and the furniture was carved and gilded in the most extravagant French style. Four crystal chandeliers were suspended from the ceiling, and their light gleamed on the white satin drapes.

The bellman said expressionlessly, 'I hope you'll be very happy together.' Collis tipped him generously and grinned.

'I suppose we'll have to sleep in the same bed,' grumbled Theodore.

Collis sat on the end of the white satin coverlet and unlaced his boots. 'Well, you know what they say.' He smiled. 'Necessity makes strange bedfellows.'

'Are you going to ring for some drinks, or shall I?' Theodore asked. 'I'm thirsty enough to drink the East River.'

'Champagne?'

'Why not? If we're going to be divorced, we might as well celebrate.'

Collis went over to the cinnunciator, and pressed the button that would send a metal disc marked 'Room Service – Bridal Suite' down to the first-floor office. 'I'm surprised they didn't put any flowers in our room,' he remarked. 'A blissful couple like us.'

There was a knock at the door. 'That was quick,' Collis said to Theo. 'I must have gotten used to the slow pace of life in Sacramento.' He walked across the silvery-grey carpet to answer it.

It wasn't room service, though. It was a messenger boy from the hotel's telegraph service. He saluted, and said he was sorry the message hadn't been waiting for Mr Edmonds when he arrived, but the Rebels had temporarily interfered with the telegraph lines from Washington, and they had only now been repaired.

Collis took the telegraph, saluted the boy in return, and tipped him two bits. Then he walked slowly back across the room, tearing open the envelope with his thumb.

The message was from Colonel Merritt 'Bones' Bonham, who had opened a letter addressed to Collis by mistake, and was sending it on; but who thought that the wartime postal system was erratic enough to warrant a telegram of confirmation, too. After all this wordy preamble, the telegram simply read: 'Your wife is dead.'

Theodore frowned. 'Collis?' he asked. 'Collis – what is it?'

Collis found a chair somehow and sat down. He felt as if he had been hit very hard with a spade handle. He put his hand up to his face and then back to his lap again. There were tears running down his face, and he didn't even know it.

Hannah, dead: *Hannah?* He couldn't believe it. And yet here it was, in a telegraph, and a letter would follow later. He turned his head towards Theodore, and he felt as if the whole bridal suite had become a blur of white satin, and pale sunlight, and pain.

'Hannah's dead,' he said, not for Theodore's benefit, but for his own.

Theodore came over and took the telegram out of his hand. He read it, and then said, 'My God. Collis, I'm sorry.'

Collis shook his head. 'I can't believe it. It doesn't even say why.'

Theodore laid his arm around Collis's shoulders. 'Do you want to go back to Sacramento? I can book you a steamer.'

'There's no point,' said Collis. 'It must have taken that letter a month to arrive in Washington, and it's going to take me at least six weeks to get back to Sacramento. She's been buried now, Theo, and a grave can wait.'

'I see,' said Theodore. 'Well, I suppose that's practical.'

'Practical!' shouted Collis hoarsely. 'The only reason I don't want to go back is that a grave is all there is. No Hannah. No wife. Just a mound in the local graveyard with a marker sticking out of it. Would you want to go back, if that was all that was left of Annie?'

'Collis, I didn't mean – '

'I don't know what the hell you meant!' yelled Collis. 'I don't know and I don't care! But it's about time that someone told you that you don't have exclusive rights on morality, or propriety, or human righteousness! It's about time that someone told you that a dream like yours isn't sacred! It's more than sacred! It's the actual stuff that this country is made of! Raw! and vital! And when you try to sanctify it, you take all of the guts out of it! The morality isn't in the dream, Theo! The morality is in getting it done! This country needs a railroad to grow, and to keep its people alive, not to satisfy some snow-white vision that some clever engineer has been keeping inside of his head!'

'I'm sorry,' Theodore said, tight-lipped.

Collis, still full of steam, still full of annoyance and grief, said, 'For Christ's sake,' and then found that he couldn't say any more. He covered his face with his hands and sobbed – huge, agonising sobs that compressed his chest and hurt his throat. Theodore didn't know what to do except stand beside him in silence.

A little while later, when his weeping had subsided, Collis took out his handkerchief and blew his nose. There was another knock at the door, and Theodore went to answer it.

'It's room service,' he said. 'You still want that champagne?'

'Why not?' asked Collis, the words sticking in his throat.

Theodore said to the boy, 'Two bottles of champagne, will you? And as quick as you like.'

Then he quietly closed the door, and stood there in the absurd celestial whiteness of the St Nicholas bridal suite, too fat, too untidy, too tired, and too regretful; unable to speak even one word that would give Collis comfort.

After a while, he sat down, his head lowered and his hands clasped together, and wished to God that he was back in Sacramento.

At first, Collis felt a sense of loss that was smashed and fragmentary; as if a framed daguerreotype of Hannah had been accidentally trodden on and broken. Because he hadn't seen her dead with his own eyes, he couldn't imagine that she was really gone. All he could picture in his mind was the way she had sat in the carriage at the Front Street levee, under her lemon-yellow parasol, one hand raised in a sad goodbye.

Only when the effects of four bottles of champagne began to wear off did he begin to understand that the broken frame was empty now, and that the daguerreotype had been taken away from him. He could search the world for the rest of his life, and he would never find Hannah again.

He went through a day of total grief and misery, during which Theodore stayed well away from him. He walked across town to the

578

shore of the East River, and sat for an hour on the grassy knoll at the foot of Fifty-third Street, smoking and looking out at the Whitehall boats and the sailing smacks.

A little after four o'clock in the afternoon, he took a cab to Washington Square, to Henry Browne's house. He felt like talking to somebody friendly, somebody who would be prepared to sit back and let him talk his grief for Hannah out of his head and out of his heart. He asked the cab to wait while he climbed the steps of Henry's Greek Revival house and knocked at the door.

It was almost a minute before anyone came to answer, and then the door was opened just four inches to reveal a thin, sallow, suspicious face.

'Yes?' asked a vinegary voice.

Collis raised his hat. 'I'm looking for Mr Henry Browne. Does he still live here?'

'Yes. Who are you?'

'I'm an old friend of his. My name's Collis Edmonds. Is Mr Browne at home?'

'Yes. Mr Browne is always at home.'

There was an awkward pause. 'Well, that's fine,' Collis said. 'Do you think you might be good enough to tell him I'm here?'

'I might be. But it won't be of any use.'

'What do you mean?'

The doorkeeper looked him up and down. 'You're a friend, you say?'

'That's right. I used to drink with Mr Browne at the Gem Saloon.'

'Ah. Well, I suppose so.'

'What do you suppose so?' asked Collis, confused.

'I suppose that I might tell you what has befallen Mr Browne. Why don't you come inside for the moment?'

'Thank you,' said Collis.

The door was opened, and Collis was conducted into the hallway by a very tall, spidery man in a dusty black frock coat and a green satin vest that looked as if it had been used for polishing silver. The house smelled unusually musty, and there was another smell in the air, too, like carbolic arnica salve. A medical smell. A smell of sickrooms and fever.

'My name is Whitworth,' said the spidery man, leading Collis through to the living-room. 'It is my allotted task to take care of Mr Browne.'

579

'Is he unwell?' asked Collis.

Mr Whitworth hesitated and stared at Collis with moist blue eyes.

'You could say that,' he remarked, after considerable thought. 'You could certainly say that.'

The sight of Henry Browne caught Collis completely by surprise. Henry was sitting in the middle of his living-room in a wheelchair, draped in a grey blanket. His head was on one side, and he appeared to be asleep. The room was still the same as Collis remembered it – with the cut-glass decanters and the pipe rack and the oil paintings of gun dogs flushing out wild turkey – yet none of the decanters or the tobacco jars appeared to have been used for a very long time. There was a thin film of dust on everything except for the small table that stood beside Henry Browne's chair, a table that was crowded with medicine bottles, syringes, pill packets, eyedroppers, and jars of ointment.

'Henry?' said Collis softly. The name fell unnoticed in the twilit room, like a bird settling on a telegraph wire.

'He can probably hear you, but I'm afraid his ability to answer is – well, limited,' said Mr Whitworth.

Collis circled slowly around his friend's chair, and gradually realised the horror of what had happened to him. The side of his face which he kept turned away from the door was almost completely missing. There was no cheek; only bare teeth protruding form a gnarled red confusion of flesh. The right eye was milky and sightless, and bulged from its socket. There was no hair on that side of his head, and his ear was nothing but a scrap of gristle.

Mr Whitworth watched Collis carefully. Then he opened a small oval box, took out a pinch of snuff, and thrust it deep into his left nostril.

'The tragedies of war,' he said, in his sharp, off-key voice.

Collis said nothing. All he could do was stand staring at the grotesque ruin that had once been his drinking partner and friend. He remembered running with him that night through the Bowery. He remembered moments of hilarity and fun and mischief. He remembered Henry Browne.

Mr Whitworth blew his nose and inspected his handkerchief closely. 'Mr Browne answered the President's call to arms at once,' he said. 'He went straight to Washington to join the Army of the Potomac, and they made him a lieutenant. So they tell me, anyway.

580

I was only employed to take care of him, out of the proceeds of his private income, and his estates.'

'What happened?' asked Collis.

'What happens to any of them? If they're lucky, they die right away. He was wounded at Manassas Junction, after Bull Run. A Confederate shell landed close by, and took half of his head off. I don't even know if he understands English anymore. He never speaks.'

Collis waited for a few minutes. Then he said to Mr Whitworth, 'I guess there's no point in my staying here.'

'Not really,' said Mr Whitworth.

Collis rubbed his eyes. He felt as if he hadn't slept for a week. He left the living-room, with Mr Whitworth following a short distance behind, and let himself out of the front door.

'There's enough money, is there?' he asked Mr Whitworth.

'Oh, yes,' said Mr Whitworth. 'The doctor doesn't expect him to last longer than six or seven months, and there's plenty.'

Collis reached into the pocket of his coat and handed Mr Whitworth a card. 'That's my address in California,' he said. 'I'd appreciate it if you'd write me when he dies.'

'Yes,' said Mr Whitworth.

Collis walked down the steps and across to his cab, which was waiting for him at the kerb. It was one of those warm, strange afternoons when you feel as if you've somehow stepped through the wrong door, and the whole world has altered without your knowing it. He looked back at Mr Whitworth, and for some reason Mr Whitworth was waving.

Collis and Theodore spent the next three days trying to raise money for the Sierra Pacific Railroad Company. They spent hours in echoing bank offices on Wall Street, waiting for bank presidents to finish their lunches and talk about finance. They talked to brokers, investors, adventurers, and gamblers. They talked to engineers and steelmakers. They talked to anybody who would listen.

Towards the end of their first week in New York, they knew what they were up against – indifference, caution, and sheer disbelief. Many investors simply wouldn't believe that a transcontinental railroad could be built; or that, if it could, that anybody would want to ride on it. Others frowned and asked them to come back when the war was over. Still more just blinked at them over their desks and shrugged.

One bank president told them fiercely that he had once travelled by express train, and that at forty miles per hour it had been impossible to read, or think, or hear himself speak. Even when Collis assured him that Sierra Pacific trains would travel at twenty-five miles per hour at the very most, he firmly repeated that men were intended to travel on foot, or on horseback, but certainly not by steam locomotive.

'Man was not meant to be tugged around the continent like a toy, by a monstrous teakettle on wheels. It isn't natural.'

Collis had an unnerving experience on Second Avenue one afternoon when he glimpsed a woman who looked just like Hannah. He called the cab driver to stop, and jostled his way through the crowds for two blocks before he saw the woman standing on the corner of Stuyvesant Square, about to cross the street. She was blonde, and there was something about the uptilt of her nose that reminded him of Hannah, but that was all. He walked back to his cab with embarrassment and bottled-up grief. Hannah was dead, he told himself. And even if she weren't, she wouldn't be here in New York. Not unless her spirit was trying to make contact with him through another woman. But that was insane. At least he hoped it was.

The most disturbing moment of all, however, was when he saw his mother. He had just spent a vexing lunch hour with A. G. Harriman, of the Harriman Investment Trust. They had eaten an impossibly heavy meal at the Collamore Hotel at Broadway and Spring Street – a bowl of thick pea soup, followed by salted cod in brandy and hot meat pie – and even after cakes and brandy they were still no nearer reaching an agreement on how much Harriman's should invest in the Sierra Pacific. So they shook hands on the steps outside the hotel, and agreed to meet in two days' time, and as they did so Collis saw his mother walk obliviously through the hotel lobby on the arm of a strange man.

His first reaction was to step forward and greet her. But then he took hold of A. G. Harriman's pudgy hand and forcibly pulled him around, like an overweight ballet dancer, so that the banker's bulk would obstruct his mother's view.

'What the devil are you doing?' demanded Harriman.

Collis touched his finger to his lips and said, 'Sshh.'

His mother was sweeping along more self-importantly than ever, and even if Collis had walked straight up to her and taken her hand she probably would have needed reminding who he was. Her attention was quite obviously all on herself, and on her flamingo-pink dress with matching cape, which made her look florid and fussy and strangely masculine, like a man dressed up as a woman

The man beside her was bulky and tall, with shaggy muttonchop whiskers in a vivid shade of Myron Parker's Hair Dye ('any colour from brown to jet black'). He wore a grey morning coat and carried himself with great pomposity. As they reached the sidewalk, he raised his cane, and a private brougham drew up beside them, decorated in a particularly offensive maroon livery. Collis kept hold of A. G. Harriman's hand and watched his mother over the banker's shoulder as she was assisted into the carrage (smiling and nodding and smiling and nodding in the manner which she had always thought was the height of gentility), and as the bulky man climbed in after her. He was so bulky, in fact, that the carriage displayed a distinct list to starboard as it was driven away.

'I wish you'd tell me what's going on,' said A. G. Harriman crossly, twisting his hand free.

'I wish I knew,' said Collis, and for the first time since he had heard of Hannah's death, he felt amused. He wondered what his sister, Maude, was doing, and decided that she was probably living in a row house on Second Avenue with a stiff-collared Episcopalian husband and complaining bitterly about the influx of poor immigrants into the avenue during the war. Maude had always had plenty of faith, but very little hope, and no charity at all.

Back at the bridal suite of the St Nicholas, he found Theodore sitting at the bureau, writing a long letter to Annie. Theodore covered the letter with his hand when Collis came in.

'You look cheerful,' Theodore had said. 'Did you do well with A. G. Harriman?'

'I did badly with Harriman,' Collis told him, pouring himself a drink. 'But I did particularly well with my mother.'

'You saw your mother?'

'Yes, but she didn't see me. And that was just the way I wanted it.'

Theodore scratched his beard with his pen. 'You're an odd one, Collis. If I didn't distrust you so much, I think I could even learn to love you.'

They returned to Sacramento in August – weeks of steaming down the East Coast under a glaring sun, days of delay in the jungle of

583

Panama, and then more weeks of steaming northwards on an ocean the colour of pewter plates. Five passengers died of yellow fever; one went mad and threw himself overboard. A dark-haired Mexican girl kept eyeing Collis through the black tracery of her shawl, but he ignored her. He was keeping his thoughts for Hannah.

Jane McCormick and Mary Tucker were waiting for them on the levee when their paddle steamer docked in Sacramento. Annie arrived a few minutes later, breathless and apologetic.

'I'm sorry, Collis. I can't tell you how sorry I am,' she said.

Collis took her arm. It was midday, and the sun was so bright and hot that nothing seemed to have any colour or substance. Even the shadows shrank out of the sun. 'You gave her a Catholic burial, I hope?' asked Collis.

Annie nodded.

Later, Collis went to the Catholic church on J Street, swinging open the white paling fence and walking across the baked soil of the graveyard under an afternoon sky as black as a Bible. He found the marker around the back of the church, under the scant shade of a small tree. There were some wilted flowers lying on the mound, and an empty urn. Collis knelt down and straightened the urn, and then slowly reached out and traced with his fingertips the letters that had been carved in the wood of the marker.

Hannah Amelia Edmonds. Beloved Wife of Collis. 1862.

Underneath, already curled from the sun and the rain, somebody had pinned a text from Revelation. 'And there shall be no night there; and they need no candle, neither light of the sun; for the Lord God giveth them light: and they shall reign for ever and ever.'

When Collis read these words, his mouth shuddered with grief, and his eyes filled with tears.

'Hannah,' he said, out loud. 'Oh, God, Hannah.'

On a wet January afternoon the following year, 1863, they gathered on the outskirts of Sacramento to dedicate the beginning of the Sierra Pacific Railroad. Leland, who had been elected the first Republican governor of California after eleven years of Democratic administration, was even windier than the weather, and full of his own importance to the point of explosion. He stood on a raised wooden platform in his tall black silk hat, his whiskers beaded with rain, and directed everybody to his place.

584

Even Leland was upstaged by the locomotive, however. It was a wood-burning 4-4-0, with a huge megaphone-shaped smokestack, and a bell that was suspended in curlicues of polished brass. It had been burnished up for the ground-breaking ceremony, but the wet cold weather had given its boiler a silvery metallic bloom, and its driveshafts and couplings sparkled with greasy droplets. The engineer and the fireman worked busily and importantly in the red-painted cab, and every now and then they would let out a little toot of steam from the whistle.

It was around the magnificently splayed cowcatcher and the huge wheels of the locomotive that the crowd had gathered, with their umbrellas shining as black as a colony of beetles, and their shoes smothered in mud. It was the locomotive which embodied the wild and breathtaking idea of the Sierra Pacific Railroad, not Leland McCormick, for all his oratory. And this was in spite of the fact that the locomotive had nowhere to go, for Collis had been able to lay enough track only to accommodate the steam engine itself, its tender, and one passenger carriage which still hadn't arrived from New York.

Collis himself stood at the back of the platform, bareheaded, his hat in his hands. He was looking thin and drawn, and his sidewhiskers were now smudged with grey. Theodore was standing beside him with Annie, and after years of travelling to Washington and back, after endless hours of struggling for his dream of a transcontinental railroad, Theodore's appearance was startling. He was bowed, and unhealthily plump, and his beard seemed ragged and unkempt, making him look like a mangy dog.

Andy Hunt was there, in an unexpectedly sober suit; and Charles, with Mary on his arm, smiling at everybody who passed. There were also several uncomfortable-looking gentlemen in the crowd who had obviously been sent from various banks and transportation companies in San Francisco, to report back on the opening ceremony to the Pacific Mail Steamship Company, and to Wells Fargo, and to interested parties like Laurence Melford and Arthur Teach. Later, Collis sent Kwang Lee around to each of these men to give them a good cigar and fifty dollars in gold.

The editor of the *Sacramento Union* wrote of the ceremony, 'It was both festive and alarming; for while we could not help ourselves from being awed by the prospect of beginning a railroad that will stretch all the way from Sacramento to Omaha, and excited by its commercial possibilities, we realised at the same time that we were

585

witnessing an irrevocable change in the course of our lives and in the history of the nation.'

Not many Californians agreed with him. They had all turned out to see a new steam locomotive, and to hear some of Leland's speechifying, but for the most part they were disinclined to believe that Collis and Leland and Andy and Charles were actually going to go so far as build this railroad all the way over the Sierras. One critic had written in the San Francisco newspapers that the Sierra Pacific was 'nothing more than a swindifulous scheme to milk money out of innocent investors, and the State of California, too.'

Leland in particular had refrained from answering such criticisms. At Jane's suggestion, he had recently persuaded the California legislature to grant the railroad $10,000 for every mile of track laid within the state boundaries, and he had used his influence as governor to coax the county authorities along the railroad's right of way to subscribe half a million dollars in bonds. Now he was drawing up a proposition for a state bond issue which would give the company $600,000 in cash – and this would go before the voters of San Francisco in April, so Leland wasn't exactly keen as mustard to get into a messy public scrap about swindles or confidence tricks.

Nonetheless, the Sierra Pacific was already running dangerously short of money. In 1863, the greater proportion of native Americans had never travelled further from their homes than a good day's walk, and the notion of riding in a train for days on end at twenty-five miles per hour was too fantastic to be imagined. Even railroad experts were sceptical, particularly in the East, where the vast expanses of the western frontier seemed as remote as the moon. Commodore Cornelius Vanderbilt, who was in the middle of taking over the New York Central and Erie Lines between New York and Chicago, said, 'Building a railroad from nowhere to nowhere at public expense is not a legitimate enterprise.'

Even as the first Sierra Pacific locomotive whistled a shrill note of celebration, and the wet bunting snapped in the cold afternoon wind, Theodore stood with his gaze directed at nothing further away than the damp planks of the platform beneath his feet. Annie held him as if she were supporting him, keeping him up under the great weight of his disillusionment and exhaustion.

Leland raised his hand for silence and said loudly: 'Ladies and gentlemen of Sacramento . . . and visitors, surreptitious or otherwise . . .' at which there was general mocking laughter. 'I shall not speak for long, because of the vagaries of the weather . . . but I do

586

wish to say that this day marks a practical beginning to the greatest social and mechanical enterprise ever undertaken by man . . . This locomotive is only the first of a whole fleet of glittering iron horses which will draw passengers and valuable freight into and out of this city of Sacramento . . . and later into San Francisco . . . these few feet of track are only the first of miles of shining rails which will span deserts, canyons, mountains, and rivers . . .'

Leland went on for ten minutes, and Collis listened in silence. The fine rain ran down his face and made it look as if he were crying. Actually, he was thinking about Leland's boasts of building up a fleet of trains, and of crossing the West with track. They were fine boasts, but the truth was that the war had led to massive inflation and chronic shortages. The small locomotive which chuffed and steamed in front of them now had cost him $13,688 – compared with the pre-war price of a big ten-wheeler of $10,000. A ton of rails which had previously cost $60 had risen to well over $112, and that was the price he had to pay in Boston. Freight charges around Cape Horn were extra, and punishingly high.

Shovels, wheelbarrows, picks, rail spikes, explosives, and signalling equipment were all in desperately short supply, and there was the ever-present risk that they would be requisitioned by the army for use against the Confederacy.

Collis had tried only yesterday to sell a block of S.P. securities to a syndicate of Sacramento businessmen; but after 'due discussion' they had decided to 'wait and see how far the railroad goes.' If every potential investor reacted the same way, Collis doubted if the railroad would stretch any further than Roseville, only a few miles outside of Sacramento. Going over the company accounts the previous night, he had estimated it would cost them over $12 million just to extend the tracks a good buggy ride out of town. Leland's $600,000 would pay for little more than a couple of miles of track.

Charles had blown out his cheeks in resignation and said, 'We're going to have to work damned hard, that's all, Collis. If people are hesitant about investing, we're just going to have to peel off our coats, jump off the dock, and say, "Come on, boys."'

Collis had closed the accounts. 'Right now,' he had told Charles, 'I'm tempted to take a clean shirt and get out for good.'

Theodore had said nothing at all.

Leland now stood with one hand raised, and the other clutching his lapel. This was a recognisable sign to anybody who had been obliged to suffer his oratory before that he was reaching the climax of his speech, and that he would mercifully soon be finished.

'My friends,' he said, 'from this day forth, California and Sacramento can do nothing but prosper, for the Sierra Pacific Railroad will in one adventurous stroke bring the peoples of America, East and West, in almost instant communication with each other, and out of that can come nothing but happier understanding, flourishing commerce, and human progress towards that ideal society which is Paradise on Earth.'

There was a light patter of applause, and then Leland said, 'I name this locomotive the *Governor McCormick*, and I ask the Lord to bless her endeavours and to keep safe all those who travel with her.'

Collis glanced at Jane. She had been promised that the locomotive would be christened for her; but at the last moment, Leland had declared that it would not be 'protocol' for the governor of California to have a locomotive named for his wife. It would smack of nepotism, or something like that; and in any case *he* was president of the railroad. Collis hadn't argued about it. The locomotive would be too small for long-distance hauls, and would probably end up ingloriously shunting freight cars around, and that struck Collis as a fitting finish for anything called the *Governor McCormick*.

The rain slicked the locomotive's boiler, and the wind blew the dark smoke out of its funnel and across the street. A small silver band, which had been sheltering in a striped marquee, struck up with 'Clear the Way!' and Leland joined in, in a wavering baritone.

Collis left the platform and walked across the churned-up street. He had almost reached his carriage when someone called his name, and he turned around to see Mrs Pangborn making her way towards him, her skirts lifted out of the mud, her bonnet stained with damp.

'Mr Edmonds,' she said breathlessly, catching him up. 'Mr Edmonds, I must congratulate you on your wonderful locomotive.'

'Thank you, Mrs Pangborn,' said Collis. 'I'm glad that somebody around here has faith in what we're doing.'

'There was something else,' said Mrs Pangborn.

'Something else?'

'Yes – rather personal, in a way.'

Collis looked around at the crowds, but nobody seemed to be showing any interest in them.

'Do you want to tell me now?' asked Collis.

'Well,' said Mrs Pangborn, 'I was wondering if you wouldn't rather call by my house this evening. You see, I have a guest staying with me at the moment who knows you, and has expressed an interest in meeting you again.'

'A guest? Who is it?'

Mrs Pangborn raised her finger to her lips. 'I'll see you tonight, Mr Edmonds. Nine o'clock would be ideal.'

It was a few minutes after nine when Collis knocked at Mrs Pangborn's door. The door was opened right away, by a silent Chinese girl, and Collis was led through into the perfumed front parlour. Mrs Pangborn was waiting for him, playing with a small white kitten with a pink bow around its neck.

'Ah . . . Mr Edmonds,' she said, rising to her feet, and curtseying. 'I'm delighted you could come.'

'I don't have a great deal of time,' said Collis edgily. These days he didn't like to be seen at Mrs Pangborn's. There were too many fundamentalists in the Sacramento business community, and too many anti-railroad lobbyists who would seize on the slightest moral misdemeanour as evidence that Collis was not fit to run a railroad on which women and children might travel.

'Well,' said Mrs Pangborn, smiling, 'I'm sure this won't take very long. Lin Lee, would you ask the new girl to come down, please.'

Collis stood in the centre of the room, tall and formal in his dark-blue topcoat, his silk hat in his hand. Mrs Pangborn asked him if he cared for a glass of champagne, but he shook his head. He was too taken up with the day's railroad business and the problems of finance to be giving this little circus act of Mrs Pangborn's much serious thought.

It was only when the door opened and she walked boldly and coquettishly in, dressed in vivid crimson, with crimson ostrich feathers bobbing in her curled-up hair, that Collis forgot about the *Governor McCormick*, and how he was going to raise twelve million dollars in a month. He saw the pearl necklaces and the diamonds and the large emerald resting in the pale creamy cleavage and he felt as if time had stopped, as if the past six years had closed up like a Chinese lantern.

'Well, Collis?' said Delphine, dropping him a little curtsey. 'You seem surprised to see me.'

'Did you expect me to be anything else?' he asked her. 'And here, of all places.'

589

Delphine looked around. 'It's clean, and respectable, and very well spoken of. They say the customers are gentlemen, and that most of them have religion.'

'I can scarcely believe it's you.'

Delphine walked slowly around him, smiling to herself. 'Because that bearded monkey of yours threatened Alice's father with blackmail? Because he said he would hold me up in public as Senator Carslake's pet whore? Because you believe that once a young lady's reputation is sullied, she melts away, like a piece of dirty ice?'

'You're as forward as ever,' said Collis. 'I'll certainly give you that'

'And you're just as self-interested as ever, by the look of you. I saw you today at the ceremony. I don't believe you even thought once of where you were, or what was going on around you. You live inside your own head, Collis Edmonds, and nowhere else.'

'I believe I'll change my mind about that glass of champagne,' Collis said to Mrs Pangborn.

Delphine came over, took Collis's arm, and looked up into his eyes. She was older, of course, but still just as pretty; and he could remember what he had felt about her that day she had first lifted her face to him in Taylor's.

'As a matter of fact,' she said, in a hushed, confidential tone, 'you and your bearded crony did me a considerable favour. Instead of wallowing in misery and humiliation for the rest of my life with Senator Carslake, I decided that if my reputation was so thoroughly soiled that it could be used to blackmail a member of government, then I might as well not trouble with it any more. I borrowed money from the Senator and rented myself a suite on Pennsylvania Avenue, and did very profitably, thank you. Senators, Congressmen, and then soldiers, when the war broke out.'

Mrs Pangborn handed Collis a glass of cold champagne, and he swallowed half of it in one gulp. 'So,' said Collis, wiping his mouth, 'you slid down the slippery slope.'

'I didn't slide,' said Delphine. 'I was pushed.'

'And so what are you doing here in Sacramento?' he asked her.

'The same as Eleanore Dumont, or any other lady who has visited Denver and Nevada City and Kansas. The same as Martha Jane Canary, or Carla Amorata.'

'You're a parlour-house girl?' asked Collis, although the flat tone in his voice made it more of a statement than a question.

'Does that upset you?'

He looked at her and shrugged. 'It's your life. Why should it?'

'You don't feel responsible for my tragic downfall?'

'I don't think so. The crash of 'fifty-seven was your downfall, wasn't it? That, and your forward behaviour, and Senator Stride.'

'You, of course, only used the fact of my downfall for your personal benefit,' said Delphine. 'You weren't actually so gross as to contribute to it.'

Collis finished his champagne and handed the glass back to Mrs Pangborn. 'Whatever you say,' he told Delphine sharply.

'Collis,' said Delphine.

'What?'

'I might as well be frank with you. I don't think I've ever been as restrained, or as moral, as a girl ought to be. It's always been in my nature, something I've been fighting against. Well, you must have noticed it yourself. Degradation – sexual degradation – somehow that's always held a strange fascination for me.'

Collis didn't move. Delphine stood there with her head slightly on one side, her hands up under her breasts as if she were about to sing in opera. Her face was flushed, her eyes bright, and Collis had the feeling that she was intoxicated either with champagne or with opium.

'Well,' said Collis, 'I think I have to be going.'

'You're not going to listen to me?' Delphine wanted to know. 'You're not going to hear me out?'

'Delphine, there isn't any point. I'm not the same man you met in New York. I have responsibilities now. I have business partners to protect. I'm a widower, still in mourning.'

'Yes, I know,' said Delphine. 'I'm sorry.'

'Thank you for your sorrow. If you want my regrets in return – if you want my abject apologies – then you can have them.'

Collis turned to Mrs Pangborn and said, 'Thank you for the champagne. And thank you for arranging this reunion. I'm afraid it wasn't quite what I expected.'

'*C'est la vie*,' said Mrs Pangborn, in an appalling French accent.

Collis went to the door. Delphine stayed where she was, her eyes fixed on the place where Collis had been, or perhaps on the past. At the door, Collis paused, and then said softly, 'Delphine?'

She didn't look at him.

591

'You grow to learn that the West is a small place,' Collis went on. 'You can easily find old friends or old enemies just by asking after them. Everybody knows almost everybody, in spite of the distances, and the wildness of it.'

He hesitated, and then he said, 'You grow to learn too that sometimes those old friends or old enemies are better left alone, especially when life hasn't been particularly kind to either of you.'

Delphine didn't answer. Collis stayed a moment longer, and then put on his hat, nodded to Mrs Pangborn, and left.

Chapter 14

The crucial stipulation of the Pacific Railroad Act of 1862 had been that forty consecutive miles of track must be laid by the company on any part of the railroad route before the government would start paying subsidies and handing over land titles. Collis hadn't worried too much about it at the time, but now it was proving an impossible sticking point. The Sierra Pacific owned a locomotive, a tender, one passenger carriage, and about two miles of rusting track – which took it just out to the city limits.

The roadbed had been graded for about a mile further on, but they simply couldn't afford to go on. With only four rails to the ton, and a ton of rails costing $115, it cost $11,500 to buy the 400 rails that each mile of track consumed, and that didn't include timber, or spikes, or wages, or anything else at all.

Leland began to talk of taking the road no further than Nevada, and possibly laying no tracks on it at all, but simply grading it as a wagon road, and charging a toll for each loaded wagon that wanted an easy route over the Sierra. Theodore argued hotly for a few weeks and then became silent and morose again. In October of 1863, he came to Collis's house and announced that he was going East again, and taking Annie with him.

It was evening, and Collis had been working all day in his library. Although he had kept on the servants after Hannah's death, he rarely used any part of the house except the library, the dining-room, and the small back bedroom. He wasn't keeping the house as a shrine. There were no pictures of Hannah anywhere. It was just that he was concentrating all his attention on the railroad these days, and all he needed was a room to work in, a room to eat in, and a room to sleep in.

Charles would often pass his house after a late lodge meeting and see his lamp still burning after midnight. 'If the Sierra Pacific could be built with sheer dedication, and nothing else, then we would have crossed the Sierras by now,' he used to say. But it couldn't, and they hadn't.

Theodore sat sheepishly in one of Collis's large library chairs while Collis finished a column of entries in his accounts books. Then Collis took off the small blue skullcap which he had grown into the habit of wearing while he worked, and smiled at Theodore in a way that made Theodore feel that he was not quite there, that he was only a shade of his real self.

'Well,' said Collis. 'Annie tells me it's eastward ho for you again.'

'Yes,' said Theodore.

'You're going to try to do what you've always threatened? Buy us mealy-mouthed merchants out?'

'Yes,' said Theodore.

'It hasn't occurred to you that we may be the only men on earth who are actually capable of carrying this venture through? That more squeamish men might have backed out years ago?'

'Leland's talking of ending the road in Nevada. That doesn't do much to inspire me.'

Collis opened the humidor on his desk, took out a long cigar, and cut it. 'You can't blame Leland for that. He's simply looking for a practical solution to our present financial problems. A short-term plan to balance the books.'

'The transcontinental railroad was never meant to be a short-term plan, ever,' Theodore said angrily. 'It was conceived on the grand scale, and only men of grand vision can ever complete it.'

Collis lit his cigar slowly. 'You know something, Theo?' he said. 'You and I could still be friends, and working partners.'

Theodore shook his head. 'You're probably right when you say that you and Leland are the only men on earth who could ever build the Sierra Pacific. I hope you're not, and I'm going to Washington to raise enough money to buy you out, and try to *prove* that you're not. But it's the only course left open to me, Collis. I cannot be party to building a railroad that may or may not be completed, according to the temperament of its owners; or to a railroad whose tracks will be laid on so much bribery, and blackmail, and plain human suffering.'

Collis thought about that, and then walked around his desk. He extended his hand to Theodore as if he were congratulating him on twenty years' service with the company, and wishing him a happy retirement. Theodore couldn't help noticing for the first time the deeply engraved lines around Collis's eyes, and the way that his hair was beginning to recede from his forehead. He looked like a man of forty, rather than a man in his early thirties.

The room seemed to be suddenly much darker, as the last

diffused light of the sun faded away outside. Theodore gripped Collis's hand in both of his and said, 'Goodbye, Collis. I hope we shall never turn out to be enemies.'

'You and I?' Collis smiled. 'You and I have always been enemies. We always shall be. Take good care of Annie for me.'

Theodore went to the door, opened it, and raised his hand in a last awkward salute. Collis said nothing; but when Theodore had gone, he sat for a long time in the gloom of his library, wondering what would become of him.

A month later, he found out. A telegram reached Andy Hunt's office from Washington, on the new transcontinental telegraph line, which had only been opened the previous November. Andy Hunt sent it on the next day's Sacramento steamer, and it was delivered to 54 K Street just as Collis was leaving to ride to Roseville, to talk to the citizens there about the railroad.

The telegraph read: 'Theodore Jones died today from yellow fever contracted in Panama. Please inform all concerned. Annie Jones.'

Collis read the telegraph twice, and then walked back into the store. Charles was there, helping Kwang Lee to make out an order for black powder. He saw the expression on Collis's face at once, and came towards him with his hands raised as if he was expecting Collis to fall.

'What's happened?' he asked.

Collis showed him the telegraph. Charles read it, and then puffed loudly, and leaned on the counter, and put his hand on his hip.

'Well, I'm damned,' he said.

'It's ironic, isn't it?' said Collis. 'He died of the lack of a transcontinental railroad. He died because his own vision hasn't yet been fulfilled.'

'Is there anything we can do?' asked Charles.

Collis thought, and then nodded. 'Sure there is. We can build the Sierra Pacific Railroad for him.'

'Us and whose millions?' Charles wanted to know.

By the spring of 1864, the Sierra Pacific had reached the end of its credit. Collis was personally in debt by nearly five million dollars, more than he had ever owned or earned in the whole of his life – all in interest guarantees and bank notes. Although the roadbed was prepared almost as far as Newcastle, thirty-one miles away, there were only eighteen and a half miles of track laid, far from the token forty miles which the federal government required; and Leland, who had been talking in the fall of limiting the line to Nevada Territory and no further, was now talking of going into liquidation, and saving whatever they could.

But Collis was determined. Not for the sake of Theodore's memory, because he realised now that Theodore had gone that the workings of the company were no longer trammelled by the moral scruples of a religious and engineering visionary. Nor yet for the sake of Hannah's memory, nor his own vision of crossing the High Sierras by rail.

The battle had become too basic for morals or visions to count for anything. It was now a battle for financial survival. What was more, Abraham Lincoln, who had enthusiastically supported the Pacific railroad from the beginning, was up for re-election in November; and while Collis didn't doubt that he would win, especially after Gettysburg, he was too cynical to trust the whole of his five-million-dollar debt to whims of the federal electorate. Better to take advantage of Lincoln's amenable presence in the White House right now than to risk having to deal with a McClellanite or a War Democrat in the new year.

The partners met in the living-room above 54 K Street on a chilly evening in March. Charles and Collis laid out all the company's accounts on the floor, and the four of them smoked and argued and drank bourbon until eight o'clock at night.

Collis, in his shirtsleeves, said, 'There's nothing left to do. I'm going to have to travel to Washington again and see if I can't have this forty-mile qualification reduced.'

Andy Hunt pointed to the accounts books. 'Even if you do that, you still won't be able to raise enough money to carry on. It's over thirty miles to the Sierra foothills from Sacramento, and because the land is dead flat, we only get a federal loan of sixteen thousand dollars a mile. That's hardly going to cover our wages bill.'

'At least we'll have a chance,' said Collis. 'I reckon I can still raise enough personal credit to lay another fifteen or sixteen miles of track.'

'And then what?' said Andy.

Leland, deep in his armchair with a large glass of whisky, gave a sage and patronising nod. 'Andy's right, Collis. We could build forty miles of track and what possible good could it do us? We'd only get sixteen thousand dollars a mile for the greater part of it,'

596

and the way our finances are going, that just doesn't make economic sense.'

Collis stood up and walked to the window. Outside, on K Street, a wagon was being loaded with fencing wire from the store downstairs, which was still open. He could see Kwang Lee talking to a tall rangy farmer. The night air was thick with dancing moths.

Suddenly, he turned around to Leland. 'Don't I remember someone saying somewhere that the base of the Rockies is located somewhere on the banks of the Mississippi – because of the rock and soil formations they found there?'

Leland shrugged. 'Maybe you do. So what? It just sounds like one of those preposterous scientific oddities to me.'

'Maybe it is,' said Collis. 'But maybe it could help us, too. You're the governor of California, Leland. Supposing the state geologist was to be obliging enough to say that the base of the Sierras was somewhere rather further to the west than it actually appears to be?'

Leland frowned. 'You mean . . . re-draw the map, geologically?'

'Why not? Every mountain range has its outwash soil – rocks and mud that have been carried downstream on to the plains by erosion. If the state geologist could positively identify soil from the Sierras on the plains, then who could argue that the Sierras didn't begin at the outskirts of Sacramento?'

'It would have to be legitimate,' Leland said dubiously. 'I'd have to send the geologist along to make indisputable tests.'

'Sure you would,' said Andy. 'But maybe Collis has got something. The government's going to lend us forty-eight thousand a mile for every mile of track we lay over the Sierras; and if the Sierras start right here in Sacramento, then we're going to make ourselves nearly a million dollars in extra cash. And let's face facts, we could use it.'

'If you have a word with the state geologist,' Collis said to Leland, 'I'll have a word with Congressman Watkins by telegraph. I'm sure he'd be only too happy to present our reports to the President.'

'All right,' said Leland. 'It's kind of a humbug, but I guess it's worth a try.'

'The trouble is,' put in Charles, 'it still doesn't solve this forty-mile qualification problem. Even with some of the track attracting forty-eight thousand dollars a mile, we're still not going to be able to lay forty miles without some kind of extra financial help.'

'That's what I was coming to,' said Collis. 'I'm planning on making another trip to Washington, to see what I can do about amending the 1862 Railroad Act. This time I'm going to take some money with me, and I'm going to pass it around wherever it's needed. Straight, no-nonsense bribes. I've learned by now that Congress is nothing but a wolf-pack, and that the only way to sway the opinions of a wolf pack is to throw it some raw meat.'

'How much do you reckon it's going to cost?' asked Charles.

'A quarter of a million dollars. But, believe me, I'll get results.'

Leland raised his eyebrows, and Andy Hunt whistled.

'A quarter of a million?' said Charles. 'That's a hell of an expensive risk to take.'

'It's either that, or bankruptcy,' said Collis.

'But we could use that quarter of a million to lay track,' put in Leland.

'How much track? Three miles? Four miles, at the most? No, Leland, there's only one way we're going to get out of this, and that's to buy our way out. That's the way Congress works. If you want legislation, you have to pay for it.'

Leland sighed. 'Very well. I believe you know what you're doing. I just think it's a very sad reflection on the integrity of the administration.'

'Wouldn't you take a bribe, if it were offered?' asked Collis.

Leland looked at him huffily. 'Only a decent one,' he said. 'And only from somebody I liked already.'

Collis saw Delphine twice in the next few weeks. He didn't get close enough to talk to her, and he wasn't sure that he wanted to. But from the way she was riding with Mrs Pangborn and two or three of Mrs Pangborn's prettier and more favoured parlour girls, all decorated and frilled in a shiny green landau, he guessed that she had made up her mind to stay for a while in Sacramento before moving on.

He found it difficult to believe that she was the same pretty and provocative girl he had known in New York; but then she had always been sexually uninhibited, and he supposed that once her father had gone bankrupt and her family life had collapsed, the parlour circuit was all she had left. It was a pretty rough and degrading way to go, though. All the myths about college-educated girls and famous French dancers going on the parlour circuit to amuse themselves during their vacations were based on nothing more than male fantasy. The kind of men that a girl had to entertain in Nevada City and Alder Gulch were demanding and crude, and even a high-spirited girl like the notorious Martha Jane Canary was soon worn down. Miss Canary had won herself the nickname Calamity Jane. Collis wondered what they would be calling Delphine in years to come.

The second time he saw her, on K Street near the post office, she turned towards him, nodded her head, and smiled. He gave her only the briefest smile in return, but he found when he thought about her afterwards that his feelings had softened towards her, and that he was quite inclined to see her again. He decided to look her up again when he returned from Washington.

The journey to Washington in the spring of 1864 was tiresome and uncomfortable. In Panama, it rained for days, and the railroad was delayed by mudslides. There was Confederate shipping action off the coast of Georgia, too, and the steamer had to heave to for eight hours in a heavy swell.

In Washington, Collis had to stay at the second-rate Capitol Hotel, although he spent most of his time lobbying for votes for a fresh and improved Railroad Act, and saw his room only when he needed sleep, or a shave, or a change of clothes. In the hotel opposite was Thomas Durant, the vice-president of the Union Pacific Railroad – a thin, energetic man with a dark goatee beard – and he was in Washington for the same purpose and with just as much money for buying Congressional votes.

Collis had dinner with Durant one evening, and they discussed in detail how they should most effectively hand out their 'educational funds', as Durant liked to call them. The Union Pacific, which had been granted a charter under the 1862 Act to build a railroad westward out of Omaha, was completely bogged down by debt. They hadn't even reached the city limits, although Omaha in 1864 was not much more than a couple of square miles of wooden houses on the banks of the Missouri.

Durant wrestled with a veal cutlet for a while, and then drank a very large glass of red wine. 'We have a divine duty to force through this railroad by whatever means at our disposal,' he told Collis. 'We cannot be judged by the same legal or moral standards as other men. Our task is too great and too urgent. And, besides, if we conduct ourselves too scrupulously, we'll never make a profit.

Collis smiled. 'I think you're a man after my own heart

Durant shook his head. 'Not me. I'm not a visionary. I believe in

599

the pursuit of wealth by the few, because that's what brings the larger benefit to the many. This railroad can make us rich, Collis, beyond any imagination. That will be our just reward for our efforts. The nation's reward will be to have a fast and effective means of transporting its people and its goods from one side of the continent to the other.'

Collis spent almost all of his $250,000, and gave out promises of special bonuses and favours to every Congressman he met. Durant did the same, even more professionally and even more energetically. He had come to Washington with $437,000 of U.P. funds, and although he was later accused of having pocketed the larger part of it for himself, he was proved to have spent nearly $19,000 entertaining Congressmen at Willard's Hotel.

Collis himself was particularly proud of having enlisted the enthusiastic support of Congressman Oakes Ames of Massachusetts, by promising the contract for all the Sierra Pacific's shovels to the toolworks owned by Congressman Ames's brother Oliver.

By early summer, Collis and Durant had the situation fixed. President Lincoln was as eager as anybody to get the railroad started; and Congress had been happily paid off. A Pacific Railroad Act of 1864 was drawn up, passed through Congress 'like a bullet through butter', and signed by the President without a single qualm or query. It gave Collis everything he wanted.

Land grants for the railroad would be doubled. Instead of ten square miles in alternate sections on either side of the track, they were to be granted twenty square miles. Best of all, the federal loans of $32,000 and $48,000 a mile would not be deferred until the company had actually laid track. They would be given two-thirds of their money as soon as each twenty miles of roadbed had been prepared, and only one-third would be held back until later.

The Act of 1864 gave the Sierra Pacific and the Union Pacific between them the potential of becoming the largest private landowners in the country. They would eventually own more than twenty million acres – more than Connecticut, Massuchusetts, and Vermont all put together. It also gave them the ready money to start laying track.

Congressman Watkins came to the Capitol Hotel the night the act was signed and handed Collis an envelope.

'You needn't open it,' he said, with a fat and satisfied smile. 'It's just an official confirmation that the Sierras rise where the state geologist of California alleges that they rise. The President himself has agreed to it.'

'Well,' said Collis, 'you must let me buy you a drink.'

Congressman Watkins raised his hands, as if to ask how he could possibly refuse. 'It seems as if my pertinacity and Abraham's faith has moved mountains,' he said.

Collis telegraphed Andy Hunt in San Francisco at once. He was to use Collis's credit with the San Francisco Banking Trust to lay as much extra track as he could. The *Governor McCormick* was already running between Sacramento and Roseville for the one-way fare of $1.85 – now Collis wanted to push it ahead as quickly as possible to qualify for all the federal loan money he could get.

He took the first steamer back to Panama. The war was going badly for the Union, and he was lucky to get away so quickly. Thomas Durant had breakfast with him the morning he left, and they shook hands on the steps of the Capitol Hotel.

'We may meet again,' said Durant. 'Out there somewhere, on the plains, or on the Great Basin, wherever our two railroads conjoin. I hope by then that both of us will be happier and richer men.'

The Panama steamer caught the tail end of a hurricane off Florida, and Collis was ill for two days. At Aspinwall, the train was delayed yet again, and he had to spend three days in a seedy hotel, shivering with influenza, nausea, impatience, and the effects of unlimited Kentucky bourbon. He thought of Theodore, dead of the yellow fever, and he wondered if God intended to mete out the same punishment to him.

But late in May, he arrived back in San Francisco, and immediately called on Andy Hunt to find out how the railroad was going. Andy's office was closed and locked, but he found Andy in the Bank Exchange Saloon, drinking with Sam Lewis and Lloyd Wintle. The saloon was thick with smoke and noise, although several conversations quieted and several eyebrows were raised when Collis walked in. News of the revised Railroad Act had reached San Francisco on the day that it was signed, and more than half of the regulars were uncomfortably remembering that they had wagered Collis two or three thousand dollars or more that he couldn't cross the Sierra by train.

'Sam, Lloyd, how are you?' said Collis, shaking their hands.

'Tolerably well, considering the latest reports from the war,' said Lloyd. 'You look as sick as a dog.'

'I am, as a matter of fact. But it's nothing that a couple of days' rest and a few stone fences won't put right. Andy – how's the railroad?'

'We're getting along slow, but sure,' said Andy.

Collis raised his hand to the barman for a drink. The barman already knew his taste in alcohol and nodded as unnoticeably as a horse trader.

'That wasn't what I wanted to hear,' Collis told Andy. 'The more miles we've laid, the quicker we'll get hold of our federal loans.'

'Well, we can't work miracles,' said Andy. 'Charles has been out on the track night and day, and he's managed to take it as far as Newcastle. We should be open for passenger business next month, a dime a mile.'

Collis reached past Sam Lewis and took his drink off the counter. 'I suppose that's better than nothing. At least we qualify for the first payment. But I want him to push the roadbed ahead, too, as well as the track-laying. It's the roadbed that gets us the loans.'

'We've had labour problems,' said Andy. 'Charles telegraphed me just yesterday asking for more men. We've got a couple of hundred Irish labourers grading the roadbed beyond Newcastle, but they're slow, and they drink a lot, and they've started complaining about the wages already.'

Collis nodded. 'That's a difficulty I've foreseen for years. And that's why I'm staying here in San Francisco for a few days. I'm going to have a word with Mr Yee, and see how many Chinese I can get together.'

Andy finished his beer. 'You're not serious about the Chinese? I always thought it was some kind of a joke. I know Charles won't like it.'

'Charles doesn't know what the Chinese can do.'

'But they're pretty skinny and weak, aren't they?' put in Lloyd Wintle. 'I mean, you take your average Chinaman and put him alongside your average Irishman, and there's no comparison. Your average Irishman has muscle. Your average Irishman can move mountains. But your average Chinaman, what is he? You're not going to build a railroad over the Sierras with funny little men in dishpan hats and blue pyjamas, are you?'

'They eat queer, too,' said Sam Lewis. 'You wouldn't be able to feed a Chinese crew on pork and beans. All that rice and seaweed and bamboo. How are you going to feed them on that?'

Collis gave them all a courteous but dismissive shake of his head. 'None of you know what you're talking about. I was close to Wang-Pu, remember, and I'm even closer to Kwang Lee. I know what the Chinese can do, and what they think about this railroad. I know about their food, too, and that's no problem because they'll bring along their own cooks. You wait until the day I can take you on a train ride to the summit of the High Sierras, and *then* tell me your average Chinese doesn't stand up to your average Irishman.'

As he had promised, Collis called that afternoon at Dear's restaurant, where he ate a simple meal of chop suey and pork, and waited for Mr Yee. Mr Yee arrived with a family from Canton, but he excused himself for a few minutes and came to sit next to Collis.

'It is many months since I saw you,' he said. 'Are your enterprises going well?'

'Have you heard about the new Pacific Railroad Act?'

'Yes,' said Mr Yee. 'Was that your doing? Are you ready to push ahead now and build your railroad?'

Collis nodded. 'I'm going back to Sacramento in two days, and we're going to start laying track like you never saw.'

'And you will keep your promise?'

'You bet I'll keep it. I want one hundred labourers now, and I shall want more later. Many more. Pass the word around that every able-bodied Chinese man is welcome to volunteer for work on the new railroad, and that they can reach me through you.'

'I am pleased,' said Mr Yee. 'I hope that Wang-Pu is aware that you have kept your word.'

Collis looked at Mr Yee through the steam from his cup of green tea. 'I don't think that Wang-Pu ever doubted it, Mr Yee.'

He had one more call to make in San Francisco, to the house in South Park called Colusa. He took a cab out as far as Happy Valley and then walked the rest of the way, under a hazy, golden sky.

South Park was already showing signs of deterioration. Many of its houses were empty now, vacated by Southerners whose fortunes in cotton and tobacco had been ruined by the Civil War. The grass in the oval gardens was weedy and unkempt, and the railings needed a fresh coat of paint. The isolation from the city that had once been one of South Park's most desirable features now made it seem abandoned and derelict.

Collis walked straight to the Melfords' house and knocked He waited for a long time before their black servant opened the door and said, without surprise, 'Mr Edmonds. Come in, sir. Mr Melford saw you walking up here, and asks you to come inside.'

Collis held back for a moment. He had only come up to South park to enquire after Sarah's health; and he had doubted if the Melfords would even speak to him. But the servant was patiently holding the door open, as if Collis was welcome, and after a moment or two, Collis decided it was probably safe to step in.

He found Laurence Melford in his drawing-room, standing by the French windows which gave out on to his neat and almost mathematical back garden. The drawing-room was severe, but opulent. There was an eighteenth-century English cabinet filled with rare Worcestershire dishes, and above the marble fireplace there was a dour portrait by Frans Hals. The drapes were rust-coloured velvet, and the carpet had been hand-woven in Belgium.

Laurence Melford himself was dressed in a black tailcoat and black tie, and wore a black ribbon around his left arm. He appeared older by ten years – white-haired, bent under the weight of sorrow and of war, and with skin like an apple that has been left to lie in a dish for days too long.

Collis bowed slightly and said, 'Mr Melford.'

Laurence Melford turned and acknowledged Collis's appearance with a nod of his head.

'Would you like a drink?' he asked Collis. 'A cigar?'

'No, thank you.'

'Then sit down, at least. I won't take up much of your time.'

Collis looked behind him, raised his tailcoat, and sat on a small English sofa, buttoned and braided in the same rust colour as the drapes. 'You're in mourning,' he said to Laurence Melford.

Laurence Melford nodded. 'Yes. Grant was killed six weeks ago, in Tennessee.'

'I'm sorry. I really am.'

Laurence Melford stood against the light of the French windows. 'Yes,' he said, in a strangely slurred voice. 'I believe you probably are.'

Then he came forward across the room. 'You know something, Collis – I always believed that you were an upstart, a most objectionable young man, one of the new generation of settlers who had come to California to do nothing but exploit her natural wealth and give her nothing in return.'

604

'I can understand your feelings,' said Collis. 'I think I would have thought the same myself, if I had been you.'

'But,' said Laurence Melford, 'but . . . I now believe I was wrong. You weren't dangerous or objectionable in yourself. Oh, I wouldn't say I ever liked you, and quite probably I still don't . . . but what you said to me about each of us acting out our historical roles . . . well, that was right. It wasn't you I was frightened of. It wasn't you yourself who alarmed me. What really frightened me was the prospect of those changes of which you were nothing more than the harbinger.'

He thought for a moment, stroking his cheek as if he wasn't sure who he was. Then he said, 'You weren't the disease. You were nothing more than a symptom. The disease is greed; the exploitation of everything this land has to offer, regardless of its traditions or its natural beauties or the memory of those who fought to make a paradise out of a wilderness. It wasn't really your fault at all. You were unscrupulous, of course, but then your destiny gives you the licence to be unscrupulous. I have been watching your progress, Mr Edmonds, and I am sure now that you will cross the Sierra by rail.'

Collis waited for a moment, and then said hoarsely, 'How's Sarah?'

'Sarah? Oh, she's quite well. She's gone to stay with friends in Calistoga. She's gotten over her . . . difficulties.'

'Do you still blame me for what happened to her?'

'Partly, I suppose,' said Laurence Melford. 'It was my fault, too, of course. I tried to keep her captive in her own home. I never allowed her to go to the parties she wanted to attend, or walk out with the boys she liked. But then I expected her to behave like a well-bred girl from Virginia, instead of a tomboy from Northern California with a mind of her own. I educated her one way and expected her to behave in another, and there isn't any wonder she got confused. But you weren't much of a friend to her, either, were you? You and your calotypes.'

Collis looked at him for a long time. 'You know it was me?'

'Who else could it have been? Who else has your particular brand of ruthless ingenuity? But Sarah told her mother everything about it, in the end, and how she volunteered to pose as a model. It was that confession of hers more than anything else that helped me to understand what was happening to California, and what was happening to me.'

Collis said nothing. Laurence Melford walked around his chair and stood over him, his hand up to his face, and smiled.

'I suppose you're wondering how I feel about the fifty thousand dollars I gave you. Well – I just want to reassure you that it can stay where it is – invested in the Sierra Pacific Railroad. After your little bit of chiselling in Washington, and the way you've gotten this railroad started, I do believe that the money might be as safe there as any place else. But I would like my stock certificates, in case you try to pull another one of your stunts on me.'

Collis smiled back at Laurence Melford and nodded his head. 'Very well. I'll have our attorneys draw them up in the morning.'

He got up to go, and Laurence Melford saw him to the door. As he put on his hat and turned to say goodbye, Laurence Melford said, 'I hope you won't take this conversation the wrong way.'

'What do you mean?' asked Collis.

'I hope you won't take it to mean that I approve of you, or of what you have done. I don't – not for one moment. All I am telling you is that I have learned to accept the inevitability of your destiny, and the history of this state; and the inevitability of the fact that if I try to stand against you, I will most certainly be broken.'

Collis thought about that, then pulled a face. 'I guess you're right,' he said. 'History can't be helped.'

He walked off, and Laurence Melford stood by the open front door of his house watching him go. Collis turned back twice, but didn't wave. The third time he turned back, Laurence Melford had gone inside and closed his door behind him.

He stood at last on the track beyond Newcastle, watching the Irish and Chinese labourers levelling the roadbed with their picks and shovels, and looking around at the impossible clutter of makeshift huts, sagging tents, smoking cooking fires, and rows of flatcars with their loads of iron rails. He wore riding boots and a thick plaid coat, for it was September now, and the railroad was gradually making its way up the lower slopes of the Sierra foothills.

A few yards up ahead of him was the *City of Sacramento*, the largest and most powerful locomotive they owned. It was a ten-wheeler, especially built for them in Philadelphia. They had needed it so desperately that Collis had ordered it taken to pieces on the East Coast, shipped to Panama, unloaded at Aspinwall and carried on flatcars as far as Panama City, then loaded on to a Pacific steamer and shipped as far as San Francisco before it was eventually loaded on to lighters and brought up the Sacramento River. It had arrived quickly. It had taken only thirty-five days from the works at Philadelphia to the railhead in the Sierra foothills, but it had cost the S.P. more than $37,000.

Collis had another severe cost problem. The federal loans were coming through at a steady rate, but they were being paid in paper dollars. In California, the only trusted currency was gold, and he was having to exchange the paper money for bullion before he could pay his wages, his expenses, or even the price of railroad ties. The exchange rate was right down to fifty-seven cents for the dollar, and that meant that more than forty per cent of their precious $48,000 a mile was being wasted.

He had done his best to make up for losses. The S.P. graders had prepared a supply road as far as Dutch Flat, and since 1 July Collis had been charging wagon teams a heavy toll to carry their loads along it on their way to Washoe, Humboldt, and Reese River. But the company was still broke, and every morning Leland and Collis and Charles would sit around the table at 54K Street over coffee and decide whether they were going to continue or not.

That Thursday morning, the accounts had shown that business was picking up a little; the thirty-one mile route they had opened between Sacramento and Newcastle was beginning to show a profit. And that was one of the reasons why Collis had taken the 6.15 train from Sacramento to the Sierra Pacific terminus, and then ridden out on horseback to see how work was progressing further along the track. He also wanted to talk to Charles about Chinese labourers.

The air was crisp, although Collis suspected it would grow hot during the afternoon. The dull clanging of rails being dropped from their flatcars was immediately followed by the furious metallic clatter of hammers on railroad spikes. The men who were lifting and placing the rails in position hardly spoke.

Charles came out of the dusty tent marked 'Construction Chief' and walked across the track to where Collis was standing. His red face was beetroot-coloured from a summer spent outdoors on the tracks, but his mood was confident and cheerful. There was nothing he liked better than to spend his time in the company of men, eating, drinking, swearing, and smoking; and although women were in short supply in the mining camps of the Sierra foothills, an occasional visit from a dogged and devoted Wappo woman was enough, as he put it, 'to keep my juices in good condition.'

Best of all, he was away from Mary on legitimate business, and for what could turn out to be years.

'Well,' said Collis, as Charles approached him up the railroad embankment. 'How's it going?'

'That cut up ahead is slowing us down,' said Charles. 'We've got eight hundred feet of aggregate to excavate there, at an average of sixty-three feet deep. I've tried digging, but that stuff's almost as hard as granite, so I've started blasting with black powder. Trouble is, black powder's damned short.'

Collis shaded his eyes and looked up ahead. The wooded Sierra foothills rose sharply here, and to maintain the level grade of the railroad they were going to have to blast out a sharp V-shape. He remembered the place from the time they had ridden out here to survey the mountains with Doc Kates. It hadn't occurred to him at the time that the trail they had followed with their wagon would be impassable for a locomotive.

'How much powder do you need?' Collis asked Charles, with his eyes half closed against the bright sunlight.

'Four, five thousand kegs. There's going to be more blasting up ahead.'

'All right,' said Collis, 'I'll see what I can do.'

Collis spent the rest of the day inspecting the railroad camp's facilities, and watching the labourers at work to see how efficient they were. He ate a rough lunch of pork and biscuits out of a tin bowl, washed down with whisky out of a coffee mug, so that the labourers wouldn't realise he was drinking. Before he left to catch the five o'clock No. 3 Freight Passenger train from Newcastle back to Sacramento, he took Charles aside.

'You've got a hundred Chinese now,' he said. 'You haven't told me how they're making out.'

Charles tugged at his nose. 'I'm not sure that I like them too much,' he said.

'Don't they work hard?'

'They work very well,' said Charles. 'When the whistle goes, they're up and ready, which is more than I can say for the Irish. But they keep themselves to themselves. They cook their own food, drink their own drinks, and about the worst I've ever seen them do is smoke a pipe of opium ash.'

'Charles,' Collis reminded him, 'we're trying to get ourselves a railroad built here. This isn't a travelling circus, for your own personal entertainment. This railroad has to be built, and in my opinion the Chinese are the best men to do it. Now, I'm sending a hundred more up by the middle of next week, and I want to hear that you've treated them well.'

Charles said nothing, but rubbed his hand around the back of his sunburned neck, and turned towards the railhead, where yet another rail was being slid off a flatcar on to the ties. Again, there was that deep, clanging sound, that sound you can only ever hear around a railroad construction camp; one of the sounds of America. 'I'm going back to Sacramento on the five o'clock train,' Collis said. 'I'll get your powder as soon as I can.'

Charles raised his hand in silent salute, and Collis turned immediately and walked away.

It took Collis five weeks to secure all the kegs of gunpowder that Charles was going to need for Bloomer Cut. At first, his telegraphed request to the Secretary of War, Edwin Stanton, was turned down. Stanton thought that railroad contractors were 'profiteers, and adventurers', and said so.

Collis was left with only one option. Without Stanton's knowledge, he wrote to President Lincoln, asking for the gunpowder. Lincoln, who knew nothing of Stanton's feelings about railroaders, signed the requisition order at once, declaring it 'very proper'.

As late summer faded into early fall, Charles and his workmen blasted their way through the cut, and continued their slow progress up towards Dutch Flat and the distant peaks of the High Sierras. It was a cold winter, and again and again they had to dig away snowdrifts just to get down to the roadbed.

Charles sent a testy note to Collis: 'It is cold, and the going is very difficult. What's more, my Wappo lady has ceased her visits, on account of the weather and the distance. Incidentally, I shall need more Chinese. At least a hundred more, as soon as you can.'

As the Sierra Pacific pushed ahead, Charles's need for Chinese labourers grew increasingly more urgent. The deep ravine of Sailor's Spur was filled in entirely by hand-quarried loads of granite and shale, excavated from the ridges ahead by the blue-pyjama'd Chinese and carried back to the ravine by horse wagons. Collis went to San Francisco in March 1865 and arranged with Mr Kwang for labour contractors to visit farms and villages in Canton, in China, and to recruit young men and boys for immediate shipment to California.

The contractors would lend the recruits their steamship fare – forty dollars – and recover it, with interest, from the wages on the railroad.

Charles, grudgingly, had to admit that Collis had been right about the Chinese. 'They refuse nothing,' he wrote. 'When we were filling in Sailor's Spur, I had them working twenty-four hours a day, and there were no complaints at all.'

Collis, on his next visit to San Francisco, went to the Kong Chow temple on Pine Street and lit incense for Wang-Pu. He told nobody, and nobody ever knev., except those deities in whom Wang-Pu had believed. Later, he ate alone at the International, and for the first time in his life he was conscious that diners at other tables were whispering about him. He heard the murmur of 'railroad millionaire' and 'Sierra Pacific'; and somehow it was only then that he realised just how extraordinary the task that he had set himself was.

Even now, with the tracks laid as far as Dutch Flat, there were still many serious politicians who didn't believe that the railroad could ever be completed. A Democratic adversary of Leland's in the California senate had declared that he wouldn't risk his money on a ticket for the Sierra Pacific Railroad, even for his grandchildren. It was all a fantasy, and the directors of the railroad company were either fools or swindlers.

Collis knew about the accusations of swindling, but he kept his temper. He had a grave marker to go back to, in the cemetery of Sacramento's Roman Catholic Church, and he knew how binding his commitment to that grave marker was always going to be.

During the fall of 1864 and the spring of 1865, the war news which reached Sacramento from Washington began to show signs of a Confederate collapse. The weeks after Collis visited Charles at Bloomer Cut, William Tecumseh Sherman, whom Collis had first seen worrying a pork chop in San Francisco, captured Atlanta, and burned it. The following month, Sheridan swept through the Shenandoah Valley. This sudden turn in the Union's fortunes on the battlefield guaranteed President Lincoln's re-election in November, and also an administration that would still be sympathetic towards the speedy completion of the Pacific railroad.

Throughout the winter, Collis heard reports that Sherman was savaging his way through the Confederate heartland, burning houses and farms and wrecking factories in an all-out attempt to break both the economy and the spirit of the South. On 3 April, a hot, idle day in Sacramento, a telegraph message came through that Grant had at last captured the secessionists' capital of Richmond; and six days later, the news arrived that Lee had surrendered to Grant at Appomattox.

The most stunning message of all, though, came five days after that – on Good Friday, 14 April. President Lincoln had been shot and killed at Ford's Theatre, Washington, while watching an undistinguished play called *Our American Cousin*. His assassin, John Wilkes Booth, had declared that the killing was an act of vengeance for the fall of Virginia.

And so it was that on Easter Sunday, 16 April, when the people of Sacramento gathered in silent crowds outside the fundamentalist church to bow their heads in respectful memory of their dead President, Collis saw Delphine again.

They had both arrived late for the service. Collis had been working on accounts for the railroad until late at night; Delphine had spent the evening entertaining two staunch Republicans who had wanted to forget their sorrow at the death of Lincoln in drink, cigars, and a double act of fornication. These two gentlemen were now sitting in the front pews of the church with their wives and their families, models of respectability and Christian humility.

The church was so crowded that Collis had to stand outside in the porch. Delphine stood a little way back, by the fence, her head bowed in prayer. She was dressed in an expensive black coat and a black bonnet, with a veil. She carried in her hand a black prayer book, and all her ornaments were jet.

It was almost impossible to hear what the preacher was saying inside the church, so at last Collis crossed the dusty churchyard and stood next to Delphine, his hands still held together, his head still bowed. The sky above them was whipped with tails of light cloud, and a faint breeze ruffled the black feathers on Delphine's bonnet.

'Delphine,' he said.

She raised her head. Her face remained veiled behind dark traceries of lace, embroidered with tiny black moths. He could see the serious beauty of her eyes, though, and the childishly pink softness of her lips.

'I came to pay my respects to Abraham Lincoln . . .' she said, in an unfinished sentence that sounded as if it should have continued, ' . I certainly didn't come to pay any respects to *you*.'

611

Collis gave her a brief, lopsided smile. 'It's a great tragedy. He won't even live to see the society he fought for.'

'Does that matter, do you think?' asked Delphine.

Inside the church, the congregation began to sing Psalm 24. 'Who shall ascend into the hill of the Lord? or who shall stand in his holy place?' A few of the latecomers in the churchyard began to sing, too.

'Why are you staying in Sacramento so long?' Collis said to Delphine. 'I thought you would have moved on to San Francisco by now.'

'I'm staying because I feel like staying,' Delphine told him. 'Do I have to give you any other reason?'

'You're not staying because of me?'

'What on earth gave you that idea? Why should I stay anywhere in the whole world because of you?'

Collis looked away across the street, where men and women were gathered under the flickering shade of the trees, the men in their Sunday frock coats and the women in their bonnets and churchgoing dresses.

'I had the idea that you loved me once,' he told Delphine. 'The same way that I loved you. I thought maybe that had something to do with your staying.'

'Oh, I see,' she said. 'The revival of a childhood romance, just like the two-bit storybooks.'

'Do I have to remind you that I came after you once, in Washington?' asked Collis. 'And do I have to remind you what you said to me then?'

Delphine looked down at her clasped hands. 'No,' she said. 'You don't have to remind me. Any more than I have to remind you that you dismissed me then as a human being, because you couldn't have me; and that you carelessly destroyed what little self-respect I had left, for the sake of your railroad.'

Collis gripped her arm. 'If you dislike me so much, then why do you stay in Sacramento?'

'I told you – because I want to.'

'I don't believe you,' Collis insisted.

She looked up at him. He couldn't understand the expression on her face at all. 'You can believe what you like,' she said. 'But this is scarcely the place to talk about it. Why don't you call by to see me tomorrow evening, at Mrs Pangborn's?'

'I can't be seen at Mrs Pangborn's.'

'Then why shouldn't I call on you? I know where you live.'

Collis hesitated. He could see that several of the more inquisitive members of the congregation were turning their heads and whispering about him now. Delphine was well known in town as one of Mrs Pangborn's fancy girls, and it wasn't socially healthy for Collis to be seen in her company.

'Very well,' Collis said, under his breath. 'At nine tomorrow, well after the sun has set.' And then he said loudly, 'I hope that answers your questions on our dear President's death, Miss Spooner,' and stepped away from her with a courteous bow. Delphine dropped him a sarcastic curtsey in return.

She was late. It was almost ten before he heard her carriage drawing up outside, and the jingling of the bridle as she tied the horse to the rail by the side door. He had been drinking whisky and smoking cigars with a kind of steady fury, and he sprang to the door and opened it even before she could raise her hand to the bell.

'Well,' he said, quite breathlessly, 'you came.'

She stepped inside. She wore a maroon gown sewn with small seed pearls, and a black shoulder cape with maroon piping. Her hair was tightly curled with tongs, and she smelled of some flowery French perfume that Collis couldn't place. It reminded him of something, or of someone . . . but he wasn't sure what, or who.

He followed her into the drawing-room. It had hardly been used since Hannah had died, and it seemed cold. Delphine walked in a circle around the room, touching books and ornaments and vases with her fingertips, and arriving at last by the gilded mirror over the fireplace, where she stopped and smiled at her own reflection.

'Would you like a drink?' Collis asked her.

She nodded. 'A glass of sweet white wine if you have it.'

Collis went to the side table, where four bottles of wine and a bottle of champagne were cooling in a bucket of crushed ice. He poured Delphine a drink, then returned to her, holding it up in his hand.

'I suppose I owe you a very deep apology,' he said.

She took her drink. 'Why? Because you're lonely?'

'Lonely?' he asked her.

She took off her bonnet and sat down on the sofa uninvited. 'I can't think of any other reason why you might be interested in renewing our friendship, can you?' She smiled.

Collis looked at her cautiously. 'I owe you an apology because of

613

what I did to you, and that's all. The reason I asked you to come here – the reason I wanted to talk to you – well, this is simply for old times' sake. We loved each other once. Why should we be hostile to each other now – especially after everything that's happened?'

Delphine stared back at him and then let out a high, loud laugh. 'For old times' sake? Collis, you must be going soft in the head! Do you still believe that I'm that coy and passionate little innocent you knew in New York? Is that the fantasy you have of me still? After all the parlours and cathouses I've entertained in? After Virginia City, and Denver, and Kansas? After all those sweating sodbusters and land agents and half-drunk deputies have climbed on top of me and – '

'Stop it!' shouted Collis. 'What the hell are you trying to say?'

Delphine shrugged and sipped at her wine. 'I'm simply trying to spare you the embarrassment of courting a whore in the way that you would a fruity but virginal young girl.'

Collis took a deep breath. 'Well . . .' he said. 'What I'm trying to say is that I'm willing to forget all those men.'

Delphine was open-mouthed. 'You're willing to forget all those men? *You're* willing? What in a hog's ass does it have to do with you? *I'm* willing to forget all those men, too! More than willing. But my problem is that I *can't*. Don't you think that's a pity? Somehow my stubborn little memory won't bring itself to erase all those squeaking mattresses and all those stinking pricks and all that tobacco juice and whisky and strange men's seed.'

'For Christ's sake, Delphine,' snapped Collis. 'This is Easter Monday, and you're talking like a – '

'A whore?' challenged Delphine, in a strong, clear voice.

Collis lifted his hand helplessly. He hadn't expected it to be like this. 'I'm sorry,' he said. 'I'm sorry for everything. There isn't anything else I can say.'

Delphine put down her glass and stood up. She came over to him and laid her small hands on his hips. When she looked up at him, her eyes were soft and concerned and blurred with tears.

'I'm sorry, too,' she said. 'I would have done anything to be able to turn back the clock, and come to you tonight the way I was in New York. But I can't. I've seen too much, Collis, and experienced too much; and what I told you before – that's true, too. I'm only living the kind of life I was always destined to lead, the way you are.'

The pendulum of the clock on the mantelpiece reflected the

lamplight into Collis's eyes like a monotonous message from an unremembered time. He bent forward and kissed Delphine gently on the lips. When he raised his head again, her eyes were still closed and her lips were still parted, and so he kissed her again.

She touched his face with her fingertips. 'Collis . . .' she said, in a dreamy whisper. 'Do you really believe that it's possible for people to forget?'

'I don't know,' he said. His chest felt tight. 'I just don't know.'

'I don't think it is,' she told him. 'We can forgive, perhaps, but we can never really forget.'

Collis leaned forward to kiss her again, but somehow she averted her face, and scratched him instead with the plumes on her bonnet. He frowned at her and tried to hold her hands, but she turned away from him and swept across to the other side of the room. She stood there, straight-backed, self-assured, and raised one hand. Then, stiffly, she tugged on her glove, pushing each finger well down.

'I believe one day that I will find it in my heart to forgive you, Collis,' she said, 'but you can be assured that I will never forget what you did to me, and what you must have done to so many people who stood in your way. Your mind was set on a famous achievement, wasn't it? To cross the High Sierra by rail, and to make your fortune. Well, you and the Sierra deserve each other. You're both cold, both haughty, and you both have hearts of flawless granite.'

'Delphine . . .' said Collis.

'No, Collis,' she said. 'I have something to say . . . something I think you ought to know. Perhaps I'm saying it for the sake of my own revenge on you; but perhaps you'll learn something about yourself, too.'

'I can't believe that anything you can tell me can possibly teach me anything about myself,' retorted Collis. He was feeling frustrated now, and he was growing angry. This wasn't just Collis Edmonds the gambler and rake that this cheap young whore was talking to. This was Collis Edmonds the railroad millionaire. Or potential millionaire, at least.

'Just listen,' said Delphine. 'I talked to Mrs Pangborn about you last week, quite by chance, and Mrs Pangborn told me something which shocked me more than anything I have ever heard in my whole life. Mrs Pangborn told me that soon after you were married to your widow woman, Hannah, you gave her a child.'

'A *child*?' said Collis. 'What are you talking about?'

'She became pregnant, that's what I'm talking about. She became pregnant, but she didn't tell you. Instead, she took herself to Mrs Pangborn, and Mrs Pangborn was obliging enough to end her pregnancy for her, before you could even find out.'

Collis stared at Delphine in horror. 'A child?' he repeated. 'But that was later . . . that was what killed her – '

'No,' said Delphine. 'It wasn't later at all. What you don't seem to understand is that there were two children. The first, which Mrs Pangborn successfully aborted . . . and then the second.'

'Hannah was pregnant with two children of mine and she didn't even tell me? I don't believe it! You're talking nonsense! Vicious, incredible nonsense!'

'Maybe I am. You can easily find out for yourself. Ask Mrs Pangborn. She'll tell you, as long as you pay her enough, and don't threaten to take her to the law. Your first child ended up in a paper parcel, floating down the Sacramento River to the sea; your second child presented complications. Mrs Pangborn accidentally pierced the womb with her instruments, and killed both your wife and your baby-to-be. She covered up her little accident by taking Hannah out of town in her buggy and leaving her there, so that her death would look like a natural miscarriage. But she killed her right enough; or rather your child did; or rather *you* did.'

Collis was white. He could feel the blood shrinking away from his face and his hands, and he could hardly find the co-ordination to speak.

'*I* did?' he grated. 'What do you mean? I didn't even *know*. My God, Delphine, she didn't even tell me.'

Delphine slowly moved around the drawing-room. 'She didn't tell you because she was afraid for any baby of yours – afraid that it might be rated second-best to your precious railroad.'

'I don't understand.'

'Neither do I, quite. But that's what Mrs Pangborn told me. Your wife didn't want to have any children until the railroad was completed. Mrs Pangborn said she'd promised you that on your wedding day.'

Collis suddenly sat down. 'My God,' he said. 'My God, I can't believe it. Hannah, and two unborn babies, just for the sake of forty miles of railroad track. Oh, my God.'

Delphine watched him for a while. He was plainly too stunned even to cry. 'I had to tell you, Collis. It wasn't the kind of intelligence I could have kept to myself, even if I hadn't wanted to hurt you.'

'Well, you've hurt me,' he said, in a choked voice.

She came across and stood beside him for a moment. Then she kissed him, very lightly, on the forehead.

He looked up at her, his eyes unfocused. 'Are you going now?' he asked her.

'Do you want me to?'

'I'd prefer it if you stayed.'

'What for? So that I can hurt you some more? Haven't you had enough, thinking of your baby floating its way down to San Francisco, and your wife bleeding to death in her carriage – all because of you and your obsession?'

Collis was silent for a long time, but eventually he whispered, 'Stay.'

Delphine shook her head. 'I'd have to charge you, and you wouldn't like that. You're costing me money as it is.'

'Stay,' he repeated.

'No,' she told him. 'You deserve to be on your own. You deserve to realise just for one evening where your grand scheme has finally got you. No place at all, but alone.'

'You whore,' he said, with pain and disgust.

'Yes,' she said, with dignified pleasure.

For more than a year after Easter Monday, 1865, Collis worked on the railroad with an intensity that frightened even Leland. Although Charles was officially in charge of construction, Collis would visit the railhead two or three times a week, pale-faced, dark-eyed, in his tall black silk hat and his black tailcoat. He was so sharp and emaciated these days that the Irish labourers called him the Raven, and the Chinese called him Yama, after the thin and elegant oriental demon who presided over Pitris, or hell.

The first challenge to Collis's freshly-fired obsession with completing the railroad came fifty-seven miles out of Sacramento, where the graders were confronted with a huge bulk of shale, protruding out of the slope of the Sierras nearly two thousand feet above the foaming cleft of the American River. It was here that Collis and Theodore and Wang-Pu had stopped with Doc Kates to share a picnic lunch; but to the railroad engineers, the outcropping looked so forbidding and impassable that they quickly christened it Cape Horn. It fell at an angle of seventy-five degrees straight down to the river gorge, and yet somehow they were supposed to cut a ledge into it to carry a railroad.

Collis went to inspect it on a windy afternoon, with Charles plodding silently beside him. Kwang Lee came too, a few steps behind Collis, dressed in a very long brown tweed overcoat.

'This is typical of Theodore,' said Charles, pointing out Cape Horn on the survey map. 'He was always seeing soft digging dirt where there was nothing but solid rock.'

Collis lifted his eyes towards the summit of the outcropping. It was grey, and rugged, and sparsely scattered with trees. From close up, it looked like one of the shoulders of the world.

'You need to blast, right?' Collis asked Charles.

Charles nodded. 'The trouble is, how are we going to get a blasting crew to perch on a seventy-five-degree slope while they bore the holes for the charges?'

Collis thought for a while, and then beckoned Kwang Lee forward. 'This is just an idea,' he said. 'Supposing the Chinese climbed to the top of the rocks and built winches up there. Then supposing they were lowered in baskets down the face of the shale, so that they could drill anywhere they liked. Do you think they'd do it?'

Charles raised an eybrow. But Kwang Lee took a careful look at Cape Horn and then said, 'I think they would find great pride in blasting that rock, Mr Edmonds. Do you want me to pass the instructions on?'

'I'd be grateful,' said Collis.

Charles watched the Chinaman go and then said, 'Well, I'll be damned.'

During the following weeks, Chinese workers were winched down the rocky spur until they were dangling fourteen hundred feet above the American River. With hand drills, sledgehammers, and barrels of black gunpowder, they gradually blasted a ledge across the uncompromising spur, until they reached the far side.

The Chinese took huge delight in cutting the fuses of their gunpowder charges to different lengths, so that when they signalled that they were ready to blast, and their colleagues hauled them up the face of Cape Horn to be safely out of the way, all their explosives went off at once, with a massive echoing bang. Collis brought several bankers and their families up from San Francisco to see the blasting of Cape Horn. It was a spectacular sight, and good for investment.

During the summer of 1866, Collis saw Delphine only once, and then she ignored him. A week later he heard that she had left Sacramento and had gone to San Francisco to work in a parlour house on Dupont Street. He often heard about her after that, from Maria-Mamuska in particular, but he never saw her again, ever.

By the winter of 1866, the Chinese railroad gangs had started work on the last and the longest of the six tunnels which took the Sierra Pacific up to the very summit of the mountains. Once they were over the top, there were still nine more tunnels to be bored before the railroad could reach the flatlands of Nevada, and Charles had already assigned digging to be started on these tunnels, night and day. But the Summit Tunnel was what he always called 'the pig', and both he and Collis took personal charge of the excavations.

To complete the Summit Tunnel, they had to bore a hole 20 feet high through 1659 feet of totally solid granite, over 7000 feet above sea level. It would have been a pig in the summer, but in the harsh winter of 1866–7, it was a struggle that drove Collis to the limits of his physical and emotional endurance. There were over forty blizzards that winter, and drifts so deep that the Chinese had to tunnel their way through the snow just to reach the face of the rock.

Three times during January, Charles asked Collis to let up; to wait until the thaw. But each time Collis refused. If *he* could stay up in the High Sierras in the bitter cold, then so could the Chinese, and so could Charles, for that matter. Every day Collis would visit each tunnel heading – the crew that was gradually blasting its way uphill and the crew that was equally gradually blasting its way downhill. Every day he watched drill bits breaking on the impossibly hard granite, as the workers sweated to bore holes that were deep enough to take an effective charge. Every day he restlessly paced his timber hut by the western heading of the tunnel, with his maps and his charts spread out on the table, and the windows blind with snow.

In March, Leland made the journey up to Summit Tunnel and brought with him a large smoked ham, a pound of good Virginia tobacco, and a bottle of nitroglycerin. Nitroglycerin had recently been invented in Europe, he had heard, and was an admirable explosive. In fact, European engineers called it 'blasting oil'. Collis ignored the ham and the tobacco and immediately called on his Chinese powder monkeys to make some tests with the explosive. For the next three weeks, to Collis's increasing excitement, the Chinese blew out foot after foot of granite with the new oil, and by

15 April, Charles was predicting that they could be through the mountain by the end of July.

The day after, they heard by telegraph from San Francisco that a consignment of nitroglycerin which had been stored in the back of the Wells Fargo office in San Francisco had exploded for no apparent reason, killing twelve passers-by and tossing a gory arm into the street. And by the end of the week, in spite of hours of argument and wheeling and dealing in the state capital by Leland and his friends, all shipments of nitroglycerin into California were indefinitely suspended. Collis was furious.

Alone, he took out a buggy and drove back along the roadbed as far as Dutch Flat. It was a sunny afternoon, and for the first time in months he wore a beige linen coat and a flat white hat. He reined in his horse outside of Doc Kate's pharmacy and drugstore and stepped inside.

The place hadn't changed at all. There was still the smell of coughdrops and soap that he remembered from the first time he had walked in with Theodore. And there behind the counter, measuring out bath salts, was Doc Kates himself.

'Doc?' Collis said.

Doc Kates peered at him hard through his spectacles, then smiled in recognition. 'Collis Edmonds. Well, I'll be. I thought you'd be sitting in a fancy office in San Francisco by now, not out here in the wilds.'

He finished serving the bath salts, and then he beckoned Collis through into his back room. 'What would you like? Coffee, tea, or a belt?'

'Coffee will do fine. I've got a hard day ahead of me.'

'The way that railroad's cutting its way through the mountains, I'm not surprised,' said Doc Kates. 'I went out to the tracks a week ago, and I could hardly believe that those rails were lying along the same old path that you and Theodore Jones penciled down on your maps.'

'The path that *you* found, Doc,' Collis reminded him.

Doc Kates put the coffee-pot on the stove, sniffed, and wiped his hands on his apron. 'I sure was sorry to read about Theodore in the *Union*. He was a fine young man. Inspired.'

'Yes, you could say so,' said Collis.

Doc Kates sat down. 'Well,' he said, 'what brings you back to the old drugstore? You didn't just come here to chew the fat, did you?'

Collis shook his head. 'It's the tunnel we're digging through to the summit. We made very slow headway during the winter, because all we had was black powder. Then Leland McCormick brought us some nitroglycerin. Blasting oil, they call it, and *that* cuts through the mountain like cheese.'

Doc Kates nodded. 'I see your problem. They've banned it now, haven't they, after that big bang in San Francisco? So how are you going to blow your way through to the pass?'

Collis sat back in his chair. Through the window, he could see Doc Kates's vegetable garden growing, just as it had last year and the year before, and always would do, until he died. 'As far as I understand it, nitroglycerin's made out of sulphuric acid, and nitric acid, and glycerine.'

'That's right,' said Doc Kates, looking at Collis warily.

Collis looked right back at him. 'Supposing someone was to bring these three ingredients – which aren't illegal when they're brought into the state of California separately – supposing someone was to bring them up the mountain, just as they are, and then supposing someone was to mix them together right up by the tunnel we're blasting out and give us a ready supply of the stuff?'

Doc Kates took off his spectacles. His eyes were watery and pale, faded by years of Sierra sun and years of Sierra snow.

'You're asking me to do it?' he wanted to know.

'Only if you're willing.'

'It's pretty volatile stuff. One mistake and you're a damned sight higher in the air than Summit Pass.'

'You're a careful man.'

'Yes, I guess you could say that I am.'

'Then you'll do it?'

'Let's have ourselves a cup of coffee first,' Doc Kates said. 'Do you fancy a ginger cookie? I've a fresh-baked batch in from Mrs Elias.'

Collis stood up, pushing back his chair. 'I don't have much time, Doc. That tunnel has to be bored, and bored quick.'

Doc Kates frowned at him. 'All right,' he said, slowly bringing the cups to the table and setting them down. 'All right, I'll do it. Do you have time for a cup of coffee now?'

All during the long summer of 1867, the tree-lined mountains below Summit Pass shook and echoed with the sound of explosions. Inside the solid granite tunnel, it was stifling and dusty and intolerably hot, but the Chinese blasters drilled incessantly into the rock face, laid their charges of freshly-brewed nitroglycerin, and gradually blew the inside of the mountains out.

Collis had to return to Sacramento in late July to tidy up months of neglected business; but in mid-August he came back to the Sierras again in a rather rudimentary private passenger car pulled by the *City of Sacramento*. He climbed down a few hundred feet away from the entrance to the west portal of the Summit Tunnel, and Charles came across to greet him.

'How's it going?' Collis asked. 'Have we licked this goddam mountain range yet?'

'You came just in time,' said Charles. 'We're drilling the last of the charge holes right now, and we reckon the two headings should meet up this afternoon. I sent a couple of Chinese foremen back to bring some champagne.'

He followed Charles into the tunnel, and together they walked uphill through the gritty dust of drilled-out granite and the deafening clamour of sledgehammers. Collis took off his hat to wipe the grimy sweat from his forehead with his handkerchief, and coughed.

They arrived at last at the face of the west heading, where thirty or forty blue-pyjama'd Chinese workers were drilling at the granite with hand drills. The white foreman, with his tall cowboy-style hat and drooping moustache, came across and said, 'Good morning, Mr Edmonds. We should be ready for blasting in a half hour or so. Then you'll be able to see daylight all the way up to the summit.'

Collis looked around him. 'You know something?' he said hoarsely. 'They said it couldn't be done. When I first swore that I'd take a railroad over the Sierras, they said it couldn't be done. Well now, dammit, we're right on the edge of showing them just how backward and blind they were. We're almost there, Charles. Can you understand what that means? These mountains I used to look at from my back veranda in Sacramento, we've licked them and we've licked them good.'

Charles took his arm. 'Come on, Collis. Let's go find ourselves a drink. You look like this heat and this dust aren't doing you any good at all.'

Collis wiped his mouth with the back of his hand. His face was glistening with sweat, and he looked appallingly haggard.

'Yes,' he said, 'you're right. But you just make sure I'm the first to see this hole blasted right through. You hear me? I don't want any blasting without my knowledge.'

'Okay, Mr Edmonds,' promised the foreman.

Together, Collis and Charles walked back down the tunnel until they were out in the daylight again. They crossed the tracks to Charles's hut, and Charles unlocked the door and ushered Collis inside. There was a rough-and-ready living-room, with a carpet, and a chaise longue, and an ugly mahogany cabinet, and even a lithograph of San Francisco Bay; through a curtained doorway, Collis could see a brass bed and a set of framed daguerreotypes of nude French models.

Charles went to the cabinet, produced another bunch of keys, unlocked it, and brought out a bottle of bourbon. 'You know, Collis,' he said, filling up two glasses, 'you really ought to take it easier. You don't look well.'

'I'm not sick,' said Collis.

'Maybe you're not now, but if you go on pushing yourself this way, you soon will be. You mark my words, if you keep working as hard as you are now, without a let-up, then you're going to be lying in your grave by the time you're forty.'

Collis sat down and took his drink. 'Do you really think that matters?' he asked Charles.

Charles sat down beside him. 'Of course it matters. You're the inspiration behind the whole of this railroad. You've changed the history of this nation in a matter of a few years, almost single-handed. How can you say it doesn't matter?'

'Hannah should have been here today, Charles. Hannah and two young children of mine.'

Charles looked uncomfortable. 'Well,' he said. 'That's the way life is.'

Collis put down his glass and rested his head in his hands. When he spoke, his voice was graver and more measured than Charles had ever heard it.

'I want to finish this railroad, Charles, because I can't go back. But if there was any way in which I could trade this railroad, and all its locomotives, and all its ties and its spikes and its rails – if there was any way in which I could trade this railroad for one day with Hannah, one more day with Hannah, then I would do it gladly.'

He lifted his head, and when he did so, Charles was shocked to see that he was crying.

'I was prepared to see people die for the sake of this railroad. I was prepared to ruin people's reputations, their happiness, their whole lives. That was the price of progress, I thought. You can't

623

make omelettes without cracking eggs. Well, it's true, you can't. But of course I wasn't bright enough to understand that it wasn't *I* who was in charge of cracking the eggs. It was God, or the destiny of America, or whatever you like to call it, and I was just as vulnerable to the twists and turns of this destiny as everybody else.'

He took out his handkerchief again and blew his nose. 'I've lost everything, Charles. I've lost more than a man can reasonably be expected to bear. And this railroad is nothing more nor less than a monument to my vanity and my pride and my human foolishness.'

'Collis – you're tired,' Charles said softly.

'Yes,' said Collis, 'I'm tired. But I'm not mad.'

At twenty minutes of noon, the foreman in the cowboy hat knocked at the door of the hut and announced that the Chinese crews were at last ready for the final blasting. When Collis and Charles stepped outside, there was a festive atmosphere around, and the workers who were assembled around the mouth of the tunnel were laughing and joking and talking excitedly. Boring the Summit Tunnel had been one of the hardest and most dangerous feats of civil engineering in American history, and they all knew how well they had done. Collis saw Doc Kates in the crowd, in shirtsleeves and a wide-brimmed hat, and he gave him a friendly salute.

'How would you like to fire the charges, Mr Edmonds?' asked the foreman. 'The box is right over here, if you'd like to do it yourself.'

Collis shook his head. 'I think Mr Tucker ought to have that pleasure. He's the chief of the construction.'

A loud whistle blew in the tunnel to warn any workers who were still left inside to clear out, and then the foreman raised his arm. A hush fell over the crowd, and a photographer with a black cape over his head took a picture of them all, with their dusty britches and their muscular arms and their hands raised against the glare of the sun. Then the foreman dropped his arm, and Charles gave a grunt of satisfaction and pressed the plunger.

There was a whirr, and then silence. Somebody laughed out loud.

'Misfire!' called the foreman. 'Yo Huang – you wanna get back in there and see what the hell's gone wrong?'

A tall Chinese began to make his way across the railroad ties towards the tunnel. But Collis held the foreman's arm and said, 'Isn't that kind of dangerous? Couldn't those charges go off at any time at all?'

624

'Well, sure it's dangerous,' said the foreman. 'But then blasting oil always is.'

'Then I'll go,' said Collis.

The foreman shook his head. 'I'm sorry, Mr Edmonds, I can't take that responsibility. That's nitroglycerin in there, not brandy and cigars.'

'You don't have to take the responsibility,' snapped Collis. 'This is my railroad and I'll do whatever I damned well choose.'

'Collis – don't be absurd,' Charles said. 'What do you know about blasting? You can't go in there. It's dangerous and it's out of the question.'

'I'm going,' said Collis, pulling off his linen coat and handing his hat to the foreman. 'I know enough about blasting to know that there's probably a loose connection. A child could fix it.'

'Collis,' warned Charles, 'if you attempt to go into that tunnel, I'll have you forcibly stopped.'

Collis smiled at him. 'No you won't, Charles. I'm going, and that's all there is to it.'

There was a disturbed murmur from the blasters and graders as the foreman beckoned to the puzzled Yo Huang. Then Collis walked along the roadbed as far as the tunnel entrance and went inside without looking back once.

Now that all the drilling had stopped, the tunnel was almost completely silent. His footsteps made a brittle echo on the solid granite, and he could hear himself breathing as if he were someone else altogether. Well, he thought, perhaps I am. Perhaps I've turned out to be someone very different from the boy who woke up alongside an Irish whore in the Monument Hotel, all those years ago. Perhaps I've come of age.

He followed the shining line of the detonator wire out of the corner of his eye. He was two hundred feet into the tunnel now, and it was still unbroken. He coughed and cleared his throat. He didn't once wonder why he had elected to do this. It had just seemed natural that he should. Fitting.

He was sweating, and so he pulled out his handkerchief to mop his face. There was a decorative CE on the edge of the handkerchief, and he had an odd momentary vision of the very day when Hannah had embroidered that for him, sitting on the veranda of their house in Sacramento, on a warm evening in May. She must have been pregnant then, he thought, with a painful feeling of loss. At that very moment, she must have been carrying my child.

He heard a whistling sound and so he raised his head and peered back along the sloping tunnel. It was at that instant that one of the priming charges went off with a loud, smart blast, and Collis felt as if his head had been smacked between two planks. Then a hailstorm of fragmented granite knocked him off his feet and half-buried him in dust and showering grit.

Epilogue

The band was playing 'Clear the Way', but all that Collis could hear from inside his private parlour car was the monotonous thumping of the drum – his right ear had been deaf since the accident. His back had also been injured and he still walked with a cane. He had arrived at last in this dry desert basin, surrounded on three sides by heat-hazed mountains, like a man who keeps a long-standing appointment with a woman he is no longer sure that he loves. Yet he knew that he had to be here. The destiny he had talked about with Hannah and Knickerbocker Jane had been fulfilled.

The iron cowcatcher of the *Jupiter*, the locomotive which had pulled Collis's car over the Sierras and across the empty wastelands of the Humboldt Sink, was now only fifty feet apart from the cowcatcher of the Union Pacific's *Engine 119*. Here, at Promontory Point, Utah, the two railroads had at last joined, spanning the continent.

Collis had been exuberant on the way from Sacramento, inviting newspaper reporters and giggling young girls to share iced champagne in his parlour car. But now he was more subdued. Every now and then he would part the blinds and stare out into the bright Utah morning, squinting as if he had a migraine. From the window he could see the two locomotives, buffed-up and shining in the sunlight and steaming softly. A line of more than a hundred soldiers of the 21st Infantry, in blue dress uniforms and dazzling white gloves, waited beside the track. A crowd of reporters and photographers shuffled impatiently in the sand and the sagebrush, their wooden tripods all set up for the track-joining ceremony, sharing cigarettes and warm bottled beer.

It was 10 May 1869, a glaring Monday, two years after Collis's men had blasted a pass through the High Sierras. After that, the speed of track-laying had been furious. With the Union Pacific frenziedly putting down rails from the east, Charles had driven their Chinese and Irish graders to the limit, trying to beat the U.P. into the heart of Utah, and as far as the rich commercial prize of Salt Lake City. Each mile of track they laid brought them more federal loans and more land grants, and Collis needed every dollar and every acre of land he could get.

627

Charles had boasted that it was almost impossible for visiting spectators from California to catch up with his track-laying gang at the railhead; and a San Francisco newspaper reporter wrote with awe that he had seen a half mile of rails laid in under twenty-eight minutes.

On 27 April, as the rival railroads neared Promontory Station, Collis had shared a picnic lunch with Thomas Durant, of the Union Pacific, under a flapping tent. With a flash of his old challenging spirit, he had bet Durant ten thousand dollars that his gangs could lay ten miles of track in a single day Durant, with his mouth full of game pie, had accepted.

The following day, in a dreamlike ripple of heat and a blur of desert dust, a handpicked crew of gaugers, rail carriers, bolters, and spikers, with Charles Tucker urging them on, had beaded down 25,800 ties, spiked 3250 rails, and between them laid over 250,000 pounds of iron. As dusk fell, they had passed the ten-mile mark, and they laid fifty-six feet more for good luck. Ten Mile Day, they called it afterwards, and put up a sign to commemorate their achievement.

Even when the Sierra Pacific's graders had met up with the Union Pacific's graders approaching in the opposite direction, Collis had ordered his men to continue preparing a parallel track – at least until it was officially decided where the two railroads should join. As they passed each other, the Sierra Pacific and Union Pacific gangs had showered each other with dug-up clods of earth, and almost blown each other up with nitro-glycerin.

Collis had spent five days arguing and wrangling with Durant and federal officials before both of them had grudgingly accepted Promontory Station as the point where the railroads should be linked. And at last, at eleven-thirty on this hot morning in May, the last few feet of roadbed were graded, and a polished laurel-wood tie was put down to carry the last rails.

The door of Collis's parlour car was opened, and Leland stepped in, wearing a severe Sunday coat and a tall shiny black hat. He looked hot and agitated.

'We're ready at last,' he said. 'I've just had the most ridiculous argument with Grenville Dodge, about hammering in the last spike. *He* wanted to do it, of all people. A common-or-garden engineer. Where was he when we were lobbying for land grants, I wonder, and scratching around for funds?'

'Have you finally settled it?' asked Collis, in a flat, disinterested tone.

'Well, yes, of course,' puffed Leland. '*I* brought the ceremonial spikes, and *I* shall drive the first one in. Two golden spikes, a silver spike, and a spike made of iron, silver and gold, that's what I brought. And the laurel-wood tie, with the silver plaque. All Dodge wanted to do was bang in any old iron spike, as if the last rail were any old rail.'

'The last rail is no different from the first,' said Collis. He looked up at Leland with a faint smile.

Leland fussily brushed at his lapels. 'Half the trouble with you these days, Collis, is that you don't seem to understand the importance of what we've achieved. We've spanned the continent! We've changed the life of this nation forever.'

'Yes,' said Collis, standing up. The band outside was playing 'The Star-Spangled Banner' for the fifth time. 'I suppose we'd better go. I wouldn't want you to miss your ceremony.'

They stepped down from the train to the dusty roadbed. There was a crowd of six or seven hundred people gathered around now, and a good deal of laughing and jostling. Two or three whisky tents had been set up, and most of the spectators were drunk. Thomas Durant, waiting by the last gap in the rails in his finest black velvet jacket, looked extremely pale in the sunlight.

It was just after noon. The two railroad engines had been uncoupled from the trains they had brought with them, and eased closer to each other, sighing and hissing as they came. A Union flag fluttered loudly from a nearby telegraph pole, and an extra wire had been brought down from one of the pole's insulators to connect up with a telegraph key, which was set up on a wooden table not ten feet away from the last rail. At the table, a young telegraph operator with shiny hair was tapping out the news to both sides of the continent that the last spike would be driven in less than twenty minutes.

'The idea is that the last spike is going to be wired up to the telegraph,' said Leland. 'When I hit it with my silver-plated sledgehammer, one single telegraph transmission will announce to all the globe that America has been bridged by a railroad at long last.'

Jane McCormick, who had been talking to Mary Tucker, came across and offered her arm to Leland like a San Francisco salami on to which someone, for a joke, had tugged a lady's white glove.

Leland took it, and patted it, and gave Collis a patronising smirk.

Thomas Durant was waiting for them. He shook them all by the hand and then said, 'You must forgive me. I have a rather severe headache.'

'Too much champagne,' remarked Jane McCormick, and continued to look pleased with herself even after Collis had scowled at her.

Grenville Dodge remained in the background, watching the directors of the Sierra Pacific with animosity. He had always thought that Leland McCormick was a windbag, and frequently said so.

The band music died away. The crowd pushed closer, laughing and clapping and singing. Collis found that he was being pressed so hard on all sides that he could hardly keep his balance.

A tall thin preacher with a single tuft of grey hair that was blown upright by the wind like the feather in a red Indian's headband came forward through the crowd. This was the Reverend John Todd, who had come to Promontory on behalf of two religious magazines. He raised both his hands and said a prayer of thanks in such a soft voice that nobody could hear him except Leland, who was standing right next to him, and who kept nodding as if the prayers were personally addressed to him.

Collis pushed his way over and stood next to the telegraph operator. As the Reverend John Todd sang out an almost inaudible 'Amen', he watched the operator tap out the words, 'We have got done praying. The spike is about to be presented.'

Charles Tucker stepped up and handed Leland's two gold spikes to Thomas Durant, who accepted them with a hungover nod. Durant then knelt down and slipped them into the pre-drilled holes in the laurel tie. The reflected inscription on the tie's silver plaque shone on his cheek: 'The last tie laid on the completion of the Pacific Railroad, May 1869.'

Leland spoke for more than five minutes, while the crowd restlessly stirred and pushed. Finally, he raised one hand and called out in his most melodramatic voice, 'Now, gentlemen, with your assistance we shall proceed to lay the last tie, the last rail, and drive the last spike.'

Grenville Dodge, who seemed to have cheered up, thanked Leland for his oratory and said, 'Gentlemen, this is the way to India.'

The silver-headed sledgehammer was brought up. Leland smiled to everyone around and gave what Collis always called his 'Presidential wave'. A telegraph wire was attached to one of the golden spikes, and Leland took the hammer and playfully swung it around. Jane McCormick was pink and glistening with glory.

'Well, I'm ready,' announced Leland, and swung his sledge-hammer at the last spike. He missed it altogether, hitting the roadbed. There was a huge roar of laughter from the track layers at the back of the crowd, who had already drunk one whisky tent out of supplies and were ready to move on. Leland, scarlet, stood back.

Now Thomas Durant, pulling on a pair of workman's gloves to protect his hands, took a turn with the sledge. He swung hard, with a grunt of effort, and also missed. The track layers were almost hysterical with glee.

Collis leaned over the telegraph table. 'What's your name, friend?' he asked the operator.

The operator glanced at him. 'Shilling, sir. Walter Shilling.'

'Well, Mr Shilling,' said Collis, 'I think it's going to be up to us to complete this great transcontinental railroad, don't you?' And he reached across the table and tapped the telegraph key himself, just once.

Shilling stared at Collis in surprise. Then, quickly, he chattered out the message, 'Done.' Collis grinned at him, reached into his vest pocket, and gave him a gold five-dollar piece.

A great cheer went up from the crowd, much to Leland's confusion. Hats were tossed in the air, and the two locomotives blasted their whistles until Collis felt as if he were going to go permanently deaf. The band struck up with 'The Star-Spangled Banner' again, and somebody fired a pistol into the afternoon sky.

Slowly, the locomotives were brought closer and closer, until their pilots actually touched. Engineers and track layers and whooping bystanders climbed up on to the piston rods and the shining pipework, and bottles of champagne were jiggled up and down and sprayed over the crowd.

At last, the spectators were held back long enough for the formal photographs to be taken. Grenville Dodge, grave and bearded, shaking hands with Charles Tucker. Leland, with Jane on his arm, trying to look expansive and statesmanlike. Only one of the historic pictures caught Collis; and that showed him next to the telegraph operator's table, with his head turned away from the camera.

He was actually asking Shilling to send a personal message to Mr

631

Charles Frémont, of San Francisco. It said simply, 'You owe me a party. Invite Melford, too.'

All across America that afternoon there were wild celebrations. In San Francisco, the whole city took to the streets and danced and drank until the following morning. In Chicago, a seven-mile parade of cheering people kept the traffic blocked for hours. In Sacramento, within hearing distance of 54 K Street, thirty new locomotives of the Sierra Pacific Railroad lined up to blow their whistles in triumphant unison.

And in Utah, Collis Edmonds was standing apart from the hoop-la all around him, leaning heavily on his ebony cane, when a red-cheeked boy came running towards him. The boy held up a handful of telegraph messages. 'They're for you, sir. Shilling took them down this morning but Mr McCormick said we should wait until now for you to have them.'

There were three envelopes. Collis tore them open one by one.

The first read: 'Congratulations and warmest regards from your fellow directors of the Sierra Pacific Railroad.'

The second read: 'A grand and meritorious achievement. Best wishes, President Ulysses S. Grant.'

The third telegraph read: 'You are the talk of the town. All San Francisco salutes you and even Father is impressed! I am back at home now, much improved, and shall persuade Father to invite you to dinner. Your favourite, Sarah.'

The locomotive blew its shrill whistle as Collis flung Sarah's telegraph exuberantly into the air and made his way into the crowd, in search of champagne. Behind him, the telegraph floated gracefully to the ground and was trampled, obscuring Shilling's handwriting so that all anyone could have read were the telling words 'Your favourite'.

WHAT TURNS MEN INTO
MEAT-HUNGRY SAVAGES . . . ?

FAMINE

by GRAHAM MASTERTON

When the grain crop failed in Kansas it seemed like an isolated incident and no one took too much notice. Except Ed Hardesty. Then the blight spread to California's fruit harvest – and from there, like wildfire, throughout the nation . . .

'The Greek-looking man said: 'This food in here – you think that you're going to keep it all to yourself? All of it? Just because you're a store-keeper you think you've got some God-given right to survive while everybody else starves?'

Nicolas didn't even want to think about it. He said: 'I'm giving you three. You understand me? Three, and then I shoot.'

The first shot missed. The revolver bucked in his hands, and he heard the bang of broken glass at the back of the store, followed by a sudden rush of green olives from three broken jars. He fired again before he could allow himself to think, and the Greek's shoulder burst apart in a spray of gory catsup. And then there was a deep, deafening **bavvooom**! and Nicolas realized with strange slow horror that the Greek had fired back at him with his shotgun, and that he'd been hit, badly hit, in the belly and the thighs . . .'

GENERAL FICTION   0 7221 6003 8   £1.75

A SELECTION OF BESTSELLERS FROM SPHERE

FICTION

LOVENOTES	Justine Valenti	£1.75	☐
VENGEANCE 10	Joe Poyer	£1.75	☐
MURDER IN THE WHITE HOUSE	Margaret Truman	£1.50	☐
LOVE PLAY	Rosemary Rogers	£1.75	☐
BRIMSTONE	Robert L. Duncan	£1.75	☐

FILM & TV TIE-INS

FORT APACHE, THE BRONX	Heywood Gould	£1.75	☐
SHARKY'S MACHINE	William Diehl	£1.75	☐
THE PROFESSIONALS	Ken Blake	£1.00	☐
THE GENTLE TOUCH	Terence Feely	£1.25	☐
BARRIERS	William Corlett	£1.00	☐

NON-FICTION

OPENING UP	Geoff Boycott	£1.75	☐
SCIENCE IN EVERYDAY LIFE	William C. Vergara	£2.50	☐
THE COUNTRY DIARY OF AN EDWARDIAN LADY	Edith Holden	£4.50	☐
WHAT THIS KATIE DID	Katie Boyle	£1.75	☐
MICHELLE REMEMBERS	Michelle Smith & Lawrence Pazder M.D.	£1.75	☐

All Sphere books are available at your local bookshop or newsagent, or can be ordered direct from the publisher. Just tick the titles you want and fill in the form below.

Name _____

Address _____

_____

Write to Sphere Books, Cash Sales Department, P.O. Box 11, Falmouth, Cornwall TR10 9EN

Please enclose a cheque or postal order to the value of the cover price plus:

UK: 45p for the first book, plus 20p for the second and 14p for each additional book ordered to a maximum charge of £1.63

OVERSEAS: 75p for the first book plus 21p per copy for each additional book

BFPO & EIRE: 45p for the first book, 20p for the second book plus 14p per copy for the next 7 books, thereafter 8p per book

Sphere Books reserve the right to show new retail prices on covers which may differ from those previously advertised in the text or elsewhere, and to increase postal rates in accordance with the PO.